Fawn wandered throu[ ] ing for the family albu[ ] shop with a bit of ev[ ] ......g bicycle, an old dress form, baby furniture . . .

Suddenly Fawn felt a surge of nausea. The ceiling seemed to be squeezing down around her shoulders, and she felt the dizziness that always preceded one of her panic attacks. Her heart pounded. Even the floor seemed to shift, and everything was closing in on her.

"What's wrong?" Scott asked, peering at her worriedly.

She stared at him, fighting for control. "Scott, did . . . it happen here?" She meant her parents' murders, but she couldn't say the words.

He understood immediately, and put his arm around her to steady her. "No, Fawn, not here."

"But I . . . there's something . . . God, get me out of here."

"Come on, we'll go upstairs." His voice was gentle; maybe coming back to this house with its horrifying history was too much for her.

But suddenly she was afraid to take another step. She felt trapped—afraid where she was and afraid to move. There was something horrible at the top of the stairs, in the kitchen . . .

FAMILY SECRETS

Marly Chevalier

LYNX BOOKS
New York

FAMILY SECRETS

ISBN: 1-55802-095-0

First Printing/July 1988

This book is published by Lynx Books, a division of
Lynx Communications, Inc., 41 Madison Avenue, New York,
New York, 10010. The name "Lynx" together with the
logotype consisting of a stylized head of a lynx is a
trademark of Lynx Communications, Inc.

Printed in the United States of America

0 9 8 7 6 5 4 3 2 1

Dedication

For my mother, in gratitude for her unfailing faith and encouragement

FAMILY SECRETS

Chapter 1

Fawn Travers slowly opened her hands, staring in surprise at the red welts that crossed her palms where her fingernails had dug into the flesh. How long had her fists been clenched, she wondered. She'd been too nervous even to notice the pain. Again Fawn glanced up and down the long, empty hallway. She'd been pacing outside the offices of Bromley, Reswick, and Christensen, attorneys-at-law, for the past ten minutes—rehearsing what she'd say to Colman Bromley. Fighting the temptation to ring for the elevator and escape.

Now, she hesitated once more before the wide teak doors and checked her watch. "Ten forty-five." She was still fifteen minutes early. "And eighteen years late," she whispered, an anxious half-smile flitting across her features. The polished brass nameplate attached to the door bounced the smile back at her, and she took note of her appearance. It was crucial she make a good first impression. Quickly she smoothed back her silky straight blond hair so that it fell sleekly to her shoulders and brushed a bit of lint off her crisply tailored navy-blue suit. Carefully, she checked to make sure that her pale pink lipstick hadn't smeared.

Then, once more, she opened her purse, reassuring herself that the small jewel case was still tucked safely inside. The case was faded with age; over the years its plush covering had been rubbed slick, almost bare in spots, but it held her most important possession, her only proof—a miniature gold locket.

"If it is proof . . ." Fawn reminded herself. Would it be enough to convince Colman Bromley? Would he tell her what she needed to know?

In a few more months she'd be celebrating her twenty-fifth birthday, but at this moment she felt like a child again. A lonely, frightened six-year-old. Just as she had been after that night eighteen years ago, the night that had so violently split her life in two that she had no memory of what had happened before. A child suddenly alone in the world, unable even to remember her own name, where she belonged, or to whom.

Opening the jewel case, Fawn Travers stared at the tiny gold locket engraved with the initials "K.D." This was all she had left to bear witness to that time, to her childhood before the night that had sent her terrified into the streets away from her home. This and the tangled hints of her nightmares, the sudden, inexplicable daylight terrors . . . What had happened that night?

With an abrupt, almost fierce gesture, she shoved the case back into her purse. Maybe it would be better to let the past stay buried. Maybe she should walk away right now. And what? . . . Until she knew the truth, she'd never feel free to live her life.

Reluctantly she faced the door. For a last brief moment she hesitated, like a skier readying herself to hurtle down a steep, perilous slope. Then she opened the door and stepped inside.

And blinked. This wasn't at all what she'd expected. Her eyes widened as they took in the gleaming rosewood paneling of the reception lobby, the high, coffered ceiling, the antique furniture. High, arched windows lined one wall, providing a spectacular view of Wall Street and the sooty spire of Trinity Church. A magnificent Aubusson in shades of moss-green, cream, and rose carpeted the floor. Large gilt-framed portraits and wing-backed armchairs gave the room the air of an exclusive men's club. There was even a hint of cigar smoke, mellow and rich, in the air.

Fawn was suddenly very aware of how far from home she was. At this time of the morning she should have been at work in her darkroom developing prints. The newspaper she worked for was just a small, struggling weekly. The office was a cluttered, rather scruffy-looking place, but right now she felt a sharp longing for it.

"May I help you?" the silver-haired receptionist asked, breaking into her thoughts. The woman readjusted her glasses on the bridge of her nose with a perfectly manicured nail and smiled at Fawn expectantly.

Fawn gave her name, adding that she had an appointment with Mr. Bromley. The tightness of her throat made her voice a shy whisper, but she was grateful any sound came out at all.

The receptionist consulted her calendar. "Which . . . oh, yes, here it is. If you'll just wait a few minutes . . ."

Fawn nodded. "Thank you." More waiting.

But at least she understood now why it had been so difficult to get this appointment. Bromley, Reswick, and Christensen obviously didn't spend their time chasing ambulances or lurking in the halls of the criminal courts to snare clients. Plainly they could afford to be choosy about whom they represented. Even someone like herself, growing up in a small, impoverished town, couldn't mistake the aura of wealth, power, and complacency in the air.

Yet surely Colman Bromley hadn't been this successful eighteen years ago? As if in answer, a pair of burning black eyes glared down at her from one of the old portraits. Fawn edged closer, transfixed by the tall, handsome, aristocratic figure in his elegant frock coat. He seemed to vibrate with impatience, as if, even after all these years, he itched to prod the painter with his knobby, gold-headed cane, to make him go faster, faster.

"That's Zachariah Bromley," the receptionist said, noticing Fawn's interest. "The founder of the firm, Mr. Bromley's great-great-grandfather."

"He looks very . . . determined," Fawn murmured. It was the most polite way she could think to phrase her reaction to the imposing portrait. Privately she was saying a prayer of thanks that she didn't have to deal with this ogre. But how could anyone from this man's family possibly be connected with her own past?

The receptionist stared at the painting, focusing on the jaws that looked as if they could crush a Brazil nut in one snap. "From what I understand, he was a real terror," she whispered. "In fact, that stubborn streak runs in the family, but . . ." Just then the buzzer sounded on her desk. She rose. "Mr. Bromley will see you now."

She led Fawn down a long hall, past a law library where clerks sat hunched over leather-bound volumes, to a spacious corner office with a sweeping view of the harbor. There were sailing prints on the walls and photos of a racing sloop. Two deep sofas faced each other in front of the black marble fireplace. The man behind the desk rose as they entered. He was tall and broad-shouldered, and his face carried echoes of the lean handsomeness of the face in the portrait. But the effect was very different; arrogance had been replaced by a quiet assurance. The receptionist completed the introductions, and his smile, automatic at first, suddenly warmed in surprised appreciation as he took in Fawn's clean-sculpted beauty. She seemed vaguely familiar, yet he was certain he'd never seen her before. He wouldn't have forgotten the glowing amber depths of those brown eyes, that thick mane of gold-blond hair, that intriguing mix of strength and vulnerability in the way she carried herself.

But Fawn was looking past him and frowning. He saw her glance flicker around the office, and thinking she was puzzled by the clutter of legal briefs and correspondence stacked around the room, he explained, "Just clearing up some last-minute business. I'm leaving on a long-postponed vacation tonight. Please sit down," he added, gesturing to a leather armchair that faced the desk.

Fawn sank into the chair, bewildered. This wasn't the man she'd traveled halfway across the country to see. He couldn't be. She stared at his thick black hair falling across his forehead—there wasn't one strand of gray. And there was no hint of jowls marring his strong jawline, no tiredness in his lively blue eyes. His body seemed as lean and muscled, as fluidly graceful as an athlete's. He couldn't be much more than thirty years old. The man she was looking for would have to be at least fifty.

Suddenly she wanted to laugh, or cry from the frustration, the disappointment. Dammit . . .

But he was already seating himself behind the desk as if nothing was wrong. "Now then," he said briskly, "how can I help you?"

"I'm afraid you can't." Good grief, how was she going to get out of here? She could feel her embarrassment flooding her face a bright red. "I'm sorry, I've made a mistake. I'll pay for your time, of course." She started to rise.

"Please, as long as you're here . . ." he said quickly. Now that he'd seen her, he was no longer so eager to get this appointment over and done with. His gaze lingered on the silky sheen of her skin, the way her perfect teeth nibbled nervously at her full bottom lip. "At least tell me what the problem is," he suggested. "If I can't help you, perhaps I can refer you to another attorney."

She hesitated. When she'd seen the name Colman Bromley listed in the telephone book, she'd simply assumed it was the man she was looking for. The one mentioned in the old newspaper clipping. That clipping was the only lead she had to locating the man who would know who she was. But that newspaper was dated eighteen years ago.

Still, she was here. And she couldn't just give up.

On the other side of the desk, Colman Bromley waited, realizing it would be better not to rush her. He'd been practicing law for seven years now, first with the D.A.'s office and then here, and he'd learned long ago the art of patience, to keep his emotions in check.

"Perhaps there is some way you can help me," Fawn said. Now that she'd decided to tell her story, her voice was firm and level. "First of all, my name isn't Fawn Travers. At least, that isn't the name I was born with."

"Then we'll start over," he suggested, leaning toward her. "Who are you?"

"I think . . . I have reason to believe, I might be Kendra Dalsworth."

The effect was immediate. Suddenly the atmosphere in the

room seemed to crackle as if an electrical storm had been let loose. Colman Bromley stared at her, old memories blurring his vision. Then abruptly he turned away, his face at once closed, wary. After a moment, he turned to her once again, but his eyes did not meet hers. "You said 'might be.' "

"That's what I've come to find out—whether it's true."

"That you should happen to be the girl every reporter, every cop, one of the best detective agencies in the country has been looking for all these years?. . ."

His words confused her. Someone had been searching for her? But she felt too relieved to worry about it now. "Then the name does mean something to you?" she asked eagerly. She had barely noticed the cold disbelief in his voice.

"Of course." The ties between his family and the Dalsworths went back several generations; they were more than just friends. He himself had only been twelve when Kendra Dalsworth disappeared. Yet the echoes of that tragedy still reverberated in his life. But for most people the Dalsworth name conjured up only visions of greed. Even pity tends to be forgotten when forty million dollars are at stake.

"Please, whatever you can tell me . . ." She took a deep breath, bracing herself. "Is is true my parents were murdered?"

"Kendra Dalsworth's parents were murdered," he corrected her. The timing was suspicious. In just six months Kendra, if she were alive, would come into her trust fund. All those millions would be hers. He forced himself to face the obvious conclusion: This girl sitting in front of him was an imposter. Harshly he asked, "Who gave you my name?"

For a moment Fawn didn't answer, didn't even seem to hear him. She'd been warned her parents were dead, and she thought she'd accepted that. It wasn't until the fact was confirmed that she realized how much she had secretly hoped they'd still be alive. She felt stunned by the pain, the sense of loss. Who had killed them? Why? There was so much she wanted to ask. But the lawyer was repeating his question. "Who gave you my name?"

"It was in an old newspaper story—just a few lines picked up from one of the national wire services." She retrieved the yellowed clipping from her purse, quoting it from memory.

" 'Colman Bromley, the family's attorney and closest friend . . .' But it doesn't make any sense—that man must be at least fifty by now.''

"Fifty-seven, to be exact. He's my father: Colman Talbot Bromley. I'm Colman Thayer. . . . People generally call me Cole.'' But it was easy to understand how the mistake had been made, especially as his father rarely saw new clients anymore. Cole eyed the wire clipping with distaste; it was no more than a dozen lines, not even from a New York newspaper. "You should have researched your claim better, if you expected to be believed,'' he suggested. "Kendra knew me. *And* my father.''

"If I could remember details like that I wouldn't be here, would I?'' she retorted. "And I'm not making any claim.''

"Oh, then you're not interested in the money?'' he asked, lifting an eyebrow.

"What money?''

"Kendra Dalsworth's inheritance. After all, that is the point of all this, isn't it?''

There'd been no mention of an inheritance in the short wire clipping, but it wouldn't have mattered to her even if she had known. That wasn't why she was here. It couldn't amount to very much, anyway—they were welcome to keep it. "Please, Mr. Bromley,'' she said, trying hard to keep the exasperation out of her voice, "Let's not spend our time quibbling over a few dollars.''

Cole shook his head amused by what he took to be the sheer artistry of her denial. "A few dollars''—she'd actually said that. It was a hell of a way to refer to forty million. "So what is it you want?'' he asked, deciding to play along for the moment.

"I need to find out what happened to me, to my family. I want to know what my parents were like, how they looked . . . what went wrong . . .'' The lawyer's face remained impassive. Good Lord, why couldn't he understand?

Cole struggled to rein in his impatience. "So you can use the information to prove you're really Kendra Dalsworth?''

He still thought she was trying to trick him, she realized. He was so damned sure of himself, so cold. Suddenly she remembered the portrait in the lobby; right now he looked just like his great-great-grandfather. Cole Bromley's eyes had the same stubborn intensity, his handsome face the same chiseled hardness. And all at once she was angry. He was so secure in his own world. He had no idea what it was like, living with these constant doubts. Dreading that one day whatever secret was hidden in her past would suddenly explode, afraid to love anyone for fear he would be destroyed, too.

"All I'm asking for is what you and everyone else take for granted. I just want my own past back." She glared at him defiantly. "And I'm going to keep searching, with or without your help."

"Exactly how do you propose to do that?"

She didn't know how she was going to go about it herself, but she wasn't about to admit that. "I suppose there must be some distant relatives still alive."

"I wouldn't advise that," he said quickly.

"Then there is someone. An aunt, an uncle? . . ."

"Yes, an aunt and two uncles," he admitted grudgingly. "But if you're thinking they'd be easier to deal with . . ."

"Please," she interrupted, "Just tell me how I can locate them."

He shook his head. "I can't do that."

"You're determined to protect them from me, aren't you?"

"Or maybe I'm protecting you," he shot back. He was surprised at his own words. He knew he was being illogical. Damn, in one more day he would have been gone, vacationing in the Caribbean, and someone else would have had to deal with this beautiful imposter. She even looked like Melissa and Joel, he realized now. Those luminous eyes, that determined lift of the chin. Of all the imposters the fortune had lured over the years, she was the best. Whoever had planned this had been very cunning. But dammit, he'd have to be the one to demolish her story. "Suppose we start with what you remember."

"But I don't remember anything . . . exactly."

" 'Exactly'?" He pounced on the word like a prosecuting attorney. He only needed one incorrect detail, one mistake.

She was staring past him, her eyes misty, focused in the

distance. "I have a vague memory of a big house, but I can't remember it exactly . . ." her voice trailed off.

"And . . ." he persisted.

"A doll, a toy tea set trimmed in gold, things like that . . ." She'd been speaking slowly, almost as if in a trance, but suddenly she leaned toward him, and her voice grew husky, intense. "You see, I've tried so hard to remember, daydreamed . . . until I don't know what's true and what's just wishing." And suddenly she was blurting out the rest, telling him what she'd never told anyone else. "I have these nightmares, horrible nightmares and panics, terrors that seem to come out of nowhere. I don't even know what I'm afraid of. Is it something from my past or am I just . . ." She looked away from him, unable to actually say the word—maybe there'd been insanity in her family.

She struggled to regain her composure, aware that he was watching her closely, his face an impassive mask. She'd come here hoping to find an ally, and instead she was facing an enemy. "Why are you so determined not to believe me?"

"Because the police are certain Kendra Dalsworth was killed." But it was more than that, he realized. He didn't want to believe her. Kendra's reappearance right now would open up too many old wounds, would be dangerous to too many people. The consequences would be devastating, especially to his own father. "Besides," he added aloud. "you don't have one piece of solid evidence to back up your story."

She opened up her purse and handed him the jewel case. "I have this. I'd like your father to see it."

The tiny locket looked even smaller in Cole's large hand. For a long moment he stared at the exquisitely engraved initials: K.D. He was remembering the Christmas before Kendra's disappearance and he could see her again, in a white velvet dress with a red sash, her blond curls bobbing, as she happily recited a list of all the presents she'd received. "And this . . ." she'd added, proudly displaying the small gold locket she was wearing around her neck. "Isn't it beautiful? I'm going to wear it all the time."

But was it the same locket? Or just a clever copy? He turned it over, studying it more carefully, and noticed the small dents along the edge of the soft metal. Toothmarks.

Kendra had had a habit of nibbling at the locket when she was nervous, he suddenly remembered—an unconscious habit, the way another child might have bitten her nails. He looked across at her in surprise. For the first time he forced himself to face the possibility that this girl might really be Kendra Dalsworth.

Fawn saw the change in his expression and realized that even if he wasn't convinced yet, he was finally taking her seriously. But then the mask came over his face again, and for some reason he seemed even more hostile now that he had before.

"I want to know everything there is to know about you," he demanded suddenly. "Where you've lived since the age of six, who raised you . . ."

"I can't tell you that."

"Why not? If you really are Kendra Dalsworth . . ." And then the thought struck him—if she was who she claimed, had she been living with her parents' murderer all this time? "There's someone you're afraid of, is that it?"

She shook her head. "I can't explain." She wouldn't buy his help by betraying anyone else. There were secrets she had to keep.

He stared at her, but she was just as stubborn as he was. "All right—for now. But there'll be no way you can stop the truth from coming out eventually," he warned. No one's secrets would be safe anymore.

"What are you suggesting?" she asked angrily. "That I just disappear again?"

He was tempted to say yes, but he knew it wouldn't do any good. She wouldn't listen to him. Yet he had to try one more time. "There are a lot of people, powerful people, who would prefer that Kendra Dalsworth remain missing forever."

Fawn suspected that Cole Bromley was one of those people. But now wasn't the time to get angry. "I want your father to see the locket," she insisted. "If you won't allow me to see him, I'll find some way of meeting him myself."

Cole didn't doubt her. He pressed the intercom button, his face grim. "Would you ask my father to step in here, please. There's someone he should meet."

Chapter 2

Kendra was putting her dolls to bed. Carefully, with a six-year-old's solemnness, she tucked in the covers and turned off the dollhouse's tiny electric lights. "Sleep tight," she whispered, then sat back on her heels and giggled, delighted.

The dollhouse, a gift from her parents, was an exact replica of their own home in Forest Hills Gardens. Though the family had a sixteen-room beach cottage in the Hamptons, a villa on the Côte d'Azur, and kept a pied-à-terre in Manhattan, Kendra always thought of the Gardens as home. It really did seem like a garden. The quiet streets were lined with flowering cherry and dogwood and tulip trees, and the carefully manicured lawns surrounding the brick and timbered Tudor homes were lush with azalea, lilac, forsythia, and honeysuckle hedges. The neighborhood was like a painting come to life, filled with bright colors and sunshine.

Kendra bent down to gaze into the dollhouse again, marveling at how perfect it was. Just as in their own home, there were five fireplaces, including the big, old-fashioned brick hearth in the kitchen. A music room with a grand piano. A greenhouse. Master craftsmen had hand-carved the tiny furniture and woven handkerchief-sized oriental carpets. Best of all, everything worked—even the fluted gold faucets in the bathrooms. Kendra flicked the lights on and off again and smiled happily. She was the luckiest girl she knew.

"Hey, buttercup, how about joining the old folks?" her father called from the stairwell. Buttercup was his pet name for her, in part because of her radiantly blond curls but mostly, he said, because it suited her sunny, buoyant personality.

She hurried to the stairs and leaned over the polished banister, staring down at his broad shoulders, sun-streaked hair, teasing blue eyes. He's so handsome, she thought, and not at all old like some of her friends' fathers. When she grew up, she planned on asking him to marry her.

"Are we going to fix hot chocolate?" she asked hopefully.

"How could we have a Sunday night without it?" he replied, pretending to be shocked.

Kendra bounced down the stairs, and her father swept her into his arms, carrying her off to the kitchen, while she giggled. Sunday was her favorite day of the week. It was the day her parents had reserved to spend with her; no business meetings or social affairs were allowed to intrude. She had them all to herself. Even the servants were gone, so meals were served right in the kitchen instead of in the long, formal, and to Kendra slightly intimidating dining room. It was like a holiday with no one frowning at her meaningfully when she used the wrong fork or tried to hide her uneaten snails beneath a sprig of watercress.

Even on a dark night like tonight, with the threat of rain in the air, the kitchen glowed with a cheery warmth. Rows of polished copper pots and pans gleaned on the walls. A fire crackled in the hearth. Her father's favorite collection of Strauss waltzes played in the background. And as always, there were flowers—at this time of year, bright pots of yellow and lavender and white crocus.

"I see you found her." Kendra's mother smiled as they entered the room. She was standing at the stove stirring a pot; a rich chocolatey aroma sweetened the air. "Good thing—I was just about to give this to the tabby next door."

"Cats don't like hot chocolate," Kendra objected quickly.

"Are you sure about that?" her mother teased, her ivory skin crinkling around her dark eyes as she smiled. She'd been working in her garden earlier in the day and was still wearing jeans and a fisherman-knit sweater. Her blond hair was pulled back into a ponytail, and she wore almost no makeup, which made the resemblence between mother and daughter even more striking.

"So, which do you prefer—marshmallows or whipped cream on top?" she asked, filling a mug for Kendra.

Kendra's brow puckered as she debated the choice, unable to make up her mind.

"Both, I guess," her mother decided, ruffling Kendra's hair fondly.

"Both." Her father nodded. "But remember, young lady, tomorrow you'll be back in the real world—no more spoiling."

"I know—school and homework and everything . . ." Kendra made a face, unwilling to admit that, for the most part, she was enjoying her first year of school.

"Tomorrow we'll all be back in the real world." Melissa sighed, bringing the mugs to the table. Six months pregnant, she moved awkwardly, her usual grace thrown off balance by the weight of the growing baby.

Joel caressed the round bulge beneath Melissa's sweater, marveling again at his good fortune. Thank God he'd ignored his father's objections to their marriage. Because Melissa's family had lost their own money years before, Joel's father had assumed her motives were calculatingly mercenary. Fortunately, Joel had refused to listen or be intimidated by threats of disinheritance. He'd known he'd found the right woman for himself. And eight years of marriage had proven him right. Even his father had become one of Melissa's staunchest admirers before he died.

And now she and Joel were expecting the second child they'd hoped for, for so long. There'd been two miscarriages in between, but the doctors said she was past the danger point now. Still, looking at her now, noticing the bluish shadows beneath her eyes, Joel was concerned. "Tired, Melly?" he asked softly.

She smiled, her hand resting on his. "It's not the baby."

She pulled a chair up close to her own for Kendra and helped her climb onto it, then turned her attention back to Joel. "Have you decided what you're going to do about Ned?"

Joel frowned. "There's no way to keep him in the firm. A brokerage house is responsible for too many other people's money to take a chance he wouldn't be tempted again. But for the sake of the family, we'll keep the police out of it. We'll make up the money ourselves."

"Do you want me to be there when you tell him? After all, he is my little brother."

"No, I'll manage. You've just been through that miserable business with Noreen. I know how your sister gets when anyone critizes her son, so I can just imagine her reaction when you suggested a psychiatrist for the boy."

"She won't take him. Noreen said the school made a mistake, Scott couldn't have done such a horrible thing. She thinks we should pressure the headmaster to take him back. She says you control a great deal of the school's private funding, the endowments."

"So, I should blackmail them?" Joel grimaced.

Melissa nodded, embarrassed. "What the hell's wrong with my family? First Ned, then Noreen. And now Nick's got this crazy scheme. . . . Is it my fault? I wanted so much to make up for their childhoods, all those years of penny-pinching and misery. The triplets were too young to even remember the good times before father went bankrupt. I've had it so much easier than they have. . . . "

"That's bull, honey. And it's just what they want you to think." When he'd married Melissa, he'd known that she'd felt responsible for her younger brothers and sister. And he'd been happy to take on some of that responsibility himself. But over the years he'd gradually come to see how the triplets manipulated her, using her generosity. It was time she started seeing it, too. "You've done everything you could for them," he insisted. "Maybe it's time you stopped bailing them out, making excuses for them."

Noticing that Kendra had stopped sipping her hot chocolate and was watching them, her eyes wide with curiosity, he said quickly, "Anyway, let's worry about that tomorrow."

"So, where should we plan on going next Sunday?" he

asked, leaning toward Kendra. "I suppose you've got your heart set on that lecture on Mayan Archeology at the History Musuem? Or maybe a Wagnerian opera?"

"Oh, Daddy." Kendra giggled.

"You don't really suppose she'd rather go to the circus with us?" Melissa asked, falling into the game.

"The circus! Really—could we go? Please?"

"Well, we'd need tickets," Joel said. "Now where do you imagine we could find a set of tickets?" He frowned, looking around the room, under the table and chairs, then suddenly he reached behind Kendra's ear and pulled out three tickets. "Suppose we could use these?"

"Oh, you had them all the time." She gasped, scrambling off her chair to hug them both. "You're wonderful."

"You're not such a toad yourself," Melissa said, tweaking her daughter's nose gently. "Hey, how about doing that trick with a bottle of something cold and bubbly?" she asked Joel.

"Good idea," he agreed. "But I'll have to disappear into the wine cellar first. Want to come along, Buttercup?" he added, and she nodded.

As they reached the steps, there was a knock on the door. "Who . . . never mind, I'll get it," Melissa said.

They were downstairs for almost five minutes. While Joel selected the bottle of champagne he wanted from the cooler, Kendra wandered through the jumble of old trunks and chests stacked against the walls. She stopped in front of the collection of baby clothes and nursery furniture that was being readied for the new arrival. "This all used to be my stuff, didn't it?" she asked.

Joel nodded. "But you're too old for it now. You wouldn't want to go back to sleeping in a crib, would you?"

"No. The baby can have it, I don't mind. But will you tell Mom to make sure it's a little brother."

"That's what we're trying for," he said, grinning. "But would you mind a sister so much?"

She shrugged. "I like being the only girl." Suddenly her brow wrinkled in a frown. "Did you want me to be a boy?"

Joel glanced at her, surprised, then swiftly knelt down so they were facing each other at eye level. "We wanted you to

be just exactly what you are. We love you just as you are—
and always will. Okay?''

She smiled widely enough to make dimples in both cheeks.
''I was only checking.''

They started up the stairs, Joel behind her. He glanced at
his watch. ''Think it's about your bedtime, buttercup. School
tomorrow.''

She started to ask for five minutes more, but found herself
yawning instead. ''I guess I am sleepy,'' she admitted reluctantly, pushing open the door to the kitchen.

The lights in the kitchen were out, the room engulfed in a
puzzling, unsettling blackness. There was no sound except
for the Strauss waltz playing in the background. Kendra could
just make out the form of her mother sitting, slumped over,
at the table. ''Guess Mom's sleepy, too,'' she whispered.

She tiptoed across the floor. ''Hey, Mom, you're not supposed to go to sleep yet.'' There was no answer.

Kendra peered around the edge of the chair, thinking
maybe it was a game, just as her father flipped on the light
switch. And in the sudden glare, the grisly vision seemed to
leap out at her—the blood, the jagged gash across her mother's throat. The wet darkness was soaking into her mother's
sweater, puddling on the table, dripping onto the tiled floor.
''Mama . . .'' she screamed. She whirled around, her eyes
searching for her father, just as his body slid, face convulsed
with pain and surprise, to the floor.

His fingers clawed at the tiles as he tried to crawl toward
her. Slowly he struggled to his feet, took a step. His legs
buckled beneath him, but he forced himself up again, still
trying to reach her. ''Run . . .'' he gasped. Blood bubbled
from his mouth. ''Run, Kendra . . .'' And then, in a silent,
twisting fall, his body slumped to the floor, eyes blind with
death.

Slowly, deliberately, a black-gloved hand pulled the knife
from his back. Kendra heard the scraping of steel against
bone.

''No . . .'' Kendra whimpered, edging closer to her
mother, her eyes locked on the dark figure standing deep in
the shadows. A large hat and scarf covered most of the face.
Still unbelieving, she stared at the thick, oversize rubber

boots, the splattered raincoat, the knife. At her father's body splayed across the floor.

"Come here, Kendra." The voice was harsh, rasping, out of breath. A black-gloved hand stretched out to her in invitation but in the other, the knife twitched impatiently. And the eyes were wild, devouring. Kendra stood paralyzed, like a rabbit trapped in the glare of onrushing headlights. The Strauss waltz ended, and the next began.

The rubber boots took a step forward, carelessly kicked Joel's lifeless arm aside, took another step. Kendra edged backward. And suddenly the figure was rushing at her, the butcher knife slicing the air.

Kendra fled. The figure lunged, missing, just as she darted around the edge of the table. "Stand still, you little bitch."

But the table was between them now, and Kendra darted to the left, then the right as the dark form started around the side. Dodging back and forth, back and forth in a desperate game of chase. Always keeping the table, with its hot chocolate mugs and the silver ice bucket ready for the champagne, between them. "Damn you," the voice hissed, breathless.

The knife whistled closer. The other's steps were longer, more cunning. Kendra doubled back, panicky.

The door—she had to get to the door, go for help. She glanced behind her, tensed to run. And in that instant, the knife ripped into her arm.

The force of the blow slammed Kendra against the table, causing the ice bucket to tumble to the floor. With a crash, ice and water skittered across the tiles. Kendra gripped her arm, helpless for a moment. But the boots were slipping, sliding on the ice. The gloved hand reached frantically for a chair and the knife clattered to the tiles, just as her mother's body toppled sideways and down.

As the hand snatched for the knife jammed beneath Melissa's body, Kendra ran for the door. With both hands she wrenched it open. Then she was outside, slamming the door against the volley of curses that followed her.

Trembling, she scurried into the tall, thick hedge that surrounded the house, branches whipping her face in the dark. The rushing of her blood roared in her ears, and she had to gag back the vomit. The door opened. . . .

Kendra froze in her hiding place. For a long moment she felt the glittering eyes rake over her, searching. "Come back, Kendra. Don't make me go after you." Kendra shut her eyes tight, not breathing. But when, at last, she opened her eyes, the door was swinging shut.

And then she saw the figure at the kitchen window, and heard the running water. The murderer was frantically scrubbing off the raincoat, washing away her parents' blood.

Kendra fled. She had to get as far away as she could before the knife came after her again. She ran, the hairs prickling on the back of her neck with the certainty she was being followed, but each time she looked around, no one was there. She never noticed the blood driping from her arm, marking her trail along the sidewalk.

At the corner she hesitated. She'd never been allowed to go any farther than this on her own. Always before there'd been someone to hold her hand, to watch out for her. She looked longingly at the turreted, gabled houses set back from the road. The golden light streaming through their lead-paned windows seemed to beckon her closer. She needed someone to hold her tight, to make everything all right again. But the memory of those wild, venomous eyes, the eyes of someone she'd believed loved her, held her back. There was no one she could trust. No one could make it all right again. Without looking, she dashed across the street.

The Gardens was a maze of quiet, twisting, turning streets, designed to ensure privacy for its residents. Tall pine oak and maple, hickory and beech trees arched over the sidewalks. The dogwood, cherry, and tulip trees that would later billow into masses of pink and white, were now still in bud, their branches spiky and menacing. Here and there, a graceful, old-fashioned streetlamp cast a dim glow, but everything else was swallowed by the darkness. Even the moon was hiding behind a bulwark of clouds. It would rain soon.

The threat of rain was keeping most people inside. Kendra drifted from street to street, ducking behind a stone wall or hedge whenever she saw someone in the distance. She had no idea where she was, where to go. No place seemed safe.

Gradually she became aware of the pain in her arm. She looked down, surprised to see the open wound. But it didn't frighten her; her emotions were too numbed to react. Still, she realized, if a grown-up saw it, he would make her go home. She took off her sweater and wrapped it around the arm so no one could tell.

But she was getting so tired. She'd fallen several times in the dark and her shins, knees, elbows hurt. It was beginning to rain, fat, cold drops, and finally she collapsed behind a thicket of honeysuckle. Pulling her knees up to her chest, she rested her head on her arms, rocking back and forth.

"Please, God, bring Mommy and Daddy back," she prayed silently. "I'll be good forever and ever, if you'll just make it so it never happened." But, recalling their bodies in the kitchen, she knew they would never come back to her. And at last she began to cry, soundless sobs that mingled with the rain.

Six feet away, a raincoated figure in heavy boots paused, scanning the darkness. Listening, waiting. A gloved hand tightened around the knife hidden in the folds of the raincoat. The rain had washed away the trail of blood but the child had to be near. Where, dammit, where . . . Just then a car turned into the street, headlights glaring. After a moment's hesitation, the figure moved on.

It seemed to Kendra that hours must have passed before she finally struggled to her feet. It was still dark, though the rain had stopped. Her corduroy jumper was soaked, and she couldn't stop shivering. Her knees threatening to buckle beneath her, she stumbled along the sidewalk, aware only of the pain throbbing in her arm.

She almost bumped into the man before she saw him.

"Well, what do we have here?" he asked, his voice slightly slurred, amused with itself. He was young, and with his long hair he looked like a hippie, but he was wearing a white tuxedo.

Kendra stepped backward, afraid to raise her eyes above his crooked bow tie.

"Hey, I'm not going to hurt you. But a pretty little girl like you shouldn't be wandering around all by herself."

"I have to go . . ." Kendra said, hiding her arm behind her back.

"You're not lost? You know your way home by yourself?"

She nodded warily, keeping her distance. Would he make her go home? No—she wouldn't. She couldn't.

"Well . . ." he hesitated, weaving slightly. "Suzy will kill me if I don't get myself home soon. . . ." He was looking past her, calculating just how late he was, oblivious of the horror that flashed in her eyes at his words. "All right, but you go straight home, and no talking to anyone. Okay?"

"Yes, sir."

She watched him amble down the street, muttering to himself. "Damn weddings . . . Suzy's going to want one next, can see it coming. What's wrong with just living together?"

The encounter had startled Kendra out of her numbness. She glanced around at the cars whizzing down the wide boulevard, the shops, and realized she was no longer in the Gardens. She'd been on this street before with her parents—it was the way into Manhattan.

The pain was worse in her arm now. It filled her head like the clanging of a giant bell. And she was getting woozy, weaker. She leaned against a car parked at the curb. With her head pressed against the window, she thought how good it would be to lie down. She tried the door handle, her small fingers fumbling with the latch. It was locked.

The next car was locked, too, and the one after that. But she kept trying; she needed a place to hide, someplace where no one would make her go home. "Please . . ." she pleaded. And on her fourth try, the door opened. It was an old battered green Chevy. The backseat was piled high with clothing. Kendra scrambled in, snuggling down beneath the layers of flannel shifts and jeans, pulling a coat over her. Her tiny body shivered once more in the dark, then was still.

Chapter 3

The old green Chevy rattled and smoked over the George Washington Bridge, leaving New York behind. Damn, she's burning oil like I had my own well, Pete Travers thought, glancing into the rearview mirror. And that muffler sounds like it swallowed a load of firecrackers.

Nevertheless, he couldn't stop himself from grinning. He was going home. And he never had to come back again. He was free; the Army was done with him. And he sure as hell was done with the Army.

It was like being sprung from a trap. The wooded slopes around his home in Colorado were littered with old, forgotten animal traps, and often Pete had pried open those hateful iron jaws from the legs of rabbits, or deer, or bobcat cubs. Now he felt the same stunned sense of deliverance that he imagined they had—the gratitude, the need to get as far away as fast as possible. And he knew, like them, a new wariness would stay with him for the rest of his days.

He'd thought anything would be better than working in the mines, hauling slag, coming up so choked with dust you couldn't even spit. But these last two years had been the roughest of his life.

A small-town country boy from the Colorado Rockies, he'd been naive enough to enlist, even lying about his age. Join the Army, see the world. But what he'd seen was how much of a fool he'd been. He couldn't stomach the endless rules and regimentation, the bullying, the callousness and stupidity that seemed an inescapable part of any large organization. It just went against all his instincts. Pete supposed he came by his contrary streak naturally. After all, his great-granddaddy had been a cattle rustler before he got religion and reformed. In fact, nearly everyone in the town Pete came from could trace his ancestry back to some outlaw or outcast. The town had originally been a hideout, a refuge for men who were tired of running and wanted to change their lives. By now it was as decent and law-abiding as any other town. But the old-time suspicion of authority had been passed from generation to generation as surely as the family Bible. It wasn't an attitude the Army appreciated. Pete's entire company had been taking bets as to whether his hitch would be up before he got a Section Eight thrown at him.

Yet Pete didn't look like a troublemaker. With his shaggy red hair, freckles, and free-and-easy smile, he hardly seemed older than sixteen. And there was a gentleness, a quick sympathy in his brown eyes. Yet often it was that ready sympathy that led him into trouble. He was always fighting other people's battles. People had to take care of one another; that's what he'd been taught, and nothing—not even the Army—would change his mind.

The jutting cliffs of the Palisades were behind him now, and he let out a sigh of relief. It was too dark to see much of the passing scenery, but he didn't mind; this part of New Jersey was mostly just a clutter of gas stations, motels, and discount stores anyway. Later the terrain would smooth out to flat wide sweeps of land—that's what he was waiting for.

He'd been away from the land too long, his vision always locked in by buildings and more buildings. That's why, instead of flying, he'd bought this old car for the trip home— to see the land again, to drink his fill of it. The green rolling hills of Pennsylvania, the gentle sinuous curves—like the waves of the ocean—of Nebraska, the pure wide vistas of Colorado. And then the heart-catching climb into the Rockies, and home.

Provided the car made it. The master sergeant who'd sold the car to him, a good friend, a man who'd taken him under his wing, had counseled him to take it easy. Referring to more than just the beat-up car, his parting words had been: "You got to learn to go along, boy—you can't change the world single-handed."

Pete was going to miss the sarge. But he was relieved to be going back where he belonged. He smiled, remembering the welcome home his mom and dad had promised him. The friends and family waiting. The girls . . .

He stretched out his long arm to turn on the radio, hoping to find a country music station. Then he remembered the radio didn't work, either. When he got home, Pete decided he'd give this rattletrap a complete overhaul. He had so many plans, so much to look forward to. . . .

In the backseat, hidden beneath the jumbled pile of clothing, Kendra stirred in her sleep and woke. Her hands clutched at the dark, terrified. Where was she? A sudden instinct warned her to remain silent, hidden. Not to remember; memory was pain, danger. And a bottomless, aching grief she couldn't face. She shut her eyes tightly, struggling against the panic, afraid even to breathe. But slowly the motion of the car soothed her. She was safe in the dark; no one could find her here. A numbing exhaustion weighed down her limbs. As the car sped on, she fell back into a troubled sleep.

Pete was having a hard time staying awake. And he was hungry, too. He was hungry most of the time, but in fact it had been several hours since he'd eaten. Somewhere in New Jersey he'd finished off the ham sandwich and bag of corn chips he'd picked up at his last stop in New York. Now he was about an hour into Pennsylvania. He needed a cup of coffee at least.

His eyes strayed to a motel at the side of the road. But his budget didn't include money for motels—not if he wanted to arrive home with more than lint in his pockets. "Beds are probably lumpy anyway," he told himself.

Cracking open the window a few inches, he breathed in the reviving cold. It helped. He could make a few more hours this way.

But the chill stiffened his shoulders after a while. Without looking around, he stretched his arm over the backseat and felt around for his jacket in the jumble of clothing.

Kendra, halfway between sleeping and waking, was having the same dream again and again. The gloved hand was thrashing through the bushes where she was hiding, clawing at her, gripping her arm in a tight vise. She whimpered, pulling the coat tighter around her in the sudden chill. Something tugged back at the coat. Her eyes flashed open. The hand was hovering right above her. She screamed.

"Jeez-sus H." Pete choked. The car swerved, careening across the lane, bouncing off the road, gravel hitting the bottom like machine-gun fire. He fought to regain control; in the backseat the screaming keened higher, hysterical. At last, brakes squealing, the car skid to a stop. Dazed, his lip bleeding where his face had slammed against the steering wheel, Pete swung around to the backseat. A little girl with blond hair and frightened brown eyes was cowering in the corner.

Kendra had been badly shaken up, but the jumble of clothing had saved her from serious injury. She clutched the coat in front of her like a shield and tried to scramble farther back, as if she could work herself into the upholstery.

Pete stared at her, his face stretched in disbelief. When Kendra saw the blood on his lips she screamed again.

"What the f— Please, I won't hurt you. Hush, don't cry, honey, Please . . ."

Slowly Kendra quieted, though her chest still heaved convulsively. For a moment they stared at each other in mutual bewilderment. "Wherever did you come from? How did you get in here?" Pete asked. But then he noticed the sweater wrapped around her arm, and his eyes widened. A spreading circle of red was seeping into the stiffened wool. The jostling she'd received had opened the wound.

"Oh, God . . ." he said, shaking his head. He leaned over the seat, trying to get closer to see how badly she was hurt. But as soon as he moved, Kendra's sobs rose to a terrified pitch, the tears washing through the streaks made by her earlier tears. It was plain she wouldn't allow him near her.

"I just want to help you, that's all."

She stared at him warily, hiccups punctuating her sobs now.

"Well, we have to do something," Pete said, consciously making his voice soothing, as normal as possible, just as if he were gentling a colt. He had no idea where a hospital might be. But suddenly he remembered the motel he'd passed a few miles back. "We'll go someplace and take a look at that arm, okay? Now don't you worry, you're going to be all right," he continued, restarting the car and turning it around. "I'm a pretty fair hand at patching people up."

All the way back to the motel he continued talking in a low, soothing voice. As much to distract himself as her. He didn't want to think about the questions a doctor would be asking him soon. And the police . . . They sure as hell wouldn't believe his story. What story? Where in hell had she come from? She must have hidden in his car when he stopped at that deli in New York, he realized. He'd been inside at least fifteen minutes, getting his sandwich. That was the only explanation he could come up with. Yet even to him the story sounded cockeyed. He needed time to think, figure this mess out. But the first thing to do was take a look at the child's arm, stop the bleeding.

"Now you stay in the car," he told the girl as he pulled into the motel lot, parking as far away from the office as possible. "I'll be back in a few minutes."

She nodded uncertainly, sniffing. "Where are you going?" As wary as she was of him, she suddenly seemed more frightened of being left alone.

"I'll be right back," he assured her. He pulled a handkerchief from his pocket for her runny nose. "I promise, I'll come back."

As he walked away, he could see her eyes worriedly peering at him through the window. He smiled confidently, but inside he was wondering what story he could tell them in the motel office if they questioned him. He was lousy at lying; already he could feel a wide-eyed guilty look stiffening his face.

At least, he told himself, he wouldn't be facing a large

audience. Out of the twelve rooms that made up the motel, only one had a car parked in front. The place obviously wasn't bustling with customers. Even in the dim, predawn light it was easy to see why. From its peeling paint and rusty, bulging screens to the faded VACANCY sign on the crooked front door, the whole place looked like it was ready to fall apart.

"Now remember, don't say anymore than you have to," Pete cautioned himself as he opened the door and smiled, cheerfully he hoped, at the bony, middle-aged woman behind the desk.

Upon seeing him, the woman gasped, the stack of yellowed bedsheets in her arms fluttering to the floor.

Oh crap, she knows . . . Pete thought. Had the police been here already? Were they searching for him? How many years did a man get for kidnapping in this state?

"Your face . . . what happened to you?" the woman whispered, still staring at him.

He wiped at his face, and his fingers came away crimson. He'd forgotten he was still bloody from the accident. Quickly he dabbed at his chin with his sleeve. "Just a little fender-bender—nothing serious," he mumbled. But his lips were trembling so badly he had to cover them with his hand.

"You're sure you're okay?" she asked doubtfully.

"I'm fine—really just fine."

She nodded, content to go back to her own problems. Stooping as if her back hurt, she gathered up the fallen sheets. "Ain't got a pay phone, if that's what you're looking for."

"No, I wanted a room. You do have rooms available?"

She snorted. "Mister, rooms we always got. Nothing else, just plenty of empty rooms." She seemed to struggle with her conscience for a moment, then added, "There's one of them new chain motels just down the road a bit—you know, with the little paper ribbon around the john and the matador picture over the bed. Most people prefer to go there."

"No, this will suit me just fine." He grabbed the registration form and hurriedly began to fill it out, doing his best to make his writing an indecipherable scrawl. "How much do you want?"

She glanced appraisingly at him, then at the clock. It was a few minutes to six. "Well, I should charge you for the full night. . . . '' She waited to see if he would object, and when he didn't, she added more confidently, "It'll be twelve fifty. But I'll bring you some extra towels.''

"No,'' he said quickly. "I mean, I just want to get to sleep.'' He handed her the money and took the key.

"You don't smoke in bed, I suppose?'' she asked as he started out the door.

"No, never.''

"Too bad,'' he heard her mutter as he closed the door. "Ain't never going to get that insurance money.''

His room, Pete was pleased to discover, was at the end of the court. And when he returned to the car, the child actually seemed relieved to see him. From the look on her face, he could see she'd thought she'd been abandoned. Although she tensed when he first reached for her, she allowed herself to be picked up and carried into the room. She seemed to weigh almost nothing at all.

He settled the tiny form on the bed. She looked so fragile, so pale. His heart ached for her. She belonged at home, with her own people. Wherever home was for her . . . And he knew that somehow he'd have to get her there. Even if it meant going to the police, putting his own neck in a noose. But for now he could see that she was in no condition to answer questions. He'd have to see to her arm first, win her trust. And maybe, if he was lucky, he could get her home without involving the police.

Slowly, with infinite care, he begun to unwrap the sweater. "Just try to stay as still as you can,'' he told her. "I'm not going to hurt you.'' Since he'd been a child, he'd been bringing home wounded animals and nursing them back to health. He had a gentle touch, which she seemed to sense.

He was relieved to see the wound had stopped bleeding. Maybe she wouldn't need a doctor, after all. He dug his scissors and first aid kit out of his duffel bag and cut the rest of the fabric away. Despite the amount of blood she'd lost, the cut itself wasn't too deep.

But something else was bothering him—something he would have noticed right away if he hadn't been so shaken up himself. She hadn't been injured in the accident—whatever had happened to her had happened hours before. Most of the blood on the sweater was dried, caked. Someone had attacked her—with a knife, he guessed, from the way the flesh was gouged. And her arms and legs were mottled with bruises, already purple.

A sudden anger boiled up inside him. Damn. What kind of monster would attack a child? He wanted to ring his neck, snap him in two.

"Who did this to you, honey?" he asked, forcing himself to keep his voice calm. "Tell me . . ."

She shook her head. "I don't know."

"But you must remember . . ."

"Maybe I fell down," she suggested. Her eyes were as honestly puzzled as his own. "Am I going to die?"

"Good Lord, no." Where had she gotten such an idea? What could a child like this know of death? Yet someone had done this to her. Dear God, why?

Deftly, and as gently as possible, he cleaned out the wound and sterilized it with sulphur powder. It would take her a long time to recover; she must have been bleeding for quite a while. And she would always carry the scar. But it was the internal scar—the damage to her trust—that worried him more. No wonder she'd been so terrified of him.

For the moment, he decided, what she needed most was rest, a chance to let her body heal. His questions would have to wait. He pulled the blanket up over her and turned off the light.

"No . . ." she objected quickly, struggling upright. "I don't . . . like the dark."

"All right, we'll turn the light back on."

"And you'll stay right here, too?" she asked.

He nodded. "I promise."

By the time he'd pulled a chair up next to the bed and settled himself into it, she was asleep.

Pete, you're taking an awful chance, he told himself. Why hadn't he called the cops right away? And told them what? . . . Honest, Officer, I never saw her before . . . Sure. They'd weld his jail door shut.

But there was something else holding him back. That desperate look of terror in the girl's eyes. How could he turn her over to strangers, just dump her? She was in a fragile enough state now—that might break her. No, it would be best for them both if he could find out where she belonged and take her home to her own people himself.

At least she was peaceful now. He watched the tiny chest rising and falling in the slow rhythm of sleep. She looked so innocent, so terribly vulnerable. For the first time he noticed the delicate beauty beneath the layers of grime—and remembered Lori and realized she'd been in the back of his mind all along. His little sister, Lori, his favorite among his brothers and sisters. Lori had been sickly all her life; the doctors had poked and prodded and stuck her with needles and suggested countless operations. And still Lori had died before her eighth birthday. Pete had been helpless to do anything but watch.

This girl had something of Lori's sweetness. She hadn't whined or complained at all while he was cleaning out her wound. Perhaps he was imagining it, but he thought he saw a physical resemblence. Lori, too, had had those long, sweeping lashes, that slightly upturned nose, that stubborn chin . . . though this girl was probably prettier than Lori ever had been. He wondered if she'd have the same merry, bubbling laugh—if she'd ever laugh again.

Damn it, he swore, the anger flashing through him. And the thought suddenly struck him like a physical blow. Would he be delivering her back to the same people who had done this to her? No, he couldn't do that. But did he have any choice?

Chapter 4

Colman Talbot Bromley strode through the gaggle of reporters waiting outside the police station, moving so fast they had to run to catch up with him.

"Hey, they find the girl?" a reporter called out.

"Any leads on the murderer?"

"Come on, Mac, give us a break—our editors are breathing down our necks. What's the lowdown?"

Colman halted, glaring at the reporter who was blocking his way, a potbellied man with cigar ash sifting down his shirtfront. Colman wasn't used to being addressed as Mac, but that wasn't what tightened his lips and made his eyes glitter. "Your editors?. . ." he snapped. "A little girl is missing. And you're sitting around here waiting for a few gory details to stick between the girdle advertisements and the football scores. Why the hell aren't you out there searching the streets, helping to find her, instead of behaving like paid ghouls?"

"Then there's been no ransom note yet, huh?" the reporter asked, unperturbed by the attack. Get their hackles up, then they'll talk in spite of themselves. That was the way he worked.

Immediately the other reporters followed up the lead. "Can you confirm that? Will the family pay? Are you from the FBI?"

Colman recognized he'd been suckered. "I don't have any answers for you now," he said, his tone suddenly reasonable, almost friendly. "Maybe after I talk with Detective-Lieutenant Almafi . . ."

The reporters watched him disappear into the lieutenant's office. "'Mac' . . ." one of them repeated, shaking his head, turning to the potbellied cigar smoker. "I bet you'd call the frigging chief justice 'Mac.'"

"So this guy's wearing a four-hundred-dollar suit—so what? Who the hell is he?"

"Lawyer. One of the big guns down on Wall Street. Believe me, he's got all the right connections."

"And no more idea than we do what happened to that little girl."

Detective-Lieutenant Salvatore Almafi was heading up the investigation in the Dalsworth case. His office looked like a bunker under siege. In addition to the mounds of files stacked everywhere, two plainclothes detectives, three uniformed patrolmen, and a secretary were crowded into the small, windowless room. The phone was ringing, but no one was answering it. The secretary was busy taking down orders from Almafi, and the men were gathered around a sectioned map on the wall. "Be with you in a minute," the lieutenant said to Colman Bromley as he entered. "The rest of you, get going—and try to keep the civilian search teams from dragging every girl between the ages of three and fifteen back to the precinct."

Bromley waited impatiently. It had been over eight hours since Melissa's and Joel's bodies were found by the cook returning from her day off. She'd called Colman first, babbling hysterically, and he'd notified the police at once.

His glance fell on the desk, and he averted his eyes immediately, but not before the scattered photographs had been imprinted on his mind. Photographs of Melissa with her lovely proud neck slashed, blood everywhere. He felt as if the breath had been knocked out of him. Melissa . . . but with all her radiance smothered, gone forever. It had happened so quickly, and now it could never be undone.

Against his will, his eyes kept straying back to the photographs. They were so clinical, so matter-of-fact. He remembered the way he'd first seen her, floating down the steps of the sorority hall, dazzlingly beautiful, her pink chiffon dress swirling around her; how her wide dark eyes had been flirtatious and shy at the same time. She'd been his date that night.

And he'd said to himself. "This is the one. This is the woman I was meant to spend my life with."

And Melissa would have married him, he was sure of it, until suddenly Joel came between them. Before Colman realized what was happening, Joel had stolen her away. There was nothing he could do but rage silently. It would have been easier to try to separate a man from his shadow as pull those two apart.

Yet, strangely, he hadn't broken off his friendship with Joel. He knew it was wrong, but he'd always hoped that someday Melissa would change her mind and come back to him . . . especially after his own marriage—a hasty affair, strictly on the rebound—had failed. It had only been recently, when Melissa was pregnant again, that he realized she would never leave Joel.

He was grateful when Lieutenant Almafi at last broke into his thoughts. "Sit down, Mr. Bromley," the detective said, maneuvering a chair through the clutter for him, and settling himself behind the desk.

For a moment Almafi's dark eyes bored into him, impassive, measuring. The lieutenant was a fleshy, barrel-chested man a few years short of middle age, though there were already heavy pouches beneath his eyes. The eyes themselves were as sad as a bloodhound's but harder, with a glint of suspicion in their depths. "Tell me why you're here," he began.

"To help in any way I can. I'm a friend of the Dalsworths. And their attorney. If you're holding anything back, if there's been any contact by the kidnappers, I want to know now."

"Are you representing the immediate family?"

"No, there is no immediate family—just an aunt, and the triplets. Melissa's younger brothers and sister." He thought of Nick and Noreen and Ned, and frowned. He'd always believed Joel and Melissa were too indulgent with those three. "Anyway, I hope you're not counting on them."

Almafi's expression was bland, unreadable. He'd already interviewed each of the triplets, and while he wasn't about to share his opinion with Colman Bromley, he'd been less than impressed with their expressions of grief. He doubted if they cared one way or another whether the murderer was ever caught—or if the girl was found.

"Especially don't expect them to help pay a ransom demand," Bromley continued. "Of course, they'll share—generously—in the estate, but at the moment they're probably broke. They made a habit of living on Melissa's handouts."

"You're the executor of the estate?"

Bromley nodded. "Yes. But as far as a ransom is concerned—if the money has to be gotten together quickly, faster than the legal machinery works—then I want you to come to me personally. I'm sure I could meet any demand out of my own funds."

Almafi stared at the attorney's lean, patrician face, his expensively tailored suit. His watch alone cost more than the detective made in a month.

Meet any demand. Shit, he bet this guy could—and without even feeling it. Still, it was a generous offer. Then again, why was he so hot to get the girl back? Was there some other motive than friendship for the family? Bromley hardly looked like the softhearted type. And the girl had been a witness. The analysis of fingerprints and blood stains in the kitchen indicated she'd been right there. She knew who the murderer was.

The lieutenant had a habit, when he was considering a new angle on a case, of unconsciously tugging at his skin, pulling his round, fleshy face into shapes usually only seen in a fun-house mirror. And now, as he continued to contemplate Bromley, his fingers strayed irrepressibly to his cheeks, stretching the skin. "Tell me, Mr. Bromley, where were you last night?"

Bromley started, leaning forward and then finally back into

his chair. Despite his angry words his tone was even, controlled. "That's a damned impertinent question, and I fail to see its revelance to your investigation."

"I was simply curious," he said. Curious as to whether the question would get a reaction—and it certainly had.

"I should think you'd be concentrating on getting the girl back. And finding the murderer."

"We've got a net of men spread all over the city, searching. Plus we've put out bulletins to the surrounding areas. If she's out there, we'll find her."

Bromley rose. Suddenly he felt exhausted and badly in need of a drink. "I want to be kept informed every step of the way."

The lieutenant nodded. He'd already been made aware of this man's power, and the sort of pressure he could apply through City Hall. So, if Bromley wanted progress reports, he'd get them. But there was a limit to how far Almafi would play the game. When—and if—the girl was found, he had no intention of letting anyone else near her. And that included Colman Bromley.

Long after the lawyer had left, Almafi sat silently at his desk, cursing the rain that had washed away the clues he needed . . . wondering what sort of future Kendra Dalsworth would have even if he did find her. Her aunt and uncles didn't seem to care anything about her, and there was something strange about Bromley's concern. Granted, the lawyer might have been a friend of the family as he claimed, but studying his face Almafi could barely detect signs of grief. And he seemed so certain that the girl was alive when apparently her own relatives had written her off as dead. Almafi tugged at his earlobe and sighed; it was a hell of a case.

"No . . . no, stop. Don't hurt them," Kendra whimpered, her tiny fists pummeling the pillow.

Instantly Pete was at her side, gripping her hand, soothing her. "It's all right, honey. It's just a dream," he whispered. And slowly she quieted.

Pete had spent the last eight hours sitting next to the bed while Kendra slept. He was exhausted and stiff and hungry.

while Kendra slept. He was exhausted and stiff and hungry. His unshaven cheeks itched, and his eyes were gritty from lack of sleep. There were moments when he wondered if he was hallucinating the whole thing. Even his own actions didn't seem quite real to him.

What the hell had happened to her, he wondered again. Where had her parents been? Maybe she didn't have any parents . . .

He saw her stir on the bed and tensed, thinking she was having yet another nightmare. But then he saw her eyelids flicker, then shut tightly. And he could tell from the change in her breathing that she was awake. Good—it was time they talked. Time he took her home. "Feeling better now, honey?" he asked softly.

Her eyes stayed stubbornly shut.

"Playing possum?" he asked, making his voice playful. "Hey, anybody in there? Come on, don't make me talk to myself."

Kendra's eyes opened cautiously. The afternoon sun, filtering through the faded, sagging curtains made her blink. She stared at him as if she'd never seen him before.

"Hello there. My name's Pete," he said with a smile. "You haven't told me who you are yet."

She looked around confused, as if the answer might be written somewhere for her. She knew she must have a name, but then why couldn't she remember it? And who was this man who smiled as if they were friends? He looked like a cowboy with his shaggy hair and red-checked shirt. Except he had freckles—she was sure cowboys didn't have freckles.

"What do they call you at home?" he was asking.

She frowned, suddenly tense without knowing why.

"Sleeping Beauty, maybe?" he suggested, and his eyes were teasing and kind, but still he couldn't get her to talk.

"Well, we have to call you something."

She nodded, watching him timidly. Her luminous brown eyes, so large and thickly lashed, reminded him of a doe. She had that same delicacy, that skittishness. "Fawn," he said aloud. "I'll call you Fawn, okay? Until you're ready to tell me your real name. Is that all right?"

"Good," he said. He just had to keep talking, gradually lead her out of the nightmare she'd been trapped in. At least she'd begun to respond. If he was patient, eventually she would relax.

"Are you hungry?" he asked. "I didn't want to leave to get food while you were sleeping, but I did find this candy bar. It's a little crushed, but I think it should taste okay." He held out the candy bar for her and after a long moment she reached for it, her eyes never leaving his face.

He watched her eat, pretending to himself he wasn't hungry. Neither of them had eaten all day. But her hunger concerned him more. Just as she was about to take the last bite, she stopped and abruptly held out what was left to him. "For you . . ." she whispered. His heart flip-flopped in his chest.

"Thank you, Fawn," he said softly. "That's very sweet of you. But you finish it yourself."

He brought her a glass of water and a washcloth to clean her tear-streaked face. "Will you let me look at your arm now?" he asked.

"It hurts," she said. But she allowed him to change the bandage. She seemed to be puzzled by the wound.

The flesh was beginning to heal, he was relieved to see. There didn't seem to be any infection. She gritted her teeth while he was working, but she didn't make a fuss or complain. Again he thought how much she was like his sister Lori. For a moment it was almost like having Lori back. And he prayed that he'd be able to help her; he couldn't bear to think of this child being lost, too.

"I think it's going to be fine," he said. "But your parents can have a doctor look at it when you get home. Where do you live?"

She turned her face away, suddenly rigid.

"You remember where your home is, don't you?" he asked gently.

She shook her head, her blond curls bobbing back and forth quickly. A dark, terrifying form hovered at the edge of her consciousness; she pushed it away. If she didn't remember, she would be safe. If she didn't remember, maybe it wouldn't be true anymore.

"Fawn, I want to take you home." He could feel her slipping away from him. "Don't you want to go back?"

"No . . . Please, don't make me. I can't . . ."

"What about your parents? They must miss you very much."

"No . . . they're gone . . ." she whispered, beginning to tremble.

"Are they dead? Were you in an orphanage? A foster home?"

She stared at him, eyes panicky. He was going to punish her for running away, she thought frantically. Didn't he know? But grown-ups knew everything. She had done something wrong, something bad had happened, and now he was waiting for her to tell him herself. If she didn't confess he would punish her. She tried to see her mother's face, tried to remember . . . But all she could see was the darkness, the blackness ready to swallow her up. And she knew her mother couldn't save her ever again.

"Please, you have to tell me, honey. What happened to your parents?"

"I don't know . . ." she sobbed. "Gone . . . a monster took them away." Her voice rose in panic. "I don't know."

And suddenly he was holding her tightly, cursing himself for pushing her too hard. "Shh, it's all right now," he murmured, rocking her in his arms, feeling the wild flutter of her beating heart. "I didn't mean to frighten you, I promise I didn't."

Fawn clung to him, sobbing. His body was warm and strong, but still it couldn't ease her grief. She needed her mother's arms, the familiar softness, the scent, the gentle voice, to comfort her. But her mother was gone forever. What had she done to make everyone leave her? Why had they gone and left her all alone?

After a while Pete said so gently his voice was barely a whisper, "Someone's looking for you. They must be very worried."

Fawn jerked away from him. "You won't let them find me, will you?"

"But you can't stay here . . ."

"I won't go back." Fear widened her eyes. "Won't, won't . . ."

"All right." He sighed, holding her close again. "We'll talk about it later."

"Won't . . ." she whispered, clinging tightly to him.

Dear God, he thought, what was he going to do now? Turn her over to the police? They would just haul her right back to whatever she was so afraid of. And she'd run away again—if she could. He thought about her bruises, the knife gouging into her flesh. It seemed more and more likely she'd been in an orphanage. Or maybe she was one of those children shuffled from foster home to foster home, no one really caring for her—just another number in some file. The thought tore at his insides.

After a while she moved away from him and began wiping her tears. Her eyes were wary again. He was all she had, he realized, and that was why she'd clung to him, and yet it wasn't possible for her to trust even him. Not after he'd threatened to take her back.

"Can we still be friends?" he asked.

She nodded, but he could still see the conflict in her eyes. "I have to go to the bathroom," she said.

"It's that door over there," he said, pointing. "Can you manage by yourself?"

"I'm not a baby," she said quickly, scrambling off the bed. He smiled. Well, at least that was a normal reaction. She was getting her spirit back.

While she was gone, he closed his eyes wearily. What was he going to do with her? Right now he was too exhausted to think clearly. Maybe there was someplace else he could take her. He recalled his own eagerness to get home, the happiness he felt just thinking about home . . . What had this girl's home been like that the mere thought of it upset her so?

She came back, making a wide circuit around his chair, and sat down again on the bed. "What are you going to do now?" she asked.

"I was just wondering that myself."

Fawn nodded and continued to stare at him in silence. There was a gold locket around her neck, and as she waited, she nibbled at it nervously with her teeth.

"You know what's wrong with us?" he spoke up suddenly. "We're both just hungry. Why don't I go get us something to eat?"

He wondered if he should bring her with him, but she still looked exhausted. Besides, until he solved the problem of where she belonged, it was safer for both of them if she remained hidden.

"Now, I'll be back as soon as I can," he told her. "I'll see if I can't find a hamburger place close by. You'll be all right by yourself?"

She nodded.

"Good. I'll lock the door so nobody can get in. And you try to sleep. I'll be back before you know it." And with one last smile, he hurried out.

Fawn listened to his steps fade away. She waited a long time to make sure he was really gone. Then slowly, cautiously, she edged off the bed. She knew what she had to do. She was sorry he hadn't understood. He was a nice man, with his cowboy shirt and his crinkly, gentle eyes. But she couldn't let anyone take her back.

Chapter 5

Ned felt like he was suffocating. He hated crowds and was allergic to flowers. The funeral parlor was jammed with both. Melissa and Joel's friends must have bought out half the florists in Manhattan. He stared at the blankets of white orchids—ordered by Colman Bromley—that covered the coffins and shook his head at the waste of money. The funeral had been arranged so quickly in order to minimize publicity. He hoped the lawyer had at least taken a few minutes away from his grief to read the damn will.

The will . . . He was certain Joel hadn't had time to change it. Almost certain . . . Shit, where was Bromley? Ned had to know—today.

A perfectly manicured hand wearing a heavy ruby ring suddenly clasped his arm. "You look so pale. Are you feeling faint?" the black-suited woman asked, leaning solicitously toward him.

Ned blinked, forcing himself back to the business at hand. "I'm fine."

"You're Melissa's brother, aren't you?" the woman continued. "One of the triplets. We met at the party she gave for you when you graduated from Harvard. And of course, she talked about you a lot. She was so proud of you, so pleased when you joined Joel's brokerage house.''

Ned nodded vaguely, searching the crowd. Where was Bromley?

"This must have been a terrible shock to you." She shook her head. "I keep thinking, I'll go talk with Melly, she'll make me feel better—as if my mind refused to accept the fact she's gone for good . . . Any news on the little girl?''

"No," he answered.

"I'm sure they'll find her. Between the police and the newspapers, they're turning this town upside down." She patted his hand. "Is your sister, Noreen, here?"

"Sitting over there on the couch." Holding court, he added to himself. He glanced at Noreen, surrounded by Melissa and Joel's friends. As usual, she had one arm locked around her son Scott, hugging him close. And as usual Scott was trying, unsuccessfully, to wiggle away. The boy, only a few months older than Kendra, looked bored. But Noreen was the perfect image of the brave, grieving sister in her little black veil, daintily dabbing at her eyes. But never disturbing her make-up, Ned noticed. Yes, she was enjoying herself. For once she was the center of attention.

"I'd better go talk with her," the woman said, giving his hand one last motherly pat. "It was good of you to remember the white orchids—they were always Melissa's favorite.''

But Ned didn't hear her; he'd just caught sight of Colman Bromley. The lawyer was just coming through the door, and Ned was startled, and not at all pleased, to see Detective-Lieutenant Almafi at his side. Quickly Ned started across the room, using the large bulk of his shoulders to push everyone else aside.

From a distance Bromley looked much the same as usual—immaculate in his English-tailored suit, his silk Sulka tie, everything about him subdued, conservative, yet elegant. But as Ned reached his side, he was shocked to see how much older Bromley looked today. The strong, handsome, patrician face was haggard. And there even seemed to be more gray in his thick mane of hair.

Bromley acknowledged Ned's greeting with a curt nod,

then went back to talking with the lieutenant. Aside from a frowning glance, Almafi ignored Ned completely.

Without appearing to, Ned concentrated on the conversation between the two men. They were discussing the joint statement they'd just made to the reporters gathered outside.

"Hope you weren't offended by my offer," Bromley was saying. "I just felt I had to do something."

Almafi shrugged. "It would have been better to leave it to the police. A reward like that is going to draw crackpots from all over. The phone lines will be jammed."

"What reward?" Ned interrupted, forgetting his pretense of not listening.

"Mr. Bromley has just offered a five-thousand-dollar reward to anyone who gives us information that helps us find your niece."

"Five thousand dollars," Ned repeated.

"Of course, you—or Nick or Noreen—are welcome to add to the amount if you'd like," Bromley suggested.

"Oh, I'm sure that's more than enough," Ned said quickly, but as he looked at their grim faces, he added, "Of course I'll propose it to the others."

Just then the funeral director announced that the service was about to begin and asked everyone to take their seats in the chapel. Ned saw his chance to question Bromley evaporating.

"Come sit with the family," he suggested. "After all, who was closer to Melissa and Joel than you. It's only proper."

Bromley was about to reject the offer but finally agreed, misconstruing the naked pleading in Ned's eyes.

"I think we should get the practical considerations out of the way as promptly as possible. I'm sure you agree," Ned said as the two men made their way toward the front pew. "You've filed the will, I suppose?"

"That's done automatically."

"There won't be any problems about it—no last-minute changes that might cause difficulty?"

Bromley stared at him. "Surely this can wait . . ."

"I'm only thinking of Joel's company. After all, I have a responsibility no matter how I might feel personally."

Bromley turned away from him, even pulling in his shoulders slightly—as if there were something unclean about me, Ned thought. Well, screw you and your damned superior attitude. I'm going to have just as much money as you ever had. Even more.

The service had started. Ned tuned out the words. He had other things to think about. Again he went over the conversation with Bromley. "No last-minute changes . . ." he'd said, and the lawyer hadn't contradicted him. Bromley was too honest to mislead him. Joel hadn't had time to change the will—or to tell Bromley about the embezzlement. Certainly Bromley wouldn't be sitting here beside him if he knew. Ned began to relax. No one would ever find out about the embezzlement now. He'd make sure of that.

But the details of the will . . . he needed to know the details. He had to be sure he'd been left in charge of the company. Nick and Noreen would be grabbing for everything they could get. He had to find a way to block them.

Thinking of his brother made Ned realize that Nick's place in the pew was empty.

And, as if on cue, Nick strode down the aisle. He was resplendent in a dark cashmere suit, French-cuffed white silk shirt, and gleaming Italian loafers. He flashed his perfect teeth in an apologetic smile at his lateness—as charming and irresponsible as always.

With a shock, Ned regarded the woman who accompanied his brother. She was a blonde, thin and expensive-looking. Ned had never seen her before, and now Nick was helping her into the pew beside him, blind to Noreen's frowns. "Only Nick would bring a date to a funeral," Noreen hissed in Ned's ear.

Ned nodded glumly. Nick's mere presence never failed to unsettle him. Even if they were triplets, Ned had never felt he belonged with them. Nick was handsome and charming enough to get just about anything he wanted. And Noreen was an almond-eyed beauty, glamorous in a hard-edged, rather intimidating way. But Ned knew, if it weren't for his bulk, no one would even notice that Ned was in a room. At least he was a big man, built like a linebacker. But his eyes were a weak, watery blue, his complexion was pasty, and he had a face like a peasant. By now Ned was used to that awkward, surprised pause when people who knew his family first met him. He expected their disappointment, even their pity for him. But it still hurt.

Still, Ned reminded himself, he was the one with the brains. All Nick could do was chase skirts. His brother hadn't even been able to hold on to his job with Joel's company, though Joel had given him chance after chance.

The service was ending. People started to leave. Little Scottie made one more futile attempt to escape from his mother's grasp, but Noreen pulled him back by his shirt collar.

"Aren't you going to introduce us to your friend, Nick?" she asked. Her voice was brittle, and her eyes glittered as she stared at the blonde.

"Of course." Nick beamed. "This is Annette Courtland. I'm sure the Courtland name is familiar to you from the newspapers and the Social Register. Annette and I are engaged to be married."

"And just when did this happen?" Noreen asked, not registering her surprise.

Nick gazed fondly into Annette's eyes. "Just last night."

"Really? I wonder what Melissa and Joel would have said."

Ned wondered, too. Melissa and Joel hadn't approved of Nick's fortune hunting. They'd categorically refused to lie for him. Ned wondered if Annette knew her new fiancé was penniless. But then he remembered—thanks to Melissa's and Joel's death, Nick wasn't penniless anymore. And it even looked as though he might satisfy his lifelong ambition to get his name into the Social Register.

From the corner of his eye Ned saw that Bromley was leaving. He ran after him, calling his name. The lawyer turned around reluctantly.

"I'm sorry to bring this up right now," Ned began, "But Melissa's death has been such a shock, such a terrible loss, I've been thinking of going off for a few months. You know, just to get away from everything. But of course, if Joel left me in charge of the company . . . well, I couldn't let him down. So, if you could just tell me . . ."

He waited, while Bromley weighed his bluff.

"Maybe you'd better stick around," the lawyer said at last.

Ned nodded, as if he'd been forced into a distasteful duty. But inside he was jubilant. "If you think it's best . . ."

"At least until we find Kendra," Bromley added. "I'm sure it'll only be a matter of a few days. The police are expecting a break in the case soon."

"Then we'll just have to keep hoping, won't we?" Ned said blandly.

"Chow's on," Pete called merrily as he opened the door, a large bag of hamburgers, French fries, and milk in his arms. And then he saw the empty room and his stomach plummeted. She was gone. Frantically he rummaged through the blankets on the bed, as if he expected to find her hiding somewhere in the tangle of bedding. He hurried to the bathroom, hoping . . . But it was empty.

"Dammit to hell, she's out there all by herself. Anything could happen to her." He was already reaching for the car keys. He had to find her. And quickly.

He didn't even know which way she'd gone, he realized as the motor sputtered to life. There were no other buildings or houses around—nothing but a hilly, desolate stretch of road. And she was so young. He marveled at the determination in that tiny body. She was willing to face anything rather than be taken back home.

At least she couldn't have gotten very far, he told himself. Unless someone picked her up . . . the thought made his insides curdle.

Turning onto the highway, he drove slowly with his face pressed close to the window, his eyes searching the tangle of tall weeds edging the roadside. The afternoon sun was low in the sky, casting long shadows, confusing the eye, and he kept thinking he'd sighted her, but it always turned out to be a trick of the light. A horn honked loudly behind him. He pulled to the side, impatiently waving the other driver past him.

Somehow he must have missed her, he decided. She couldn't have gotten this far. Was she hiding from him? He remembered how small she was. And her hair was the same pale blond as the winter-bleached weeds.

He wheeled the car into a U-turn. The sun was in his eyes now, blinding him with its glare. He squinted, desperately searching the thick undergrowth. It would be dark soon. He had to find her.

Fawn stumbled wearily through the tall weeds. Instinct had warned her to stay far from the wide, graveled shoulder of the road. It would have been easier to walk on the level surface, but someone was sure to see her there. She was determined not to get caught.

She'd already fallen once, skinning her knee. And her short, bare legs were scratched from the burrs and thistles. It seemed she'd been walking for hours. Yet when she turned around, the rooftop of the motel was still visible in the distance. She trudged on, her lips clamped in a stubborn line.

She didn't know where she was going. She had nowhere to go, no one who was waiting for her . . . Only someone to run away from.

A car whizzed by on the highway. Three children bounced around happily in the backseat, and a spaniel was poking his nose out the window, ears flapping. No one in the car saw her. But once the danger was past her relief was tinged with disappointment. She didn't want to be alone anymore. She needed someone to hug her, to take care of her, to tell her what to do now.

She remembered how nice Pete had been to her. His eyes had been so friendly. Maybe she shouldn't have run away. She turned back to look at the motel, but it had disappeared in the distance. She was all alone. And it was getting dark.

"Alone . . ." The word reverberated over and over in her head, keeping time with her short, clumsy steps. She was so tired and thirsty, and her arm was hurting. She bit her lip to keep from crying. And then she saw it—a small brick house near the road. She noticed the signs out front and the brightly colored pumps. It was a gas station. And a thin, balding man was lounging in the doorway.

She stared, pushing the hair out of her eyes. She knew she should hide, not let him see her. But already she was hurrying toward him.

"Shee-it, what do we have here?" the man said, looking down at her in surprise.

Fawn smiled uncertainly. He had a rough, gravelly voice and his eyes weren't as nice as Pete's, but he did seem friendly.

He glanced around. "You all by yourself, sweetie?"

She nodded.

"What's your name? You live around here?"

She shook her head.

"Cat got your tongue, huh? Or maybe you can't talk . . . that it?" He tilted his head, studying her. And then he smiled. "You're a real pretty little thing, aren't you? Real pretty. And not any more than five, six years old, I bet."

He noticed her staring at the soda machine. "Want a soda pop?"

She opened her mouth to say please, but her throat was too dry for the word to come out, so she nodded again.

"Whatever you want, honey. We're going to get along real good." He dropped a slug into the machine, hit the side, and a bottle rattled out. Again he looked around to see if anyone else was there. "Come on, let's go inside."

"Come on," he insisted when she hesitated, holding out the orange soda to tempt her. She followed him inside and he shut the door.

The small office smelled of oil and grease and stale cigarette smoke. The pay phone was surrounded by telephone numbers written on the wall, and a fly-specked pin-up calender hung over the cash register.

"Let's put you up here," he said, suddenly grabbing her and lifting her onto the desk. He pulled up a chair right next to her, sitting so close she could feel his breath on her cheek. She leaned away from him.

"Gonna be shy, huh?" he laughed. "Here, drink up your soda."

He rocked back and forth impatiently in his chair, his eyes never leaving her, while he waited for her to finish. As she put the bottle down, he noticed the bandage beneath the sleeve of her sweater. "What happened here?" His fingers brushed against her arm, then slipped down to her knee. "So pretty . . ."

Fawn, recognizing a new feeling of fear, tried to slide away from his touch, but she was already at the edge of the desk. She couldn't move any farther without falling off. His hand closed possessively on her leg, and started slowly to move up. "Want to play a game?" he whispered.

She shook her head, frightened, pushing helplessly at his hand.

Just then a bell sounded, startling them both.

"Hey, anybody here?" a voice shouted.

"Son of a bitch," the man swore, quickly yanking his hand out from under her skirt and wiping his sweaty palm against his pants. He peered out the window and turned toward her again, a frown on his face. "A customer . . . I'll be right back. You wait—don't you move."

As soon as he'd gone, Kendra scrambled off the desktop. But there was only one door. How could she get out without his seeing her? She glanced out the window and her eyes flashed wide with surprise. And relief.

It was Pete. He was talking with the man. She forgot she'd been running away; all she could think was that Pete had come to take her away from the man. In a second she was through the door.

"There she is," Pete cried, opening his arms as she ran toward him and scooping her up in a hug. "Thank God."

Tears of relief trickled from Fawn's eyes.

"Thought you hadn't seen her," Pete said, staring hard at the man.

"Oh, is she the one you meant? Sorry, I just figured . . ." He backed up, watching Pete nervously. He held up his hands. "Hey, I didn't do anything."

"Are you all right?" Pete asked her.

"Yes," she whispered. "Please, can we go?"

He nodded. He would have liked to belt the gas station attendant into next Tuesday, but for once caution won out.

He settled her in the front seat next to him, and they drove away.

"You scared me silly," Pete admonished.

"I'm sorry." She smiled up at him, glad to be beside him. He made her feel safe again. He had worried about her, and she was sorry and at the same time happy that he had. "Are you angry with me?" she asked.

"Of course not. I understand now." He turned to look at her. "But I want you to promise you won't run away again."

She wanted to shake her head yes, instead she said, "Will you promise you won't take me back?"

He stared at her for a moment. "That's the deal, huh?"

"I want to stay with you. Please?"

"Fawn . . ." What could he tell her? She had no idea what she was asking. Yet there had to be some solution. And he knew he couldn't send her back. Or abandon her to strangers. He thought of his own home, and slowly an idea formed in his mind. Maybe . . .

But aloud all he said was, "Let's go back to the motel. Maybe after I've had a night's sleep I'll think up a solution. But for now, we stick together." Unless the police track us down, he thought suddenly, and felt his stomach knot.

But Fawn was smiling up at him as if the problem was settled.

Chapter 6

A_s the first light of morning slipped through the motel's skimpy curtains, Fawn stirred in her sleep and woke. Immediately her eyes flashed to the other twin bed where Pete was sleeping. He was still there, she saw with relief. He hadn't left her alone.

They were going to start on their trip today, she remembered happily. He'd promised to take her along. And Pete wouldn't break his promise.

She watched him contentedly for a moment. With his red hair and freckles he looked more like a big kid than a grown-up. He'd been so sleepy the night before. She smiled, remembering how he'd tried to tell her a bedtime story but his eyelids kept drooping shut. But then her smile faltered. He was so quiet, so still. Why didn't he move? She wiggled out of bed, frowning. He'd given her one of his shirts as a night gown, and she tripped over the long hem as she scrambled up on his bed and leaned over him. "Pete, are you okay?"

There was no answer.

"Pete . . . Please be okay. Say something," she pleaded. Determinedly she pried open one of his eyelids.

"Hey . . . what . . ." he sputtered, suddenly awake. "Oh, Fawn, it's you." He grinned. "Hey, what's wrong? You're white as a ghost."

"I thought you were dead, too," she whispered.

He hugged her, folding his long arms protectively around her. "Oh Fawn, honey . . ." What could he say to her, how could he help her? Her world was so filled with violence. The monsters and terrors that other children only imagined had come close to actually destroying her. And as she snuggled close to him, he realized he was all she had left.

"How's your arm today?" he asked, inspecting the bandage.

"It hardly hurts at all," she assured him.

"Good," he said, though he suspected it was more painful than she was admitting. She just wasn't a complainer. He helped her out of bed. "Let's get dressed. It's time we were on the road."

She nodded happily. When she smiled like that her brown eyes seemed to light the whole room. She was such a beautiful child. Someday, he thought, she was going to be a real heartbreaker.

But for now what she needed was a loving home, friends her own age, a normal life with sandlot baseball games, Easter egg hunts, snowball fights. She deserved a world where her biggest worry would be if she was going to be invited to a schoolmate's birthday party.

He laid out her sweater, corduroy jumper, and blouse for her. He'd washed her clothes the night before, even scrubbing the mud off her shoes. He wanted her to start out fresh, as if that would somehow undo part of the damage that had been done to her.

"Can you dress yourself?" he asked.

"Of course."

"Sorry, silly question," he said with a smile. He was pleased to see her so self-sufficient. In the same circumstances another child might demand to be babied. But there was nothing weak or spoiled about her.

Pete paid the motel bill, frowning at how little money he had left, and they were on the road before the sun was fully over the horizon.

They kept to the back roads, and Pete scrupulously obeyed the speed limit and traffic signs. He couldn't afford to be stopped by the police. The time when he might have contacted the authorities, turned the girl over, was past. He had no defense at all now. But somehow that didn't matter. Seeing Fawn smiling beside him, her face so trusting, he felt a sudden wave of happiness wash over him. He'd risk anything to keep the smile in those eyes.

"Getting hungry, Fawn?" Pete asked after a while.

She nodded enthusiastically, her curls bouncing. She was beginning to think of the name Fawn as her own. It gave her a feeling of belonging somewhere.

"Let's stop and get a real meal," Pete suggested. A grocery store might be safer, but there were none open this early. And they'd had nothing to eat the day before but a few cold, greasy hamburgers. Besides, the deserted, rolling countryside they were passing through seemed isolated enough. The few towns they'd driven through amounted to no more than a scattering of wood-frame houses and stores. They seemed to be in the middle of nowhere.

Fifteen minutes later Pete spotted a roadside café in the distance. As they approached, the neon sign out front flashed on. "Must be just opening," he said. "Shouldn't be any crowds, at least."

"Good morning," the waitress called as they entered. She and the cook were sitting in the back booth, finishing their own breakfasts. She waved at the rows of empty tables. "Sit wherever you want."

Fawn chose a table near the window and sniffed the air hungrily. "Can I have pancakes?" she asked.

"Anything you'd like."

"Well, you folks are sure up bright and early." The waitress grinned as she brought them their menus. "Where you coming from?"

"Boston," Pete answered quickly.

"Never been there myself. You going far?"

"Not really." He hadn't counted on such a friendly, inquisitive waitress. Perhaps stopping wasn't such a good idea. Hoping to head off any further questions, he asked for a cup of coffee for himself and milk for Fawn.

While they were placing their orders the door opened and a deliveryman dumped a stack of newspapers next to the cash register, then seated himself at the counter.

Pete stared at the papers with dread. With the car radio

broken, he hadn't heard the news for several days, and he'd had too much on his mind to think of buying a paper. But damn, it should have occurred to him. Fawn's disappearance might have made the papers.

"Just leave the money next to the register," the waitress called as he picked up the paper. She was leaning over the counter joking with the deliveryman, obviously a regular. Pete nodded numbly, grateful that she was too busy to notice the shock on his face. His eyes ran down the page, stopping at the headline at the bottom of the page. "SEARCH CONTINUES FOR MISSING GIRL. STORY ON PAGE 4." Could it mean Fawn? He turned quickly to the inside page and felt as if he'd been kicked in the stomach as he saw the photograph. It was Fawn. She looked a bit younger, but perhaps that was simply her smile—a smile that glowed with complete confidence in her world. Her hair was shorter than it was now, and she wore a delicately embroidered dress with ruffles. But there was no question in his mind. It was Fawn.

Somehow he managed to get himself back to the table, even smiling at the waitress as he passed.

"I think we'd better forget breakfast," he told Fawn. "I'll explain in the car," he added, jumping as a bell sounded behind him.

"Your breakfasts are ready," the waitress called, and he realized the bell had been for her. He frowned. They couldn't leave now. It'd be too suspicious. He quickly folded the paper over, hiding the photograph, as the waitress approached.

"Can I get you anything else? More coffee?"

He shook his head quickly. As soon as she'd left, Pete slipped the paper back onto the table. He couldn't be sure what Fawn's reaction would be if she saw her picture, but luckily she was too busy eating. He stared at the photo again, realizing how these last days had marked her. He wondered if her eyes would ever be as innocent again . . . If there would ever come a day when she'd be able to smile so easily.

The door of the café opened, and three more men entered. Pete swore under his breath as each of the men stopped and picked up a newspaper. And another car was pulling into the parking lot.

"Eat fast," he urged Fawn, forcing himself to take a bite of egg, completely unaware of what he was eating. He'll have to take her back now. They were searching for her. But if he just walked into a police station with the kid . . . Pete knew he should have expected this, and yet all he could feel was a sudden emptiness inside.

He began to read the article quickly, his frown deepening as he read on. Suddenly he understood what the child had been trying to tell him. Her parents had been murdered, and she had been a witness. No wonder she'd blocked it out of her mind. Yet the article puzzled him, too. There was no mention of any other relatives. The only one who seemed to want her back was some lawyer by the name of Colman Bromley. And the police—so they could force her to relive the whole nightmare again and again. They couldn't find the killer themselves; how could they be trusted to protect her?

And what did this lawyer want with her? Why had he offered a five-thousand-dollar reward? He probably figured he could use her in some sort of a scheme. Leave it to a lawyer to try to get money out of a tragedy.

"What's wrong, Pete?" Fawn asked. "Don't you like your eggs?"

He forced himself to smile. "Everything's fine."

And as he spoke it was clear to him what he had to do. He wasn't going to take her back where a bunch of reporters and lawyers and cops could tear her apart. He wasn't going to let her be stuck in an orphanage or fobbed off on some distant relative (if any existed) who didn't want her. Something—God or just dumb luck—had put her in his keeping. He wasn't going to turn his back on her.

But first they had to get out of there. He thought again of the reward. Dammit—for five thousand dollars any of these people might turn them in. He nervously scanned the other tables. By now half a dozen people had their noses in the paper, but so far no one else seemed to have seen the article. At the counter a trio were arguing sports, checking the scores. But at another table a truck driver was methodically going through every news item—and he was on page 3 now. When he turned the page . . .

Pete signaled to the waitress for a check. "Be with you in a minute," she called back.

Pete stared helplessly at the open newspapers. "Look, why

don't we save the rest for a snack," he suggested to Fawn, wrapping up her toast in a napkin. "We'll have a picnic in the car."

The waitress still hadn't come with their check. Please, God, he prayed, just get us out of here in time. If they catch us . . . He saw the truck driver turn the page, and stare right at the photograph.

At last the waitress brought the check. Pete hurriedly scooped out enough money and left it on the table, and in a moment they were heading for the door—right past the man whose paper was open to the picture of Kendra Dalsworth. And then they were outside. But it was at least five minutes before Pete could breathe normally again.

In the café the waitress was leaning over the counter, frowning at the picture in the newspaper. "Did you notice that little girl that just left?" she asked.

The deliveryman shook his head. "I like 'em a few years older." He grinned. "Say just about your age."

"I think it might have been this girl," she persisted, pointing at the photograph.

"You're letting your imagination run away with you. This girl, she's kidnapped in New York, what's she going to be doing in a jerkwater town like this?"

"She's got to be someplace. Why not here?"

"Yeah, she did kinda look like this girl," he agreed, craning his neck to get a better view of the picture. "Nahh, couldn't be. It's just a coincidence, that's all."

"Oh, men—you're too busy looking up skirts to notice anything else. I'm going to call the police, and tell them I saw her. And if I get that five-thousand-dollar reward, I'm going to spend it all by myself, too."

Pete stopped in the next town and parked the car. He checked in his wallet to see how much money he had left.

"What are you going to do?" Fawn asked.

He turned and looked at her, and his voice was very serious as he asked, "Fawn, do you want to come home and live with my family?"

"Forever?" she asked.

"Yes, forever."

"Would they let me?"

He smiled. "They'd be crazy about you. Mom's always saying she doesn't know what to do with herself now that the rest of us are grown-up. And she's taken in other kids before—when there was an emergency at the mine or sickness in town"—though that had always been a temporary arrangement. But he knew his parents would love this girl. And that she would be as good for them as they would be for her. At least, that's the way he hoped it would work out.

Fawn looked up at him, her eyes glowing with excitement. "Can we go see them right now?"

He laughed. "It's a long trip. But are you sure?"

"Yes, I'm sure."

"Okay, then we have to do one thing first. You wait here in the car, and I'll be right back."

When Pete returned he was carrying a large paper bag. They drove to a deserted picnic area and he gave her the clothes in the bag—a pair of boy's jeans and a cowboy shirt—and told her to put them on.

While she was changing he dug his scissors out of the duffel bag. He hated the thought of cutting off all her curls—she had such pretty hair—but they couldn't take a chance someone would recognize her. And luckily, she didn't seem to mind at all.

Afterward she looked in the mirror and giggled. "Now we're both cowboys."

He hugged her, grateful that she was willing to go along with the masquerade so good-naturedly. He'd had to guess on the size of the clothes, and they were at least two sizes too large. It made her look even smaller and more fragile. But she gave him a spunky grin, and his heart melted.

He hadn't been able to resist one other purchase, and now he held it out to her—a fuzzy, bow-tied teddy bear. Her eyes widened.

"Oh, I love it," she said. She hugged the bear tightly. "I'm not going to let anything happen to it." And he knew it was worth every penny he'd paid for it. Even if he had to hock his watch to pay for gas.

And they'd be safer now. With her new clothes and her short hair, a casual observer would be sure to take her for a boy.

Now, if they could just get home . . . .

* * *

Colman Bromley seated himself across from the lieutenant, tossing his Burberry over a spare chair. It was raining again today, and the weather matched his mood. "Any progress?" he asked.

"In finding the child?" Almafi looked glum. "Yeah, she's been sighted—in Hoboken, the Bronx, New Hampshire, Alabama, Minnesota . . ." He picked up a handful of letters from one of the open bags stacked around his office and dropped them disgustedly on his desk. "Here's one from some one-horse town in Pennsylvania. Some waitress in a café wants to know when we can send her the reward." He sighed. "And we haven't heard from Alaska and Hawaii yet."

"But you're checking them all out? One might be just the lead we need."

"We're doing everything we can. Mainly it's a matter of finding a pattern—a few letters that corroborate one another, suggest a trail . . ."

Bromley stared at the jumble of envelopes. "I'm thinking of hiring a private detective."

Almafi nodded. He'd stopped distrusting this man. And he shared his sense of helplessness, the frustration that for all the power they each wielded in the world, they couldn't find one small child. "It's your money, but . . . well, frankly, I think maybe it's too late."

"You think she's dead?"

The lieutenant only nodded.

Bromley stiffened. "And what about the fucking bastard who killed Melissa and Joel? Are you giving up on that, too?"

"Of course not." But too much time had passed since the murder. The statistics proved that if they didn't catch their man in twenty-four hours, they probably wouldn't get him at all. There was only one thing that would change that—if he murdered again. Which brought the child back to his mind again. She'd been a witness. If she were found, the murderer couldn't afford to let her live. Maybe it would be better for her if she were never found.

If she were alive at all . . .

Chapter 7

"We're almost there," Pete said. "Just one more turn in the road, and we'll be able to see the town."

Fawn sat up straighter, her nose pressed against the window. They'd been traveling for two days now—passing through the gently rolling fields of Nebraska, the wide plains of Colorado, and at last climbing into the Rockies. The car was missing on two cylinders. Both she and Pete were tired and sticky and bone-weary. But now the excitement in his voice was contagious.

"There it is . . . ." Pete said, sweeping out his arm to include the ragged collection of wood-frame houses and mine shafts that clung to the steep slopes of the valley. "We made it—Rustler's Creek."

Fawn squinted her eyes, staring. Where was the town? The scene below them looked like a model railroad setting.

"Isn't it the most beautiful place you've ever seen?"

She stared at the evergreens and bare-branched aspen. Spring was still several weeks away in the mountains. "I guess so."

He laughed. "I know it's not New York—but it'll be a lot better place to grow up. You'll see."

And then she laughed, too. If Pete liked it, then it had to be okay.

They started the descent into the valley. "There on your left is the best place to go sledding," he told her. "I'll bring you up here right after the first snow . . . And over there, that's one of the finest swimming holes you'll ever see . . ." Excitedly he pointed out spot after spot to her. All the places he'd roamed as a boy, the memories suddenly flooding back.

They drove slowly down Main Street, with its grocery and saloon and movie house. Pete rolled down his window, waving at people as they passed, and everyone's faces lit up as they waved back enthusiastically. A man sitting on a pick-up truck outside the post office shouted, "Hey, Pete, 'bout time you got back."

"See, it's a great town," Pete said, slowing down to wave to another group of people. "Everybody knows everybody else all their lives."

"But nobody knows me." Several blue-jeaned girls close to her own age stared at her curiously as Pete drove past, and then turned to whisper among themselves.

"You'll make friends," Pete assured her.

"But they're all friends already. What if they don't want another friend?"

Pete turned to her, seeing the worried frown clouding her face. She had a point, she was an outsider. And Pete knew the town was wary of outsiders. "Then you'll just have to win them over, Fawn," he said gently. "Make the first move yourself. Can you do that?"

"I'll try," she answered, but already he could see a growing spark of determination in her eyes. And he knew with her spunk and charm she was going to be just fine. "I'll make you a bet," he said. "I bet in two weeks they'll all be stumbling over one another to be your friend."

"Okay," she grinned.

Pete wondered if he should have warned his parents he was bringing her home. He'd called the night before and told them he was bringing a surprise with him, but he hadn't wanted to say any more on the phone. And it was too late to worry about it now. They were at the house.

A young, pretty woman, her hair as red as Pete's, was sitting on the wide front porch. "Hey, Ma," she shouted, scrambling up from her seat, "he's here."

And suddenly a dozen people were tumbling out of the house and crowding around the car, all of them with the same open, friendly face that Pete had, and the same wide grin. His mother wiped her hands on her apron, her eyes misty. "Well, get out of the car, boy, and let me give you a hug."

But before Pete could get out she saw Fawn. "Who's your little friend?"

"I'll explain in the house," he said, helping Fawn out of the car. He led her inside, everyone talking at once, and for a moment Fawn felt lost in the excitement. Two large, shaggy mutts trailed after them, jumping up and down and barking. It was like a party. Every one of Pete's sisters and brothers, nieces and nephews and cousins had shown up. And they all seemed to want to hug him at the same time.

The house smelled wonderfully of baking ham and sugar cookies. There were sparkling white lace curtains at the windows and lots of plants. Crocheted head- and armrests covered the comfortable, old-fashioned sofa and chairs. Toys were scattered everywhere. Fawn, clinging to her teddy bear, smiled shyly at the children near her own age.

"Welcome home, son," a man said, rising from a chair. There was a tinge of gray in his hair, and he walked with a limp—the result, Pete had told Fawn, of an accident in the mines. "Looks like you've grown up some, boy," he said as he eyed Pete proudly. "Damn, it's good to have you home."

"You don't know how glad I am to be here," Pete said. "I was beginning to think I'd never make it."

"Are you hungry?" his mother asked, gazing up at him fondly. She was a short woman, plump and rounded, and she barely came up to his shoulder.

"I knew she'd be trying to feed you right away." His father laughed. "The whole time you were in the Army, she was afraid they were starving you."

"Oh, Ed . . ." she said, blushing.

"We ate a big breakfast just a few hours back," Pete assured her.

His mother leaned down to Fawn. "But I bet you wouldn't mind having some cookies and milk anyway, would you?" Her voice was soft and soothing, and her cheeks dimpled as she smiled.

"Is it all right?" Fawn asked, turning to Pete.

"Sure, honey, you go with Mom," he said, giving Fawn's shoulder a reassuring squeeze. And a few minutes later Fawn and the other children were settled at the big oak kitchen table with a heaping plate of cookies before them.

"Who is she, some neighbor's kid you offered to drop off?" Pete's sister Kate asked. "I don't recognize her."

"Well . . . uh . . . it's a long story."

Pete's mother returned to the living room in time to hear his answer and gave him a look searching enough to make his ears burn red. "I think we'd all better sit down," she said. As usual, she hadn't raised her voice, but something in her tone instantly cut through the hubbub. Everyone immediately sat down. "Pete, you have something to tell us?"

He looked around at his waiting, suddenly hushed family and for the first time wondered if he was expecting too much of them. How could he make them understand? "Look, I know you're going to think I'm crazy . . ." he began, telling the whole story, just as it had happened. Fawn's hysteria in the car, how she'd run away when she thought he was going to take her home, finding the article in the newspaper. He passed around the clipping so they could all read it. "Her folks are dead; no one seems to want her back but this lawyer."

"That poor, sweet child," Kate said. "It makes you want to cry."

"Yes, we all feel for the girl," his mother agreed. "No wonder she looks so lost. But, Pete, you took such a chance . . . You've always been impulsive, but to bring her all this way . . ."

"Now, Emma, stop worrying about him. He got her here safe, didn't he?" Pete's father pointed out. "The thing is, what should we do now?"

Pete looked at him gratefully. His father was already thinking of the problem as one the whole family would share. But still, that didn't mean they'd be willing to take the child in. And Pete felt he shouldn't force the idea on them. They had to want her or it wouldn't work.

"Well, I think we'd better send her back, and right away," Frank spoke up; he was older than Pete by four years and had always been the more cautious, more sensible brother.

"Oh, you would. . . ." his sister Kate sputtered. "What are you going to do, hang a tag around her neck and ship her to the New York police department?"

"Anyone got a better idea?" Frank retorted. And everyone, it seemed, thought he or she did. Or at least they all had an opinion. Suddenly they were all talking at once, their voices low, urgent whispers so the children in the kitchen wouldn't hear.

"Enough," Emma commanded, casting a stern, motherly eye over her brood. "Kate, it's fine of you to offer to take the child yourself, but you've got your hands full now, especially with another baby on the way. And as for sending her back, well, I just don't know. . . . Anyway, we don't have to decide right this minute, do we?"

Pete sighed with relief. If they could just have the time to get to know Fawn, to see how much she needed them . . .

The rest of the day was an agony for him. At supper it made his heart ache to see how well-mannered Fawn was, sitting up so straight at the table, eating everything on her plate, saying "please" and "thank you" with almost painful conscientiousness. She wants so desperately for them to like her, he realized.

After supper, his father took Fawn on his lap for a bedtime story. And then, just as he'd done with each of his own children, he held up his old gold pocket watch to her ear so she could hear the chimes. For the first time that day her large, uncertain eyes filled with light, and she giggled. And Pete suspected, as far as his father was concerned, the battle was won.

But his mother hadn't made up her mind yet. Pete had noticed how she'd kept watching the girl all afternoon and evening. And he could almost hear the argument going back and forth in her head.

Long after everyone had gone to sleep that night, Emma was still struggling with her thoughts. "Might as well get up," she told herself at last. "Not going to sleep anyway."

Slipping into a robe, she started down the hall to check on Fawn. They'd put the child in Lori's old bedroom. In so many ways this girl reminded her of Lori. "But no," Emma warned herself, "don't start pretending. . . . " This was a different girl with needs of her own.

A dim light still shone in the room; the child had insisted on it. But the bed was empty. Fawn was gone. Emma suddenly felt sick, thinking of how the girl had run away before.

She hurried to Pete's room; he was sleeping as soundly as a rock, his first good sleep in days. And there, curled up on top of the comforter at the foot of the bed, was Fawn—asleep, clutching her teddy bear.

"Thank God," Emma breathed. She started to pull a blanket over the girl. But suddenly Fawn bolted upright, her small body rigid with fear. "It's just me, child," Emma whispered soothingly. "What are you doing here?"

"I had a bad dream . . . I got scared all alone." Despite the warmth of the room, Fawn was shivering. "Are you mad at me? Are you going to make me go away?"

"Oh, precious . . ." Gently Emma smoothed back the tumble of curls from Fawn's forehead and caressed the trembling cheek. "I think it's time we had a talk," she whispered. "Just you and me."

"Everything all right?" Ed asked sleepily when Emma returned, having watched Fawn till she was safely asleep again.

"Do you really think they'll send that child to an orphanage?"

"What do you expect, Emma?"

She was silent for a while, frowning up at the ceiling. "You know, we've got that spare bedroom," she said suddenly. "And we're both still young enough . . . the child needs a home, anyone can see that."

"Can't argue with that," Ed agreed quietly.

"She let me hold her. She put those tiny arms around my neck and clung like she was holding on for dear life." Emma's eyes filled with tears at the memory.

Ed struggled upright in bed, watching his wife closely. "Emma . . ." he began, but she interrupted quickly. "You're the one that's always saying people should help each other, not stand around waiting for someone else to do it. And we could love her—dear God, how could we not? So what's the problem?" She stared at him almost defiantly. "Well . . ."

He grinned. "Honey, I agree. I was just trying to tell you I left some extra money on top of the dresser. Figured the first thing you'd want to do tomorrow is take her out and buy her some new clothes. Maybe a few toys."

"Oh, Ed, you knew all along. . . ."

He pulled her into a hug. "I just know you."

Emma settled contentedly against his shoulder. Suddenly there was so much to talk about, so many plans to make. It was going to take time and a lot of love before Fawn could learn to trust freely again. And somewhere in her memory she would always carry the pain of this last week. Would the child be able to live with that? Or would it come back to haunt her someday?

Chapter 8

An hour before dawn, the snow-covered mountain slopes gleamed palely in the moonlight, and the sky was a deep velvety blue. In the distance, an owl swooped low and rose again, a mouse dangling from its talons. Fawn adjusted her backpack and started up the steep, almost perpendicular trail.

The crusted snow crunched beneath her boots. It was as loud as the beating of her own heart. She could feel the first tingling of fear and reminded herself not to look down. The trail rose steadily upward. Even in the summer it was a difficult climb, but now the snow made every step precarious. Fawn found herself moving almost on hands and knees, grasping stunted pine trunks to pull herself forward. Her boots slipped on a patch of ice—an early melt had partially thawed the snow before it froze again—and she slid back, grabbing for a firm hold to stop her fall. She waited a moment, catching her breath, while the snow tumbled past her and down the slope.

She moved more slowly now. Under her ski jacket, the sweat was trickling down between her breasts. The wind whistled past her, growing stronger. She had almost reached the top. But now came the tricky part. The cliff cantilevered out, meaning she had to swing her legs up and hoist herself over the ledge to the top. For a moment she would be hanging in space. As she prepared to ascend she felt her insides tense and her breathing quicken. The thought flitted through her mind that no one knew where she was. She hadn't even told Gram or Pete. It wasn't fair to make them worry. And she couldn't explain to them why she was continually drawn to taking these chances. It was the one thing that she couldn't talk to them about. But if she fell it would be days before someone found her. . . .

For a moment she was tempted to give in to the fear, to stop now and make her way down the mountain—to safety, to home. But then, with a sudden, decisive effort she began to swing herself up. Muscles straining against her own weight, and the precipice glittering wickedly below her, she pulled herself onto the ledge and rolled away from the edge.

She'd done it. And as she struggled to catch her breath, she grinned. For the moment there was nothing in the world she was afraid of—she'd beaten the fear. She wished there was someone with whom she could share her triumph and her sudden joyous sense of release. But these feelings she had weren't something she had ever been able to talk about with anyone else.

No one else knew of her fear. Her friends thought of her as a daredevil because she was always racing her horses over the highest jumps, spending weeks alone in the wilderness, skiing the toughest trails at breakneck speed. They would never understand the terror that sometimes came to her for no reason at all—even when she was snug in her own bed. So she took chances like these because it was the only way she could think to tame the fears inside her that she didn't understand. If she learned to prepare for the fear, control it, and teach herself that it would pass, then she felt she would survive.

She frowned, remembering the last time it had happened. She and Pete and Gram had been on a weekend trip to Denver. They'd had a wonderful time, shopping in the big department stores and wandering around Larimer Square. The last night they'd decided to treat themselves to dinner in one of the best restaurants in the city. They'd even ordered champagne and Pete had waltzed her around the dance floor, kidding himself about his two left feet. But when the waiter had come to their table to carve their prime rib dinners she had suddenly felt faint. As her heart speeded up, the whole world seemed to shift and grow distorted. She couldn't even hear the waltz music anymore for the rushing in her ears. And each second seemed endless, as if she were frozen in time. She'd forced herself to smile and pretend nothing was wrong. But she felt trapped, suffocated, terrified. Finally she'd excused herself and stepped outside, yet even the night sky had seemed oppressively low and heavy.

In time the attack had passed. And she'd returned to the table, insisting she was fine, that it had just been all the excitement. But she wondered how much longer she could hide the truth from Gram and Pete.

Fawn shook her head, forcing herself back to the present. The sky was beginning to lighten, and in a few minutes the sun would edge over the horizon. She'd have to hurry if she wanted to get the photograph she'd come for. Shrugging off her backpack, she gently lifted out the camera, which she'd carefully wrapped earlier to protect it against the cold and damp. Now she undid the plastic and set up her tripod. It was going to be a beautiful picture, with the snow-covered mountains surrounding her and the first rays of the sun splashing them with light.

Three hours later Fawn was back in the darkroom at the *Rustler's Creek Journal*, developing her film.

"Magnificent . . ." Sam breathed beside her as they watched the print emerge in the developer. He was part owner and editor of the *Journal*. They'd been friends ever since they were both in grade school, and lately they'd become more than friends. Sam was just a year older, a large, sandy-haired man with gently inquisitive green eyes. "I wish you hadn't gone up there by yourself," he said, leaning closer to study the prints, "but these really are fantastic."

"Another unbiased opinion," she teased, smiling at him as she started to hang the prints to dry.

"So I can't be objective with you . . ." he said, nuzzling

her neck. "But this is good stuff—and I'd think so even if you looked like Horace Greeley." His eyes lingered on her blond hair and graceful, willowy figure. "As, thank God, you don't."

"Oh, I've been thinking about growing a beard," she teased. "Thought it might make you take me more seriously."

"Believe me, I take you very seriously now."

Sam turned his attention back to the photographs, selecting the one he thought was best. It was one of her favorites, too. The sun just skimmed the horizon, and the snow-covered slopes glowed gold and pink. "I wish we could afford to print this in color," he said.

"We're lucky we can afford paper. But it'll work fine in black and white," she said. She knew how careful Sam had to be about their budget. Theirs was the only paper in town, and despite its popularity it still was a struggle taking in enough money to produce each weekly edition. The town's population was just too small and now, with the mine laying off workers, things were only going to get worse.

Fawn had been working for the paper for the two years since she'd returned from college in Denver. She was the paper's only photographer, and like the secretary, and Billy the part-time stringer, and even Sam himself, she did whatever else was required. Often that meant writing stories, doing page layouts, fixing a broken press, even soliciting advertising. And she enjoyed it all.

"You know what I think?" Sam said, still looking at the photographs. "I think you should hold some of these back, see if you can't get them published in a national magazine. They're certainly good enough."

Fawn smiled at Sam's encouragement. He was always pushing her to expand.

She hesitated. "I'll think about it." She was nervous about being too ambitious for herself, though she wasn't sure why. Maybe because it would eventually mean leaving Rustler's Creek.

But she was proud of her photographs, and she'd already had a number published nationally: studies of lined, weary miners' faces and their families, and small-town life, and a few mountain scenes. Fawn had a knack for sensing the right moment, the most expressive moment to shoot, and the patience to wait for it. And her pictures always showed great respect for her subjects; their own dignity always came through.

Fawn's personal favorite was the series she'd done on families. It was a subject she returned to again and again: the physical and spiritual resemblances among kin, the subtle ways they mirrored each other. She didn't need a textbook on psychology to understand the fascination she felt, but she knew, too, that her keen curiosity gave her photos an edge that set them apart.

"You look tired," Sam said suddenly. "I'll bet you didn't get more than three hours sleep last night."

"Two. I wanted to be in position before the sun came up."

He shook his head. "Come on, I'll drive you home."

"Sounds good," she said gratefully.

Fawn lived in a small Victorian-style house not far from Gram's. The house was no more than a dozen years from falling down, but the rent was cheap and in two years she'd managed to make it livable.

Stopping his Jeep in front of her house, Sam leaned over and kissed her slowly. She smiled, feeling the warm, comfortable feeling his touch always gave her.

"I could come in," he suggested, brushing back her hair and nibbling along her neck.

"That's a very tempting offer," she said, snuggling closer to him. She was about to say yes, when suddenly she found herself stiffling a yawn instead. "I'm sorry. I really am tired, and I've got that big story to cover tonight. The Firemen's Annual Fish Fry, remember?"

"Right. I wouldn't want you to nod off there and be trampled by a horde of hungry firemen." But his bantering tone didn't quite hide his disappointment, and he turned his face away for a moment.

"I'll see you later, Sam," she said, kissing him quickly. But before she could get out of the car, he'd gripped her hand and gently turned her so she was facing him. His eyes were very serious. "Fawn, don't you think it's time we started talking about getting married? How long are you going to keep avoiding the subject?''

"I don't know . . . I wouldn't blame you for getting tired of waiting. But right now I just don't know what I want. The problem isn't with you—it's me. I feel so unsettled inside . . . I can't explain it."

"Maybe we're too close," he said after a while. "Hell, I'm almost the boy next door. Maybe you can't feel a grand passion for someone you traded baseball cards with. Maybe if you were farther away, I'd look better."

"Farther away? . . ."

"You have too much talent for this little town, anyway," he continued. "Maybe you should get out, test yourself . . . then if you came back, it would be your choice, you'd be sure."

"What about you?"

"I belong here. I've always been sure of that," he said. "And I'd be waiting for you. I'll always be waiting for you."

"Oh, Sam." She hugged him quickly and hurried out of the Jeep before he could see her tears. As she walked up the path she called over her shoulder, "I'll see you tonight, okay?"

Fumbling with her keys, she heard him drive off; and for a moment she rested her head against the door, shivering in the chill wind, the tears streaming down her face. Why did everything have to be so complicated? Why couldn't she just settle down and get married like everyone else?

At last she managed to get the key in the lock and open the door. Two years ago, when she'd first moved into this house, it had been a complete wreck. She'd gotten it for a ridiculously low rent, with the understanding that she would make repairs herself. And she had. She'd sanded the scarred, gummy floors and laid down a clear coat of varnish to accentuate the beautiful old planking. She'd replastered and painted, and even tiled the bathroom. And she'd turned the mud room into a tropical garden that looked as if it had been lifted right from the Riviera—all with paint. It was a *trompe l'oeil* fantasy. She'd painted it herself, not even using a picture for a guide, just seeming to know how everything should look. The effect was stunning; it warmed her now as she shrugged out of her ski jacket and rubbed her hands together. But again she wondered how she'd known what a garden on the Riviera looked like. Because after it was done, she checked at the library, and the plants and flowers she'd painted really did exist. It was just another strange bit of knowledge tucked into her mind that she couldn't account for.

She made herself a cup of tea and settled into a chair in the living room. This was her favorite room. The walls were a warm buttercream, and the room was dominated by a large stone fireplace. All the furniture was of antique oak with hand-carved scrollwork and brass fittings. The light-filled windows faced out toward the snow-laden pines and the mountain slopes in the distance.

But today none of it had its usual soothing effect. Maybe Sam was right; perhaps she should think of leaving. But she loved Rustler's Creek. It had given her an almost idyllic childhood. Fourth of July picnics and catching fireflies at dusk; bicycling to the ice cream stand with friends; skiing and horseback riding and swimming and hiking. And always Pete was there whenever she needed him. And Gram and Pops, too, right up to the time he had died of a heart attack the year before. She was comfortable here. Or was she just hiding? Frowning, she went to her bedroom and lay down for her nap.

By one o'clock she was awake and up. She dressed in a clean pair of jeans and a black turtleneck that emphasized the luminous depths of her eyes. She pulled her blond hair up into a topknot, then hurriedly slipped on a pair of dangling, hand-crafted silver earrings. Pete and his wife, Sue, were expecting her for a late lunch in their restaurant.

Pete had begun working in the restaurant soon after his return from the Army, and now he owned it. Over the years the three of them had gotten into the habit of eating together after the lunch rush was over. Fawn had been nine when Pete married, and from the start she and Sue had been close. They'd even asked her to come live with them, but by that time she was settled in at Gram's. Yet they always had kept a room for her, and she'd spent the night there often.

A few customers were still lingering over the last of their lunches when Fawn entered the restaurant. Pete and Sue were seated at their usual table in the corner. The air was rich with the aroma of simple American cooking—steaks and hamburgers, fried chicken and brook trout and chili. And all of it Fawn knew would be delicious.

Fawn leaned down and kissed Pete's cheek and gave Sue a quick hug. There were a few strands of gray in his hair now, but to Fawn Pete looked the same as he always had. He had been so good to her. She was just sorry that he and Sue hadn't been able to have any children of their own.

"How are you, Princess?" he asked, pulling out a chair for her.

"Starved." She smiled at the waitress ready to take her order. "I'll have a bacon and egg salad sandwich, Betty, and some coffee, please." She hadn't had breakfast yet.

"Eighty-six on the egg salad. Chicken, maybe?"

"That'd be fine." Fawn nodded. "How's your little boy—feeling better?" she asked when Betty returned with the coffee.

"Yeah. Must have just been the flu. He'll be fine—until it's time to go to school tomorrow morning."

Fawn smiled, remembering the times she'd tried, unsuccessfully, to con Gram into letting her stay home from school. Gram had been indulgent with her, but she hadn't let her get away with any nonsense either.

"Drop by the house for a visit sometime soon," Betty suggested. "You won't believe how the kids have grown."

"This week," Fawn promised.

She and Betty had worked together as waitresses each summer while Fawn was attending college. She'd been a bridesmaid at Betty's wedding and thrown a baby shower for her when her first child was born. And now they were both twenty-four, Betty had two children, and Fawn was still waiting—for what she didn't know.

In fact, almost all Fawn's friends in Rustler's Creek were married and starting families. In her weaker moments, Fawn envied them. Their paths ahead were as clear and straight and uncomplicated as their pasts. There were no mysterious time bombs waiting to go off in their futures. No fears that their children wouldn't be . . . normal.

For years Fawn had known there was something horribly wrong in her past. Try as hard as she could, she couldn't remember anything at all of her life before her sixth birthday. And Pete and Gram were obviously reluctant, uncomfortable, about discussing her adoption. In a relationship that was otherwise so open and easy, that would have been clue enough, even if she hadn't had her own nightmares to confirm her worries. As a teenager all she could guess was that there was some inherited illness in her family.

During her senior year of high school, she'd made a determined effort to brace herself for the various possibilities. She'd haunted the medical-journal shelves at the library and taken out every book on genetics she could find. There were so many terrifying diseases that could pass from generation to generation—Hodgkin's disease, hemophilia, schizophrenia . . . It was a horrifying list, especially as there was so little a person could do to protect herself against them.

And as she read of each new illness, she felt the initial symptoms already taking hold. Till at last her innate humor came to the rescue—she couldn't have everything. Even Edgar Allan Poe's heroines hadn't been that doomed. And when weeks later, the romantic white dress she'd ordered, perfect for sad farewells, arrived from the mail-order house, she wore it to the Christmas dance instead.

From then on, she'd lived determinedly in the present. And there'd been one other lasting effect: She felt an even greater gratitude to Pete and Gram. Whatever the secret in her background, they loved her fully. And they'd done their best to protect her from it.

Fawn reached across the table and squeezed Pete's hand. "When the weather gets better, why don't we plan a camping trip?"

His eyes sparkled. "Sounds great to me." If he could have afforded the time away from the restaurant, he would have spent most of the year traipsing around the back country.

Sue nodded enthusiastically. "And maybe we should take Sam along this time, too." Even if she never brought up the subject directly, Sue was definitely on Sam's side.

"Sounds fun," Fawn answered at the same moment a bell began tolling in the distance. One of the mine workers, Harry Logan, his face was ashen with shock, burst through the café doors. "One of the tunnels just collapsed," he gasped.

"God, no. Any men down there?"

He nodded. "Sixteen, we figure."

"Damn," Pete said, the word lost in the sudden scraping of chairs, the rush to the door.

Sue was on her feet, too. "The teams will need food and hot coffee. Let's get it packed up. And put in a couple of bottles from the bar, too."

Fawn slung her camera, always with her, over her shoulder and headed for the kitchen, although the important thing now was to help in any way she could. The photos for the paper could wait.

Fawn and Sam were sitting in the back booth of the Painted Pony Tavern. It was late afternoon, two days after the mine collapse. The last miner, broken legs dangling uselessly beneath him, had been lifted out of the tunnel several hours before.

"Another?" Sam suggested, picking up Fawn's empty beer bottle. He looked exhausted, and his hands were bruised and rope burned from his efforts during the rescue.

Fawn nodded, moving her head slowly, with a slightly exaggerated care. She was already beginning to feel the effect of the beer. Or perhaps her wooziness was just the result of the sudden drain of adrenaline now that the crisis was over. She'd been on the move almost constantly for the last two days. But now the last cup of coffee had been served, the last photograph developed, and she felt strangely empty, tired. Yet she wasn't quite ready to go home yet.

"We got good stuff," Sam said, referring to her pictures.

"Hell of a way to get it." In her mind she could still see the miners' wives standing in the cold, their faces pale and set, as they waited to find out if they were widows. There had been two deaths. She saw again the women hugging each other in a

futile attempt at comfort, the animal greediness for touch when
in pain . . . the men turning away; it was easier to face the
malignant blackness of the tunnel than the women's grief. And
she saw again the men who had survived being lifted out, their
eyes stunned and opaque-looking. The rescue teams had gone
back down into that dark void again and again, clumsy with
exhaustion but gallant in their refusal to give up.

She shuddered. The scene had been like one of her nightmares. She could feel so clearly· what it was like to huddle
in the darkness, waiting for death—to feel alone and abandoned. To Fawn, it was too real.

"Hell of a way," she repeated.

Sam took her hand. "It's over now, Fawn," he said, and
she nodded, but still she couldn't shake the memory of death
waiting in the darkness.

"This the press table?" someone asked.

They looked up to see the two stringers the wire services had
sent out. The two men had arrived the second morning: a tall,
curly-headed kid who kept breaking his pencil point in his nervousness, and a balding, sad-faced man whose red-veined nose
showed he was as much a veteran of the bottle as the news desk.
They'd only occasionally gotten in the way and kept their intru-
sions into the grief of the widows to a minimum. The older
one's name was Aaron, and the younger one's was Ted.

"Sit down," Sam invited, moving over to make room.
Fawn did likewise, and the curly-headed kid sat next to her.

"Thanks," Aaron said, sighing as he settled heavily into
the booth. He already had a glass of Scotch in his hand. A
double. "And thanks for all the help you gave us. A lot of
local papers resent it when we show up. Don't like their only
shot at glory snatched away from them."

"I think any glory belongs to those men in the mine,"
Fawn said. "And to the ones who were waiting. Not us."

The older man raised his glass of scotch. "Good for you,
beautiful. To them, then . . ."

"Are the newspapers going to carry the story?" she asked.

He nodded. "Front page, most cities. It's been a slow news
week. Why?"

"I'd just like the major stockholders to see the effect of
their cost cutting this year."

Aaron drained his glass and leaned toward her. "They will. And you know what sold the papers on the story? Not, I hate to say, my friend's"—he gestured at his companion—"or my colorful, hard-hitting prose. It was your pictures. That shot of that miner seeing sunlight again after thirty-two hours—you're going to make a mint on that, lady."

Fawn felt uncomfortable. She was proud of the shot, very proud. But she'd agreed to let it be distributed nationally not because she wanted to make money, but because she wanted the story told. The reporter didn't seem to understand—these people were her friends.

"You're wasting your time here, honey," Aaron continued. "You could get yourself a nice berth with a national publication just like . . ." And he snapped his fingers. He must have felt Sam stiffen beside him, because he added quickly, "Of course, if you're happy here . . ."

"I've been suggesting the same thing myself," Sam said, but there was little enthusiasm in his voice.

"I'm comfortable here," Fawn said. And to change the subject she asked, "How long have you been in the business?"

"Nearly thirty years now. Started out for the old *New York Herald*—that's gone now." He paused with an old newsman's sentimentality for a folded paper. "Unions keep shooting the papers out from under me. Finally decided the wire services were the safest bet. But I've seen it all in my time. . . ."

And he was off, reminiscing and telling anecdotes, lubricated by several more glasses of Scotch. He was a good storyteller and no one else felt like talking, or leaving yet. In a few hours they were all feeling like old friends.

Fawn laughed along with the rest, the drinks and the relief from the tension of the last few days perhaps making Aaron's stories seem funnier than they really were.

"That's better," he said. "The lights are back in your eyes now. Don't mind me," he said, turning to Sam, "I'm not poaching, so this isn't a line. But, Fawn, you really do remind me of someone. I've been thinking that all night . . ."

"Who?" she asked.

He suddenly seemed to have second thoughts. "Oh, it isn't important. She's not even alive anymore."

"Who?" Fawn persisted, grasping her glass so tightly her fingers ached.

"Melissa Dalsworth." He looked around the table. The name seemed to mean nothing to any of them. "You're all probably too young to remember. It was a story I did, let's see—about eighteen years ago. It made a big splash in all the papers. With your hair up, you're almost the exact image of her."

"Who was she?" Sam asked.

"Wife of a brokerage house tycoon in New York. She and her husband were murdered—never did find the killer. As I recall, there was a little girl involved in the case. Murdered, too, I guess, though her body was never found." He looked at Fawn speculatively. "How old are you?"

"Twenty-two," Fawn said hastily, deducting two years from her age. She risked a quick look at Sam, warning him not to give her away.

Aaron shrugged. "Oh well . . . can't blame an old newshound for hoping for a long shot."

She smiled. "Of course."

Aaron offered to stand them to one more round of drinks, but Fawn said it was time for her to be getting home and stood to leave.

"Why did you do that?" Sam asked as he drove her home. "Lie about your age?"

"Oh, Sam, he was just telling a story to pass the time. And he was half-drunk anyway."

"Doesn't it make you curious, though?

"Let's just forget it, okay?" Fawn said curtly. But she was more upset than she was willing to admit. And the first thing she did when she entered her house was turn on every light in the place.

Fawn woke up the next morning wondering why she'd been so foolish as to let Aaron's words upset her. But the story stayed with her for the next few days, and she couldn't shake it. Every time somebody said she reminded him or her of someone else, she went through this. But this time she decided she was going to find a way to lay these questions to rest for good.

Sunday morning she had breakfast with Gram and Sue and

Pete. Afterwards, while they were still in the kitchen, the women washing dishes while Pete puzzled over the crossword, Fawn decided to get it over with.

"The strangest thing happened," she began, trying to keep her voice light as she told her family what Aaron had said.

Gram was rinsing a plate under the running water, and she suddenly stood frozen, listening to Fawn, as the water continued to cascade unheeded down the plate.

"Gram? . . . I know it's foolish, I mean it couldn't . . ."

Gram stared at her, then turned to Pete. His face had turned the color of cold ashes.

Suddenly, Gram, with a quick and decisive motion, set the plate in the drain and turned off the water. "Let's go in the living room. Pete, would you fetch that little jewel case? It's in my dresser."

Fawn followed them into the living room, suddenly doubtful that she wanted to know.

"Maybe we should have told you this a long time ago," Gram began. Her eyes were troubled and she seemed very nervous. "But we didn't want to upset you."

"I guess we should be grateful to this newspaper fellow for giving us a push," Pete added. But he didn't seem grateful; he seemed miserable. "I wanted so hard to protect you from all of this, but you're grown up now. You're strong enough to know."

He handed her the clipping cut from the newspaper he'd bought so many years ago in the café in Pennsylvania. And he told her how he'd found her and as much of the truth as he'd been able to piece together. "You were wearing this locket when I found you. You were so terrified . . . you'd been hurt. . . ."

Fawn could hardly believe what they were telling her. She felt stunned. And she had so many questions—questions they couldn't answer because they'd never known the full truth themselves.

"Maybe what you should do," Pete suggested, "is go see this lawyer, Bromley. Maybe he can give you the rest of the story."

"Go to New York? . . ." Fawn repeated. She felt as if her life had been turned upside down. Somehow knowing half the truth seemed more painful than knowing nothing at all.

"We'll pay," her grandmother said. "I've been saving up the money for a while, figuring someday you'd need to know more than we could tell you."

"No, I have some money," Fawn objected. "And once the checks for these last photos I sold clear the bank, I'll have enough." Although she was speaking, her mind was a blank. She looked at the newspaper clipping again. There was no mention of any relatives worried about her return. And why had she been wandering in the streets, abandoned? She glanced at the locket, then at her arm; the scar was still visible after all these years. "Do you want me to go?" she asked. She wasn't sure she wanted to go.

"It's your choice, Fawn," Pete said. "But maybe you do have some relatives back there, even if they didn't come forward at the time, try to get you back. How else will you ever know the truth?"

"You're my family," she said.

"Honey, we're never going to lose what we have together," Gram said, putting her arm around Fawn's shoulder. "We're not afraid of that; the love between us is too strong. But we understand that you need more than that now. There's a peace that comes from knowing your own place in the world. I guess we didn't realize we were depriving you of that."

"You'd be going for us, too," Pete said quickly, trying to make it easier for her. "I always wondered if I'd done the right thing, and I don't want to carry that guilt to the grave."

"Guilt? You saved my life."

"Fawn, can you look me in the eye and tell me you never wondered about the people you were born to?"

"I thought you'd be hurt if I asked," she said very softly. And suddenly she knew she wanted to go. Knew she had to go.

Pete hugged her tightly, then released her. "We'll be waiting for you, whenever you want to come back. But maybe that world is where you belong now. At least if you see it you'll know."

C h a p t e r 10

It was a very unhappy trio that sat in Cole's office in the glare of the noonday sun: Colman Bromley, his son Cole, and Fawn.

"Where can we contact you—should we need to?" Colman Bromley asked. Physically there was a great resemblence between the two lawyers; they both had the same tall, rangy build and the same strong jawline. But there was no humor or understanding in the older man's eyes. In fact, Colman Bromley was so lacking in any human warmth as to seem glacial. From the moment Cole had called his father into his office and showed him Fawn's locket, it had been a grueling interview. An inquisition. He seemed to believe she'd stolen the locket.

"Why would you be contacting me?" Fawn asked. "You obviously don't believe my story."

"Is there some reason you . . . hesitate to tell us where you're staying?" There was a nasty edge of insinuation in his voice.

"Balfort Hotel, room four-twelve," Fawn answered defiantly. She set down the glass of Chivas Regal, still full, that the father had almost forced into her hand. A strange bit of hospitality considering his attitude, she thought. Perhaps he'd hoped the alcohol would make her careless, that she'd slip and reveal she was a fraud.

She rose from her chair. "Thank you for your time, anyway," she said stiffly.

Only Cole reached out his hand to shake hers. She thought she glimpsed a hint of, what, sympathy, in his eyes. They were very nice eyes, she realized, and felt a quick regret that she'd never see him again.

Wall Street was a noisy swirl of traffic and rushing pedestrians, but Fawn barely noticed. She was too angry. When she'd entered Cole Bromley's office, she had still not quite believed that she was Joel and Melissa Dalsworth's daughter. The idea was too new, too unexpected. Yet as she answered his father's hostile, rapid-fire questions, two truths had taken hold in her mind: He wasn't able to disprove the story at any point, and more importantly, Pete wouldn't have lied to her. If Pete believed that she was Kendra Dalsworth, then she wasn't going to give up just because Colman Bromley didn't like the idea.

Stepping into the street, she hailed a taxi with such fierce determination that immediately a cab pulled over for her. "I need to go to the library," she told the driver.

"Which one, lady? We got hundreds."

"The biggest."

He nodded. "Forty-second Street." And he whipped back into the traffic, cutting close enough to a passing car to knock the dust off it.

Fawn recognized the Forty-second Street library as soon as she saw it; she'd seen pictures of its high marble columns and twin stone lions out front, and it was even more impressive in actuality. She hurried past the guard and into the high, ornate lobby. "Where do I find the old newspaper stacks for nineteen sixty-seven?" she asked the clerk at the information desk.

Ten minutes later, she was seated at a long, old-fashioned table as one of the aides explained how the microfilm machine worked. He was a young man, wearing a tie but with his shirtsleeves rolled up, and he was very helpful.

Pete had told her that he'd found her on the ninth of April, so Fawn started with the papers dated several days before that. She turned the dial, flipping past stories of muggings and protest marches and rock concerts. There were ads for everything imaginable, all at unbelievably low 1967 prices. But there was no mention of Melissa and Joel Dalsworth.

At that moment, Colman Bromley was being ushered into Captain Salvatore Almafi's office at One Police Plaza. He was carrying, very gingerly, a brown bag. "Thank you for seeing me right away," he said as he took a seat.

"You said you might have some new information on the Dalsworth case? . . ." Almafi responded. The case still rankled in his mind—it had been one of his few failures—and he was having trouble restraining his curiosity. His gaze fastened on the paper bag that Bromley set carefully on his desk.

"You still have Kendra Dalsworth's fingerprints on file, don't you?"

"Sure, we keep everything when it's an unsolved murder case."

"Then can you have someone analyze this?" Bromley took a glass out of the bag, careful to handle it only by the rim. "It should have at least one set of clear fingerprints on it."

"Holy Mother, you've found her?" Almafi fairly leaped out of his seat. "After all these years?"

"Perhaps. Probably she's just a very clever con artist."

Almafi doubted Bromley believed that; if the lawyer really thought the girl was an imposter he wouldn't be so nervous. And there was something else that was puzzling Almafi. He felt certain Bromley would have chosen to keep the girl's reappearance a secret. "Why did you come to me?"

"It was my son's idea. He thought this would be the quickest way of confirming the girl's identity."

"And maybe you thought I'd find out about it sooner or later anyway?" the captain suggested, tugging thoughtfully at his earlobe.

Bromley nodded. He hadn't been able to convince the girl or his son of the need for secrecy. But his son was probably right. Almafi was bound to get wind of the situation; maybe she'd even come to him herself.

"What's she like?"

"Beautiful . . . maybe even more beautiful than Melissa." He frowned, reining in his thoughts. "I mean, the facial configuration is right, I can see traces. . . . And she's got Joel's temper. But then, maybe it's only a coincidence. Or a clever make-up job, even plastic surgery. Some people would go to any lengths to get their hands on that money.''

''Well, let's find out one way or the other.'' Almafi hurriedly gave orders for his secretary to have the Dalsworth case file pulled and sent to the lab and a block of time frozen for the test. Then the two men strode down the hall together. ''If she is Kendra Dalsworth, I want to talk with her right away.''

Bromley scowled. ''She doesn't remember anything from that night.''

''I still want to talk with her. She's my only chance to catch the killer. If you won't cooperate, then . . .''

''All right,'' Bromley agreed reluctantly. ''But give her a few days first. And for God's sake, keep it out of the newspapers.''

''Of course. We're not the only ones who know she was a witness—the killer knows, too,'' Almfafi assured him grimly.

The motion of the microfilm was making Fawn feel slightly sick. And it didn't help that her nerves were tying her insides in knots.

And then she found what she'd been looking for. ''WEALTHY GARDENS COUPLE FOUND MURDERED'' the headline screamed. And below was a photograph of Melissa and Joel. She knew it was they immediately, even before she read the story, recognition thudding into her so hard she felt as if the wind had been knocked out of her. For a long time she stared at the picture. Melissa's blond hair was arranged for evening in a graceful cascade of curls, and there was a sparkling necklace of diamonds at her throat. She was a stunningly beautiful woman. But it was her eyes that held Fawn, the gentle smile and tenderness in them. Joel had his arm protectively around his wife. He seemed to radiate vitality and confidence and an unquenchable love of life. They looked like the perfect couple.

Gazing at the image of her father, Fawn could remember his eyes, teasing, merry, filled with love, looking into hers. She stroked the cold, unyielding screen, remembering warm flesh. A tear slid down her cheek. And then she was crying unstoppably; the tears that had been pent up inside her for so many years suddenly spilling forth. She ran for the rest room, unaware of the curious eyes that followed her.

Why? she asked herself. Why should they have died? How could God have been so cruel?

For a long time she leaned against the tiled wall, clasping her arms tightly around herself, mourning the touch she would never feel again. At last her tears slowed, leaving her with a cold eddy of grief inside. She splashed her face with water and combed her hair, and as she stood before the mirror, she thought for an instant she glimpsed Melissa—and then realized it was herself.

Fawn understood now that Pete had been right; Melissa and Joel were her connection to the world, and she needed to acknowledge that link. She had to learn what she could about them. Already she felt so close to them both. Yet she realized with a start that she still knew nothing, could remember nothing about these people. She was flesh of their flesh, yet they were strangers to her. She needed to know exactly what had happened the night they'd been killed. According to the lawyers she did know. But, until she could force herself to remember, the newspaper files were the only source of information she had.

Fawn left the rest room with a quick, determined stride. She had a lot of work to do this afternoon. As she sat down at the microfilm machine again, and saw those doomed, innocent faces, so ghostly in the light, smiling up at her, she thought she was going to be ill. With the aid of her newspaper training, she forced herself to put emotion aside. She took the notebook she always carried by habit out of her purse and began making notes.

She read that Melissa and Joel had been married for eight years. There were no other children. Joel's family dated back to the Revolution, and Melissa's father had been involved in a bankruptcy scandal while she was still a child. The police were guessing that the murders had occurred during a botched kidnapping attempt, or perhaps the murderer had been a burglar surprised in the act. Or maybe he was just a psycho. The police seemed to have a lot of theories, but not much else. No fingerprints of the killer, no witnesses—except her.

She turned her head away, shaken. Now she knew what had tormented her all these years. She'd seen it happen. But wasn't there some way she could have stopped it, gone for help? How could it be that she'd lived and they'd died?

She stared at the scar on her arm, feeling hopelessly guilty, resolved to discover the truth.

And then Fawn read something that made her gasp. At first she thought it was a typographical error. Or a newsman's fantasy hype. Quickly she searched through the next day's paper, and there it was again: "The Dalsworth estate is estimated by reliable sources to be in excess of forty million dollars".

Fawn sat back, the figure wavering before her eyes. Forty million dollars. In excess of forty million. No wonder the story had been such big news. And no wonder everyone assumed she'd been kidnapped. But who had gotten the money? Could it have been the motive for the murders?

She turned the dial, flipping to the next day: the day of the funeral. There was a photograph of Colman Bromley; he looked much younger, but his face was a mask of exhaustion and grief. Despite her earlier anger, she softened at the sight of him; he'd obviously been badly shaken by the deaths. Next to him was a stocky, black-haired police lieutenant who evidently was in charge of the case. But it was the second photo that held her interest, and for a long time she stared at the picture of the three people emerging from the funeral home—Melissa's two brothers and her sister. Their faces were decorously arranged in expressions of mourning, yet Fawn felt a strange sense of uneasiness looking at them. She shook off the feeling. These were her only blood relatives. Here was a living link to Melissa and Joel.

She felt a gentle touch on her shoulder and jumped. "The library's closing now," the young man explained almost apologetically.

Fawn looked around; everyone else was already heading for the door. She'd been too lost in concentration to notice. "Yes, I'm sorry. I'll leave."

He caught the chagrin in her voice. "We'll be open again tomorrow," he said. "And I'll keep all this stuff handy for you, if you want to come back."

"Thanks. I will." She stood up, refocusing her eyes after the fuzzy whirl of the microfilm. The young man touched her elbow for a second, as if to steady her.

"There's a coffee shop a block away. I'll be done work in

a few minutes." His ears reddened, and he hurried on. "I could buy you a cup of coffee . . . maybe dinner?"

She smiled. "Thank you, but no. I really need to be alone now."

The library was only a dozen blocks from her hotel, but Fawn decided against returning to the hotel immediately. She was too filled with conflicting emotions to sit quietly in her hotel room. Besides, she thought best while she was walking.

She turned left on Fifth Avenue, heading uptown into the flood of pedestrians hurrying home and soon found she was matching her steps to their brisk, almost frantic pace. In Rustler's Creek, no one moved that fast unless there was a fire. Yet it was pleasant to be caught up in the general bustle.

The sun was just setting and the streetlights going on. She passed Saks Fifth Avenue, Cartier, Tiffany, and a host of pricey, elegant boutiques. Peddlers had spread their wares out on the sidewalks—sunglasses, purses, paintings, umbrellas—and called to her as she passed. It was like a carnival ground. Yet she walked on, hardly seeing any of it. She was too busy thinking of the photograph of the three people on the steps of the funeral home. Her aunt and uncles. It seemed strange to think of them in that way. She wondered how soon she could meet them. But she was hesitant to just appear on their doorstep—even if she'd known where to find them. Perhaps she should write first. But would they believe her any more than Colman Bromley had?

Colman Bromley had left Captain Almafi's office in a state of near shock. He still didn't understand how the child had survived, but somehow she had and it was time to accept that.

As soon as he'd conferred with Cole, Bromley asked his secretary to set up an appointment at the Dalsworth house for that evening. Bromley wanted all three of them—Nick, Ned, and Noreen—together when he gave them the news. But Nick couldn't be found. Apparently he'd left his office early and no one knew where he could be reached.

In fact, Nick was still sitting in the private executive garage of the Dalsworth Building. He was slumped down in the seat of his new Alfa Romeo, and despite the evening chill, his burgundy blazer was stained with sweat. He felt sick, and the scent of his cologne, thick in the closed car, was only adding to his nausea.

He crumpled a note between his fingers. But its crude block lettering was still imprinted on his mind: TOMORROW IS YOUR LAST DAY TO GET THE MONEY. REMEMBER I CAN ALWAYS SELL THE TAPES ELSEWHERE. IT'S YOUR FUNERAL. The note had come in a black-edged envelope, like an old-fashioned mourning card. Evidently his blackmailer had a sense of humor. And he'd enclosed a photo of Nick entering a motel room with another man's wife.

Nick glanced at his Piaget watch. It was too late to get to the bank today. This was the second demand; the first he'd ignored, hoping it was a joke.

He'd found the first note a week ago—sent in a black-edged envelope—among his morning mail at the office. It was marked "personal and confidential" and there was no return address. The message was short, but succinct:

Fools die young. Especially if they fool with a certain man's wife. I have videotapes of you and the lady, at the Madison Motel. You have five days. Go to the bank and withdraw twenty-five thousand dollars and wait.

A silly, juvenile letter. Nonetheless, Nick had sloshed coffee all down his shirtfront when he read it. And he'd blithered around the office all morning, and returned from lunch so soused Ned had sent him home.

But then he decided to ignore the note. It was Nick's favorite way of dealing with trouble, and in the main he found it worked very well. Either the problem went away on its own, or someone else eventually was forced to deal with it.

But obviously this problem wasn't going away. And there was no one else who could fix it for him.

And how had the blackmailer known he hadn't withdrawn the money from the bank? That's what frightened Nick most. And then another thought occurred to him: Somehow the man had managed to get into his car and deposit the note on the dashboard. Nick's car was always locked, and access to the garage was restricted. What if the blackmailer had planted a bomb while he was there, too? Nick scrambled out of the car and yanked open the hood. Everything seemed all right, but then what did he know about the inside of a car? Cars were a mystery to him. He would buy one, run it till it started to fall apart from the abuse, then buy another. He jiggled a few wires, feeling like a foolish matron, then gave it up and climbed back into the driver's seat.

There wouldn't be a bomb, he decided. Not yet. The blackmailer wanted to play him for a while, make him sweat, get his money. Nick wondered if the real aim, however, was to torment him, not to extort money. The people he'd antagonized—it was a long list—didn't need a paltry twenty-five grand.

Nick's car phone buzzed, and he jumped. He didn't feel like talking with anyone. It was probably just Jolene, anyway. By now he should have been in her arms, feeling the tantalizing musky smoothness of her skin, with those incrediably long legs wrapped around his waist. Hearing her whimpers. He shook his head. Sex just turned his stomach at the moment. He wished fervently he'd never met Jolene.

He glanced again at the jewelry case on the seat. It was from Cartier—topaz and brilliants to match Jolene's smokey, scintillating eyes. He prided himself on his ability to always pick the right gem for each of his women. It was how he categorized them—sapphires for Priscilla, pearls for Beth, tourmaline for Babette . . .

God, there'd been so many . . . All married, all the wives of men who thought they were better than he was. Powerful men. But he'd vanquished each, before the man even understood that there was a contest. And as a sign he'd won, he always, the last time he slept with her, gave the wife a "small remembrance."

It gave Nick a special kick to be at a charity ball, or the race track, or a gallery opening, and see his jewels around a woman's neck. Her hand might be on her husband's arm, she might be staring adoringly into his eyes, but the brand she wore was Nick's. She knew; Nick knew. He smiled. At one especially memorable cotillion, no fewer than five women in the room had been wearing his emblem.

Nick quickly brought himself back to reality. He'd been a fool. He'd known Jolene's husband was "connected": His name was prominently featured in Senate subcommittee hearings, printed in the newspapers as a "reputed mob boss," and mentioned in connection with half a dozen unsolved murders. This was the man Nick had chosen to humiliate.

He was an idiot, and he'd have to pay the twenty-five thousand. Even a public disclosure of this escapade would be enough to shake his position in society, and to Nick that thought was almost as frightening as the idea of what Jolene's husband would do to him if he found out. He'd pay, and somehow try to get hold of the videotape. But he doubted the blackmailer would be satisfied with just one payment. No, he'd probably have to keep paying until he could figure out a way to effect a more permanent solution.

Thank heavens August was only five months away; then he'd have all the money he'd need. His share of the trust. In the meantime, he'd have to manage somehow. For years Nick had been living far beyond his income. There'd been the houses, the cars, two disastrous divorce settlements. And he'd had to buy his way onto the best charity committees and into the best clubs. A bitter frown crossed his face. After Melissa's and Joel's deaths, he'd thought at last he'd have everything he'd always wanted. But it hadn't worked out that way.

Well, when the fucking trust was dissolved, he'd have millions to play with. And he'd find a way of making sure the blackmailer got none of it.

The car phone sounded again, and this time he picked it up, just to escape his own thoughts.

"Nick, you've got to get home right away. Now. " It was Noreen, and her voice was an hysterical whisper.

"What's wrong?" he asked, not bothering to hide his irritation. It was probably just something about her son, Scott, getting in trouble again, he assumed.

"Bromley's here, and he says he's found Kendra."

"No. He can't have . . ."

"Just get back here, and as quickly as you can."

C h a p t e r   11

The hotel lobby was jammed with tourists, but Fawn barely saw them as she walked in. She was staring at Cole Bromley, settled in a chair in the lobby waiting for her.

"More questions?" she asked, frowning, remembering the hostile grilling his father had put her through and becoming angry all over again. "Did you bring your rack along? Or did you just plan on pulling out my fingernails one by one?"

"I knew you'd be happy to see me," Cole said, smiling. But then he added more seriously, "Actually, we do owe you an apology; that's one of the reasons I'm here."

"Please, let's just forget it." She looked away from his warm blue eyes, wishing things had turned out differently— wishing they could have been friends. She badly needed a friend right now. "It doesn't matter anyway," she said. "I'm just going to do it on my own."

She started to walk away, and he reached for her arm. "Kendra . . . Fawn . . ."

She stopped, confused and wary. He was standing so close to her she could smell the clean, masculine fragrance of his cologne, and the scent of his skin. His hand on her arm was very gentle, but insistent. "Please, just listen to me. . ." he began.

"Maybe we should go somewhere else to talk," Cole suggested, glancing around the busy lobby. "Someplace more private . . ." He stopped, noticing how pale Fawn had turned. "What's wrong . . . are you going to faint?"

Fawn shook her head, but she had to lean against the wall for support. Everything seemed to be spinning, and there were colored spots floating in front of her eyes. "I just stood up too quickly," she said. But she felt horribly woozy. The day's events and the lack of food were beginning to catch up with her.

"Come on, I'll take you up to your room." He put his arm protectively around her shoulder, holding her tight.

She let herself be led into the elevator. "Fourth floor . . . Really, I'm all right," she protested, embarrassed.

He didn't argue, but at the door he took her key and opened the door himself, then gently guided her to the nearest chair.

"Really, I'm fine. . . ." she insisted as he brought her a glass of cold water from the bathroom.

"It's been a rough day for you."

And he'd been partly responsible for that fact, she thought to herself. She tilted her head up defiantly, expecting another cross-examination. "Why are you here?"

Cole sat down on the bed facing her. They were so close their knees were almost touching, and for a moment he remembered what she'd felt like in his arms. But he forced his mind back to business. There was too much at stake for him to allow his feelings to get in the way. "Today, after you left, my father and I did some checking on your background."

"But why? You both made it quite plain you thought I was lying."

"Can you blame us for being cautious? But you remember that glass of Scotch my father gave you in the office? He took it to police headquarters and had the prints analyzed. Meanwhile I went through the old files, and even spoke with the goldsmith who'd made your locket. Everything corroborated your story; you really are Kendra Dalsworth."

"That news must have pleased your father," she suggested wryly.

"You don't understand; he's not your enemy. It's just that he's waited so long for you to come back. He was afraid to believe it was true. He was forcing himself not to hope, not to be taken in by false sentiment."

Fawn searched Cole's face, wondering if he was telling the truth. Perhaps he really believed what he said. But even if Cole didn't question his father's motives, she still did. She couldn't help feeling there had been something else behind the older lawyer's reaction to her claims.

Cole realized she was still wary of him. "I brought a peace offering," he said, opening his briefcase and handing her a framed photograph. "This is from my father's office. We thought you'd like to have it."

Fawn stared at the picture, holding it so tightly her fingers whitened. It was Melissa and Joel at the beach, barefoot, both wearing white duck pants rolled up to their knees and T-shirts. The wind was blowing through Melissa's hair, and both of them were tanned and laughing. And between them, one tiny hand clasping each of theirs, was a small, tousle-haired child, giggling happily. "Is that me?" she asked.

Cole nodded.

"Where was this taken?" She didn't even remembered being at the ocean.

"Your family's beach house—out in the Hamptons. It was on the Fourth of July. Our houses were next to each other, and we always celebrated the holiday together with a big picnic. You and Melissa were both crazy about fireworks, so Joel always arranged a big private show for you and invited the neighbors from miles around."

"Our own fireworks?" Then she remembered reading that her parents were rich. But no matter how hard she concentrated she couldn't bring back the memory of that Fourth of July. She felt a terrible, searing sense of frustration. Somewhere there had to be a key that would allow her to unlock the past. "We all look so happy," she whispered, still staring at the photograph.

"You were. When I was a kid I used to spend as much time as I could at your house because Melissa had a way of making everything seem wonderfully funny and exciting. I think everyone loved her. Both your parents were very special people.''

"Why didn't the police ever find whoever killed them? Certainly there must have been some way to track the killer down, a witness who saw something . . .''

He gently took her hand. "Only you. And that's why it's so important for you to tell us anything you might remember.''

Fawn shook her head, guilt flooding her. She couldn't remember. She couldn't help them then, couldn't now.

"Fawn," he said sharply, reading her thoughts, "don't blame yourself. You were a child for heaven's sake. It's a miracle you were able to escape.''

"By running away, saving myself," Fawn voiced her thoughts.

"You were six years old. There was nothing you could have done to prevent their deaths.''

"But the murderer's still out there somewhere, Cole. That's my fault.''

"None of it is your fault." He sighed, realizing he couldn't convince her. "Maybe in time you'll remember something . . .''

"I have to." She said fiercely. "I owe them that.''

"Well, in a few days the police will come by and talk with you. "You'll be able to go over it with them.''

She nodded. "And I want to read the police records, too. That might help.''

"I don't think that would be a good idea, Fawn, even if the police would allow it. Why don't you just let them handle it?''

"Well, they haven't done a very good job of it so far, have they?''

Cole frowned. "We'll talk about it some other time. Why don't we concentrate on the good things now? After all, you're home again." He smiled and smoothly changed the subject. "Have you eaten dinner yet?''

"Actually, I haven't even eaten breakfast yet," she admitted.

"Breakfast? No wonder you nearly fainted. Where would

you like to go? Twenty one, Windows on the World, the Four Seasons?''

Fawn hesitated. Why was Cole suddenly acting so friendly? It was such an abrupt about-face she couldn't help questioning his sincerity. When had she stopped trusting people?

''I'll take you anywhere you'd like,'' he offered, waiting for her to choose.

''Just someplace quiet. And quick.'' Even if she didn't trust him, at least by having dinner with him she'd have a chance to question him about her family. Right now he was her only source of information. Besides, now that the subject of food had been raised, she realized she was famished.

''How about right here? Room service?''

She nodded. ''I think I'd like that best. The menu is next to the phone.''

By unspoken agreement, they both avoided the emotional subject of her past during dinner.

''So,'' he said pouring her a cup of coffee, ''what have you seen of New York so far?''

''Not much—I've only been here one day.''

Cole launched into a description of all the things there were to see and do in the city. Broadway and Lincoln Center. The South Street Seaport. The nightclubs and museums. SoHo and NoHo and the Village and Chinatown and Little Italy. He talked as if he would be the one to show her the city.

''I don't think I'll be here long enough to see half of all that,'' she objected, shaking her head and feeling slightly overwhelmed.

By the time they'd finished their hamburgers Fawn felt herself beginning to relax a bit. Despite her misgivings, it was difficult not to like Cole. He was perceptive and witty and sensitive. But she had to be careful not to let herself be lulled by those deep blue eyes and that wide, handsome grin of his.

''Where were you all these years?'' he asked suddenly. ''Whom were you living with?''

All Fawn's wariness returned into a rush. ''I don't want to talk about that.''

''Was it as bad as all that?'' he pushed.

''What are you imagining—that I spent my childhood

blacking boots or some other horror out of Dickens? I had a marvelous childhood. And a family anyone would have felt lucky to be part of.''

He looked at her speculatively, obviously not convinced. But he had to admit, ''Well, you seem to have turned out all right.''

''Thank you.'' She smiled. ''That seemed to be a compliment.''

''It was. In fact, you've turned out spectacularly. But you'll have to forgive me if I believe it wasn't due to the people who stole you away.''

''Cole,'' she cautioned, her voice suddenly sharp, ''please don't.'' Had all his friendliness only been a calculated ploy to get her to let down her guard? She couldn't be sure. But as long as there was so much suspicion about her disappearance, she couldn't tell him or anyone else about Gran and Pete. She had to protect them. Once the murderer was discovered, perhaps everything else could be explained, too. Until then, she couldn't put Pete in danger.

Suddenly she remembered all the questions she needed to ask. ''I read about Melissa's brothers and sister in the old newspapers today,'' she said. ''I want to meet them. Are they still here in New York?''

Cole nodded, thinking how the triplets had immediately moved in after their sister's death and taken over her parents' house. It would have taken dynamite to get them out. ''In fact, my father is with them tonight. He thought he should break the news in person.''

''Break the news? I don't exactly hear champagne corks popping in that phrase.'' A frown darkened her eyes. ''I suppose my coming back will be a surprise for them. I guess in my pleasure that they existed I forgot: I'll be reminding them of a dreadful time.''

''Maybe they'll be pleased, too,'' Cole said. And maybe tigers will start eating at vegetarian restaurants, he thought silently. But perhaps he was letting his own dislike for them color his judgment.

''You have to understand,'' he told her, ''The situation is . . . complicated.''

''How?''

"Basically, it's the money."

"I don't want anything from them, not financially," she said emphatically, her chin tilting up.

"But it's your money. It was left to you. They each got a healthy bequest, but the bulk of the estate was left in trust for you." He went on quickly to explain the trust arrangement. Each of the triplets was a trustee, along with his own father. The money had been in their control, and they had been managing it all this time. Nick was the president of her father's brokerage house and Noreen worked there, too, but it was Ned who actually ran the operation. Now that Fawn was back, however, it would all be hers—as soon as she reached her twenty-fifth birthday, which was only a few months away. At that time the trust would expire, and she would assume control of the assets. She could do anything she wanted with the money, and as long as she kept her shares, she would be the brokerage house's major stockholder.

Fawn listened silently, still unable to believe it could be true. "I just can't grasp it," she said, shaking her head, when he had finished. "It's just too abstract, too much money." She hadn't made much money working at the paper, but it hadn't really mattered because no one in Rustler's Creek was wealthy. All she could think of was that from now on she wouldn't have to worry about meeting her rent payment on her house.

Cole smiled. "Let's put it this way," he said. "Did you see something you liked in any of those shop windows you passed today?"

"There was an emerald ring at Tiffany's . . . I dont' know how much it was."

"It doesn't matter what it costs—you could buy it, and a new outfit at Bergdorf's to match, and maybe a sable coat to go with it—you'd look great in sable—and then you could buy a limousine to take you home. And you could come back the next day and spend just as much, and every day after that . . . and still you'd be rich."

"And bored eventually. Not to mention running out of closet space." She laughed.

"Well, there are a lot more sensible things you could do with your money. The point is, it's yours."

"And my relatives?"

"They each got three million from the will. And they've been living in your parents' house all these years. Ned and Noreen, anyway. Nick split off the open lot next door—your mom's garden—and had his own house built."

"Well, I'm certainly not going to kick them out; is that what they think? After all these years, it's more theirs than mine. What are they like?" she asked.

"First off, they're triplets. But it would be better if you didn't mention it. Nick, especially, doesn't like the idea. He says it makes them sound like freaks."

"I'd think it'd be nice; they've always had a companionship, built-in friends."

"Maybe it's the selection he objects to," Cole murmured to himself. "Anyway, Ned's the sharp one, though he doesn't look like much. He's obsessed with the business. In the last eighteen years, I don't think he's taken one vacation. He's steady and cautious and . . . well, frugal would be the polite word. But he's uncomfortable around people. He leaves the glad-handing to Nick."

"And Nick?"

"Very handsome. He's big on all the charity committees and always has his name in the society columns. Nick is very concerned about his social position. I don't think he'd marry anyone who didn't have ancestors on the *Mayflower*."

Fawn's eyebrows rose. "How many wives has he had?"

"He's on his third, and I don't think that's going well." Cole remembered how Nick had protected himself this time, having a prenuptial agreement drawn up before the wedding. His first two wives had walked off with everything but the silver. And probably deserved it, Cole thought.

"What about Noreen?" Fawn asked. So far it didn't sound too hopeful. But maybe Cole was biased against the triplets for his own reasons, and when she met them she'd be pleasantly surprised.

Cole seemed to be hesitating. "Noreen's harder to pigeon-hole. She can be very warm and very cold. But she's dedicated to her son, Scott. You don't remember him, I guess, but he's just about your age.''

"What would have happened if I hadn't come back?" Fawn asked suddenly. And she saw immediately from the expression that he tried to hide and couldn't, that he didn't want to answer. "What?" she persisted.

"The trust would have been dissolved on your twenty-fifth birthday—this August eighth.''

"August eighth?" They'd always celebrated her birthday in July. But then Pete had had to guess at the date from the clues she could give him as a child. "And once the trust had been dissolved?"

"The most likely course of action would be that your relatives would have you declared legally dead. And then they would inherit the whole pie.''

"Oh . . ." No wonder they wouldn't be pleased by her return. "Damn," she said suddenly. "Damn the money." She wasn't even sure she wanted it, and now it was going to make everything impossibly tense.

"Maybe it will all work out," Cole said, but there wasn't much conviction in his voice. "Try to forget about the money for a while.''

"And do you think they will?"

"No, I don't. But remember, I'll always be there to help you.''

Will you? she wondered; but she didn't voice her doubts out loud.

"I promise I'd call my father after I'd spoken with you," he added. "I'd better do it now.''

Cole spoke on the phone for a few minutes, his frown deepening, and then turned to her. "Do you have any plans for tomorrow evening?"

She shook her head.

"We'd like to to stop by the office then. Say about eleven o'clock? It's important.''

Reluctantly she agreed and after a few more minutes, Cole hung up. "I have a few papers here for you to sign, too," he said. "We want to get the legal proceedings out of the way as quickly as possible." He took a thick sheaf of papers from his briefcase and handed them to her.

As Fawn began to read through the pages of affidavits and legal forms, she became less certain that she should sign anything yet. After all, she didn't really know anything about the Bromleys. She didn't want to be railroaded into anything she'd regret. The telephone rang again. "I'll get it," Cole offered. "It's probably my father calling back." Fawn, lost in a thicket of legal verbiage, nodded.

"Hello," Cole said, picking up the phone. There was a silence at the other end, and then a man's voice asked. "Is this Fawn Travers' room?"

"Yes. May I tell her who's calling?" It didn't sound like Nick or Ned, but there was a strained, tense quality to the voice, and Cole couldn't be sure.

"Tell her it's Sam." The tone was distinctly unfriendly.

"Fawn . . ." Cole held out the phone for her. "Sam." Her face lit up in a happy smile.

"Hi, honey," she said, swinging her hair back and nestling the receiver against her ear. There was a cozy contentment in her voice, and her eyes were glowing.

"Oh, him, . . ." Cole heard her say. Obviously Sam wasn't the sort to restrain his curiosity. "He's a lawyer. I'll explain later."

"Oh, him" drifted over to the window to give them a change to talk privately. Not that he wasn't already forgotten, he thought ruefully. Well, what had he expected? Fawn was too beautiful, too vibrant, not to have a lover. The only surprise any sensible man should feel was that he was experiencing such an unjustifiable needling of jealousy—just as his father had been jealous of Melissa and Joel, he thought suddenly. The thought made him uncomfortable.

"It's good to hear your voice, too. Sam," Fawn was saying, her voice soft and intimate. "I'll call you tomorrow. Good night, Sam."

She turned back to Cole. "I'm really very tired. Could you leave these papers with me? I'll read them later."

"We'd hoped to get everything signed tonight. . . ." he began, but it was obvious she wasn't going to change her mind. It wouldn't help matters to push her. Picking up his briefcase, he headed for the door. "We'll see you tomorrow morning, then. Try to get some rest."

Long after he'd left, Fawn sat on the bed, her knees pulled up under her chin, rocking softly back and forth. She was remembering the dazzling way Cole had of smiling at her and the gentleness in his eyes. She'd never met a man who'd had such an effect on her. But could she trust her reaction? Obviously he'd been trying to win her confidence tonight, and the thought made her feel like a pawn in a game of which she didn't know the rules. It was all so complicated, and she had the distinct impression that Cole had been holding back, that he hadn't told her everything. She sighed, shaking her head. What was she getting into?

"You mean this girl, this stranger, suddenly . . . remembers," Noreen said to Bromley sarcastically. Nick had joined them at last and he was smiling idiotically, as if determined to view the whole episode as a bad joke.

"No, she really doesn't remember anything at all," Bromley answered. "But, as I explained, the locket and the fingerprints should be conclusive enough for any court."

"And how did she know to come to you?" Ned asked. He'd spent the last half hour nervously pulling at his frayed suit-coat cuff. Like most of Ned's clothing, the suit was at least ten years old.

"From an old newspaper clipping," Bromley explained. "Apparently the people who took her away had kept it all these years."

"Just who are these people, anyway?"

"She won't tell us."

"How convenient," Ned said. "What are you trying to pull, Colman?"

The lawyer shoved the computer printouts he'd gotten from the lab toward Ned. "Look for yourself; she's definitely your niece. There'll be no problem proving it. I'd just hoped your response to the news would be a bit more positive. You should be pleased and relieved she's alive, for heaven's sake." He was tired of arguing with them. He'd been there nearly two hours, and he felt that he was making no progress.

But, confronted with the proof, Noreen smiled at him. "Colman, give us a chance. Surely you must realize what a tremendous shock this is for us. We'd given up on the poor child, and now you suddenly tell us . . . You understand, don't you?'' The bitter, stubborn lines had disappeared from her face, and she was all charm. Colman had seen this act before; he and Noreen had a long and turbulent history together—a history Colman had come to sorely regret. How could he ever have imagined himself in love with her? And he knew that, when she turned sweet like this, it meant she thought she couldn't win by a direct attack.

"Noreen . . ." Nick whined, confused by her quick change of attitude. He never had had her subtlety.

"Come now, Nick—think," she said sweetly. "We certainly want to start this relationship right. Wouldn't it be foolish to antagonize her?" She turned to Bromley before Nick could answer. "So you see, you have nothing to worry about. As a matter of fact, I'm sure we're all very eager to welcome her home."

Chapter 12

Fawn had only been awake for a few minutes the next morning when the telephone rang in her room. She glanced at the clock; it wasn't quite eight-thirty yet. Who could be calling her at this hour, she wondered, still feeling a bit groggy. She had lain awake for hours after Cole left the night before; but at last she'd fallen into a deep, almost drugged sleep and now felt as if she were still groping her way through a fog. Finally, she picked up the phone.

It was only the desk clerk. "You have a visitor," he told her. "A Mrs. Noreen Wescott. Shall I send her up?"

In her shock, Fawn nearly dropped the phone. Her aunt—here? She was the last person Fawn had expected. "Do you wish to see her?" the desk clerk asked.

"Yes," Fawn managed to get out at last. "Of course I'll see her."

"I'll send her right up, then."

It was only when she hung up that Fawn realized she was still in her nightgown. Her hair wasn't combed yet, and she hadn't even brushed her teeth. She made a quick dash for the bathroom.

Three minutes later Noreen was knocking at the door. Fawn tugged her comb hurriedly through her hair one last time, and slipped into her bathrobe. This wasn't at all how she'd planned to look when she met her aunt. But then Fawn realized it probably wouldn't have mattered if she'd had more time; her hands were shaking too badly to apply makeup or even button a blouse. Smiling to hide her nervousness, Fawn opened the door.

For a moment both women stared wordlessly at each other. Fawn's first thought was that Noreen's picture in the newspaper hadn't done her justice. Her aunt was a beautiful, unmistakably elegant woman. Tall enough to tower over Fawn, she wore her height with an air of pride and self-assurance. A magnificent lynx coat was tossed casually over her broad shoulders, and a black pearl necklace gleamed at her throat. As if to emphasize her height, her ash-blond hair was pulled up into a tight knot at the top of her head. Her smokey, uptilted eyes were unreadable.

"So," Noreen said with a small smile that seemed to stretch her skin even tighter across her prominent cheekbones, "you're Melissa's daughter."

Fawn nodded. "I'm so glad you came."

Noreen shook her head, smiling. "What are we being so formal about, child? I've waited a long time to hug my only niece. You wouldn't mind, would you?" And suddenly Fawn found herself enveloped in a long, perfumed, furry hug.

"There, that's better," Noreen said. For a moment she held Fawn at arm's length, studying her face. "What an exquisitely beautiful child you are. It's too bad Melissa can't see you now. She would have been very proud."

Fawn blushed with pleasure, then suddenly remembered her manners. "Please, come in—and I apologize for the mess," she added, thinking of the unmade bed and the clothes scattered around.

"There's no one else here, is there?" Noreen asked as she entered. Her gray eyes quickly swept the room.

Fawn shook her head. "I hardly know anyone else in New York."

"That's right, you don't."

Fawn thought she heard a hint of satisfaction in her aunt's

voice. Carelessly Noreen shrugged off her lynx coat. She was wearing a full-sleeved deep purple blouse and perfectly cut black wool slacks; pearl cuff links matched her necklace, and a huge marquis diamond ring glittered on her hand.

"I'm sorry I'm not dressed," Fawn said. "I wasn't expecting . . ."

"Oh, I wanted it to be a surprise." It would be a surprise to Nick and Ned, too, Noreen wasn't sure how they'd react when they found out. But she'd decided it was worth the risk. "I just felt you and I should have a little talk before everyone else got into the act." She looked at Fawn intently. "Do you remember me at all?"

Fawn shook her head. "I don't really remember anything from those years."

"Nothing?"

"Nothing."

"Well, that's all right," Noreen said briskly. "Don't worry about it. We'll have plenty of time to get to know each other."

"I'd like that."

"Good. Now that you're back, we don't want to lose sight of you again." Noreen glanced around the small hotel room. "But you can't stay here—this is barely big enough for a closet. You'll come and stay with us," she said decisively. "It's your home, after all, where you belong."

"I don't think . . . I mean, I don't want to impose . . ."

"Nonense, everyone's dying to meet you. Especially my son, Scott. Do you remember Scottie?"

"No.' Her aunt didn't seem to believe that she remembered nothing about them, Fawn realized. But it was probably natural. It must have been as disconcerting for Noreen to deal with as it was for her.

"You and Scott were so close, almost inseparable," Noreen told her. "He's almost the same age as you are. I'm sure you'll be great friends again. Anyway, pack up your things and we'll leave right after breakfast."

Fawn hesitated. She yearned to see her parents' home. She was certain it would bring back the memories buried in her subconscious. Yet this was all too sudden, too forced—as if Noreen were acting out a script. But then Fawn wondered if she wasn't being overly critical. Under that smooth, self-assured veneer, her aunt was probably just as nervous as she was. And maybe she was letting Cole's negative comments about her relatives influence her too much. Contrary to everything he'd said, Noreen was doing her best to be friendly.

Noreen noticed her hesitation. "Honey, it'll be better for us, too. It's hardly convenient to keep running into the city every time one of us wants to see you."

"I hadn't thought of that. Of course I'll come, then. And thank you. But I can only stay a day or two."

"We'll talk about that later. And don't worry that you'll be crowding us. It's a big house. In fact, you can have your own apartment over the garage."

Fawn remembered that she was supposed to be at the lawyer's office at eleven o'clock. "Call up and cancel," Noreen suggested. "I'm sure they'll understand."

Cole hadn't come in yet when Fawn called. Vaguely disappointed, she left a message, apologizing for canceling the meeting and explaining where she'd be.

"You know, you really don't need them anymore, anyway," Noreen said. "I'm sure we can work out everything between us."

So the animosity between Cole and her relatives was mutual, Fawn realized. She wondered what was behind it.

While Fawn dressed, Noreen wandered around the room, inspecting everything. "Is this all you brought?" she asked, obviously surprised as she peered into Fawn's closet.

"I wasn't planning on staying very long."

"But not even one cocktail dress?" Noreen laughed. "How . . . uncomplicated. I can't go anywhere without three trunks full of clothes."

Fawn looked at the row of jeans and simple skirts and blouses. She'd brought only one suit and no evening clothes at all. It was the way she packed for a newspaper assignment; she hadn't expected to find herself suddenly tossed into such a monied environment. "Too casual?" she asked.

"Just a bit. But that's easily fixed. We'll just pop over to Bergdorf's and pick you up a few dresses. A simple black sheath would be perfect for you, with your complexion. Or maybe something in pink silk . . ."

"Oh, no, I couldn't." Fawn objected quickly.

"If you don't like Bergdorf's, we can go someplace else."

Fawn laughed. "It's not that. It's just that I don't have much money. I couldn't afford a store like that."

Noreen looked at her in surprise, then shook her head, chuckling. "Fawn, you could buy out the store if you wanted to. You are rich. R-i-c-h," she spelled it out. "I thought Colman told you."

Fawn had been dreading this moment, when the subject of her inheritance first came up. Yet Noreen didn't seem disturbed at all. If anything, she seemed pleased for her. Maybe Cole had misled her—maybe the family had never counted on collecting the rest of the estate. Still she hesitated. "I can't really think of that money as mine yet."

"So, we'll put everything on my charge," Noreen said as if the matter were settled. She suddenly seemed very cheerful. "I probably won't be able to resist a few new things for myself, anyway. I love to shop." She gave Fawn a quick hug. "Let me help you finish packing. We don't want to keep all those beautiful new clothes waiting."

In a few minutes the suitcase was almost full. "What's this?" Noreen asked, holding up Fawn's portfolio and starting to leaf through it. "Why, you take pictures . . . and very good ones. I love this shot of the mountain lion sunning himself. You're very talented." She looked through a few more of the photographs. "I'd guess from these that you grew up out West. Am I right?"

"West of the Hudson, anyway, " Fawn admitted reluctantly. She felt ungracious being so secretive after Noreen had shown such an interest. But she knew she had to keep that part of her life hidden. She should never have brought the portfolio with her. It had been Sam's idea; he wanted her to show it to some editors in the city. But she should have realized how the pictures might lead someone to Pete and Gram.

"Somewhere in the mountains?" Noreen persisted. "A small town, I'll bet."

"Aunt Noreen, I don't want to be mysterious, but I can't talk about those years. Not yet. Please don't ask me any questions."

"My dear, I didn't mean anything." Noreen looked hurt.

"I know you didn't," Fawn agreed quickly. "But ever since I've been here, everyone's been trying to find out where I was raised, assuming I'd been kidnapped."

"By everyone, I imagine you mean Colman, and Cole. They're very clever. And you're right to be careful around them."

"You sound as if you don't trust them."

Noreen shrugged her elegant shoulders. "Frankly, I always thought Colman's relationship with your parents was slightly . . . unhealthy. And who knows what financial mischief he's been up to with your inheritance all these years. As for Cole— no matter how charming he is, remember his first loyalty is to his father." Noreen paused. "I bet when Cole was explaining the will to you he didn't mention that his father would also share in the estate if you . . . hadn't been found before your twenty-fifth birthday."

"No, he didn't. . . ." Fawn said reluctantly. So she'd been right. Cole hadn't told her the complete truth. "How much would Mr. Bromley get—if something happens to me?"

"Ten million dollars."

No wonder Colman had been upset when she suddenly returned. Ten million dollars was a fortune.

"I probably shouldn't have said anything," her aunt was saying. "Please don't repeat it. But I just can't help feelig a little protective of you." She gave Fawn a warm smile. "Now, if we're just about ready, I'll call the car around."

It was a beautiful spring day, warm and breezy. Most of the people on the streets had shucked off their coats, and the sunlight reflected off the freshly washed store windows filled with displays of colorful warm-weather clothing. On the corner outside the hotel, a peddler was selling balloons.

Noreen directed the driver to take them to the Plaza, and they almost seemed to float through the traffic, enveloped in the scent of rich leather and a purring silence. It was the first time Fawn had ever ridden in a limousine. She smiled, recalling the "limousine service" run by old Mr. Findley in Rustler's Creek; his fleet consisted of two ancient Chevys with torn upholstery and rusty fenders. It was quite a contrast between that and Noreen's gleaming white Bentley and uniformed chauffeur.

The Plaza Hotel is situated at the edge of Central Park. As they approached they drove past a large, splashing fountain and a line of horse-drawn carriages waiting for passengers, stopping at the front steps.

"I thought we'd have breakfast in the Palm Court," Noreen said, as the doorman helped them from the car. "Then we can go right across the street to Bergdorf's."

Fawn nodded. She was wondering what Pete would think of all this. She hadn't called him the night before to break the news because things still seemed too unsettled, but he'd have to be told soon. It would be a shock, that was for sure. He'd just naturally assumed her parents came from the same sort of world as he did.

Bergdorf's main floor was a collection of small, elegant boutiques, all displaying the latest in fashion; at one end was Van Cleef and Arpels. On the way to the elevator, a blue silk scarf, delicately embroidered with gold, caught Fawn's eye. She looked at the price tag. It was $285.00.

"Do you want it?" Noreen asked casually.

Fawn quickly shook her head no. How could anyone spend that much for a scarf? Yet all around her, salesclerks were wrapping up purchases that were just as expensive.

In the dress salon, a salesclerk named Yvonne greeted Noreen as an old and valued customer. "Let me show you this lovely little knit we just got. It'd be perfect for you . . ."

"Maybe later," Noreen said. "First we need to pick up a few things for my niece." She hugged Fawn. "Now, what do you suggest? Something in a dinner dress, first, I think. But I warn you, I suspect she has very simple tastes."

The salesclerk brought out three dresses, all gorgeous, and Noreen wouldn't even let Fawn look at the price tags. As Fawn slipped the first one on, a creamy white crepe that accentuated her every curve, she almost gasped. She hardly recognized the image in the mirror, and for a moment she nearly regretted all the years she'd spent in blue jeans and flannel shirts.

''She wears that well, doesn't she?'' Yvonne commented. ''Such a lovely figure . . .''

Fawn blushed and glanced at Noreen's face in the mirror. For a second her spine seemed to turn to ice. There was such a look of loathing and envy distorting Noreen's face that she seemed almost hideous. It was a look of pure hatred. But immediately Noreen's face shifted back to its usual smoothness, and she smiled. ''Yes, she's very like her mother,'' Noreen agreed. ''Let's try that peach silk next.''

Fawn stood silently while Yvonne unzipped the dress, still staring at Noreen. But her aunt was smiling as if everything were fine. Her face was as bland as a baby's.

As she tried on the second dress Fawn began to wonder if she'd imagined the vision in the mirror. Perhaps it was a trick of the light. Yet she couldn't stop glancing warily at Noreen. Fortunately Noreen didn't seem to notice; she chatted happily with Yvonne and urged Fawn to take every dress she tried on. She was as cheerful as if they were two schoolgirls getting ready for a date. And gradually Fawn found herself forgetting her doubts.

They finally settled on two dresses with the matching accessories for Fawn and a mauve watered-silk evening suit for Noreen. As they began to leave with their arms piled high with packages, Noreen decided Fawn should have some perfume to go with her new outfits. ''Something French and very romantic . . .''

''Aunt Noreen, I can't accept it . . . It's too much,'' Fawn objected.

''Nonsense. Think of it as making up for all the Christmas and birthday presents I missed giving you all these years.''

A few minutes later they were in the backseat of the limousine, heading for the Gardens. ''Wear one of your new dresses for dinner tonight,'' Noreen suggested, ''I told the cook to make a real feast. And Scottie will be there. I can't wait for you two to meet again.

Noreen was determined that she and Scott would be friends, Fawn realized. Her aunt hadn't mentioned Nick or Ned all day long, but she'd brought Scott into the conversation several times.

''What does Scott do?'' Fawn asked.

"Why, he works for Dalsworth, Inc. I thought you knew. He's put his soul into that company. In fact, we always assumed that one day he would be running the company himself."

Fawn saw that Noreen was watching her closely for her reaction. And suddenly she understood why it was so important that she like Scott.

"Of course, that's up to you now," Noreen added quickly, still studying Fawn's face. "It's a horrible burden to have pushed on you all of a sudden—expecting you to make all these business decisions when you don't know anything about that world. So much responsibility . . ." Noreen's eyes were so pitying it was as if Fawn had just contracted some fatal disease.

I don't want to take anything away from Scott, Fawn nearly said. But there was something about her aunt's obvious attempt to manipulate her emotions that kept her silent. She could understand Noreen's worry, and she really didn't want anything from them that was rightfully theirs. But they'd always understood that the money had been left to her. And right now she was too confused about everything to know what was the right thing to do. Cole had only spoken in generalities the night before; she'd have to know a lot more before any sort of decision was possible.

But she was sure Noreen would be right there advising her, pushing Scott's claim. And maybe it would be best to leave the company in their hands. The idea made a lot of sense. But she'd have to see. . . .

And again Fawn wondered what she was getting into.

C h a p t e r 13

A_s soon as the limousine crossed the Fifty-ninth Street Bridge, they were in Queens, Noreen explained. Everything looked different here; this was an industrial area. Instead of the skyscrapers of Manhattan, they were surrounded by dingy gray warehouses and factories and old-fashioned brick apartment buildings. And cemeteries.

"Queens was originally the burial ground for all of the city," Noreen explained as they passed another cemetery.

Fawn realized she had no idea where her parents were buried. Before she left the city she would find out and take flowers to their graves. But more important than that, she prayed she would have remembered enough to see their killer brought to justice.

Gradually the landscape became more suburban. They passed small parks and row after row of brick houses with neatly trimmed lawns. "We're almost there," Noreen told her, laughing as she added, "Everyone's going to be so surprised." She had a gloating look in her eyes, as if she'd beaten everyone to the big prize in a treasure hunt.

But Fawn was too busy with her own thoughts to really

notice. She was nervously wondering what the rest of the family would think of her—and what it would feel like to see the house again after all these years. Melissa and Joel's house . . . Now it was the closest she could come to touching them and the love they'd shared together. Yey it was also the house where they'd been murdered, and the thought made her shiver. Part of her wanted to escape right then, yet at the same time she could barely control her impatience to get there.

Noreen, sensing her uneasiness, patted her hand soothingly. "If you find this difficult, if you start remembering then you just come straight to me. I want you to know you can always confide in me."

They'd been traveling on a wide boulevard for the last several minutes, but now they turned off to a side street. The shops were more expensive-looking here, and the architecture was mostly English Tudor. As they passed through a charming, old-fashioned square, with the buildings connected by walkways high above the streets and a graceful clock tower silhouetted against the sky, Noreen told her, "That used to be the old Forest Hills Inn. The tennis players used to stay there while they were competing in the tournament. The clubhouse isn't far away."

"It's lovely," Fawn said. "The whole scene looks like it was lifted right out of an English village."

They were turning down a maze of winding streets now. Fawn stared at the three- and four-story houses, with their turrets, red-tiled roofs, and lead-paned windows, and at the seemingly hundreds of cherry and dogwood and tulip trees. They'd just begun to flower, and their branches were soft clouds of pink and white that almost took her breath away. The lilac was in bloom, too, and the first of the forsythia, and a dozen other blossoms she couldn't identify. Bright yellow daffodils and tulips and crocus nestled against the fresh green of the hedges and the carefully tended lawns. It was like a fairy tale come to life. How could she ever have forgotten this?

"We're here," Noreen said, as the limousine pulled into a drive.

It was a beautiful house—and huge, four stories high—with massive chimneys at both ends, a thick oaken door, and gleaming double French windows leading to a terrace on the third floor. There was even an attached greenhouse. Yet despite its size, there was nothing forbidding about the house. It seemed to welcome her.

And as they started up the walk, Fawn heard the cheerful twittering of birds in the air; there were wrens nesting in the ivy climbing up the brick walls. She smiled. It seemed like a good omen.

But Noreen grimaced. "I keep meaning to have that damn ivy cut down one of these days."

Suddenly the front door opened, and a man stood glaring at them in the wide archway. His broad shoulders almost touched both doorposts. From the way he was dressed—the knees were nearly worn out of his baggy pants, and his shirt was gray with age—Fawn guessed he was one of the help. But Noreen smiled nervously and determinedly pushed Fawn forward. "Ned—say hello to Fawn. I've brought her home to stay with us."

Awkwardly Fawn held out her hand to shake; but for a moment Ned ignored her, gazing over her head at Noreen, and a look passed between brother and sister that was anything but friendly. At last Ned shoved out his hand toward Fawn. "Excuse me, I wasn't expecting you. Come in," he added abruptly.

"Isn't that nice?" Noreen said. "I was afraid you'd still be at work. But now we'll all have a chance to get acquainted."

"Of course, you're including me, too, aren't you?" a second man asked, entering the foyer. His voice had a brittle, strained quality to it, but his face was all smiles.

Fawn remembered Cole's description of Nick and realized that this handsome man in the three-piece suit with a bright yellow silk handkerchief flowing from his breast pocket must be her Uncle Nick.

"Welcome home, Kendra . . . I mean, Fawn. That's what you want to be called, isn't it? Well, whatever you want. I just want you to know how happy I am personally that you're here." And he pumped her hand enthusiastically. His handclasp was sweaty, and almost painfully hearty.

Nick's eyes traveled over her appreciatively. "You're quite

a looker.'' A thought seemed to occur to him, and for the first time his smile reached his eyes, too. ''I bet you have a lot of boyfriends. In no time at all, I'll bet you'll be running off to get married.''

''Don't be an ass, Nick,'' Ned hissed through his teeth.

Noreen took Fawn's arm. ''Come on, let's go in the living room and have a drink. It'll be more comfortable talking there.''

It certainly couldn't be any *less* comfortable, Fawn thought to herself. There was so much tension around her, she felt the air might suddenly ignite. It was obvious the brothers were unhappy about her showing up without warning and Noreen kept glancing at Ned, her face stretched into a placating smile, almost as if she were afraid of him. Or, at least, of what he might say.

''Well, what do you think of it?'' Noreen asked Fawn as they paused at the entrance to the living room. Her hand gestured toward the high-ceilinged, light-filled room. ''We've left everything just as Melissa had it.''

Fawn's gaze traveled slowly over the gleaming, brass-handled antique furniture and around the creamy yellow walls hung with soft, misty Impressionist paintings. Two cream-colored sofas stood parallel to the large fireplace, and the pillows piled on the sofas picked up the fresh pinks, yellows, and greens of the paintings. A collection of porcelain vases, carefully back-lit, was displayed in a high lacquered Chinese cabinet. Everywhere she looked there were beautiful things—fanciful, hand-blown paperweights, rich-hued Tiffany vases, an antique silver writing set on the desk. But more important, it was a comfortable room, a room that welcomed you and instantly raised your spirits.

''It's beautiful,'' Fawn said. ''I've never seen anything so perfect.''

Nick was already heading for the bar. He grabbed one of the large Baccarat glasses and filled it nearly to the top with Scotch. Although (as she had learned from Cole) Nick lived next door, he seemed to treat this house as his own, too.

''You are going to fix something for the rest of us, aren't you?'' Noreen asked.

Nick took a long swallow from his glass before answering. "Sure, what will you have?"

Fawn didn't really feel like having a drink, but it might seem rude to refuse, and things were strained enough as it was, so a minute later she found herself sitting on the sofa with a glass in her hand.

"Welcome home," Noreen said, raising her drink in a toast. She turned to Ned. "Where's Scott?"

He shrugged. "Who knows?"

"But I told him to . . ." Noreen began, frowning, then suddenly shut up.

They were all silent now. They were facing one another on the sofas—Nick and Ned on one, and Noreen beside Fawn on the other. It was like a standoff at the beginning of a game, the two opposing teams lining up, Fawn thought. The silence was getting awkward. Nick cleared his throat and smiled around the group nervously, but when he opened his mouth it was only to finish off his drink.

Fawn used the time to study the two men. She noticed that, for such a large man, Ned's movements were very precise, almost fussy. And he seemed painfully shy. Perhaps his brusque, cold manner was simply a cover for his shyness. She remembered he had never married. He was a very plain man: his face was broad and unusually flat, he was balding, and his shabby clothes seemed to emphasize his thick, paunchy middle. Noreen and Nick were both so good-looking, it must have been difficult for him growing up in such a family. Perhaps the clothes and his abrupt manners were his way of announcing he would't compete in a contest he couldn't win.

Nick, on the other hand, seemed very aware of his good looks. He had the air of a man who'd traded on his face and his charm most of his life—like the college quarterback who's never grown up. It was strange how different the two brothers were: anyone looking at them would swear Ned was at least ten years older than his brother.

"So, you're going to be staying with us . . . here," Ned said at last. "That's good. The only sensible solution . . . "

"It won't be a problem?" Fawn asked.

"Not at all. Not at all. Stay as long as you want," Nick

said, finally finding his voice. Fawn smiled, remembering that it wasn't his house he was being so generous with.

"I thought we'd put Fawn in the apartment over the garage," Noreen explained. She turned to Fawn. "It was originally set up for the couple that ran the house. It has its own separate entrance. But we haven't had live-in help for years, so it hasn't been used. I hope you like it. I've had the maid arrange everything for you."

Fawn thanked her, and they all lapsed into an awkward silence again. Given the circumstances, it would have seemed foolish to make small talk, to chat about the weather or how bad the traffic was, and none of the three seemed willing to say what was really on their minds. No one wanted to mention Melissa's and Joel's deaths, or the money, or ask Fawn why she'd come back. And Fawn herself had decided it would be better to wait and give them time to react to her in their own way. She was grateful, at least, that they didn't seem compelled to pretend to an affection they didn't feel. After all, with all the years that had passed, they were really strangers to one another. It would take time for them to get to know one another again.

At last Ned stood up. "Well, I'll see you at dinner, I guess."

Nick quickly added, "We'll be there, too—my wife, Suzanne, and I."

Fawn nodded. It was going to be a long meal, she suspected.

Dinner was served at eight. Noreen had told the cook she wanted something special, and the food was marvelous: salmon mousse, Bibb lettuce with Stilton cheese, white asparagus, a crown rib roast with chestnut stuffing, and lemon sorbet in between the courses. For dessert there were fresh raspberries with crème fraîche. Scott had finally shown up, looking dour and a bit drunk, and all during dinner he concentrated more on his wine than the food. He was a good-looking young man, tall and athletic. He had Noreen's dark eyebrows and heavily fringed eyes, but the resemblance ended there. Fawn thought he reminded her of someone else, but she wasn't sure whom. Perhaps it was Cole; Scott had the same sort of clean-cut handsomeness. Despite the fact that Noreen had seated Fawn next to Scott, she barely had a chance to talk with him. He was not exactly antagonistic; it was more as if he were trying to distance himself from everyone at the table. The constantly refilled glass of wine in his hand seemed to be a shield to hide behind.

"Doesn't your cousin Fawn look nice in her new dress?" Noreen asked Scott at one point, trying to get him to talk. "We went shopping today, and I think we did very well."

Scott turned to stare at Fawn. She was wearing the peach silk dress, and she did feel very good in it. The others had dressed formally for dinner, too. Even Ned was wearing a suit—though it looked like something he'd grabbed off a rack at Robert Hall twenty years ago.

Scott leaned closer to Fawn, his eyes not quite focusing. "Be careful," he whispered. "She'll try to make you over, too." And then he went back to his glass.

As he'd promised, Nick's wife, Suzanne, was there as well. But after a while, Fawn wondered why he'd brought her along. He ignored her during the entire meal. And on the few occasions when he did comment on something she'd said, it was only to contradict her. And Fawn noticed they never touched; there was none of the casual physical affection that people in love unconsciously express. Yet she was a beautiful woman. Her hair was a deep glowing red, and she was wearing a low-cut yellow dress that showed off her slim, lush figure. She was much younger than Nick, and Fawn recalled that Suzanne was his third wife. But whatever had drawn them together seemed to have died out a long time before. Nick even seemed oblivious of the anger smoldering in his wife's green eyes.

Nevertheless, the meal went better than Fawn had hoped. The triplets were obviously trying hard to make her feel welcome. They talked of the happy times they'd all enjoyed together when she was a child, and how close-knit the family had been. It sounded like an idyllic time, filled with laughter and love. Nick and Ned and Noreen almost seemed to be competing to prove which of them had been closest to her parents, but it made Fawn warm to them all.

As they moved to the living room for coffee and brandy,

Noreen took Fawn's arm. "You haven't really had a chance to see the house yet. Why don't we have Scott stay home tomorrow and show you around?"

Fawn wasn't exactly eager for Scott's company, but she did want to see the house, so she thanked Noreen for the offer. "And I'd like to see the old family albums, too," Fawn added. It would be another way to bring back the good times they'd talked about at dinner.

Nick frowned. "God, have we still got those? I imagined someone must have thrown the albums out years ago."

"I didn't," Ned said quickly.

"Of course, you never throw anything out."

"Is my dollhouse still here?" Fawn asked. The words were out of her mouth before she even knew she was going to ask the question. Immediately three heads turned to stare at her.

"I thought you didn't remember anything from your childhood," Ned said, eyeing her suspiciously. He obviously thought she'd been lying to them.

"I don't—except suddenly I knew I'd had a dollhouse built exactly on the plan of this house." She was as surprised as they were. Why had that popped into her head? But she was pleased she was at last beginning to remember. The triplets didn't seem to share her pleasure, though, and that was puzzling.

"I doubt we would have kept a dollhouse all these years, even if there was one," Ned said. His large hands seemed about to crush the delicate brandy glass he was holding. "Anyway, there's been a lot of changes made in the house since then. You couldn't expect us to leave everything just as it was."

"Ned had several of the rooms on the second floor made into an apartment for himself," Noreen explained. "He had the carpenters up there for weeks, doing Lord knows what . . ."

"I only had a few cabinets put in," Ned retorted. "No need to be so mysterious about it."

"Well, a woman can't help being a bit curious," Noreen said, smiling stiffly. "After all, you never let anyone up there . . ."

"They're my rooms." Ned was as defiant as a two-year-old hugging a toy to its chest.

For a moment no one said anything. And then Ned grudgingly apologized, Nick suggested another round of drinks, and the conversation shifted to a safer subject. They were all beginning to feel the strain of the evening.

When the clock chimed ten, Fawn gratefully excused herself. She suspected that Nick and Ned were as relieved to see her go as she was to escape. Before she left Noreen gave her a quick hug and whispered, "Just give it time, Fawn. People at our age get a little set in their ways. . . . But it's all going to work out."

Fawn nodded. "I understand. And thank you for being such a help."

Noreen smiled. "Well, I want you to be happy here. And remember, if you need to talk, you just come to me."

The maid had already turned down the bed in Fawn's apartment, and a small tea service had been laid out for her in the tiny kitchen in case she wanted a hot drink before she went to bed. Fawn smiled at the thoughtfulness of it and reminded herself to thank Noreen in the morning.

It was a pleasant apartment. One wall of the bedroom was exposed brick, and there was a brass bed with a bright blue-and-white quilt and an old-fashioned armoire of bleached pine. A pitcher beside the bed held a fragrant bouquet of white lilac. The decor reminded Fawn of a country inn, and she felt almost at home here.

Maybe tomorrow would be better, she thought—once everyone had gotten over the shock of her return. She was sure Noreen was right. She just had to give it time. Fawn wanted to like these people and to have them like her. After all, they were her only blood relatives in the world. And her only link to her past—to Melissa and Joel.

For a while she wandered around the apartment, too keyed up to sleep. Suddenly it occurred to her that Pete didn't know where she was yet. He might be calling the hotel now, trying to reach her. She didn't want him worrying.

It would only be eight o'clock in Colorado, she realized, because of the time difference—early enough to still call tonight. And it would be so good to hear Pete's voice. But as she reached for the phone, her hand stopped in midair. She didn't want to place the call from the house. Until she could convince everyone that Pete had had nothing to do with the murders and hadn't kidnapped her, she'd have to keep his identity a secret. And if she called from the house, his phone number would appear on the bill.

The apartment had its own separate entrance, so there wouldn't even be any need to let the others know she'd gone out. Quickly she pulled a coat around her shoulders and slipped out the door. She remembered that the limousine had passed a row of small shops and cafés not far from the house. She headed in that direction. She'd make the call from a public phone.

"*Pete* . . . Pete? Are you still there?'' Fawn clutched the phone tighter, wishing there weren't so many miles between them.

"Just picking myself up off the floor, honey,'' he said, trying to cover his shock with a joke. "There must be something wrong with this line. I could swear you just said forty million dollars. . . . ''

"I did. It's hard to believe, isn't it?'' They'd been talking for nearly ten minutes now, and Fawn had told him about her interview with Cole Bromley, and that everyone was satisfied she was Kendra Dalsworth. She'd explained that she'd been invited to stay at the house for a while and described the triplets. He'd been pleased for her, though he wondered why the triplets hadn't made the plea for her return instead of the lawyer. And not wanting him to worry, she'd been careful not to mention the tension her return had caused. But at last she'd had to tell him about the inheritance.

"Sweet Jerusalem—forty million dollars,'' he repeated. He was thinking of all the things that much money would buy— and how little he'd been able to give her while she was growing up. "I guess I should have never taken you away like I did," he said. "They could have given you everything you ever wanted."

"No," Fawn said quickly. "You did the right thing. I couldn't have gone back then." She thought of the noisy, happy dinners at Pete's house, remembered the strained faces around the table this evening, and knew that the money could never have made up for the love she'd had all through her childhood. It would have been wonderful to have the money, too, but if she had had to choose, she'd rather have had Pete and Gram. Besides, the triplets might not even have wanted her. And if they had taken her in, there would have always been the friction caused by the money.

"Don't you like these people, Fawn?" Pete asked. He knew her well enough to guess there was something she wasn't telling him. Certainly the discovery that she was suddenly rich should be making her happier than she sounded.

"I don't know whether I like them or not yet. I'm still confused about everything."

"Anybody would be. It's a lot to adjust to all at once." He sighed. "Damn, Fawn, when I think of everything you could have had . . ."

"Pete, the world's full of poor little rich kids," she interrupted, thinking of Scott. He'd been raised with all the money anyone would need, and it didn't seem to have done him any good. "Besides, what do you think the murderer would have done if I'd come back? After all, I am the only witness." She hadn't meant to tell him that—it had just slipped out. She bit her lip. It was bad enough that he felt guilty about the money, now he was going to worry about her safety, too.

"But you can't identify the killer. You don't remember anything."

"But maybe I will." She didn't tell him about remembering the dollhouse. But now there was no question in her mind: In time it was all going to come back to her.

"Fawn, you be careful. Don't take any chances." He shook his head, knowing she wouldn't listen to him. Once she got an idea in her mind . . . But this time it could get her killed. "Hey," he said suddenly, trying to pump some enthusiasm into his voice, "I've been thinking about coming East myself. Be great to see the old town again. Why don't I just hop on the next plane . . ."

"Pete, you're so transparent." She smiled. She knew he'd rather bounce down the Colorado River in a barrel than come to New York. And there was the very real possibility he could end up in a New York City jail. Until the killer was found, even Pete was a suspect.

He listened patiently while she explained it all to him. And then just as if he hadn't heard a word, he said, "I still think I should come. Somebody's got to watch out for you."

"But I'm fine. And I'll be careful. And if I need help, I'll call you."

"That's a promise?"

"Don't you have enough gray hair already?" she teased. "Stop worrying."

"There you go, making fun of your elders again." But the teasing was back in his voice, too. "I'll be sitting by the phone waiting to hear from you. Got my ear trumpet all polished up. And, Fawn," he added, "We all love you. Remember that."

"I love you, too."

She was smiling as she started back to the house. It had been good to hear Pete's voice. She could picture him in front of the fireplace, poking at the logs to get the fire just right, while Sue worked on her needlepoint. There was such contentment in the scene, for a moment she wished she were with them— or snuggled in Sam's arms, listening to the warm rumble of his voice and laughing at his jokes. But she'd be back there soon. And when she returned, she'd have the answers she'd been waiting for all her life.

It was a beautiful night. The moon was almost full, and the breeze sifted through the flowering branches that glowed against the dark night. Here and there a few petals were fluttering softly to the earth. As she passed a newly mown lawn, the scent of fresh grass after the long winter made her smile. The streets were almost deserted at this time of night. Fawn spotted a man walking his dog in the distance, but he turned down another street before she reached him. She walked for two blocks without even a car passing her.

Gradually it began to occur to her how dark these streets really were. And at the same time she started to wonder if she was lost. The streets seemed to twist and turn in on themselves, so that by now she wasn't even sure in which direction she was heading.

She was beginning to feel very uneasy. All the stories she'd heard about crime in New York suddenly crowded into her consciousness. She kept turning around, unable to shake the feeling that someone was following her; but there was never anyone in sight. Yet the hair prickled at the back of her neck.

She began to walk faster. A fallen branch snapped beneath her feet, and she jumped at the sound. Again she whirled around, searching the shadows behind her, straining against the darkness. Something moved. But was it someone slipping back into the shadows or just the wind rustling through the trees?

A sudden feeling of helplessness washed over her. She was alone and lost, like an animal trapped in a maze. The sound of her own heartbeat, ragged and quick, was aloud in her ears. The thought flashed through her mind. She had to hide.

She stopped, confused and panicky. What had made her think that? Why was she so sure someone was chasing her? And, looking down, she realized she was gripping her arm right where her old scar was. It must have been on the same streets that she had fled in terror from her parents' murderer. Here, in the darkness, she had tried to escape. Was she simply reliving that night again? Or was someone following her? Had her parents' murderer discovered her already? She leaned against a tree trunk, fighting to force herself back to reality. And then she saw the car.

Her first reaction was relief. She'd ask the driver where she was, how to get back to the house. But then she frowned. There was something wrong; the car was slowly edging along the curb, searching for someone. Had the killer returned to these streets also, hoping to find her and silence her forever?

She began to run. But she was still wearing the delicate high-heeled sandals that matched her new dress, and each step threatened to turn her ankle, to spill her onto the sidewalk. The car had speeded up behind her. It was less than half a block away now. She couldn't outrun it. And there was no place to hide, no one to help her. She looked at the darkened house nearby. Nobody was home.

She turned to face it.

"Fawn . . . Is that you?"

An almost hysterical laugh bubbled up in her throat. It was Cole; he was the one driving the car.

He pulled over to the curb in front of her. "My God, I've been looking all over for you. Thank heavens you're safe." He opened the door. "Get in and I'll take you back to the house."

"What the hell were you doing out alone this late at night?" he asked, when she was sitting next to him.

"You sound more like my nanny than my lawyer," she told him. "Do you baby-sit all your clients like this?" She could still feel the adrenalien pumping through her. She felt jumpy, angry at her own foolishness, and couldn't stop herself from turning it against him.

"Don't you read the newspapers?" he demanded. "This is a dangerous city."

"All right, all right. It was a dumb thing to do." And yet it wasn't a street mugger that she'd been afraid of. She knew she'd been fleeing from some memory in her past. She couldn't tell him that. But she was grateful he'd been so concerned for her.

"Just don't do it again," Cole admonished.

She noticed the small, tight knot that had formed at the edge of his jaw, and she had an urge to reach over and smooth it, to ease away the tension. She twisted her fingers together to stop herself. What was she thinking of?

For a moment neither of them spoke. And then he turned to her, and his voice was soft and gentle. "Sometimes I'm a real idiot, and I guess this is one of those times. What I was trying to say is, I don't want anything to happen to you."

"You don't have to apologize," she said. "I think we came out of this one about even. So, I'll forget all about it if you will."

"Agreed," he said with a grin.

"But first, why were you trying to find me? I didn't think anyone knew I'd left the house."

"I stopped by, apparently right after you'd gone, to deliver some more papers for you to sign. I've spent most of the evening in a negotiating session on another case, and couldn't get out here here any earlier. Ned suggested I just hand the papers over to him, but I thought it might be wiser to give them to you myself. So Noreen went to your room to call you.''

"And found out I wasn't in my room." Damn. Now they'd be wondering where she'd been.

"I've been looking for you ever since," he explained. "I thought you might get lost. These streets can be a bit confusing."

"I noticed. And yes, I was lost." She waited for him to ask where she'd been. She intended to dodge the question. But he was being careful not to ask. And she was so grateful he wasn't prying that she found herself saying, "I wanted to call home."

He nodded. "That's what I figured."

He started the car to drive her back to the house. "How's the homecoming been so far?" he asked.

"A little strained," she admitted. "But they're all trying."

"Hmmm," he said noncommittally. He didn't mention that none of the triplets had seemed very concerned that she was out alone on the streets. Maybe he was being too cynical. But then, a fatal mugging would have solved all their problems. It was still true that if she didn't survive until her twenty-fifth birthday, all the money would end up in their pockets.

"It's just a lot different than I expected," she said. "I mean . . . I don't feel the connection I thought I would." Her voice was tentative, and he realized she was trying to reason through something that was still a puzzle to her. "I thought I would recognized them, somehow. I don't mean like an old friend, exactly. But when I look at the pictures of Melissa and Joel, I feel that I'm part of them. And I don't feel that with the triplets."

"You mean, as if you came from two different tribes?" he asked. He knew what she was getting at, though he wasn't sure how to express it. It wasn't so much physical characteristics as a resemblance of the spirit that was missing.

She nodded. "But maybe I'm being too impatient. I guess in time I'll find the threads that connect us together."

Cole looked at her earnest, puzzled face and kept silent. In his mind she was as different from the triplets as day and night, and she always would be.

Fawn, observing his thoughtful expression, realized that she was talking too much; the fright she'd had must have loosened her tongue. She certainly hadn't meant to share her doubts with Cole. Yet she needed someone to confide in, and he was so easy to talk to. He really did seem concerned. But then she remembered Noreen's warning not to trust Cole or his father. And she remembered what else Noreen had told her.

"Cole, why didn't you tell me about the ten million dollars?"

Cole stared at her blankly, as if he didn't know what she was talking about.

"The money your father would have inherited from Joel and Melissa's estate," she reminded him. "If I hadn't returned . . . or if something happens to me . . ."

"Nothing's going to happen to you," he said quickly. "But you're right—I should have told you about the money right away. It just didn't seem that significant. And you were already so set against my father; I thought knowing about the money would just make things worse."

Ten million dollars, insignificant? She wondered why Cole was so intent on protecting his father. And what else did he know that he hadn't told her? She hated all these secrets, but then she reminded herself that she, too, had secrets to keep. And despite everything, she found herself wanting to give Cole the benefit of the doubt.

"You have to trust someone," Cole said softly. They had reached the house by then, and he parked in the driveway, then went around to open her door.

"I guess I'd better go in and let them know I'm all right," she said.

He nodded, and they began to walk to the house. "Are you sure you want to stay?" he asked suddenly. "I could take you . . ."

But she was already shaking her head. "No. I'm not ready to leave yet."

"Well, I'll see you the day after tomorrow, at least," he said. "They've called a general board meeting to acquaint you with the company's holdings, and I'll be there."

For a moment he leaned closer to her, and she thought he was going to kiss her good night. She lifted her face to his, and their eyes met. He was so close she could feel the soft warmth of his breath on her cheek. But then he quickly brushed a fallen petal from her hair, and stepped back.

"Good night, Fawn," he whispered, and then he was striding down the walk.

She waited until his car was out of sight before finally turning and entering the house.

C h a p t e r   15

She'd overslept. When she awoke at last the sunlight was pouring through the windows. She glanced at the clock. It was nearly ten. She must have been more tired than she realized.

She slipped out of bed and stretched, smiling at the view from her window. A family of squirrels was playing chase up and down the trunk of an oak tree, and a plump golden tabby was sunning itself atop a stone wall. The blossoms were so thick on the branches of the cherry trees they seemed like soft pink clouds. It was a perfect day. And it was the day Scott was going to show her the house.

Fawn hurried to take her shower and get dressed. She was glad none of the triplets had decided to stay home with her. This day apart would give all of them, including her, time to adjust to the situation. And maybe tonight they'd be a little less tense, the conversation less strained. It was just an awkward situation for them all, she felt. Yet they were adamant about insisting she stay. They'd made that clear last night when she'd returned to the house, as if they'd been afraid that she wasn't coming back. She was welcome here for as long as she wanted to stay; in fact, they'd talked as if they hoped she'd stay for good.

Thinking about the night before reminded Fawn of Cole. She smiled, remembering how concerned he'd been about her. It made her feel a lot less lonely. The papers he'd brought were sitting on her night table, and she brushed her fingers over them as she remembered how serious and protective he'd been. And how gentle his touch had been as he stroked her hair.

She wondered why he'd decided to deliver the papers last night. Surely they could have waited until the meeting. Or he could have had them sent to the house by messenger. Was it possible that he'd just wanted to see her again?

Stop it, she told herself sternly. It was just as likely that Cole had been checking up on her. Perhaps his father had asked him to keep an eye on her.

And yet, despite all her misgivings, one stubborn idea kept bobbing to the surface: She was still looking forward to seeing him tomorrow.

She slipped into a pair of jeans and a turtleneck, then added a soft mulberry wool vest and a wide belt. The belt's large silver buckle had been designed by one of her friends who was a silversmith, and wearing it was like carrying a bit of home with her. She braided her long blond hair into a plait down her back, tugged on her boots, and then she was ready. And suddenly she felt very hungry.

Quickly she crossed the lawn to the house and let herself in. As she passed the living room, the large painting over the fireplace caught her eye. It was a French country scene, and with the morning sun on it, it was breathtaking. She moved closer, feeling she could almost sense the breeze rippling through the flowers, the warmth of the vibrant blue sky. And then she saw the name painted in the lower corner—Monet. My God, she wondered, was it real? She looked around at the other pictures; there was a Seurat, a delicate Cassatt, a Dufy watercolor . . . It was like living in a museum.

The stereo was on, and she entered the dining room humming along with the love song that was playing. Scott was sitting, shoulders hunched together, at the dining room table. "Shit, she sings in the morning," he groaned, staring morosely into his coffee. "Send her back, she can't be one of us."

"Sorry. Bit of a hangover?" she whispered.

"Definitely not one of us—she's too nice," he informed his coffee. Then noticing her startled expression, he flushed and added, "I'm just kidding. Don't mind me. Sit down and have some coffee."

Fawn poured herself a cup of coffee from the silver service and took the chair next to him. She noticed that his normally attractive face had a greenish pallor and his thick hair stood up in unruly clumps, as if it had been combed with his fingers.

"I realize that my showing up here so unexpectedly is going to cause some problems," she said. She decided she was done with tiptoeing around the subject. And considering Scott's behavior at dinner the night before, she didn't think she had much to lose. Maybe if they faced it, they might still have a chance to be friends.

" 'Problems'?" he repeated. His eyes slowly focused on her. "For me, you mean?"

"I guess, especially for you." After all, Noreen had said they'd all expected him to eventually take over the company.

He grinned. "Not for me. In fact, Princess, your coming back is exactly what I would have prayed for—if I ever prayed."

"Why?" she asked, puzzled. It occurred to her he might still be drunk. But he seemed sober enough.

"Because"— he leaned toward her—lowering his voice to a whisper—"if I'm lucky, they're going to stick you with the fucking company. In a few months, legally, you'll be the president. And that means I'm off the hook."

Now she was truly confused. "Off the hook?"

Scott nodded, explaining, "Mother, in a determinedly misguided sense of mother love—or something—has always had very clear ideas about my destiny. I wouldn't be surprised if she had my diapers embroidered, 'President, Dalworth, Inc.' The thing is, she hasn't been able to convince anyone else—including Nick or Ned."

"Or you?"

"Well, she's working against great odds there. I know myself." He grinned, but then turned serious. "Don't listen to her, Fawn. I know she's started campaigning already. Very subtly, I'm sure, but she'll keep up the pressure. Listen to me—I'd make an abysmal company man of any sort, let alone president."

"Scott . . ." It disturbed her to see anyone so down on himself.

"No." He waved off her concern. "I'd be good at something, if I ever got the chance to find out what—besides surviving Mother. And I'm hoping, Fawn, that you're going to give me that chance. What is it Henny Youngman says, 'Please, take my job . . .' "

"Why don't you just tell her yourself?"

He glanced at her sharply, then turned away. When he spoke, his voice was harsh. "You haven't been around for the last eighteen years, Fawn, so maybe you'll refrain from making judgments. . . ."

Fawn felt her face reddening, but she wasn't angry. He was right. What did she know of Scott's life?

Leaning close to her, his expression contrite, he said, "I'm sorry. But you see how hopeless it is. How could you have a president with such a big, smart-alecky mouth? Anyway, if your return is going to be rough on anyone, it's you. And I don't want to make it any worse."

"What are you saying exactly?" she asked. He knew the family, he could tell her what to expect.

But he obviously wasn't going to.

"Oh, Lord, all these questions before breakfast," he moaned, shaking his head. He gestured toward the line of chafing dishes on the buffet. "Come on, eat up . . . The cook's feelings are very easily hurt. And you have no idea—yet—how hard it is to get a decent cook."

Fawn decided to let it drop. But it occurred to her that this was hardly the conversation Noreen had envisioned when she'd so eagerly volunteered Scott to be her companion today.

While they finished their breakfast of eggs Florentine, Scott asked her what she'd like to see first. Now that he'd had a chance to say what was on his mind, he'd settled into an easy familiarity with her. He seemed like a different person. She was surprised by his wry wit and by the odd bits of knowledge he'd collected on dozens of different subjects. She was beginning to like him, and when they left the table they were laughing.

"If you'll just follow me, " he said, holding out his hand. "Considering the size of the house, we usually provide rollerskates for the tourists, but I'm afraid the wheels are out being goldplated at the moment."

She'd told him she was most interested in those rooms that were unchanged from Melissa and Joel's time. So they started with the large library. "No one really comes here but me," he told her. She wondered why. It was a wonderful room, with bookcases from floor to ceiling, and deep leather armchairs and a fine view of the garden through the double French doors. And in the corner there was a miniature armchair, just the right size for a six-year-old. Her chair. On the lower shelves, where a six-year-old girl could have reached them by herself, were several dozen children's books—fairy tales, picture books, and a complete collection of Winnie the Pooh.

She tried to picture the three of them sitting here together in front of the fireplace in the evenings, tried to see her parents' faces, but nothing would come. She couldn't remember.

"Are the family albums here?" she asked finally. Maybe they would help.

Scott shook his head. "The maid looked for them this morning, but they seemed to have disappeared." Seeing her disappointment, he added, "Maybe they're down in the basement. We could look there."

She agreed quickly, and they walked back through the kitchen and down the stairs. The basement had the musty, rather pleasant smell of old wood and perfumed clothes locked in trunks. Dust covered everything. The floor was a clutter of boxes and trunks and furniture. In the corner by the stairs long wine racks were carefully arranged in rows.

"A lot of this stuff belonged to our grandparents—Melissa's and the triplets' parents. It was stored here after they died. I don't think anyone's even been through it," Scott told her.

Fawn wandered through the jumble, searching for the albums. The cellar was like an old junk shop with a bit of everything—there was a rusting tricycle, an old dress form, baby furniture . . .

And suddenly Fawn felt a surge of nausea. The ceiling seemed to be squeezing down around her shoulders, and she felt the dizziness that always preceded one of her panic attacks. Her heart pounded. And now even the floor seemed to shift, and everything was closing in on her.

"What's wrong?" Scott asked, peering at her worriedly.

She stared at him, fighting for control. "Scott, did . . . it happen here?" She meant her parents' murders, but she couldn't say the words.

He understood immediately, and put his arm around her to steady her. "No, Fawn, not here."

"But I . . . there's something . . . God, get me out of here."

"Come on, we'll go upstairs." His voice was very gentle; maybe coming back to this house with its horrifying history was too much for her. "It's all right now. I'll hold your hand."

But suddenly she was terrified to take another step. She felt trapped—afraid where she was and afraid to move. There was something horrible waiting at the top of the stairs, in the kitchen . . .

"Fawn, it's all right now. It's only a memory." The memory of her parents being stabbed right in front of her, of the killer going after her . . . But he had to lead her back to the present. "Nothing is happening upstairs—except the cook is probably in the liquor cabinet. You know, Ned marks the bottles, but she just washes the lines off and remarks them after she's had a few. The woman is wasted as a cook—think of the tax accountant she would have made."

Fawn hung on his words, knowing he was trying to distract her. But everything was muffled by the frantic rushing in her ears.

She leaned against the banister. "Just let me stand here for a minute. It'll pass; it always passes." That's what she had to grab hold of, keep repeating—it always passed. And after a time—she had no idea how long—she felt the tension easing in her chest, and her heart slowed to a more bearable pace.

"I'm fine now," she said, starting up the stairs. The cook was still finishing up the breakfast dishes in the kitchen, so Scott led Fawn outside. They sat side by side on a lounge chair. Around them the morning was clear and bright and completely peaceful.

"Did you remember his face?" Scott asked. "Whoever it was that killed your parents . . ."

She shook her head. "No. But I know now that I was there, in the basement, sometime that night. And that whoever it was was waiting upstairs. But eventually I'm sure I'll see the face, I'll remember it all."

He shuddered. "Are you sure you want to stay, Fawn?"

She tried to laugh. "Part of me doesn't want to stay at all. There's a little voice in my head whispering, get the hell out of here. But that's why I have to stay."

He looked at her curiously. "I can't say I understand. But then I'm a specialist in running—while standing still."

"Come on," she said, getting up and holding out a hand to pull him to his feet. She even managed to inject a little enthusiasm into her voice. "Let's get back to the tour. I'll be fine now."

An hour later they'd been in every room except Ned's suite. That was locked. Fawn felt she could imagine much more clearly what living here must have been like. She was impressed with how light-filled and cheery the rooms were and how carefully each detail had been thought out. Melissa's and Joel's tastes had been impeccable and wide-ranging, and there was often a playful element in the way they'd chosen to combine the treasures they'd brought back from their travels all over the world.

But a great deal had been changed over the years, too, as Scott told her. Especially in the bedrooms. Everything had been moved out of her old bedroom and gotten rid of. It was Scott's room now. Of course, there was no reason why they should have kept any of her things; they'd thought she was dead. Yet somehow she'd hoped one small trace of her childhood would have survived to call up the past.

"I guess that's everything," she said as they started down the stairs.

"Except the greenhouse."

The air in the greenhouse was moist and warm and fragrant with the scent of a hundred blossoms: creamy white gardenias, delicate orange blossoms, rows of roses in all colors and varieties, and pots of pink and red and white parrot tulips with their ruffled, scalloped edges. It was a dazzling display.

"Your mother used to spend hours here. She could make anything bloom," Scott said. "And she used to let us help her, though I imagine what we mostly did was get in the way. But she never scolded, even when we used the sprayer to have water fights."

"I wish I could remember . . ." Fawn said. She frowned as if trying to hear some echo of those childish giggles still in the air.

"Noreen just has a gardener come in now," Scott said.

Fawn had been strolling up and down the aisles, and as she stopped to admire a tray of paper narcissus she suddenly glimpsed the leather spine of a book thrust behind the table. She tugged it free, thinking the moist air would ruin the binding.

"What's this doing here?" she asked.

"That's a good question," Scott said, staring at the large, flat album. "That's the family picture album that we've been looking for."

Whoever had put it there, obviously hadn't wanted it found. But which one of them had hidden it? And why?

She carried the album to the living room, and with Scott sitting next to her, they began to leaf through the pages. The first photographs dated back to the year before her parents' marriage. There were pictures of Melissa and Joel holding hands and smiling at each other with such love and hope in their eyes, it was almost painful to see. There were snapshots of their honeymoon in Venice; the first photograph of her as a baby in her mother's arms; and scenes of holidays through the years, with Noreen hugging Scott, Nick always with a different girl, and Ned standing awkwardly to one side.

Years slipped by in a few pages. And as Fawn studied the photographs, a puzzled frown began to cloud her eyes. Fawn had had a lot of experience photographing families together, and she knew how clearly the camera could capture the hidden relationships among people. She'd taken pictures herself where the evidence was unmistakable: the stiffness between a husband and wife who weren't getting along; the spoiled bully who insisted on being in the center of every picture; the scornful posture of a teenager who was ashamed of his parents. It was all there for the camera to see.

And as Fawn's eyes scanned these pictures, she began to sense there had been something very wrong in her own family. The night before, the triplets had tried to give her the impression it had been a carefree, loving group, without a hint of discord. Yet she noticed in picture after picture how Nick and Ned unconsciously leaned away from each other . . . and the way Noreen had of edging in front of Melissa . . . and how Ned was always watching Joel out of the corner of his eye. Only Melissa and Joel seemed comfortable and loving—and unaware of the discord around them.

Theirs was hardly the happy family everyone had portrayed last night. And Fawn knew that she'd only believed them because that was what she wanted to believe. She had excused away all the tension and animosity in the air; she told herself it was all due to her sudden, unexpected return. But there'd been something ugly beneath the surface even before the murders.

Scott was staring down at a picture of Noreen and himself and frowning, and suddenly Fawn realized there was someone missing from the album. "Isn't there a photograph of your father?" she asked.

Scott shook his head. "Not one. Mother says he was very handsome, distinguished-looking. They were only together a short time. I guess the memory's still pretty painful for her."

"You never saw him?"

"He died before I was born—in a car accident, Mom says. But I'm not even sure that's the truth. She tells such vague, contradictory stories about him. Anyway, after my father supposedly died, your parents took her in, and we lived here until I was nearly two years old. Even after that your folks pretty much watched out for us." He turned away, slightly embarrassed. "I used to pretend Joel was my father. And later I thought it might be Colman."

He saw her surprise and said, "It's not such a ridiculous idea. My mother has always been very attracted to Colman. It's true he was married back then, but who knows what happened between the two of them? And there's always been a strange sort of tension there." Scott shrugged. "The problem is, when you don't know the truth, you can't help making up stories. I guess you must have done the same thing."

He would have gladly traded all his fantasies for just a few facts he could be sure of—details as simple as how his father and mother had met, what his father did for a living, whether he was happy with his life. But Noreen wasn't much help. Sometimes just bringing up the subject made her furious. Fawn's return had raised all the old questions in his mind. He tried to laugh it off.

"Hell, I don't even know if I should celebrate St. Patrick's day, or take offense at Polish jokes. While I was at college I lived on pizza . . . maybe I'm Italian."

Fawn was silent, feeling the hurt beneath his words. She'd spent most of her life trying to bury the same pain.

"Maybe someday I'll have the courage to do what you're doing," he said. "You went out looking for the answers you needed." He turned to her, and there was a shy new affection shining in his eyes. "Anyway, we've found each other. That's something to be grateful for."

"Yes it is," she agreed, smiling. Suddenly she knew they were going to be friends. And that alone would have been enough to make her glad she'd come back.

"It's funny, but when we were kids, I hated you," Scott said. "You were so much better than I was in school. You didn't get into trouble the way I did all the time. Mom was always throwing it in my face, as if we were in some sort of competition. But I want you to know, I'm on your side now."

"You sound as though you're expecting some sort of battle."

"The board meeting tomorrow is only the first round," he said. "But I'll do what I can to help."

She nodded, dreading the next day. But at least Scott would be there. And Cole . . .

C h a p t e r   16

The headquarters of Dalsworth, Inc., were housed in an elegant, turn-of-the-century building just off Wall Street. With its high, coffered ceilings and carved mouldings, it looked like a bank. The tall marble columns in the lobby were a dark green color—just the shade of money, Fawn thought to herself. And that's what they'd all come here to discuss: the money. Colman Bromley had felt it was time she became acquainted with her holdings, though she would not gain control over the fortune until her twenty-fifth birthday.

Nick was at her side as they entered the private elevator. They'd had to fight their way through a crowd of reporters outside the building; somehow news of her return had leaked out, and the reporters were almost climbing over one another to get a few words from the heiress. But Nick muttered "No comment," and strong-armed his way through the crowd. Fawn hadn't thought of Nick as a big man—next to Ned everyone looked small—but she'd been impressed by his strength. That wasn't padding filling out the broad shoulders of his perfectly tailored pin-striped suit, she realized. With his arm supporting hers, he'd propelled her through the crowd as if she'd been a doll.

"Now I'll be at your side every minute," Nick told her at the door to the conference room. "Don't let all this financial jargon throw you. And you don't have to make any decisions today, remember that." He sounded more nervous than she was.

"Thank you, Uncle Nick," she said. "But I just expect to listen today."

"Good, good." He nodded his head in approval. "Don't let anybody hustle you into anything."

"Who would do that, Uncle Nick?" she asked, meeting his eyes, and he suddenly turned away. "Aren't we all family?"

He chuckled, not at all good-naturedly. "I suppose the others have already warned you against me. But, Fawn, when you need a friend, you'll find I'm the one you can count on."

Ned and Noreen had already made the same sort of assurances to her that morning. All the attention made her feel like the only kid on the block with a baseball. But she knew now that they were all deadly serious. The carefully presented veneer of happy family life had begun to split, revealing the wormy surface beneath it.

The other board members were already seated when Fawn entered, and there was a rush to greet her, everyone standing up at once. Cole gave her a reassuring wink, but there was no chance for them to talk. Bromley handled the introductions; in addition to Nick and Ned and Noreen, several accountants and senior executives were attending the meeting.

Fawn was given the chair at the head of the long, polished mahogany conference table. And just as they were about to start, Scott rushed in and slipped a chair in right next to her, ignoring Nick's glare. "Told you I'd be here," he whispered.

"Nick, would you like to begin?" Bromley asked, and Fawn remembered that Nick was actually the president of the company, though Ned was the one with the financial talent.

"This is your idea, Colman," Nick said. He seemed miffed that Scott had wedged himself closer to Fawn. "You do the talking."

"All right," Bromley agreed evenly. He gave Fawn a

friendly smile. "We'll try not to throw everything at you at once. The actual details of the trust arrangement with an accounting of the assets can be gone over later, for example. But we wanted to give you an overview of the company and try to fill you in on what's been happening for the last eighteen years."

"I'm sure you'll see how carefully the company's assets have been managed," Ned said stiffly. He looked as nervous as if he were on trial.

The next two hours were filled with a dizzying recital of facts and figures. The accountants had brought charts with them, and they flipped over page after page of graphs and long columns of sums. And they seemed to be speaking a foreign language: noncumulative preferred . . . debenture . . . floating supply . . . composite quotation system . . . variable ratio plan . . . round lot. Cole had often interrupted and tried to explain as much as possible in everyday terms, but then the accountants just plowed ahead. Fawn was lost. It would take her weeks of study to make sense of what she'd just been told.

"Well, that about wraps it up," Nick said at last, smiling broadly. "You see, Fawn, we're delivering the company to you in excellent financial health."

"Meaning he wants to keep his job," Scott whispered.

Nick's face turned a mottled red and white, and the cords in his neck tensed, straining against his shirt collar. "I was working for this company when you were still in diapers, Scott," he said angrily. "Joel brought me in himself. You might just remember that." The unmistakable fury in his voice produced a sudden silence around the rest of the table, and the others looked at one another uncomfortably.

"Nick, this is no place for a brawl," Noreen said sharply. "When are you going to learn to control that temper of yours?"

"Just tell your son to keep his mouth shut," Nick retorted sullenly. "And I'm not the only one in this family with a temper."

"Let's get back to the business at hand," Bromley suggested. "Now that Fawn's back, I think we should order a complete audit of the trust funds. She should know exactly how much she'll be inheriting in five months.''

"Surely that can wait a few months," Ned objected. He had already started to gather up his papers as if the meeting were over.

"No . . . I think now would be best. Don't you, Fawn?" Bromley countered, putting the question directly to her.

"It sounds sensible to me," Fawn said. The money was such an explosive issue that before today she'd been willing to postpone any detailed discussion of her inheritance until the shock of her sudden return quieted down. But now she wondered why Ned was so opposed to an audit. He actually seemed frightened of the idea.

"I think what Ned means," Noreen said, "is that audits are expensive. Why have it done twice—now and again in October? Certainly Fawn would be willing to trust us for a few more months."

"Of course she would," Ned said quickly.

Nick nodded in agreement and smiled around the table; he was all charm again, and it was difficult to believe that a minute ago he'd seemed ready to throttle Scott. "I'm sure when Colman says now, he doesn't really mean right now," Nick said smoothly. "Just that we should think about it . . .''

Bromley handed a page of legal print to Fawn, but his eyes never left Nick's face. "No, Nick, that's not what I meant. . . . In fact, I've brought the authorization papers with me today." He turned to Fawn. "All you have to do is sign at the bottom."

Out of the corner of her eye, Fawn could see Nick tense beside her. His face was frozen in an awkward—and unconvincing—smile. At his end of the table, Ned wasn't even trying to smile; his fists were clenched, and the look he shot Bromley was filled with pure venom.

"Maybe Fawn would like to think about it for a few days," Noreen suggested smoothly. "These last few days have been a horrible strain on her. There's just so much anyone can take. And, Colman, I think it's very unfair of you to expect her to make this sort of decision now."

"Fawn's perfectly capable of handling the situation," Bromley answered. "I think you're underestimating her."

Fawn had kept silent because she wanted to be sure where each of the triplets stood; she'd wanted to hear it from their own lips. And what she'd heard disturbed her. Why were they all so opposed to this audit? What were they hiding? This was Melissa and Joel's company; she had a responsibility to make certain it was being run the way they would have wanted it to be. It wasn't just her own inheritance at stake; the company was entrusted with a lot of other people's money. There were retirement funds, small family nest eggs, trust funds for widows and orphans . . . If someone was stealing from the company, those people would be the losers. Was someone stealing? Were they all? Ignoring the frowns around the table, she picked up the pen and signed the authorization. "Can you start the audit immediately?" she asked Bromley.

"This afternoon," he assured her.

Nick shrugged. "Well, I guess that closes the meeting with a bang." He started to rise.

Fawn stood up, too. "Now, if you'll just show me where my office is . . ."

Ned stopped dead in his tracks. "Office?"

And immediately Nick protested, "Fawn, we don't actually expect you to work her."

"True," Scott whispered, low enough so only Fawn could hear. "Nick doesn't even expect Nick to work."

"I won't require anything large," Fawn said, meeting their obvious shock with a calm smile. "Just someplace where I can study all these reports more thoroughly. After all, I have a lot of catching up to do."

"Of course we'll find an office for you," Noreen said. But she didn't look pleased, either.

Scott grinned, flashing a victory sign to Fawn as the others stood up to leave. "I think you're going to be good at this."

"Yes, she is, isn't she?" Cole agreed. He was suddenly standing beside her, and there was a warm smile in his eyes. "You did beautifully today."

"I was lost most of the time," she admitted with a laugh. She had to tilt her head up to look into his eyes, and she thought how strong and sturdy and capable he was. And handsome in his three-piece suit. There was something very reassuring about his presence; it seemed he could handle anything. As much as was possible, he'd guided her through the confusing fusillade of financial terms; while the others seemed to be trying to overwhelm her with masses of facts and figures, Cole's explanations had always been clear and to the point. "I'm glad you were here," she told him. "Nobody else seemed to be speaking English."

"I think they were trying to impress you, maybe even scare you off," he said. "Frankly, I doubt they expected you to understand half what you did." But she'd done better than she realized. He'd noticed how impressed the executives were with her; and he'd seen, too, how startled and uncomfortable the triplets had been by her astute questions. Not to mention how unhappy they were when she agreed to the audit; they'd obviously expected her to be no more than a puppet with them pulling the strings.

Fawn was thinking about the audit as well. The others had left now, so she and Cole were alone, and she felt free to ask him, "Why did they object to the audit so much?"

"I haven't been involved in the trust management up till now, so I don't know for sure," he told her. "And maybe it's nothing more than that they don't like the idea of someone checking up on them—just a matter of pride. Or maybe there's been some petty pilfering over the years—dipping into the company funds for their own use, having the business pay their personal expenses." Or maybe it was something much worse, he thought to himself. But whatever had prompted them, it was the first clear sign there was going to be trouble ahead.

"So, one of them could have been stealing from the company all these years?"

"It's unlikely. They had to file quarterly reports, and my father's kept as close an eye on them as possible." Still, if one of them was really clever, maybe there'd be some way . . . And all these years, everyone expected that the money would eventually end up in their pockets anyway, so no one had suspected they would be embezzling their own funds. But perhaps one of them had been preparing for her return all along.

She still looked worried, so he tried to reassure her. "If

there's anything wrong, Fawn, we'll find it. But there's no reason to be concerned yet.''

She smiled. ''You're right. And I've got enough to worry about already.''

He knew that was true. She was still coming to terms with the fact of her parents' murders, and trying to untangle her own past—while at the same time she had to deal with a brand-new family and an inheritance she never suspected existed. It was a wonder she was able to smile at all, considering the strain she was under. And she looked so fragile today. Her black suit emphasized how slim she was and the delicacy of her build. And her skin was almost as pale as her white, high-necked blouse.

''How about some lunch?'' he asked as casually as he could. Maybe he could at least spend a few hours with her. ''And I could show you a bit of the city afterwards.''

She started to say no, then changed her mind. She needed a few hours of respite, a chance to get away from everything. ''Lunch sounds fine,'' she said. ''But what if all those reporters are still waiting downstairs?'' She didn't feel like answering a lot of questions; she still had too many questions of her own.

''We'll sneak out the back way,'' Cole explained with a grin. ''Where would you like to go?''

''For lunch . . . anywhere you choose.'' Suddenly she was looking forward to the hour ahead. She would have enjoyed seeing the city with him, too, but there'd be no chance for that today. ''I won't be able to spend much time,'' she told him. ''I have another appointment this afternoon.''

''Where?'' he asked quickly.

''Captain Almafi called the house yesterday. He wants to talk with me.''

Cole looked grim. ''You've had a rough day already—why don't you postpone that? I'll call him myself if you'd like.''

''I have to go. Captain Almafi thinks now that I'm back there's a good chance he'll be able to find my parents' murderer. I have to do everything I can to help.''

''Then I'll come with you.'' he insisted.

''I'm not sure that's a good idea.'' Why was he so opposed to her seeing Captain Almafi? she wondered. Was he just trying to protect her from more hurt, or was there something else he was afraid of? He certainly seemed to have been on her side today at the meeting. And his father—insisting on the audit—seemed also to be looking out for her best interests. So why was she still reluctant to accept Bromley as the caring, family friend his son had painted him as? And why, just when she was beginning to trust Cole did she hold back?

"We can talk about it after lunch," Cole suggested, taking her arm. "Right now, I'll bet you're starved."

He was smiling again, and she shook off her dark thoughts. For the moment they were just two people going out to lunch together. She was going to forget everything else and enjoy herself.

Chapter 17

As soon as the board meeting was over, Nick had hurried to his car. The blackmailer had sent another note the night before to tell him when and where to make the $25,000 payment. And Nick would have to move quickly if he wanted to arrive on time. The blackmailer had been painfully specific about the consequences of being late.

As Nick jockeyed through the crowded midtown streets, ignoring the shouts of the drivers he cut off and racing the car's motor at every red light, his face was set in a petulant frown. He felt as though the whole universe were against him. First the blackmail, then Fawn's return, and now this business about the audit. So, a few dollars had stuck to his fingers now and then. The money should have been his, anyway. Damn her for coming back. He'd been so fucking close to getting everything he wanted, and now his whole world was crumbling.

And there'd been damned little in his bank account after he'd withdrawn the twenty-five thousand dollars the blackmailer had demanded. It was as if the blackmailer had known just how much Nick had. And he had nothing more to draw on; he'd borrowed against just about everything he owned. The mortgage company, the tax man, and a dozen creditors were after him already.

Shit, he'd just have to live more carefully until . . . when? The inheritance wouldn't be coming to him now.

No, he refused to believe that. Fawn couldn't steal the money he'd waited for all these years. She was a kind-hearted girl, and she seemed to like him. Surely he could talk her into handing over his share. Or the others would think of something. That's what they were all waiting for—for one of the others to come up with a way of getting rid of her. Of course, there was always the way her parents had been gotten rid of. . . .

But that would be too suspicious. The girl had only been dumped on their doorstep four days ago. No, the police would never buy an "accident" or a "kidnapping" so soon.

His mind twisted around in the maze, unable to find a way out. Better to deal with one thing at a time, he decided. Settle with the blackmailer. Then find some way to handle Fawn.

The blackmailer had chosen an old, abandoned Catholic church for their meeting. The structure seemed ready to collapse, and the side door he'd been instructed to use was almost rusted shut. As he slipped inside, his jacket rubbed against the dusty wall, and he stopped to brush off his sleeve, swearing to himself. Of all the damned fool places to meet.

It took his eyes a minute to adjust to the dim interior of the church. Only the faintest bit of sunlight streamed through the soot-encrusted stained-glass windows, though here and there a section had been shattered and the light fell in a jagged pool on the floor. Gradually he began to make out shapes. The church seemed to be a hangout for the neighborhood hooligans, he saw. Empty beer cans and cigarette butts littered the floor, and obscenities, mostly misspelled, were carved into the backs of the pews. And what hadn't been destroyed had been carried off. Even part of the altar railing had been ripped out.

Nick shivered. He'd never been religious, still the place gave him the spooks. He wanted to get out of there as quickly as possible.

He'd been told to enter the confessional—another example

of the blackmailer's taunting sense of humor. But as he stared at the dark, enclosed booth, he hesitated. Maybe Jolene's husband had already seen the videotapes. Maybe a few of his goons were waiting for him. . . .

It was too late to worry about that now, he realized. And with a violent yank at the door, he hurried into the small, pitch-dark booth.

"I knew you'd come," a voice said from the other side of the ironwork screen. It was a high, squeaky voice that didn't seem human at all, more like a cartoon character's. And whoever it was seemed very amused with himself.

"Who are you?" Nick demanded, trying to bluff his way through his nervousness. He couldn't see past the screen at all. Yet something in that eerie, inhuman voice tugged at his memory; he'd heard it somewhere before. "Just tell me who you are," he insisted again.

"You're going to have to figure that out for yourself, Nick." The blackmailer's laugh echoed crazily through the small booth; the sound made Nick's flesh crawl, as if he'd been touched by something slimy and cold. "Tell me about Jolene. . . ." the voice demanded.

"It's over," Nick said quickly. "I haven't seen her again. It was just a few afternoons in a motel, anyway."

"So you say . . ."

"She never meant anything to me," Nick insisted, suddenly angry at Jolene for getting him into this mess. "She was just a silly, oversexed broad."

"Maybe you should tell her husband that," the voice taunted.

"Dammit, what do you want from me? I brought the money."

The partition separating them slid open an inch. "Yes, the money . . . Give it to me."

For one desperate moment Nick considered making a grab for the shadowy figure. But the opening was too narrow to get his fist through. And the blackmailer, as if reading his thoughts, cautioned, "You'll never get those videotapes if you try anything foolish."

"How do I even know you have any tapes? Where are they?"

"Nowhere that you can get your hands on them."

"I'm not going to give you the money until I see—" Nick began, but he was interrupted by the sound of his own voice coming through the screen: ". . . afternoons in a motel . . . She meant nothing to me. She was just a silly, oversexed broad." The blackmailer had taped the whole conversation. It was as good as a confession. Now his own words were all the proof Jolene's mobster of a husband would need. Shit, how could he have been such an idiot? "Turn it off," he shouted. The sound of his own voice, so craven and pleading, was making him sick.

"The money, Nick . . ."

Silently he slid the envelope with the money inside through the opening.

"Now, about your next payment . . ."

"No. I want the tapes now."

"Nick, a man of your—shall we say—experience shouldn't be so naive." Again the grotesque laugh made his skin crawl. "All right, we'll make it just one more payment—for one hundred thousand dollars. A nice round figure—and you're a man who appreciates figures."

"You're crazy."

"Let's just call it getting-away money. You do want to be rid of me, don't you Nick?"

"But I don't have that much," he protested.

"You'll get it. When you're cornered, you always find a way."

"In a few months . . . I'll be able to give you twice that much, more even, then."

"From your niece's inheritance? No, Nick, I'm not going to buy a ticket in that lottery. You have ten days to get the money, or I start playing show-and-tell. Now get out of here."

Nick stumbled out of the booth.

Outside, the sun was shining in a cloudless sky, and two young boys were playing ball against the steps of the church. Nick walked past them blindly. It had suddenly come to him how the blackmailer had been able to alter his voice so completely. Helium. You could buy helium balloons all over the city. It was a trick he and Ned and Noreen had delighted in themselves as children, inhaling the gas and giggling over the way it transformed their voices.

For a moment he wondered . . . then quickly discarded the possibility. Blackmail wasn't their style. Still, if the blackmailer had altered his voice, it must mean that Nick would have recognized it. It was someone he knew. But who?

He suddenly turned to the boys playing ball. "Is this the only door that works?"

"Naah, there's a couple doors in the back, and one over on the other side."

And the blackmailer had undoubtedly already sneaked out one of them, Nick realized, cursing himself for not thinking of the idea earlier.

He'd better start worrying about how he was going to get the money. Now that Fawn was back, he was going to have a hell of a time persuading anyone to lend him another cent. Damn her. It was all her fault he was in this fix.

Colman Bromley was frowning as he strode through the halls of Bromley, Reswick, and Christensen. And as his mind went back over the meeting, his frown deepened.

The office staff exchanged worried glances. Had one of them screwed up? "The Old Man looks like he could chew daggers today," a junior clerk whispered. But he was careful not to let the "Old Man" hear him. No one called Bromley that to his face.

It was a term of affection and respect, but it was based on fear as well. When Colman Bromley was in a mood like today's, no one wanted to draw attention to himself. The experience of being called on the carpet by Bromley was enough to turn a man's bones to jelly.

"Is Davis still handling the accounting for the Dalsworth trust?" Colman asked his secretary. She nodded.

"Get him in here. And start bringing in everything that deals with the Dalsworth estate."

"Everything? There're two full filing cabinets and . . ."

"Everything, please."

He settled himself behind his desk, drumming his fingers impatiently. Damn, he should have kept a closer eye on the estate. The triplets' reaction at the meeting this morning was proof enough of that. But he had such limited oversight powers. His hands had been tied by the terms of the trust.

He remembered how he'd objected to the wording of the will when it was first drawn up. But Melissa and Joel were so trusting, and they'd worried that the triplets' feelings might be hurt if there was any suggestion of their being checked up on. Bromley had finally stopped trying to convince Melissa and Joel that there should be more safeguards, that his power of attorney should be utilized to the fullest.

He tried to tell himself how unlikely it was that any of the triplets had actually been doctoring the books. Up until Fawn's return, everyone had expected the money to go to them, anyway. All they had to do was wait—unless one of the three was after it all. Maybe he'd counted too much on their suspicions of each other to keep them in line; he'd been so sure they'd been watching one another, each one protecting his stake in the inheritance.

Bromley looked up to see Davis entering his office.

"I hope you didn't have any plans for this evening."

"Well, actually . . . I did . . ." Davis stuttered.

"Cancel them. We're going to do a little digging."

Ned returned to his office in the early afternoon. Given the mood he was in, he didn't feel like talking with anyone. The morning—the board meeting—had been a disaster. As he passed the metal file cabinets that lined one wall of his office, he gave them a savage kick, then sank wearily into his chair, rubbing his balding temples. "Damn that Colman," he whispered. "And damn the girl."

There was a knock on the door. "What now?" he muttered. But it was only his secretary, Rose.

"How did it go, sir?" she asked timidly. "The meeting, I mean . . ." He shrugged; he never told her any more than was absolutely necessary. Rose had been with him for eleven years now. He remembered giving her a bonus—a little pot of ivy—on her tenth anniversary with the firm. She was no beauty, but she was a good secretary—efficient and quiet and not given to prying. But now it was obvious that she was worried. Her pale, slightly bulging eyes seemed close to tears.

"They won't? . . ." She hesitated. "There won't be any change in the management of the firm, will there?

"I don't have to start cleaning out my desk just yet, if that's what you mean," he answered grimly.

"I'm glad, sir."

Ned was suddenly touched by her concern, surprised by her loyalty. He wasn't used to any woman, even one as plain as Rose, taking an interest in him. And then he decided she was probably just worried about her own job. Angry with himself for thinking it was anything more than that, he said roughly, "I'm sure whatever happens they'll keep you on."

"Oh, I wouldn't stay . . . without you. It wouldn't be the same at all." And suddenly her face flooded with color. "Can I get you some coffee or something?" she asked quickly in an effort to hide her embarrassment.

"No, I'm going out again." he answered without looking at her. He was suddenly as uncomfortable as she was. She really had been concerned about him, and he didn't know how to handle it. Yet, he was pleased, too.

Rose nodded, her cheeks still pink, and hurried from the office. Ned stared after her. Despite her drab clothes and stiffly curled hair—even *he* knew women had stopped wearing their hair like that fifteen years ago—she'd seemed almost pretty for a moment. And there'd been real devotion in her eyes. Was it possible? He'd never suspected she had any feeling for him at all. She should wear rouge or something, he thought. That little bit of color in her cheeks made all the difference. . . .

But as he glanced at the clock, he forgot Rose entirely. He had an appointment to keep. He had to move ahead quickly with his plan—especially now, with Colman poking around, Ned realized. He might not have much time left. . . .

Grabbing some files from his desk, he left the office immediately. And, despite the expense, he changed buses twice on his way uptown, watching over his shoulder to make sure he wasn't being followed.

The old printing shop was in a section of town given over to junkies and cheap hotels. The windows were covered with fly-specked advertisements for engraved wedding invitations and photocopying while-you-wait. Only the door looked new, and that was of thick-plated steel.

As Ned entered, the frail, gray-haired man behind the counter was arguing with a female customer. "So, go somewhere else. I think you only come in here to get out of the cold, anyway," the man said to her, motioning for Ned to be patient.

"I will," the woman answered defiantly.

"Good, good." He ushered her to the door, locking it as soon as she'd left. "People wander in. . . ." he said apologetically, turning to Ned. He shrugged, his palms lifted, as if to say, what could he do? "But tell me, how did the meeting go?"

"Not great—but I'll be able to handle it."

"It's a sweetheart of a set-up you've got."

Ned nodded, accepting the compliment. But after all, wasn't he the boy wonder, the financial genius?

"You're sure this girl isn't going to make trouble?"

"That's my worry, Franz," Ned replied, just a bit curtly. The old man was beginning to think of himself too much like a partner, rather than a hired hand.

"Okay, okay—so you handle her," Franz agreed quickly, leading Ned into the back room. "I got the new paper right here, all ready." He adjusted his wire-rim glasses and began to open the bulky floor safe. His fingers were long and delicate, and as they gently twirled the dial their elegance seemed at odds with the rest of his appearance. He was dressed no better than a street bum, in pants that were baggy and threadbare at the knees and a moth-eaten, shapeless sweater. But his hands were perfectly cared for.

At last he lifted a square package out of the safe and set it on the counter. He stepped back and, with a gesture of triumph, motioned for Ned to unwrap the brown paper.

Inside was a quarter of a million dollars in phony stock certificates and negotiable bonds. Exact duplicates of the genuine stocks and bonds that were at that moment locked in Ned's office safe. As Ned rifled through the certificates, his motions slowed, becoming as gentle as a man with a newborn baby. "Beautiful," he breathed.

"I do only the best—that's why you choose me, no?"

Ned nodded, still staring at the engraved certificates. "But you're going to have to work faster. He took an envelope filled with cash and a list out of his pocket and handed it to Franz. "Here's what I'll need next. You should have masters on all these by now."

Franz studied the list. "No problem. When you want?"

"By next week."

"That quick? There's so many. . . ."

"I'm not going to have as much time as I thought."

"So, she is giving you a scare." But when Ned frowned, he added quickly, "Okay, I do my best." He fingered the cash in the envelope. "Maybe a bonus in it for me, huh?"

Ned ignored the suggestion, didn't even seem to hear it.

Just then there was a noise at the door of the shop, and both men jumped. A young girl on roller skates had rattled the door handle as she passed. Franz laughed as Ned hurriedly rewrapped the package. "We're too nervous."

"I don't intend to go to jail," Ned said, then asked, "What about the painting? Is it done yet?"

"The Monet? My friend is almost finished. A real artist this man is—you won't be able to tell from the original."

"You're sure? After all, I'm paying enough."

Franz shook his head sadly. "This will make you millions, and still you argue over a few dollars. But don't worry, it will be perfect."

"I expect it to be." After all, that painting hung right over the mantelpiece in the living room. The fake had to be good enough to fool the others. Now that Fawn was back, there was no margin for mistakes. And Ned hadn't liked the way Colman Bromley had looked at him during the meeting. But he was prepared to deal with that. Ned reminded himself that this was just another case for Bromley. While he had devoted his life to this alone.

And he wasn't going to let anything, or anyone, stand in the way now. Not when he was so close to the realization of his dream. When he got done, there would be nothing left of the Dalsworth estate but an empty husk.

"*I feel* like a kid playing hooky from school," Fawn said, gazing around the restaurant with a mischievous smile. She was having a marvelous time. Cole had taken her to the South Street Seaport for lunch, and she'd loved the collection of old brick buildings and shops that made up the area. The Seaport had been New York City's first harbor and dated back nearly four hundred years, Cole had told her. A few graceful old sailing ships were docked at the pier in memory of the time when this port was the bustling, busy entryway to the city. In the last few years the area had been completely reconstructed and renovated, so that it sparkled like new. But all the old charm had been kept. There were delightful rows of shops selling old-fashioned toys and books, hand-knit sweaters, and seashells. Large tubs of evergreens lined the wide brick walkways, and peddlers offered their wares from gaily painted carts. Cole and Fawn had wandered up and down the streets, looking into the small sailing museum and stopping to enjoy the street magicians and mimes.

They decided at last on one of the restaurants in the renovated Fulton Fish Market. The Market was an enormous three-story building that seemed to have been lifted right out of the past. Its ground floor was filled with dozens of stalls piled high with appetizing, intriguing displays of gourmet food—fancy chocolates, all sorts of cheeses, fresh cracked crab and lobster, pasta in a myriad of different shapes and colors. The air was fragrant with the scent of freshly roasted coffee beans, baking bread, and flowers. "It's marvelous," Fawn said. "You don't know where to look first."

Cole grinned. He was glad she was enjoying herself so much. She was entitled to some pleasure after these last few days. And he was enjoying himself, too. He'd often come here for lunch—the Seaport wasn't that far from his office on Wall Street—and grabbed a quick bite at one of the stands on the second floor that offered every sort of food from pizza to sushi to Indian tandoor. But that wasn't the same as being here with her; she made everything seem special and new and wonderful. Just watching her made him smile. She was so alive, and there was such a sparkle in her eyes. Compared with her, most people seemed to be sleepwalking through life.

He couldn't remember the last time he'd been so happy. He wanted the afternoon to last forever. It was dangerous to feel this way about her, he knew. There were too many complications. And soon she'd be going back to wherever she'd come from. Back to Sam.

Cole noticed that he wasn't the only one who couldn't seem to keep his eyes off her. Everywhere they went, heads turned; and the look he saw in other men's eyes were pure envy. But Fawn was unaware of the interest she was attracting. She was beautiful enough to make a man's heart ache, but it was a totally unspoiled, unself-conscious beauty. And perhaps that was as much a part of her charm as her shimmering gold hair and her creamy, flawless complexion.

In the restaurant they'd been seated at a table with a panoramic view of the East River and the graceful towers of the Brooklyn Bridge. They'd both ordered cold lobster salad, and Cole had introduced her to a New York egg cream, which he explained, following the crazy logic of the city, contained neither eggs nor cream. But Fawn had thought it was delicious, anyway. Cole realized he was trying to sell her on the city. If he could somehow make her love New York, maybe she would stay a little longer. It was a futile hope and he knew it, but he couldn't face the thought of losing her so quickly.

"We should do this every day," he said, as he ordered coffee after they had finished eating. "I haven't had so much fun in a long time."

"That's because you're always working," she teased. "Maybe you should play hooky a little more often."

He nodded, suddenly serious. He knew he put in too many hours at the office, using work to fill the void, the empty place that should have been filled by a wife and family. "The strange thing is," he said, "that I always promised myself I wouldn't be one of those men chained to a desk. My father let his work consume his entire life. Maybe it was one of the reasons my parents divorced."

"How old were you when they divorced?" she asked.

"Eleven. It was the same year your parents were killed. After their deaths everything seemed to change. It was the end of the good times. Dad spent even more time in his office, and my mother made a new set of friends and was always flitting off to Newport or Palm Beach or Europe."

"And you?"

"Boarding school during the year, and summers I was shifted back and forth between them like a hot potato. There just wasn't room for me in their lives. So, I started to fend for myself pretty early." He said it lightly, almost shrugging it off, but the sense of loss was evident in his eyes. He hadn't had much of a childhood, she realized.

"But you're close to your father now, aren't you?" Fawn asked.

"It was my taking up law that brought us together," Cole explained. "I'd planned on being anything but a lawyer. But gradually I got interested in my father's cases, fascinated by finding the right solution to a legal puzzle. And I saw the good a person could do."

"So you joined your father's firm? . . ."

He shook his head. "I wasn't interested in defending big corporations, or helping some millionaire rook the government out of a few tax dollars or writing a rebellious nephew out of a will. No, up until last year, I'd been working for the D.A.'s office—going after drug dealers, putting organized-crime figures behind bars. Not exactly what Dad had in mind for his son . . ." he added with a rueful smile.

But she could see his work had meant a great deal to him. And she wondered why he'd given it up.

Cole sensed the question she wanted to ask and said playfully, "You see it's all worked out for the best. If I hadn't been at Bromley, Reswick, and Christensen I would never have met you. And that's an opportunity I wouldn't have wanted to miss."

She smiled at the compliment. But she realized, too, that he was dodging the real issue and couldn't help saying so.

"The fact is, I'm all my father has left in his life," Cole explained reluctantly. "Which means I have a special obligation to him. I don't want to disappoint him. And more than anything else, I don't want to see him hurt anymore. He's suffered enough." As Cole spoke, his face hardened and determination deepened the timbre of his voice. "I'll do whatever I have to, to protect my father."

"It sounds as though you think your father is in danger. From whom? Does it have something to do with my coming back?"

"A lot of the past is being dredged up." Cole shrugged his shoulders. "Who knows what the consequences will be? Maybe you should consider that a little more."

He was warning her, she realized. Somehow, before this was all over, they might end up as enemies. The thought disturbed her more than she wanted to acknowledge, and she tried to push it aside. Suddenly the day had lost all its joy.

The waiter stopped by their table to ask if they wanted more coffee. Fawn shook her head. "It's time for me to leave," she said. "I don't want to keep Captain Almafi waiting."

"Fawn, can't you just let it rest? Hasn't there been enough pain already?"

"I have to do this, Cole. Please, I don't want to argue about it."

Cole stood up, his face grim. "All right, let's go and get it over with."

"If you'd rather not come . . ." Perhaps it would be better if she saw Almafi by herself. Yet she didn't really want to face this interview alone. It was a relief when Cole insisted on accompanying her. She wasn't sure how far she could trust Cole, but for the moment he was the only friend she had.

* * *

Captain Almafi's office was located at One Police Plaza. The building was in modern design, built with a dark, cheerless brick, and reminded Fawn of a fortress. As she and Cole walked through the long corridors on their way to Almafi's office, a number of police officers and public defenders greeted Cole like a long-lost friend.

" 'Bout time we saw your ugly puss down here." A sergeant grinned, slapping Cole on the back. "Where you been?"

"Flattery will get you nowhere, Callahan," Cole answered, as he shook the man's hand. "And I just decided it was time I started keeping better company."

The sergeant gave Fawn an appreciative glance. "I guess you are, at that."

"No leering, Sergeant," Cole warned playfully.

"Me? I'm a perfect gentleman," he protested, then leaned closer to Fawn and added with a wink, "But I'd watch out for him if I was you, Miss."

"Pay no attention to him, Fawn," Cole grinned. "He's a notoriously bad judge of character."

"Well, I was all set to vote for you, so I guess that proves it." Suddenly the sergeant looked more serious. "You are going to run, aren't you, Cole?"

"I haven't decided yet." Cole shrugged. "Anyway, right now we've got to get up to Almafi's office. He's expecting us."

"Then you don't want to be standing here talking to me. But just let me say we all wish you'd come back to work. These new guys they got have their heads up their—" He stopped suddenly, blushing. "Excuse me, ma'am."

"Maybe we'd better talk about it some other time," Cole suggested, rescuing the sergeant from his embarrassment.

The two men shook hands again, and a minute later Cole and Fawn were riding the elevator up to the captain's office.

"What was the sergeant talking about when he said he was going to vote for you?" Fawn asked.

"There was some talk of my running for Congress," Cole said, shrugging it off.

"Do you want to?"

"I haven't really made up my mind," he said. It was a decision he had to make soon. Right now the nomination was his if he wanted it, and everyone expected that he'd win easily, but there were other considerations to take into account. His father wanted him to stay at the law firm to carry on the family tradition.

Captain Almafi was waiting for them at his door. His bulky frame seemed to almost quiver with impatience, and he'd chewed his cigar down to the nub.

"Are we late?" Fawn asked.

"Not at all. But I've been waiting eighteen years to see you, and I just couldn't stand to wait another minute more." He held out his hand to her, studying her carefully. Colman Bromley hadn't exaggerated, he realized. This girl glowed with that special beauty that was evident in all the photographs he'd seen of Melissa Dalsworth. She had the same shining mass of blond hair, the lively, expressive eyes, the gentle smile . . . But he glimpsed a streak of independence and determination that he hadn't seen in the mother. And he was relieved; he'd worried that what she'd been through might have crushed her spirit. But it seemed to have made her stronger. And she was going to need that strength to get through what he was about to ask her to do.

"Come on in and sit down," he said gently. He arranged the chairs for them, putting Fawn immediately across from his desk and Cole farther away. Almafi was not enthusiastic about Cole's presence; he would have preferred to have Cole wait outside. But he guessed, correctly, that Cole wouldn't agree to that. He could see how protective Cole was of the girl. And he was worried that it might cause problems.

"First of all, let me thank you for coming here," he began.

"I want to do everything I can to help," Fawn said quickly. "But I might as well tell you right away that I don't remember anything about that night. I'm trying to, and I thought being in the house would help, but so far . . ."

The captain nodded. He was disappointed but not really surprised. He'd already spoken with the department's psychologists, and they'd warned him not to expect much. The trauma of that night was simply too severe; the memory had to be repressed or it would have overwhelmed her. Still he had to be absolutely certain. "Isn't there some detail . . . anything that you remember?"

She focused inward, weighing something in her mind, then said hesitantly, "Yesterday, I thought I remembered that I was in the basement before . . . it happened. That the murderer was waiting upstairs for us. But I can't be certain . . . it was only a feeling." But she recalled how strong the sense of dread had been and wondered how it was possible that she'd been mistaken. Still, she couldn't see how that would help him. What he needed was a clear-cut identification of the murderer. She had to see the face in her mind again.

"That's good," he said, leaning closer to her, willing it all to come back to her. "It's a start. . . ."

"But if I'm wrong . . ."

"You're not," he assured her. "We spent days going over the house. Your father had been carrying a bottle of champagne. And in the basement we found fresh prints, so I think we can assume that your memory is accurate."

"But what if I don't remember anything else?" She felt as if she were failing him—and, more important, Melissa and Joel.

"There's one thing we can try, something that might bring back that night," he suggested cautiously. "Would you be willing to be hypnotized?"

The captain glanced at Cole and saw that he was frowning. But Fawn was already agreeing. "I'll do anything that might help," she said.

"Fawn, maybe you should think about this for a while," Cole told her. "It might be dangerous for you, being forced to relive a horror like that."

"It's dangerous for her having the killer still out there, knowing she's a witness," Almafi retorted. He didn't like asking her to go through this, either, but damn, he didn't see any other way. "Once the newspapers discover she's back, it'll be splashed all over the paper. And just what do you suppose the murderer's reaction is going to be?"

"The newspapers already know she's come back," Cole said grimly, remembering the crowd of reporters in front of the Dalsworth headquarters this morning. He wanted to wring the neck of whoever had leaked the story.

"Then I guess we don't have any time to waste," Fawn said calmly. Somehow knowing a killer might soon be stalk-

said calmly. Somehow knowing a killer might soon be stalking her didn't frighten her as much as the buried memories of her past. "When do you want me to see the hypnotist?"

Almafi smiled; she had guts, that was for sure. But he wished there were a less painful way of finding the truth. "The theory is that it would be most likely to be successful if the hypnosis were conducted in the house itself. In the room where . . ."

"All right," she agreed. "Do you want to do it this afternoon?"

"Tomorrow morning would be better. I'd prefer that no one else was in the house." He was thinking specifically of the triplets. He'd never been able to definitely link any of them to the crime, yet he'd never been totally convinced of their innocence. And they—along with Colman Bromley—were the ones who'd benefited most by Melissa's and Joel's deaths.

"I'd like to be there, too," Cole said quickly. He was opposed to the idea, but if Fawn was set on going through with it, at least he wanted to be there.

Fawn reached over and took his hand. "That's all right, isn't it?" she asked the captain.

Almafi saw the way that Cole was looking at Fawn and decided it might be a good idea to have him there. He knew Cole was a good man to have when the going got rough, and it was obvious that Fawn had come to the same conclusion. And there was no reason why she should have to face this alone. "As long as you don't get in the way, you're welcome," he told Cole. "But I don't want either of you mentioning this to another soul. And that includes your relatives."

Cole and Fawn agreed, and they all set a time to meet at the house the next morning. As Fawn rose to leave, the captain held her hands in his for a long moment. "Thank you," he said. "A lot of people wouldn't have agreed to help."

"Just catch whoever killed my parents," she said. "That's all I want."

C h a p t e r 19

It was nearly dusk when Fawn started back to the house in the Gardens. As her taxicab crossed the Fifty-ninth Street Bridge, she glanced back at the towering Manhattan skyline. It was a magnificent sight at this time of the evening; the setting sun seemed to gild the buildings with its golden light, and each window reflected the glory of the sunset, turning them into shimmering rose-hued mirrors. Fawn smiled in spite of herself. She was beginning to understand what drew people to this city and held them here.

But as the taxi rattled over the potholed streets of Queens, a frown settled on her face again. Cole had wanted to drive her home, but she'd insisted on taking a cab. She needed to be alone for a while. She had a lot of thinking to do. And she was finding Cole's presence very distracting, even if it was in the pleasantest way possible.

She wondered if she should even go back to the house. After the board meeting this morning, she might not be welcome there. The triplets would probably still be upset over the audit. But nothing could be settled by running away, she'd decided. She'd have to face them. They were still her family, she reminded herself.

Besides, she had to be at the house tomorrow morning for the session with the police hypnotist. She was beginning to wonder if she'd make a mistake in agreeing so quickly to Almafi's suggestion. She was about to open doors that had been locked for eighteen years, and she was suddenly afraid of what she would find. But it was too late to turn back now. And she owed it to Melissa and Joel.

"We're almost there," the driver said. "What was that address again?"

Startled, Fawn looked out the window. She'd been so lost in her thoughts she hadn't realized how close they were to the house. And she didn't feel ready to go back yet.

As the taxi passed the café where she'd phoned Pete several nights before, she realized she hadn't called home since. Somehow, with everything that was going on here, she'd almost forgotten Rustler's Creek. "Stop here," she told the driver quickly, opening her purse to pay him.

She needed to talk with someone from home. Not Pete—he would just worry. But Sam. And as she remembered the afternoon she'd spent with Cole, she felt a little guilty. It was illogical; she'd never made any promises to Sam, and she was perfectly free to see whomever she wanted to. Yet she couldn't shake the feeling that she was betraying Sam.

In the café she got a few dollars' worth of quarters from the cashier and checked her watch. Back in Colorado it would be four in the afternoon; Sam should still be in his office. As she dialed, she almost wished she could be there with him.

Billy, the young part-timer, answered the phone. He seemed very relieved to hear her voice. "Thank God you've called," he whispered.

"Is something wrong?" she asked, instantly worried.

"Wrong? Sam's been a bear ever since you left—a *magna cum laude* graduate of the Attila the Hun school of charm. Hold on a sec, I think that's his roar now . . ."

"Hey," she teased when Sam came on the line, "are you abusing the help?"

"And myself," he added, his deep voice rumbling over

the line and seeming to wrap around her. "I miss your body. When are you going to get it back here?"

"I wish I were there now, but . . ."

"So do I. Believe me, you're talking to one very horny guy."

"Oh, Sam." She laughed. For a moment it was as if nothing had changed in her world, and it was a wonderfully comforting feeling. "I'm sure Rustler's Creek is full of girls who'd love the opportunity to help you out of your . . . problem," she teased.

"As a matter of fact, I have had a few offers. But next to you, they're all . . . And besides, I can't find anything in the office. How did I ever manage to get a newspaper out before you started working here?"

"What's missing?" she asked.

"The obit file, among other things."

"It's in the top drawer of the desk in the corner—the one hidden under all the old pizza boxes . . ." Fawn went through the list with him, pleased she could remember where everything was. In her mind's eye, she could see the dusty, jumbled office again, and it seemed like the most wonderful place imaginable.

"Okay—maybe we'll even get an edition out this week," Sam said, when she'd answered all his questions. But then his voice took on a serious note. "Fawn, are you all right?"

"Of course," she answered quickly. "I'm fine."

"This is Sam you're talking to, remember. I want the truth. You sound a little shaky. And Pete's told me most of the story."

"Everything's just a little confused right now. But I'm muddling through." She tried to keep her voice light. She was grateful that Pete had explained the situation to him, but at the moment she didn't feel like discussing the triplets, or her parents' murders, or any of the rest of it. She especially didn't want to tell Sam she was the only witness to the murders.

But he already seemed to know. "Fawn, you've got to think about yourself. There's a killer out there somewhere, and sooner or later he's going to come after you . . ."

"Sam, stop it. Just don't worry—I'm fine. Good God, I'm not a child anymore."

"You're not John Wayne, either. I don't want you getting into a situation you can't get out of. The calvary isn't running rescue operations anymore."

"I'll be careful," she promised. "But this isn't something I can walk away from. I can't let the killer get away with it."

He sighed. "I figured it'd be hopeless trying to talk you out of it, but I had to try. At least I want to hear from you more often. Can you give me the number where you're staying so I can call you?"

"It's better if they don't know where I've come from," she told him. "Not until this whole thing is settled."

"There's got to be someplace I can contact you," he insisted. And to hide the fear in his voice, he added lightly, "Just in case I forget where the extra beer is stashed . . ."

"I'm sure you'd never forget that." But she knew he was concerned, and she didn't want him worrying about her. "I suppose you could call the lawyer's office," she said reluctantly. "But only if it's absolutely necessary."

"The lawyer, that's the fellow who was in your hotel room?"

"Yes. His name's Cole Bromley."

"You two are spending a lot of time together, I guess." Sam said, then added quickly, "Well, of course, that's to be expected. What's he like?"

She hesitated. "It's difficult to say . . . I'm never quite sure what he's thinking."

"You like him, don't you?" It came out sounding more like an accusation than a question.

"I don't know how I feel about him. Why are you so determined to pin me down?"

"That's answer enough," Sam said softly, and for a moment neither of them spoke. "You don't owe anything to me, Fawn," he said at last. "You're completely free. I don't want you coming back to me just out of a sense of obligation. That would make us both miserable."

"Sam, nothing's happened," Fawn insisted. And that was true. Yet she couldn't help remembering Cole's arm around her waist as he'd guided her through the crowds at the Seaport, and how exciting it was to be with him and how their eyes had met when they'd laughed. For the first time, she faced the fact that what she felt for Cole was more complicated than mere friendship. The thought disturbed her. What did she really know of Cole? He, too, had kept secrets from her; and his father, although he seemed to be on Fawn's side, was going to lose a lot of money due to her reappearance. Cole's father was the real mystery. He'd been a close family friend, yet Fawn had never felt any particular affection from him. And Cole, she knew, would go to great lengths to defend his father. What if she was falling in love with a man who would someday betray her?

And she didn't want to hurt Sam. He was such a warm, loving man, so honest and uncomplicated. He'd been her best friend since they were both children. Yet she couldn't help what she was feeling for Cole. And Sam seemed to understand, perhaps even more than she did.

"It's all right," he said, his voice suddenly husky. "I know everything's all confused for you right now. Your whole world's been turned upside down. After a while, things will sort themselves out. And whatever you decide, I'll understand. In the meantime, I just hope this guy's doing a good job of taking care of you."

It was exactly what she would have expected Sam to say, but Fawn knew it hadn't been easy, and she felt a sudden rush of gratitude toward him. For a moment she was tempted to tell him she'd catch the next plane home. But she knew that would be a mistake. And in the end, it would be unfair to him, too. There was no way of pretending that her life hadn't changed. She could still go home, but not until everything here was resolved.

She gave Sam Cole's office number, and he offered to telephone Pete and let him know she was all right. Promising that she'd phone them both again as soon as she could, she said good-bye.

"Be careful," he told her before hanging up, and then added. "If you need me, I'll be there in a flash."

Long after she'd hung up, Fawn, feeling herself near tears, stood motionless, thinking of Sam and wishing things were different.

* * *

Her eyes were still clouded as she walked through the Gardens and toward the house. She'd thought coming back to the city would clear up the mysteries that had tormented her, yet now she was more confused than ever. It seemed as if there were no place where she truly belonged anymore—not back home, and not here among relatives she couldn't trust. If the triplets wanted to dispute her claim to the inheritance, why hadn't they announced the fact right away? And why had she been invited to stay at the house? Why all the pretense about how close they'd been to Melissa and Joel? Most importantly, why was she still unable to remember anything about that night?

As she passed along the winding, tree-lined streets, Fawn noticed again how quiet and peaceful and serene it all seemed. Lights twinkled cheerily in the windows of the solid, stately homes. The mingled scent of lilacs and woodsmoke from a dozen fireplaces was fragrant in the air. And the red-tiled roofs seemed to glow as the last rays of the setting sun touched them. How could these quiet streets have been the scene of a brutal double murder? It seemed almost impossible to believe.

But as she made her way toward the house Fawn realized that behind those graceful brick walls, people were probably right now reading the story of those long-forgotten murders. No doubt it would all be rehashed in afternoon newspapers, along with the news of her return. The crowd of reporters she'd had to fight through before the board meeting was proof of that. Now the murderer would know she was back. Fawn shuddered. Perhaps at this very moment he was planning how to silence her. For good this time.

Who had leaked the news of her return? she wondered. Hadn't they realized they were putting her life in danger? Now the only sure way she could protect herself was to remember the identity of the killer—to find him before he found her.

All the lights were on downstairs as she approached the house. Ned and Noreen were already home, she realized. For a moment, she hesitated on the walk, bracing herself to meet them. As she stood there, she felt something brush against her leg and jumped, her heart in her throat. But it was only a kitten. Shaking her head at her jumpiness, she bent down to pet its soft, white fur. "You nearly turned my hair as white as yours," she laughed. The kitten purred and rubbed itself against her legs.

"You'd better get on home," she said. "I'll bet somebody's waiting for you." She scratched under its soft, delicate neck once more, then stood up. "And maybe they're waiting for me, too."

But as she entered the house, she didn't see any of the others. Then she heard voices coming from the dining room. Scott and Noreen were arguing. They obviously hadn't heard her come in.

"I'm sick of talking about that damned board meeting," Scott was saying. "I was just trying to help Fawn out. Anyway, I don't have to act like a stuffed shirt anymore. All your plans for my running the company just went into the toilet."

"The hell they did," Noreen retorted.

"The money—and the company—belongs to Fawn. You had no right to go making plans with it, anyway."

"Forget Fawn, can't you?" The dismissal was plain in her voice; it sounded as though Noreen were talking about no more than a minor inconvenience.

For a moment there was silence, and then Scott asked her, "You're up to something, aren't you?"

"Well, someone has to do your thinking for you. Just leave it to me, Scottie. Haven't I always taken care of you?"

"I won't let you harm her," he said. His voice was very quiet, but there was a new firmness in it.

"Don't you threaten me, young man. You owe everything you've ever had to me. Everything you are. You're my creation."

"Right . . . I forgot that, " he snapped. "I suppose I don't even have a father."

"No, you don't." Noreen seemed close to hysteria. "I've scrubbed out every trace of him in you. It's as if he never existed. You belong to me."

"But why . . . Who was he that you can't tell me the truth about him?"

"You're never going to know. No one ever will."

"You truly hate him, don't you?" Scott asked. "Sometimes I used to think you hated me, but it was because you could see him in me, and you couldn't stand that."

"Stop looking at me that way, as if there were something wrong with me. I've done what should have been done. And now, when we're so close to the final triumph, I won't let your weakness ruin it." There was the angry rattle of dishes being pushed across the table. "The subject is closed. That girl had no business coming back here, shoving the past in our faces again."

"Mother . . ."

And suddenly Noreen sounded contrite, tearful. "Oh, Scottie, you wouldn't choose a girl who's almost a stranger over your own mother who's given her life for you."

"It's not a contest. I just feel sorry about the rotten deal Fawn's gotten. And I like her," he added.

Fawn had heard enough; she turned and left the house again, hurrying across the lawn to her own apartment above the garage. She hadn't meant to eavesdrop, but at first there hadn't seemed to be any way to announce her presence without embarrassing them all. But now she was glad that she'd overheard them. At least she knew for certain where she stood.

She wondered how Noreen planned on getting her to give up her claim to the inheritance. Did Noreen think she would be so easily manipulated? Perhaps her aunt expected her to be satisfied with only part of the estate.

Fawn frowned, remembering how hesitant she'd been even to move into the house. And it was her own house, left to her by Melissa and Joel. Fawn had a right to be here. But she hadn't wanted to take anything away from the triplets. Yet apparently Noreen didn't feel the same way. She just wanted Fawn out.

Still wondering what Noreen had in mind, Fawn opened the door to her room. And stopped on the threshold. Someone had been in her room. Nothing was quite as she'd left it that morning. The suitcases, the articles scattered across the dresser, had been rearranged. And her portfolio of photographs from home, which she'd tucked under the bed, had been pulled out—a corner of it was still visible.

For a moment, Fawn thought perhaps it had just been the maid cleaning. But as she searched through the dresser drawers, she realized her locket was missing—the miniature gold locket Melissa and Joel had given her—the one she'd been wearing that night. The locket that had convinced Cole she really was Kendra Dalsworth. She looked everywhere; it was gone.

Quickly she pulled the portfolio out from under the bed and flipped through the pages, already knowing what she'd find. At least a dozen pictures were missing. And two of them were of Pete. Worse, several of the other missing photos were of the town itself. There would be enough clues in those pictures to lead someone right to Rustler's Creek if he was clever enough.

Suddenly she was angry—with herself for having brought the portfolio along in the first place, but more with whoever it was who'd taken the pictures. And it had to be Ned or Noreen. Or Nick, she realized. He had a habit of walking in and out of this house as if it were his own.

Scooping up the portfolio, she started for the door, ready to confront them. But then she stopped. She was sure none of them would admit the theft, and her anger would only confirm that whoever had taken the pictures had chosen the right ones. If she didn't say anything, the thief couldn't really be sure. He was probably counting on her confirmation.

Even working with a detective, the thief would need time to trace those photographs to Rustler's Creek. Perhaps by then she would have remembered the identity of the killer. Then Pete would no longer be under suspicion.

Did the thief really believe that Pete had committed the murders? Or was he hoping to use Pete to discredit her story, to somehow cast doubts on her claim to be Kendra Dalsworth? Was that why he'd taken the locket, too? Was this how he'd planned to get hold of her inheritance?

It was time she got some answers to her questions, Fawn decided, clutching the empty jewelry case. Beginning right now. And as she stepped out of her room, she saw a narrow shaft of light under Ned's door. He was home, then. Her knuckles rapped sharply on his door. She'd start with him.

C h a p t e r 20

She had to knock three times before Ned came to the door. But at last the bolt was slowly drawn back and the door opened a few cautious inches. "Oh . . . it's you, Fawn," he said, his large frame blocking her view of his room. He seemed very uneasy at the sight of her.

"I have to talk with you, Uncle Ned."

"I was just . . . napping." But he didn't look drowsy. In fact, his eyes had an almost feverish brightness.

She ignored the hint to excuse herself and leave. "Could I come in, Ned?"

He didn't answer. But slowly a vacant smile spread over his face, as if to cover the awkwardness of the silence. He seemed to be waiting for her to change her mind and go away. Ned never let anyone into his rooms; it was the one part of the house she hadn't seen yet, and obviously he didn't want her to see it now. But she was too upset over the loss of the locket to give up.

"Ned, can I come in?" she persisted.

He glanced behind her as if to make sure she was alone, then nodded reluctantly and stepped aside.

Ned had three rooms of his own: a bedroom, bath, and sitting room. It was the sitting room that Fawn entered now, though in fact there was almost no place to actually sit. The room was a jumbled clutter of extra furniture and odds and ends. It looked like an old attic or a junk shop. The walls had been paneled in a cheap-looking knotty pine and covered with pictures. Even the floor seemed strange; like the rest of the house, it was of wide, pegged-oak planking, but here it didn't seem as solid as it did in the other rooms. The floor was almost springy beneath her feet.

Ned was watching her nervously, so she tried to smile. The room was so unlike what she'd expected that, for a moment, she forgot why she'd come. "This is quite a collection of . . . things you have here," she said. There didn't seem to be any other word to describe the curious, motley assortment of frayed pillows, cracked porcelain figurines, old clocks, and lamps with mismatched shades propped everywhere she looked. But she remembered how important this room was to Ned, how possessive he was of it. And scattered in among everything else, there were a few very fine pieces.

A lithograph on the wall caught her eye: a picture of the Dalsworth Building on Wall Street. It was yellowing now, but the workmanship was excellent. She took a step toward the wall to study it more closely, but Ned quickly slid in front of her, blocking her way. He reminded her of a big sheepdog, as he herded her back into the center of the room. His actions made it clear that he didn't want her to touch anything.

And she wondered if her locket was now hidden somewhere in the room. Was that why he was so nervous? She turned and looked straight into his eyes. "Ned, something's been stolen from my room." But, on purpose, she didn't tell him exactly what was missing.

She watched him, waiting for his reaction, but strangely there was none at all. His face was even blander than usual, perfectly smoothed of all expression. It reminded her of the times as a child when she'd feigned innocence to some lie or misdeed. Ned was meeting her gaze with the same forced, unblinking stare. "Why did you come to me?" he asked at last.

"I thought you might know who took it."

"Why should I know that?" And suddenly he seemed frightened. He tried to cover it by acting offended, but Fawn was certain he was hiding something.

"Aren't you even going to ask me what was taken?"

"I'm sure whatever it is, it's just been misplaced," he said hastily, stumbling over the words. "You must have made a mistake."

Fawn shook her head. "I haven't. Someone stole the gold locket my parents gave me. It's the only link I have from my childhood, Ned, and it's important to me. I want it back."

"I'll look for it," he promised quickly as he started to move her toward the door. "Really, I will—just leave it to me." His large hand closed around her arm, as if she were a troublesome child being escorted from the room. "Maybe the cook or the maid took it."

"No, Ned. I don't believe it was any of the help." Fawn met his eyes, and this time he turned away from her. She couldn't be sure if he was the one who'd taken the locket, but she was certain now that he had some guilty secret and that she couldn't trust him. From now on, she'd have to be on her guard against them all.

After Fawn left, Ned stood for a long time with his ear pressed against the door, making sure she was really gone.

She was beginning to grow suspicious, he realized. And that was dangerous. Damn, all this fuss over one stupid little locket. When millions were at stake . . .

He never should have allowed her into his room. He strode back and forth across the floor, and his eyes swept over the walls and the clutter of furniture, making sure nothing was out of place, that there was nothing that might have caught her eye. His fingers itched to reopen the secret compartment concealed beneath his feet. In a minute . . . he promised himself. And superstitiously, as if some trace of her consciousness might remain in the air like perfume, he forced himself to wait.

Impatiently he straightened the shade on a ceramic clown lamp. It was originally intended for a child's room and part of the clown's hat had chipped off, but the lamp was still perfectly good. Ned had picked it up off a heap of castoffs strewn at the curb awaiting the garbage collection. That was how he'd acquired almost all his treasures. He couldn't believe what people would throw away—perfectly good, valuable things. Throwing things away not only outraged his sense of thrift, but he also couldn't resist the idea of getting something for nothing; it was another little victory against the world.

At last Ned could wait no longer. Kneeling down on the floor, he pushed aside a small rug and began undoing the intricate spring latch concealed in the planking. Slowly the planking slid apart, revealing the compartment below stuffed with bundles of stock certificates and negotiable bonds, and this paper was the real thing, not the counterfeits in the Dalsworths' company safe. There was another secret cache in the room, built into the paneled wall, which housed the authentic paintings he had replaced with forgeries.

Gently Ned lifted the contents out, spreading them over the tables and chairs and sofas. They were so beautiful—with their elegant engraving, the old-fashioned words . . . And they added up to a fortune. It was worth the danger to keep them here. For a moment Ned felt totally satisfied as his hands reached out and stroked the parchment lovingly. A warm tingling, strangely similar to sex but much better, spread through his body. He felt larger, stronger; his very being seemed to have expanded through all these signs of his power. The Dalsworth fortune—at least the biggest chunk of it—was right here, right in front of him, surrounding him. It was his. His . . .

Accumulating it bit by bit had been a long, nerve-wracking process. But his plan, like all the best plans, was simplicity itself. Joel hadn't moved quickly enough to remove him from his position in the company. And after Joel's death, there'd been no one to oppose him. Nick and Noreen were no match for his cleverness.

It had been fortunate that Melissa had wanted the terms of the will written so trustingly. But Ned was sure that no matter what, he would have found a way. For the money was his— he understood it, he'd devoted his life to it. All the others cared only for what the money could do for them, could buy; Ned alone cared about the money itself.

At first he'd moved cautiously. He'd had to be careful not to arouse Bromley's suspicions. And he'd been generous with his brother and sister so that slowly they became content to let him manage the business with very little interference. It had taken him four years to find the perfect forger.

But gradually he'd begun to replace each company stock and bond with a counterfeit. He'd kept scrupulous records, seeing that the interest was paid on time and ensuring that the counterfeits were never cashed in; that would have alerted the authorities immediately. There had been a few difficulties: the other executives in the company had sometimes questioned his methods, and Bromley in particular had wanted the company's assets entrusted to a bank, but as long as he was still in charge of the company there was nothing anyone else could do. No one had ever guessed the truth.

Ned grinned, letting his fingertips trace the crisp parchment. His relatives—those fools were fighting over an inheritance that virtually wasn't even there anymore. In a few more weeks, the company would be sucked dry. It might have been safer for him to leave now, to be satisfied with what he had so far—especially with Bromley threatening a complete audit—but Ned couldn't bear the thought of leaving without it all. It was impossible for him to even pass a penny in the street without stooping to pick it up, so how could he abandon any part—even a small part—of the fortune he'd worked so hard for?

It depressed Ned to think of leaving at all. He'd enjoyed the game, but it was almost over now. Soon he'd be in South America. He already had his escape route planned, and he'd chosen South America because there'd be no threat of extradition. Of course, he could never come back . . . But why would he want to? At last he'd have the money to really begin living his life. The future he'd imagined for so long was almost within his reach; yet the closer he got to it, the more unreal it began to seem.

Instead his mind drifted back to the past. He saw his father struggling over column after column of figures: every night his father had sat hunched over his books, adding, subtracting, muttering to himself. A pale, thin-lipped, broken man. "Don't make any noise, your father's trying to concen-

trate . . . Go away, your father's busy." His father was determined to pay back every one of his creditors in full, even
though the law would have excused him. But he never gave
a thought to what he owed his son.

Everyone had told him his father was so honorable. After
all, the bankruptcy wasn't even his fault—his partner had run
off with everything that wasn't nailed down, leaving only
stacks of debts and unfulfilled contracts that had already been
paid for. But Ned felt only shame for his father. His father
was a fool, and a loser. A mark. Ned had promised himself
he would never be as vulnerable, never be humbled as his
father had been. By paying off these debts of honor his father
had meant to teach him another lesson entirely, but what Ned
had learned was that there were winners and losers and it all
came down to money. And Ned was going to be a winner.
He wasn't going to be like his father.

All during his youth, Ned had dreamed of making a fortune on his own. He would dump the stacks of crisp green
bills in front of his father, and his father would look up,
blinking and dumbfounded. "It's yours," Ned would say casually as his father stared at him. And then for the first time,
his father would see him, really see him. But his father had
robbed him of that dream, too, just as he'd robbed him of all
his childish dreams. The old man had died too soon. And
Ned had cursed him at his funeral for all that had been lost.

Ned frowned. He'd proven he was a winner, but now there
was no one to acknowledge it. No one knew. None of them
saw him for what he really was. He'd heard the condescension
in their voices, caught their amused, patronizing smiles. He
had a right to their respect, dammit. He was richer, stronger,
more cunning than any of them. But he was forced to pretend, to hide his secret—and allow them to go on smirking
behind his back. . . .

He thought suddenly of his secretary, Rose. How he would
love to show her all this. He imagined her gasping in surprise, her eyes suddenly lit with a new respect.

Yes, if he could only show Rose . . .

She was the only one who seemed to have guessed there
was more to him than the comic, dull accountant.

But then his smile stiffened on his lips, and his habitual

caution reasserted itself. Rose hadn't somehow already guessed, had she? Was there some motive behind her sudden display of regard? Could she be after the money for herself?

Nervously he began scooping up the papers, then stopped. No, she couldn't know. He'd been too careful, too sly for any of them. What Rose saw was just his natural strength, his true self.

Still, for a while he would have to maintain the charade. Even with her. The risks were too large. But someday, maybe he would bring her here and show her his secret. He would prove that her faith in him was more than justified. He smiled, his fingers idly fondling the stacks of certificates, as he let the daydream take over.

And suddenly he was imagining himself in Rio, with her by his side. Tanned, and in new clothes, she would be quite attractive. She wasn't the sort to run wild with money, clothes, was she? No, she was a sensible girl, not the demanding sort at all.

Maybe—he held his breath at the idea of it—should he, when the time was right, ask her to come with him? He wouldn't have to tell her exactly how much money he had. . . . She would be so grateful to be lifted out of her gray, mundane life.

The thought frightened and pleased him at the same time. And what if she turned him down?

He shifted fretfully, pulling in his shoulders. He would think about all this later. There was no need to make any decisions now. For a while yet, his life could go on as it always had.

He turned his attention back to the stacks of bonds and certificates with which he'd surrounded himself. There was a lot of work to be done; the final hand of the game hadn't been played yet. And as for Fawn—her future as a heiress was going to be unexpectedly short.

C h a p t e r   21

"You don't have to go through with this, Fawn, if you don't want to," Cole said softly. For a moment he glanced around the kitchen table as if daring Captin Almafi and the psychiatrist to disagree, but when he turned back to Fawn his eyes were gentle. "No one will think badly of you if you change your mind."

"But I would," she told him. She was relieved, and a bit surprised, at how calm her voice sounded. Inside the panic was whispering through her veins like the humming in a telephone wire.

Cole had arrived at the house promptly at ten that morning, and Almafi and the police psychiatrist had shown up several minutes later. The psychiatrist, Dr. Woodlawn, was a short, plump man with a pink scrubbed face and a fringe of absolutely white hair. He had an intense, professionally avuncular manner. "Well, we sit and talk for a while, huh? Get comfortable with each other," he suggested. "In the kitchen, I think. That's where the . . . incident took place, yes?"

So they had all sat around the kitchen table while the cook,

Martha, served them coffee and pretended not to listen to their conversation.

"So, we start almost from scratch," the doctor began. "You remember nothing of that night, yes?"

"I'm afraid not," Fawn answered.

"No, you mustn't apologize," he said quickly, waving his plump white hand in the air as if to erase her words. "Repression of a memory as distressing, as overwhelming as this is not a deliberate act. You, your conscious self, had nothing to do with it. Your body simply reacted in the only way possible to prevent itself from being destroyed. There is a limit to the pain a system can stand without collapsing. If your mind hadn't defended itself against this pain, it wouldn't have survived."

"But you're asking her to relive it now," Cole pointed out, his face grim.

"But you're no longer a child now," Woodlawn said, turning back to Fawn. "And you're in good health, yes? No heart problems, anything like that? I will just take your pulse." His fingers felt for the pulse in her wrist. "You understand, as we get closer to the pain the body will react, the system will mobilize to defend itself. The muscles tense, the blood pressure skyrockets, and the heartbeat gets faster and faster."

Fawn nodded. The symptoms sounded like those she'd felt during the anxiety attacks she had experienced throughout her life. Somehow she'd always managed to get through those. And maybe, if they were successful today, this would be the last time. "But afterwards, I'll remember everything?"

"The memory is buried very deep. We mustn't expect too much. All we can hope is that you will begin to resolve the puzzle, begin to understand . . . The thing to keep in mind is that as a child you were completely vulnerable, powerless, but that's not true anymore. And we'll be right here with you." But of course, once the hypnosis took effect, she wouldn't even be aware of their presence; the past eighteen years would simply cease to exist for her.

Martha had returned to the table with a fresh pot of coffee. "More coffee, honey?" she asked Fawn, pointedly ignoring the others. Her lips were set in a thin, tight line, expressing disapproval of these visitors.

"No thank you, Martha," Fawn said. "If you wouldn't mind, we'd like to be alone for a while now."

Martha glanced suspiciously at Almafi and the psychiatrist. "You want me to leave?" she asked Fawn.

"Please." Fawn nodded.

"If that's what you want . . ." the cook agreed reluctantly. "I'll just sit a spell in the living room."

Fawn smiled at the older woman's protectiveness. Martha hadn't even been employed by the household while Melissa and Joel were alive, yet she'd almost immediately taken Fawn under her wing. She'd done everything she could to make Fawn feel welcome. Even if Scott was right about her nipping from the liquor cabinet, Fawn didn't care—she was too grateful to her.

"Are you ready to start now?" Almafi asked Fawn once the four were alone. He tugged at his jowls nervously. He wasn't happy about this whole business, but there was still a murderer to be caught—a murderer he'd waited eighteen years for.

Fawn nodded. She wanted to get it over with.

She expected the psychiatrist to use a prop—a pocket watch slowly swinging in front of her eyes, perhaps, as the hypnotists did in the movies—but he simply instructed her to close her eyes, and he began talking in a low, soothing voice. And gradually she felt herself relax; her breathing slowed, and her limbs grew heavy. She was aware of nothing but his voice, guiding her back through the years. To that night . . .

"Your name is Kendra Dalsworth, and you're six years old. It's Sunday night. You're in the kitchen with your parents. Is anyone else there?"

"No, just us three," she answered, her voice suddenly childlike. She smiled contentedly. Sunday was her favorite day; her parents always saved it for her. And she could feel the smooth gentleness of her mother's fingers as she brushed back her hair. They were all laughing, and her father was holding up three tickets, a mischievous grin lighting his eyes.

"What are you talking about?" the voice asked.

"The circus. Daddy says we can go to the circus next week."

Her fingers closed together, as if around an object, and Woodlawn asked her what she was holding.

"Mama made hot chocolate." The mug, her own special porcelain mug with the gold rim and the painting of Winnie the Pooh on the front, was warm in her hands. The sweet smell of the chocolate mingled with the light, flowery scent of her mother's perfume and the fragrant hickory smoke from the brick hearth.

"What's happening now?"

"I'm going down to the basement with my father to get a bottle of champagne from the cooler." She said it reluctantly; she wanted them all to stay together. Just the three of them, safe and happy and nothing ever changing.

"And now you're coming back up the stairs. . . ." the voice prompted.

"No . . ." She shook her head, beginning to feel queasy. Her heart was thudding fast and faster in her chest as if it would explode. Her skin was suddenly clammy, glistening with sweat. She didn't want to go any further; everything in her fought to hold back. But one step after another, the stairs fell away behind her and she couldn't stop herself. The door loomed forbiddingly before her, growing larger.

"The door is opening now. . . . What do you see?"

"Nothing," she whispered frantically. But her skin, so flushed with color a moment before, was suddenly ashen. "I hear the music. . . ." The waltz, but it sounded strange, as if someone were playing it on the wrong speed; it was so slow compared to the racing of her own heart. "It's dark, black. . . ."

"Where's your mother?"

"Mama . . . are you sleeping?" But she knew that wasn't true, yet she couldn't stop herself from leaning closer, reaching out a hand to her mother's still, silent body. And then the lights flashed on, and there was blood everywhere. Blood and the sharp glisten of white where her mother's windpipe had been severed. Blood darkening the rounded curve of her mother's belly, a jagged slash where the baby had been growing. Kendra shrieked. It was a cry of such shock and rage and anguish that it was almost unbearable to hear.

Without thinking, Cole reached for her, but Almafi grabbed his arm, roughly pulling him back.

"What is it?" the psychiatrist asked, leaning forward intently. "Tell me who else you see."

"She's dead . . . I have to help her," Kendra sobbed; she was a child now, unable to understand the horrible finality of death, refusing to accept it.

"Tell me who else you see," Woodlawn repeated insistently.

"Daddy . . ." She looked around wildly. "Daddy, help her. . . ." Huge tears ran down her cheeks; she was sobbing uncontrollably now, choking on her tears.

"My God . . ." Cole breathed. "Enough, godammit. You've got to stop now." He didn't care if he had promised not to interfere—this was too much of a risk.

Almafi glanced at him, then back at the psychiatrist uncertainly. This was much worse than he'd expected. How much more could she take? "Dr. Woodlawn . . . ?" he whispered hesitantly.

The psychiatrist hushed him with a curt wave of the hand, his eyes still locked on the girl. "We're close," he insisted. "Almost there . . ."

The shadowy figure pulled the knife from her father's back. "Come here, child." A black-gloved hand beckoned her closer, but in the other hand the knife twitched impatiently.

"Who is it?" Woodlawn demanded.

"I can't . . ." Kendra whispered. Beneath the brimmed hat, the face was shrouded in shadow. But suddenly she knew that the faceless killer wasn't a stranger. Knew it in the same mysterious but unmistakable way one knew something in a dream. The figure in the bloody raincoat was someone she'd loved, someone she'd trusted. Desperately she tried to deny the truth. But the figure was edging closer now, coming after her. Kendra shrank back in the chair, paralyzed with fear. "No . . ." she whispered frantically. "No . . ."

"My God, what are you doing to that poor child?" Martha exploded, rushing into the kitchen. Her eyes were blazing. From the start she'd been suspicious of these strangers—so she'd crept back to listen at the kitchen door. And it was a good thing she had; someone had to put a stop to this.

"Martha's right—it's gone far enough," Cole said grimly. He looked at Fawn's face; it was so white it seemed like a death mask. "Don't you see she can't tell you anything?" Gently he took Fawn's hand in his own, willing her back to him.

Almafi and Woodlawn stared at each other helplessly. They'd been so close. . . . But had they pushed her too far? Captain Almafi turned away, shaken and suddenly disgusted with himself.

"Fawn, listen to me now," the psychiatrist said. "You're safe. There's no one to hurt you any more." Slowly he began guiding her away from the terror, bringing her back to them.

And at last Fawn looked at them with a flicker of recognition. But immediately her gaze strayed to the cellar door, as if she still expected the murderer to be hiding there.

"It's over now, Fawn," Almafi said. But he knew that wasn't true. Until the killer was caught, she would never be safe.

Martha hurriedly brought her a glass of brandy—a triple— and Fawn sipped it slowly, her hand still unsteady. "I just couldn't see the face. . . ." she said once she had her voice was under control. "It didn't work, not well enough."

Woodlawn sadly shook his head. "No, perhaps hypnosis is not the answer. The repression is too strong. Sometimes we must let these things take their own course, wait for an event that will trigger the memory."

Fawn nodded. She was exhausted, drained. She felt bruised all over. And when she closed her eyes she saw her father struggling to reach her, falling and forcing himself back to his feet as the life flowed out of him.

"In its own time it will all come back to you. But now you should rest."

"Yes," she agreed. "I'd like to be alone, please." But not to rest. She had to think. Because suddenly everything had changed.

Captain Almafi stood up. "We'll go, then. But I'm going to station a man outside to watch over the house." He felt guilty, as if he were running out on her, leaving her to deal with the horror alone. But there was nothing he could do— except try to protect her from a killer without a face.

"Do you want me to stay?" Cole asked once the captain and Woodlawn had left.

She shook her head. "I need some time alone."

"All right. Call me if you want to talk."

She tried to smile; it was a hesitant, wavering smile.

"You've done everything you could, Fawn," he told her. "Try to forget it all now."

That wasn't at all what she intended to do, but she nodded, not wanting him to worry.

"Well, I guess I'd better go." He started for the door, but suddenly turned around. For a moment they stared at each other, and then wordlessly they moved into each other's arms.

"Oh, Fawn, I don't ever want you to have to go through anything like that again," he whispered, holding her tight. And she clung to him, her eyes closed, wanting to tell him the truth yet knowing she couldn't. But for a moment just having his arms around her was enough.

"I'll call you tomorrow," she said finally, pulling away from him.

"I'll take that as a promise," he said.

She watched him stride down the walk, surprised at how much she'd come to depend on him. But what she had to do now she had to do alone.

"You want me to fix you another brandy?" Martha asked, breaking into her thoughts.

"No, but have another one yourself if you'd like," Fawn said, noticing that Martha was just finishing up a snifter of her own.

"Maybe just a short one. And then I got some grocery shopping to do. If you'd like the house to yourself . . ."

"That'd be fine. And, Martha, I'd appreciate it if you wouldn't tell any of the others what happened here today."

Martha nodded. She'd finally figured out what the police captain had been up to with this hypnosis business, but she couldn't understand why Fawn had agreed to it. Why would anyone be willing to relive an experience like that? To Martha, it was like getting your hand caught in a meat grinder and then, knowing how it felt, volunteering to stick the other one in, too.

But Martha promised she'd keep her mouth shut in front of Nick and Ned and Noreen.

"Not a word to any of them," Fawn insisted, wishing she could explain but knowing that would only endanger them both. She just had to hope that Martha would keep silent. It was crucial that none of the triplets suspect she'd begun to remember.

Alone at last, Fawn sank wearily into a chair, slowly rubbing her hands up and down her arms as if she were chilled. She felt limp, empty even of her tears.

She gazed around the kitchen blankly. The brick hearth still remained, but everything else had been changed since that night. New furniture, different wallpaper, even her mother's collection of blue-and-white Staffordshire plates had disappeared. But the evil was still here; it seemed to have seeped into the walls, it lingered in the air.

And again she saw Melissa's and Joel's lifeless bodies. And the black-gloved hand beckoning her closer, calling her to her death. "Come here, Kendra. . . ." It hadn't been a stranger at all; the voice had been as familiar to her as her own parents'. It must have been one of them . . . Ned or Noreen or Nick. She knew it now—knew it without understanding exactly why she was so sure.

But which one, dammit? She tried to force a face onto the shadowy figure. And couldn't. It was as if she were blinded somehow, by the horror of it and the confusion and sense of betrayal.

Whoever it was, she wanted to hurt as badly as she'd been hurt. She wanted to make whoever it was pay for everything—all the years Melissa and Joel had been robbed of, all the years the three of them should have had together. And she knew she'd been carrying this rage and pain with her all her life. It was a relief to let it finally explode.

The killer had betrayed them all. But she was going to get him. Or her. She promised herself that. No matter how long it took. No one could make her leave now. Not until she'd found out the truth; that was why she hadn't told Almafi or Cole. If she'd even hinted they should look for the killer in her own family, they would have insisted she leave the house immediately. They would have told her it was too dangerous to stay. But Fawn didn't care about that now. If she ran away the murderer would have won. And he might track her down anyway, she realized, recalling the photographs of home that had been stolen from her room. It was too dangerous to let her live, to gamble that she'd never remember enough to identify him. It was probably only due to the fact she was being watched so closely—by the police and Cole and the press—that she was still alive now. Her death would be sure to cast suspicion on the three, if only because of the money she was about to inherit. But how much longer would she be safe? The killer had already gotten away with two murders; he'd be certain to try again sooner or later.

She'd have to work quickly.

But which one was it? Which one . . .

C h a p t e r 22

"Is something wrong, Fawn?" Noreen asked. The entire family was seated at the dining room table, eating breakfast. "You don't look well this morning," Noreen said to Fawn, and all of them turned to look at her.

"I'm fine," Fawn answered, pouring herself some more coffee from the large silver coffeepot.

"You're not eating," Ned commented.

It was true. There were fresh raspberries and cream, smoked salmon, shirred eggs in black butter, baked ham, and scones hot from the oven with thyme honey—and Fawn had't touched any of it. "I'm just not very hungry this morning," she said. The excuse sounded feeble, even to her ears, and they were all still watching her. She forced herself to take a bite of buttered scone. But the thought that she was sitting at the same table, eating with her parents' murderer nearly made her gag.

"Maybe you're coming down with something," Nick suggested. Fawn wondered if that wasn't a hopeful glint she saw in his eye.

"If there's anything on your mind, Fawn, I hope you'll

come to me," Noreen said, frowning. She twisted the huge emerald ring back and forth on her finger, nervously watching Nick and Ned out of the corner of her eye. "I'd prefer to think you'd confide in me, rather than . . . strangers."

Strangers . . . Did Noreen know about Almafi and the psychiatrist's visit yesterday? Fawn was sure Martha hadn't said anything. But she realized now that she'd forgotten to caution the maid. Or maybe Noreen had found out some other way. Fawn stood up quickly, forcing herself to keep her voice calm. "Thank you for your offer, Noreen. But it's really nothing. . . . I'll just take a few aspirin before I leave for the office."

"There's really no need for you to bother yourself with the company yet." Ned objected quickly.

"I just thought I'd go in for a few hours, and look around. You don't mind, do you?"

"Of course not. We're glad you're taking such an interest in the company," Noreen said smoothly before Ned could answer.

Fawn smiled, convincingly she hoped, and hurried out of the room. She didn't want to give them a chance to ask exactly what she was going to be looking into at the office. Her life depended on not arousing their suspicions.

She'd spent yesterday afternoon, after Cole had left, going through the house again room by room. She wasn't sure exactly what she was searching for, but there had to be some evidence somewhere linking one of the three to the crime. But she hadn't found anything that seemed at all suspicious. Noreen's closets and drawers were filled to overflowing with a breathtaking array of clothes and furs and jewels. Noreen enjoyed spending money. But Fawn had already known that. And Noreen's acquisitiveness had a thoughtless, rather childlike quality to it; Fawn couldn't see her murdering because of it. As for Ned, his rooms were locked, and he alone had a key. There was no way Fawn could find out what he was hiding inside. In the basement Fawn had stumbled on a few of Nick's old trunks, apparently forgotten. But all they held was old clothes.

At last Fawn had given up. If the answer was here, she couldn't find it. And she felt guilty rummaging through their belongings, spying on them. Even if one of them was the murderer, the other two were innocent. But until she found the truth she had to suspect them all. Later she would find a way to make it up to the other two. After the murderer was caught.

Perhaps she could find some clues at the company, she'd decided. There might be something in the old records. . . . She planned on starting back eighteen years ago, at the time of the murders. It would be a long day.

She waited at the window in her room until she saw the limousine pull out of the drive and disappear around the corner. Certain they'd all left, she hurried back into the house.

And right into Nick's arms.

"Hey, I'm glad I caught you—literally." He chuckled. "Where are you off to in such a rush, beautiful?"

"I'm a bit late, Nick." She was in no mood for his gushing friendliness, and she didn't particularly like his arm around her.

"Just give me a minute; this won't take long." He steered her into the living room. "I need you to do me a little favor— nothing important." He gave her a smile suggesting it really was nothing at all. "Just sign a paper for me."

"What sort of paper?"

"Right here on this line. Here's a pen."

"What sort of paper?" she repeated.

"Just a little loan agreement. You know how banks are, all these tiresome formalities. Now that you're a member of the family they need your name, too."

Fawn pulled away from him and he tried to take her arm again, but she deftly stepped out of his reach. And suddenly he noticed Martha was watching them from the kitchen. "Come on, Fawn, it doesn't mean anything." He smiled. "Just sign . . . "

"In other words, you want me to co-sign a loan for you?"

"Yeah, I suppose that's the term." His tone suggested she was being unreasonable, pedantic. "Hey, what's a family if we don't trust each other?"

"You tell me, Nick."

He looked into her grim eyes and suddenly began back-pedaling. "Look, maybe this isn't the best time. I mean, hey,

I can get anybody to sign this. I just thought maybe you'd want . . . We'll just forget it.''

Fawn sighed tiredly. 'I'm sorry, Uncle Nick. Let me look it over later, and ask Cole. I'm not sure I should be signing anything yet.''

"No, no, that's okay. I probably shouldn't have asked.'' He gave her a fatherly pat on the back. "You go have a good time today. See you later, huh?''

"Why don't you just leave the paper with me?'' she suggested. "I'll talk it over with Cole.'' She suddenly felt sorry for Nick, guessing that beneath all that flash and the expensive clothes, he was lonely and vulnerable, maybe even frightened. He was his own worst enemy, it seemed, a boy who had never grown up.

"No, it's okay.'' He quickly tucked the paper into his pocket. "Hell, I wouldn't even bother mentioning it to Cole, he's pretty busy right now. And as I said, it's really nothing.''

She added. Why was Nick so nervous about her telling Cole? And how much had the loan been for? He hadn't let her see the figure. "I'll be at the office all day,'' she called over her shoulder, starting for the door.

"Don't forget the charity gala tonight. I want my whole family there to see me get my award,'' he called after her. Nick was being honored as "Man of the Year'' by the charity organization sponsoring the ball, and he'd insisted that Fawn as well as the rest of the family attend.

He gave a quick, lighthearted wave as she closed the door, but once she was gone his smile faded immediately.

"Bitch . . .'' he muttered.

"Look, this is the last time . . . if you could even let me have ten thousand . . .'' Nick could hear the whine, the pleading in his voice. He'd been on the phone for the last hour, and by now he was sweating so hard he was having difficulty holding the receiver to his ear. The man on the other end of the line was his last hope. Nick took a deep breath, trying to get his old carefree manner back. "It's a good investment for you. When I inherit . . .''

"You're not going to inherit, from what I hear,'' the voice on the other end said. There was no room for bargaining in his tone. "You're out of credit; don't you get it?" There was a dry laugh. "That's it, you don't get it." And the phone went dead.

Nick swore, pushing his fingers distractedly through his hair. Without a loan, there was no way he could meet the blackmailer's demand, no way he could raise the money. But he had to. If he didn't he'd be ruined.

All these years he'd been so cavalier about paying his debts; after all, he'd told himself, a gentleman didn't have to concern himself with anything as mundane as payment schedules. Hell, the nobility carried debts for generations. But now his indebtedness was killing him. He shuddered at the thought of what Jolene's husband might do if he found out about their affair. And since no one would lend him enough to get his shoes shined, now that everyone knew Kendra Dalsworth had been found, he had no money to keep the blackmailer silent. One of his prospects this morning had jokingly suggested that Nick might as well use the trust documents for toilet paper, that's all they were good for now.

Suddenly he realized he was being watched. He glanced up. His wife, Suzanne, looking cool and crisp in an ice-blue linen dress, was standing in the doorway to the study. There was a small smile on her carefully made-up face. He wondered how much she'd overheard.

Her first words immediately dispelled his hope that she'd not been there long. "Another turn-down? You seem to be having a bad morning."

"It's just business," he said brusquely.

"Do you want to tell me about it?" She sat down on the other side of the desk, arranging her skirt carefully to show off her legs. She'd always been proud of her legs, though Nick had stopped noticing them a long time ago.

"No, I don't want to talk about it," he said, trying to dismiss her. "It's not important."

"It's only that you look so worried, dear." Yet she seemed calm, totally unruffled herself. And it occurred to Nick that if he went under, he'd go by himself. Suzanne might look prettily concerned for a minute or two, but she wouldn't really care. Somehow she'd manage just fine without him. In fact, with her green eyes and red hair, she'd look great in black; she'd probably find some new man at the funeral. He shuddered. He was getting morbid.

There had to be some way out of this. If it hadn't been for Fawn . . . if she'd just stayed away . . . it was all her fault.

"Would you like some tea—or maybe something stronger?" Suzanne offered, as gracious as a hostess at a garden party. Nick shook his head no impatiently; he was still immersed in the unfairness of it all. If Fawn would just disappear . . .

"Maybe you'd like me to rub your neck . . ."

"No!" he shouted. "Just leave me alone. Go get your hair done or something. . . ."

"All right, Nick." She rose. But as she reached the door, she turned. "By the way, I noticed someone had opened the wall safe in my bedroom last night. But you don't have to worry about my jewels; I've put them in a safe deposit box at the bank."

"You what?"

"It occurred to me how easily they might be stolen if they were in the house. But they'll be safe now. No one can get to them but me." She smiled blandly and was gone before he could say another word.

So that's where all her jewelry had gone. Dammit, he should have gotten to it first. There was no way he could get his hands on it now. Suzanne wouldn't sacrifice one seed pearl to help him out. In fact, she seemed to be enjoying his predicament.

He should have dumped her a long time ago. And he would, after all this was over. But right now he had other things to concentrate on. Like Fawn . . . and how he was going to get rid of her.

Chapter 23

By two o'clock Fawn still hadn't found one useful piece of information. She'd gone through every quarterly and annual report for the last twenty years, had studied the minutes of the board meetings, and read hundreds of intra-company memos. But there was nothing that pointed to the identity of the murderer. All she'd learned was that Ned was as secretive and closemouthed at the office as he was at home—and that Nick's main interest in the company was in using it to further his position in society.

Fawn sighed and swiveled her chair around to face the window. She had the feeling that if she had to read another row of figures, she would go blind. The office that had been provided for her was a small cubicle—just temporary, she'd been assured—but the view from the window was magnificent. All of lower Manhattan was spread out before her, and beyond the waves of the harbor sparkled in the sunlight. It was a perfect spring day, the sky cloudless and a brilliant blue. But Fawn barely noticed any of it. "Which one?" she asked herself again. "Which one had held the knife?"

Ned? Was that the secret hidden behind his evasive eyes?

Of the three of them, he'd seemed the most upset by her return. But her parents had put him through college, paying all his expenses, and then taken him into the company. His future had been assured.

And Nick? He certainly seemed to like the comforts money could buy. Joel had set him up in a cushy job, too. And besides, Nick had been about to marry an heiress, so what would he have needed with the Dalsworth fortune?

In fact, all three of them had been taking handouts from her parents for years. She remembered that her mother and father had even invited Noreen to live with them after the birth of her son. Joel was just like a father to the boy, Noreen had said.

But one of them had wanted more. One of them had been greedy enough to kill to get it. And now she, too, was standing in the murderer's way, Fawn realized. All the more reason to kill her.

The phone rang, and Fawn reached for it, frowning. But as soon as she heard the voice on the other end, her face lightened. It was Cole.

"I've been sitting by this phone all morning, willing it to ring," he said. "I finally couldn't stand it anymore."

She smiled. She knew how busy he was, how there were always clients calling him, but he made it sound as if her call was the only one that mattered. "I'm sorry," she said, "I know I promised to phone, but . . ." Her voice trailed off. It was impossible to explain that she'd been hoping to find some piece of evidence, some clue, before she spoke with him. Half a dozen times she'd reached for the telephone, wanting to tell him everything, but then forced herself to wait a little longer.

"Are you all right?" he asked.

"Of course." What else could she say to him? She tried to tell herself it wasn't a lie; certainly it would be too dangerous for the killer to make a move against her so soon after her return. Unless the killer suspected she'd begun to remember . . .

"Look, have you eaten? Maybe we could get together for a late lunch." Cole suggested. "Just to talk . . ."

"You don't know how much I'd like that," she began.

That was the truth, at least. "But I promised myself I'd spend the day at the office. There's so much here for me to learn."

"Okay." He sounded disappointed, and for a moment she almost changed her mind. It would be so good to see him. "Anyway, we'll have a chance to talk tonight," Cole said, "if Nick's speech doesn't last all night."

Fawn had been dreading the thought of the award dinner for Nick that evening, but now, remembering that Cole would be there, she was glad she was going.

Just then the secretary entered the room, her arms piled high with the latest batch of reports Fawn had requested. "I'd better get back to work," Fawn said, with a sigh. She was aware that the secretary was watching her curiously, obviously wondering who was on the other end of the line.

"At least, save me the first dance tonight," Cole asked before he hung up, and Fawn agreed, pleased and a little surprised by the request. She'd expected that Cole would arrive with a chic, stunning socialite on his arm, but maybe . . . Realizing where her thoughts were heading, she forced herself to stop. As soon as she was anywhere around Cole she started acting like a schoolgirl with a crush. He undoubtedly had that effect on almost every woman he met. But she couldn't afford such foolishness right now. There was no room for anything in her life but unmasking her parents' killer.

When Fawn looked up, the secretary was still waiting uncertainly in front of her desk. The girl's name was Debbie, and she was a pretty, giggling girl about the same age as Fawn. For a moment Fawn almost wished they could trade places. But then she smiled, realizing Debbie might be wishing the same thing. After all, for all the rest of the world knew, Fawn's biggest problem was deciding how she was going to spend the magnificent inheritance that had suddenly been dumped in her lap. Debbie was probably wondering why Fawn wasn't turning cartwheels up and down the halls.

"Can I get you some more coffee?" Debbie asked.

"Thanks, that'd be nice," Fawn said, as she began leafing through the new batch of records. None of it looked very promising. Just the same bland promotional brochures and financial memorandums.

"Here's your coffee," Debbie said, placing the mug on the desk and craning her neck to see what Fawn was reading. "Mr. Froebush says pretty soon you'll have the whole file room up here."

"Who's Mr. Froebush?" Fawn asked.

"He's the head of the file department. Kind of a fussy guy—you know, the way some old people get." Debbie giggled. "You almost have to sign in blood to get anything out of that room."

Fawn suppressed a shudder at the image. But suddenly she had a thought. "How long has Mr. Froebush been with the company?"

"Forever, I guess. I think they built the building around him."

"Then he was here when my father was alive?" Fawn asked.

"I'm sure he was."

Fawn smiled. She'd been going about this all wrong, but now she knew what to do. They might be able to whitewash and edit the company reports, but no one could tamper with an old employee's memory. She rose. "I think I should thank Mr. Froebush in person then, for all the trouble I've put him to this morning. Where's his office?"

"Down in the basement. I'll take you down if you'd like."

Fawn shook her head. She wanted this to be a private conversation. "That's all right. In fact, we're done here, so why don't you take the rest of the afternoon off."

"You wouldn't mind?" Debbie asked, her eyes eagerly straying to the sunny spring scene outside the window.

"Go on, have a good time, " Fawn said. "I'll see that all these reports get back where they belong," she added, picking up some of the files and heading for the door. "Oh, but don't lock up the office. I'll be coming back here."

"Have a good weekend," Debbie called after her happily. And then she hurried to straighten up her desk and run a comb through her hair, humming as she thought of the free afternoon ahead of her. There was a sale at Bloomie's—that's where she'd start.

But just as she was about to leave, a messenger stuck his head into the office. "Package for Miss Fawn Dalsworth," he announced. Under his arm he was carrying a large white box with a bright red ribbon.

It must be flowers, Debbie decided. "I'll sign for it." She wished someone would send her flowers, and for a moment she was almost jealous. Some people got all the breaks. But she couldn't help liking Fawn, even if she was an heiress. And maybe this would cheer Fawn up; she'd certainly seemed worried all morning.

Carefully Debbie set the big, ribboned box in the middle of Fawn's desk, where she'd be sure to see it when she came back. She fluffed up the bow again, thinking it must be quite a bouquet from the size of the box. Hesitantly her fingers played with the lid; it wouldn't hurt to take just a peek inside. But the lid was securely fastened. She shrugged. It was none of her business. Besides, there was that sale at Bloomie's to get to. She hurried out of the office. But all weekend long she knew she was going to be wondering what was in the box.

Cole knocked at the door of his father's office, then poked his head inside.

"Yes . . ." Bromley said impatiently, then saw it was his son and smiled. "Come in, Cole."

It was almost two o'clock, and Bromley and Rod Davis, the lawyer who handled the Dalsworth estate, had been going through the files since early morning. By now Davis had an exhausted, beleaguered look on his red, beefy face. Rod was a former football player, and in the dozen-odd years since he'd graduated from college he'd softened and run to fat. Despite his expensive suits, he usually had a disheveled air about him. But today he looked even worse than usual; his suit jacket was accordioned in wrinkles, and there were ink stains all over his shirt cuffs. His soft round gut rolled over his belt buckle.

"You two haven't stopped for lunch yet, have you?" Cole asked, knowing that once his father started on something, he forgot everything else. It was a trait both father and son shared.

"No time . . . " Bromley said, but Rod looked up hopefully.

Cole held up the brown paper bag he was carrying. "Triple-decker turkey, roast beef, and ham with Russian dressing. From your favorite deli," he tempted. "Why don't you take a few minutes off? You'll be fresher when you come back."

"Makes sense," Rod agreed instantly. Even Bromley nodded grudgingly. "Guess maybe I am hungry."

Rod was immediately out of his chair and putting his notes away when Bromley's voice stopped him. "No reason we can't work while we eat." Rod's face fell.

"Sorry, I only brought one sandwich," Cole said. "I wasn't sure what you'd want, Rod. And I thought you might want to get out for a few minutes anyway."

"Sure." Rod looked at Cole gratefully. They both knew if Cole had brought a sandwich for him, too, he would have been stuck working right through lunch.

"Just don't be too long. . . ." Bromley said as the heavy-set attorney scurried out of the office. And when he turned back to Cole he was frowning. "You'd think Davis would be as eager to get to the bottom of this as I am, wouldn't you? But for some reason he's resisting every step of the way."

"It is his neck on the chopping block," Cole commented. "If somehow they've managed to get a fraud past him . . ." But ultimately, Cole knew, if there'd been an embezzlement from the Dalsworth estate, the entire law firm would be held responsible. "Have you found anything yet?"

"Nothing," Bromley said, glumly taking a bite of his sandwich. "So far everything's in order, every paper, every entry. Hell, every *i* is dotted, every *t* crossed."

"But? . . ."

"I can't shake this instinct, the feeling I got at the board meeting." He leaned forward in his chair, his eyes earnest, worried. "Something's wrong. It's probably staring me right in the face, and I can't see it."

"Can I help somehow?"

Bromley shook his head. "Rod's nervous enough as it is. Besides, it's just a matter of slogging through the paperwork."

Cole nodded, hoping this time his father's instincts were wrong. Rod was no legal genius and there was some question as to whether he'd ever be made a partner in the firm, but certainly he was competent enough. If there was a problem, he should have caught it.

"Have you spoken with Kendra . . . Fawn lately?" Bromley asked suddenly.

"This morning." Cole remembered the strain in her voice; he hadn't been able to stop worrying about it since. But maybe he was imagining it. She'd said she was all right. He'd been hoping at least he'd be able to tell her there was nothing to worry about as far as the money was concerned. But he couldn't even do that now.

"She's a fine girl," Bromley said, seemingly to himself, but his eyes were focused keenly on his son's face. "She's very much like Melissa. She would have been very proud."

Cole nodded. "She's an exceptional woman."

"Mmmm . . ." Bromley pursed his lips, frowning. "Exceptional is the best you can do? Carrie Nation, Eleanor Roosevelt, even Lizzie Borden were all exceptional."

Cole grinned. "All right, I like her. Is that what you wanted to hear?"

Bromley shook his head sadly. "When I was your age—all those centuries ago—and I met a girl with Fawn's beauty and spirit and laugh and everything that girl has . . . well, I sure as hell wouldn't have been satisfied with just saying I 'like' her."

Cole nodded, thinking of Fawn's mother. His father had lost her—twice—and yet he had never forgotten Melissa. Was he destined to travel the same route as his father? His father had never gotten over the pain of Melissa's love for Joel. Fawn obviously had a boyfriend back home: someone she would go back to when all this was over. He didn't want to feel the same intense jealousy that had ruined his father's life.

Cole gazed out the window for a moment, seeing Fawn's face before his eyes. Did his father still see Melissa's face, even now, eighteen years later? Looking back at Bromley, pushing aside the sandwich and returning all his attention to the papers in front of him, Cole was afraid that he did . . .

Fawn was beginning to lose hope. She'd spent the last several hours listening to Mr. Froebush's reminiscences and drinking cup after cup of the weak tea he brewed on his own private hot plate. He seemed delighted to have the chance to talk about Joel; it was obvious he'd had a great deal of affection for her father. He'd recounted funny stories and fond memories of business triumphs and examples of her father's loyalty and generosity to his employees. Fawn was glad she'd come; she was seeing a side of her father she'd been too young to appreciate herself. But nothing Froebush had said helped answer her question: Which one of the three was the murderer?

"And you say all my father's papers were destroyed right after his death?" she asked. That puzzled her.

Froebush nodded. "Your uncle insisted on it."

"Which uncle—Nick or Ned?"

"Ned, of course. Nick wasn't even with the company then."

She frowned. Certainly Nick had told her he'd worked for her father's company for over twenty years.

"Oh, Nick was here for a couple of years before," Froebush explained quickly. "And he came back real quick after your father's death. Moved right into the executive suite. But the whole year before Joel died, your uncle wasn't working anywhere from what I heard."

"Why did he leave?"

Froebush looked embarrassed. "Can I get you another cup of tea?" he asked, busying himself with filling the kettle and clicking his dentures together nervously.

"They had a fight, didn't they? Nick and Joel."

When Froebush turned to face her, his face was mottled in angry red blotches. "Your father carried Nick for years, waiting for the boy to find himself, to settle down. But finally enough's enough. And it wasn't fair to the rest of us, Nick waltzing in three hours late, leaving early, pushing off his work on everybody else. And trying to lay every secretary in sight, if you'll excuse my language, miss. If it was my decision, I'd have kicked him out years before."

So Nick had lied to her. Had he simply been too ashamed to admit he'd been fired? She knew how touchy Nick's pride was. But had Joel's ousting him from the company—perhaps his desire to get back in—been the motive behind the murders?

"What about Ned?" she asked. "Were there any problems between him and Joel?"

"I don't know that I should be telling you any of this," Froebush said uneasily. He seemed to feel he'd gone too far.

"Please . . ." Fawn insisted. "I have to know."

"You probably think I'm a cranky old man making up stories."

"I think you're the only one who can—or will—tell me the truth."

He smiled. "And you're right. Anyway, if there was anybody else who figured out what Ned was up to, I'd be real surprised. 'Course, Joel probably knew. . . ."

"Knew what?" Fawn asked, gripping the table to try to control her impatience.

"About all the ghosts on the payroll." Froebush had lowered his voice to a whisper, and now he sat back looking very satisfied with himself. It'd been a long time since he'd had a beautiful young girl hanging on his every word. And he couldn't hide his pride at figuring out what no one else had.

"I don't understand. . . ."

"The week after your father died, a funny thing happened to the payroll; there were a dozen fewer people on it," Froebush explained.

"Ned fired them?"

Froebush shook his head. "Nope. Because, you see, they never existed in the first place. See, Ned was in charge of the payroll, and he was adding extra salaries to the list. Making up names and writing checks for them. In an organization this size, no one knows exactly how many people are employed week by week. Then he probably cashed the checks himself at a check-cashing service, using phoney IDs."

"But wouldn't he have gotten caught?"

"Inside the company he could protect himself. And he was always careful to take the taxes out so the government wouldn't come after him. You probably couldn't get away with it now, with all these computers and such, but back then . . ."

"Do you think Joel suspected?"

"You couldn't put anything past your daddy for long. And

those extra checks were adding up to quite a bit of money. Anyway, something was on Joel's mind that last week.''

''Did you tell the police about this?''

''They never asked.'' Froebush looked uncomfortable. Maybe he should have told someone. But he couldn't have proven anything, and anyway Joel was dead, and Ned was firmly in control of the company. So what did it matter, he'd told himself. All he would have accomplished would have been to talk himself right out of a job. Which is maybe what he'd done just now. ''You're not going to repeat any of this, are you?'' he asked Fawn.

She shook her head, feeling sick to her stomach. Had her father been about to expose Ned? If so, then Ned had had a motive, too—motive that he'd managed to conceal from almost everyone all these years.

She rose shakily to her feet. ''Thank you for telling me. It's more important than you could know.''

Froebush patted her hand. She looked so upset, he almost wished now he could take it all back. But he didn't want anyone to take advantage of her, either, and in a way he felt he owed it to Joel to warn her. ''I'm glad you've come back,'' he said. ''But just be careful. I wouldn't put it past any of them to try and steal the company right out from under you.''

Fawn nodded, wishing that was all she had to worry about.

She made her way back to her office slowly, still thinking of what Froebush had told her. It seemed the closer she looked at the past, the uglier it got.

As she walked into the office, the first thing she saw was the large white package on the desk. It had her name written on the outside, but there was no indication of where it had come from or who had sent it.

Quickly she untied the big red ribbon and lifted off the lid. And suddenly her breath caught in her throat as she dropped the lid; she thought she was going to be sick. Nestled on the blood-soaked tissue paper was a small white kitten, its throat slashed, its dead eyes staring up at her.

She jerked backward, feeling as if she were about to faint. For a moment it was as if she were back in the house that night, reliving the horror of it again. "No . . ." she whispered. "Please, no . . ."

Slowly she sank into a chair, her hands clenched together, forcing herself back to the present. Someone was trying to frighten her, to make her run away. But who? Which one of them?

She looked again at the small, still body. Despite the blood matting its fur and the horrible slash across its throat, there was something familiar . . . And then she realized this was the kitten she'd petted on the walk several nights before. "I'm so sorry . . ." she whispered. But she knew now that she was right; the murderer had to be one of the three. This was a warning.

Angrily she jammed the lid back onto the box. She wasn't going to be frightened off. The killer had just made his first mistake.

Chapter 24

The charity ball at which Nick's award was to be presented was being held at the Pierre, one of the finest hotels in Manhattan. Outside on Fifth Avenue a line of shiny black limousines slowly inched up to the portico, and the women emerging from the dark interiors in their colorful gowns and shimmering jewels seemed like butterflies released from their cocoons. Immediately the reporters and photographers crowded around them, flashbulbs popping.

Fawn had hoped that her own arrival would pass unnoticed, but as soon as Nick helped her from the car, they were surrounded by reporters shouting out questions. Photographers elbowed one another aside to get the best shot. "Are you happy to be home at last?" "What's it like to suddenly find out you're about to inherit millions?" "Have you given the police a description of your parents' killer?"

"Ignore them," Ned hissed. And as he grabbed for her arm, it took all her self-control to keep herself from flinching. But he was too busy propelling her through the crowds to notice.

Inside, the gilded, high-ceilinged ballroom had been transformed into a fantasy of red and white. Thousands of red tulips were banked against the walls and spilled from the balconies. Here and there climbing roses and grapevines had been woven into cozy, romantic arbors. At one end of the huge room a waterfall splashed into a pool filled with flashing silver-white *koi*. The tables were covered in a deep, rich red and at the center of each stood a towering arrangement of white lilacs.

"Well, what do you think, Fawn?" Noreen asked. "I don't suppose you ever saw anything like this back wherever it was you came from."

Numbly Fawn shook her head. It was spectacular, she thought, gazing at the men in their tuxedos, the women in silk and satin and lace and chiffon. The room seemed to blaze with the fiery sparkle of diamonds, rubies, emeralds, sapphires. But nothing could ease the chill she felt in her heart. It was becoming more and more difficult to hide her feelings, to smile and pretend.

"I just love all this red and white. It's so dramatic," Noreen said gaily. "I'll have to be sure to compliment the decorating committee."

But Fawn was remembering the white box with the red ribbon, and what was inside. She hadn't mentioned the kitten to anyone. She'd hoped her silence would prod one of them into asking about it, but so far nothing had been said. Whoever had sent the package wasn't going to be tricked into an admission. But at least Fawn could deny them the satisfaction of knowing how much it had upset her.

"Come on, let's go get a drink," Nick said. This was the night he'd waited for, for so long, yet he seemed strangely uneasy. Maybe he was just nervous about the speech he was to give, Fawn told herself.

As they started across the room, they were stopped again and again by people wanting to congratulate Nick on his award. "I haven't gotten it yet," he protested. "Who knows, they might still change their minds." He said it as if he were joking, but there something very close to fear in his eyes.

Noreen, however, was in a festive mood. She looked stunning tonight in a one-shouldered midnight-blue gown with ruffles cascading down the front. And her eyes glittered with the same hard brightness as the diamonds at her neck, wrists, and fingers. She'd arranged to be escorted by one of the senior executives from the company, a handsome, gray-haired man. Fawn felt a little sorry for him; Noreen was treating him as no more than a servent while her gaze obviously raked through the crowd searching for someone else.

Scott had a date for the evening, too, so Fawn had been paired with Ned, who was grumbling again about the cost of the tickets—four thousand dollars for the party of eight.

"Shut up, Ned," Nick whispered. "It's for charity. Besides, none of the money came out of your pocket."

"You're damned right. I'm not that much of a fool," Ned answered. The thought seemed to cheer him up, and from then on he looked around the ballroom with an air of smug satisfaction. It was as if he had a secret that made him superior to everyone else there.

Just as they took their seats at their table, the orchestra began playing. Fawn, remembering her promise to save the first dance for Cole, looked around for him, and with a quick lightening of her heart, saw that he was already making his way through the crowd toward her. But before he could reach their table, Noreen had grabbed Fawn's arm and was pulling her up. "Come on," Noreen said, putting her arm possessively around Fawn's waist, "I want to show off my pretty new niece to all my friends." Fawn shrugged apologetically to Cole and the next minutes were lost in the swirl of new faces and names.

At least, Fawn realized gratefully, it wasn't necessary for her to do anything more than smile and look politely interested. Noreen did all the talking: Yes, it had been such a surprise . . . but Noreen had never given up hoping . . . Yes, they were inseparable, just like sisters . . . Again Fawn marveled at how completely Noreen could switch personalities. Her aunt seemed to believe every word she was saying. Or was there something else behind all this? Was Noreen trying to divert suspicion from herself in advance, so that if something happened to Fawn, no one would suspect she'd had anything to do with it?

At last the black-coated waiters began serving the first course, and everyone settled down to dinner. Except Nick. He was too nervous to eat. He couldn't get it out of his mind that tonight was some sort of elaborate practical joke on him. Everyone here knew his secret, he was sure of it. They were all laughing at him behind his back. His ears burned a dull red, and his face was growing more flushed with each drink he gulped down.

Fawn, at her end of the table, was aware of Nick's stare fastened malevolently on her. Why was he suddenly so furious with her? She turned away, shivering, as the speeches began. It was the first time she'd glimpsed the soul behind the charming, carefree mask Nick kept so firmly in place. And she wondered if the desperation she saw in him would stop at anything—even murder?

His name was being called from the stage, Nick realized. He stumbled up, only vaguely aware of hands patting him on the back, pushing him forward. There was no place to hide. And then he saw the audience rise to their feet . . . and they were applauding him. They were applauding him. No one knew the truth about him. He was safe, it was all right. Tears of relief blinded his eyes. He'd done it, he'd fooled them all—for now.

As he returned to the table after his speech he saw Fawn's eyes, curious and thoughtful, on him, but he only grinned. He felt invincible. He could handle anything now, even her.

The orchestra had begun to play once more, and slowly couples drifted out onto the floor. Immediately Fawn found herself surrounded by young men asking asking her to dance.

"Sorry, fellows, but she's already promised this one to me," Cole said, seeming to appear out of nowhere and holding out his hand to Fawn. "Unless you've changed your mind?" he asked her.

"I haven't," she said, smiling, and for a moment, as they stared at each other, everyone else became as insignificant as mannequins in a store window.

"I knew there was going to be a rush for you," he whispered as he led her onto the floor.

"I guess I'm a bit of a curiosity." She laughed. "All this returning-from-the-dead business."

Cole glanced at her quickly and realized that she believed what she was saying. She was so unconscious of her own beauty, so innocent of the fact that she was raising every male pulse beat in the room. And as she moved into his arms, he felt his own heart lurch with a sudden foolish, uncontrollable happiness. "You look lovely tonight, Fawn," he whispered.

"Is that your considered legal opinion?" she teased. But

she couldn't help blushing happily; and to cover it, she added quickly, "This is one of Melissa's gowns." There hadn't been time to shop for a dress, and so Noreen had suggested she wear this. It was a beautiful gown—filmy, shimmering white chiffon in a timeless Grecian style that skimmed lightly over her curves and swirled around her legs. With it she was wearing delicate emerald drop earrings, and her blond hair was pulled up into a loose fall of curls.

"It's perfect for you," Cole said. "You look as though you've stepped straight out of a vision."

Fawn nodded, her eyes suddenly somber. She'd thought almost the same thing when she'd first seen herself tonight in the mirror. It hadn't seemed quite real. It was almost as if she'd somehow become Melissa. And without meaning to, Fawn glanced toward the table where the triplets were sitting.

Following her gaze, Cole frowned. "I wish you had come with me tonight," he said.

"I couldn't. It was important to Nick that the whole family show up together." Besides she had to keep watching them; sooner or later there would have to be some clue, one of them would make some slip, and she would know who the murderer was. That's what she had to keep concentrating on. But just being in Cole's arms made it difficult to think of anything but him. She was so conscious of his hand against her bare flesh pulling her close, the warmth of his breath against her cheek. Her body seemed to respond to him with a will of its own. It was unfair that he was so handsome, so distracting. "Why do you think Nick was so nervous tonight?" she asked suddenly, determined to force her thoughts away from Cole.

"What does it matter?" Cole asked, shrugging impatiently. He didn't want to talk about Nick tonight. Or Ned or Noreen. He'd waited for this moment for so long. It was perhaps the only chance he'd ever have to hold her close. For just this one evening he wanted to pretend . . . But even now he could sense that she was distancing herself from him— even as they touched she was somewhere far way where he couldn't reach her. His mouth set in a hard line.

"Is something wrong?" she asked quickly.

"No, why?"

"All of a sudden you got this look on your face . . ."

"It's nothing," he said, forcing a smile and drawing her nearer to him.

Yet she could feel the tension in his body. Beneath the broad shoulders of his dinner jacket, his muscles were taut, and there was a strained, controlled edge in his voice that she'd never heard before. It was the first time she'd seen him less than totally self-assured.

Nervous about the growing silence between them, she tried to think of something to say. But she felt as shy as a girl at her first dance—except that she'd gone to her first dance with Sam, and she hadn't been shy at all. In fact, they'd spent most of the evening arguing the merits of a battered old Chevy that Sam hoped to buy and ended up out in the parking lot peering under its hood. Gram had just shaken her head when Fawn returned home with her frilly net formal covered with grease stains. Fawn smiled at the memory. There was nothing distracting or unsettling about Sam.

"What's the smile for?" Cole asked.

"I was just thinking about home. About Sam." She remembered that she'd given Sam Cole's office number to call if he needed to get a message to her. "I guess you haven't heard from him?"

Cole's smile was rigid and thin lipped. "As a matter of fact, I have—twice. But he asked me not to mention it unless you inquired." His voice had taken on the clipped, impersonal tone of a lawyer advising a client about a case, and he was leaning back to study her reaction to the news.

"What did Sam want?" she asked nervously.

"Just to make sure you were all right." He hesitated, then added, "Apparently he worries a great deal about you."

"But why the secrecy?"

"He didn't want you to feel he was prying."

Fawn nodded—that was just like Sam. She was relieved that the explanation was so simple. At least she didn't have to be anxious about what was happening at home. Yet, someone had stolen the photographs from her room . . . "I'll call him tomorrow," she said. "And thank you, Cole, for telling me. It's good to know I can count on you."

"Just remember that," he whispered. He smiled to hide the ache inside. Good old Cole, he thought bitterly. The guy who doesn't get the girl. It was a new role for him, and he might have been amused by the irony of it, if it hadn't mattered so damned much. All his life he'd always gotten everything he'd wanted. Every woman he'd ever wanted. But he would have traded it all for Fawn. She was the one he'd been waiting for all his life, without even knowing he was waiting. Until she'd walked into his office, so radiantly beautiful and determined.

But he couldn't even tell Fawn how he felt. She was counting on him to be a friend. Was this how his father had felt? Cole wondered. And right now her life was too confused for anything else. She was struggling to make some sense of a suddenly untrustworthy world, and he was perhaps even more conscious of her vulnerability than she was herself. He was determined not to take advantage of that vulnerability. But maybe when this was all over . . . And in the meantime he would grit his teeth and be a friend and nothing more.

The dance was ending. He began escorting her back to the table. "About tomorrow . . . what time shall I pick you up?" he asked, then saw by the look on her face that she'd forgotten their trip. "We're going to Long Island. I promised you a surprise, remember?"

"I'm not sure I should go. . . ." She was thinking of the triplets again. And after the kitten today, she wasn't sure she could take any more surprises. "Would you mind if we postponed it?"

"Of course not. But I'm afraid your Great-Aunt Lavinia is going to be very disappointed."

She glanced up at him, startled. "My . . . who?" She hadn't realized there were any relatives she hadn't met yet.

"Your mother's aunt," Cole explained. "She's very old now and not up to making the trip into the city." He didn't add that since Melissa's death it had been Lavinia's strict policy never to be in the same room as the triplets. "She's very excited about seeing you. She's been peppering me with questions about you all week. But I'm sure she'll understand if you want to put off meeting her. I'll just explain . . ."

"But I do want to see her," Fawn interrupted. Surely Lavinia would be able to fill in some pieces of the puzzle.

Cole grinned. "I'll pick you up at ten, then?" At least they would have the long drive out to the Island together. "She's expecting us around teatime. Lavinia still serves an old-fashioned tea, with buttered cucumber-and-watercress sandwiches. But we'll stop somewhere earlier in the afternoon for lunch, first. I know a great seafood restaurant . . ." Suddenly he couldn't seem to stop talking. In part, it was just his relief that Fawn had agreed to come along, and partly it was to keep her close to him. The orchestra had begun playing again—a loud, thumping Rolling Stones song—and she had to bend close to him to hear. Her lips were only inches from his. Suddenly he couldn't trust himself to say another word. He was almost dizzy with the sense of her, the long sweep of her lashes, the graceful, inviting curve of her neck, the perfume of her silky skin.

Fawn looked up, puzzled by his silence. And it was as if they were both caught unaware; their eyes met, and everything else faded away to nothingness. It had happened in an instant, like a photographer's flash that illuminated them and left everything else in darkness. Even the air between them seemed to vibrate.

After a moment Fawn blushed and looked away. But in that instant something between them had changed.

But even if Fawn and Cole weren't aware of anyone else, there were others watching them. Ned and Noreen and Bromley; and of the three only Bromley seemed pleased.

"They make a fine-looking couple, don't they?" Bromley said, nodding at Fawn and Cole. He sighed. "Just looking at them makes you wish you were young again."

"I hardly think of myself as old," Noreen answered sharply, wrapping her arm possessively around his. "Anyway, Colman, I thought you were going to dance with me." She hadn't invited him over to her table just so he could watch Fawn.

But even as he led Noreen onto the dance floor, his eyes kept straying back to Fawn. He couldn't get over how much she looked like Melissa tonight. It brought back so many memories. She was too like Melissa—too fragile and beautiful and vulnerable. And as the music played on, he was filled with a terrible foreboding.

Chapter 25

"What are you doing here?" Ned demanded as he opened the front door and saw Cole waiting.

"So pleased to see you, too, Ned," Cole answered easily, but his eyes glimmered with a steely hardness.

"What are you doing? Checking up on us?"

Before Cole could answer, Fawn—in a sweater and skirt, her hair pulled back in a braid—hurried down the stairs. "Didn't mean to keep you waiting."

"That's all right; Ned's been making me feel right at home," Cole said. Ignoring Ned's glare, he took Fawn's arm and they started down the sidewalk.

"I'll be home late, Uncle Ned," she called over her shoulder. "Don't wait dinner for me."

"Where are you going?" Ned asked suspiciously.

"Out," Cole said, opening the car door for Fawn. And as he backed down the drive, he saw that Ned was still eyeing them with a frosty stare. "Why's he so set on keeping us apart?" Cole asked Fawn.

"I don't know." It was just another in a long list of things she didn't know. Was Ned afraid of what Cole might tell her?

Or what she might tell him? Maybe Ned believed Cole was trying to get his hands on the inheritance. It was the sort of thing Ned would think. She shook her head, and she could almost hear all the questions rattling around inside.

"Be careful, your face is going to freeze like that," Cole teased, and she realized she'd been frowning. Quickly she tried to rearrange her features into something that might pass for a smile.

"That's better. You don't want to go around scaring little kids."

She grinned. "Is it really that bad?"

"You tell me, Fawn. Is it?" And she saw that his eyes were studying her with real concern. "Just what the hell's going on in that house?"

Oh, Cole, please don't ask, she pleaded silently. It was bad enough that she had to keep up this act in front of the others. And she was so tempted to rest her head on Cole's shoulder, that nice, broad, capable shoulder, and spill out the whole ugly mess. But if she did, wouldn't he make her leave? So she just shrugged and said, "Let's just forget about Nick and Ned and Noreen for today, all right?" The words came out more sharply than she'd intended, and she blushed. He would think she was angry with him now. But it was only that she felt so frustated . . .

Yet he didn't seem offended. They'd stopped for a light, and he very gently reached over and took her hand. His eyes stared intently into hers. She was reminded of the way Pete looked at her when he thought she was coming down with a fever. Protective, worried, and angry with a world that threatened her. She glanced away, suddenly feeling unsteady.

A car horn sounded impatiently behind them; the light had changed. Cole sighed and turned his attention back to his driving. "All right, Fawn," he said softly. "I don't know what else I can do to make you trust me."

"Cole, I do trust you. It's just . . . just that I'm confused about a lot of things right now, and I need some time to sort it out on my own." It was as close as she could come to the truth.

"If that's what you want . . ." he said, and for a while they were both silent.

He'd released her hand, and she was surprised by how

alone she suddenly felt. But she was the one who'd put the distance between them. She smiled sadly, remembering the night before, that moment when the rest of the world had disappeared and for an instant they'd known each other with the intimacy of lovers. Damn, Cole, she thought, if you only knew how confused I am . . . Confused by you, by emotions I shouldn't be feeling. By thoughts I have no room in my life for. Why did this have to happen now?

Right now she should have been concentrating on the meeting with Lavinia, rehearsing the questions she'd ask. And instead, all she could think of was Cole.

Ten days ago she didn't even know this man existed, Fawn reminded herself. As if she could fight what she was feeling with logic . . .

And suddenly she wished she could remember the boy he'd been. He'd only been eleven when she disappeared, and he'd probably thought her a terrible nuisance—a six-year-old tagging after him, pestering him when he wanted to be with his friends. Still, she would have liked to remember. She wanted to know everything there was to know about him.

But wasn't it bad enough that, now that they'd met again, she'd never be able to forget him? The way his hair curled just the slightest bit at the back of his neck, his gentle, searching blue eyes, the planes and angles of his face . . . He was wearing a heathery tweed jacket and jeans today, and his collar was open. All at once she realized how much she wanted to touch him, to stroke that small vunerable hollow of his collarbone.

She glanced away quickly. "It's a beautiful day for a drive, isn't it?" she said, almost cringing at the inane words, but knowing she had to say something. Anything but what she was thinking.

"Yes, the weather's fine," he agreed. And such a safe topic, he thought to himself. Obviously, whatever was on her mind—and he was sure it had to do with the triplets—she was going to keep to herself. But if that's what she wanted . . .

"They say it might rain before night, though," he added. "But maybe we'll be back before then."

Fawn nodded, unable to think of anything else to say. It looked as if it was going to be a long, silent trip. And as she met Cole's eyes, she realized he was thinking the same thing.

And then, for no reason—or maybe just because it suddenly seemed ridiculous that they should be so stilted with each other—they both began to laugh.

"Why don't we just relax," Cole suggested, "or the next thing you know, we'll be asking each other what's your sign and do you come here often?"

"I thought all you lawyers were so glib," she teased.

"Only when we're charging by the word," he retorted. "Anyway, this is supposed to be my day off. And yours, too, So we don't have to make conversation if we don't feel like it."

"Of course not."

"We'll just enjoy the scenery."

". . . in companionable silence," she agreed.

"And are you enjoying the scenery?" he asked after a minute.

She looked around; the sky was a brilliant, shimmering blue, the trees were in full leaf, and a soft, fresh-scented breeze made the whole world seem buoyant and new. "It's very nice," she said.

"I'm glad you like it. I had it flown in especially for you."

"Ah, you see—you are glib. Please remember, I'm just a small-town girl."

"I won't say another word," he promised.

But of course, he did. Now that the tension had been broken, neither of them could stop talking. It was a holiday, and for a few hours they felt free to enjoy each other's company without thinking about the past . . . or the future.

By the time they stopped for lunch, the conversation had skipped from which part of the country they liked best, to sailing on the Sound, to favorite movies, to what was the worst joke they'd ever heard. They'd discovered they both loved horses and riding and confessed their most embarrassing moments. Fawn's cheeks were aching from laughing so hard. And Cole noticed the sparkle had returned to her large brown eyes.

The restaurant was situated right on the ocean. Cole had called ahead to arrange to have a table set up for them on the terrace overlooking the water. There was a fresh bouquet of wildflowers on the table and a bottle of Dom Perignon already chilling in the silver ice bucket.

"It's beautiful," Fawn said. "You're going to spoil me."

"Impossible." He grinned.

They had the terrace to themselves. Even the waiters were careful not to intrude on their privacy any more than necessary. "They must think we're on our honeymoon or having an affair or something," Fawn whispered. The waiter who'd just brought their coffee had noisily cleared his throat before approaching their table, as if warning them of his presence.

Cole glanced at her sharply, then looked away. "It's a logical assumption, I suppose," he said. "Can I order you anything else?"

She shook her head. She hadn't even been able to finish her strawberries Romanoff. "It was a perfect meal."

Yes, perfect, he thought to himself, and perfectly friendly, innocuous. He would have given anything if the waiters had been right about them. It was agonizing not even being able to touch her. She looked so beautiful today. She was wearing a soft cashmere sweater the color of ripe apricots and a dark brown suede skirt, and for hours he'd been trying not to think of the gentle curves and hollows and silky flesh that lay just beneath the fabric.

"Cole," she said suddenly, and he looked up, wondering if she'd read his thoughts. The tension was back in her face, and her fingers were knotted tightly around the coffee cup.

"What's wrong?" he asked.

For a moment she just stared past him, her eyes focused on the silver ice bucket and the nearly empty bottle of champagne. And then she shook her head. "It's nothing," she said trying to quell her anxiety. "Could we go now?"

He motioned for the check, wondering what had suddenly made her so nervous. "You're not worried about meeting Lavinia, are you?" he asked.

"In a way . . ." She frowned. "Why didn't anyone tell me about her before?"

"She asked us to give you a little time to get settled in, without being mobbed by relatives," Cole explained. "As for the triplets saying anything, they'd just as soon forget she exists. Not that she cares much for them, either."

"And what do you suppose she'll think of me?"

"Well, she won't keep you guessing." He grinned. "Lavinia always says exactly what's on her mind. Some people find her intimidating, and I guess she can seem awfully fierce. But if she likes you, she's for you one hundred percent, no fine print, no holding back.''

"Then I'll just have to hope she likes me."

"It really matters to you, doesn't it?"

Fawn nodded. She was depending on Lavinia more than she could admit. She was convinced that somewhere in her great-aunt's memory lay the key to the identity of the murderer, even if she wasn't aware of it. But would Lavinia be willing to discuss the past, to face all those painful memories again? Fawn knew she would feel guilty about asking—but she also knew she didn't have any choice.

Lavinia's house was a rambling old Victorian with an octagonal tower and a wide, welcoming front porch. Delicate white scrollwork trimmed the gables and eaves, and the house itself was painted a soft blue-gray that matched the ocean lapping at the sandy beach in back. It reminded Fawn of her own place in Colorado—except it was obvious that this house's roof never leaked and the shutters weren't ready to take off in the next strong wind. No, her house was just a scruffy urchin compared to this grand old Victorian. Still, for a moment she felt a little homesick.

Cole parked the car in the drive behind a lovingly polished antique Bentley, and glanced at his watch. "We'd better hurry," he said. "We're two minutes late now."

Quickly Fawn checked her reflection in the rearview mirror. "Do I look all right?"

He grinned. "I don't think it's possible to look any more all right than you do."

He whisked her up the walk of crushed white shells and rang the bell. "We won't stay any longer than you want to," he whispered, giving her hand a reassuring squeeze.

The door swung open, and a slim, petite woman with silver-white hair stood on the threshold. "You're late, Cole," she admonished, but there was a twinkle in her eye.

"Guilty." He laughed, leaning down to kiss her cheek. "But I know you'll forgive me. I've brought Fawn . . . Kendra.''

"Well, then, step aside and let me see her, for heaven's sake."

The lively brown eyes fastened on Fawn, curious and searching. And for a moment Fawn felt the queerest tumbling sensation; aside from the delicate tracery of wrinkles, the face she was looking into was a mirror image of her own. The same wide-set eyes, the same high forehead and stubborn chin. And, looking at Lavinia's face, Fawn knew that she'd been waiting for this moment for years; she'd finally found the link that bound her to the rest of the world.

"Come in, child," Lavinia said, her voice quavering just the slightest bit.

She led them into a parlor decorated in soft pinks and yellows, with masses of flowers arranged in Chinese porcelain bowls. The windows opened out onto the ocean and outside the sky had begun to cloud over while the ocean foamed restlessly, promising a storm. But inside everything was comfortable and cheerful and cozy. A fire crackled behind the gleaming brass fire screen, taking the chill from the air.

"Sit down beside me, Fawn, so I can take a good look at you," Lavinia said, patting a spot on the sofa next to her.

Nervously Fawn sat down. Suddenly she very much wanted this woman with the wise, inquisitive eyes to approve of her.

"Turn on the lamp, please," Lavinia asked Cole, never taking her eyes from Fawn's face. Fawn met her gaze squarely, and for long moments the two women stared at each other wordlessly, all the grief and fears of the past revived, and the hope that had never died . . .

And then, with infinite gentleness, Lavinia's hands reached toward Fawn and she held the young face between her trembling fingers. There were tears in Lavinia's eyes as she whispered, "Thank God. I could never believe you'd be lost to me forever."

She caressed Fawn's cheek as if reassuring herself the miracle was real. "Will you let me hold you, child?" And it seemed the most natural thing in the world for Fawn to be enfolded in those arms, for her to rest her head on Lavinia's shoulder.

When they separated at last, they were both crying. "Are you all right?" Fawn asked.

Lavinia nodded, smiling. "I've been waiting for these tears for eighteen years. They're pure happiness, that's all."

Cole, forgotten till now, handed Lavinia his handkerchief. Despite his smile, his own eyes were misty. "Should I leave you two alone?"

Lavinia looked back and forth between Fawn and Cole. "No, I think you belong here. But you could pour us all some brandy, if you would."

"He's awfully handsome, isn't he?" Lavinia whispered mischievously, while Cole was pouring the drinks.

Fawn nodded, blushing in spite of herself, and wondering how Lavinia had recognized Fawn's feelings so quickly.

"And she's every bit as beautiful as you said," Lavinia continued, raising her voice to include Cole in the conversation. "Frankly, I thought you were exaggerating."

Cole grinned and handed Fawn her glass. "No need to exaggerate."

"Please . . ." Fawn objected, thoroughly scarlet by now.

"Your mother was just as shy about her looks," Lavinia told her. "In fact, I can see a lot of Melissa in you. And if you wouldn't think me too vain for saying so, you look remarkably like I did at your age."

"I'm glad." The way the two women resembled each other seemed a marvelous, unexpected gift that neither of them could quite believe. And for the first time, Fawn realized, she had some idea of what she would look like as she grew older. It was comforting not to have to wonder anymore.

"It's mostly the eyes, I think," Lavinia was saying, still studying her. "What I used to be able to do with those eyes . . ." She smiled fondly, recalling her youth. Despite the years, Lavinia's eyes were still wonderfully compelling, filled with life and joy. And a sudden quick sorrow. "We never had any children of our own, my husband and I. He's dead now, bless his soul. But it's nice to know something will continue . . ." But abruptly her voice harshened. "What have those three told you about Melissa and Joel?"

She was obviously referring to Ned and Nick and Noreen. And from the sound of her voice, there was no love lost there. "They really haven't talked much about my parents," Fawn said.

"That's what I expected."

"I was hoping you'd be willing to tell me more."

"Just what is it you want to know?"

Fawn hesitated. She was very aware of being on delicate ground. Arousing Lavinia's suspicions might only put her in danger, too. And out of the corner of her eye, Fawn could see Cole leaning forward in his chair, paying close attention to the conversation. But she couldn't afford to lose this opportunity. "It's about the triplets . . ." she began. "I get the feeling they resented Melissa and Joel."

"So it still shows, does it? But it wasn't Joel they resented so much; he was their free meal ticket. It was their own sister, Melissa. They blamed her for everything."

"Why?"

Lavinia sighed. "It all seems so long ago now, but I don't suppose anyone quite gets over the hurts he or she suffered as a child. And those poor children—there were times it was impossible not to ache for them. So, in a way, I can't blame the triplets for not forgetting, not forgiving . . ." She frowned, her eyes focusing on the past. "Emmaline should never have told her husband."

Fawn was thoroughly confused by now. She knew that Emmaline was her grandmother—Melissa and the triplets' mother—but as for the rest . . . "What shouldn't Emmaline have told her husband?"

"That the triplets weren't his, of course." And then Lavinia saw the surprise on Fawn's face. "I forgot, you wouldn't have known that. Perhaps I shouldn't have mentioned it."

Fawn stared at her. "You mean Emmaline had an . . ."

"Affair. Yes. And she got pregnant. I loved my sister, but there's no sense trying to pretty up the facts. She could be an awful fool at times. Any other woman would have seen through that man right away. He was a predator, the kind of man that smells of danger and sex. But he was very handsome, in a swaggering sort of way. And she was bored. After the excitement of her debutante year, all the spoiling and attention a pretty girl gets, I suppose marriage seemed dull, flat, stale . . ."

Fawn thought back to the pretty, petite blond woman she'd seen in the family album. There'd been such an expression of melancholy on that face, such a look of wilted hopes; she'd seemed to fade into the background, ghostlike, as if whatever

ties had bound her to life had already been irrevocably severed.
"Wouldn't her husband give her a divorce?" Fawn asked.

"In spite of the scandal—and the gossips would have fed
on the bones of it for months—I think he would have. But as
soon as Emmaline realized she was pregnant, she ran to tell
her lover. Lord knows how she could have believed he'd be
pleased . . ." Lavinia turned away, blinking unsteadily.
"That bastard . . ." she whispered.

"They were in a hotel room. Emmaline had brought a
bottle of champagne and glasses, to toast the news. She'd
always liked to make little ceremonies out of things, and she'd
wanted this to be a celebration. He hit her, that huge, knobby
fist of his splitting open her lip, slamming her against the
wall. And he kept hitting her and hitting her . . ."

"Lavinia . . ." Fawn said, thinking she should stop her,
but Lavinia shook her head. "Someone has to know. Emmaline and her husband are dead now. And for all I know,
he's dead, too. I hope so. And I won't live much longer.
Someone has to know."

"The triplets were never told?" Cole asked.

"No. Though it's possible they found out some way on
their own. I've always wondered about that."

"Then Emmaline's husband raised them as his own?"
Fawn asked.

"He fed them and clothed them and gave them his name,
if that's what you mean. But he couldn't love them, couldn't
touch them. It wasn't that he meant to be cruel, but. . . .
there'd always been a rigid, overly intellectual quality to him.
And after this it hardened into bitterness. Maybe it would've
taken a saint to forget."

Cole was thinking back to the snatches of family history
he'd heard. "His company went bankrupt just before the triplets were born, too, didn't it? He must have thought his whole
life was collapsing."

Lavinia nodded. "While he was staying home for months
with Emmaline—nursing her back to health from what he at
that time believed had been a street mugging—his partner
was looting the company."

"A fine partner," Cole said.

"But don't you see? It was the same man. Emmaline's

lover. And by the time the truth came out, he was gone, had disappeared without a trace, leaving nothing behind but years of debts to be repaid.''

''Legally, your grandfather could have gotten out of paying most of those debts,'' Cole explained to Fawn. ''But he wouldn't. In the end, he cleared every debt to the penny.''

''I think perhaps it was his way of trying to set things right,'' Lavinia suggested. ''He had his own streak of romanticism, too, I guess. But it was a futile gesture; there was no way of undoing the past. All he really accomplished was to work—and worry—himself into an early grave.''

Outside the rising wind whipped the gray expanse of sea into a froth. The storm that had been building all afternoon was going to strike soon, Fawn realized. But it wasn't that that made her shiver. She was thinking about the past and imagining what it must have been like for the triplets to have grown up in such a household: with a mother who'd retreated from life, and a father to whom they were constant reminders of the man who'd ruined him. Yet it couldn't have been a happy childhood for Melissa, either, she realized. ''Why did the triplets blame my mother? None of it was her fault.''

''But they couldn't know that. All they could see was that Melissa was loved and they weren't. That if there were a few dollars left over for a new toy or a new dress, Melissa always came first. And when she tried to share, somehow it only made it worse. Melissa herself never understood why she was treated so much better. She felt guilty about it—and they all used her guilt like a blank check. Spiteful they were, too.''

Had one of them hated Melissa enough to commit murder? Fawn wondered. Had jealousy, rather than greed, been the motive?

The distaste was evident in Lavinia's voice as she spoke of the triplets and, as if suddenly aware of it herself, she asked Fawn, ''I suppose you think I should have more sympathy for the three of them? I did at one time, you know.''

Fawn nodded. She was sure that Lavinia wouldn't have blamed the triplets for the circumstances of their birth, and had already guessed that her great-aunt would have done everything she could to befriend them. Yet, at some point, she'd turned against them. And maybe her harshness now had as much to do with disappointment as anything else. "What happened?" she asked. "What changed?"

"I suppose it was partly the way they treated Melissa, though perhaps I could have forgiven, understood, that. But there were other . . . incidents." Lavinia hesitated, obviously reluctant to go on. But then, as if mentally squaring her shoulders, she continued in a brisk, controlled voice. "When the triplets were about twelve, there was a boy in their neighborhood who used to taunt them. He was undoubtedly a bully, the sort who enjoys humiliating and making fun of those more vulnerable than himself. It was a wealthy neighborhood—the family was still living in the same house, the only thing saved in the bankruptcy—but of course the triplets didn't have money as the other children did, and they were constantly having their noses rubbed in the fact.

"Anyway, this boy was passing their house one afternoon and suddenly a dozen heavy stone blocks came tumbling over the parapet; he was struck in the head. It was just luck that his skull wasn't cracked wide open. But maybe not good luck—he lived, but his mind was never right again. That afternoon the triplets had been playing on the roof. And the workmen, who'd brought the stone blocks up to repair the chimney, swore the blocks had been piled in the center of the roof, far from harm's way, when they left the day before."

Cole lifted his head sharply, frowning. "You're suggesting . . ."

"Nothing was ever proven," Lavinia said. "The triplets were questioned, of course, but they were all wide-eyed innocence. And eventually they were believed. Melissa, who should have known them best, was the most stubbornly loyal."

"But you weren't satisfied?"

Lavinia sighed. "It wasn't the only . . . accident. The worst, but not the only one."

Fawn felt sick to her stomach. Lavinia's story had smothered the last wistful doubts she might have had. "Which one of the three do you think it was?" she asked.

"That question had tormented me for years," Lavinia told her. "And I still don't have an answer."

"But the other two would have known the truth probably,"

Cole said. "They shielded the guilty one, didn't they? If in fact, only one of them was guilty."

Fawn had had the same thought. And she was remembering the edgy, apprehensive way they watched one another. How Ned and Noreen had both warned her about Nick's temper.

She turned to Cole. "Why wasn't I told about this before? Didn't your father know? Didn't the police?"

Lavinia answered for him. "Colman didn't even know the family then. And you see, it was hushed up right away. I'm probably the only one who even remembers. And it could be—I hope it is—that I'm wrong." She hesitated, and when she spoke again her voice was no more than the whisper of someone in a confessional. "There was such a fierce, unholy anger in me against their father, against what he did to Emmaline . . . perhaps it made me too suspicious."

"But, still, you told me . . ." Fawn said. "Why?"

"Because of the inheritance. It may not be easy to pry that money away from them, and I want you to be prepared. It's true they're not children anymore; undoubtedly they've learned to fight their battles in a more civilized fashion. Endless lawsuits, for instance . . ." she added with a glance toward Cole.

"They wouldn't have a chance in court," Cole said quickly.

And Fawn realized that both he and Lavinia were unconsciously backing away from the uglier implications of the situation. Neither of them was prepared to accept that one of her relatives was a murderer.

"Maybe this will all turn out much better than we expect," Lavinia suggested. "In the end, most of our worst fears prove to be no more than shadows on the wall, don't they?"

Fawn agreed, and was relieved when Lavinia didn't seem to notice the lack of conviction in her tone. There would be no civilized court battle . . . not when another murder—her own—would offer a much more certain solution.

Chapter 26

"Good evening, sir. You're working late," the security guard said, quickly sliding his half-eaten liverwurst sandwich out of sight under the counter and standing up straighter.

Colman Bromley flicked a few raindrops off the lapel of his double-breasted gray suit. "Just wanted to check up on a few things," he said.

"I'm afraid you'll have to sign in. Company policy on weekends." The guard pushed a lined notebook with Dalsworth, Inc., and the date printed on the top of the page.

Bromley bent over the page, seeming to fumble for his fountain pen, and signed at last. There were only a few employees' names on the list; according to the check-out times the last of those had left an hour before. "Looks like you have the building to yourself."

"Just the cleaning crew. Guess everybody else is home getting into their dancing shoes." The guard sounded wistful. "Will you be long, sir?"

"Not if I find what I expect to find."

The days of poring over bales of financial records had finally paid off. For a long time it had seemed like a hopeless game of connect-the-dots, but at last a picture had begun to emerge. Bromley's suspicions had been right on target. And now he knew where to look for the proof.

As he pushed the elevator button for the executive floor, he wondered again if Nick or Ned or Noreen was in the building. Their names hadn't been on the guard's list; he'd made certain of that. But any of them could have entered their offices via the private board members' garage, which meant the guard would never have seen them. It might have been wiser to wait until Cole returned from his day at Lavinia's. But Bromley was in no mood to be prudent. He was too angry, and his nerves were stretched as tightly as a loaded crossbow. If his suspicions were correct, much more than Fawn's inheritance might be forfeit. Her life itself was in danger.

The executive offices were housed on the third floor. As the elevator slowly opened, Bromley thought he saw a light wink off in one of the offices. He hesitated. But there was no sound except the faint crackling of the heating system, noticeable now in the silence. He rubbed his aching eyes; perhaps he was just over-tired. When this was over he was going to sleep for a week.

Slowly he approached the half-open door. The vault holding all the company's most valuable papers—including securities—was inside. Dammit, let's get it over with, he told himself, pushing open the door. His hand swept across the wall, searching for the light switch. And suddenly a blinding flare of light engulfed him and he heard, distinctly, sickenly, the sound of his own skull being crushed. Even as he began to turn, his knees buckled beneath him. And his hand slowly raked down the wall as he fell heavily to the floor.

"What are you thinking?" Cole asked softly.

They'd started back to the city half an hour before, and in all that time Fawn had spoken barely a dozen words.

"What am I thinking?" Fawn repeated, breaking out of the web of her thoughts. "Nothing of much use, I'm afraid. Just stumbling around in a fog."

He glanced at her. "Sometimes it helps to talk things over," he said pointedly.

She made a small *mmm* sound, neither agreeing nor disagreeing, and went back to staring out the window.

"God, you're stubborn." That won him an apologetic smile and nothing else.

A few more miles went by in silence. He noticed how Fawn's fingers kept straying back to the amethyst ring on her finger. Just before they left Lavinia had given her the antique ring, and now it was almost as if Fawn were touching it for luck. He cleared his throat and tried a different approach. "So, what did you think of Lavinia?"

"You know the answer to that." Fawn laughed. "How could I not like her? She's marvelous."

"She seemed to have a pretty high opinion of you, too."

Fawn turned to him, tucking her legs up underneath her on the seat. "You know, for the first time this afternoon, I felt I'd really come home. It was just as I'd dreamed it would be . . ."

"You used to dream about coming back?"

"Sometimes. It didn't have anything to do with not being satisfied with the family I had. They'll always be part of me, and that's the way I want it. But still, occasionally I did wonder, hope . . ." A new thought made her frown. "It's sad, though, all those years Lavinia and I missed together."

"But you have each other now," Cole reminded her.

Fawn nodded slowly, accustoming herself to the idea. "Sort of the silver lining . . ." she suggested, smiling contentedly.

"And the triplets are the cloud, right?" he asked.

Reluctantly she nodded her head yes.

"You know, there's no reason that you have to go back to the house. In fact, after the character references those three got today, you'd be crazy to . . ." He saw her stiffen and knew he was in for an argument. "Fawn, I'm speaking as your legal counsel—and your friend. Let me get you a hotel room."

"But I want to go back," she said stubbornly. "Please, let's just drop it." She was having enough trouble keeping her courage up as it was. Last night she'd slept—or rather lay stiffly in her bed—with a chair jammed against the door.

Tensing at every sound. And that was before she'd heard Lavinia's cautionary tale.

Cole was watching her closely. "I'm not going to drop it. Maybe you and I have a different definition of friendship, but in my book friends confide in each other. For instance, why did you ask Lavinia all those questions about the triplets? You were obviously looking for something."

"Cole . . ."

And all at once he suspected the truth. "Fawn, you don't have the idea in the back of your mind that one of those three murdered your parents?"

"Why not?" she whispered. It was a relief to admit it at last.

"Because it doesn't make sense. The police were firmly convinced that it was a botched kidnapping attempt."

"I wasn't kidnapped," she insisted.

"Maybe you don't want to believe . . ."

The storm that had been threatening all evening suddenly let loose. Rain pelted the hood, and lightning cut jagged arcs through the sky. Fawn shivered, remembering how it had rained that night, too. The rain, the blackness surrounding her, even the motion of the car triggered a flood of panic in her. But this time she wasn't going to run away. "I wasn't kidnapped," she repeated. "There was no ransom note, was there?"

"And no one left to send it to, anymore," Cole replied. And he added more softly, "I've never thought much of the triplets myself, but the police checked them out. They all had alibis."

"Alibis can be manufactured. And if the police were looking for a kidnapper, I doubt they spent much time on the triplets."

Cole sighed. "If it had been one of the three, then the motive must have been the money. Which means you would have been killed, too. After all, they couldn't get the money with you still alive."

Fawn pushed up the sleeve of her sweater and leaned over so that the lights from the dash shone on her arm. Even in the dim interior the scar traced a long white line along her flesh. "How do you think I got this?"

"That night?" Cole said, feeling sick. "That son of a bitch . . ."

"Maybe I should have told you right away, the day the hypnotist came. That's when I first really remembered. I knew it was one of them."

He was silent for a moment, too angry to speak. Whoever had done that to her . . . "Which one?" he asked at last.

She shook her head. "I can't see the face. . . ."

"But that's why you're staying at the house—hoping you'll remember."

"Cole, please understand . . . I have to do this."

He didn't answer. Instead he slowed the car and eased it over to the shoulder of the road and stopped. "Come here," he said gently, holding open his arms. And for a while they held each other wordlessly. The tears ran down her cheeks and he stroked her hair, whispering her name again and again. "Fawn, I couldn't bear losing you."

She leaned back, looking into his eyes, touched by the emotion in his voice. His fingers gently brushed away her tears, and she smiled. "I wouldn't want you to lose me." The breath caught in his throat; he pulled her close, suddenly overwhelmed by his need for her. And without either of them knowing quite how it happened, their lips met in a long, lingering kiss.

Afterward, she nestled her head against his shoulder, simply content to be in his arms. Outside the rain still drummed against the car, but now the sound seemed cozy and comforting. She felt that she could stay there with Cole forever.

"We have to talk, Fawn," he said at last.

"I know." She sighed, watching the raindrops roll down the window. For a moment neither of them said anything.

"Maybe we'd better sit up and behave ourselves," Cole suggested at last. "I don't have a hope of making any sense with you so close."

She slid over to her side of the car. "Better?"

"Worse." He smiled. "I miss you already. But I think it's time for a little cold logic. The first thing we have to decide is how to keep you safe. Nothing else matters as much as that."

She started to open her mouth to object, but just then the car phone buzzed. Cole reached for it.

The voice on the other end was hysterical. Cole recognized it as his father's housekeeper, but it was a few minutes before he could calm her down enough to understand what she was trying to tell him.

"Your father's been attacked. They took him to the hospital, but . . . Just come back quick . . . please, I don't know what to do."

"Mr. Colman Bromley?" the nurse at the emergency desk repeated, checking her list with maddening slowness. In the background a child cried and a group of orderlies were making bets on a baseball game. "Yes, Mr. Bromley was brought in two hours ago."

"Is he all right?" Cole asked. He and Fawn were still out of breath from running all the way from the parking garage.

"Are you relatives?"

"I'm his son." For God's sake, why couldn't the woman just tell him what he needed to know? "Can I see him?"

"I'm afraid that's impossible," the nurse answered, shaking her head. Cole's heart plummeted.

"Dr. Findley will be able to give you the details. He was the attending physician when your father was brought in." She caught the eye of a burly, white-coated man with a beard and signaled for him to come over.

"Is my father still alive?" Cole asked as soon as the introductions were finished.

"He was alive when we wheeled him upstairs, yes. He should be in surgery now," Dr. Findley said cautiously.

"What happened to him?"

"Your father sustained a blow to the head. He has a depressed fracture of the occipital area, and we suspect a subdural hematoma which is bleeding into the cranial vault. I ordered a C.T. scan—that's computerized tomography—for confirmation. That will show if there's damage to the brain. Also due to the site of the trauma, he's lost vision in one eye, and of course he's unconscious."

"My God," Cole breathed. He'd gone white around the mouth and Fawn gripped his hand. The doctor's recital had been so matter-of-fact, as if he were discussing a machine that was malfunctioning. But perhaps it was his way of blunting the shock.

"He was put on an I.V. immediately, of course," the doctor continued. "Mannitol to relieve the fluid build up and Decadron to prevent swelling of the brain tissues, plus the usual antibiotics."

"But he is going to recover?" Cole insisted.

"It's not possible to make a definite prognosis in cases of this sort, I'm afraid."

Cole wasn't interested in cases of this sort—only in his father. And he was beginning to suspect all this medical terminology was just a way to avoid telling the simple, painful truth. "What are you saying—that my father might not make it?"

"I'm sorry. I really don't know. If he survives the first forty-eight hours, then we can be more hopeful. But even then there might be permanent brain or spinal damage. You should be prepared for that."

Cole nodded. His face was perfectly controlled now, but his skin was an ashen-gray. "If you'll just tell us where we can wait . . ."

Dr. Findley directed them to the Intensive Care waiting room on the fourth floor. "And you'll have to stop in the administration offices first and sign a few forms," he added. "Just follow the blue line painted on the floor."

Cole thanked him and started to turn away, then stopped. "Can you tell me how it happened?"

Findley hesitated. "Well, he might have fallen . . . but frankly, I'd guess he turned his back on someone he shouldn't have."

"You mean someone tried to kill him?"

"And probably believed they'd succeeded. The police are at the scene now, searching for the weapon."

"Where did it happen?"

"At the Dalsworth Building."

Cole's head snapped up. "That's where it happened—the Dalsworth Building? Are you sure?"

"Executive offices, as I understand," Findley said. "Look,

we'll do everything we can for him. But try to be patient. It'll be a long wait, if we're lucky . . .''

Or he could be dying, dead, right now, Fawn thought. And she hoped that Cole wasn't thinking the same thing.

"It looks as though I'm going to be here all night—probably longer," Cole said to her once Findley had left. "But I don't expect you to stay. We'll get you a hotel room somewhere . . .''

"Of course I'll stay," she interrupted. "I want to . . . please." It was so little to offer; at that moment she would have made any sacrifice to reassure him his father would recover.

A quick flicker of gratitude shone in his eyes, and he hugged her. "Okay. I could use some company."

Three hours later they'd still had no word from the operating room. The hospital was beginning to quiet down for the night, and they had the waiting room to themselves. The nurse at the desk had promised to notify them the moment Bromley was out of surgery, nonetheless Cole kept pacing back and forth from the waiting room to the desk, checking. His frustration radiated from him like heat waves; he wasn't used to being helpless, to facing a problem he couldn't do something to resolve.

Cole looked up expectantly at a sound in the hall. But it was only the porter, mopping the floor.

"I'll get us some coffee," Fawn volunteered. "Would you like a sandwich, too?"

"Couldn't keep it down."

She nodded. She didn't have any appetite, either.

She couldn't get it out of her mind that it was her fault Cole's father was fighting for his life. She should have warned him about the triplets. It had to be one of them—hadn't Bromley been attacked in the executive offices of Dalsworth, Inc.?

The doctor's words came back to her: Colman Bromley had turned his back . . . And she saw again her own father sliding to the floor, the stunned expression on his face, the horrible pain in his eyes. Dear God, it had happened again. She should never have come back. A terrible rage threatened to overwhelm her; it coursed through her veins like acid. She clenched her fists, battling for control. There was no time for her anger now; Cole was depending on her calm. But later . . .

As she returned from the vending machine with the coffee, she nearly bumped into a doctor wearing surgical-green leaving the waiting room.

Afraid to breathe she looked into Cole's eyes. And saw that the news was good.

"He's out of surgery," Cole told her. "It went reasonably well—something about decompressing blood clots. At least now he's got a fighting chance."

"Thank God."

Cole nodded, a new worry furrowing his brow. "Now if he can just get through the next forty-eight hours."

"He will," Fawn promised, praying she was right.

There was a large clock on the wall of the waiting room; Fawn and Cole spent the next hours trying not to stare at it.

"I think those hands must be glued down solid," Cole muttered at one point. But slowly time did pass.

There was no question of anyone being allowed in to see Bromley yet. In any case, he was still unconscious. But one of the doctors was stopping by with hourly progress reports. He explained that a neurologist had been called in for consultation. And the neurosurgeon suggested an ophthalmologist be brought in, too, if the damage to Bromley's vision didn't spontaneously reverse itself. "He still doesn't have any vision in one eye," the doctor said.

"How can you tell that if he's unconscious?" Fawn asked.

"The pupil doesn't react to light. Even when you're unconscious the pupils should contract if someone shines a light in your eyes."

"And his mind?" Cole asked. "Is there going to be permanent damage?"

"We won't be able to tell that for a while," the doctor explained. "But I assure you, we're doing everything we can."

"At least he's in good hands," Fawn said once the doctor had left. "Half the staff seems to be at his bedside."

"Yes," Cole agreed, then smiled wryly. "And it doesn't

hurt that my father donated a sizable chunk of money to this hospital, either.''

Outside the sky was still a rolling mass of storm clouds. But the sun was just coming over the horizon, sending bright shafts of pink and gold through the clouds. Fawn and Cole stood at the window, their arms around each other, watching the new day burst forth.

''A sign . . .'' Fawn whispered, and he nodded.

''And time for you to be thinking of getting some rest, too,'' he added. ''Why don't you take the keys to my apartment? I'll be fine here.''

''If you're staying, I'm staying.''

''Stubborn . . .'' He shook his head in mock despair.

But she frowned. ''Maybe I'm too stubborn.'' She was suddenly remembering the triplets and how she'd kept the truth to herself. ''Cole, I think we should call the police. Tell them what we know—or suspect, anyway.''

''We'll talk with Captain Almafi later. He's probably still in bed now. And when Dad wakes up, maybe he'll be able to identify his attacker.'' Though the doctor had told him it would be unlikely that Bromley would be able to answer questions for a few days.

A nurse brought in two trays of food for them. Scrambled eggs and bacon and toast. As soon as the aroma hit her, Fawn felt famished. But a twinge of guilt made her hesitate; how could she think of food right now?

''Eat,'' Cole ordered, smiling. ''Starving yourself isn't going to do my father any good.''

''All right. But you, too . . .''

He took a piece of toast. But his eyes were still on her. ''Fawn, none of this is your fault. Do you understand that? My father has always been a man who does just what he wants.''

''I should have warned him.''

''And then he would have been more careful? Perhaps. Or maybe he would have tried to personally shake the truth out of those three. Considering the way he felt about Melissa and Joel—and the way he feels about you—that seems more likely. But I can tell you this for sure, he wouldn't have backed off. So stop trying to blame yourself.''

She nodded, but she still wasn't convinced.

A few minutes later they heard steps approaching along the hallway. It was a sound they'd both developed an exaggerated awareness of these last hours. Cole glanced at the clock, suddenly tense; it was too early for their hourly report. Had something happened? The doctors had warned him that his father was only clinging to life moment by moment.

And so when Noreen, wearing a mink coat and a wide-brimmed hat appeared in the doorway, the first expression on their faces was relief.

"You might have called me and let me know," Noreen said crossly as she entered the room.

Cole shot Fawn a cautionary glance. "I'm sorry, Noreen. We were a bit preoccupied."

"Downstairs they said he was still in critical condition."

Cole nodded. "By the way, how did you find out?"

"I realized that Fawn hadn't come home last night. I was worried." She sat down next to Fawn, patting her hand. "Didn't you realize I would be? Anyway, when I couldn't reach you, Cole, I called your father's house. His housekeeper broke the news."

"It's very good of you to come all the way down here," Cole said.

"Your father . . . means a great deal to me." But her attention suddenly seemed distracted by the ring on Fawn's finger. "That's Lavinia's ring, isn't it?" she asked, frowning. "Is that where you've been?"

"Yes. We had a wonderful day there. Lavinia knows so much about the family's history."

"She watches too many soap operas. I certainly hope you didn't believe everything she told you. In fact, I think she's getting senile."

"I suppose so," Fawn agreed, not wanting to give anyone a reason to go after Lavinia, too. Already she could see that Noreen wondered just what Lavinia had told her.

There was an awkward silence for a moment, and then Noreen said, "I'd like to see Colman for a few minutes."

"That's out of the question—they're not allowing any visitors," Cole said. And then realizing how abrupt he'd sounded, he added, "The doctor should be coming by soon to give us a progress report. You can talk with him."

Noreen started to object, but Cole said, "That'll just have to do. No one is getting in to see my father. And if you'll excuse me, there's a phone call I have to make."

He returned five minutes later wearing a relieved expression. He gave Fawn's shoulder a quick, comforting squeeze. "Did I miss anything?"

"We were just discussing the . . . accident," Noreen said. "Apparently no one has any idea what happened?"

"So it would seem," Cole answered. "We'll probably never know; the doctors say my father won't ever be able to remember anything himself." Though, in fact, they didn't know whether or not he would retain his memory.

The doctor stopped by shortly afterwards and told them the patient's condition was unchanged, but the staff was remaining guardedly optimistic. "Look, I'm going home for a few hours," he said, first rubbing the back of his neck, then his bloodshot eyes. "Why don't you do the same? We'll call if there's any change."

"I'd prefer to stay," Noreen said, after the doctor had gone.

Cole shook his head. "I appreciate it, but really there's no need. Besides, Fawn has offered to wait with me."

Noreen eyed Fawn coldly, irritation pinching her features into a stiff mask. "Of course. I suppose you'll let Nick stay, too."

"Nick isn't even here," Cole said wearily.

"But I saw . . . I guess it must have been someone else . . . I just assumed it was he."

"No one is staying but Fawn and me."

"Well, if I'm not wanted, I'll go. But at least it wouldn't be too much trouble to keep me informed, would it?"

"If you'd like . . ."

Noreen gave them both a brittle smile that disappeared instantly, and fluffing her mink collar, she turned on her heel and left.

Cole watched her until she was safely in the elevator. "Well, what do you think?" he asked Fawn.

"I don't know . . . She was obviously worried, upset about

being left out. I think she really is in love with your father. Which makes it unlikely she would have tried to kill him.''

"Maybe she didn't know her own strength," Cole suggested sardonically. "Maybe she's worried because he's still alive and might identify his assailant.''

Fawn shook her head. "I just can't believe she's the one.''

"Well, at least I made sure that she—or Ned or Nick—isn't going to get a second chance. I called one of the investigators that the law firm employs occasionally, Joe Mazzini. He's a retired Treasury agent, runs his own security firm now. A very reliable man. He's going to see that from now on there's a twenty-four-hour guard on my father.''

Fawn smiled tiredly. "I'm glad one of us is still thinking.'' The tension of Noreen's visit seemed to have sapped the last of her strength. Including the last fretful night she'd spent in the house in the Gardens, she'd only had a few hours sleep in the last two days. She was so sleepy her eyes felt gritty.

Cole put his arms around her. "I'm taking you home. Come on, no arguments.''

"Home? . . .'' She didn't know where home was anymore.

"My place. You'll be safe there.''

They stopped at the desk, and he left his telephone number with the nurse. "We'll call if there's any change," she promised.

The lobby was more crowded this morning. At the door to the street, Fawn and Cole had to wait while a flustered young man helped his very pregnant wife into a wheelchair. "Honey, I'm not going to have the baby right here," the woman laughed. "Go take care of the car. I think you left the motor running.''

"I'm not leaving you," he insisted, and then, realizing they were blocking Fawn and Cole's way, he smiled apologetically and moved aside. "Our first," he explained, as if it weren't obvious.

"Congratulations." Cole grinned.

It had started to rain again—a thick, heavy downpour that made it seem as dark as night. The gutters ran full, already swollen by yesterday's storm, and an empty garbage can rolled noisily down the street, chased by the wind. "I'll go get the car and bring it around," Cole offered.

Fawn shook her head. "Why don't we wait? It's bound to let up soon." As long as they stood under the portico that covered the hospital driveway, they could stay dry.

"All right. As long as we're waiting anyway, why don't I try to pick up a newspaper. There might be something about what happened to my father." He hurried back into the lobby.

Fawn stood at the curb, too tired to think. Too tired to see the car suddenly bearing down on her, gaining speed. It was the sound of the wheels bouncing over the curb that finally alerted her. She froze, unbelieving, as the car raced along the sidewalk, aiming right at her. Time seemed to slow down, as if everything were happening in slow motion, and with perfect clarity she saw the tiny baby booties swinging from the rearview mirror; the tan, brimmed rain hat pulled low over the driver's eyes, hiding his face . . .

And then, with the bumper almost touching her, she stumbled backward, knowing already it was too late. She felt herself lifted in the air, hurled sideways, and waited for the sound of her own bones splintering. It was a moment before she realized the car had already skidded past her, and her feet were still dangling in the air. And then she felt Cole's arm around her waist and knew he had whirled her out of harm's way.

The driver had swerved back into the road. But not in time to avoid an ambulance parked at the curb. There was a solid thud as the fenders collided, the sound of glass shattering and metal ripping. They could see the driver's head snap sideways with the force of the impact, hitting the rearview mirror and for an instant the car shimmied, out of control. Then it straightened, speeding away, and a moment later it was gone.

Cole had set Fawn back on her feet, but his arm still hugged her waist protectively. "Are you all right?" he asked.

She nodded. "Thank God you were . . ." And she hiccupped.

"Take a few deep breaths," he told her, as she hiccupped again. "It's just a reaction to the fright."

Fawn tried, but it seemed as though her body had forgotten how to breathe normally. Now that she was safe, the full shock of it all had finally hit her. If Cole hadn't been keeping a watchful eye on her and rushed over to pull her out of the way . . .

"I think you'd better sit down for a few minutes," he said, leading her back into the lobby. His arm was still around her as if he intended never to let loose again.

"Did you see who it was?" he asked when the normal color had begun to return to her skin.

She shook her head. "He had a hat pulled down to hide his face. Or her face . . ." she added suddenly, realizing she'd just assumed it was a man. Noreen could have stayed around a few extra minutes, seen them leave . . . She realized Cole was thinking along the same lines. "Maybe we're jumping to conclusions," Fawn suggested. After all, it could have been anyone—New York is full of crazies."

He smiled wryly. "For once that's an almost comforting thought."

But neither one of them believed it had been a demented stranger. Which meant that Fawn was the next target. . . .

"Welcome home," she whispered to herself.

C h a p t e r   27

*F*awn woke with a start, fleeing from her dreams. And in that instant between sleep and wakefulness, she knew she wasn't alone. Panicked, she kept her eyes shut tight, trying to remember where she was, why she should be so frightened. Slowly the night before came back to her—the hospital, the car racing toward her—and then she remembered Cole bringing her to his apartment. But Cole had gone back to the hospital after making sure she was safely locked in. The presence moved closer; she could feel its warm breath on her cheek, knew it was leaning over her.

Her eyes flashed open and she was staring directly into an inquisitive pair of large brown eyes. She laughed. It was Cole's Irish setter. The dog, seeing her awake, began to wag his tail and nudge her hand with his cold, black nose.

"Time to get up, huh?" Fawn asked with a grin. She glanced at the clock; it was 7 P.M. already. She'd slept the whole day away. Maybe sometime during the day Cole's father had passed through the crisis and was on his way to recovering; she hoped so. Absently she stroked the dog behind his ears; his name was Toby, she remembered now. "All right, Toby," she agreed, struggling out of the sheets.

The dog stretched his front paws along the floor, his back end in the air and his tail wagging, and barked once. "Trying to start up a game of fetch, are you?" she asked. She found a tennis ball on the floor, threw it, and he bounded after it. He was a beautiful dog, a glossy mahogany red with blond feathering along his legs and tail and ears. Obviously he came from a long line of champions. But despite his regal looks, Cole had told her, he was a bit of a clown. And she suspected that's what Cole liked best about him.

The second-floor bedroom was open along one wall and overlooked the living room; The soft evening light gleamed on the polished antique furniture and suffused the Tabriz rugs with a vibrant vari-hued glow, and one wall of glass two stones high looked over the harbor. It all looked completely peaceful. Fawn checked that the locks on the door—as in most New York apartments there were several, including a Fichet—were undisturbed.

In the bathroom she found a note Cole had taped to the mirror. "You're beautiful when you're sleeping. And you don't snore. Marry me." Laughing, she read the postscript, "Please, Fawn, don't take any chances."

Toby had returned with her shoes held gently in his mouth. He dropped them in front of her and sat down, an expectant look on his face.

"You want to go out?"

His ears perked up, and he wagged his tail.

She hesitated; she really shouldn't leave the apartment. But she couldn't explain that to Toby, and he hadn't been out since Cole had walked him this morning. Fawn vaguely remembered something about a dog-walking service, but there was no telling when, of if, they would be by today. Toby waited patiently for her to think the thing through, seemingly confident she would come to the right conclusion.

"All right, fellow, but just once around the block."

She hurried into her clothes, Toby prancing excitedly around her the whole time. At least at this hour of the day, she reflected, there should still be plenty of people on the streets.

The long rain had washed the city clean. As she stepped outside she sniffed the fresh air appreciatively. A soft breeze was blowing in from the harbor, and the sky glowed with that intense blue that came just before sunset. It was good to be out again.

Still, she couldn't help being nervous. She stayed close to the buildings, well away from the curbside and the traffic whizzing by; she scrutinized every approaching stranger and kept turning around to make sure no one was following her. Toby, weaving happily at the end of his leash, seemed puzzled by her caution.

"You want to romp, don't you, fellow?" she said. And suddenly she was angry; this was just like being in a cage. And she didn't intend to spend the rest of her life looking over her shoulder, worrying . . .

"So far all the advantages have been on the killer's side; he must be feeling pretty confident by now, sure we'll never catch up to him," she said as she locked herself back in the apartment. "I think it's about time we shook him up." But how was she going to accomplish that?

The question stayed with her as she showered and toweled her hair dry. How could she panic the killer into making a mistake? Could she bluff him into believing she'd remembered his identity? But there was no guarantee he'd fall for it. No, there had to be another way. And sooner or later it would come to her.

She dressed in one of Cole's robes, a big terry cloth one that drooped over her shoulders and hid her hands until she rolled up the sleeves. It still carried his clean, masculine scent, making her realize how much she missed him.

She tried calling the hospital, but all they would tell her was that Colman Bromley's condition was still critical.

For a while she wandered around the living room, studying the pictures, especially a set of horse-racing scenes in water-color done by Raoul Dufy. A collection of small, framed family photographs on a table caught her eye, too. Propped right in the center was a photo torn from a newspaper: her own picture, taken the day of the meeting in the Dalsworth Building. She smiled to think that he'd saved it.

She was browsing through the shelves of books that lined one wall when the buzzer sounded. It was Cole.

"Are you all right?" he asked as soon as she opened the door.

"Everything still in one piece and working," she assured him with a smile.

He hugged her. "So I see. I think you're just what that robe needed all along. In fact, the effect is quite . . ." He let the sentence trail off, just grinning.

"How's your father?" she asked, confident the news would be good.

"Out of danger. He's still not awake, but he's beginning to respond to all the medical prodding and poking." Cole hugged her again. "He's going to make it, Fawn. He's going to make it."

"Thank God."

Toby yipped, nudging Cole for a little attention himself. Cole reached down and patted his head. "Sorry, fellow. I'll take you out right away . . ."

"I already did." And seeing Cole begin to frown, she added quickly. "I was careful. It was perfectly safe."

"Nothing's perfectly safe. Not till we catch that bastard."

"But I can't spend the rest of my life cowering under the bed covers," she said. "Anyway, what do you want to do now—sleep or eat?"

"Eat. I grabbed a catnap at the hospital. Can you cook?"

"Anything but pheasant under glass," she answered with mock indignation.

"Well, I was getting a little tired of pheasant, anyway. Something simple will be fine. I'm going to take a shower, scrub this hospital smell off. Thanks." At the stairs, he turned. "And, Fawn, would you make enough for three? I've invited Captain Almafi over."

After inspecting the cabinets and refrigerator, Fawn decided to make French Dip: sliced roast beef on a crusty French roll served with a cup of hot *au jus* to dunk it in and creamy horseradish sauce. It was a Western favorite—Pete served it in his own restaurant—though she hadn't seen it on the menus in New York. She fixed a pot of thick corn chowder to go with it.

Cole was just coming down the stairs, shaved and in a clean sweater and slacks when Almafi arrived.

"Smells wonderful." The captain sighed, his large nose leading him into the apartment. They had no difficulty convincing him to join them.

"I want you to know how sorry I am about your dad, Cole," Almafi said when they'd sat down at the table and Cole had opened a beer for each of them. "I've butted heads with your father a few times, but I've always felt he was one of the best."

Cole nodded. "He feels the same about you. Are you supervising the investigation?"

"Not my precinct. But, yeah, I've been poking my nose in, so to speak." He took a spoonful of the corn chowder, and his jowly face lit up appreciatively. "Wonderful . . ." he said to Fawn.

"Thank you. Do they have any leads in the case? Are they close to an arrest?"

"Not with a ten-foot pole." The captain's dark eyes were mournful again. "They've got no witnesses. Not a single fingerprint that shouldn't have been there. Nothing but a lot of theories without a peg to hang them on."

"Who's conducting the investigation?" Cole asked.

Almafi gave him the name, and Cole snorted. "Great. He couldn't find his ass without a manual."

Almafi concentrated on his sandwich, his face bland, but Fawn suspected he agreed with Cole's assessment. "Has anyone bothered to ask where my relatives—Nick and Ned and Noreen—were during the attack?" she asked.

She suddenly had the captain's full attention. "Of course you're about to explain why that's important," he suggested.

She took a deep breath. "Because I'm certain now that one of the three of them killed my parents—and that Coleman Bromley had begun to suspect which one." Once she'd started, she told him everything: the images that had come back to her during the hypnosis, Lavinia's warnings, the attack on her outside the hospital.

Almafi let the words tumble out, never interrupting. And afterward he was silent, distractedly pulling at his chin, tugging at his ear lobes and nose, as if they, too, were facts that suddenly had to be arranged in a new order.

"Maybe . . ." he allowed at last. He leaned toward her. "Let's go over it again." He started at the beginning, questioning, double-checking, debating each point with her.

Half an hour later, he sat back and sighed. "Son of a bitch—I've been had. They were right here under my goddam nose the whole time, and I'm out running around the countryside looking for a flipping kidnapper. I guess that makes me chump of the year."

"No one else guessed the truth, either." Cole said.

"No excuse." He pushed back his chair, suddenly in a hurry to leave. "I'm going to have to start back at square one. Go over everything in the files . . . dammit, I'm going to get that bastard."

At the door he turned, as a new thought hit him. "And just how do you two plan on spending the next few days?"

"At the hospital, I imagine," Fawn replied.

He nodded slowly, frowning. "Nothing else, you understand. It's bad enough when a cop starts believing he's Wyatt Earp and thinks he has to go out and set the world right all by himself. But for a civilian, it's just plain suicide. So, you two steer clear of it. Besides, I'm sure to have a lot more questions for you, and I'll want you around to answer them."

"I'll help in any way I can," Fawn assured him.

Once they were alone Cole hugged her. "You're pretty impressive, you know that. Most people would be gulping Valium by the handful by now."

"I just want it to be over," she said.

"Maybe it will be soon—now that Almafi knows where to look."

Fawn broke off a bit of her sandwich and fed it to Toby; she'd lost her own appetite. "Just how much chance do you think the captain has of identifying the killer now? After all, it's been eighteen years."

"My father obviously found something suspicious. He wouldn't have been at the Dalsworth Building otherwise. Perhaps that's the place to start. What was he searching for? And who nearly killed him to prevent him from finding it? I think, for the time being, we can assume the same person tried to run you over. Maybe there's some way to tie one of the three to that."

Fawn smiled. "So we start with the present and work backward . . ."

"We? . . . Didn't you hear the captain's lecture?"

Her eyes, filled with bland innocence, met his. "I said I'd help. I don't recall promising anything else."

Cole frowned. "I think it'd be better if you stayed here."

"Why? Where are you going?"

"Back to the hospital," he said, not quite looking at her.

"And . . ." she prompted. "Where else?"

"Aren't you sleepy or something?"

"No. You're the one who hasn't been to bed in over thirty hours."

"I couldn't sleep," he said. She realized it was true. His eyes were overbright, feverish, and every bit of him seemed to thrum with energy—the sort of nervous energy that takes over after the body has been pushed past the point of exhaustion. He was riding on pure adrenaline now. She figured she'd better be there when he finally crashed.

"You can tell me where we're going while I get dressed," she said.

"Fifth Avenue," Cole told the taxicab driver and gave him the number of the building.

"Fif' Avenue?" the driver repeated, looking down at a map on the seat beside him. He muttered a few words in a foreign language and scratched his head.

"By the park . . . Central Park," Cole explained impatiently.

"Not go over the bridge?" The driver sounded disappointed. "No airport?" It was also obviously the only route in the city the driver had learned so far.

"Just go uptown," Cole told him. "I'll tell you how to get there." They'd decided to take a taxi rather than Cole's car to avoid the hassle of trying to park in Manhattan, but now Cole was beginning to think they'd made a mistake. He sat back and sighed. "What we need is a preservation group to save the old New York cabbies. There wasn't a block of the city they didn't know, and they could explain the state of the world while they were getting you there.''

"Speaking of explanations . . .'' Fawn said. "Exactly who is this Rod Davis we're going to see?''

"He works for Bromley, Christensen. In fact, he was the one in charge of supervising the Dalsworth trust. If anyone knows what alerted my father's suspicions, he should be the one. They've been living in each other's pockets for the last week.''

"What's he like?''

"A hard worker, but not brilliant—a plodder. He's a few years older than I am, but he hasn't made partner yet, and I think it's finally dawned on him that he never will.'' Cole frowned. "It's been hard on him, seeing the men he started with pass him and realizing he'll never catch up.''

A few minutes later, following Cole's directions, the driver made the turn onto Fifth Avenue. They stopped in the middle of a block of elegant, carefully maintained apartment buildings on the edge of the park. "This is a nice neighborhood,'' Fawn commented.

"This is an expensive neighborhood,'' Cole said. "Especially considering Rod's salary.''

A doorman with more gold braid and gleaming buttons on his coat than an admiral stopped them at the entrance. "I'll have to announce you,'' he explained. "Whom did you wish to see?''

As the doorman called up to the apartment on the intercom, Fawn looked around the lobby. The floors were of polished marble, four-feet-high arrangements of flowers filled the urns flanking the elevators, and a tapestry looking as if it dated from the Middle Ages covered one wall.

At last the doorman told them they could go up. The Davis apartment was on the fourteenth floor, or actually what would have been the thirteenth if the builder hadn't superstitiously skipped that number. Cindy Davis, Rod's wife, had already opened the door a crack, waiting for them to emerge from the elevator. She was dressed in a robe and wasn't wearing any make-up.

"Hello, Cindy,'' Cole said. "Thanks for seeing us on the spur of the moment like this. Is Rod in?''

"He's sleeping," she whispered through the narrow open-ing in the door. "Is something wrong? I could give him a message . . ."

"I'm sorry. We really need to talk with him. We'll only be a few minutes."

"I can't wake him up." She glanced nervously from Cole to Fawn. "Can't you tell me what's wrong?"

Just then there was a high-pitched shriek, and a child's voice wailed, "Mama, he took my toy." "Did not . . . It's mine," a second child shouted.

"I imagine Rod's awake now," Cole suggested.

"I . . . oh . . . what the hell, might as well get it over with . . ." Cindy sighed, moving aside for them to enter. She waved a hand toward the living room. "Just sit any-where. I'll go quiet the kids."

The apartment was furnished in a starkly modern style. A huge mirrored block, faceted to catch the light from different angles, served as a coffee table. The floors were bare, littered with old newspapers, clothes, toys. More clothes, mostly children's, were strewn haphazardly across the oversize ox-blood leather sofa and armchairs. A number of glasses, crusty with dried whiskey dregs, were scattered around the room.

Cindy came back alone and sat uneasily on the arm of one of the chairs, waiting. She was a pretty, gamine-faced woman. Cole remembered that she'd been a cheerleader in college; that was how Rod, who was a football player, had met her. But there was nothing pretty about her today, no sign of her usual perky, giggly personality. Her eyes were rimmed in red, and her hair hung limp and tangled around her pale face.

"Rod isn't here, is he?" Cole asked gently.

She shook her head. "No."

"Where is he?"

"I don't know." She started to cry. "He's left me." And she slid down into the chair and wrapped her arms around herself, sobbing. Fawn reached out her hand in sympathy and Cindy grabbed it, clinging to her, the tears still rolling down her cheeks.

But when she raised her head at last, there was anger in her eyes. "That bastard just walked out on us. Packed his bags and left. What's he done?"

"Didn't he tell you?" Cole asked.

"He never told me anything. I trusted him and now look . . ." The sounds of the children playing drifted through the apartment. "They don't know yet . . ." Cindy said, starting to cry again.

"When did he leave?" Cole asked.

"About six o'clock, yesterday afternoon."

Just about the same time his father had gone to the Dalsworth Building, Cole realized.

"Came in, shirttail flying," Cindy continued, "his eyes all wild, and just packed up. Said Bromley was going to figure it out any minute now, and he—Rod, I mean—wasn't going to get stuck with the dirty end of the stick. He was always crude, you know. Said he hadn't been paid enough to . . ." she stopped, searching in her pockets for a tissue.

Cole gave her his handkerchief. She blew her nose, pushed the hair out of her face.

"I should have seen it coming," she said, calmer now. "He was so on edge these last few days, always yelling at the kids, at me. And if I came in the room when he was making a phone call . . . Is there another woman?"

"I don't think so," Cole said.

She shrugged. "Well, that's something, I suppose."

"Do you know who he was talking to on the phone?" Fawn asked.

"No. I'm sorry. But he took a lot of money with him. I guess he stole it? . . ." She looked up at them, a new worry suddenly pinching her face into wrinkles. "Will I have to pay it back?"

"No, I wouldn't think so," Fawn assured her. If Rod Davis had been stealing, then the money could only have come from one place: the Dalsworth estate. And Fawn had no intention of seeking retribution from this lost, frightened woman.

"Thank God," Cindy said, but her relief started a new trickle of tears. "I'm sorry—I'm not usually like this."

Fawn stood up. "I think it's time we left, Cole."

He agreed, and after a few words of comfort and offering to help in any way they could, they headed for the door.

Cindy trailed after them, seemingly torn between her desire to be by herself and her fear of being alone.

"Please call me if you hear from Rod at all," Cole asked her. "There's more at stake here than just the money."

She nodded. "You know he couldn't have thought whatever it is up himself. He's never had what you might call a creative mind."

"Damn!" Cole exploded once they were in the elevator. "Rod was our best chance of clearing this up, and now he's gone."

"Maybe the police will find him."

Cole nodded. "I'll talk with Almafi, explain the situation. He'll request a customs watch at the airports right away, and maybe one of the agents will pick Davis up—if he isn't already out of the country."

"I wonder if it's just the police he's running from," Fawn said, frowning thoughtfully. She saw the puzzled look on Cole's face and explained, "Maybe he's more afraid of the person who engineered this scheme, the person he was talking to on the phone."

"One of the triplets . . . it's got to be."

"But which one?"

"Fawn, I think you'd better brace yourself for the fact that one of your trustees has been embezzling from your parents' estate. My father's suspected it ever since the board meeting last week, and it's obvious now he was right. I don't know how they did it or how much is gone, but . . ." He stopped, realizing she wasn't listening. "Fawn, do you understand what I'm saying?"

"Someone's walked off with a large chunk of the Dalsworth fortune."

"You don't seem very upset."

She nodded absently. "I was just thinking of something . . ." And she closed her eyes, seeing again all the locks on Ned's door, remembering how nervous he'd been the whole time she was in his room. She'd thought then he was hiding something, and now she had an idea what. Somehow she had to get back into the house and search that room . . .

* * *

Cole wanted to check in on his father at the hospital before they went home. "If you don't get some sleep they're going to put you in the hospital," Fawn told him, but he insisted he was fine. Then he promptly dozed off in the taxi. Luckily this time they had a driver who knew where he was going.

Colman Bromley had finally been moved up to a bed in the Intensive Care ward. He was still connected to the monitors, but his condition was improving all the time. He'd even regained consciousness for a few moments. Fawn was glad to see the guard Cole had arranged outside the door. Now that Bromley was recovering, his attacker might try again.

Normal visiting hours for the hospital were just ending, but those rules didn't apply to Intensive Care. Visitors were allowed in at any time of the day or night, but only one at a time and only one an hour. And the visits were to be kept short.

Cole spoke to the guard, who assured him that, following his instructions, no one else had been allowed in to see his father. "I'll just be a few minutes . . ." Cole told Fawn.

She nodded. "I'll be in the waiting room."

She bought herself a cup of coffee from the vending machine, took a sip, and grimaced. Funny, the night before she hadn't noticed how bad it tasted.

The waiting room wasn't empty. A tall figure stood staring out the window, his shoulders hunched and a bouquet of daisies dangling from his hand. Slowly Fawn realized it was Scott. She touched his shoulder gently, and he jumped.

"Fawn . . ." He looked at her as if she were his only friend in the world. "They won't let me in to see him. The guard wouldn't even tell me why."

"Because someone tried to kill him."

Scott shook his head. "No. It must have been an accident . . . he fell . . . or maybe it was just someone trying to steal a few typewriters. That happens all the time."

"Is that what Noreen told you?"

"She was too upset to discuss it. I've always known that she cared about Colman more than she was willing to admit, but I'm still surprised . . . She's worrying herself sick."

That he was going to die . . . or that he was going to live, Fawn wondered.

"What is it you wanted to ask Colman?" Fawn asked, suspecting she already knew the answer.

"I need to know if he's really my father," Scott said. "And if they won't let me see him now, I'll just keep coming back until they will. It's time I started getting my life in order."

"Scott, why don't you insist that Noreen tell you the truth? If she knew how you felt. . . . She does love you very much."

"She gets almost hysterical if I bring up the subject." He sat down wearily on the couch and leaned back his head. "Maybe I should have left home a long time ago. There's something about our family that just isn't normal. Like my mother and Ned still living together . . . Doesn't that seem odd to you?"

"Maybe . . ."

"They don't even like each other," Scott continued. "It makes you wonder if there's more going on there than we can see."

"Perhaps Ned just stays because it's cheaper." She glanced at Scott. "Haven't you ever, even once, been in Ned's room?"

"Never." He grinned. "Ned's probably got the place booby-trapped when he's not there."

Fawn smiled, but silently she was hoping Scott was wrong. She wouldn't put it past Ned to rig up some trap.

There was something else she wanted to ask, but she wasn't sure how to bring it up. Scott noticed her frown and commented, "This has been a pretty rough homecoming for you, hasn't it?"

"It's just that I'm still having trouble remembering," she said, realizing he'd given her the opening she needed. "I think if I could just go back to when it all started . . . maybe if you told me what you remembered from that time . . ."

"You mean when your parents were murdered?" He squirmed in his seat. "To tell you the truth—this is going to sound horrible—it didn't make that much of an impression on me. I mean, not right after. I was only six myself, I didn't understand. And at the time I was a lot more concerned with just having been kicked out of school."

"You were expelled? What did you do?"

"They had a pretty good reason." Scott seemed to want to let it go at that, but after a moment he continued, "I was in the office, alone, being punished for something or other—I was always in trouble—when the school yearbooks were delivered. I don't know why, but I took a pair of scissors and went through each book and gouged out my own picture. No one else's picture, just my own. It sounds sick, doesn't it? And it cost a fortune to replace all those books. So, I wasn't very popular—at school or at home. Anyway, that's why I can't remember much. I'm sorry . . ."

"That's all right," she said, trying to hide her disappointment. It had been a long shot, anyway, hoping he would remember something that would confirm her suspicions. "Did they let you back in school?" she asked.

"Yeah. Mom pulled some strings—something to do with an endowment that was part of your parents' estate. Since she had become one of the trustees, I guess they didn't want to offend her."

Fawn saw Cole coming down the hall toward them and rose. The tension had at last faded from his face, but it had been replaced by a numb weariness. These two days of worry, of asking questions and getting nowhere, had finally taken their toll. He looked near collapse.

"I'd better get him home," she said.

Scott nodded. "Call me tomorrow, we'll talk some more. And, Fawn, try to forget the past, okay? It's all over now."

But it wasn't.

Chapter 28

"*Come* on, move, dammit," Nick swore, staring at the meter on the directional finder. A steady beeping pulsed through the car, indicating the bug he'd planted in the blackmailer's satchel was working, but so far the blackmailer seemed to be staying put. Unless, of course, he'd already found the bug, discarded it, and was halfway across the city by now.

"Why can't just one damned thing go right for me?" Nick asked himself. It had seemed like such a brilliant idea when he'd thought of it; by hiding a bug in the payoff satchel he could tail the blackmailer and discover his identity. And once he knew who it was, Nick was sure he could figure out some way of getting the money back.

Up to this point the plan seemed to be working. It had been surprisingly easy to get the hardware he needed. He'd just looked in the Yellow Pages under surveillance equipment, which had led him to security control equipment and systems, which led him to a small shop in one of the city's seedier neighborhoods. The salesman had been careful not to ask too many questions, as if afraid of scaring off a customer, but there'd been a knowing smirk on his face, an air of smarmy complicity, that had set Nick's teeth on edge.

"Ever worked one of these things before?" the man asked as Nick looked hesitantly at the equipment spread out on the chipped Formica counter.

Nick shook his head.

"All right—this is your bug," he explained picking up an instrument about the same size and shape as a disposable cigarette lighter with a tiny antenna protruding from one end. "You stick this in whatever he . . . or she"— again there was the sly look—"is going to be carrying."

"And this is your receiver." He flipped open the lid of a briefcase; it was made of cheap imitation leather, Nick noticed with a frown. Inside there was an on-and-off switch, a flashing light to show the unit was working, and a meter with a needle that moved to the left or the right, "according to the direction in which your party is moving," the salesman explained. "And, of course, the beeper gets louder when you're closer and weaker when you're losing the trail." There were also two small antennae, one to be affixed to either side of the car, to pick up the signal.

"Seems simple enough," Nick had said.

"It takes some getting used to. Out in the open country it has a range of about a mile. But in the city, especially going around corners, you can lose somebody in a few blocks. And it doesn't work if they're inside a building and you're outside. Maybe you should consider hiring an experienced operator. In fact, I just happen to be available at the moment . . ."

"I'll manage," Nick said curtly. The last thing he wanted was a witness.

The man shrugged. "Your business . . . Good hunting."

Now as Nick slouched lower down in the car seat, he wondered if perhaps he'd made a mistake in trying to handle this alone. Maybe at this very moment the blackmailer was laughing at him . . .

His face flushed hotly, as he remembered the derisive tone of that horrible, helium-distorted voice—the way it echoed through the deserted church.

"Bonds, Nick? I told you to bring cash, didn't I?"

"They're just the same as money," Nick had insisted

"Fully negotiable, payable to the bearer . . . you can cash them anywhere . . ." he babbled, arguing with the figure behind the grillwork to take the satchel. After all he'd had to go through to get those damned bonds in the first place, the risks he'd taken, to satisfy the blackmailer's demands, and now the voice was telling him it wasn't good enough.

"It's either take this or nothing at all," Nick had said at last, gambling on the blackmailer's greed.

"All right—leave the satchel and get out."

"What about the tape? You promised you'd give me the tape."

Again that eerie laugh had filled the confessional. "Maybe I'll send it to you—after I've cashed the bonds. So you just better make sure there's no problem."

"No . . ." Nick began, but the voice cut him off.

"I'm making the rules. Now get out of here."

Nick had left. But he'd only gone half a block, to where his car was parked on a narrow side street, and waited for the blackmailer to emerge.

Now he was wishing, for the twentieth time, that he'd thought to bring a hip flask with him, when suddenly the needle wavered, then began to veer off sharply to the left. For a moment he stared at the meter dumbly, surprised that it was actually working. The beeper signal grew louder, more distinct, then quickly began to fade. With a frantic grinding of gears, Nick pulled out of the parking place. He floored the gas pedal, raced to the corner, and made the left turn without even slowing down. Once again the signal came in strong and steady.

Guided by the volume of the beeper, he stayed a careful distance behind his prey. He didn't yet know which car he was following. Still, he scanned the traffic ahead, searching for someone he'd recognize. But the night was too dark to identify anyone. Yet that would work to his advantage, too. Even if the blackmailer was checking the rearview mirror, watching for a tail, he wouldn't be able to see Nick.

They were in SoHo now. Narrow, twisting streets, artists' lofts, coffee shops. Nick concentrated on watching the meter, ignoring the colorful, six-story-high murals painted on the solid brick walls of the old buildings.

He had to retrieve that tape—and the bonds—before Ned found out. He didn't even want to think about what Ned would do if he discovered the theft. That frightened him even more than the police. When it came to money, Ned could be so . . .

The beeper signal was suddenly fading. Nick realized he must have missed a turn. Quickly he wheeled around in a U-turn, doubling back, not breathing until the signal strengthened once more.

He was passing through the Lower East Side now, cutting across Delancey and Hester streets. During the day these sidewalks would be crowded with shoppers, and there would be "collarers" stationed outside the stores to entice customers in. But at night the area took on a more sinister character as the parks were abandoned to the junkies and an occasional cheap prostitute.

The idea of shopping reminded Nick of his wife. Not that she would ever stoop to buying anything in one of these little discount shops, he thought bitterly. No, here he was drowning in debt, and suddenly she was buying out every store on Fifth Avenue. She obviously intended to squeeze every penny out of him that she could. Good old loyal Suzanne. But he had a surprise for her—for all of them; he was going to come out of this thing on top. Somehow he'd find a way to handle this blackmailer. And after that, Fawn . . .

It was Fawn who was to blame for all this. Fawn who'd made him a thief. After all, what had he done but simply "borrowed" a small part of his share of the inheritance—or what would have been his share if she hadn't come back. He'd waited all these years for that money; he had a right to it. But apparently it was going to take a little more convincing to make her see it.

He was crossing the Williamsburg Bridge now, still following the signal. And all at once it occurred to him that he'd seen the dark-colored sedan ahead of him several times before that night—near the church and in SoHo. It couldn't be just coincidence he told himself; that had to be the blackmailer. He stepped on the gas—if he could only get a glimpse of the face. But just as he was getting close, the sedan picked up speed, increasing the distance between them. Fortunately

Nick had at least caught a glimpse of part of the license plate. He frowned. It was a "Z" plate, which meant a rental car. Why would the blackmailer rent a car? Unless Nick would have recognized the blackmailer's own car? . . .

There was no chance of his catching the sedan again; the beeps had faded and the car was several minutes ahead of him now. But he was sure that they were heading into Queens, toward the Gardens. And the nagging suspicion that Nick had had all along suddenly settled into a certainty: The blackmailer was someone he knew, someone he was close to.

Nick needed a drink. A good stiff drink. And time to think, to decide what to do now. To calm down.

Just as he'd suspected, the blackmailer had led him straight back to the Gardens. When he'd arrived, the sedan was parked on the street, directly between his house and the one shared by Ned and Noreen and Scott. The lights were on in both houses, blazing out onto the sidewalk as if there was a party going on. For a moment he wondered what his wife, Suzanne, was doing still up; she was usually in bed, pretending to be asleep, when he came home late. But the thought quickly faded from his mind; he had more important things to think about.

He let himself in, heading directly for the bar in the study. First the drink, then the gun . . . This time he was going to be the one making the rules. He rummaged around in the desk, looking for the automatic that he kept in the top drawer. It was gone.

Suddenly he heard a loud thump overhead, and the staccato rhythm of high heels on the parquet floor above. And what sounded like a trunk being dragged across the bedroom.

He hurried up the stairs. "What the hell's going on?" he began, but the words faltered in midair.

Suzanne was standing by the bed, folding one of her new evening dresses, a beaded red satin, into a steamer trunk. There was a look of settled determination on her face, a hardness he'd never seen before. "Good evening, Nick," she said calmly. "I was hoping we'd have a chance to say good-bye."

He stared at her, at the already filled suitcases covering the bed, and finally at the familiar black satchel sitting incongruously on her dressing table. The satchel he'd stuffed with bonds.

"Suzanne? . . ." He took a step into the room, his mind fumbling desperately for another explanation. "No, it couldn't have been you."

"If you say so . . ." she agreed, as if humoring a child. But there was a smug smile in her eyes. She tucked several jewel cases into the trunk.

He just stared; even with the evidence right in front of him he couldn't believe he'd actually let himself be blackmailed by his own wife. He was the one who was going to dump her; it had never once occurred to him that she might walk out on him. Or that she was capable of such a piece of calculated, cold-blooded trickery.

Oblivious of her husband's growing anger, Suzanne had calmly gone on packing. Her movements, quick and efficent, were multiplied in the mirrored closet doors that lined the room, so that there seemed to be dozens of her, all silently taunting him. And gradually he realized that the other image repeated over and over in the mirrored doors was his own— pop-eyed, his mouth working in and out and out like a goldfish's, gasping for air.

"You bitch," he whispered. "You don't think you'll get away with this?"

She grinned. "It's worked out pretty well so far. In fact, better than I hoped. You must have even more guilty secrets than I suspected, to be willing to fork over a hundred grand. Just what else is it you're hiding, Nick—besides all those afternoons in bed with other men's wives?"

"I didn't realize you were so jealous," he said, hoping to distract her as he began to slowly, cautiously circle around behind her.

"You never thought of me at all. And I was so damned much in love with you. So gullible. For years I refused to believe all the hints my 'friends' kept dropping, ignored all the pitying looks."

He'd reached the fireplace now. His hand closed around the poker, silently lifting it behind his back. He took a step forward.

And suddenly froze. The automatic—the one he'd searched for downstairs—was pointing straight at his heart.

"You're not being a very good sport, Nick," Suzanne said, keeping the gun leveled at him. "But I'm not going to let you stop me. So you might as well just drop that poker."

He tensed, considering what his chances would be if he rushed her. But the automatic seemed very much at home in her hands.

"I mean it, Nick. You wouldn't want to get blood all over your beautiful silk shirt, would you?"

And as they stared at each other, the doorbell rang.

"That must be the men to pick up my luggage," she said. "Be a doll and let them in." And when he didn't move, her gun hand gestured impatiently. "Now, Nick."

He stumbled downstairs and opened the front door. From the landing, Suzanne called out to the men, "Almost done— just give me a minute."

By the time he got back to the bedroom she was just zipping up the last suitcase. The gun was out of sight. She read his thoughts. "Forget it, Nick. There are witnesses now, re- member?"

She was right, he realized; she'd outmaneuvered him. "Go, then," he said bitterly. "But you're not taking all this stuff with you." Now he knew why she'd been running up charges all over town; there was a small fortune in furs, jewels, de- signer clothes here. Not to mention the bonds she'd tricked out of him.

Her eyes glittered, and for the first time he clearly saw the hate behind them. "You're referring, I suppose, to that clever prenuptial agreement I was naive enough to sign. If you'll recall, I get to keep my clothes—even if you haven't paid for them. And as for the bonds—well, whom did you plan on telling, Nick? It should make a wonderful little item for the gossip columns. And the police. They'll all be laughing so hard, they'll barely be able to turn the key in your cell."

"I'll find you," he promised, anger thickening his voice, mottling his face.

"No, I don't think so." She swept past him, crisp and elegant in one of her new Saint Laurent suits, the black satchel tucked demurely under her arm.

At the door she turned. "I'll send the men up for the rest. I think we're even now, Nick. By the way, there never were any videotapes." And with one last gloating smile, she was gone.

Long after the house had fallen silent, Nick stood alone in the center of the room, boxed in by his own reflection everywhere he looked. For the first time in his life he couldn't stand the sight of himself. Without thinking, he grabbed a heavy crystal perfume flacon from the dresser and smashed it against one of the mirrored doors. The mirror shattered, glass and crystal flying everywhere in iridescent arcs, crashing to the floor. The room was drenched in her scent. And suddenly he was grabbing anything he could reach—lamps, pictures, chairs—and hurling them into his own mirrored reflection. Splintering glass slashed his skin, but he didn't notice. He wasn't aware of anything but his own rage. When he was finished, the room looked as if it had been hit by a bomb.

For the last fifteen minutes, Noreen had felt the urge to throw something, too. Something large and quite heavy. At Ned. It seemed the only way that she could get him to pay any attention to her demands.

They were alone in the living room; earlier in the day Scott had returned from the hospital, looking exhausted, and had gone straight to his room. And the servants had retired for the night. Noreen was sitting on the couch, her feet tucked up under the wide folds of a black velvet caftan. Her fingers picked nervously at the gold embroidery work around the hem, but her eyes never left Ned, who was standing with his back to her at the window. He was staring at Nick's house.

"Ned, for God's sake, the show's over for the night. Come sit down; I want to talk."

"What do you suppose finally made her do it?" Ned asked, not moving from the window. "After all these years . . ."

Noreen yanked angrily at a gold thread, and one of the embroidered rosettes disintegrated. "I don't give a flying fuck why she left him, and I can't understand why you should, either. Maybe Suzanne just got fed up with his catting around.

Everyone has their limits, you know, even her. Anyway, it's not going to make any difference to us.''

"Still, it's interesting . . . the timing . . ."

Noreen tried to rein in her impatience. The last thing she wanted to do was start a quarrel. If Ned had any idea how close her temper was to breaking, he'd simply burrow down inside his skin and refuse to talk with her at all. "I just won't deal with you when you're crazy like this," he'd told her once, as if she could help it. He didn't understand what it was like for her. No one did.

She forced herself to take a couple of deep breaths, mentally stepping back from the edge. She had to stay calm, had to make Ned listen to her, agree.

She'd planned the whole evening so carefully. She'd arranged with the cook to have Ned's favorite dinner served—roast goose with apricot stuffing and coconut cream pie for dessert—and she'd sat through an old Hitchcock movie with him—*Strangers on a Train*—parts of which had been filmed in the Gardens at the Forest Hills Tennis Club. And the whole time they'd watched the movie, she'd been refilling his brandy snifter.

But none of it seemed to have done any good. Despite all her flattery and coaxing and wheedling, she still was no closer to getting what she wanted. "Ned, please," she said now. "Just give me the paper."

At last he turned and looked at her. "This is getting to be a very old, very boring, subject, Noreen."

"Then why don't you just give it to me?"

"I explained why years ago. It's safer with me. And nothing's changed to make that less true."

"Everything's changed!" she exploded. "Dammit, I know Almafi spoke with you today, too. He's reopening the old investigation. Who knows who he's going to question this time, what he'll find out."

Ned stared at her for a moment. "What are you suggesting—that I'd tell him something? Or maybe show him the decree?"

She shook her head quickly.

"Then what are you so worried about?

"Please, I'd just feel more secure if I were the one who

had the paper. Or maybe we could destroy it? That would be best, wouldn't it—just to burn it?''

''I thought you trusted me,'' he said. ''And now some old potbellied, dim-witted police captain asks a few questions, and suddenly you decide you can't depend on me anymore? All right, if that's what you want, I'll give the paper up. To Scott.'' He smiled. ''You do trust Scott, don't you?''

''No . . . I mean . . . I don't want Scott to know about this. Not Scott.'' She shut her eyes tightly, fighting for control. ''Please, Ned, don't do this to me.''

Ned came and sat down next to his sister on the couch. In a coldly clinical way he seemed satisfied, as if an experiment had turned out the way he'd expected. ''And you think you're strong enough to stand up to Almafi all by yourself,'' he said after a while. ''Look at yourself, you're falling apart. Don't you realize what would happen to you, what would have happened to you already, without me?''

''You won't give the paper to Scott? Please?'' she whispered.

''Of course not. Now let's just forget the whole thing.''

''But what about Almafi?''

''He can't force you to answer his questions. And as soon as Fawn is out of the picture, he'll stop coming around, bothering us.'' He stood up. ''Now, why don't you get some sleep? You look like hell.''

''I don't understand why you're not more worried,'' she said. ''Fawn isn't going to simply disappear.''

Ned was staring out toward Nick's house again. A slow smile formed on his lips. ''Oh, I think she is—one way or the other.''

''Just because we want her to . . .'' Noreen shook her head. But she realized that Ned wasn't paying attention to her anymore. He'd reached into the pockets of his baggy trousers, pulled out a beige rain hat, and was twirling it on his finger.

''What the hell is that?'' she asked, not bothering to hide her irritation.

Ned grinned, the hat still spinning on his finger. ''Just something I picked up in the trash . . .'' He gave her a peck on the cheek, and she looked up at him in surprise. He neve showed any affection unless he was feeling extremely pleased about something.

"Hold on for a few more days," he told her. "And after that, I don't think Fawn—or Almafi—is going to be a problem anymore."

With a puzzled frown on her face, she watched him climb the stairs and heard his door slam. And then the familiar clicking of the locks, all three of them, turning.

And somewhere hidden in that room, she remembered, was one yellowed piece of paper that could destroy her life. She should have known he wouldn't part with it. She shivered, recalling his threat to show it to Scott. Clearly that was a warning to her not to bring up the subject again.

Dammit, it wasn't fair. Somehow she had to get that piece of paper. To hell with Ned and his assurances, she had to start protecting herself.

After all, it wasn't Ned's past that was going to be unmasked for the whole world to see.

C h a p t e r 29

The answer was there when Fawn woke up. It was as if it
had come to her in a dream, though she didn't remember
dreaming at all. But even before her eyes were open, she
realized she'd already decided to go back to the house in the
Gardens to search Ned's room. And she knew how she was
going to get everyone out of the house while she did it.

Cole was still asleep on the sofa in the study. The sofa
wasn't quite long enough for him, and his feet were propped
up on one of the armrests, his toes sticking out from underneath the blanket. It was the first time, she realized, that
she'd ever seen him looking defenseless and awkward, and
she felt such a rush of love for him it frightened her.

"This is a hell of a time to fall in love," she reminded
herself, but still she stood there looking at Cole until Toby
finally nudged her hand with his wet, black nose. Wagging
his tail, he dropped his leash at her feet.

She grinned. "You're the only sensible one here, aren't
you, fellow? All right, I'll take you for your walk."

When she returned, she put a call in to Colman Bromley's
office and spoke with his secretary. The woman seemed hes

itant at first, but at last she agreed to do as Fawn asked. "Is there any word on Colman's condition?" Fawn asked before hanging up.

"I've just spoken with the hospital," the secretary said. "He's doing better all the time. When you see him, tell him everyone here's pulling for him."

"I will."

Afterward she called Captain Almafi. "Do you have any plans for one o'clock today?" she asked him.

"Nothing that can't be changed if it has to. Why?"

"I've arranged to have a board meeting called for this afternoon at the Dalsworth offices."

"And you want me there, too?"

"I'm not sure yet. It depends on . . . what happens this morning. But if I call you, will you come?" she asked.

"Of course. But what makes you believe the three of them will show up?"

She smiled mischievously. "They're being told we're going to discuss splitting up the inheritance."

Almafi laughed. "They'll be there," he agreed. "But Fawn, you're not going to try anything on your own, are you? I'm paid to take chances, you're not. Remember that."

"I know," she said gently. "You gave me the lecture before." But it still came down to the fact that she was the only one who could get into the house. The police would need a search warrant, and there was no evidence to convince a judge to issue one yet. And someone had to get into Ned's room before the evidence was destroyed or hidden where they'd never find it. Besides, as long as the house was empty, what could happen to her?

Fawn considered waking Cole to tell him where she was going, but she knew he'd have a dozen arguments against it. And he still seemed so exhausted. She decided to let him sleep. After all, this was the first time his head had hit a pillow in the last three days, and it was going to take him more than a few hours to recuperate.

She scribbled a quick note, asking him to meet her at the Dalsworth Building that afternoon. Then after giving Toby a few dog biscuits—and getting her face washed in thanks—she hurried out of the apartment.

* * *

"Aren't you going to the board meeting?" Ned asked. He was wearing his "best suit," a tatty-looking blue serge with egg stains on the lapel and cuffs that dragged along the floor. Noreen wondered what Goodwill bin he had picked that out of.

But then she forced her mind back to his question. "Of course I'm going to the meeting," she said. "I'm just running a little late." She was still in her bathrobe. "But I don't want to hold you up. Why don't you go ahead and take the limo in, and I'll drive in once I'm dressed."

"It wastes gas, taking two cars."

"Just this once, I think we can afford it," she said sharply. "Of course, if you want to wait . . ." She yawned, stretching her arms over her head. "I think it's going to take another cup of coffee this morning to wake me up."

"Oh, for God's sake," Ned said irritably. "Nick's already left. I saw his car pull out fifteen minutes ago."

"Maybe he wants a chance to work on Fawn before the meeting," Noreen suggested. "Who knows what he might decide to tell her?"

Ned frowned. "Fawn's up to something, you know that," he said after a minute.

"And it's killing you that you can't guess what."

"I'm glad you find it so amusing," he said stiffly. "Go ahead—sit there and drink your coffee. I'm leaving."

Noreen waited until she heard his car pull out of the drive. And then slowly she set down her coffee cup, her fingers trembling slightly. It had worked—he was gone.

Standing up she shrugged off her bathrobe, revealing the navy-blue Aldolfo suit and white blouse she was wearing. Reaching into the pocket, she clipped on a pair of large pearl button earrings. Aside from her lipstick and mascara, which she could put on in the car, she was ready.

There wasn't much time. If she didn't show up at the Dalsworth Building in time for the meeting, Ned would certainly know something was wrong. It didn't take much to arouse his suspicions.

She hurried out to the garage, rummaging around until she located a hammer and a pair of pliers. Then she took a chair from the kitchen and lugged it up the stairs, setting it down in front of Ned's door. Luckily, she'd thought to send Martha out shopping earlier in the morning, so there was no one in the house to ask questions.

"Please let this work," she whispered, as she lifted the hammer and brought it down hard on the top pin in the door hinge. The pin inched slightly out of the hinge. She swung again. Missed. "Dammit."

It would have been a lot easier if she could have gotten the keys from Ned. But he never let them out of his sight; they were attached to him like barnacles. And she didn't know how to pick a lock. So this was her only chance: if she could knock the pins out of the hinge, she should be able to get the door to swing open on the other side.

And slowly she was making progress. The first pin broke free and clattered to the floor. But by now her nervousness was making her movements clumsy; she was trembling so much she could hardly aim. She was running out of time. And afterward she'd have to put everything back together again. And hope that Ned didn't notice the chipped paint.

Finally the last pin slipped free. She gripped the hinge with the pliers and began pulling. And the door swung open.

She stepped inside, her eyes widening as she took in the chaotic jumble that spilled over the furniture and littered the floor. She'd been vaguely aware of Ned's sneaking things up to his room for years, but this . . . It was a madman's attic. She shook her head. "You'd need a machete to get through this."

How was she ever going to find one small piece of paper in all this mess? But she didn't have time to think about it. There was a battered imitation Louis XIV desk leaning against the far wall. She waded across the floor toward it, kicking old newspapers and magazines out of her way as she went; she'd start there.

Half an hour later she still hadn't found what she was looking for. "Dammit, Ned, where the hell did you hide it?" she swore. If all this had been for nothing . . .

"Think," she told herself, fighting the desperation that was welling up inside her. "Think . . . where would you hide it?" She'd been pacing back and forth across the floor, and suddenly she stopped, and with a puzzled frown on her face, pounded her heel against the floorboards. There was an odd springiness to them, a hollow ring in the sound of her foot against the boards. Looking up, she realized that the ceilings seemed lower in this room. She grinned.

In an instant, she was down on her hands and knees, pulling away the threadbare rug. It took her a few minutes to figure out how the trick spring worked, but at last the planking slid aside.

A half-strangled gasp escaped her lips, as she stared into the compartment dumbfounded, her eyes bulging. "What in the world? . . ." Noreen whispered.

She reached out a hand tentatively and ran her fingers over the raised lettering on one of the bonds. "That louse . . . that frigging, penny-pinching louse . . . there must be millions here," she said rifling through the stacks of bonds and certificates, noticing the denominations. Not one of them was under twenty-five thousand dollars.

But where had it all come from? Ned's share of Melissa and Joel's inheritance had been safely banked all these years. She knew that for a fact; she'd seen the monthly statements. He hadn't withdrawn one penny from his portfolio in years, if ever.

She held up a handful of bonds, splayed open like a deck of cards, and frowned. So where had this come from? And suddenly she knew. This was the Dalsworth inheritance. This was the money that should have come to them after Kendra's birthday. Good old smiling, shuffling Ned was planning on waltzing out with the entire inheritance. She should have guessed.

Suddenly she began to laugh. It was a jerky, abrupt, almost hysterical sound; and once she started she couldn't stop. For once she'd outsmarted Ned. All the years of work he'd put into this scheme, all the calculating and plotting, and now it was all blown to hell. She giggled. It was just like Ned to keep all this here where he could drool over it and gloat. No wonder he'd spent so much time in his rooms. She imagined the look on his face when he found out his secret had been discovered.

But the thought abruptly sobered her. There was no telling

what he might do. She glanced quickly at the door, shuddering, suddenly terrified that she'd see him standing there watching her. But she was alone. Still, she felt her flesh crawl.

Quickly she grabbed a couple of pillow cases from the bed and began scooping the bonds into them, frantic to get away before she was discovered. "Burglars . . . an intruder breaking into the house." That was it—she could blame it on strangers, she told herself.

And as she hurriedly stuffed the pillow cases, her fingers caught on a small gold chain. Puzzled, she held it up, and the tiny gold filigreed locket sparkled in the sunshine. Fawn's locket. And the photographs were there, too, the pictures that had been stolen from Fawn's room. So it had been Ned. But why had he wanted them, and badly enough to sneak into her room to take them? What was he up to? She remembered again his assurances that Fawn wouldn't be a bother to them much longer.

She didn't have time to wonder about it now. It was absolutely crucial that she show up at that board meeting on time. And she would leave the door off its hinges. That might add some credibility to the story of a break-in.

Casting one last hectic look around the room, making sure there was nothing that would prove she'd been there, she spotted a beige rain hat—the one Ned had been twirling on his finger the night before. She picked it up and tossed it onto the desk. She shook her head; Ned would steal anything.

There wasn't time to straighten up the mess she'd made, she decided. But it didn't matter. Burglars could hardly be expected to be tidy.

Quickly she lugged the bulging pillow cases into her room—it took three trips—and stuffed them under her bed. She'd find a better hiding place for them later. At least there was no danger of Ned's calling in the police. What could he tell them?

A few minutes later she was in her car, racing toward Manhattan. It wasn't until she reached the bridge that her pulse began to return to normal. And then she remembered for the first time that she hadn't found the one thing she'd gone to Ned's room to look for.

C h a p t e r 30

If Fawn had looked out the window of her taxi just as it was entering the Gardens, she would have seen Noreen, flushed and breathless, speeding the other way. But Fawn was too busy worrying about how she was going to get into Ned's room. Would there be another set of keys somewhere? Could she pick the locks?

Planning to slip up to her room first and change, she told the taxi driver to let her off several blocks away. The day was turning hot and muggy; the heat seemed to seep into her bones, slowing her steps. The billowing cherry blossoms were all gone now, and the trees were in full leaf. But new blooms had taken their place: iris and tulips and azalea and honey-suckle and showy rhododendrons that towered over her in the still air.

As she crossed the lawn in front of the house, she took off her jacket, wishing there were a breeze, wishing she were on her way to the beach—wishing she were going anywhere but where she was going. She was wearing her new clothes. Jeans, she'd realized, would hardly be appropriate in the Dalsworth boardroom; and if she found what she expected to find, she intended to dump the evidence right in the center of that long, polished mahogany conference table for all three of them to see. So, she'd decided on a crisp, tailored pair of cream-colored linen slacks and matching jacket. With it she was wearing a high-necked, café-au-lait crepe blouse; and her blond hair was pulled up into a neat knot at the top of her head.

She approached the house cautiously from the back. For a few minutes she hesitated, alert for any signs of life inside. No one seemed to be home. She hurried up the stairs and edged into the silent hall, nervously glancing at her watch. They should all be assembling for the meeting in just a few minutes; soon they'd begin to wonder where she was. She'd have to call before long—make some excuse about being delayed—to keep them there, waiting for her. But right now, the problem was how to get into Ned's room.

And then she saw the door . . . the hinges unfastened, the door itself leaning open at a slight angle. Certainly Ned wouldn't have forced the door this way. Which meant someone had beaten her here. Someone perhaps who shared her own suspicions?

Treading as softly as a ghost, she approached the door and peered inside—and saw the floor boards gaping open, the empty compartment beneath. She remembered the first night she'd come to this house and Noreen had talked about how no one was ever allowed in Ned's room; how Ned had had a carpenter completely rebuild the room. The conversation had made Ned very uncomfortable. No wonder, Fawn thought.

Pushing the door closed behind her, she walked around the edge of the hole, measuring it with her eyes. It was a square, she guessed about five by five feet, and over two feet deep. Whatever Ned had been hiding must have been quite bulky. It had to have something to do with the Dalsworth inheritance. But what was it exactly? Money, phoney account books? And without the evidence, how could she prove anything at all?

She sank down on the sofa, pushing aside a few pillows. Who had gotten here first? "Damn . . ." she whispered. There was no way to prove anything, but it must have been Ned who attacked Cole's father, who tried to run her down outside the hospital; Ned who had killed her parents. It all fit together—the greed, the embezzlement, the anger he'd shown at her return. But she had to have proof, something more substantial than a hollowed-out cavity hidden beneath the floorboards of his room.

As she considered the problem, her eyes swept across the tangled collection of odds and ends that took up every available inch of space. But she wasn't really paying attention to anything but her own thoughts. It was unlikely that there would be anything here to help her, anyway. Not after someone else had just searched the room.

She wished Cole were here to see this, to offer suggestions. For a moment she considered calling him. And then she had a better idea. She hurried back to her own room and picked up her camera case. A few photographs would be proof at least that Ned had gone to a great deal of trouble to hide something.

She set the focus on the camera, checked the light meter, and began clicking. It felt good to have a camera in her hands again. But something was nibbling away at her consciousness, and she found it difficult to maintain her usual concentration. There was something very disturbing about Ned's room. Perhaps it was just that it was such a silent testimony to greed—a ravenous, consuming greed totally divorced from any sense of need or usefulness or value. But it was more than that, she realized. Somehow she had the feeling she was missing something.

With the viewfinder to her eye, she scanned the room again, focusing on one small section at a time: the desktop piled high with old clothes, the cracked clown lamp, an empty fish tank, a beige rain hat, a stack of magazines . . . Suddenly she jerked the camera away, her eyes riveted on the rain hat. A hat just like the one the driver had been wearing that night outside the hospital.

But how could she be sure? There had to be hundreds of hats exactly like this in the city of New York. Was she so anxious to have this horrible business over with that she was jumping to conclusions? Very carefully she picked up the hat by one edge—and saw the dried blood inside the hatband. A chill whispered down her spine as she remembered how the

car had careened into the side of the ambulance; the driver's
head had slammed against the rearview mirror, and the force
of the blow must have gashed his head. And the blood would
have marked the band in exactly this position.

She grabbed the hat and her camera and started for the
door. This wasn't the evidence she'd come for, but it would
do, at least for a bluff. With it perhaps she could convince
Ned she knew the whole story. Maybe at last the nightmare
was almost over.

"Important meeting today, huh?" the guard at the Dalsworth
entrance said as Fawn hurried past him.

She nodded grimly. "Is everyone else here?"

"They've been cooling their heels for a while now," he
said as if the idea pleased him. Obviously he didn't care much
for the triplets.

As the elevator doors closed, Fawn checked her watch.
Before she'd left Queens, she'd stopped at a phone booth and
made several calls: one to Almafi to ask him to meet her
here, another to the Dalsworth offices to say that she'd be
late, but that there would definitely be a meeting this afternoon and it was crucial that they all attend. She'd tried to
reach Cole, too; he was out, but she left a message on his
answering machine.

Now, as she entered her office, she asked the secretary if
Captain Almafi and Cole had shown up yet. Debbie shook
her head. "I haven't seen them. Is something wrong?" she
added.

Fawn tried to smile. "Nothing for you to be worried
about."

"Maybe I should fix you a cup of coffee?" Debbie suggested, still concerned. And as Fawn caught a glimpse of
herself in the mirror, she understood why. Her skin was
drained of all color, and her eyes, so dark they were almost
black, seemed huge in her face. But coffee wouldn't help.
She already felt as if all her nerves had been pulled taut. And
her stomach was growing more queasy by the minute.

"I'm supposed to tell everyone when you've arrived,"
Debbie said hesitantly.

"Go ahead," Fawn agreed. "We'll start the meeting in

fifteen minutes." And as she watched the secretary walk out of the office, she added a silent prayer: Please let Captain Almafi and Cole be here by then. She didn't relish the idea of confronting Ned alone.

While she was waiting, she paced nervously back and forth in her office. Someone had opened the window—the building had been constructed before the time when they started sealing windows shut—and she paused to let the cooling breeze play over her. Far down on the street below, the crowds scurried past with that frenetic New York rhythm that had at first seemed so strange to her, but now looked natural. All those people rushing to appointments, to close a deal, to meet someone they loved, she thought, wishing she were down there with them. She took the rolled rain hat out of her pocket and for one crazy moment imagined it sailing out the window, floating on the breeze until it landed where no one could ever find it. But then she quickly shook her head. There was no way she could make the truth go away, no matter how ugly it was. She had to face it.

"You're not thinking of jumping, are you?" a voice said behind her.

She whirled around, startled. It was Nick. There was a strained smile on his face, and although he had dressed with even more care than usual, in a brown sharkskin vested suit with a yellow-and-white pin-striped shirt and silk tie, there was something unsettled, not quite right, about his appearance.

"I didn't hear you come in," she said suddenly, realizing she'd been staring at him.

"Your secretary's gone. There was no one to announce me." All the while he spoke, his eyes were focused on the hat she was holding in her hands. "What's that?"

She hesitated, wondering how much she should tell him. But he'd know the whole story soon anyway. And maybe if he understood he'd be willing to help, to back her up.

"Fawn . . ." he prompted. "The hat? . . ."

She took a deep breath. "Nick, someone tried to kill me, to run me down in a car, several nights ago. I couldn't see his face clearly, but the driver was wearing this hat."

"You're sure?"

"Almost positive." She turned the hat inside out to show him. "There's blood on the band. The police should be able to run some tests to make a positive identification. After all, there are only a few suspects."

"Suspects? . . ." he repeated, frowning.

"Yes. Whoever tried to kill me must have attacked Colman Bromley, too. And murdered my parents . . ." she added softly. She stopped for a moment, not sure how to tell him the rest. How to tell him his brother was a murderer.

"Fawn . . ." he whispered, his voice filled with sympathy. He moved toward her as if to comfort her, but at the same instant his hand jerked out to grab the hat. Instinctively she'd yanked it back out of his reach, and his hand pawed at the empty air. She moved back a step.

"I only wanted to see it," he said stiffly. He held out his hand and smiled at her as if she were a foolish, mistrustful child. For a moment he was almost convincing, but then his expression seemed to splinter and she saw the desperation, the hate and fear underneath.

"Give me the hat, Fawn. Now."

She edged backward another step. Her shoulder was pressed against the window frame. Frantically she looked toward the desk, thinking if she could just push the intercom button, call for help. But she was too far away. And Nick was blocking her path.

For a while, they stared at each other as the sounds of traffic drifted up to them from the street far below. And then Nick's glance shifted to the open window. A smile twitched on his lips. "I'm sorry, Fawn, but I guess you're going to jump after all."

My God, she realized, she'd been wrong about Ned. It had been Nick. Somehow she'd been taken in by that smooth, friendly manner of his, the college-boy face. But then she remembered his temper; hadn't Ned and Noreen tried to warn her? But she'd been so sure it was Ned. And suddenly she saw one last chance to save herself. A way to stall him . . . to confuse him.

"I don't understand why you're defending Ned," she said quickly. Nick had already been moving toward her, but now he stopped, frowning in puzzlement at her words. "I don't think Ned would care this much about protecting you. Do you?" she asked.

"What does this have to do with Ned? You're not making any sense."

"But don't you see, I found the hat in Ned's room. And he had this secret compartment hidden under the floorboards, too. That's why he would never let anyone in his room." Nick was still looking at her warily, suspecting a trick, but at least he was listening. "I know it'll be a scandal, Ned's being arrested, but no one will blame you. There's no way you could have guessed. Ned fooled us all, even the police. That's what I've been trying to explain to you."

She could almost see the wheels clicking behind Nick's eyes as he tried to decide whether to believe her or not; he was obviously tempted by the idea of putting all the blame on his brother. And for a moment she thought she'd won. But then Nick shook his head. "It was a good idea, Fawn. But unfortunately the blood on that hat is mine. And as you said, the police will be testing it . . ." He looked at her sadly. "Why did you have to be so much trouble, Fawn? I tried scaring you away. But it seems there's only one way to get rid of you for good."

She glanced out the window, imagining her body hitting the concrete far below. She recalled hearing somewhere that a person was mercifully unconscious long before her body hit and wondered if it was true. "Someone will know you were in here with me," she reminded Nick.

His eyes had taken on a strange, manic glimmer, and when he answered he seemed to be talking to himself. "I'll tell them I was here—that I struggled with you, tried to stop you. Unfortunately . . ." He nodded decisively, satisfied with the story. And she knew she couldn't stall him any longer.

As he started for her, she flung out her arm and spun the hat past him. He blinked, distracted. And in that instant, she dashed toward the desk. Her fingers were already funbling desperately for the intercom button when he lunged at her from behind and began dragging her across the room to the window. Her feet dug into the carpet and she clawed at his hands, but he was too strong for her.

My God, he is going to kill me, she thought frantically.

And suddenly she felt her body being lifted up into the air as she struggled to break free of his grasp. But he was too strong.

Neither one of them noticed the door opening, heard the secretary begin to announce that Captain Almafi and Mr. Bromley had arrived, and stop halfway through the first words, dumbfounded, her mouth agape. But suddenly Cole was plowing into Nick's body, knocking him off balance and freeing Fawn who fell to the carpet. Almafi, moving surprisingly swiftly, was right behind Cole. It was all over in seconds. Nick, arms flailing, lay pinned beneath Almafi's bulk.

"Are you all right, Fawn? Did he hurt you?" Cole asked worriedly. His arms were wrapped protectively around her, and his eyes glowed with a mixture of fierce concern and gentleness. It reminded her of a picture of a guardian angel she'd seen once as a child. All Cole needed was a flaming sword. Certainly he was handsome enough. It struck her that that was hardly an appropriate thought, considering the circumstances, and she realized she must be in shock. It had all happened so quickly.

She heard a loud thud behind and flinched, thinking Nick was coming after her again. But there was no chance of that. The captain had slammed him against the wall and was holding him there, tightly and none too gently, by his shirt collar.

"What happened?" Cole asked.

"He was going to throw me out the window." And for a minute it sounded so impossible she wondered if they would believe her.

"That's a lie," Nick shouted. "She was going to jump, I was trying to stop her . . ." But something in Almafi's expression told him it wasn't going to work. "Oh, shit . . . I want a lawyer."

"Cole, he's the one who . . ." she stopped, still a little light-headed, then forced herself to go on. "I found the hat, the one he was wearing the night he tried to run me down. But I didn't know it was his at first . . . If you hadn't come when you did . . ." While she was fighting for her life, she had managed to keep her wits, had not panicked, but now that it was all over, her mind seemed to have shut down completely. All she could think of was how close she'd come to death.

Cole seemed to be thinking the same thing. Again and again he gently touched her hair, caressed her cheek, as if convincing himself she was really there in his arms, safe and unharmed.

"We're going to need a statement," Almafi said.

Cole nodded. "Give her a little more time. I'll bring her down to the station later myself." And then he glanced at Nick, his face abruptly hardening. "Can't you get him out of here?"

"Good idea," Almafi agreed. He began unfastening the handcuffs that dangled at the back of his belt. As soon as Nick saw the cuffs, he started shaking his head violently. "No, you can't put those on me. Don't you realize who I am?"

"From now on you're just going to be a number, bud," Almafi said.

"No, I'm somebody. Ask anyone, read the newspapers . . ."

Almafi nodded. "Sure. And this time you're going to make page one. Just think of the headlines."

A shudder ran through Nick's body as the handcuffs snapped shut, and his muscles went rigid and stiff. He glared at Fawn with undisguised loathing. "This is what you wanted, isn't it, you bitch? But I'll make you pay for every line those reporters write. You wait and see . . ."

"That's enough," Almafi growled, roughly hauling Nick out the door.

But Nick went on shouting hysterically. "I'll make you all pay . . . My lawyer will get me out, they won't be able to hold me . . ."

The commotion in Fawn's office had brought Ned and Noreen out of the boardroom. They stared at Nick being led away, shocked. "Dammit, what has that fool done now?" Ned hissed. "They're arresting him."

Noreen gripped his arm. "Do something, Ned," she demanded. "For God's sake—"

"Stop panicking." Ned interrupted, shoving her back into the boardroom. "We need time to think this over . . ."

Captain Almafi had dragged Nick halfway down the hall by now, but Fawn could still hear him shouting. "You better run back to wherever you came from, Fawn. If I find you . . ."

"It's just bravado," Cole told her. "Forget it."

She nodded, but she couldn't stop herself from asking, "Are you sure? He'll have a good lawyer. And maybe the lawyer will get him out."

"I don't think so." But there was just the slightest doubt in Cole's voice, and when she glanced up at him, his eyes were worried.

C_ole_ knocked gently on the door to the bedroom. ''Breakfast in bed?'' he called out.

Fawn sat up in bed, quickly smoothing back her tousled
blond hair. ''Sound great,'' she called back, grinning as Cole
opened the door. He was carrying a huge bamboo tray; and
the aroma of fresh, hot muffins and coffee wafted across the
room to her. Toby was trailing behind him, bounding back
and forth, tail wagging.

Cole set the tray down on the bed and kissed her.

''The waiters are very forward around here, aren't they?''
she teased.

He grinned. ''Considering how marvelous you look, you
got off easy with just a kiss. In fact . . .'' And he leaned
down and kissed her again, this time very thoroughly and
with a passion that blotted out the rest of the world and left
them both breathless. ''Fawn . . .'' he whispered, touching
her cheek, tenderly tracing the outline of her chin.

''Yes? . . .'' Her voice was as soft as his as she gazed into
his eyes.

''I . . .'' He stopped suddenly and seemed mentally to shake himself, as if he'd just remembered something. "I guess we'd better eat our breakfast," he said at last. But there was still a huskiness in his voice that his brusque manner couldn't disguise.

She nodded, a little puzzled. And she looked so beautiful with her hair curling softly around her face like a halo and her eyes shining with the morning sun, that for a moment his will power almost deserted him. He had to keep reminding himself how vulnerable she was. She'd just been through a hellish time, topped off with a grueling, traumatic interview at police headquarters. She needed time to recover, to be sure of her own feelings. Perhaps then . . . But he didn't want her ever to look back with regret, to think that when she had most needed someone to trust he had abused that trust.

But damn, it was difficult. She was wearing one of his shirts as a nightgown, and he couldn't help noticing the delicate hollow at the base of her throat and wanting to caress it . . . couldn't stop thinking about the swelling curves beneath the thin cotton fabric. His hand as he poured out the coffee was not quite steady.

"Mmmm . . . that's good," she said as she took a sip out of the large, hand-crafted pottery mug. "Different . . ."

"It's a special blend—Dutch Chocolate Almond," he told her.

Sitting there with the blanket tucked around her, holding the mug with both hands, she suddenly seemed very much like a child, he thought. And he remembered how little time she had had to be a child, carefree and innocent, before her whole world was shattered. Last night at the police station they'd forced her to go over that night eighteen years ago again and again. And there had been nothing he could do but hold her hand and silently ache for her; he'd been helpless to protect her against the horror of her own memories.

Even now, there was an echo of that pain in her eyes, and for a moment he thought she was about to remember again. "I hope you're hungry," he said quickly to distract her. "I spent hours in the kitchen baking." He whisked the napkin off the tray, and her eyes opened wide as she saw the basket of huge, golden muffins, the platter of crisp bacon, and a bowl of the largest, most perfect strawberries she'd ever seen.

"You have a choice," he said, holding out the basket to her. "Blueberry, coconut, apple and walnut, or honey bran.

Or you can have one of each if you want to make a pig of yourself. I think that's what I'm going to do.''

"I'd never be able to move again.'' She grinned, her fingers hesitating over the basket as she tried to decide. "Did you really make these yourself?''

"Well, actually . . . I did at least call up and order them.''

"That's what I thought.''

"I can make you eggs if you want, though,'' he offered. "If you like them scrambled. It seems no matter what kind of eggs I start out to cook, they always end up scrambled.''

Fawn shook her head, a half smile on her lips. "I don't think I'll risk the eggs.''

She moved over to make room for him on the bed, and he sat down cross-legged on the other side of the tray from her while they ate. Toby was lying at her feet; he wasn't exactly begging, but there was such a soulful expression in his brown eyes as he watched the bacon disappear that Fawn eventually sneaked him a few pieces. "I think he practices that look in the mirror,'' Cole said. "But don't you believe it, he's already had a good-sized breakfast of his own.''

She nodded vaguely, and he realized her thoughts were somewhere else. She'd been gradually growing quieter for the past ten minutes. And now as Cole looked at her closely, he knew it was no use trying to pretend none of it had happened: she was attempting to be cheerful for his sake, but there was no way she could shake off the memory of these last few days. "Maybe we should talk about it,'' he suggested softly.

She glanced at him, knowing exactly what he meant, and once again a little surprised by how easily they read each other's thoughts. "I keep feeling I've failed someone,'' she said, relieved to be able to talk about it.

"Who? You mean Nick? He did himself in, Fawn, with his own greed.''

She'd been tormented all night with the image of Nick being dragged away in handcuffs, and she knew it would be a long time before the shock wore off, but that wasn't what she was referring to now. "I was thinking more of Captain Almafi and your father. And my parents. Unless I remember more than do now, even Captain Almafi doesn't think they'll be able to convict Nick for my parents' murders. And that's what this whole thing was about—catching Melissa and Joel's killer.''

Cole heard the frustration in her voice, the despair, and took her hand, forcing her to look at him. "The important thing is that they have Nick in custody now. You can testify that he tried to kill you. And eventually I'm sure they'll find the link that ties him in with your parents' deaths, too.''

"Maybe . . .'' She'd been certain, once they knew which one of the three was guilty, that the memory of that night would at last be released from her subconscious. But they'd spent hours questioning her, and she still couldn't swear to one new detail. Her memory was like a spool of film that broke just as she was looking into the killer's face. Without a positive identification from her the police might never be able to charge Nick with her parents' murders. And Nick was still swearing he was innocent, insisting he'd never even been near the house the night her parents were killed.

"Do you think they'll let Nick out on bail?'' she asked worriedly. "I mean, without the murder charge . . .'' The thought of Nick free frightened her more than she could admit.

"Almafi's determined to hold him,'' Nick assured her. But privately he had his doubts as to how long it would be possible to keep Nick locked up. Fawn was right; there was no real evidence yet against Nick in connection with Melissa's and Joel's deaths. Although he was charged with attempted murder, he would probably be released on bail. And he had retained a sharp, first-rate lawyer, a man Cole had come up against several times when he was with the D.A.'s office. Nick's lawyer had a reputation—a well-earned one—for finding new ways of twisting the law to his clients' advantage, of scooting through loopholes and perverting precedent to suit his own ends. Considering Nick's clean record up till now and his position in the community—and if they drew a symphathetic judge—who knew? That was one reason Cole had insisted that Fawn continue to stay at his apartment. If they were going to let Nick out on the streets again, Cole wanted Fawn where he could be sure she'd be safe.

"I suppose I should call Ned and Noreen,'' Fawn said reluctantly. She'd run into them last night at the police station Almafi had wanted statements from them, too—but they hadn't had a chance to do more than exchange a few words. Both Ned and Noreen had appeared to be in a state of shock. Ned had acted suspicious of everyone, his face wary and closed. Noreen had just seemed frightened. But both of them had eyed her coldly, almost with loathing, as if she alone were responsible for all this.

"I'm surprised you're willing ever to speak to those two again," Cole said. "After the way they turned away from you last night . . ."

"This has been horrible for them, too—their own brother arrested . . . And they are my relatives. I guess I owe them even more of an apology than they owe me. After all, I suspected them, too."

"Why don't you give it a few days," Cole suggested. "Let the dust settle. There'll be plenty of time later to set things right between you."

Fawn nodded in agreement. In a few days perhaps everyone could approach the situation with a little less emotion. And secretly, remembering the anger in their eyes, Fawn was glad for the reprieve.

The doorbell rang, interrupting her thoughts. "Why don't you start getting dressed," Cole suggested. "I'll go see who it is."

Fawn was still tidying up the breakfast dishes and brushing the crumbs out of the bed when he returned a few seconds later. "Who was it?" she asked.

"Reporters. I took the phone off the hook first thing this morning, but now they're camping outside the door." He grimaced. "I think we'd better sneak out or they're going to be pestering us all day. Unless you want to talk with them? . . ."

She shook her head quickly. "Last night at the police station was more than enough," she said, recalling how the newsmen had mobbed her, shouting questions, sticking microphones in her face. "Just give me ten minutes, I'll be ready to go. But how are we going to get out without their seeing us?"

"I'll show you," he said and grinned.

A long, brick-walled terrace, really more of an enclosed garden, ran the length of Cole's apartment. At one end there was a iron-studded wooden door. "It's always kept locked," Cole explained as fifteen minutes later he opened the door and helped her onto the fire escape. "No one should see us go out this way."

"Sneaking down fire escapes . . ." she said with a smile of complicity and a shake of her head. "Life has certainly gotten complicated lately." But then she looked back up at the door and frowned. If they could get out undetected this way, maybe someone could get in. Cole, seeing the look of worry on her face, realized she was thinking about Nick and the threats he'd made.

"All the doors, including this one, are wired into the alarm system," Cole assured her. "And there's an iron bar that goes across the door, too. Someone would need a battering ram to get in this way." He'd originally had the security system installed when he was working on some very sensitive cases with the District Attorney's office and bringing the work home with him every night. Later he'd kept it just to protect his paintings, antiques, and family heirlooms. But now, seeing the sudden relief on Fawn's face, he knew that none of that mattered half as much as her safety. He'd never been entrusted with anything that was as worth protecting as she was.

"Where to? . . ." he asked as they reached the street.

She knew right away where she wanted to go. "Let's visit your father in the hospital."

It was a sunny, golden day, without the mugginess of the day before. Even the gray haze of smog that had hung over the city for the last few days had finally drifted out to sea. As Cole and Fawn sped across town in their taxi, their driver whizzing through lights just turning red with a cheerful insouciance, Fawn began to feel her mood lighten. The parks were filled with children playing and mothers wheeling carriages. Fountains splashed, and pigeons strutted along the sidewalks. And every intersection seemed to have its own group of street musicians, magicians, and mimes. Best of all, Cole was there beside her, with a warm smile in his eyes that was just for her. He was wearing white slacks and a pale yellow polo shirt and carrying a navy-blue blazer, and she thought he looked more elegant, more handsome than any mannequin in any of the expensive stores they passed.

"Should we get something for your dad in the gift shop?" Fawn asked as they entered the hospital lobby.

"Why don't you pick it out?" he suggested. "I've got to make a few phone calls. There was no way I could call from the house with all the reporters jamming the line."

She nodded, watching him stride across the floor to the phone booths, and noticed that there were a few other women who had stopped to admire the gleam of his black hair, the graceful, confident set of his shoulders. And she suddenly giggled, remembering something Gram used to say when she thought someone was eyeing Pops: "Eat your heart out, girls. This one's taken." And in the same instant she knew that she wanted with Cole all that Gram and Pops had shared—the lifetime together of laughter and love and comfort through the hard times. Without even realizing it, her decision had already been made.

As she crossed to the gift shop, she caught a glimpse of the driveway through the wide glass double doors—the driveway where Nick had nearly run her down. A chill zigzagged down her spine. Strange that the memory hadn't disturbed her as they emerged from the taxi. Then she knew why: Cole had been in the middle of telling her a long, elaborate, and very funny story about a sailboat race as the two of them had gotten out of the taxi. And she realized now that he'd done it on purpose, timing the story perfectly to distract her.

But even in the gift shop it was impossible to stop thinking about Nick. His picture, looking very elegant and "chairman of the board," was splashed across the front page of every newspaper on the rack. Almafi was right. Nick had made the headlines, and in a big way. And Fawn realized he might hate her for this more than for anything else that had happened to him. All his years of social climbing had been destroyed in one morning.

She forced herself to buy an edition of each paper for Bromley, knowing he'd want to follow the case closely, even from his hospital bed, and selected a few crossword puzzle books and a small green plant in a brass pot. By then Cole had joined her.

"How did you know Dad was a crossword puzzle nut?" he asked, smiling. But beneath the smile he seemed upset.

"You spoke with Captain Almafi?"

He nodded. "Nothing much has changed since last night. Nick is still insisting he had nothing to do with Melissa's and

Joel's deaths . . . that it was all a conspiracy, a scheme to defraud him of his share of the inheritance. Obviously his attorney has informed him that if he were convicted he would lose his right to any share of the Dalsworth estate. By law, a killer is not allowed to profit from his victim's death.''

"At least he's still in jail," Cole said.

Fawn nodded. "For now . . .''

Bromley had been transferred from Intensive Care to a private room, an indication that his recovery was progressing smoothly. It was actually a suite, Fawn saw as they entered, with fine modern rosewood furniture and original lithographs on the walls. But at the moment nothing much could be seen but the huge arrangements of flowers stockpiled everywhere. It almost seemed as if the hospital bed had been set down in the middle of the flower fields of Grasse. She looked at the small green plant she was holding and almost laughed; talk about carrying coals to Newcastle, she thought.

Bromley had been catnapping when they entered, but as soon as Cole touched him, he sat up, his eyes blazing with their old intensity. Aside from the bandages wrapped around his head he looked almost like his usual self, and Cole told him so with a relieved grin.

His father chuckled. "You should know by now what a hard head I have. Now if I can just convince the doctors . . . they seem to have me booked in here permanently."

"Just a few more days. And I agree with them. It's about time you took a bit of a rest, anyway."

Bromley snorted, ready to object, but then he saw Fawn standing in the doorway. His expression suddenly softened, and he motioned for her to come closer. "You've brought me the very best medicine you could, son," he said as he smiled at her. "I've been so worried . . .''

"There's nothing to worry about anymore," she told him quickly. Together she and Cole filled him in on everything that had happened since he'd been found unconscious and nearly dead in the Dalsworth Building. He was livid when he heard about the attack on Fawn. "That son of a bitch Nick," he swore. "I never much cared for him but . . . I still can't quite believe it."

Fawn nodded. She was still have trouble believing Nick was a killer herself.

Suddenly Bromley frowned, remembering what had brought him to the Dalsworth Building that night. "There's something else we have to talk about. Someone has been embezzling from Fawn's trust fund."

"I know," Cole said. "Rod Davis has skipped—apparently he was involved in the scheme. We talked with his wife."

"Damn . . . Well, was it Nick, was he the one behind it? Nick's always been a greedy bastard, but frankly I wouldn't have thought he had the brains to pull off a thing like this. Even with Rod's help."

"There are a lot of answers we don't have yet, Dad. And Nick isn't admitting to anything. He's still hoping his lawyer can get him out."

"We've got to recover that money," Bromley insisted as he started to struggle out of bed.

Fawn looked at Cole, aghast. "Stop him . . . he's not supposed to be moving around."

But Cole was already gently but firmly easing his father back onto the pillows. "Just relax, Dad. Let the police handle this. It's not going to help Fawn to have you collapse."

"He's right," Fawn added. "Another few days won't make any difference."

For once Bromley let himself be persuaded. Just the effort of trying to get out of bed had left him light-headed and weak.

"Maybe we should leave," Fawn suggested.

"Not yet," Bromley said, gripping her hand. "There's something else I want to tell you." He paused for a moment to catch his breath, then went on. "Did you know Scott's been to see me? We had quite a talk. He had the damnest notion—but then you know all about that, don't you Fawn?"

She nodded, suddenly embarrassed.

"I want you to know. I'm not Scott's father." Cole looked up in surprise, and Bromley blushed. "It's true Noreen and I . . . Well, I made it plain to Scott that before he was born nothing ever happened between his mother and myself, and I want you both to know that, too."

"Then Noreen was telling the truth? Scott's father really was killed in an automobile accident?"

"I don't know for sure. But I think it's time Scott started concentrating on his future, rather than the past. I suggested he get out on his own, travel a bit perhaps, find out what he wants to do with his life."

Fawn thought Bromley was right; Scott had lived in Noreen's shadow too long. "Did Scott agree?" she asked.

"Yes. In fact, I think he'd just about come to the same conclusion himself. He's a fine young man, and a lot stronger than he realizes. I think he'll do very well on his own. And I told him, if he ever needs any help, all he has to do is come to me."

"I'm sure that meant a lot to him," Fawn said, remembering how fond Scott was of the older man. And she realized she'd become very fond of Bromley herself. She understood now, at least partially, why he'd been so upset at her return. It had opened up so many painful old wounds for him. And he'd been afraid of what might happen to her—for him it would be almost like losing Melissa all over again. So he'd tried to hide his fears beneath a gruff, forbidding exterior.

He had worked so hard since she came back to trying to protect her inheritance, and she could see how exhausted he was. It occurred to her that she hadn't yet mentioned the secret compartment hidden beneath the floorboards in Ned's room. But they could discuss it another time. There'd been enough unsettling news for one day.

Cole, too, realized it was time to leave. "We'll be back tomorrow," he promised. "Is there anything we can bring you?"

"How about getaway clothes and a rope ladder?" Bromley joked.

"Out of the question," Cole said with a laugh.

"All right, all right . . . Then at least call up the Four Seasons and have them send over a few trays of decent food. This hospital stuff could make you sick."

Cole grinned. "Done. Anything else?"

Bromley stared at them both fondly for a moment. "One more thing. Stop worrying about me. Go out and have a good time. Let the police straighten out the past. You two start enjoying the present."

Chapter 32

Despite Colman Bromley's advice to Fawn and Cole to forget the past, it wasn't that simple. "For the next twenty-four hours neither of us will even think about Nick or the police or any of the rest of it, right?"

Fawn looked doubtful. "Do you believe we can really do that?"

"I think you have to," he told her. "You've been through enough harrowing experiences to last a lifetime in these last two weeks. It's time you gave your nerves a rest. Let the police tie up the loose ends. You've done what you set out to do—filled in most of the blanks in your past and ensured that your parents' murderer will finally stand trial for their deaths."

She still looked troubled. More than anything she wanted to put all this in the past. Yet something about the way everything had worked out didn't feel quite right. She didn't know what it was that was bothering her, and maybe, it suddenly occurred to her, it was no more than the fact that she'd been living with this horrible mystery for so long that even now that it was over, she didn't know how to let loose. If she could only see the killer's face, could remember for sure . . . But perhaps she should be grateful that she couldn't recall the details of that night; perhaps it would be more than she could stand.

"Fawn . . ." Cole said softly, "Let it go."

She nodded slowly. "You're right," she agreed and saw the relief on his face; he'd obviously been more concerned about her than he'd admitted. "There's just one more thing . . ." she said as he took her hand. "I have to call Pete. If he hears about this on the news, he'll be worried about me."

Fawn dialed Pete's number, and she could tell from his voice that so far the news hadn't reached him. It was cheering to think there was someplace where life was tranquil and uncomplicated. And for a few minutes she let him ramble on, as he filled her in on the gossip and told her about the deck he was building on the back of the house.

"We all miss you, Princess. When are you coming home?" he asked at last.

Fawn took a deep breath. "It's going to be a while yet." As briefly as possible she explained the situation, sloughing off the attacks against Bromley and herself. But even the little bit she told Pete made him incoherent with shock and anger.

"I should never have let you go by yourself," he said at last when he could finally string a sentence together. "Look, I'll get on the next plane out . . ."

"No—" she interrupted quickly. "I'm all right, perfectly safe. There's nothing more to worry about. Besides, until the the police are completely satisfied as to what happened that night, I think it would be better if you didn't show your face around here."

But it took another five minutes to convince him that he shouldn't start packing his bags. At last he agreed, but only on the condition that she promise to send for him immediately if there was any hint of further trouble. "And I mean immediately, young lady," he added, trying unsuccessfully to disguise his apprehension by being stern. She wished she were there to hug him and rumple his graying hair and tease him into one of his wide, crooked grins—to prove to him that she was all right.

"Look, there's someone else here who'd like to talk with

you,'' Pete said. "If you want . . ." he added hesitantly, and she knew immediately he was referring to Sam. It was a conversation she'd been dreading for a few days now, but she owed it to Sam; they'd always been honest with each other.

"What's all this stuff we're not supposed to worry about?" Sam asked as soon as he got on the line. "I could only hear half the conversation. What's going on there?"

She gave him the same abbreviated version she'd given Pete and promised to fill in the details later. "It's all finished, done with," she assured him.

"But you're not coming home yet, are you?" he asked very softly.

"No . . ." She hesitated, unsure of how to tell him about Cole, about how suddenly everything had changed for her. But Sam seemed to know already. "You found what was missing for you here, haven't you, Fawn?" he asked. "I think I knew even before you did. In a way, I guess I knew even before you left how things would turn out."

"I'm sorry . . ." she said, thinking of all the years that Sam had been her best friend, all the rough spots they'd helped each other over. And he was still being her friend, still helping her. "You're one of the best men I've ever known," she said.

"But I was never right for you—or it would have happened between us a long time ago." He paused, and she could hear him taking a deep breath; when he continued, there was a determined note of acceptance in his voice. "It's that lawyer, Cole Bromley, isn't it? Well, just make sure he takes good care of you." Sam sounded like a fond older brother, and Fawn realized that he was telling her the affection between them hadn't been lost, but had only settled into a new course.

"You take care of yourself, too," she whispered.

Cole was waiting for her outside the bedroom when she emerged. "Anything wrong?" he asked, seeing her expression. "Is someone sick?"

She shook her head, and he didn't pry any further.

"Would you like to just go out and walk for a while?" he suggested.

She nodded, still subdued, and they made their way out of Cole's apartment and into the sunshine. Fawn was thinking of Sam and Pete and Gram and the life she had lived in Colorado—and realizing she wasn't the same person who'd left home with such trepidation and uncertainty only a few weeks before. But she knew, too, that no matter what happened from here on in, she would always treasure the past they'd shared together.

"You look like you're a million miles away," Cole said.

She smiled. "Only a few thousand." She wanted to say more, but she remembered how fiercely Cole had disapproved of Pete right from the start. He had never been willing to believe that Pete's involvement in her disappearance so many years before had been simply an accident; that Pete had been guilty of nothing more than the innocent desire to protect a distraught, terrified little girl.

"Maybe it's time we discussed Pete," Cole said, as if he were reading her thoughts. "After all, we can't go on avoiding the subject forever."

She glanced at him and was relieved to see the scowl that usually appeared on his face whenever Pete was mentioned was absent now. Instead Cole seemed simply curious, ready to listen with an open mind.

So as they walked, she told him what she remembered—how she had woken up in Pete's car, hysterical with fear, the wound on her arm bleeding again. And how Pete had been as startled, and almost as scared as she was. Neither of them had known how she'd gotten there, and as she talked about Pete bandaging her arm, Cole for the first time glimpsed the panicky confusion of that night, not as an outsider, but as Fawn herself must have experienced it. Even after all these years, her voice still trembled with relief. "Pete saved my life," she said. "Or at the very least, my sanity. When I think what could have happened . . ."

Cole nodded; there was no need for her to finish the sentence. "But didn't he try to find out where you'd come from, take you back to your family?"

Fawn shuddered, aware that Pete would have been sending her right back into the murderer's arms. "I got hysterical every time he talked about it. And when I thought he was going to take me back anyway, I ran away. Then later, when he found out my parents were dead and no other member of

my family had stepped forward, asking for my return . . .''
Her mouth twisted into a wry smile as she thought how well
her disappearance had suited the triplets, how handsomely
they'd profited from it.

"So Pete decided to adopt you, in a matter of speaking?"
Cole asked.

Fawn smiled again, but this time there was genuine pleasure in it as she told him about Gram and Pops and how
they'd taken her not only into their home but also into their
hearts. And as she described those years, she sensed a change
in Cole's attitude as it moved from suspicion to surprise to
something close to approval.

"They're not at all what I imagined . . . especially Pete,"
Cole finally admitted. "In fact, I'm looking forward to meeting him."

"I know you'll like him. And I owe him so much, more
than I'll ever be able to repay."

Cole hugged her. "From what you've told me about Pete
I think he'd be satisfied just knowing you were safe and
happy." With his arm still around her waist, he added, "And
it's about time we started working on that project. The whole
day's ahead of us, let's enjoy it."

"What do you suppose is going on in there?" a reporter from
one of the national tabloids asked as she stared at the Dalsworth house in the Gardens and frowned. She was getting
frustrated. She'd been watching the house for hours now, but
so far she had nothing to file except a few paragraphs on
getting the massive oaken door slammed in her face.

A second reporter, lounging against a parked Mercedes
shrugged. "What do you think is going on in there? They're
gnashing their perfectly capped teeth and wishing we'd go
away." He grinned. "And for two cents I would."

The first reporter dug into her purse, brought out two pennies, and held them out. "My treat . . ." she said with a
mischievous smile, as the other reporters laughed. "You going to buy us all out?" someone joked.

But she didn't answer; she was sure she'd just seen a movement at the drawn curtains in the living room across the street.
She stared intently, willing the face to appear again. But th

window remained shadowed and blank. She sighed. It was going to be a long wait.

Inside the house, Noreen gave one last nervous tug at the curtains, assuring herself that not even a sliver of light could get through. "They're still out there," she said, her voice rising hysterically.

"Dammit all, will you forget the frigging reporters," Ned shouted.

Noreen whirled around to face him. "You said everything was going to work out, that there was nothing to worry about. And now look—we've got reporters practically camping on our front lawn, the police calling us in for questioning, Nick about to be indicted for Melissa's and Joel's deaths . . ." Something in Ned's expression made her stop suddenly. She'd never seen him like this before. His face and neck were suffused with an angry beet-red flush; in the lamplight even his ears glowed a dull red. But it was his eyes that frightened her the most; he was staring at her with a blind, fanatical intensity, and she realized he hadn't heard a word she'd said.

He smiled at her in a calm, thoroughly disconcerting way. "Come sit next to me," he said, gesturing to a spot on the couch beside him.

Reluctantly she crossed the room and sat down gingerly on the edge of the couch as far away from him as possible. With the curtains drawn and only one small lamp lit, the room made her feel slightly claustrophobic. It was so dim and airless and silent. Despite the bright sunshine outside, in here it seemed like the middle of the night—or as if time had stopped altogether.

Ned continued to stare at her, and she nervously ran her fingers through her uncombed hair. Ned was dressed, but she was still wearing her nightgown and robe, her face not even made up yet; and somehow that seemed to put her at a disadvantage.

"What did you do with the bonds, Noreen?" he asked at last. His voice was so low she thought—she hoped for a moment—that she hadn't heard him right. "All the stock certificates, the bonds you took out of my room . . . where did you hide it all?" he insisted.

"You're not going to blame me because someone broke

into the house? I was as shocked as you were." At least she'd pretended to be, and it was so late when Ned got home from the police station, everything was so confused, she thought she'd gotten away with it.

"I've searched all over the house" Ned said. "Obviously you've hidden them very well. But now you're going to tell me where."

"Are you so sure *I'm* the one who took them?" she asked and then realized by acknowledging she knew what he was talking about she'd tacitly admitted her guilt. But it didn't matter; he'd never be able to find her hiding place. And she breathed a sigh of relief that she'd managed to beat him back from the police station last night and remove the pillow cases from under her bed. Everything was now safely stashed in a large steamer trunk at the airport. She'd driven it there herself, then mailed the claim ticket to herself in care of Colman Bromley's office, being sure to mark it "personal" so he'd save it for her unopened.

Ned sensed her new confidence and glowered. "You don't want to play games with me, Noreen. I want it all back."

"Half that money's mine—mine and Scott's," she retorted angrily, and the shock on his face was so great it was almost as if she'd driven her fist into his stomach. For a moment he was too apoplectic to speak; he'd never intended to share the money. "Don't worry, you'll get your half back," she reassured him quickly. "But only after this whole thing is over."

Silent rage radiated from him in waves, like heat. But she knew as long as she had the money, he had to listen to her. To get the money back he would do anything, even swallow his own anger.

"All right, you want to bargain," he said at last, his voice hoarse but controlled. "Spell out the terms."

"First of all, I want you to give me the paper you've been 'keeping' for me."

He reached into his pocket and withdrew a folded, time yellowed document. "This? It's what you were looking for when you searched my room, isn't it?"

She nodded. "Aren't you sorry now you didn't give it me when I asked? Where was it?"

"Hidden inside the lamp base—the one of the clown with

the big crack in it.'' He smiled maliciously. ''I thought it was a nice symbolic touch.''

''That's not funny.'' Her hand jerked out for the paper, but he'd already unfolded it and was staring down at the words.

''You don't think you're a little cracked, Noreen? Obviously Melissa and Joel thought so. Or they wouldn't have signed these commitment papers to have you put away. Maybe you should have gone. Maybe the Sunnybrook Institute was the place for you—so quiet, so isolated, such nice thick bars on the windows . . .''

She shuddered. ''Stop it, for God's sake. You know I'm not crazy. It was just a plot of Melissa and Joel's to get rid of me, to push Scott and me out of their lives.''

Ned was staring at her with a thoughtful, speculative expression, and she dimly realized through her panic that he was baiting her on purpose, just to see her reaction. But she had no one else to turn to. ''Ned, you've got to help me. You've always been the clever one, you can get us out of this.''

''Us? . . .'' He turned his cold fish-eyes on her. ''It's Nick who's going to be on trial, or in your hysteria have you forgotten that?''

''But Nick expects us to testify for him. That's all he kept saying last night. And if we refuse, they'll just subpoena us anyway. Don't you see, his lawyer will try to get him off by blaming us. And once they get us on the stand, they'll ask about everything and all those people will be watching, listening, and they'll try to trick you and you have to answer and . . .''

''Noreen, stop it,'' he said sharply. She was immediately quiet, but she was still trembling and her eyes had grown so wide the whites showed all the way around the iris. ''Go pour yourself a drink,'' he said. ''You're no good to either of us this way.''

She rose numbly, obediently. ''We have to do something.''

''Just let me think,'' he said. But he already knew she was right about one thing; they couldn't risk a trial. Just a moment ago Noreen had been almost raving with fear. And that's what she'd be like on the stand—or worse, much worse. She'd never be able to withstand a determined cross-examination.

One question about Scott's father and what had happened to him, for example . . . Ned shut his eyes, forcing the thought away.

Shit. First the money, then this. Everything was falling apart. He had to concentrate, find a way out.

Noreen had returned to the couch and was huddled at the far end again, a glass in her hands. She was getting to be a real problem, a debit now. Ever since Fawn's return . . . And suddenly Ned stopped, realizing how simple the answer was. His lips twisted into a shrewd, thoughtful smile. He'd just use one problem to solve the other.

"This is all Fawn's fault, you know," he said softly to Noreen. "It's Fawn who's trying to take our money away from us, Fawn who wants this trial. She's trying to get rid of you just as her parents did."

"Then you have to help me, Ned. Please . . ."

He moved over next to her and took her hand. "Didn't I help you before? Wasn't I the one who warned you?"

Noreen looked at him and suddenly shuddered. "Oh, God. Why did she have to come back? It was all forgotten . . ."

"Once Fawn isn't around anymore, it'll be forgotten again." His voice was soothing, hypnotic. "I was right before, wasn't I? Didn't everything work out just as I said it would after Mellisa and Joel were taken care of?" He waited for her to nod. "Then you know what has to be done."

"I can't . . ."

"Would you rather be locked away? Do you want Scott to find out the truth?"

"Scott's gone," she whispered. "He left a note. He said he had to get away from here . . . He didn't even say when he was coming back."

"That's Fawn's fault, too."

She nodded. "Yes . . . Ever since she showed up, he's been asking questions, talking about finding out about his father."

"She's trying to take away everything that's yours."

Noreen was silent for a moment, and Ned waited. "But if anything happens to Fawn, they'll suspect us right away," she said at last.

"Not if they have someone else to blame."

"Who? Nick's in jail."

"I wasn't thinking of Nick," Ned said. "It'll take a few days to arrange, but trust me, it'll all work out fine. For us, anyway . . ."

Noreen nodded, but her eyes remained glued to the paper lying on the coffee table—the paper bearing Melissa's and Joel's signatures that was to have locked her away forever. "We have to burn that," she said suddenly. "Now, before anyone else sees it."

"All right, whatever you want," Ned agreed. He watched her crumple up the paper and put it in an ashtray, then set fire to it.

"Don't you think you should tell me where you've hidden the money now?" he suggested casually.

Her gaze never wavered from the flames, the slowly curling, blackening paper. "After," she said. "After it's all over."

C h a p t e r   33

It was nearly ten o'clock at night before Fawn and Cole
returned to his apartment, their arms filled with packages.
They'd lingered over a long dinner at a sidewalk café, then
slowly strolled home, enjoying the night air.

"Do you think the reporters are still here?" Fawn whispered as they started up the walk.

"You wait here, I'll scout ahead," Cole whispered back
in a very creditable imitation of a cowboy in an old B western. She giggled, thinking perhaps they shouldn't have had
that last brandy after dinner; they were certainly in no condition to meet an assemblage of reporters. Yet it had been
such a relief to be able to relax at last; after the tension they'
both been under for the past few weeks, they'd needed th
chance to unwind.

Cole was back in a few minutes. "All clear," he reported
"I guess we're old news now. They're onto something else."

"Thank heavens," she said with a sigh. Cole unlocked th
door, and she dumped her packages on the carved ironwoo
table—a relic from an old sailing ship—in the entrance hall
"Flip a quarter for who gets the shower first?" she sug

gested. She suddenly felt sticky and dusty from their hours of traipsing around Manhattan under the bright sun.

"Or we could save water . . ." He didn't finish the sentence, but there was a wicked gleam in his eye and they both laughed. "No, you go first. I'll wait."

"I won't be long," she promised and, picking up one of the packages, she headed for the bathroom.

The shower produced a marvelous cooling tingle all over her body, but it was nothing compared with the delicious, and very new, sensations she felt deep inside herself as she thought of Cole and the night ahead. All day long they had been aware of what was happening between them and where it would end. The anticipation had heightened their every moment together. It had lent a special tenderness to their playful bantering and made each touch seem sensuous and meaningful. It was like the night before Christmas when she was a child, like all the nights before rolled into one, but better.

And as she quickly emerged from the shower and glanced in the mirror, she saw that she even looked different. There was a glow to her smile that had never been there before. She pulled back her thick blond curls and stared at herself. "So that's what it looks like to be in love," she whispered.

They had spent part of the afternoon buying new clothes for her—her old clothes were still at the house in the Gardens—and now she slipped into a sheer, very soft white nightgown that had been imported from France. The delicate fabric flowed gently over her curves, hinting at what was beneath, and the embroidery-edged bodice dipped just low enough to delineate the swelling of her breasts.

In the bedroom, she brushed her hair, letting it fall free to tumble around her shoulders, then traced perfume along her quickening pulse points. She could hear the water running for Cole's shower. He was singing, loudly but not well. She paused, shaking her head and smiling, as his deep, resonant voice cheerfully mangled the melody.

"We just got a telephone call from the man who wrote that song," she called through the door. "He's rushing right over to suc you."

"Wait till he hears the second chorus," Cole shouted back. "I get worse as I go along."

"Impossible," she said with a laugh.

She wandered out to the terrace, suddenly feeling as if her happiness was too great to be contained indoors. The night had turned cool, but a warm breeze still wafted gently over the city, carrying with it the heady green scent of spring, fresh and alive. The cool bricks felt good beneath her bare feet, and the breeze made the long folds of her nightgown whisper softly against her legs.

The terrace had been bordered with miniature evergreens and pots of climbing roses. Here and there a wisteria vine in full bloom spilled its blossoms over the brick wall. It all had a natural, unstudied charm that Fawn found very appealing. But slowly her gaze traveled beyond the walls to the lights of the city—hundreds of thousands of lights blazing at once, so many that the sky itself had taken on a rose-tinged hue. For a long moment her eyes drank in the sight. Despite everything that had happened here, she'd come to feel a fondness she'd never expected for this city. There'd been pain and disappointment but joy, too, and perhaps the joy outweighed all the rest. If she hadn't returned, the memory of Melissa and Joel and the love they'd shared together would have been lost to her forever. And she would never have met Lavinia or Captain Almafi or Colman Bromley or Cole. Especially Cole . . .

Suddenly he was there beside her. Fresh and clean and still slightly damp from his shower. He was wearing the terry cloth robe she'd had on a few days ago; on her it had been so large it had seemed to swallow her up, but it fit his broad shoulders and tall, rangy frame perfectly. "Mind company?" he asked softly.

She shook her head, and gestured out toward the lights. "I was just thinking how beautiful it is."

"Incredibly beautiful," he whispered, but he wasn't looking out at the city at all, only at her. He pulled a small velvet-covered box out of his pocket and held it out to her.

"What's that?" she asked, surprised.

He grinned. "What did you think all that ear tugging was for at the auction at Christie's today?"

She looked at him in amazement. They'd wandered through a number of art and photography galleries that day, ending up at the famous auction house to see the current exhibit and watch a jewelry auction. But she hadn't realized he'd bought anything. Now that she thought about it, though, she did remember his acting strangely during the auction. And afterward he had disappeared for ten minutes. Her fingers trembling, she opened the case. And then her eyes widened as she saw the shimmering crystal heart on a delicate gold chain; inside the crystal was a smaller heart carved from a flawless carat of glowing ruby.

"It's exquisite," she breathed.

"Like you," he whispered. He lifted the necklace from its case and gently fastened it around her neck. He had wanted to give her something to replace the locket that had been stolen from her. And as soon as he'd seen this, he'd known it was what he was searching for: a way of telling her his heart was as firmly held by hers as the ruby heart inside the crystal—that his future and his hopes were as indissolubly linked with hers.

"Thank you," she said and reached up to kiss him. And as their lips met, tentatively at first, and then with a growing, quickening passion, they were suddenly filled with an impatience, a hunger for each other, that left them both breathless. He pulled her closer, aware of nothing but the silken feel of her skin beneath the thin nightgown, the warm responsiveness of her touch. Trembling, his lips caressed her throat, and she arched with pleasure. "God, I love you, Fawn," he whispered, his voice suddenly husky.

She held his face gently in her hands, looking into his eyes, and said quietly, "And I love you." And then as her arms slipped around his neck, he swept her up and carried her into the bedroom. Moments later her silk nightgown and his terry-cloth robe lay forgotten in a heap on the floor.

And Fawn and Cole were lost in a private world all their own, a world of eyes and lips and hands reaching out, touching, discovering, drawing each other deeper and deeper into pleasure, all the need they'd felt suddenly blazing in a white heat. It was as if they were intoxicated with delight and wonder . . . with each other. Slowly Cole's tongue traced the full curves of her breasts, her nipples, the satiny smoothness of her stomach and down to the moist, pulsating cleft between her thighs. And her own hands were exploring, caressing, pulling him closer, her tongue teasing and greedy. Until neither of them could bear to wait another moment. With a slow, deliberate sensuousness he entered her, their rhythms matching, growing ever more urgent, until at last she cried out and heard him moan her name, and it was as if their very souls had fused together.

For a long while afterward, they lay on the bed, hushed and breathless . . . and overcome by a marvelous, melting sense of exhaustion and peace. Silently they stared at each other and smiled. A soft, golden glow from the lamp haloed the bed. Even the stars seemed to sparkle through the window with a wonderful new clarity.

Fawn rested her head on Cole's shoulder and heard his strong, sure heartbeat mingle with her own. "We fit together perfectly," she whispered.

"I checked with the factory," he said with a smile. "We were made for each other."

She nodded happily. She still felt slightly stunned, overwhelmed by the intensity of their coming together. She'd never felt like this before; it was as if the whole world had been made new and fresh. And yet at the same time, it seemed this moment had existed forever, waiting for her. And she could see by the expression in Cole's eyes that it was the same for him.

She felt too happy to stay still a minute longer. "Let's do something," she said, taking his hand and pulling him upright.

He grinned. "What did you have in mind? Bowling, tightrope walking, another shopping spree?"

"Anything—as long as it's with you."

They settled on a foraging trip to the kitchen. Cole found a package of Brie in the refrigerator, and Fawn sliced up some French bread and arranged it all on a platter. There was also a bottle of Moët in the refrigerator that Cole opened.

Fawn felt totally relaxed for the first time in weeks. And they couldn't stop smiling at each other. Or touching. No matter where they went in the large kitchen—to the refrigerator, to the cabinets to get the glasses—they found themselves brushing against each other, touching shoulders and hips, as if they'd become each other's good luck charm.

They brought the cheese and bread and wine into the living room. While Cole lit the fire already set in the fireplace, Fawn tossed a few pillows on the floor for them to sit on.

"Now then, what should we talk about?" Cole asked as they spread out in front of the fire.

"You choose," she said.

But suddenly, as he looked into her huge, luminous eyes, he wasn't interested in talking at all. And, after a moment, neither was she.

"You should have known it was too dangerous," Pete told himself for the thousandth time that morning. "You should never have let her go all by herself. You are the world's prize jackass."

Still muttering, he marched into Stapleton International Airport, totally oblivious of the people turning and staring at him. A fierce noon sun was beating against the huge windows, and Pete had packed so hurriedly he'd forgotten his sunglasses. He squinted, further deepening the frown that had been on his face for hours, and looked for a phone booth. He had to reach Fawn. He had to warn her. She was still in danger. The man who had called Pete at his home that morning had refused to identify himself, but there'd been no doubt about his message. Someone meant to hurt Fawn. His little girl . . .

Pete's jaw clenched even tighter as he remembered how vulnerable and unsuspecting Fawn was. Hadn't she just called him two days ago to tell him there was nothing more to worry about, it was all over? He had to warn her—tell her not to trust anyone, go anywhere, until he arrived.

He tried her New York number again. By now he knew it by heart. Eight, nine, ten rings and still no one answered. Where the hell was that young lawyer she was staying with? More importantly, where was Fawn? Had something happened to her already, Pete wondered as the phone continued to shrill in his ear.

He glanced at his watch. He was booked on United's Flight

162 into LaGuardia. It was scheduled to leave at 12:25, and it was already ten minutes past twelve—just enough time to pick up his ticket and get to the gate. Scowling, he hung up the phone. He couldn't chance missing this flight. As it was, he wouldn't arrive in New York until 6:00 their time. As he hurried out of the phone booth he prayed that would be soon enough.

"Maybe we should have answered that," Fawn said as she and Cole dashed down the stairs. Letting a phone ring unanswered made her feel vaguely uneasy. But they were already outside, and Cole had been locking the door before the first ring sounded.

"If it's important they'll call back," Cole said, tucking her arm in his.

"Or they could leave a message, I guess." What if it was something important? The caller had been so persistent. The phone had still been ringing when they walked away.

"Can't leave a message—I didn't turn the machine on. Anyway, it was probably just someone selling magazine subscriptions. And if you don't stop worrying, all that beautiful blond hair of yours will turn gray."

"You wouldn't like me gray?" she asked.

He stood back and studied her in mock seriousness. "Tell you what, you stick around for fifty or sixty years and I'll decide then."

"That's an awfully long time to just had around waiting for you to make up your mind, sir."

"Well, I was actually thinking of a slightly more formal arrangement—something to do with orange blossoms and a minister and marching down an aisle. You know how we lawyers like everything signed on the dotted line."

"Cole . . ." she breathed, her eyes suddenly wide and sparkling.

"This is not a proposal," he cautioned her. "For that you get champagne and a candlelight dinner and anything else can think of to make you say yes. If I'm only going to do once, I want to do it right." And very gently his fingertip brushed her cheek, and his voice was suddenly serious. "I've known for a long time, Fawn, that you were the one I was looking for. But I want you to have time to think about it, too, to be sure that I'm what you want. . . .''

She nodded. But there were no doubts in her mind at all; she already knew what her answer would be.

Cole cleared his throat, seeming to pull himself back from the seriousness of the moment, and said lightly, ''Now I'd better get myself to the office before they rent out my desk to somebody else. And you were planning on doing a little work this afternoon, too, as I recall,'' he added with a nod toward the camera case slung over her arm.

''Slave driver . . .'' she retorted, shaking her head and smiling. But actually she was itching to capture a bit of New York on film. She and Cole had spent a marvelous few days together, an indecent amount of it in bed and the rest wandering around the city, browsing through shops and museums, and feasting in one fabulous restaurant after another. Even their breakfasts would have made Diamond Jim Brady pause. Being in love certainly seemed to be good for her appetite. But now it was time to get back to the real world. Cole had work that just couldn't be put off any longer; he'd already warned her that after spending a few hours at the office this afternoon, he'd probably be bringing home a full load of work to go over tonight. And if she was going to be showing her portfolio to editors in New York, she wanted to include at least a few pictures of the city along with her work from Colorado.

Cole's office was just a short walk from his apartment, and Fawn decided she'd accompany him there and then stroll around until she found something that caught her interest. Afterwards they would meet back at his place and decide where to to go dinner.

''I'll see you at seven,'' he said, giving her a quick kiss as they reached his office building.

''Are you really going to stay that late?''

He grinned. ''That's early. When I first started you couldn't pry me away from my desk before nine or ten. And I'll bet most of the associates will still be there when I leave.'' He frowned. ''You'll be all right, won't you? If you'd rather I got home sooner . . .''

She shook her head quickly, not wanting him to worry. "I'll be fine."

He still hesitated.

"Now who's worrying? Anyway, Nick's still in jail. What could happen? Go to work."

He grinned. "Independent cuss, aren't you? But be careful, all right?" And with one last hug, he turned and entered the building.

It was nearly seven when Fawn returned to the apartment. She'd had a very productive afternoon photographing the harbor and the children in the park and the old men lounging on the benches, smoking and gossiping together. Contentedly Fawn patted the pocket of her jacket where the rolls of exposed film nestled safely next to her light meter and flash attachment. Until she found a darkroom to develop the prints she couldn't be sure of how they'd turned out, but she felt optimistic.

Cole wasn't back yet, and as she started for the bedroom to change for dinner, she wondered where they would eat tonight. So far she'd fallen in love with every place Cole had taken her. She noticed Toby was no longer following at her heels. But he was back an instant later and dropped a tennis ball at her feet. He sat down, obviously waiting for her to throw it.

"All right," she agreed, laughing. "A short game of fetch. But then I have to get ready."

Toby was just bringing the ball back the third time when the phone rang. Remembering the call they'd missed earlier, she ran to answer it.

To her surprise it was Noreen, on the line. And she sounded upset. "Well, it's about time," Noreen said. "I was beginning to wonder what I was going to do if I couldn't reach you."

"What's wrong?" Fawn asked.

"Is Cole there?"

"No. But why . . ."

"Never mind, it doesn't matter," Noreen said quickly. "But I think you'd better come out here quickly."

"Noreen, what's happened?" The obvious tension in Noreen's voice was beginning to make Fawn very uneasy.

"You have to come out here. Some man has shown up. He says his name is Pete Travers, and he wants to see you . . ."

"It can't be." And if it really was Pete, why hadn't Noreen put him on the phone? Why wasn't he the one making the call?

"That's who he says he is . . . a tall, wiry man, red hair going gray, cowboy boots," Noreen added, impatient with Fawn's doubts. And Fawn knew it had to be Pete. Dammit, what could have gotten into his head, showing up like this?

"The problem is," Noreen was saying, "he no sooner got here than he started to feel ill. I don't think it's serious, probably just something he ate on the plane, but I don't think he should be wandering around the city on his own."

"I'll come out there right away," Fawn said quickly. She could bring him back here to Cole's.

"Please hurry," Noreen said, already sounding relieved.

"I'm on my way," Fawn assured her.

Halfway to the door, Fawn realized Cole wouldn't know where she'd gone. She thought of calling his office, but he'd probably already left. A note would be quicker. Hurriedly she scribbled a few words on the note pad by the phone and propped it up on the counter where he'd be sure to see it.

"Cole, you're finally going to meet Pete. I've gone to pick him up now. Explain when I get back.

Love, F."

And a few seconds later she was out the door, never even seeing Toby sitting with the tennis ball in his mouth, patiently waiting for her to resume their game of fetch.

Chapter 34

"*Fawn* will be here very soon," Noreen told Pete as she came back into the kitchen.

"Thank you, ma'am. I really could have called her myself. It was kind of you to insist on doing it for me. In fact, I guess I should have gone straight to where she's staying, but I didn't think to get the address. Luckily that man on the phone—the one I told you about—gave me this address."

He smiled, trying to think of something else to say. It wasn't that he felt like talking—he was too worried about Fawn—but he couldn't think of any other way to calm this woman down. And again he wondered what was wrong with her. From the moment she'd answered the door she'd been a bundle of nerves, all wired up like a race horse at the starting line. No, worse, he corrected himself—like a race horse shot full of amphetamines or something. Even now her eyes were moving nervously around the kitchen, her hands clenching and unclenching spasmodically.

"This is a real pretty house you got here," he said at last. "Never seen anything quite like it."

Noreen jumped, then forced herself to smile. The effort

was obvious—all the muscles in her face seemed to resist, and the smile kept threatening to turn into something closer to a snarl. It was an expression Pete had seen before in animals that felt trapped. But certainly she had nothing to fear from him. He'd tried his best to make that clear.

"You haven't drunk your coffee," she said suddenly. "You have to drink your coffee."

He brought the cup to his lips. He didn't really want it; his stomach was close to rebelling as it was. But if it would make her feel better . . .

Her eyes never left the cup, and when he put it down, he noticed she checked to see how much was left. It was almost empty.

Suddenly he had an idea what might be troubling her. Maybe it was this room. The newspaper had said this was where Fawn's parents were murdered. Perhaps all the talk about the murders lately had made Noreen nervous about being in this room.

"What are you thinking?" she asked abruptly.

"Just that . . ." he stammered awkwardly, then decided things couldn't get any worse. "This is where they were murdered, isn't it?"

To his surprise she seemed eager to talk about it. "Yes, in this room. Melissa was sitting right where you are now. And Joel was over by the door. He was coming up the stairs, you see. He'd been in the basement."

Pete tried to nod; for Fawn's sake it was important that he learn as much as he could about that night, and he wanted to encourage Noreen to continue. But all of a sudden even the smallest gesture seemed to require more energy than he could muster. His head was beginning to ache, and he felt lethargic and confused.

Noreen was still talking, but her voice seemed to be coming from a distance now. "It's not easy to kill someone with a knife, you know. You need to study a book of anatomy first, know just where to make the thrust. Melissa was harder. She was the first. Her throat had to be cut. But with Joel the knife hit home the first time."

Her face had a horribly smug look on. And there was a reckless, almost rabid glitter in her eyes. An appalling sus-

picion began to penetrate Pete's dulled mind. No, it couldn't
be. . . .

"It was really a case of self-defense, you know," Noreen
continued. "Melissa and Joel were trying to get rid of me.
Me and my son, Scott. To make room for their new baby.
'The doctor thinks it's going to be a boy,' " she mimicked,
her mouth pursed nastily, then dropped back into her own
petulant voice. "So they looked around for a reason to get
rid of us—and found it. I knew what they were up to. No
warned me." She leaned across the table and whispered con
fidingly, "All their talk about how I should take Scott to a
psychiatrist—just because he'd been kicked out of school—
that was only a trick. An excuse. It was me they wanted to
have locked away, committed."

Pete shook his head, trying to clear it. Surely he couldn't
have heard her right. Fawn had told him they already had the
killer locked up, hadn't she?

"I should have guessed from all the questions Melissa and
Joel were asking," Noreen went on. "They'd always wanted
to know who Scott's father was, but when Scott started hav
ing problems . . ." Her voice rose hysterically, "There wa
nothing wrong with him—he wasn't anything like his father
I'd made sure of that. Scott was mine, all mine. And he loved
me. He was the only person in the world who loved me."
She looked at Pete angrily. "You don't understand. Meliss
and Joel didn't understand, either. Somehow they must hav
found out the truth, and when they did all they could thin
of was locking me away . . . hiding the dirty, ugly truth. W
were too tainted to be around their precious little Fawn o
their new baby . . . But I was too smart for them."

Good Lord, she's crazy, Pete thought as he listened to he
wild, incoherent ramblings. None of it made any sense—
except for one unmistakable fact: This woman had killed
Fawn's parents. And she intended to kill again. There coul
be no other reason for her admitting to all this now; sh
didn't expect him to be around to repeat it. But why had sh
lured him here in the first place? The answer came to hir
with a sickening certainty. It wasn't he she was after at al
It was Fawn. He was only the bait in the trap.

He had to get away—somehow stop Fawn before sh

reached the house, before Noreen could get to her. Frantically Pete struggled to stand up. But his legs refused to work. They were numb, seemed paralyzed.

Noreen, watching him, smirked. "You might as well give up. You're not going anywhere."

Pete ignored her; all his concentration was focused on getting out of his chair. But he was growing weaker by the moment. It was becoming an effort even to remain upright.

"Stop fighting it," Noreen said sharply. "I put enough sedative in your coffee to knock out an elephant."

He stared; her figure was no more than a blur to him now.

"Haldol," she explained. "It's used to treat psychotic disorders. It's odorless, colorless, tasteless . . . There's no way you could have known. And it won't even show up in their tests later. You see, we thought of everything. This time nothing's going to go wrong."

Leaning on his arms and trying to force himself up, Pete made one last stubborn effort to rise. But all he managed to do was knock the coffee cup to the floor; it hit the tiles with a clatter, and the little bit of coffee still left in the cup puddled on the floor.

"Looks like this isn't your day to be a hero," Noreen said as she watched Pete's body slump back against the chair. His helplessness seemed to amuse her.

It was growing dark outside. "Where the hell is Fawn?" Noreen asked suddenly. She stood up and began pacing the kitchen, yanking at the blinds to make sure they were shut as tightly as possible and flipping on lights. She came over to the table and propped Pete's sagging body back up, then nodded as if satisfied with the effect. "Can you hear me?" she whispered.

Pete's eyelids flickered, but he remained silent. He had to save his strength. Somehow warn Fawn when she arrived . . .

"This is her fault, not mine," Noreen insisted; a pulse had begun to twitch in her forehead, and her voice was rasping and harsh. "Everyone had forgotten until Fawn came back and started poking her nose where it didn't belong. Just like her mother—all sweetness and innocence and the whole time she was trying to destroy me." Noreen stopped suddenly and raised her head; the doorbell had just rung.

"She's here," Noreen whispered as the bell chimed again. "And this time I've made sure she won't be able to run away."

Noreen glanced once more at Pete, saw he hadn't moved, and hurried to the door. She appeared perfectly composed. "Come in, Fawn. We've been waiting for you."

"Where's Pete?"

"In the kitchen—go right on in."

"Is he feeling better?"

"Why don't you go see?" Noreen answered, locking the door behind Fawn, who was already on her way to the kitchen. There were three separate locks—not unusual for a house in the city—and Noreen made sure she locked them all as well as put the safety chain on. The other doors and windows were locked up just as tightly, the telephone wires cut. Yes, everything was ready. Noreen patted the long, sharpened knife in her pocket; she was wearing carpenter's pants and the deep pocket hid the blade perfectly. Afterward she'd have to remember to burn her clothes. It would, she knew, be impossible to get all the blood out of them. . . .

In the kitchen, Fawn had forgotten all about Noreen. "My God, Pete, what happened?" she asked frantically, kneeling beside his slumping figure. His face was slack and expressionless, and there was no color in it at all. He looked as if he'd had a heart attack or stroke. Why hadn't Noreen told her, called for an ambulance? They had to get him to a hospital.

But as Fawn clutched Pete's hand, a hint of life returned to his eyes. He opened his mouth, trying to speak, and she leaned closer, straining to hear the slurred, laboriously formed words. "Run, Fawn . . ." he whispered. "Get away . . . she killed your . . ."

"Parents," Noreen finished for him, suddenly appearing in the doorway. "That's what you're trying to tell her, isn't it, Pete? But your warning's just a little too late."

"No . . ." Fawn whispered. But as her eyes met Noreen's she knew it was true. Nick hadn't murdered her parents—Noreen had. Noreen, who stood there now with a long, flashing butcher knife clenched in her fist and her eyes narrowed in a feral, malevolent eagerness. All at once Fawn felt as she'd been hurled back in time; she was a child again, terrified, paralyzed with horror and disbelief, staring into the face of her parents' killer. A face she'd trusted, but now warped and hideous with rage. Noreen's face.

But the memory's returned too late to save me, Fawn realized. Or Pete . . . And with that thought anger exploded inside her. No, not this time, she vowed. Not Pete, too.

"What did you do to him?" she demanded.

"He's just drugged. You see, you two are going to have a little falling out—a fatal one," Noreen explained. "The police will assume he got impatient for his cut of the inheritance. It should be an easy story to sell. They still haven't entirely given up the idea that whoever you've been living with might be an accomplice in your parents' deaths. And neither of you will be alive to say any differently."

While Noreen talked, Fawn glanced around the kitchen, searching for some way to save herself and Pete. The door to the outside was triple-locked, but she couldn't have left Pete anyway; he was totally defenseless, too groggy now even to understand what was going on. She would have to stop Noreen by herself. But how? Noreen was bigger than she was—taller, heavier, undoubtedly stronger. If Fawn was going to have any chance at all, somehow she had to throw Noreen off balance.

"Are you sure you thought of everything, Noreen?" Fawn asked. "All it will take is one small mistake for the police to figure out it was you." But even as she spoke the words, Fawn wondered if there was even one small speck of rationality left in Noreen to appeal to.

Noreen laughed. "Ned worked out every detail. He's out right now establishing our alibi. And do you really believe I'm stupid enough to think you're worried about me, about what happens to me? You're just like your mother. You'd like nothing better than to see me locked up for the rest of my life. I knew right away what you were after with all your poking around, prying into the past."

Fawn started to shake her head, but Noreen wasn't about to be stopped; the words spewed out of her, harsh and guteral and filled with hate. "Yes, you're just like Melissa. My sweet sister, everyone loved her. Joel . . . Even Colman.

And now you have Cole. But nobody ever cared about me. I never understood. Why did my father love her and not me? I was just as pretty. I tried harder to please him than she ever did. But he couldn't stand to even look at me. And then I found out why; he wasn't my father at all. You probably found that out, too, didn't you?'' Noreen asked abruptly, her eyes fixed on Fawn.

Fawn nodded, remembering Lavinia telling her the story—the man who'd beaten Noreen's mother when he discovered she was pregnant, who'd embezzled every penny from the company the family owned.

"So I went looking for my father," Noreen went on "You're so eager to know the truth, to go digging around in other people's secrets. Let me tell you the rest of it. I was only eighteen when I found him. He'd come back to my mother, wanting money. He'd gone through all his. Drank it I imagine. He was living in a cheap hotel—I can still remember the smell of mildew and urine in the hall, the cockroaches running across the floor. He wasn't even handsome anymore But I didn't care. I thought at last I'd found someone who'd love me. Me . . .'' She clenched the knife so tightly her knuckles turned white, but her eyes were no longer focused on Fawn; she was seeing another time, another place.

"He pretended to be glad to see me. I don't think he ever knew who I was—or cared. I was just some young girl who would buy him drinks, let him touch her. He took me up to his room. I tried to explain how I'd waited for him to come back for me, but his hands were pawing at . . . He pushed me down on the bed . . . I didn't understand. . . .'' And suddenly Noreen was looking at her beseechingly. "Don't you see, I'd never . . . It wasn't my fault.''

Fawn nodded, and for just a moment she hoped . . . but then Noreen gripped the knife tightly again, and the hardness returned to her eyes.

"I didn't mean to kill him. He was trying to keep me from leaving after . . . afterward, and he was drunk, and his head hit the bed post. But no one would have believed me. No one has ever taken my side.''

"You didn't tell anyone?'' Fawn asked.

"Just Ned, after I found out I was pregnant. I knew Ne

wouldn't try to take Scott away from me. Scottie's the only thing I've ever had that was all mine. I won't ever let him find out who his father was. After you're gone, he'll come back to me. He'll stop asking questions.

"Yes." Noreen nodded, her lips twisting into an odd smile, "Once you're dead, everyone will forget all about this." Her eyes fell on Pete, slumped over in his chair. "Once you're both dead. . . ." And she began to close in, her eyes as cold and hard as the blade in her hand.

Desperately Fawn tugged at Pete's shoulder, trying to rouse him, but he was unconscious. He was too heavy to lift, and she couldn't abandon him. Noreen was counting on that; by immobilizing Pete, she'd trapped Fawn, too.

Think . . . Fawn urged herself frantically, trying to fight down her panic. But the word echoed uselessly inside her head; there was no way out.

Noreen was still advancing. She was only a few feet away now. Fawn tensed, her whole body trembling; somehow she had to get the knife away from Noreen, stop her.

"Forget it, Fawn," Noreen hissed, taking another step forward. "You're no match for me."

For a moment the two women faced each other. Fawn gripped the back of Pete's chair, fumbling frantically in her pocket with her other hand for something, anything to use as a weapon. And as her hand closed around a small, squared object, she knew there was a chance. One chance . . .

Noreen was already raising the knife, rushing forward. "I'm going to show you how your mother died, Fawn."

But just as the knife slashed toward Pete's throat, the room exploded in a blinding white flash of light. Noreen fell backward, staggering, the knife clattering to the floor as her hands flew to her suddenly sightless eyes. And in that instant Fawn slammed into her, driving her against the wall before she could recover. Together they tumbled toward the basement steps. Noreen clawed blindly at the doorjamb, but Fawn was already pushing her down the stairs. With the last of her strength Fawn slammed the door shut and locked it. And as she leaned against the door, fighting to get her breath back, she could hear Noreen on the other side pounding to get out.

"My God, it worked. . . ." Fawn told herself, still not

quite believing it. "It worked." And she blessed the luck that had prompted her to spend the day shooting photographs, that had kept her from emptying her pockets at Cole's apartment. If she hadn't been carrying that automatic flash . . .

As soon as she'd felt it in her pocket, she'd known it was her only chance. Like most photographers, Fawn usually carried a separate flash gun that worked independently of the camera. And it had a voltage power that was temporarily blinding—especially if it went off right in someone's face. And Noreen had taken the full force of the flash; it would be a while before her sight returned to normal. Enough time, Fawn hoped, for help to arrive.

Her knees still weak, Fawn crossed the kitchen and put her arms around Pete. She'd have to get to a phone, call the police. But right now she just needed to reassure herself they were both safe. She felt drained, sickened by what she'd done and by the memory of the tortured hate she'd seen in Noreen's face. And she could still hear Noreen cursing and raging through the thick locked door.

But suddenly a new sound made her raise her head. The sound of the front door opening. Relief washed over her—it was Cole; he'd gotten her message and realized something was wrong. But then she knew it couldn't be Cole. She hadn't told him where she was meeting Pete; he'd just assume she'd gone to the airport. And Cole didn't have a key . . . There was something she'd forgotten.

The answer was there in the open doorway. Ned. And he had a gun in his hand.

Chapter 35

For a long moment Ned and Fawn stood staring at each other. He seemed as startled as she was; obviously he hadn't expected her to still be alive. Keeping his eyes on her, he used his foot to push the door behind him closed, while he kept the gun still trained on her. "Where's Noreen?" he demanded.

Fawn shrugged, pretending not to understand. Somehow she had to keep him away from the kitchen, away from Pete. And she silently prayed that the lock on the basement door would hold, that Noreen wouldn't somehow manage to get free.

"I know Noreen's here," he said, his eyes darting warily around the room. He frowned, trying to figure out what had gone wrong.

Fawn began cautiously edging the wide, curving stairway that led to the second floor. If she could just get upstairs . . . he would have to follow. And with all those rooms, it would take him forever to find her.

Ned, too distracted by his own thoughts, seemed almost to have forgotten her. She took another step. And suddenly the

cut crystal lamp on the table beside her exploded in a thousand flying fragments, and a split second later she heard the
solid, deadly thud of the bullet embedding itself in the wall.
A gray wisp of smoke was coming from the silencer at the
end of the gun barrel. "You're not as smart as you think you
are, Fawn," Ned said, smiling as he watched the color drain
from her face. "In fact, you've done me a favor getting rid
of Noreen—however you managed it. I never planned for her
to survive this little family bloodbath."

Fawn stared at him, chilled by the brusque, businesslike
tone of his voice, the inhuman blankness of his eyes. Noreen
had been all hot rage, but he was as cold and soulless as a
balance sheet. And that made him twice as dangerous, Fawn
realized.

"I knew Noreen was close to breaking; she always was
unstable," he went on. "All that guilt she was carrying
around; it was so easy to make her believe that Melissa and
Joel had discovered her sad little secret. There's nothing like
guilt to foster an active imagination. She was pathetic
really."

"Then Melissa and Joel never planned on having her committed?"

Ned choked on his laughter. "I had those committment
papers forged. It was just the right touch to drive Noreen
over the edge." He seemed eager to let Fawn know how
clever he'd been. "The whole plan would have worked to
perfection—if only you hadn't gotten away that night."

"But why?" Fawn asked. "Joel had taken you into the
company. . . ."

"And he was going to fire me," Ned interrupted harshly.
"Couldn't have a thief working for him, he said. But I beat
him. I'm going to end up with every penny of the Dalswort
fortune. Noreen was stupid enough to think she could get
half, but just last night she made the mistake of telling me
where she'd hidden the bonds she'd taken from my room."

So he'd been hiding the money he'd embezzled in his room,
Fawn thought. Keeping it handy so he could gloat over it.
But the knowledge wasn't going to do her any good now. He
only wanted her to know how thoroughly he'd beaten them

all before he killed her. "Did you try to kill Bromley, too?" Fawn asked, stalling for time.

Ned laughed. "No, that fool, Nick, got caught with his hand in the till. It's quite funny, really. That society wife of his was blackmailing him, and he was stealing the bonds. Only he didn't know they were fake. I have the real ones.

"As next of kin, I shouldn't have any trouble getting the letter Noreen sent to Coleman's office with the claim ticket. Then I'll have everything." Ned told her. "Even the art. Noreen never found that. So you see, at this point, Noreen would have just been in the way. Sooner or later she'd have cracked, babbled the whole story."

Fawn remembered Noreen's crazed ramblings and knew he was right; the careful facade Noreen had maintained all these years was disintegrating. If the police ever questioned her, everything would spew out like a geyser: a sulphurous, poisoned stream that would reveal Ned's secret to the world. How he had manipulated her, played on her fears, how he was the one behind Melissa's and Joel's deaths. But Ned would make sure Noreen never got to the police. . . .

The antique grandfather clock in the study began to toll the hour and Ned frowned, suddenly gripping the gun tighter.

"Your time's up, Fawn."

She edged backward, trying to keep the fear from showing on her face. "You've been *too* clever, Ned. With Nick in jail and everyone else dead, you're the only suspect the police will have left."

"But everyone knows I'm spending the day at the office. I was very careful to sign in, make sure I was remembered," he said calmly. "No one knows I slipped out through the executive garage. Especially as I left a tape running. Right now they can hear me moving around, dictating letters . . ." He took a step forward purposefully. "Now tell me where Pete is, and we'll get this over with."

Fawn ran, desperately sprinting toward the darkened study as Ned fired. The shot whistled past her, whining in her ears and ricocheting just inches from her head. She dove toward the floor.

And as she listened to Ned's steps coming closer, the front door crashed open and Cole was barreling through it, heading straight for Ned. Ned whirled around, firing wildly. But Cole was already slamming into him, the two men grappling together, Cole twisting Ned's wrist until at last the gun clattered to the floor. Ned scrambled for the gun but Cole yanked him back. For a moment it was just a blur of bodies, and then Cole's fist connected solidly with Ned's jaw and Ned slumped to the floor, his head hitting the marble with a loud thud. Cole stood over him, still panting, but Ned wasn't moving; he'd been knocked unconscious.

"Fawn? . . ." Cole called, his eyes worriedly searching the room for her. Slowly, her knees still weak, she stood up.

"How did you know?" she whispered.

"I called your grandmother in Colorado. It didn't make any sense that Pete should suddenly come here against your advice. Someone must have talked with him. Your grandmother didn't know who had made the call, but she knew Pete was told to come to this address. As soon as I heard that, I was sure something was wrong." Cole picked up the gun and dropped it into his pocket, checking to make sure Ned was still out cold. "Where is Pete?" he asked.

"In the kitchen. They drugged him."

"They? . . ."

"Ned and Noreen . . . I locked her in the cellar. Oh God, Cole, it all came back to me; I remembered everything. It was Noreen that night . . . she hated us. . . ."

"Hush," he whispered, rocking Fawn gently in his arms. "It's all over now."

He led her to the couch as tenderly as if she were a fragile, long-lost treasure, and sat down next to her. In a few minutes they would call the police, but right now all she wanted was to feel Cole's arms around her. "It's over," she whispered, still not quite believing it.

Softly Cole brushed her hair back and caressed her cheek. "It's over," he assured her. And then he smiled, and there was such love in his eyes that the rest of the world seemed to melt away to nothing. "And for us, it's just beginning. . . ."

Be sure to look for the next sizzling novel of romantic suspense coming to you in August from Lynx Books

THE SABLE NIGHT

Ernestine Hill

When beautiful Aunica Shaw returns to her waterfront home on Galveston Bay, little does she suspect the grave danger that awaits her there. Through the long, dark hours of night, she listens terrified to the sounds of boats and footsteps along the coast, to the eerie thunder of the relentless tropical storms, and to the ominous voices of her dreams, wondering at their veiled message.

Not knowing whether to trust the handsome man who has taken over her home, Aunica's fear builds. Even as she gives in to her desire for him—the same mesmerizing emotion that draws others to her land in search of buried pirate's treasure—she is wary of the dark secrets shrouded in the cloudy golden depths of his eyes. And as the nightmare closes in on her she struggles to make sense of the confused haze of her emotions before she loses her heart *and* her life.

DESIRE

Scandalous world of the elite.

Susannah Erwin

More Than Rivals...

Seven Years Of Secrets

MILLS & BOON

MORE THAN RIVALS...
© 2023 by Susannah Erwin
Philippine Copyright 2023
Australian Copyright 2023
New Zealand Copyright 2023

First Published 2023
First Australian Paperback Edition 2023
ISBN 978 1 867 28205 1

SEVEN YEARS OF SECRETS
© 2023 by Susannah Erwin
Philippine Copyright 2023
Australian Copyright 2023
New Zealand Copyright 2023

First Published 2023
First Australian Paperback Edition 2023
ISBN 978 1 867 28205 1

MIX
Paper | Supporting
responsible forestry
FSC® C001695

Published by
Harlequin Mills & Boon
An imprint of Harlequin Enterprises (Australia) Pty Limited
(ABN 47 001 180 918), a subsidiary of HarperCollins
Publishers Australia Pty Limited
(ABN 36 009 913 517)
Level 19, 201 Elizabeth Street
SYDNEY NSW 2000 AUSTRALIA

Cover art used by arrangement with Harlequin Books S.A.. All rights reserved.

Printed and bound in Australia by McPherson's Printing Group

More Than Rivals...

MILLS & BOON

A former Hollywood studio executive who gladly traded in her high heels and corner office for yoga pants and the local coffee shop, **Susannah Erwin** loves writing about ambitious, strong-willed people who can't help falling in love—whether they want to or not. Her first novel won the Golden Heart® Award from Romance Writers of America and she is hard at work in her Northern California home on her next. She would be over the moon if you signed up for her newsletter via www.susannaherwin.com.

Visit the Author Profile page
at millsandboon.com.au for more titles.

You can also find Susannah Erwin on Facebook,
along with other Harlequin Desire authors,
at Facebook.com/HarlequinDesireAuthors!

Dear Reader,

Welcome to the secrets and scandals of the Lochlainn family! This new two-part series begins with media mogul Keith Lochlainn, who has recently been given a terminal diagnosis. He decides to hold a contest to determine which of his newly discovered grandchildren should inherit his empire by giving them each a business objective to complete. This is a tale that has been percolating in my head for a long time, and I'm so thrilled to finally share it with you.

More Than Rivals... is the story of the first grandchild, Anna, and the setting is very dear to my heart: a theme park! I had so much fun creating my own tourist destination—after years of spending my vacations at theme parks in California and Florida—and I hope you have fun, too! And what theme park is complete without a nighttime spectacular? But the real fireworks take place between Anna and her rival to control the theme park, the enigmatic—and oh so sexy—Ian Blackburn. Anna finds herself forced to choose between pleasing her recently found grandfather and her heart...while Ian has his own family secrets to contend with that might stand in the way of a fairy-tale happily-ever-after.

Please enjoy Anna and Ian's story, and please also feel free to contact me! I'd love to know your thoughts. You can find me on Twitter, @susannaherwin; on Facebook at susannaherwinauthor; on BookBub, @susannaherwin; or at my website, www.susannaherwin.com.

Happy reading!

xoxo

Susannah

DEDICATION

For Charlotte,
but not until you're old enough to read this

PROLOGUE

Six months ago

KEITH LOCHLAINN COULD no longer deny reality.

He was dying.

Oh, not today. Probably not even this year.

But the doctor's report clutched in his hand—the fifth doctor he had consulted—confirmed what he had already been told: his heart had a looming expiration date and he was out of options to push the day back. No medical procedure would save him from the inevitable.

And it was inevitable, wasn't it? This wasn't news to him. All living things had a finite amount of time.

But he'd thought he would have more time to put his affairs in order. More opportunities to arrange who would succeed him at the helm of the Lochlainn Company, the multinational media conglomerate started by his father, Archibald. Control of the company still stayed within the family, with most of the shares still held by Keith. After he died, however...

Keith crumpled the sheets of paper into a ball. This was why he preferred paper to computer files; paper was far easier to destroy. Easier to pretend he'd never read the contents in the first place.

He'd planned to leave the company to his only child, Jamie. The regret of his life was that he hadn't sired more children, followed by the regret that his desire to do so had driven Jamie away as a teenager when Keith had divorced his mother, Diana, to marry a younger woman. For decades, Keith had feared he would have no heir, as wife number two through wife number five produced no offspring and Jamie rebuffed all attempts at contact, refusing any and all financial support offered by Keith.

Then, seven years ago, his son had returned to him. Smart, driven, and ambitious, Jamie had built a famed name for himself as an investigative journalist, using an old family name on his mother's side to avoid being connected to his father. But then Jamie had met someone and, although the relationship fizzled, he'd decided the globe-trotting life wasn't conducive to eventually raising a family. He'd contacted

Keith about working for the Lochlainn Company and was welcomed back with open arms, any past grievances forgiven and forgotten.

But their reconciliation had been too good to be true.

Keith sighed, his shoulders slumping. He still had energy. He could and did run rings around the arrogant MBAs who ran the various divisions of the Lochlainn Company, who believed they could steer the organization better than he could. He'd be damned if he allowed his family's legacy to pass to that bunch of hyenas after his death.

A knock at the door caused Keith to snap his head up. His current wife, Catalina, entered the library, carrying a tray heaped with plates and glasses. Didn't see a coffee mug on the tray, damn it. No more caffeine for him. He stared at a generous arrangement of imported cheeses. She intercepted his look and brought him a salad.

"Chef made this for you." She placed a bowl filled with leafy greens on the table in front of his wing chair. "The rest of the food is for your one o'clock meeting."

Keith nodded and took a bite, chewing the spinach leaves methodically. Catalina settled into the chair next to him and fixed him with her dark gaze. "You're thinking about Jamie again," she said softly.

"You think you can read me so well? Bah." Keith stabbed a cherry tomato with his fork.

"I know what today is. It's hard to believe it's been seven years since…well. Since."

Keith put his fork down. If his wife wanted to poke the bear, he would oblige. "Seven years of idiotic bureaucratic tangling with the French authorities. Seven years of wasted investigations." He pointed at her. "I didn't want him declared dead. You pushed me into it."

She smiled sadly at him. "Keith, he was gone immediately. He couldn't have survived the explosion. The yacht was nothing but matchsticks. And even if he did, he would have drowned in the aftermath. Everyone agrees."

"You want to move on," Keith muttered. "You wanted Jamie declared dead, so you have unfettered claim to my money when I'm gone."

"You know that's not true. I'm not entitled to anything from you. Nor do I want your money." She placed a glass of water on the table and portioned out three pills from a plastic box, handing the first one to him. "But it was fun playing this game with you. Never gets old."

"Bah," Keith said again, and swallowed the pill. "Where's Bingham?"

Another knock sounded. Catalina rose and opened the door, and then turned back to Keith. "He's right on time."

Bingham Lockwood brushed past Catalina and planted himself in front of Keith, remaining standing.

Keith looked up at him. "Well?" he barked.

Bingham slid his gaze over to Catalina, who had followed him back into the library, and raised his eyebrows. She shook her head slightly.

"Speak," Keith snapped. "I can handle it. Don't pay attention to her."

After another exchange of glances with Catalina, Bingham handed a manila folder thick with printouts to Keith. He took it with trembling hands and placed it on the table next to his abandoned lunch. He couldn't make himself open it. "Just give me the news."

"There are two confirmed living results," Bingham said. "We're searching for more, but the records indicate this might be all."

Two. Keith exhaled. "Names? Ages? Genders?"

"Wait." Catalina picked up the folder. "You're sure?"

Bingham nodded. "We received much cooperation from former staff at the fertility clinic. The Lochlainn name goes a long way."

"And the Lochlainn checkbook, no doubt," Catalina said under her breath. "Please tell me you didn't violate any privacy or HIPAA laws."

Bingham kept his gaze focused on Keith. "Per Jamie's college roommate, Jamie supplemented his ability to pay for his university tuition by making sperm deposits at the fertility clinic in exchange for payment. There were two successful pregnancies attached to his identity number. We have ascertained the names and locations of the resulting children."

"I don't think—" Catalina started, but Keith spoke over her.

"Tell me everything about them," he demanded. "Now."

Keith was dying, true. But now he had heirs. And he'd be damned if he died before seeing one of them succeed him at the helm of the Lochlainn Company.

The only question was which heir should he choose?

ONE

IAN BLACKBURN AVOIDED three things.

One, large crowds of people. He preferred gatherings where one could easily converse—and easily escape the conversation, should it become necessary, which often it was. There were drawbacks to having one of the country's more recognizable surnames.

Two, holidays. In his estimation, they were trumped-up excuses to sell consumer goods and pressure people into celebrating whether they wanted to or not. Not that he begrudged the existence of greeting card companies and producers of holiday movies. Companies had to turn a profit, after all, and there was a lucrative audience for forced cheer and blatant heartstring tugging. Blackburn Amusements, his family's business better known as BBA, did its best business around federal holidays when people had extra time off work to enjoy the thrill rides and other forms of entertainment on offer. But Ian had learned all too early in his life to beware of emotional manipulation.

And third of his list of avoidances: Lakes of Wonder, the theme park owned by one of BBA's fiercest rivals, the Lochlainn Company.

Tonight boded to be a personal hell of epic proportions, considering the date on his smartwatch read October 31 and he stood amid a raucous crowd of costumed partygoers eager to celebrate Halloween, packed tightly into a hotel rooftop restaurant and adjoining terrace to celebrate the holiday. And not just any hotel: the Shelter Cove Hotel, which stood at the front gate of Lakes of Wonder.

In short, a perfect trifecta of Ian's worst nightmares.

But he was willing to overlook his aversion to all things saccharine and overly manufactured and to ignore the heavy press of attendees. If all went to plan, Ian would accomplish the goal that kept him going, day and night, despite the difficulty of the last several years. And only one thing stood in his way:

Anna Stratford. The newly appointed Lochlainn Company executive who held his future captive with a stroke of her signing pen.

If only he knew who she was.

Ian's gaze searched the other guests at the party. It was an interesting mixture. Most of the people had paid—and paid dearly—for the privilege of celebrating Halloween at tonight's party. The attendees wore elaborate getups, most of them inspired by the costumed characters who roamed the theme park during the day. While there were trick-or-treat stations set up around the terrace for the guests to help themselves to candy and soft drinks, the real draw of the event was the spectacular view of Lakes of Wonder, lit up below them and picture-perfect for selfies to be splashed across guests' social media accounts. People began staking out the perceived best place from which to watch the promised fireworks show almost as soon as the doors opened and refused to budge as the party grew more crowded, leading in one case to near fisticuffs.

Thankfully, Ian didn't have to contend with the worst of the crowds. He was in the section of the terrace cordoned off with velvet ropes for invited guests and other VIPs, the area guarded by a Lakes of Wonder executive wearing a headset and flanked by two imposing security guards. Here candy stations continued to be available but were joined by tables heaped with sugary desserts as well as several open bars. But most of the VIP guests shunned the food—although not the alcohol—choosing instead to gather in small groups, exchanging murmured conversation. Not a few turned to glance in his direction, their gazes darting away the moment he caught them looking. No doubt they were discussing why the CEO of rival amusement park company, BBA, was at a Lakes of Wonder party.

Let them look. The public would soon discover why he was there.

"You would not believe what I went through to get these." Tai Nguyen, the senior vice president of strategy and operations for BBA, appeared at Ian's side. He carried half-full glasses of neon-green liquid with light-up plastic ice cubes in the shape of Seamus Sea Serpent, the mascot of Lakes of Wonder, floating on top. The ice cube changed color as Ian stared at it, from neon yellow to fuchsia to aqua blue. A more unappetizing sight Ian would be hard-pressed to conceive of.

Tai tried to hand one of the glasses to Ian, but he refused to take it. Tai shrugged. "You're missing out," he warned.

"Humans aren't meant to consume beverages that glow in the dark. And that's without the fake ice cube." Ian turned his attention back to the theme park.

Tai shook his head. "This drink encapsulates the quintessential Lakes of Wonder experience," he said. "Whimsy. Colorful. Fantastical." He took a sip from the drink in his right hand and wrinkled his nose. "On the surface. Watered down and not as strong as it once was underneath."

"I'm impressed you got all that. Very appropriate metaphor. 'Watered down and not as strong as it once was' is an accurate description of this place." Ian's gaze was caught by the Lighthouse of Amazement; the towering icon of the park was lit in orange and purple spotlights for Halloween. The Lighthouse was once famous the world over as a symbol not only for Lakes of Wonder but as the main logo for the Lochlainn Company, the vast multimedia conglomerate that owned the theme park as well as a film studio, television networks, several news organizations and a publishing house, among other businesses. However, seven years ago, the Lochlainn Company changed its branding to be an interlocking "L" and "C," removing all trace of the Lighthouse.

And soon the Lochlainn Company wouldn't own Lakes of Wonder.

Tai followed his gaze. "It's a shame."

Ian shot him a look. "What is?"

"That the Lochlainn Company let Lakes of Wonder get so rundown in the last decade or so. To think that it was more popular than Disneyland back in the day."

"For a short day," Ian said. "The first amusement parks, like Coney Island, were more like carnivals with rides with iffy safety records and disreputable clientele. Lakes of Wonder was the first amusement park with immersive, themed areas. But then Walt Disney did it bigger and arguably better, and now everyone thinks Disneyland was the first to offer a family-friendly experience. And, of course, BBA came next, and our parks provide more thrills." His gaze traced the outline of the lighthouse. "Although the original design of Lakes of Wonder was revolutionary. The technology in some of the original rides is so advanced, it hasn't been improved." He knew that for a fact because Cooper Blackburn's name was on the patents. Ian's great-grandfather, who had been Archibald Lochlainn's original partner in Lakes of Wonder before their partnership ended in acrimony and Cooper struck out on his own, founding BBA as Blackburn Amusements.

"To be honest, I prefer Lakes of Wonder to Disneyland. I know it's smaller and not as well-maintained. But there's something about taking that slow ferry between all the different lands that I really enjoy. It's…oddly relaxing."

"Not lands, ports," Ian corrected. "Each themed area is supposed to be a different port on a different lake. Buccaneer Bayou, Valhalla Fjord, Heroic Harbour, et cetera. The exception is the Lighthouse of Amazement, which is on an island at the center where all the lakes converge." Another design by his great-grandfather, who'd gown up on Mackinac Island in Michigan and used the Great Lakes as his inspiration. Of course, if one asked the Lochlainns, they'd point to their name—Gaelic for "land of lakes"—as the inspiration for the park, but Ian knew which story he believed.

"Well, I, for one, look forward to conquering the ports." Tai saluted Ian with his second drink. "Once the park is ours, that is,"

"It will be." Ian pulled his gaze away from the Lighthouse. He'd have all the time in the world to inspect Lakes of Wonder after the deal was signed. There was only one small possible wrinkle in his plans, and he was at the party to meet her ahead of time. "When you were getting the drinks, did you ask about Anna Stratford?"

Tai shook his head. "I barely escaped the crush at the bar alive. But earlier I ran into a few Lochlainn Company execs who were also looking for her. She must be from the New York headquarters. No one associated with the park or the LA office seems to know who she is."

Ian's stomach clenched. "Interesting."

Tai shrugged. "You think so? She's probably a business development exec or someone on their legal team who finagled a boondoggle trip to California to rubberstamp the sale of the park. We've both commented on how uninterested the big guys at the Lochlainn Company seem to be in the sale of Lakes of Wonder to BBA. Sending someone like Anna out here is more indication of their lack of interest."

"Maybe." Ian didn't buy Tai's speculation. He had too much experience dealing with the Lochlainns. Hell, his family had too much experience, going all the way back to Cooper and Archibald.

The crowd was growing thicker, even in the

VIP area, as the time for the fireworks show drew closer. Ian searched the faces. One of them had to be Anna Stratford, but who? But he didn't spot anyone matching the appearance of a Lochlainn Compay executive he didn't already know.

One intriguing female guest held his attention. Too bad she was obviously a Lakes of Wonder fan who'd talked her way into the VIP area. That would also explain why she was alone and not working the crowd, hoping to build her network in case the rumors about Lakes of Wonder's future were true. She stood in the far corner of the balcony, her hands gripping the wrought-iron railing as she leaned over the waist-high barrier, her rapt expression tightly focused on the Lighthouse of Amazement.

Unlike the others in the VIP area who'd skipped wearing Halloween costumes in favor of suits of gray and black, she was dressed as a fairy in a strapless dress of shocking pink with shimmering wings attached to her shoulders. A crown of equally pink flowers sat on top of blond curls that cascaded past her shoulders. Her cheeks sparkled with glitter, her glowing skin illuminated by the strings of globe lights strung above the terrace.

She appeared utterly out of place.

She appeared delectable.

The costume suited her. The dress clung to her luscious, round breasts and full hips, the skirt flaring above her knees and revealing curvaceous calves. His gaze traveled the length of her long legs, to her metallic high-heeled sandals and up again, past the bend in her waist and the slope of her shoulders to the top of her rosy floral headpiece. He was unable to pull his gaze from her, vivid and vivacious in a sea of monotonous monotones.

Ian didn't have a "type." He thought the concept was sophomoric and not a little bit pedestrian. Love at first sight was even more laughable, a concept wholly foreign to him in its sheer ridiculousness. But he had to admit if he did have a type, then she would fulfill his every visual requisite plus ones he didn't know he had.

"Spotted your quarry?" Tai broke him out of his revery.

Ian almost jumped before he realized Tai was referring to Anna Stratford and not the current object of Ian's interest. He admonished himself to cease staring at the fairy princess. Not only was he being impolite—or worse—but he had a time-sensitive mission. And it was not to hook up with a random Lakes of Wonder superfan, no matter how fascinating he found her. "Not yet."

"You sure? Seems like you might have a different type of quarry in your sights." Tai grinned and then finished off his second drink.

Ian regarded Tai. There were advantages and disadvantages to working with his closest friend. Tai was an excellent business development executive whose financial savvy was second to none. Asking him to join BBA had been a no-brainer. However, Tai also knew where all of Ian's buttons were located and how to light them up with nimble dexterity. "I have only one reason for being at this tedious event."

"If you say so." Tai wiped off the Seamus-shaped ice cubes with a napkin and pocketed them. "Linh is going to love these. Maybe my team should create financial projections for a series of afterhours events like this one at our parks."

"When three-year-olds like your daughter are our target audience, sure." Ian's gaze returned to the woman at the railing. Now she was talking on her phone, her face turned toward the crowd as she laughed at something being said on the other end. She threw her head back to expose a creamy length of neck, her curls tumbling around her shoulders as they shook with mirth. A real laugh, deep from within. Authentic.

Ian wasn't used to people revealing their inner emotions in such an unguarded way in public. He was aware his stare verged on rudeness but he was unable to glance away.

Tai's gaze followed his and he smirked. "I'm going to mingle. Do you want to meet later tonight or in the morning?"

"Tomorrow is fine. No need to pregame our strategy. We'll meet at the conference room."

Tai's smirk deepened and he nodded toward the woman in the fairy costume before turning to leave. "Enjoy your night.".

"My night would be more enjoyable if I could find Anna Stratford." Ian grabbed a champagne flute off a passing waiter's tray. It wasn't until he was about to take a sip that he realized the champagne was colored blue. He rolled his eyes and lowered the glass.

He meant what he'd said to Tai. Tomorrow should be a mere formality, a ceremonial signing of the deal. But the introduction of a mystery negotiator into the deal at the very last minute caused all his senses to go on high alert. His hand tightened on his plastic flute, causing the stem to crack off, and he flagged down another waiter to take the pieces away.

He was letting the Lochlainns get into his head, like he had all those years ago when he was straight out of business school and handling his first negotiation for BBA. The Lochlainn Company and BBA had been locked in bitter rivalry ever since Archibald and Cooper had abruptly ended their partnership. A younger and more naïve Ian had thought surely the old family rivalry would not stand in the way of an excellent business proposition to partner on a new ride technology that both BBA and the Lochlainn Company could then customize for their own individual needs.

He'd walked into the conference room to close the agreement to discover that Keith Lochlainn had swooped in at the last minute and locked up the new technology exclusively for Lakes of Wonder. Ian had been left embarrassed and, worse, the misstep had cost him trust with the BBA board of directors, who'd been willing to install Ian as CEO a few years later but then put Ian's stepfather, Harlan Bridges, in place over him as the chairman of the board.

If there was no love lost between the Black-burns and the Lochlainns, there was even less between Ian and Harlan. And to rub salt in the wound, the Lochlainn Company hadn't used the new technology. Ironically, by buying the Lakes of Wonder, Ian would finally be able to utilize the new system—only, ten years later, it wasn't so revolutionary.

Damn the Lochlainns. Anna Stratford might be their last-minute twist, but Ian was older and much wiser now. And after the deal was successfully concluded tomorrow, the Lochlainns would be out of the theme park business – and Ian would finally have a path to removing Harlan from BBA.

He checked the time on his smartwatch. The party would be over soon. He would make one more sweep of the VIP area to see if he could identify the mystery Lochlainn executive and then call it a night.

His gaze firmly avoiding the corner where the woman in pink was now swaying to the music being piped over the loudspeakers, he spotted a clump of newly arrived guests speaking to the woman guarding the velvet ropes. He recognized the tall brunette standing in the middle and smiled. Finally, the night was turning his way. Catalina Lochlainn was here.

He may have his issues with Keith Lochlainn and his lieutenants, but he had always liked Catalina. Besides, she wasn't a true Lochlainn, just one by marriage. And since she was the one who told him about tomorrow's new addition to the negotiations, Catalina should be able to point the elusive Anna out to him.

Catalina smiled as he approached and excused herself from her companions to greet him. "Ian! Good to see you. I thought this type of event wasn't your cup of tea."

"Doing my last bit of due diligence before tomorrow's acquisition closes."

"I'll miss being invited to these parties. And having free access to the park."

"You are a welcome guest at our theme parks whenever you like."

"Thank you, but that's not the same. But you didn't come over to talk to a Lochlainn for social chitchat."

"What makes you say that?"

"Perhaps the fact that Keith still has a dartboard with your face on it after you hired away his favorite chef for your executive dining room."

He laughed. "That's minor. What about when the Lochlainn Company snatched the deal for Apex Comic characters to appear in theme parks out from under BBA? And then they never appeared at Lakes of Wonder. He did the deal to keep us from using them." That still smarted. Not as much as the first time the Lochlainns had double-crossed him, but the scar was there.

"Ah, but you disturbed Keith's stomach, and that is unforgivable. Still, I'm glad this deal is going through. So, how can I help you?"

"Anna Stratford."

Catalina's eyes widened, just for a second. "What about her?"

"What do you mean? You called to give me a heads-up yesterday."

She folded her arms and regarded him. "Is that why you are at the party? To meet Anna?"

"Due diligence," he reminded her. "Why else would I be here?"

Catalina sighed. "I'm not officially part of the Lochlainn Company. And I have nothing to do with the sale. But I don't like blindsides." There was that flicker in her expression again.

Blindside. Ian was right to be wary about the

sudden addition of Anna to tomorrow's meeting. "Anna. Is she here?"

Catalina glanced around the terrace and then her expression softened. "See the blonde standing alone in the far-left corner of the terrace?"

Ian followed her gaze then frowned. The woman in pink? *His* woman in pink? "You mean the Lakes of Wonder superfan who somehow talked her way into the VIP section?"

"What makes you think she's a superfan?" Catalina arched her eyebrows high.

"She's in costume. She's not networking. That says this is not a work function for her. She's barely taken her eyes off the Lighthouse of Amazement since she arrived. Conclusion—superfan."

Catalina bit back a smile, but not before Ian saw it. "Sounds like you didn't need me to point Anna out to you after all."

Wait. Catalina couldn't be serious. "The superfan wearing glitter is the Lochlainn Company's new shark?"

Catalina nodded, no longer keeping her smile contained. "She is the newest addition, yes."

He struggled to keep his expression intact. Anna Stratford looked as tough as the shot glasses of overly sticky butterscotch pudding now being passed around.

Then he remembered he was still dealing with the Lochlainn Company.

There had to be a catch.

Catalina regarded him, her smile fading. "I take full responsibility for my phone call, but I overstepped my place in telling you about Anna. Please don't make me regret my decision to tell you. Neither of us want to be on Keith's naughty list. Trust me."

Ian searched Catalina's gaze. There was something else. Something she wasn't saying. But then, that was the Lochlainn way. "Don't worry. The call stays between us."

"Good luck tomorrow." And with that, she was gone in a swirl of silken skirts.

Ian's gaze zeroed in on Anna. When she turned her head to accept a glass of blue-tinted champagne from a passing waiter, her beaming smile was almost bright enough to light the area all on its own.

He frowned. In his previous dealings with the Lochlainn Company, the executives had been as jaded and as cynical as Ian himself. No one else in the VIP section so much as batted an eyelash at the waiters serving food being passed.

And, may the theme park gods help him, he was more intrigued by her than before.

He straightened the cuffs of his shirt, smoothed his jacket, and prepared to unwrap the enigma Anna Stratford presented.

TWO

ANNA STRATFORD SHIVERED, unsure whether the chill came from the evening breeze or the ghostly chorus chanting Halloween music over the loudspeakers. When she'd put on her favorite sundress in her hotel room earlier that day, the temperature had been in the high eighties, not too dissimilar from the weather back home in Ft. Lauderdale. But Southern California lacked Florida's humidity and, once the sun went down, the heat disappeared. Her glass of chilled champagne—she'd texted multiple photos of the blue-hued drink to her cousin Maritza, to share with Maritza's five-year-old daughter, Pepa—was delicious, but not warming.

"Are you cold? May I offer you a hot drink?" A man spoke from her right.

Anna jumped. She'd thought she was done with making small talk with Lakes of Wonder executives who obviously wished they were anywhere else but babysitting her for the evening. She was sure she had said good-night to her main handler a while ago, reassuring Teri McWilliams, the head of corporate communications, that she would be able to find her way back to her hotel room from the party on the terrace by herself without any problem.

She turned to address whoever had drawn the short straw and had to check up on her. "I'm fi—"

Her pulse skipped a beat. Then her heart rate sped up, the rapid thump drowning out all other sound.

The speaker had to be one of the most flawless specimens of male adulthood it had ever been her privilege to view—if on the stern and forbidding side. Broad shoulders in a charcoal wool jacket designed to display them to their best advantage, the silky black shirt underneath tailored perfectly to his form. Cheekbones that could slice the wind. Bottomless dark eyes that seemed to see right through her and into the next county. Tousled black hair that was neither straight nor wavy, a touch too long for the "forbidding captain of industry" look he pulled off elsewhere, but she liked the length—it made him seem a teeny bit accessible. Human, even.

Who was he? He certainly wasn't one of the Lochlainn Company executives she'd met, nor did he appear to be on staff at Lakes of Wonder. Maybe an actor? She was in Southern California, after all, although Hollywood was a two-hour drive north of Lakes of Wonder. Or a major league athlete of some kind?

He quirked an eyebrow in question and her brain stopped processing thoughts. She could only stare at his perfection, like a Roman statue come to life in all-too-vivid color. "Is that a yes?" he asked. "They're handing out cookies and hot chocolate." He indicated a tight knot of people surrounding a nearby concession cart.

"Um…" Her mouth opened and closed a few times. Try as hard as she could, she couldn't get her lips to form words, just sounds. People who looked like him were rare occurrences in her life. People who looked like him definitely didn't walk over to her and offer her drinks.

"If you're concerned, you can watch me go to the cart and come straight back. No funny business." He held out his hands, palms up, and all she could do was notice how…large…they were. Large and well formed, with long, thick fingers and...

She found her breath. With difficulty. "I, um..." His grin started to falter. "I mean, thank you. A drink would be nice. Thank you."

He smiled, and if she thought him handsome before—well, she was wrong. The smile transformed his face, turning foreboding to panty-melting sexy. And judging by the gleam in those knowing eyes, he was aware of his effect on her. "Don't move."

Now that she'd had time to adjust to his presence, her brain could start to process again. She glanced to her left and her right. More and more people were discovering her corner of the terrace and filling in any empty space. "I have a feeling this is a 'you move, you lose' type of situation."

She was referring to the spot she had staked out on the terrace to view the upcoming fireworks, but he flashed that grin at her again, even more knowing than previously, before plunging into the cookie and cocoa cart melee. She inhaled. Did he think she was flirting?

Was she flirting?

She didn't have a lot of experience with which to compare. Having had the same boyfriend for the last six years until they'd broken up a month ago—even if the relationship had been effectively over much longer—meant she was woefully out of practice in giving and receiving romantic signals. She shook her head to clear it and grasped the wrought-iron railing with both hands, allowing the solidness of the metal to reassure her that this was indeed her life now. That she was standing on a five-star resort's exclusive rooftop terrace as part of a VIP crowd about to watch Lakes of Wonder's renowned Halloween firework show, with movie-star-handsome men asking if they could bring her treats.

She had to speak to Maritza, to ground herself in reality – or least, the reality that had been hers until that fateful knock on her office door. No one knew Anna better than her cousin, who was also her best friend and housemate. When Maritza had found herself suddenly single a month away from giving birth, Anna had moved into her small bungalow to help with newborn and never moved out. Although she had last spoken to her cousin not less than an hour ago, the purpose of that phone call had been to say good-night to Pepa. The five-year-old should be asleep by now, so she and Maritza could freely speak.

"So what's happening now?" Maritza answered. "Did you sell the theme park already? I thought that was tomorrow."

"Shh! You're not supposed to know why I'm here." But Anna had had to tell someone about the surreal turn of events that had led to her trip to Southern California, and she'd trusted Maritza with her deepest secrets her entire life. "And don't remind me about tomorrow. I haven't been told who I'm meeting or even allowed to go over the paperwork. The Lakes of Wonder people continue to brush me off, saying those are details I don't need to worry about. All I know is I sign the agreement, I shake hands, I pose for a photo, I walk out." Her gaze remained locked on the man who had offered her a drink. True to his word, he joined the back of the line at the concession cart.

"They sound awful."

"They're fine." They weren't—the managers she'd met were more condescending than any of Anna's wealthy interior design clients ever had been—but Maritza had enough stress in her life. She didn't need Anna's minor-by-comparison annoyances added to them. "The situation is...unusual."

"That's the understatement of the century. Who has someone with no prior experience or connection jump in and sign off on a massive sale? A sale that will be scrutinized by the media, and the IRS, and the Justice Department, and—"

"I guess Keith Lochlainn does," Anna interjected. "Who knows why billionaires do anything?" The man was third in line now. He wasn't really buying a beverage for her, was he? This had to be a prank. Perhaps a Lochlainn Company executive had put him up to it, as revenge for Anna being thrust into their carefully negotiated deal at the last second.

She wouldn't mention meeting him to Maritza, just in case.

Maritza sighed. "Sorry, I didn't mean to make you more apprehensive about the whole thing. You're still processing everything you learned and—"

"I'm great." Anna cut her cousin off. No need to go into how well she was dealing—or not dealing—with the major life changes that had been thrust upon her. "And tonight's party is fun." She failed to mention she was the only guest in the VIP section wearing a costume and that the other guests had no problem staring at her with visible smirks. "The desserts are amazing and the view…there are no words for how spectacular this view is. I can see the entire theme park, with the Lighthouse smack-dab in the center. But, hey, the show will start soon, so I wanted to quickly check in without little ears listening. How is Pepa?"

"She's better now that we finally have a diagnosis, although she keeps asking where you are. She wants to show you how she can make her own lunch now and not feel 'icky.'"

"I'm sorry for leaving. I wish I could be there to help as you figure out how to work with her diabetes."

"Stop apologizing. Nothing is your fault." Anna could picture Maritza's narrowed eyes and free hand on her hip as she said it. "My mom and dad are here. I've got support."

"Right. Your parents," Anna repeated through suddenly numb lips. She forced moisture back into her mouth and attempted a smile. Aren't people supposed to hear your smile even when they can't see it? Not that she could fool Maritza. "That's good."

Maritza exhaled. "I saw your dad today—"

Out of the corner of her eye, Anna spied the man walking toward her, his hands laden with mugs. If this was a prank, at least she would get a hot cocoa out of it. "I need to get off the phone."

"You need to talk to your parents. They're worried—"

"I know." Anna screwed her eyes shut. When she opened them, the man was closer. "Let them know I'm fine.

"Anna—"

"Gotta run. Love you." Anna hung up as the man reached her side. "You returned much faster than I thought you would."

"I have sharp elbows," he said dryly, handing her a sealed plastic mug and a see-through bag containing a frosted jack-o'-lantern sugar cookie larger than Anna's hand.

"Halloween marks the start of the holiday season. I'm pretty sure elbowing small children out of the way for cookies and cocoa puts you on Santa's naughty list." She opened the mug's lid and breathed in the chocolate scent before sipping. Delicious. So far, not a prank.

Here came his smile again, even more devastating than before. "You're the second person tonight who suggested I could be put on that list," he said.

"Oh?" Anna raised her eyebrow. "Why? Do you regularly elbow small children? Fleece widows out of their inheritance?"

His warm expression fled, replaced by an assessing stare. She resisted the urge to hide behind her mug the best she could. "Is that what you expect from me? A fleecing?"

"Expect? Am I supposed to expect something from you? I'm sorry, do we know each other? Or perhaps you have me confused with someone else." That would explain why he had approached her. This had to be a case of mistaken identity. He was too...well, too *everything* to be interested in her.

His stare turned quizzical then his brow smoothed out. "You're right. We haven't been formally introduced." He held out his right hand for a handshake, which she accepted. "Ian."

His touch was warm and firm, his fingers enveloping hers with their strength. Her father—well, Glenn—always said one could tell the nature of a person based on their handshake. Ian's grip said he was powerful and used to getting his own way. He was in control of how long their hands remained connected. But he was also careful not to overwhelm her with his strength.

"Anna," she responded. He released her hand, triggering a wave of disappointment that took her by surprise. "Pleasure to meet you."

Ian continued to regard her, his eyebrows raised as if in expectation. She cleared her throat. "Is it not a pleasure? I'm sorry, I'm from Florida. Do people say something different after an introduction in Southern California? This is my first time here."

He laughed. His laugh was deep and rich and sent frissons of electricity from her fingers to her toes. "Oh, the pleasure is definitely mine."

Her stomach squeezed at the light of appreciation in his gaze, while her face was hot enough to warm everyone standing on the terrace. Thankfully, the lights overhead winked out as the announcer told the guests to relax and enjoy the evening's show, sparing the entire party from seeing her blush brighter than a stoplight. In the ensuing darkness, she put her cocoa on a nearby cocktail table and hugged her arms tight across her chest, trying to appear calm and sophisticated. As if being in the VIP section and talking to men whose grin could make every panty within eyesight spontaneously combust was another day ending in "y" for her.

Her actions didn't have the intended effect. Instead, he frowned. "Still cold?"

She shook her head. Cold was the last word to describe the awareness lighting her nerves, causing the little hairs on her arms to rise to attention. He had her literally quaking in her sandals. "I'm good," she choked out.

He shook his head. "You're shivering." Before she could object, he'd taken off his charcoal-gray suit jacket and draped it around her shoulders, easily covered her costume wings. "Your dress might be perfect for a Florida evening, but it doesn't stand a chance against our cool California nights."

His jacket enveloped her like a warm hug. Her fingertips skimmed the surface of the fabric, ran along the seams. Working with textiles was one of the joys of her job as the in-house interior designer for her family's furniture store, and the fine wool outer layer and smooth silk lining were very fine textiles indeed. She inhaled, breathing his scent, redolent of pine and musk. So delicious, if the scent could somehow be bottled, he would put most perfume companies out of business within a month.

She should give the jacket back to him. Instead, she snuggled deeper into its luxurious embrace. "Thank you."

"Can't have you freeze to death, after all. His tone was light but his mouth wore a sideways twist. "Wouldn't be hospitable. Certainly not before you finish everything on your agenda."

"My agenda?" She did have an agenda—as in meetings she was expected to attend in the following days—but he made it sound as if she had an ulterior motive. And she also had one of those—but how would someone she just met know that? The Lochlainn Company attorney had assured her the reason she was at Lakes of Wonder was known only to a handful of trusted family insiders. Not even the theme park executives she'd been dealing with knew. It certainly wasn't public knowledge.

Or maybe the events of the last month were causing her to question even the most innocent of statements, and the only thing he meant was her agenda as a tourist. Maritza would tell her to relax and enjoy his company, after all—

A glorious burst of gold and silver sparks exploded over the Lighthouse of Amazement and chased her thoughts away. "Oh!" was all she could manage to exhale.

Music poured over the loudspeakers, orchestral and stirring, the fireworks timed perfectly to the beat and tonal shifts as the soundtrack shifted from stirring chants of heroic action to melodic love ballads to comedic set pieces. Anna even sang along, if under her breath, to some of the more popular songs she remembered from her childhood. She oohed as the fireworks created spinning discs of fire in the sky, and aahed when the sparking lights revealed entwined hearts. Then the soundtrack shifted to spooky Halloween music, the fireworks blazing orange and purple. Ghostly figures over the Lighthouse as the music built to a crescendo and then stopped.

The crowd on the terrace clapped. Anna turned to Ian. "That was fun—"

Out of the corner of her eye, flames streaked upward from the Lighthouse. She jumped and grabbed Ian's arm, firm and strong and warm under the silky cotton of his shirt. She dropped her hands when she realized what she was doing. He merely smiled and directed her attention back to the Lighthouse. "Don't miss the big finale."

The flames—controlled, and part of the show, Anna could see now—leaped in time to the music. The Lighthouse appeared to be on fire, but that was an illusion created by realistic projections on the building's outer walls. Then Seamus Sea Serpent appeared out of the lake. He dove back down and, when he emerged again, the magic of special effects made it look as if he expelled streams of water to douse the flames. The music started again, more triumphant than before, as more fireworks than Anna could count lit the sky brighter than daylight, one giant circular burst of color after another.

The applause was thundering this time. Anna waited a few beats before joining in. "Now that's the end," she deadpanned.

"That's the end," Ian agreed. "Impressive, although they grossly overspent on the effects and the return on investment is nonexistent. By the time the show pays for itself, the technology will be outdated, and even more money will need to be spent." The lights came up on the terrace as he turned to her. His gaze swept over her expression. "I take it you don't agree?" he asked.

"There's more to investment than dollars and cents." To some people, Anna's parents might just sell furniture. But Anna knew better. Stratford's Fine Furniture sold comfort, home, a place to form and nurture a family—

Family. Her mind stuttered on the word. Maritza knew she had to talk to her parents. But she was still processing the news that the solid foundation upon which she had relied her entire life was...well. Her parents were still her parents. Her solid foundation still stood. The Knock did not change that. Her heart knew that truth, implicitly.

Her brain, on the other hand, needed more time. And that was the real reason why she was in California.

"What about joy? Delight? The show creates memories, and those are priceless." She swept a hand, indicating the rapt crowd on the other side of the velvet ropes, chatting animatedly as knots of people began to move away from the railing and back toward the tables laden with sweets and alcohol. "See the kids? They'll still be talking about tonight when they are twice my age."

Ian regarded her as if she had grown a unicorn horn in the middle of her forehead. "Interesting argument."

"What?" Anna picked up her hot chocolate.

"Are you trying to tell me you've never thought of theme parks as places of happiness?"

"Now I know you're kidding. That's the marketing. But we know that's not the reality."

She laughed. "I don't think—"

A small child rammed into Anna's legs. Her knees buckled and she fell forward, the perpetrator bouncing off her and running away. Before she could even exclaim, Ian's large hands were there, grasping her elbows, keeping her upright. Her arms wound around his shoulders and she sank against him.

He smelled even better that his jacket. The notes were deeper, richer. Warmer.

She pulled back, suddenly aware this was the second time she had clung to him in less than a half hour. And without so much as asking for his consent. Her gaze locked onto Ian's. Was he angry? Or worse, amused that she was literally throwing herself at him—multiple times? But instead, his eyes were dark with concern. "Are you okay?" he asked.

She nodded, her breathing coming back under control. "I'm fine—"

No. Wait. She wasn't fine. She was…she sniffed and looked down.

When the child had hit her, Anna's cocoa

mug had tipped before falling out of her hand. Now she wore most of its contents. Ian's beautiful jacket was splattered and wet.

"Oh, no!" She grabbed a stack of napkins from a nearby table and started to dab at the cocoa. "Don't worry. I'll have this dry-cleaned and returned to you."

He shook his head. "I'm checking out early in the morning. My morning is packed, and then I'm flying to a conference in Hong Kong. My assistant can take it to the cleaners when I return next week."

"Next week? You can't let a stain like this sit. Chocolate and milk are a recipe for destroyed fibers. I can mail it to you after it's cleaned."

He shrugged. "It's just a jacket. No need to go to so much bother."

Just a jacket? She smoothed her fingers over the wool. The silk lining slid against her skin, causing voluptuous shivers. If she owned this jacket, she wouldn't wear anything underneath so the lining could caress her like the world's most tender lover. "You said you were checking out tomorrow—are you a guest at this hotel?"

His eyes crinkled at the corners. "I am."

"So am I. I travel with a stain removal stick. It's so miraculous, it practically walks on water.

Can I at least try to get the worst of the spill out and then return the jacket to your room?" She ran her fingers across the fine weave. "It would be a shame if this were ruined. Merino wool, I'm guessing. Italian milled."

She looked up. He was gazing at her as if the unicorn horn had regrown out of her forehead.

"What?" she asked.

"You're not—" He stopped. Then he nodded, a slight one, as if he were agreeing with an unspoken thought. "Right. So. You're proposing you remove the stain tonight."

"At least, I hope I can. It shouldn't take long."

"And bring the jacket by my room?"

Her stomach flipped at the way he lingered on the last word. "I can leave it at the front desk if you prefer. But I'd feel better if I made sure you received it before you leave."

He smiled then, a halfway smile that slightly dented his cheeks. "My room is fine. I was planning on being up, anyway. To prep for tomorrow," he clarified, his eyebrow raised.

"Right." He had mentioned he had a packed morning. "Sure, I'll bring it by."

"I'm in 3140. The Wonder Suite. Why don't we say in one hour? That should give both of us enough time." He held up an index finger in the universal sign for "one minute" at an Asian man approaching them, his hands full of jack-o'-lantern cookies. Then Ian turned back to her. "Until then."

She swallowed, trying to work more moisture into her mouth. "See you later."

Ian nodded and left, finding the other man. The two talked for a minute then they walked together toward the exit. Anna watched them until the crowd hid them from view, and then held her chilled palms to her overheated cheeks. Ian's voice had deepened and lingered on the word "then," rolling the word on his tongue like a promise of more fireworks to come—only this time, the pyrotechnics would involve only the two of them.

Unless that had been her imagination.

Anna wished she had dated more in college. Or in high school. Or any time, really. Then she would have more experience with reading people and whether they were interested in her or merely flirting to flirt or if she was making the whole thing up because she found Ian attractive. Her fingers could still feel the strength of his arm as she'd clutched him, the breadth of his shoulders. She'd practically climbed him as if he were her own personal gym equipment.

She didn't act this way with people she didn't know. She didn't act this way with people she *did* know.

She wanted to continue to act this way with Ian.

Her last relationship had been fine if predictable. Monotonous. She couldn't blame her boyfriend for breaking up with her, either. *She* was monotonous. Anna, the good student, the obedient daughter, the dutiful girlfriend.

Her life had stretched out before her in easily measurable chunks: earn a scholarship to Florida State, meet a nice man, earn her degree. Work at her parents' furniture store as the in-house interior designer, learn the clientele and their wants and dislikes. Take over the business after her parents decide to retire. Spend two weeks' vacation every summer at the Stratford family compound of lakeside cabins in the Smoky Mountains. *Noche Buena* at *Tía* Belen's house, Passover Seder with Uncle Simon and his husband. Marry the nice man and when children came along, introduce them to same cycle of holidays and family get-togethers.

She had a good life. A great life. She was lucky and privileged, in so many ways.

Then came the Knock. And everything that

she thought she knew—everything that she thought she was, down to the marrow in her bones—was called into question. Leaving her confused and, yes, still angry the life that had been hers until the lawyer had showed up on her doorstep had been based on a lie, leaving her with no idea of who or what she was meant to be.

Maybe she was someone who saw someone to whom she was attracted and went for it, potential embarrassment and social strictures to "be a good girl" be damned.

And maybe someone like Ian—someone who exuded success and command and was so devilishly handsome he made movie superheroes appear lackluster and pedestrian—could be interested in a furniture store "client customer success manager" as her business cards read.

The party was starting to dissolve around her. People streamed toward the wall of glass doors that led to the hotel's signature restaurant and, beyond it, the elevators. The cookie and cocoa cart had been wheeled away. Wait staff were dissembling the towers of sweets. The bar was still doing brisk business, but it was evident the event was over.

She pulled Ian's jacket tighter around her,

reveling anew in the soft silk of the lining and his spicy male scent—albeit now mixed with chocolate—and went to her hotel room. She was at the most Wonderous Place on the Planet, as the ads for Lakes of Wonder proclaimed. Perhaps her stain removal stick would not be the end of the magic the night had in store for her.

THREE

IAN ROLLED HIS NECK. The desk and office chair in his suite were more ergonomic than expected for hotel furniture, especially considering most guests would be spending their time in the theme parks on vacation instead of in the room working, but he couldn't seem to release the tension making a knotty home for itself between his shoulder blades.

His laptop was open on the desk, the contract in vivid black and white on the screen. He should be going through the sales agreement to see if there any loopholes he had missed. "Be prepared" wasn't just a scouting motto or a song from a Disney movie; it was the code by which he conducted his life, to the point of taking over the preparations for his twenty-first birthday surprise party. Leaving outcomes to chance was for amateurs.

But, try as he might, he couldn't focus on the

page in front of him. His thoughts were otherwise occupied by the enigmatic-and oh-so-appealing Anna Stratford.

She was not what he'd expected. At all. Nor had she batted an eyelash when he'd introduced himself. To anyone else, it would appear as if she hadn't known who he was. But that was impossible. Of course, she'd know who her opponent would be in the boardroom tomorrow.

She must be a good actress, he decided. So good, she was almost impossible for him to read. Perhaps that was the twist. Present him with a last-minute opponent so unexpected he would be taken off guard, miss a step. Pay more to acquire Lakes of Wonder or cause him to make unwise concessions.

Or maybe he had Anna all wrong. Maybe she was as guileless and transparent as she'd seemed on the terrace. After all, he'd approached her... although Catalina Lochlainn had all but pushed him in her direction.

He supposed he would find out which version of Anna was correct if she made good on her promise and came by his room. He looked forward to seeing if she would offer anything beyond his cleaned jacket. His cock grew heavy at the memory of how her lush breasts had pressed against him, her soft gasps in his ear as her hands gripped his shoulder. The hot cocoa spill had been an accident, but Ian admired people who took advantage of serendipity to press their advantage. He did the same.

But whatever happened—if indeed, she showed up—he had no illusions that Anna Stratford was anything but the latest in a long line of Lochlainn tricks and feints.

His phone rang. Tai. "Did you find anything?" he answered.

"My team has been over the supporting documents and schedules twice," Tai responded. "They're airtight."

Ian rose from the office chair and began to pace on the carpeted floor. "Have them read it again."

"Let's save time. Go ahead and tell me what the issue is," Tai suggested.

"I…don't know. Yet."

"Then why are you so sure one exists?"

"Because there is always an issue with the Lochlainns." He reached the opposite end of the room far too soon and turned around.

"Can I persuade you to stop overthinking this?" Ice cubes rattled in Ian's ear as Tai took a sip of whatever he was drinking. "I've gone over the terms so many times, I have them memorized. The agreement to buy Lakes of Wonder is straightforward."

Ian shook his head. "There's something the Lochlainns aren't telling us." A vision of Anna's eyes, shining with unfettered joy as she'd watched the fireworks, almost stopped him in his tracks. Her generous full mouth curved into a smile so broad she couldn't be faking her enjoyment—could she?

Who offered to get stains out of jackets in the first place?

Or maybe it was part of a Lochlainn ruse to spring an unsuspecting trap on him at the last minute.

Tai's sigh echoed through the phone. "Look, I wasn't raised on castle intrigue the way you were—"

"Castle intrigue. Nice. Another good use of metaphor."

"I wasn't referring to amusement parks." Tai snorted. "Although it does fit, seeing as how you were born into an amusement park dynasty."

"I wasn't raised on castle intrigue."

"No, only to look for ambushes around every corner."

"I'm thorough and prepared. That's why BBA

is the number two amusement park operator in the world." Although allowing Anna Stratford to walk off with his jacket—an obvious pretense to contact him again this evening—was not exactly erring on the side of caution. Would she come to his room in her fairy costume? He hoped so. He wondered if her skin would turn the same color as her dress when she—

Too late, he realized Tai was speaking.

"—not saying you aren't justified. You were brought up by Harlan, after all."

Ian's hand ached. He released his tight grip on his phone. "What's your point?"

"My point is your stepfather is a jackass. Since he consolidated his control over BBA's board, you've been under attack as CEO. And this is the first major deal as CEO you get to put your imprint on. So, I understand why you are kicking the tires a few more times than necessary. But maybe stop kicking them into oblivion. You can't go anywhere if the tires are shredded."

Ian made a dismissive gesture. "Forget everything I said about your metaphors. That one is tortured."

"I'm not wrong about Harlan."

"Harlan is a nonentity. Or he will be once we

close this deal. Preston and Olive have promised to vote with me to kick him off the board." And out of the family for good, he thought grimly. His mother had suffered enough.

"And that's another reason why you're spinning your wheels. Pun intended." Tai fell silent for a moment. "You know, speaking of Preston and Olive, I never asked why your uncle and cousin are joining you now when you've been trying to get rid of Harlan since I joined the company."

Ian exhaled. "We don't talk of this publicly. But my great-grandfather, Cooper, was Archibald's original partner on Lakes of Wonder. Family legend says Cooper even designed the Lighthouse, only for Archibald to kick him to the curb before the park's opening. Cooper went on to found Blackburn Amusements, so no one should cry for him. But Preston and Olive have been obsessed with Lakes of Wonder as long as I've known them. I've agreed Preston will be charge of Lakes of Wonder once the sale goes through, hands off."

"Aha!" Tai said. "I get it now. This acquisition is a family honor thing and that's why you expect the Lochlainns to screw BBA over. I knew your mother's Sicilian influence was involved somehow."

Ian smirked. "This isn't a vendetta."

"You sure? Do I need to start shopping for a horse's head to slip into Keith Lochlainn's bed?"

"This is a business deal, not *The Godfather*. The Lochlainn Company has a well-earned reputation for underhanded tricks that I'm staying ahead of. Besides, the horse's head would be for Harlan."

Tai snorted. "Can I give you advice?"

"No, but you will anyway."

"Stop borrowing trouble and get some sleep." Ice rattled again on the other end of the line. "I have an early breakfast about the San Diego expansion. See you at the meeting?"

"Nine a.m. at the Lakes of Wonder admin building. Sixth floor conference room."

Tai said his goodbyes and Ian turned to his previously ignored laptop screen. Maybe his friend was right. Maybe there wasn't a twist. Perhaps Anna didn't have a strategy up her nonexistent sleeves that would filet the sale like trout being prepared for dinner. After all, Tai was correct that Ian had learned early and often with Harlan as a stepfather—and later as chairman of BBA's board—to be wary and to watch his own back at every turn.

But to paraphrase the old saying, was it paranoia when the conspiracies turned out to be real? When Ian's mother, Guilia, divorced Harlan, Harlan had exploited a loophole in their prenuptial agreement that gave him ownership of Guilia's BBA shares and secured his seat on the board. So far, Ian had managed to sidestep the knives and arrows aimed at his back—and often, his front—but he was more than ready to remove Harlan for good. If Preston and Olive held to their end of the bargain and voted their shares with Ian at the next board meeting, he would finally have the power to do so.

A knock came at his hotel room. Finally.

He threw the door open. "I was wondering when you would come—"

A bellman blinked back at him. "Sorry for your wait." He held out an ice bucket. Condensation frosted the sides and the corks of three bottles poked over the top edge. "Compliments of the Lochlainn Company. Welcome to Shelter Cove Hotel."

Ian swallowed his disappointment and took the bucket, placing it on the table in the sitting area. He returned with a generous cash tip, which he handed to the bellman. "Thank you."

"Enjoy your stay, sir." The bellman left and Ian examined one of the bottles. Champagne. Pricey stuff, too. Well, apparently the Lochlainn Company expected him to celebrate, one way or another.

Another knock at his door, the same staccato rhythm as before. Did the bellman forget something? He wrenched the door open. "Yes?"

The person on his threshold wasn't from bell services.

"Anna," he breathed.

"Hi," she said, her smile as genuine, if a bit more tentative, than it had been on the restaurant terrace. She held up his jacket. "I'm so sorry I took so long. The cocoa was a bit more stubborn than anticipated, and I didn't want to harm the fibers. I also had to be careful of the silk lining—I didn't want to leave a water mark. But I think it's mostly as good as new?"

Her words tumbled in a torrent, but Ian barely heard them, fascinated by the vision in front of him. Anna had changed out of her bright pink dress and towering sandals into light pink joggers topped by a matching hoodie. Her hair had lost its flower crown and her blond curls flowed freely across her shoulders. The fairy-dust glitter was sadly gone from her cheeks, but a dash of fresh lipstick outlined her lips.

There was even a tiny water droplet on the tip of her nose, no doubt left from washing her face. A rather delectable nose, he noted, and then wondered when he had ever paid attention to that portion of someone's anatomy before. But in way, Anna Stratford's nose was the encapsulation of everything he found intriguing about this mystery woman: a perfectly ordinary physical feature that, by virtue of belonging to her, was made extraordinary by her animated energy.

Her rush of words had ceased. She was waiting, her eyes wide and questioning, for him to respond. "Sorry, you lost me somewhere around 'fibers.'" He held the door open wider. "Come in. I don't have hot cocoa, but the hotel supplied champagne. It's a better vintage than whatever that was served at the party."

She shook her head and continued to hold out the jacket. "I don't want to impose. You said you were checking out early and I was about to go to bed. I only wanted to make sure I returned your—" Her gaze sharpened as she focused on something over his right shoulder.

"Wait. Is that…? No way. You can see Lakes of Wonder from your room?"

He stepped to the side and indicated she should enter. "I've been told this room offers the best view. Even better than the view from the rooftop terrace earlier."

She hesitated, but only for a second. Then she walked past him and crossed the room until she was almost pressed flat against the floor-to-ceiling windows that made up the far wall. "Whoever said that wasn't wrong. Look, from this angle you can see Mythic Springs and Buccaneer Bayou as well as the Lighthouse of Amazement."

He joined her at the window, stopping briefly by the suite's wet bar to pour two flutes of champagne. He handed one to her and kept the other for himself. "It's not as centered of a view as the terrace for the firework show, but I appreciate the bird's-eye perspective. You get a better idea of the park's layout." With his free hand, he indicated a brightly lit silver flag discernable in the distance. "There's Black Hole Bay."

Her left index finger traced the spot on the glass. "It's closer to Olympic Cay than I thought. It felt like I walked forever to get between them when I was in the park earlier today."

"Illusion," he said. "The original designer created winding paths that double back on themselves to give the appearance of distance. So guests would feel as if they'd traveled through time to reach the next destination." He shrugged. "And the more time guests spend walking, the happier they are to sit and watch one of the live entertainment shows. And if guests are watching a show, then they aren't standing in line for a ride, thus decreasing the wait times for other guests."

"Really?" She turned shining eyes to him. "That's clever."

Clever? He shrugged. "It's standard operations. Create ways to keep crowds dispersed and traffic flowing." He drank from his flute, his gaze focused on Anna. "But that's theme park 101, as you know."

Anna opened her mouth then snapped it shut. Her lips made a perfect bow shape when they were closed, Ian noted, and wondered again at his apparent obsession with cataloging human features—an obsession that began when he'd opened the door. "Let's pretend I know nothing. Teach me?" she asked, her gaze focused on his.

FOUR

COMING TO IAN Blackburn's room was a mistake. Anna was sure of it. She should have trusted her first instinct and asked bell services to deliver the jacket to him. But lately, she didn't have a great track record of being right about…well, anything.

Interacting with Ian was like was staring at an enormous open box of jigsaw puzzle pieces, but the cover was missing so she had no idea what picture she was supposed to form.

Like now. She had no idea how to read him. His gaze was narrowed, but a faint smile played on his lips. "Are you quizzing me on how well I know the attractions industry?"

"Just picking your brain," she demurred. Earlier, while trying to remove the stain, she'd been racking her brain why Ian approached her. Now, she decided, perhaps fate was the reason. She needed a crash course on how Lakes of

Wonder operated, since the Lochlainn Company executives had decided not to educate her in advance of the meeting tomorrow, and the universe had provided an instructor. "I'm all ears. What else do I need to know?"

He regarded her, a speculative light in his eye, then he smiled. "Okay. I'll bite." His left arm brushed hers as he raised his hand to indicate a point in the distance. "Theme park 101 it is. Let's start with...see the tall structure in the center of the park? You know what that is, right?"

She scoffed. "That's easy. That's the Lighthouse of Amazement."

"That's the name. But do you know what it is?"

"A tall lighthouse?"

He turned to face her, leaning his left shoulder against the window. A smirk played on his lips as he bent his mouth close to her ear. She shivered. "That's the weenie," he said, and straightened.

His breath was warm and her nerves were on red alert, simultaneously craving him to come nearer yet apprehensive he would—because if did, she would have to be honest with herself about what she hoped would happen by coming to his room. She had to blink a few times before she fully processed his words. "You have to be kidding. Weenie? As in…" She indicated the Lighthouse, lit up in the distance. "It is rather phallic, I suppose."

A bark of laughter escaped him. He glanced down at her, the gleam in his eyes intensifying. She wanted to bask in his heat, like a cat finding a sunbeam. "As in the treat used to train dogs," he corrected.

"Oh." She hoped the warmth flooding from her checks to her chest wasn't visible in the room's dim light. "It doesn't look like kibble."

He gave her the same assessing stare as he had earlier on the terrace. She resisted the urge to check if a unicorn horn truly had sprung out of her forehead. Then his smirk deepened. "It's named that because dog trainers use weenies to draw dogs' attention. Park weenies are designed to draw guests' attention. Weenies at the center, like the Lighthouse, keep people moving further into the park so the entrances don't become crowded."

His eyes reflected the neon glow of the park, the pinpoints of light beckoning her closer. She immediately understood the concept. "Ah.

That's how the park gets guests to move from one place to another?"

"Testing me on techniques used to capture guests' attention?" He indicated her hoodie. "There are several ways. Bright colors, for example. People are drawn to them." His gaze dipped to her mouth, his dark eyes becoming pools of black. "As you know. Your pink lipstick makes it difficult to focus on anything else."

His rough-edged words caused an instant rush of heat between her legs. She couldn't look at him for fear of betraying how much he was affecting her. No doubt he would laugh if he knew. He probably entertained late-night guests in his hotel room all the time, beautiful, sophisticated guests who knew how to banter and lightly joke. People unlike her. Or, at least unlike her before the Knock.

She drank deeply from her flute despite knowing better. Champagne shut off her critical thinking centers. But the cool liquid was welcome as the room's temperature seemed to be increasing. "Is that why you wear monotones?"

His eyebrows rose. "Me?"

She drained her glass and set it down, turning to face him. "If people wear bright colors to draw attention, then those who wear dark colors—like you—must be dressing to avoid it. Right? I mean, Batman doesn't hunt criminals dressed in neon yellow."

He snorted. "I suppose dark clothes would be better at night. If one were a stealthy superhero, that is."

She looked down. Her flute was full again. "Considering my glass was empty fifteen seconds ago, I'd say stealth is something you excel at." She raised her gaze to him. "So? Is that why you dress the way do? To avoid detection?"

"Are you asking if I fight crime in my time off?" he said, topping off his own glass. "Sorry, no."

She looked at him from over the top of her flute. "I think I'm right. Not that you have a secret identity that fights crime, but you want to avoid attention."

"Really." His tone was dismissive, but for the first time his gaze wouldn't fully meet hers. "Why would I do that?"

She shook her head. "I don't know. Maybe it's because you know bright colors would alert your prey and you wouldn't be able to get close enough to them otherwise."

He didn't respond, but his fingers tightened on the stem of his glass.

Anna's success at work relied on reading her customers' body language. Often, a client would outwardly express delight or enthusiasm, but there would be something in their stance—feet braced as if preparing for impact, shoulders a half inch higher than normal—that told her their internal reaction was something quite different. Ian continued to lean against the window, no change discernable in his position, but his gaze now studiously contemplated the brightly colored lights of the theme park below.

Maybe she was learning how to read him after all. She smiled as she held out her half-empty glass. "Is there more? This is the best champagne I've had in…ever."

The sharp light returning to his expression, he poured what was left of the bottle into her glass. "There is. And you're incorrect."

"No, I'm sure this is the best champagne I've tasted."

His half-smile dented his left cheek. "No. About colors. Theme parks use shades of green or blue to cover buildings and objects they want guests to ignore. The colors blend into the vegetation or the sky. The guests' eyes slide over them."

"Hmm." She considered his words as her

limbs turned heavy, the stress that had kept her shoulders rigid and her jaw tight for the last several weeks now dissipating. The alcohol, she knew. Considering her dinner had consisted of nothing but desserts containing enough sugar to keep a bakery in business for a week, it was a miracle she wasn't drunk. But she wasn't, not yet, just warm and relaxed and slightly fuzzy around the edges. "Blues and greens might redirect guests' eyes, but only during daylight. After sundown…one needs dark colors to go unnoticed." She widened her eyes in mock horror. "Until it is too late for the unsuspecting."

His smile deepened as he opened a new bottle of champagne. "You make me sound like a vampire."

"So far, I've only seen you after sundown. Maybe you wear green and blue during the day. Or maybe you really are a vampire and can't go out in the sun." She looked up at him from under her eyelashes. She wasn't sure if she had the flirting thing down pat, but she would prattle on about any subject if it meant his gaze stayed riveted on her. "Are you?"

He topped off her newly empty glass. "Interesting question. What do you think?"

She took a sip. The new bottle was different. The champagne was brighter, more acidic. Bolder. Like she should be perhaps? Maybe this was where she truly belonged, drinking champagne with a man who exuded danger—not to her physical well-being, but to her mental equilibrium. As it was, he was already occupying far more of her brain space than someone she just met should be. Or rather, that was how she would have reacted before the Knock. Now? She caught his gaze. "I think whoever you bite would enjoy it very much. Even if they regret it in the morning."

His hand froze, his flute halfway to his mouth. He recovered almost instantaneously, but she knew she hadn't imagined it. "But perhaps your partner objects to you going around biting people," she continued.

He drank deeply from his glass then set it down on the side table. He took another step toward her. This close, she could see his eyes weren't a dark brown, as she'd initially thought, but a mix of amber and gold and bronzed umber. "They would. If I had one."

He was very imposing. His shoulders were broad, his black shirt slightly straining across his chest. The sleeves were rolled up, revealing muscular forearms. Forearms that looked more than up to the task of supporting her weight, holding her steady as she moved above him...

She had no idea where that image came from but now that it had found a home on the main screen of her mind's cineplex, she couldn't get rid of it. She swallowed. "I don't have anyone in my life who would object. Not that I'm a vampire. Obviously."

Here came that look of scrutiny again. She lifted her chin and met his gaze until a smile dented the left side of his face. "No. But you aren't what I'd expected, either. I'm beginning to suspect you wear bright colors to distract and disarm."

"Or maybe I just like pink," she countered.

"No one likes pink that much."

"No one likes nothing but moody mono-tones, either, yet here you are." Their breaths comingled. She could almost taste the cham-pagne in the air.

He bent his head, the space between them dissolving to scant millimeters. "I wonder. Who are you, Anna?"

She shivered at the low growl in her ear, goose bumps rising almost painfully along her arms. Who was she? She had no idea how to answer him. How could she when the answer eluded her own grasp?

But maybe she could find the answer. And the best way to start was to be direct and honest about what she wanted. Starting tonight.

She raised her head, her gaze catching his. "I'm someone who finds you very attractive. And I'm wondering if the reason why you approached me on the terrace was because you find me attractive. And if so, perhaps we should do something about it. Tonight."

She held her breath, scarcely believing she'd said the words out loud. Then her breath exhaled in a shaky swoosh as amber flames flared to life in his brown eyes.

"Fairy wings and glitter caught my attention. But I'm finding the woman who wore them to be far more intriguing." He lifted his right hand, the back of his fingers caressing her cheek, trailing sparks in their wake. "Is this why you came to my room?"

She swallowed. "I didn't spill the hot chocolate on purpose."

"Bell services could have delivered my jacket."

"True. I wanted..." Her mind spun. There were so many ways to finish the sentence. So many things she wanted, from a clean bill of health for Pepa to discovering how she fit in the world after the Knock. Then his thumb traced a path over her lower lip and all else burned away. Her breath caught, leaving enough air to exhale one word. "You."

His smile couldn't be more devilish if he were wearing a horned costume and carrying a pitchfork. "Glad to hear it."

"I leave tomorrow."

"So do I. After the meeting, of course."

Right. He'd mentioned he had a packed morning. Of course, she had a meeting of her own to attend. She nodded. "One night only. No questions, no regrets."

His left hand came up to join his right, cupping her face in his warm, generous grasp. "I guarantee regret is the last word you'll use."

She didn't doubt it. And she wasn't lying. She wanted him. So much, her knees were soft with it. So badly, she might expire from shivery anticipation alone, craving his touch on her breasts, between her legs. Still, there was something in his tone—a hint of self-satisfaction, or perhaps conquest?—that caused her to hold her chin high and stare him down. "Prove it."

The embers in his gaze flared into flames,

the amber flecks gleaming in the reflected glow of the Lakes of Wonder neon lights. Then his mouth crashed down on hers and she couldn't see, couldn't think, could only feel.

She dissolved into a molten pool of desire. Somehow her legs functioned enough to walk backward toward the large bed, their mouths never losing contact, his hands knowing exactly where she needed to be touched for the flames to leap higher. Somewhere along the way she lost her joggers, then her hoodie, revealing the lacy bra she put on in the hopes that was happening would indeed happen before it, too, was discarded. Her knees finally gave out as the backs met the cool, crisp sheets and she fell onto the bed, only for Ian to pull her toward him until she was half on the bed, half off, her legs held open in his sure grasp.

She used her elbows to prop herself up and met his half-lidded gaze with a smile. "Well?" she said. She kicked off her slip-on shoe—very glad she was no longer wearing her sandals with their multiple buckles—used her right foot to caress his calf through the fabric of his trousers. "We only have one night. Are you going to stand there and look? Or are you going to put those hands to a better use?"

She'd never talked that way to a partner before. She always let her boyfriends take the lead. But Ian seemed to enjoy her words. His wicked mouth twisted with a promise that scored a direct hit to her core, causing an answering rush of wetness between her legs. His hands played with the bare skin of her legs, raising goose bumps that had nothing to do with the room's temperature. Not that she knew if the room was cool or warm, as she was burning up from inside. If his fingers brushed a centimeter higher, she might spontaneously combust into flames from how much she wanted him.

Then his fingers did go higher, pulling aside the damp silk of her panties. He smiled up at her. "So beautiful," he murmured, and she flushed at the pleasure in his tone. He brushed the pad of his thumb over what he saw and she bucked, hard, unable to control her movements. She was going to come, just from a slight touch.

She'd always had a hard time orgasming with her previous boyfriends. Unable to relax, perhaps. Too worried about pleasing them to be able to take her own pleasure.

But with Ian…

Then his mouth replaced his fingers, his tongue drawing her in and finding her most sensitive spot, and the fireworks that erupted behind her eyelids were brighter and more brilliant than anything Lake of Wonder had to offer.

When she calmed, his hand on her stomach keeping her anchored to this world, she opened her eyes and found him lying next to her, still fully clothed, his gaze focused on her. "Wow," she breathed.

He laughed. "I'll take it."

She rolled onto her stomach and started to undo the buttons of his shirt. "That was... wow." She got his shirt open and began to play with the treasure she uncovered. Gorgeously defined pecs above a firm abdomen, flat, coppery nipples and a happy trail of crisp, dark hair leading to one of the most impressive erections it had ever been her privilege to handle once she freed him from his trousers and briefs. He growled at her touch, a deep groan that caused her insides to clench and demand his attention anew.

This was relatively new to her, to take her time, to explore and wander. Her last partner had always been so eager to get to what he called "the main event" that she'd forgotten how much fun it could be to just touch and taste, discovering what caused him to squeeze his eyes shut and his skin to shudder. She couldn't get enough of his erection, drawing him into her mouth, her tongue swirling and lapping, her hands experimenting until she found the right rhythm and pressure to make him lose control.

When he came, she reveled in the knowledge she'd caused that. She, Anna Stratford, had made this glorious human being, this accomplished, smart man far out of her usual league, fall apart. She grinned up at him. "Want to go again before the night is over? Might as well make our time count."

She shivered at the gleam in his eyes as he pulled her up and over him, his hands coming up to cup her breasts before his fingers found her tightly furled nipples. "We're going to run out the clock," he promised before kissing her into oblivion.

FIVE

ANNA GIGGLED THEN clapped her hand to her mouth and glanced around to ensure no one overheard her decidedly unprofessional laughter. The hallway of the Team Lakes of Wonder stretched out in front of Anna for an infinite distance. Or maybe that was just how it appeared to her to senses, addled by a night of truly amazing sex. Did everyone feel this...well, alive, after a one-night stand? Anna was aghast at what she had been missing all her adult life. Or maybe last night had been the perfect confluence of setting, partner and timing.

Her head pounded despite the two pain relievers she'd taken after sneaking back to her hotel room that morning while Ian showered. She needed a vat of coffee followed by an ocean of water. Her gait was unsteady and she slowed her pace despite running late. But her legs still reminded her with almost every step of her activities the night before, her thighs deliciously tender where Ian had grasped them. Her muscles ached from wrapping around Ian's solid torso, pressing into him as he pumped into her, his gaze never leaving hers, ensuring everything happening between them was with her full consent and resulted in her pleasure. Her hand flew out to brace herself against the wall as her memories triggered a rush of wetness between her legs, her nipples hardening to painful points as her knees threatened to give out.

Thank goodness she and Ian had agreed it was only night, because Anna wasn't certain she would survive many more. She certainly wouldn't have a productive life. She wanted nothing more than to return to her hotel room and relieve the pressure building fast and hot deep inside her. If only she'd brought her vibrator with her on this trip, but who knew it would have been necessary?

She took a deep breath. She had the rest of her life to draw upon last night for her wildest fantasies. She needed to pull herself together and get through today. And another side benefit of Ian occupying all five of her senses so fully? She hadn't had the time nor energy to stress about this morning's meeting. Until now.

She glanced at the numbers on the doors as she passed them. While part of her was glad she'd turned down an escort from the hotel to the meeting—she wouldn't have had the mental focus to make small talk with whomever had been assigned to babysit her—it might have been nice to be sure she was heading in the right direction. Finally, she came to a large glassed-in conference room. Several people had arrived before her and were standing in small conversational groups or availing themselves of the table laden with bagels, donuts and baskets of leftover Halloween candy. Ian would have fit right in with their tailored black and gray suits. She, on the other hand...she smoothed the skirt of her lemon-yellow dress and pushed the door of the conference room open, her pulse beating fast as her throat suddenly went dry.

Wherever Ian was, she hoped his meeting was going well. Not that she knew why her apprehension was at DEFCON levels. As had been explained to her ad nauseam the day before, her role in today's meeting was mostly ceremonial. Sign, shake hands, skedaddle.

People's heads turned as if one when she opened the door. Anna beelined toward the first Lakes of Wonder executive she recognized, her hand held out for a handshake greeting. "Hi, Teri. Good to see you again. Hope I'm not late."

Teri shook her head. "Right on time. We're still waiting for the BBA team to arrive. Can I get you anything?

"Coffee. A swimming pool of it."

Teri smiled. "Will a large cup do?"

"If I must. I can have seconds, right?"

Teri laughed and made a motion at a young man standing nearby. Before Anna knew it, a steaming mug of coffee had materialized in her right hand and Teri was directing her to a seat at one end of the very long and wide table. Anna sank into the oversized black-leather chair, the seat back looming high behind her, feeling like a kid who had been invited to sit at the grown-ups' table for a holiday dinner.

She glanced at the documents that had been placed on the table in front of her chair. She'd seen them before, but the amounts of money involved in the sale still took her breath away. Previously, Anna had never been involved in any business negotiation larger than helping a family pick out a house full of furniture. That, granted, could be a hefty bill—for a family.

But nothing compared to selling a theme park worth billions.

Family. Anna squeezed her eyes tight and then opened them to look around the room. No one was paying attention to her, per the usual whenever she interacted with the Lochlainn Company executives. No one caught her gaze. And no one else sat down at the conference table as they continued their conversations in scattered groups around the room. Phrases foreign to her such as "four quadrant release" and "value added loyalty program" were tossed around.

The message that she was an interloper and had no real place in today's discussion couldn't be clearer than if they had hired the Lakes of Wonder Marching Band to play "Hit the Road."

She took out her phone and saw she had a string of texts from Maritza, asking if she was okay, and groaned. She missed her usual call to say good morning to Pepa before kindergarten. In her defense, she had been otherwise occupied. Rising from the table, she found a corner that was mercifully free of people using jargon and called her cousin.

"You're alive, after all," Maritza answered.

"Is Pepa upset?"

"No. She's fine. She was excited to get to school to show off her Halloween toy haul to her friends."

"Careful, she might start a trend of swapping candy for toys." Anna laughed then sobered. "I'm sorry about missing the call."

"Yeah, that's not like you. So, I'm hoping the reason is really good one. As in *really* good." Maritza dropped her tone to low and breathy, the vocal equivalent of a wink wink nudge nudge.

"Um…" Anna hoped her blush would subside by the time she had to return to the conference table.

"Tell me everything!"

"I will, but not now. I'm in the meeting room. But the people from BBA haven't showed up yet." Her gaze swept around the conference room. Yesterday's meetings had been on a lower floor, in a windowless space. That was not the case here. Once again, she was overlooking Lakes of Wonder, although this view was not one meant for guests. She could see the service road that circled the park's backstage areas, and the rear of the buildings that housed the Buccaneer Bayou attractions. The Lighthouse still stood proud in the background, however, drawing her focus. Like a good weenie should, she thought, and smiled at the rush of warmth lighting her from within.

She wrenched her gaze—and her thoughts—away from the vista with difficulty. Only then did she notice the three framed photos hanging on the opposite wall.

She approached the nearest framed work for a closer look. The black-and-white photo depicted a half-built Lighthouse of Amazement in a field of mud, with a crane off in the distance. In front of the building site, both wearing hardhats, were a beaming Archibald Lochlainn, the founder of the Lochlainn Company and its subsequent empire—she recognized him from the Wikipedia article she'd read—holding a baby she could only assume was his only child, Keith.

Keith. Her biological grandfather.

"Anna? You still there?"

Anna wrenched her thoughts back to her phone call. "Yeah, I'm here."

"You zoned out. Again."

"I know. I just…it's weird, being here, you know?"

"It's been weird ever since that lawyer showed up." Maritza paused. "Are you mad at me?"

"Why would I be mad at you?"

"For asking you to send in your DNA to that company. I thought it would be fun. I had no idea—"

"*You* had no idea?" Anna laughed. The laugh sounded angry to her ears and she winced. She tried again, softening her voice. "You had no idea? That's an understatement.

Not for the first time, she wished she had never answered the Knock. But how could she have known that the pleasant-appearing man in his Brooks Brothers' suit was there to erode the solid ground upon which she had built her life?

Her parents had kept the truth of her conception from her. Her biological father was not Glenn Stratford. She did not inherit from him her blonde curly hair or her tendency to freckle, as she had assumed all her life. Instead, her parents had used an anonymous sperm donor to conceive her.

And the donor's identity turned out to be Jamie Lochlainn, the now-deceased son of Keith, who had sold his sperm to a top fertility clinic to pay for college when he had been estranged from his father and refused to touch his family's money.

"But it's okay," Anna hurried to reassure

Maritza. "I mean, look where I am. Free, all-expenses-paid trip to California."

"Yeah, that's part of the problem. You ran off without speaking to your parents. And you're still not speaking to them." Martiza's tone softened. "They miss you. Please call them."

Anna sighed. "I will. I just... Not now. Let me get through today's ceremonial signing first." When she'd answered the Knock, the lawyer—whose name she would never forget, Bingham Lockwood—had not only told her the truth of her parentage but offered her a once-in-a-lifetime opportunity: finalize the sale of Lakes of Wonder to the BBA Group. If she completed the transaction by the end of the year, she would earn a place in Keith Lochlainn's will.

Her grandfather's will.

The grandfather she'd never known existed.

She never did receive a satisfactory answer as to why Keith was insisting on such a complicated hoop for her to jump through. To her, it was simple. Either he accepted she was conceived from Jamie's sperm, or he didn't. Perhaps asking her to oversee a complicated business deal indicated he thought something else had been passed down to Anna aside from twenty-three chromosomes. Something intangible that made her a Lochlainn.

"Okay," Maritza said. "Break a leg or whatever people say in business meetings. I'm here if you need me."

"Thanks, although I should be the one there for you and Pepa."

"Hey, you earn a spot in Keith Lochlainn's will, you will be," Maritza joked. Then she turned serious. "But I know that's not the reason you accepted that lawyer's challenge. Just..." She sighed. "We all love you, you know. The Lochlainn thing, it doesn't matter. Not to us. You're still our Anna."

"I know." Anna's nose tingled and she blinked back the tears before they could form. "But it matters to me." She said her goodbyes, her gaze returning to the photo of Archibald and baby Keith, before turning her attention to the other images.

Centered on the wall was a photo in yellow-tinted saturated color. The Lighthouse was complete, soaring high into the cloudless blue sky. Looming next to it was the iconic mechanical Seamus parade float, several stories tall and rumored to have breathed real fire in its heyday, which had long ago been mothballed. In the foreground of the photo stood a much older Archibald, his back hunched but his gaze direct. Next to him she recognized Keith, perhaps in his thirties or early forties. And Keith was holding...

A toddler Jamie. Who grinned for the camera as if he knew this kingdom would all be his someday.

Before Anna knew what she was doing, her right hand reached out to trace the curve of Jamie's cheeks. She recognized the mischievous glint in his eyes. She'd seen it often enough in photos of herself as a baby and small child.

The third photo on the wall had been taken recently. The image was in high definition, the banners on the Lighthouse vivid and vibrant for Lakes of Wonder's seventieth anniversary. But no one stood in front of the Lighthouse. No Keith, no Jamie. Just the tall white tower, the surrounding grounds empty and deserted. No doubt the photo had been taken before the theme park's opening, judging by the silvery morning sunlight, but the empty landscape still made Anna shiver.

What happened? How had the Lochlainn family gone from being the proud possessors of Lakes of Wonder to selling it off? She squinted, willing the two-dimensional Keith to impart his secrets.

The photo remained silent.

The room started to buzz with conversation. "Anna?" Teri materialized next to her. "The BBA team has arrived. We're ready to get started, if you are?"

"Of course." Anna put on her brightest smile and turned around to greet the newcomers. She held out her right hand for a handshake to the nearest BBA executive, a tall, beautifully dressed Black woman. "Hello, I'm—"

"Sorry we're late. My fault."

Anna froze. She knew that voice. She'd last heard it that morning. In bed.

Ian's bed.

It couldn't be him. She must have heard wrong. Her subconscious, which was still playing erotic images from last night whenever her mind wandered, must have conjured his voice.

She peered around the woman shaking her hand. Her stomach dropped to the floor. No, she wasn't hallucinating.

Ian filled the doorway of the conference room, the last of the group to arrive. "Hi. Ian Blackburn, BBA's CEO. Good to meet everyone in person, finally."

His darkly amused gaze caught and held hers in the seconds before he was rushed by several Lochlainn Company executives eager to greet him.

"Anna." She forced her name through numb lips and then finally remembered to let go of the woman's hand she was shaking. "I'm Anna Stratford."

"Shall we take a few minutes to grab coffees?" Teri asked. The Lochlainn and the BBA factions began to drift toward the table of food, making small talk along the way.

Anna somehow found her chair at the conference table, the room out-of-focus and spinning around her. A fresh cup of coffee appeared in front of her, giving her something to focus on. She looked up to thank whoever had delivered the mug to her.

Ian was leaning over her chair. His smirk was even more pronounced as he bent down and spoke for her ears only.

"Hello again. Let's hope today's signing is as equally...pleasurable...as last night. I have to say, that was the most fun I've had dealing with a representative of the Lochlainn Company.

He was amused. No, more than amused. He was *smug*. His lips may be incredibly talented, but she wanted nothing more than to wipe that expression off them. "Did you know?"

"Know what?"

"We would be on opposite sides of the table today."

His smirk didn't falter. "Of course. The Lochlainn Company informed us last week that you would be joining today's signing."

Oh, *of course*. Her pulse sped up even as her heart sank past her stomach. "That's why you approached me on the terrace."

"I wanted to meet you before this morning's meeting." His smirk turned knowing. "And I have no regrets. As promised."

His voice seemed to come from far way. She screwed her eyes shut, hoping when she opened them again, she would be on the hotel's terrace waiting for the fireworks and this would all be a very bad, awful nightmare brought on by too much blue champagne.

How could she be so…blind? And naïve. Categorically naïve.

She had only herself to blame. Maybe if she'd taken the time to become more acquainted with the theme park industry, she would know all the players and their names, but everything had happened so fast. And she'd been so hurt by her parents keeping the truth of her parentage from her, she'd barely kept herself together to put on a brave face for Martiza and Pepa while ensuring her design clients would be taken care of in her absence before getting on the plane at the required time. Besides, Bingham Lockwood had told her she only needed to show up. Make her mark—literally—as a Lochlainn by signing the deal, and she would fulfill the challenge Keith had set her.

She suppressed her groan.

Once again, she had gone with the flow, doing exactly what others had expected of her without questioning or stopping to think the situation through. And the one time she'd thought she was breaking free from the rules by which she'd lived until now—a no-strings-attached, one-night stand with a stranger—it turned out he wasn't really a stranger. Or rather, she wasn't a stranger to him.

And yet his scent caused her breath to stutter, the heat of his arm across the back of her chair making her pulse jump in erratic leaps.

She closed her eyes to stop the room from spinning around her. When she opened them, she found Ian regarding her, his expression unreadable. She raised her eyebrows. "What?"

"You didn't know."

"That covers a lot of things," she said. "As I'm discovering."

"You didn't know I would be here today," he clarified. "As part of the BBA team."

"Of course, I knew." Her chest burned. It was one thing to realize how badly she'd screwed up by blithely going along and not paying more attention. It was another to know Ian Blackburn had deliberately played her. That last night had been…calculated, and not the result of an attraction that, damn it, even now caused heat to pool deep in her belly as her skin yearned for his touch.

She put on her most professional expression, the one she brought out for clients who insisted on ordering sofas too big for their spaces despite her counseling against it and then demanded the ensuing unworkable result was Anna's fault for not warning them. "I'm merely surprised you were told I would be here."

That wasn't much of a lie. She was a very recent addition to the proceedings.

His gaze narrowed. "We never did establish what position you hold at the Lochlainn Company. Business development, I assume?"

She inhaled deeply, hoping the oxygen would clear her brain. "Interesting question. But—"

Teri dropped into the seat on the other side of Anna. "Good! I see you've met."

Ian didn't remove his gaze from Anna. "Yes. In fact, we were discussing what Anna does at the Lochlainn Company."

Teri made a sweeping motion with her hand. "What doesn't she do?"

"Doesn't do," Anna said. "That covers it—"

"Anna is a special liaison to Keith Lochlainn." Teri spoke over Anna. "She's been sent by New York specifically to oversee today's closing. And we're honored to have her for today's signing. Isn't that right, Anna?"

Teri held Anna's gaze. Her "don't screw this up" warning was clearer than if she had spray-painted the words on the boardroom's walls. Anna nodded, avoiding looking in Ian's direction. "I am here at the request of Keith Lochlainn, yes."

"Then let's get to it." Teri opened the file folder in front of her. Everyone else at the table followed suit. "Shall we start?"

SIX

"Agreed. And...done." Ian signed the last page
with a flourish then stacked the documents
neatly together before sliding them across the
table to Anna. "Your turn," he said, the words
coming out a bit rougher than he'd intended.

Last night, "your turn" had had a different
meaning. She shifted in her chair, rearrang-
ing her legs. He smiled. It seemed he was not
the only one having a harder time than normal concentrating without being interrupted
by memories of their recent activities in vivid
detail.

His smile deepened. This meeting had gone
better than expected. Not only had he need-
lessly worried about a last-minute negotiation
twist, but he was able to spend the morning
gazing at his companion of the night before.

He preferred the Anna that had been in his
bed, all tousled curls and flushed skin and swol-

len lips begging to be kissed again and again. But the woman across the table from him was a delightful vision, today dressed in a yellow dress with a high waistline, emphasizing those heavy, glorious breasts. To his surprise, she didn't speak much during the meeting, allowing the Lochlainn Company executives to do the bulk of the talking. Instead, her focus appeared to be caught by the photos lining the wall opposite her. Whenever she did catch his gaze, her expression remained carefully schooled in a mask of calm, reminding him she was an excellent actress—except when they were in bed. That hadn't been an act, he was positive. Too bad they were currently sitting in a boardroom. Once they finished the meeting…

They'd agreed last night was a one-and-done. And he was scheduled to leave for Hong Kong tonight. But perhaps she might be amenable to a repeat in the near future. To see if they could make lightning strike twice.

Her gaze flicked over and caught his. He smiled at her, a smile informed by the delightful images in his head of her sprawled against his pillows, limbs akimbo and skin flushed hot. As if she had read his mind, a warm pink washed over her cheeks as she pulled the papers to her.

She flipped to the first page and her pen hovered over the paper. Then she put the writing instrument down and crossed her arms on the table. "Why do you want to buy Lakes of Wonder?"

He furrowed his brow. "We spent the last two hours discussing that."

"No, you spent the last two hours going over the financials and determining the price was fair. You never expressed why you want to buy the park."

The chatter in the room slowed, trickling to a stop. All eyes in the room were focused on them. He kept his expression neutral. "It's a good business decision," he said.

She shook her head. "Not answering my question."

"BBA owns amusement parks. Lakes of Wonder fits into our portfolio. Therefore, we made you a fair offer. Theme park 101," he offered, his gaze falling to linger on her mouth. Were her lips still swollen, or had they always been that delectably pillowy? The terrace and his room had both been dimly lit, after all.

She threw him a sharp glance and thinned her lips into a tight line, much to his disappointment. "But does Lakes of Wonder truly fit? It's a theme park for families. BBA's properties offer thrills for teens and other adrenaline seekers. I do know it's difficult to market to two different audiences. Like, for example...um." She hesitated and then her words tumbled out. "Like a business that sells furniture to families with large houses and a business that sells furniture to single people who live in smaller apartments. The first sells big, heavy pieces, so they need a spacious showroom. The second can sell multipurpose items that take up less room. You don't get—what's the word?—advantages from combining the two."

His smirk grew smaller the longer she talked. She was right, of course, even if her examples lacked the finesse he would expect from a Lochlainn Company executive. But what game was she playing? Why bring this up at the last minute?

"The word you're looking for is 'synergies.' But any costs associated with bringing Lakes of Wonder into BBA's operations are our problems, not yours. Another reason why this deal is very advantageous to the Lochlainns."

Her gaze focused on the large photos of Lakes of Wonder on the opposite wall. "When we last spoke," she said, and he noticed she was careful to avoid referring to when that was, "you said theme parks don't bring joy. That happy families are just a marketing gimmick. Do you really believe that?"

Yes. He did. Because he'd grown up in amusement parks and he knew from experience they didn't bring families closer. Didn't create fond memories, and certainly not ones he wanted lasting a lifetime. They did create infighting and backstabbing and heart attacks at an early age, however. "Does what I believe matter to today's negotiation? We've agreed on the terms. The financing has been approved. Unless you have a deal point we haven't covered, what I personally think isn't germane to the discussion. I leave marketing up to my marketing team." He glanced around the table at the other Lochlainn Company executives. "Any other questions? No?" He glanced at his smartwatch and then turned back to Anna. "We're scheduled to take photos commemorating the deal signing in fifteen minutes, so…"

Anna stared him down. She really did have gorgeous eyes. He could lose himself in their blue depths if he wasn't careful.

But he was always careful.

He smiled at her and indicated her abandoned pen. Her gaze narrowed. Then she reached for it—

No. She reached past the pen. Her hands instead pulled all the pages together in one neat pile, aligning them with a tap of the edges on the boardroom table. Leaving the papers in a neat pile, she pushed her chair back, pulling the strap of her purse over her shoulder as she rose and made her way to the exit. "I'm so sorry to have wasted everyone's time, but there will be no signing today."

The door slammed behind her and the room erupted into chaos. Ian could scarcely keep track of who was shouting what. Several Lochlainn Company executives jumped up, their intent to go after Anna and drag her back to finish the meeting clearly written on their expressions, but Ian cut them off with a loud, low, "No. I'll handle this."

He was almost out the door when Tai appeared at his elbow. "You sure? We have a potential breach lawsuit in the making. We should leave instead."

"No, it's my..." Ian stopped. "This might be payback."

Tai opened his mouth then snapped his lips shut. "I don't want to know, do I?"

"Can you calm things down here? Let them know we still want to go through with the acquisition."

"Sure," Tai said, but Ian was racing down the hallway before Tai finished uttering the syllable.

He spotted her waiting for the elevator. He ran, ignoring the shocked gasps from the people he passed. "Anna, wait!"

She ignored him, tapping her foot as she waited. The elevator doors opened and she scurried inside. The doors started to close. With a burst of speed, Ian managed to insert his foot into the decreasing gap between the doors, and then slid the rest of his body into the elevator cab.

Anna stared at him, her mouth slightly open.

"What was that about?" His lungs burned and he gulped air.

She huffed and tore her gaze away, staring straight ahead. "I decided not to sign."

"You can't do that. BBA and the Lochlainn Company have an agreement."

"I can, and I did."

"You've given us grounds to sue on breach of promise. We will take action."

"I didn't say I wasn't selling you Lakes of Wonder. I said I wasn't signing today."

The elevator ground to a halt. Anna flung out her arms and braced herself against the walls. "What the…what happened?"

"I pushed the stop button."

"You did—why isn't the alarm ringing?"

He pointed to a red button marked Alarm. "Separate system. It's an old elevator. This building dates to the construction of Lakes of Wonder."

She lunged for the control panel but he easily blocked her access. "You're safe."

"Trapped with you?" She scoffed.

"You didn't seem to mind being in an enclosed space with me last night."

Red flooded her cheeks. "People need this elevator, you know. What if someone with mobility issues is waiting to use it right now?"

"There are three other elevators." He unfolded his arms and closed half the space between them. "You realize today was the culmination of months of negotiating. Of time-consuming back-and-forth emails and conference calls, research, pulling numbers together…"

"I'm aware. And I'm sorry. But I…can't."

She truly was a damn good actress. He almost bought that was regret making her eyes widen, causing her to bite those plump lips. Almost. Because he also remembered those lips giving as good as they got, biting and sucking and whispering wicked words. She might play the sweet princess in her summer-colored dresses, but he'd had a taste of what Anna Stratford was capable of last night and it was far from innocent.

He was so close. So. Damn. Close. To ridding BBA of Harlan's disastrous, poisonous leadership. To freeing not only his company but his family from his former stepfather for once and for all. All he needed was Lakes of Wonder to secure his uncle's and cousin's votes on the board of directors.

This deal had to happen. And he would not let the Lochlainn Company pull the rug out from underneath him again, no matter how attractive the woman doing the pulling.

"Can't. That's an interesting choice of words." Before he knew it, he'd closed the remaining space between them. The elevator light yellowed and flecked with dust gathered over the years, but it was bright enough to illuminate the freckles bridging her nose and spilling over her cheeks. Freckles that still stood out despite the crimson still blooming in her cheeks. "Seems to me all you needed to do was pick up a pen. And as I recall, your hands are in excellent working condition. You had no problem with grasping—"

"Stop right there. Yes. I can physically sign. But I can't..." She inhaled, the curves of her breasts pushing against the flimsy yellow fabric of her dress. Breasts that had overfilled his hands, warm and satiny with dark rose tips that—

He shook his head to clear it. Reconciling the woman who stood before him with the temptress tangled in his sheets the night before would have to wait. "Why, damn it? What is wrong with the deal?"

"You are!" The words burst out of her.

"Me?" He stared at her. "What the hell... look, if this is about last night, I have a very good memory and you were a consenting participant. But this is a multibillion-dollar deal you're deciding on a whim—"

"This isn't about last night. I mean, I'm not thrilled to learn you had ulterior motives—"

"Ulterior? What are you accusing me of—" He stopped. "Wait. You really didn't know I'd be in the meeting today, did you? Do you think last night—"

She exhaled, a loud puff of breath. "Never mind. Let's not talk about last night. Ever. It happened and will never happen again."

"Then why—"

"If Lakes of Wonder must be sold, it should be to someone who cares about its history and its legacy." She rested her balled-up fists on her hips. "Not to someone who sees it as only dollars and cents."

"You can't—" He took a deep breath. He'd known the Lochlainns would throw a twist into the deal. His mistake was believing Anna, despite her fairy costume and predilection for pink, would be honor-bound to play by the normal rules of cut-and-dried dealmaking. He had to give the Lochlainns credit, however, for taking him so off guard. "If you read the deal paperwork, you'd see that BBA has laid out a very prudent offer that considers Lakes of Wonder's past and present-day goodwill—"

She shook her head. "You're babbling more MBA buzz speak. Why do you want to acquire the park? Tell me. Or better, teach me. I want to be convinced you are the right buyer."

Oh, he could teach her so many things. Things he'd wanted to teach her the night before but they'd run out of time. And theme parks had little to do with the lessons he had in mind.

He had to give the Lochlainns credit for this latest gambit, however. He'd been right. Anna wasn't the usual Lochlainn shark. She used earnestness instead of cynicism, enthusiasm instead of jaded weariness. That made her even more dangerous.

But perhaps he could make the delay in signing the deal work to his advantage. He could use the time to consolidate his position with the other directors on the board who weren't in Harlan's pocket, gain more votes to make his victory over his stepfather secure.

He smiled and placed his hand on the slick metal of the elevator wall above her right shoulder, resting his weight as he leaned toward her. "I'm happy to show you anything you want. Anytime."

Her breathing stuttered. She smelled of lemon and mint, of summer breezes and fresh air despite being trapped in an elevator on a gray November morning, and he suddenly wanted nothing more than to forget BBA, forget the Lochlainn Company, and whisk her off to a secluded bungalow with a large bed and no other furniture.

Then her gaze narrowed into daggers of dangerous light, and he was back to standing in an airless elevator cab stopped between floors in an ancient office building. "I've already experienced what you're suggesting and there will be no repeat. Unless you want me to add 'reneges on his word' to the reasons why I'm hesitant to sign."

He straightened and held up his hands, palms out. "I'm referring to Lakes of Wonder only, of course."

Her gaze searched his. What she was looking for, he didn't know, and from the frown lines appearing on her forehead, she wasn't successful at finding it. "Okay. We have our first deal."

"Second," he reminded her. "Last night. Remember?"

Her gaze flashed. "Fine, second. Here. Shake." She held out her right hand.

"Not so fast."

Her hand lowered. "Now what?"

"I can't wait around forever for you to make up your capricious mind about whether you feel like selling or not. There needs to be a time limit."

"Fair enough. How about…by New Year's Eve?"

"December first. The deal must be closed by

the end of BBA's fiscal year, which is December thirty-first." And by the next board meeting.

She pursed her lips. "Fine. But you better be prepared for a full demonstration of why I should sell to BBA."

This time he was the one who offered a handshake. "I plan to be very thorough."

Her gaze narrowed at his insinuating tone but she took his hand, her palm sliding against his. The resulting electric spark didn't take him by surprise. He already knew when they came together, lightning struck.

"Let's hope you are. I plan to be satisfied. Before I sell the park." She released his hand, but red still flew high on her cheekbones.

Oh, he'd satisfy her. He had the utmost faith in his ability to charm even a chameleon like Anna into going along with his wishes. Exhibit A, his hotel room. He pushed the stop button, releasing the elevator, and the cab began to move again. "What's your phone number?"

"What? Why—"

"We're going to be spending a lot of time together at Lakes of Wonder. It would be helpful to have a way to reach you."

The elevator reached the bottom floor and dinged open. They exited to an empty lobby.

"Give me your phone," she said. When he acquiesced, she typed furiously before handing it back to him. "There. Now you have it."

He looked at his screen. "Make me believe" read the name on his contact list. He laughed. "I have meetings I can't rearrange in Hong Kong. Shall we say a week from today? We can meet a half hour before the park opens at the VIP entrance."

She shook her head. "No. Meet at the main entrance gate. The ticket booth furthest to the left."

He frowned. "It's faster to use the VIP entrance."

"But it's not the experience most parkgoers have." She raised her eyebrows. "Have you ever visited just as a regular guest?"

He…no. Not even as a child. As a member of the Blackburn family, he'd had VIP guest privileges at most amusement parks around the world. "If you insist. Main entrance gate."

She smiled. It turned the grim lighting in the lobby into a bright summer's day. "Don't be late."

Oh, he wouldn't. He needed this deal to be done.

He wanted Anna Stratford.

He saw no reason why he couldn't be successful at attaining them both. Woo Anna, and the theme park would also fall into his hands.

He would beat the Lochlainns at their own game. Twice over.

SEVEN

ANNA CHECKED THE time on her phone, sighed, and then returned the device to her ear. "He'll be here," she insisted to Maritza, on the other end of the call. Her foot tapped a staccato rhythm on the pavement. She wasn't nervous about seeing Ian Blackburn again…was she?

She was. Nervous. And scared. She'd blown up the big deal between the Lochlainn Company and BBA. She'd risked billions of dollars on a whim, driven by seeing the photos of Archibald, Keith and Jamie, wanting to know more about this place that brought generations of Lochlainns together, only for Keith to let it fall into disrepair and to be sold.

Nervous and scared…and excited. Her stomach fluttered like it had every time she had thought of Ian in the last week. He hadn't been exactly forthcoming about his identity. On the other hand, she wasn't about to tell him she was a Lochlainn. She couldn't, per the terms of the Knock, or she would risk her place in Keith's will. But every time she tried to stir up a bout of righteous indignation at sleeping with Ian under false—no, not false, just not fully honest—pretenses, she only stirred up memories of how amazing his body had felt against hers. Hot, vivid memories causing her breath to catch and her pulse to race.

"Yes, he'll show up," her cousin agreed. "With a lawsuit. I still don't know what you were thinking."

"I was thinking..." Anna screwed her eyes shut. "Ugh. I wasn't thinking. I was reacting."

"Have the Lochlainn Company people said anything to you yet?"

"No." Anna's phone and email had been very quiet about the unsigned paperwork. Too quiet. The only item that could be termed a response was a mass email sent to all the Lochlainn Company executives who had been in the meeting, reiterating Anna was calling the shots in the negotiation and to follow her lead. "They seem to be leaving everything up to me."

"We're talking billions of dollars. That's weird."

"I know."

"And unsettling."

"I also know." Anna sighed. "But there might be a method in their madness. I think there is more going on, both with Keith Lochlainn and with Ian Blackburn. This deal isn't as clear-cut as it was presented to me."

"What makes you say that?"

Anna hesitated. "A feeling…" She winced and took the phone away from her ear. She put it back up in time for the tail end of Maritza's long-suffering sigh.

"Anna…"

"Have my feelings ever steered me wrong?" She bit her lip. Damn it, Maritza was not the person to ask.

"Do you seriously want me to answer that?"

"If that's a reference to my parents lying to me—"

"What? No!" Maritza huffed. "It's a reference to you pretending you can continue to ignore your parents. You said you'd call them."

"I know, and I—" Anna sighed. "You know what I find the most hurtful about the Knock? It's not that my dad—Glenn—it's not that he and my mom lied. Or rather, didn't tell me. It's that a family, whose only connection to me is a DNA test, is trusting me with one of their major businesses, while the people who raised me barely trust me to talk to clients on my own."

"I know you feel that way." Martiza inhaled. "But you're not playing with someone's suite of living room furniture—"

"Playing with? Now you're doing it, too."

"I didn't mean it that way. You yourself call it playing."

"Because designing interiors is fun!" Anna rubbed her forehead with her free hand. "I know you and my parents have only my best interests at heart. But I need to see this Lochlainn thing through. And I need more time before I can talk to them."

Maritza clicked her tongue, a sign that she was willing to drop the discussion. "Okay. Just remember you're making a decision about an icon of people's childhoods."

"Even more reason for me to dig deeper and understand what is going on."

Maritza snorted. "Are you sure you're not doing this because you want to dig deeper into Ian Blackburn? Like 'dig your fingernails into his back' deeper?"

To be fair, the thought had crossed Anna's mind. More than once. It might have been the starring act in her dreams the last six nights. "I was given a task to do, and I want to do it properly."

"If you say so." Maritza did not sound convinced. "I have to run. Call me after your date."

"It's not a date—" But Maritza had hung up.

"Ugh." Anna squeezed her eyes shut.

"It's not a date? Guess I shaved for nothing."

Her eyes flew open. Ian stood in front of her, his amused grin lighting the air around him, brighter than the still-rising sun.

Any stress from her phone call with Maritza fled, replaced by a new tension. The taut strumming started low in her belly and then flew along her nervous system, her heartbeat a loud timpani drum solo in her ears. Really, it should be illegal for any human being to look as good as he did, especially considering the early morning. If she thought Ian in his sharply tailored business suits and pressed suits were enough to take her breath way, that was nothing compared to Ian in black jeans that appeared to have made precisely to hug his muscled thighs and well-defined ass, topped with a dark gray Henley pullover with the sleeves pushed up to reveal his forearms. Tensed forearms that had held him suspended above her before their bodies came together in—

She blinked, the vision disappearing. Sure, that night had been fun. More than fun. But there would be no replay of that scene. She resolutely dragged her gaze from the exposed skin below the pushed-up fabric and turned to look over at the crowds starting to form. "Sorry to have caused you to waste your time. I prefer stubble to clean-shaven, anyway."

"Noted." His grin caused her stomach to jump in interesting patterns.

She rolled her eyes and looked away, hoping to appear as unaffected as possible. "I see you're still in your camouflage."

He looked down at his outfit. "I'm dressed for a day in the parks."

"Wearing an absence of color," she pointed out.

"Black is the result when all colors are mixed. I contain multitudes."

She laughed. "Shall we go in? I have a pass that allows guests."

He pulled a card out of his wallet and waved it at her. "Your pass or mine? It's amazing what perks you receive when you are prepared to spend billions of dollars, only for the rug to be pulled out from under the deal at the last minute." His tone was deadpan, but amusement gleamed deep in his dark gaze.

"The rug isn't gone for good, just…rolled up for now." They entered the park and strolled through Seamus's Seaport, then crossed the bridge that marked the boundary between the seaport and the six lakeshore ports that comprised the park. The bridge was themed to resemble the Pont Neuf in Paris but was much wider than the original to accommodate throngs of guests. However, Anna and Ian could easily meander as the crowd was sparse, mostly consisting of mothers with children too young for school strapped into strollers.

"Not a huge turnout this morning," he noted.

"It's a Friday," Anna rejoined. "During the school year. People have work, you know."

"Precisely. Fridays are a day people take off work for an extended weekend. It's one of our busiest days at BBA parks."

"It's also the start of the holiday season. People have more commitments than normal."

"And that's why the park should be more crowded than normal, with people eager to see the decorations." He looked over at her. "Point one for selling. Lakes of Wonder isn't attracting the guests necessary to stay financially afloat. BBA parks are."

"This is just one day, in the early morning. The place could be packed by this afternoon."

"Agreed. Today is only one data point. But we have the historical attendance figures. They're in the deal paperwork."

Anna pressed her lips tightly together. She couldn't blame the weather for the lack of guests. It was a gorgeous Southern California morning. The air was crisp, a reminder that colder days were coming, but also promised a warm afternoon, a reminder that autumn still brought high temperatures. Sunlight lit the faux French storefronts lining the bridge and the Lighthouse of Amazement in the distance, throwing the buildings into sharp relief, a contrast to Florida's softer, more golden glow. Not even the hint of a cloud lingered on the horizon.

She'd always thought California was desert-dry, dusty and filled with car exhaust. Now she understood why people clamored to live here.

"Let's sit on that bench." She pointed to a wooden bench festooned with intricate wrought-iron curlicues.

Ian shot her a quizzical glance. "Tired already?"

"No. But we're here to observe, right? So, let's observe."

Ian's expression was skeptical, but he followed her lead as she beelined to the bench. It provided the perfect view of both the people entering the park looking left and the Lighthouse of Amazement looking right. "So now what?" he asked once he had arranged his long legs next to Anna's.

"Now we watch."

"For how long?"

Anna turned to him. "Do you have a problem with sitting still?"

"You make me sound like a kindergartener refusing naptime."

"Well?"

"I don't know how you do things at the Lochlainn Company, but at BBA, we belong to the 'time is money' philosophy."

She rolled her eyes. "In my line of work, it's always wise to observe the customer in their setting before making sweeping changes."

"Right. Your work. What is it that you do at the Lochlainn Company again? We never established that." He leaned back against the wooden slats of the bench, stretching his arms out across the top of the bench. If she leaned back, her shoulder would fit neatly into the loose grip of his hand. His hand, so warm, so sure, so knowing...

She kept herself perched on the forward edge of the bench. "What don't I do?" She echoed Teri's words at the meeting. They weren't a lie. She literally did nothing.

His gaze narrowed. "You aren't on the business development team. I checked. There isn't an Anna Stratford matching your description registered to the California or New York bar, so you aren't a lawyer. You—"

"Look!" Anna indicated a toddler dressed in a "Lad of Wonder" T-shirt running down the wide paved road, a woman who appeared to be his mother judging by their shared bright auburn curls in hot pursuit. "He's heading straight for the Seamus balloons," she predicted.

Sure enough, the toddler came to a dead stop in front of the balloon vendor, his gaze fixed on the bright green helium-filled balloons bearing the smiling image of Seamus bobbing in the morning breeze. The mother caught up, visibly winded, and with a smile for the vendor and a frown for her son, picked him up and began to carry him away. The toddler burst into loud, angry sobs, attempting to throw himself out of his mother's grasp, his hands opening and closing in the direction of the balloons.

"Poor thing." Anna got up from the bench. Ian put his hand on her arm. His touch was warm. And electrifying. Her toes and fingertips crackled with the heat. "What?"

"She has her reasons for not buying the kid a balloon. And she's trying to bribe him with carrots she took out of her bag instead of buying snacks from a Lakes of Wonder concession cart. You need guests who will spend money at the park. Concentrate on them."

Anna couldn't keep her mouth closed. Her jaw insisted on hanging open, wider with each word Ian uttered. "She's looking after a toddler. Of course, she brought snacks for him. For all you know, he has a food allergy."

"The park sells prepackaged carrots." He shrugged.

"For ten times the cost of cutting up your own carrots at home."

"Lake of Wonder's profits in the snack category are abysmal. Guests who use Lakes of Wonder as a substitute for the city park are not profitable." He gave her a lopsided grin, the rakish angle of his lips making him seem even sexier. "You want a lesson in business? Revenues need to exceed expenses to equal profits."

And to think she'd found Ian Blackburn attractive. Still did, damn it. "Thank you for explaining basic arithmetic. I'm going to see if she needs help. Perhaps *she*—" Anna stressed the word—"would appreciate a random act of kindness." She shook off his light grasp, her skin still bearing his impression, and approached the mother struggling to get her son back in his stroller.

"A random what?" Ian called after her, but if she heard him, she didn't give any indication. He watched her go through narrowed eyes. Looked like he would need to change his tactics even more if he wanted to successfully woo her into selling the park. This was unlike any other business negotiation he had conducted and, for the twentieth time that morning, he wondered what, precisely, was her angle. Or rather, the Lochlainn Company's angle.

Still, he couldn't help admitting the view was delightful. Anna had foregone the country-club dress she'd worn to the meeting for what he could only assume was her idea of blending in with the parkgoers—because she certainly wasn't dressed as a theme park executive. Colorful leggings in shades of green outlined the curves of her legs and clung to the round globes of her ass. On top, she wore a lime green T-shirt, topped with a turquoise hoodie. Her blond hair was pulled back in a braid interwoven with green and turquoise ribbon. She literally sparkled, and it took him a second to realize she once more wore glitter on her cheeks.

Anna finished her conversation with the mother and, after a brief exchange with the balloon vendor, came back and handed the toddler the object of his desire. The toddler beamed, the mother beamed, and Anna—

Ian realized he was wrong. She didn't glow because she wore glitter. Her joy at making the small family happy lit her from within.

Anna was almost back to the bench before he belatedly understood the reason for her colorful outfit—she was dressed to remind people of Seamus, from the abstract sea-serpent-scale print on her leggings to the beribboned braid that resembled the plates on Seamus's neck.

"You really are a Lakes of Wonder superfan," he commented when she sat down. A little closer to him this time. He smiled.

"I read up on what people wear when they

come to the park. I wanted to fit in for my first time." She swiveled her head at the sound of drumbeats. "Hey, there's a drum corps approaching!"

"The park used to feature a marching band, but budget cuts eliminated it. How can this be your first time at Lakes of Wonder?"

"What?" Her eyes widened. "Oh. I mean, first time wearing a Seamus-inspired outfit. Let's go see the musicians." She rose from the bench and didn't wait for him to join her.

Ian stared after her. While he didn't doubt this was her first time wearing her outfit, he was pretty sure that wasn't the original intention of her words. He took out his silenced phone and glanced at the notifications filling the screen. Harlan's assistant sent an urgent message that Harlan was looking for him. Ian hit Delete. Simonetta Igwe, the COO, needed his attention. He texted back with a time to speak that evening. He scrolled through tens of other urgent messages, and then put the phone back into his rear jeans' pocket.

He hadn't planned on spending the whole day in the park. He'd cleared his schedule for two hours, at most, and that included a meal. But solving the ever-evolving mystery of Anna

Stratford had shot to the top of his very extensive to-do list—because he needed to close the sale to remove Harlan from BBA, of course. Not for any other reason.

Certainly not because when he'd been wide awake with jetlag in Hong Kong, he'd tried reading the most boring prospectus he'd brought with him only for his thoughts to linger on Anna, the fireworks in the sky reflected in her rapt gaze. Anna, those gorgeous eyes blinking heavily after their first kiss then closing as she'd reached for him, her mouth open beneath his and her tongue playfully teasing his until the time for teasing was over. Anna, shuddering above him…

Anna, her shocked expression when she saw him in the boardroom.

His conscience twinged and not for the first time. Perhaps he should have been more straightforward when they'd first met, but she'd literally knocked him sideways with her glitter and fairy wings. He didn't like the implication Anna thought he had been trying to play dirty, even though playing dirty was the Lochlainn Company's preferred modus operandi.

At least the postponement of the sale had had one silver lining: he had time to prove to her that while he intended to drive a hard bargain for Lakes of Wonder, the offer was a fair one and he, at least, intended to play with honor.

He rose from the bench to join Anna where she watched the drum corps when his phone rang with the ringtone assigned to Tai's personal cell phone. He sighed. He could ignore everyone else, but Tai never called unless it was critical. "Where's the fire?" he answered.

"Harlan," Tai responded. His voice echoed, as if he were standing in a stairwell or some other place where he could have privacy and not be overheard.

"Now he's using you as his messenger? His assistant already sent me a message."

"No, the fire *is* Harlan. I found out he's calling for a vote of no-confidence in you as CEO at the next board meeting. It's supposed to be hush-hush but my assistant is friends with—"

"Harlan knows." Ian wondered where the day's heat went. Then he realized the sun was still blazing overhead. He was the only one chilled. "He's going on the counteroffensive. Someone must have told him about my upcoming vote to oust him."

"He's going to use the failed acquisition of Lakes of Wonder as the pretense for the vote.

Something about how it was vital to securing BBA's future, et cetera."

"The acquisition didn't fail. It's not closed. There's a difference."

"Do you have the votes for the ouster?"

"Not fully secured," Ian admitted. "Olive and Preston will only vote with me if they're given Lakes of Wonder to run."

"Does Harlan have the votes to get you out?"

"If he wins Olive and Preston to his side, yes."

"So, you need the acquisition either way."

Ian's gaze sought out Anna, standing on the outer edges of the small crowd gathered to listen to the drum corps. She was bouncing on the balls of her feet in time to the music, her blond braid swinging. When a young child bumped into her, she whirled around. But instead of scolding him for running into her legs, she stepped back and let the child, along with the apologetic adults accompanying him, step in front of her, the better to see the musicians.

He almost didn't want to join her. He was enjoying the view far too much from where he was. The leggings she wore should be declared illegal for how they clung to her legs and ass.

"Don't worry, I'll be successful. The acquisition may be delayed, but it shouldn't take much longer to close it. When's the vote?"

"He tried to strong-arm people into a special meeting of the board, but no-go. So, next scheduled meeting in December."

"More than enough time to ensure the only one getting voted out is him." Ian ended the call and made his way to Anna's side, who moved over to make room for him with a broad smile.

Lakes of Wonder must be his. If wooing Anna Stratford into selling the park to him was what he needed to do to ensure he could oust Harlan from BBA, then that was what he would do. And if, as a result, Anna Stratford found her way back into his bed, that would be an extra—and very pleasurable—bonus.

EIGHT

Wooing Anna was taking longer than Ian had expected.

Not because the time they spent together was wasted, but because he didn't have enough time to be with her. BBA had twenty-three parks in the United States and seven overseas, with active plans to expand into additional countries. Even without the battle lines with Harlan being clearly marked, Ian would be working sixty-hour weeks across ten time zones.

He had managed to carve out a few days over the two weeks since their first meeting in the park to walk around Lakes of Wonder with her. Wandering the theme park in her company was crucial to securing the deal and therefore spending as much time with her as possible was vital to the future of BBA, or so he'd told himself. So what if he cancelled his standing meetings and his assistant now automatically said no even to urgent requests so Ian wouldn't miss his scheduled time with Anna? He only had the best interests of his company in mind.

His presence in the park today had nothing to do with the way she made him laugh. Or how her observations, which seemed to come out of left field, always contained a pithy kernel of truth he had never considered.

No. He had no other motive than to get her signature on those documents, and maybe entice her to sealing their deal over a repeat bout in his hotel room. The sex truly had been too good not to repeat. But that was all.

Or so he knowingly lied to himself.

Anna was sitting at a small round white table outside Space Alien Al's Savory Snacks. Her elbows rested on the plastic surface, her hands providing a cup for her chin. A soft smile played on her lips as she watched the crowd—still light, in Ian's professional opinion—and her gaze was warm and relaxed.

She'd looked at him that way that night. After the fireworks had dissipated and their bodies were cooling. She'd turned to him, that exact same air of contentment wrapped around her.

Wrapped around both of them.

He approached, catching her gaze, which

snapped back to her usual expression when they were together: cool, professional, guarded. He shouldn't be disappointed she automatically injected distance into their interactions; he was still in the early stages of winning her over.

But he was.

He handed her a plastic cup heaped high with berry-flavored frozen custard and decorated on top with a Seamus-shaped cookie. "Here. This is the best thing served at Lakes of Wonder. We tried to get the exclusive rights for our parks, but…it didn't work out."

Because the Lochlainns came in with a higher bid at the eleventh hour. Of course.

Anna took a bite and then another, closing her eyes as she licked the spoon, and then she stuck the spoon back in the cup for another taste. Her pink tongue swirled as she lapped up every trace of custard.

He had to look away. Otherwise, it would be apparent to everyone within eyeshot what an immediate, potent effect she had on him. Next time, he would wear his baggiest jeans. And maybe a long shirt that fell halfway to his knees.

Her sigh of satisfaction didn't help his situation. "This is delicious. Whatever Lakes of Wonder is paying for the rights, it's not enough."

He agreed. Anything that made her moan with pleasure like that was priceless. "I have the Pieces of Eight coaster next on the schedule. Ready?"

"I have a better idea. Since you said I need a bird's-eye view of the business, then why don't you provide one literally?" She rose from the table to throw the empty cup away, then grabbed his left wrist with her free hand and began tugging him toward a brightly painted sign that read "Skyroute to Valhalla."

He planted his feet on the purple brick walkway. "No."

"No, I don't need a high-level view of the business?" She tugged harder. He didn't budge.

"No, you don't need a literal one." He removed her hand gently and indicated the adjacent path that led to Buccaneer Bayou. "Next stop, the scurvy septet of scurrilous scoundrels, or so they keep singing. And singing."

She crossed her arms over her chest and propped herself against the edge of the table. "We've already spent a lot of time in Buccaneer Bayou."

"But you haven't been on the coaster," he pointed out. "I wanted to show you—"

"I know. You've said and I quote, 'The Pieces

of Eight coaster has a fast-loading capacity, making it one of the better investments in the park,'" she recited. "I get it. Instead, I'd like to visit Valhalla Fjord. Since it's one of the original and therefore most outdated sections of Lakes of Wonder, I'd like to hear your thoughts on its future should BBA purchase the park."

"Certainly." He turned to his right. "This way to the Valkyrie Bridge. We'll need to walk through Heroes Harbor first."

"Or…" She pointed overhead to a rickety bucket suspended from a thin wire. It looked barely capable of holding two kittens, much less two grown adults. "We take the Skyroute."

No. He was not going to go on the Skyroute. But then Anna shifted, and that's when he noticed she was leaning on the table, not for effect, but to take her weight off her feet. Feet that appeared red and raw where her sandals' straps met her skin.

He bit back his exclamation. When Anna had showed up in her flimsy footwear, he'd warned her they might not be appropriate for walking several miles on the park's concrete walkways. But the sandals looked great on her, showing off her curvy calves to great effect, so he hadn't argued his point too hard. "Trouble walking?"

She started to shake her head and then she sighed. "Yes. These shoes weren't as broken in as I thought they were."

Something inside him twinged. Mostly anger at himself for not noticing she was in pain earlier. "Do you want to take the Skyroute?"

She smiled. "I thought you'd never ask."

Their flimsy metal pail—Ian couldn't think of a better way to describe the Skyroute vehicles and wished he didn't have to think about this mode of transportation at all—shuddered as it left the loading station and ascended at what had to be an unsafe speed into the sky. He didn't look ahead, because he would be reminded they were suspended several hundred feet in the air, traveling on what appeared to be a rather thin and insubstantial wire. He didn't look down, as the theme park guests below them had shrunk to the size of carpenter ants. He didn't look to the right, where death contraptions like the one he was in whizzed past, traveling in the opposite direction. That left looking to his left.

Looking at Anna.

She had no trouble taking in their surroundings, her head swiveling as she identified as many landmarks as possible. "There's Heroic Harbor—so that ugly square building must be the Supervillain's Revenge ride." She paused. "I see what you mean about the lack of three-hundred-and-sixty-degree theming." She took out her phone and started to make notes. "There should be a budget to theme the entire building so guests on the Skyroute are still immersed— Oh, look! The Lighthouse! I bet this would be a great place from which to view the fireworks."

"The Skyroute is shut down at night."

"What? Why?"

The real question was why it wasn't shut down 24/7, he wanted to respond. "Smoke from the fireworks."

"Right." She typed another note. "Still, I wonder if there is some way we can take advantage of the view from up here? Maybe re-open after the fireworks are over so people can see the park's lights from this angle? Or maybe as a special event on nights when there aren't any fireworks?" She scooted on the bench so she could look over the side, making the bucket rock slightly. Ian gritted his teeth, bile sloshing as his stomach flopped. "This is spectacular."

Focus on Anna. Focus on Anna. Focus on Anna.

But keeping his gaze locked on her only made his stomach flip harder, although in a much more welcome manner. The sunlight, when it wasn't playing hide-and-seek with clouds, turned her locks to gold and created a corona around her. Her cheeks were flushed pink, her eyes sparkling as she pointed out new items of interest.

He was counting the freckles on her right cheek, the one most visible to him—a task that required much concentration and took his mind off where and how far up he was—when he noticed two things.

One, the gondola was swaying side to side far more than usual.

Two, the gondola was no longer moving forward. They were stopped, suspended in mid-air. There wasn't even a gondola stopped in the other direction with which to commiserate with its passengers across the distance. He could see the back wall of the gondola ahead of them, but that was the only indication they weren't just…dangling. He swallowed, his mouth in dire need of moisture. Damn it, he'd known better than to take the Skyroute. He should have insisted Anna go by herself, and he should have traveled on foot to meet her.

Anna turned to him. "Wonder why we stopped? Maybe there's a guest needing assistance at one of the landing stations."

He nodded, a small, jerky movement. He didn't trust himself to speak.

The wind picked up. What would have been a welcome breeze on the ground was a nerve-plucking gust that caused Ian to tighten his grip on the edges of the bench. He closed his eyes for what he could have sworn was only a nanosecond. But when he opened them, he found Anna staring at him, concern spilling from her gaze.

"Everything okay?"

He nodded again.

Her gaze narrowed. "Why don't I believe you?"

He shrugged. To avoid her perceptive stare, he took out his phone. Perhaps Park Operations would know how long the Skyroute shutdown would last.

His throat tightened, making it hard to swallow even as his mouth dried out and required moisture. His palms were clammy, causing his grip on the bench to slide. The gondola was open to the elements and the air was brisk and cool, but his lungs couldn't take in enough oxygen.

A slight breeze shook the gondola and he squeezed his eyes shut, hoping to stave off the vertigo he could feel building. He did not want to show weakness in front of Anna. Because she was a representative of the Lochlainn Company, he insisted to himself, and she would exploit any weakness against him. That's what Lochlainn loyalists did. She would find a way to use his soft spots against him in the negotiation.

But as her concerned gaze met his, he felt some of his dizziness recede. He grabbed onto the comfort of her presence and held on for dear life.

Anna regarded Ian. If she wasn't mistaken—and she wasn't—his complexion was several shades lighter than it had been earlier that day. She didn't miss his white-knuckled grip on the bench, either. She scooted along the seat until her left leg brushed his right one, letting her knee press against his, while ignoring the thrill that left her feeling somewhat light-headed at being so close to him. It would not do for both of them to pass out. "Is it the height or the type of ride vehicle or both?" she asked.

Ian's head whipped up. "What do you mean?"

"You're not having a good time."

"I—" He pressed his lips together and stayed silent. She waited, keeping her knee where it was, letting him know she was there. After a few beats, his leg relaxed, falling against hers. "I dislike being suspended in midair."

He may not be enjoying their time in the sky, but she was enjoying the press of his thigh, the brush of his shoulder as he leaned toward her and away from the edges of the gondola. "I appreciate you indulging me despite your obvious aversion to traveling in this manner."

"Your feet hurt."

"Yes, but you did warn me. You could have said 'I told you so' and continued our march across the park." She whistled a few bars of "Seventy-Six Trombones" from *The Music Man* while mimicking a marching band drum major keeping time with a baton.

The ghost of a smile appeared. "Hopefully I'm not being that regimented."

"No. But I did feel like I had to keep up or else. I'm enjoying our current enforced break, but I'm sorry this isn't enjoyable for you."

"I'll be fine."

The breeze picked up, turning into a strong wind. The gondola wobbled, just a slight swing, but enough movement to ensure Ian's expression returned to blank stone.

"I'm sure we'll start moving any second now," she offered.

Ian nodded, a short, curt bob of his head.

Anna stared at her sandals. Stupid footwear. She knew they weren't practical. But they made her legs look incredible.

A burst of static from the speaker overhead caused Anna to jump, shaking the gondola further. "Sorry!" she gasped.

"Please stay seated and keep your arms and legs inside your vehicle," a voice said from the speaker. "We are experiencing technical difficulties. Our attraction will resume shortly."

She turned to Ian. "We should be moving soon."

Ian shook his head. "No."

"Why not?"

"The message said they need more time to fix whatever is wrong."

"How do you know that?"

"The use of 'technical difficulties.' If this were a quick blip, the recording would say 'momentary stop.' It's code so the ride operators will know how to manage guest expectations without causing alarm."

Anna blinked. "That's clever."

Ian shrugged, a small, economical movement. "All parks use something similar."

Another gust of wind, stronger than the previous one, blew through the open vehicle. The sky, which had been a clear robin's-egg blue earlier that day, was now full of jagged clouds piled high. "I think a storm is coming," she said, and immediately wished she hadn't.

He glanced at the sky. His expression turned as gray as the bottom of the cloud directly above them.

Anna didn't mind the movement of the gondola—the way it shimmied in the air was rather thrilling—but the more the wind picked up in speed, the lower the air fell in temperature. Her T-shirt and shorts provided little in the way of protection. She crossed her arms over her chest, hugging them to her for warmth.

Ian glanced over. For the first time since the gondola had taken to the sky, a spark of interest flared in his gaze. "Cold?" he asked.

She was about to protest she was fine, keeping up the pretense she'd been engaged in all day, but she liked seeing a hint of the Ian she knew return to the stoic statue currently sitting next to her. "A bit," she acknowledged. "Guess my sandals weren't the only bad choice I made getting dressed."

Ian relaxed his grip on the bench, lifting his left arm in a silent invitation to move closer and share in his warmth. She knew she should keep her distance. Knew that if she allowed Ian to embrace her—even if only to ensure she wasn't chilled and numb from the wind—she would forget to be angry at him.

Forget he had lied. Well, okay, he hadn't told a bald-faced falsehood, but he also hadn't told her who he was. A lie by omission was still a lie. And thanks to the Knock, Anna had had her fill of lies of omission—but Ian's paled in comparison to her parents'.

Forget that a deal worth billions of dollars was on the line.

Instead, she would remember. Remember the heat of his mouth and the fire of his touch. Remember how he felt inside her, filling her, pressing deep, insistent, demanding...

Remember that she, too, was not who he thought she was.

So really, who was she to hold that night against him?

"Anna?" Yes, there was life back in his gaze now. "Come here. No need for us to suffer separately."

He was right. Why be a martyr? She scooted closer to him, keeping her movements small so as not to cause the vehicle to move, and allowed his left arm to gather her close.

She realized her mistake as soon as his warm hand closed over her shoulder. His touch seared her skin as if her thin T-shirt didn't exist. She inhaled, hoping fresh air would break the spell his presence was beginning to weave over her, a spell of softening resolve and building desire, and quickly realized that was a mistake when his scent filled her senses. She was instantly taken back to that night in his room, her nose buried deep in his neck, surrounded by his addictive essence that was difficult to describe in words but made her blood heat.

Like now.

Her nipples were hard and aching and the cool breeze was not the culprit. Thankfully, her bra would hide the evidence of Ian's effect on her, and her goose bumps—the tiny hairs on her arms quivering with awareness—could be attributed to the temperature. But she didn't dare look at him, for there was no disguising the want that must be naked on her face.

The breeze picked up and gondola shook again. Ian's hand tightened on her shoulder and she patted his thigh, keeping her touch light and as impersonal as possible. He only wanted the comfort of another person next to him. A golden retriever could take her place. In fact, maybe he might prefer the unconditional attention of a pet to her awkward movements right now—

"Anna." He breathed her name as if uttering a prayer. "Thank you."

On reflex, she lifted her head to respond. "Of course—"

Their gazes met with an almost audible clash. She swallowed the rest of her words, the fire in his dark eyes lighting the embers kindling deep in her belly. Licks of flame raced through her veins, until every nerve ending popped and sizzled.

She had to move away from him. Or she would do something she would regret.

She rose halfway up from her position on the bench, intending to scoot back to her original position. But the wind changed position and rocked the gondola sideways. Anna lost her balance and fell, half landing on Ian. Their legs entwined as Ian's arms came up to hold her waist while her arms instinctively circled his shoulders, seeking a secure hold as the gondola continued to sway.

Too late, Anna realized she was sitting sideways on Ian's lap. Her cheeks radiated fierce heat as she rocked herself forward to untangle her limbs from his. But Ian held fast and she gave in to her desire to relax into him. His thighs were hard and solid and they scorched her legs below her shorts.

"Anna," he repeated, and her name was no longer a prayer but a statement full of need. Their gazes continued to tangle as his right hand left her waist to stroke her hot cheek, his thumb trailing sparks as he brushed her lower lip.

He wanted her.

And she wanted him. She may not know who she really was. She may be an ocean's depth over her head with the theme park negotiations. But she knew one thing with an eternal certainty. She craved Ian Blackburn. As a friend, as a business rival, as her teacher in theme park negotiations—she'd take him any way she could have him, even temporarily, even for a stolen moment in a stalled gondola.

"Ian," she responded, marveling she could still form words when all the air had escaped her lungs. "I'm no longer cold."

"Good." His other hand began to explore the curve of her waist, discovering the sliver of bare flesh between her waistband and the hem of her shirt. She gasped. "But perhaps I should ensure this area does not become chilled."

"In fact, I'm rather warm."

"Then my efforts are working." His fingers traced abstract designs on her skin, leaving lightning bolts in their wake.

She swallowed, hard. "I propose an addendum to our deal. The first deal."

His touch slowed then stopped. She hurriedly added, "We shook hands on land. So, if we're in the air...the deal is null."

She would regret this. But up here, alone, the two of them suspended in the air on the slimmest of wires, no one to see them save for pigeons and the occasional seagull, she could pretend nothing else mattered. No Lakes of Wonder sale. No Lochlainn heritage to claim. No questions about where she belonged. Just her and him and the chemistry bubbling between them, threatening to ignite into an inferno.

He didn't answer her in words, but his left hand came up to join in right in framing her face. Then his lips were on hers and she forgot to think.

His mouth was warm and welcoming. She sank into his embrace, seeking and answering, their tongues exploring and tangling as if this was their first kiss. And in a way, it was. When they had kissed in Ian's room, the promise of sex had been thick in the air, the kiss a mere prelude—a hastily-blown-past checkpoint, in fact—on their hurried way to the main event.

But here in the gondola, with sex not even a remote possibility, they were free to focus on kissing. To learn each other's likes and preferred methods. Anna learned Ian enjoyed a gentle tug of his lower lip, shuddering as her teeth lightly grazed him. He made a sound of triumph in his throat when she moaned as he kissed her jawline and found the sensitive skin below her ear. Their mouths came together again as he pulled her to him, his hands tangled in her hair, her fingers holding on to his shoulders for support as otherwise she would be a melted puddle on the floor, nothing remaining but her treacherous sandals. They experimented with pressure and speed, learning each other's rhythm and discovering, in the end, they could ignite the other with a simple brush of lip against lip.

Making out with Ian Blackburn was a transcendent experience, turning her veins into lava and her nerves into pure electricity. The ground was literally shaking underneath her—no.

The gondola was moving.

She pulled back from Ian, keeping her eyes squeezed shut, afraid to see what might be in his gaze. Would she see triumph, for getting her to break her vow of not becoming involved physically with him again—even if it was just a kiss?

But it wasn't just a kiss. Anna was sure of that.

She opened one eye, then the other.

Ian's gaze was focused on the gondola station where they would disembark, coming steadily closer. "We're almost on the ground," he said, his tone neutral. "There's a gift shop next to the station. We can find you a pair of walking shoes and a sweatshirt before we continue with our tour."

His tone was brisk and professional, acting like a bucket of cold water on the desire still swirling in her veins.

This had been just a kiss after all. To him.

"Right. The ground." Anna swallowed. "About our deal. I, um, I…enjoyed the kiss. A lot." Her words built in speed, coming faster and faster until they tumbled one right after the other. "But it doesn't change anything. I still haven't decided what I'm going to do. About Lakes of Wonder, I mean. I don't want you to think I kissed you to lead you on or to otherwise manipulate you, because I didn't. And I know I should pretend the kiss didn't happen, but I can't pretend something didn't happened when it obviously just did happen, so—"

"Anna."

She looked up. Ian's gaze was steady and constant, his focus on her a flame without a hint of flicker. Her breath caught. "You kissed me as a distraction. I appreciate it. Nothing has changed."

She sat back on the bench, his words having an oddly deflating effect on her mood. "You think that's what happened?"

A half-smile dented his left cheek. "You wear your emotions embroidered not on only your sleeve, but your entire outfit."

"So. We're back on. You'll continue to show me why you are the best owner for Lakes of Wonder."

"Until December first." He smiled at her. "Unless you have all the information you need now and want to call an end to our bargain sooner."

No. That was the last thing she wanted. She thought spending time with Ian would buy her time to learn more about the Lochlainn family. Instead, she only grew more confused about who she was—and who was starting to matter to her, very much, in a way that did not bode well for the future stability of her heart.

Their gondola was slowing down, the station looming closer. The guests in the vehicle ahead of them were disembarking, the park staff ensuring they safely exited their gondolas. "I still have some open questions. For instance, our destination of Valhalla Fjord. I heard the Viking Longboat has dry rot?"

"Parts of the boat have been closed to guests, yes." Their gondola settled into place next to a revolving walkway. Ian jumped out and turned to give Anna a hand. She tried not to wince when her shredded feet met solid ground again. "But it's been that way for years."

"Why didn't the Lakes of Wonder management fix it?" Anna clung to the railing as they descended the embarkation station's stairs, allowing the metal balustrade to support her weight. Too late, she looked up to see Ian's speculative stare.

"I was hoping you could tell me," he said. "You're the one who works for the Lochlainn Company."

She swallowed, hoping to work moisture into her mouth. "I want to hear your theory. About why repairs haven't been done, that is."

Her heart pounded furiously against her chest walls. The terms of the challenge required her relationship to Keith Lochlainn to be kept out of the press. If the public found out Jamie was her biological father before Keith decided to reveal all, she would be cut out of the Lochlainn estate.

She wanted to trust Ian. She was enjoying his company far too much than she should. And that kiss…she was proud of how well she appeared to have recovered. She wasn't stuttering. She was controlling her breathing. Any stumbling in her gait could be put down to her uncomfortable shoes and not to the real reason: her knees turned to liquid whenever he caught her gaze. And she liked him. He was smart—his quick observations about the theme park business opened new perspectives for her—and he made her laugh.

But something held her back from telling him the real reason why she was in charge of the sale. After all, the fate of Lakes of Wonder was still in her hands. And he wanted the park.

He regarded her for a moment, his eyes searching hers. Then he shrugged as he guided her to the entrance of the nearest gift shop.

Anna headed for the clothing section, Ian following close behind. "My theory is Lakes of Wonder was the crown jewel of the Lochlainn empire when Archibald ran the company. There was talk of building more theme parks, but Archibald was exacting and the plans were never to his satisfaction. After he died, Lakes of Wonder fared well under Keith, but then he seemed to lose interest…maybe thirty years ago? He stopped investing in the park in favor of spending time and money on the Lochlainn Company's other businesses. But he also wouldn't sell the park." He slid her a sideways glance. "Until now."

Thirty years ago. Anna was twenty-seven. That meant Jamie's and Keith's estrangement must have occurred around the same time Keith decided to stop putting new money into Lakes of Wonder. "Hmm," she murmured, not willing to share the direction of her thoughts with Ian. Not yet. Maybe not ever. "Look, slip-on shoes!" She grabbed a pair in her size, uncaring they were decorated with garish cartoons of Seamus Sea Serpent's face. In fact, that was a point in their favor. "And…here's a hoodie."

"You would pick the pink one," he said.

"Of course. I'm not the one who wears camouflage 24/7. There's a matching one in dark gray if you like. It should go with everything in your wardrobe." She tossed the sweatshirt to him.

He caught it. "I think you know that shade

of pink matches your cheeks. That's why you picked that one."

"I wasn't aware you paid attention to my cheeks."

"I've paid attention to every inch of you. If you recall."

"That was weeks ago. You can't expect to recall every last detail." She did, of course.

"Refresher courses are free, you just have to ask."

She turned to grin at him. Then her smile slipped.

She was used to seeing Ian smirk at her as he delivered his cheesy comebacks. Or contemplate her silently with his eyebrows quirked as he digested something she blurted. She even knew the weight of his stare when it was hot with desire.

But an Ian who lightly teased her, his expression open and relaxed? That, she was not used to. Her pulse thumped against her eardrums, drowning out the cheerful music being pumped into the store.

She liked this carefree Ian. Very much.

Too much.

But falling in deep "like"—her mind refused

to consider the word "love"—with Ian Blackburn was firmly off her agenda.

For now.

NINE

A WEEK LATER, all Anna had accomplished was to muddy the already murky waters passing for her thoughts. She wasn't ready to sell Lakes of Wonder and return home to Ft. Lauderdale – or as Martiza put it, she was continuing to avoid her parents. And after a trip up the coast to Los Angeles, where Anna paid for a tour of Lochlainn Studios and visited the small museum on the film lot dedicated to the family's rise to prominence, she was even more conflicted about where she fit into the powerful dynasty— or if she was even meant to fit in. After all, the only thing she had in common with them was half her chromosomes. Blood may be thicker than water, but that was a low bar to pass. Blood was still pretty thin.

The one area where her conflicts seemed to be resolving was her feelings for Ian. Ever since the kiss in the gondola, he seemed to have taken up permanent residence in her subconscious. She could go about her day perfectly fine, with only the occasional stray thought—like now, and she pressed her legs tightly together in a vain effort to relieve the pressure that seemed to build every time his name even whisked across her brain. But at night, he starred in her dreams, leaving her restless and empty when she woke up and he was not physically present.

She doubted she took up nearly as much space in his subconscious. He gave no indication he felt anything for her except willingness to repeat their night together. Yet she checked the time on her phone with her breath held in anticipation for the fifth time in ten minutes. She should be seeing him in person for the first time since the day they kissed in the gondola right about—

Now. She smiled when she spotted him.

She'd asked him to meet at sunset, an hour before the park closed. It was a Friday, which meant fireworks would signal the end of the park's operating hours; Anna had learned they were too costly to set off every night. Still, crowds of people were streaming toward the exit, especially families with small children who were too tired to wait for the evening spectacular. But the packed walkways didn't slow down Ian, who was swimming against the tide with ease. He deftly dodged a double stroller holding twins while capturing an errant balloon just before the string disappeared into the atmosphere. He handed the balloon back to a small child who stopped, midcry, with an astonished look on her face. He didn't wait for the parents' gushed thanks, choosing to wave them off as he continued his forward progression without missing a step.

She applauded as he reached her side. "That was a flawless grab. Eleven out of ten."

He shrugged. "I happened to see the kid untie the string weight and release the balloon at the right time."

"You can accept a compliment, you know. Say, 'Thank you, Anna, for appreciating my chivalrous act.'"

His smirk was lopsided. "Nothing chivalrous about it. I was saving my eardrums from the kid's shrieks. I should have let the balloon go so the kid could learn actions have consequences."

Anna returned his smirk. "Right. You were being purely selfish."

"Chivalry is dead." But his smirk turned into

a smile. "So. You wanted to meet? And it had to be now?"

She took a deep breath. Although they had returned to their state of professional détente after the kiss, being near him was half pleasure, half pain as every moment brought their time together closer to an end. "Yes. You've been very generous with your time these last few weeks, and I appreciate it. But we haven't spent time at the park after dark."

He raised his eyebrows. "I have no objections to spending time with you after dark. But I thought we took those activities off the table."

She laughed, even as she repressed the shiver caused by his low tone. She knew he was just teasing. Their usual harmless flirtation that meant nothing. At least to him. "Not in that way, and you know it. But the park is a different place after sundown. The lights, the mood—everything changes."

He looked around. The area in which they were standing was starting to fill with knots of people staking their space to watch the fireworks in an hour. "Yes. It becomes a crowded mess here, while the rest of the park remains open but few guests are utilizing the rides and restaurants. A waste of resources."

She frowned at him. "Or people are thrilled to watch the nighttime entertainment and the park provides them with twenty minutes of spectacle they will remember for a long time."

"Not when they're too busy filming it to put on their social media—and impeding the view of the people behind them—to make actual memories."

"You're hopeless."

"Are you just now figuring that out? I thought you were a quicker study than that."

"I dare you to watch the faces of the kids tonight and tell me they aren't enthralled by the fireworks."

"I don't need to observe them. They will be. But they're kids. Kids are thrilled to find a stash of stale candy three months after Halloween."

"How did you get to be so cynical?'

"If by cynical you mean practical as well as profitable…" He shrugged, his gaze turning flat and cold. "Experience. A lot of it."

She turned away. He'd scored a direct hit on the one target for which she had no protection. She had no experience. Not with theme parks, and not even with running a business. Her parents rarely shared decisions about the operations of the store with her. She decided not to dwell on how shut out that made her feel—on how shut out she'd always felt. She'd untangle her emotions later, although a small part of her brain wondered if, again, this was why she refused to let Lakes of Wonder go. Despite never meeting Keith or Jamie, at least the Lochlainns were allowing her to participate in major decisions about the direction of their family legacy.

Her parents, who'd raised her from birth, did not.

For the one thousand, three hundred and forty-second time that week, she wondered at what the Lochlainns expected of her. And why their expectations seemed so unattainably high even if she had been born and bred a Lochlainn, while the family who raised her had such low ones of her.

"Well, Mr. Experienced—"

"Thank you. A bit late, but I'll take the compliment." He mock-puffed his chest.

"Ha. Ha," she deadpanned. "You may know a lot about spreadsheets and profit and loss columns. But what do you know about how people feel?"

He stepped closer to her. The teasing glint deepened, accompanied by something far more primal. "I'm very good at making people feel. As you should know."

He scored another direct hit, affecting her low and deep, a rush of warmth making her knees soft. "Not that kind of feelings. Emotions. Happiness, joy, comfort—evoking those in others."

"I've been known to create happy endings. Come with back to the hotel and I will remind you." He waggled his eyebrows and she laughed.

"You're incorrigible. And you know…" She held up a finger. "One, we have our deal, and two—" a second finger joined her first one "—not what I meant. Again."

The crowd began to build in the plaza. Parents placed small children on their shoulders. The crowd's chatter began to crescendo, drowning out the background music loop coming from hidden speakers in the bushes and building walls. The air vibrated with anticipation as the lights lining the walkways began to dim. The hairs on Anna's arms rose as she shivered. She held her right arm out to Ian, pointing out the goose bumps. "See? This is what I mean. The feeling that something magical is about to happen."

He traced a finger, slow and deliberate, down the delicate skin at the center of her inner forearm. Her blood caught fire, the flames catching instantaneously. She snatched her arm back. He merely smiled and let his hand drop. "I am aware of how to create that feeling, yes."

She was saved from having to answer when the lights winked out and a warm male voice announced over the loudspeaker that the show was about to begin. But the impression of his touch lingered far longer than it should have. Her skin ached for more of his feathery-light strokes. Who knew it was possible to become addicted to Ian Blackburn in a few short weeks? She didn't think it was possible to crave the feel of someone's skin on hers this much. To ache with want—not just desire, the demanding urge to find sexual completion—but want. Wanting his fingers to casually tangle with hers. Wanting his shoulder to brush hers as he leaned down to whisper something in her ear. Wanting the heat of his gaze concentrated on her so much she could taste it, a metallic tang equal parts hope for the future and part despair her want would never be fulfilled.

For when it came to what Ian Blackburn desired...oh, she had no doubt he would agree to a repeat of their night in his hotel room. Perhaps even a third or fourth repeat. The sex had been that good. But she was clear on what he truly wanted.

He wanted her park.

Not her.

They watched the fireworks in silence, Ian's gaze focused on the sky while hers wandered over the faces closest to her. Couples leaning on each other, their arms entwined as they lifted their faces to the bright explosions overhead. Children who'd been perpetual energy machines minutes before the show began were now still with awe, exhilaration shining in their eyes. Parents, faces taut with harried exhaustion, the lines relaxing as they oohed and aahed and held phones up, recording the night to be relived at home.

This was why Lakes of Wonder mattered. Not the thrill of the rides or the amount of profit made in the gift shops and at the concession stands: this. A communal making of memories, a fifteen-minute respite from daily annoyances and chores and even bigger issues. A chance to be dazzled by music and lights and colorful explosions and believe, if only for a split second, and then deny it forever more, that magic really could exist.

Ian remained impassive beside her, his expression never changing during the show. Not even during the grand finale, when the eruptions built and built until the night's darkness had been banished and the world was lit by purple and green and gold and red, brighter than a summer morning. Not even when the music evoked childhood wishes and dreams in a blatantly manipulative maneuver to jerk tears from the listener's eyes—and Anna obliged, her cheeks wet as the chorus sang of familial love and believing in oneself.

The lights came back up in the park and the crowd starting to move toward the exit as if one large organism. It was all Anna could do to keep her feet planted and not be swept up in the tidal wave surging for the gates.

Ian wrapped his arm over her shoulders, keeping her close. To protect her from the crush of people? No doubt. But she leaned into his strength, reveling in the feeling of his protection even though she could fight the crowds on her own. "Let's get out of here," he said low in her ear.

He guided her into a nearby gift shop, past

the displays of toys and souvenirs that were being raked over by parkgoers eager for one last purchase, and to a door in the back, almost indistinguishable from the wall. They slipped through and Anna found herself in a utilitarian hallway, white and plain and distinguished mostly by the running lights that lit the walkway.

"Service corridor?" she guessed. She'd read that Lakes of Wonder had almost an entire city built behind and underneath the theme park, allowing custodial staff, repair technicians, and staff who didn't want to be seen wearing the wrong costume in the wrong part town to move freely about the park without guests seeing them.

"Yes," Ian answered. "But they are rarely used. Some of the foundations have been compromised. This corridor is no longer in use, to avoid any potential safety issues."

"But they can be made safe again, right?"

Ian ran a hand through his hair. "I know what you want me to say. Anything is possible—"

"If you dream it, you can do it," she interjected. "Is that what Walt Disney said?"

"That quote is attributed to him, but he didn't

say it. However, Disney probably would've agreed anything is possible if you throw enough money at it. Do you think Keith will pump the necessary funds into Lakes of Wonder if you don't sell the park?"

She stayed silent.

"I didn't think so. So—"

She placed her right index finger on his lips and shook her head, not ready to let the lingering magic of the nighttime show be dissipated by another discussion on the practical aspects of the theme park business.

He frowned at her and spoke around her finger. "What? Are you ready to leave?"

No. That was the last thing she wanted to do. Every time she exited Lakes of Wonder, she was one step closer to selling it. And one step closer to returning to the mess she'd made of her life in Ft. Lauderdale. She shook off the clammy hand clenching her stomach at the thought of seeing her parents again. She knew she owed them an explanation for running off to California the way she had, without so much as a goodbye text. Yet the longer she put off the long, in-depth and no doubt emotional conversation they needed to have, the more hurt would be built up and the harder the discussion would be. And yet…

She pointed at the tunnel ahead of them with her chin. "Where does this corridor go?"

Ian followed her gaze. The safety lights were on, illuminating the passage. The tunnel was surprisingly free of dust, and he supposed the Lakes of Wonder custodial team maintained the underground passageways despite their disuse. The sound of people chatting and laughing as the cash register beeped with transactions came faintly through the closed door leading back to the gift shop. The crowds would still be thick in the park for at least another hour.

Truthfully, he wasn't ready for his time with Anna to be over. Their original deal had dwindled down to one week, and his calendar held only one more scheduled meeting. And being with Anna meant his shoulders stood their best chance of losing the knot that had held them stiff around his ears for the last week. He'd had to muster up every ounce of self-control he had to put behind him the video call with Olive and Preston that had made him late this evening.

If he shut his eyes, he could still see his uncle's and cousin's smug faces. Hear their voices.

★ ★ ★

"Harlan came to us yesterday with a very interesting proposition," Olive had begun, steepling her fingers under her chin as if she were a James Bond villain. "You know he's calling for a vote of no confidence in your leadership at the next board meeting, right?"

When they were kids, Olive had stolen his favorite Star Wars action figure and thrown it into a roaring fireplace. He had the feeling his Han Solo toy got off easy compared to what she'd wanted to extract from him now.

"I'm aware," he said.

"Right, Tai runs and tells you everything," she said with a sniff. "Anyway, Dad and I still back you. Right, Dad?"

Preston nodded.

"But!" Olive held up her index finger. "We want...guarantees...in return."

"You'll get Lakes of Wonder." Ian shuffled papers on his desk as if he were bored. "There was a due diligence issue impacting the sale that I'm taking care of, but the park should be ours soon. Once we integrate operations into BBA, it's yours to run, as we discussed."

"That's the thing." Olive examined her blood-red fingernails. "Dad and I talked it over and we don't want to run the park after all. Too much math involved. Right Dad?"

"Don't like numbers," Preston rumbled.

"Okay." This was turning out better than Ian anticipated. "BBA will run Lakes of Wonder. So what guarantees do you want? Profit sharing? Control of the entertainment?"

"See, that's the problem." Olive cocked her head to the side. "We still want all of Lakes of Wonder, only we don't want BBA to run it."

Here came the migraine, right on time. "You're not making sense."

Olive frowned. "I'm as smart as you are, Ian. I'm tired of people saying I'm not."

"You're very intelligent, Olive," Ian agreed through his teeth. "Please tell me what you want."

"To shut down Lakes of Wonder."

"What?" Ian's gaze ping-ponged between Olivia and Preston. "Why? It's still a moneymaking proposition. Under BBA, the park would turn a tidy profit."

"And Dad and I have an opportunity to develop the land into a live/work/retail opportunity." She shrugged. "I'm tired of theme parks. And Lakes of Wonder is perfectly situated to be retail destination."

"You said you don't like numbers," Ian said slowly. It was the only argument that sprung to mind.

"Oh, we'll hire people to do that. Right, Daddy?"

"Right," Preston said.

"Preston." Ian appealed to his uncle. "You know what Lakes of Wonder means to our family. Surely you don't want to destroy—"

"That's our deal," Preston said. "We get Lakes of Wonder, no questions asked. You get our votes. Or we vote with Harlan and get what we want from him anyway, he doesn't give one flying damn about the theme park biz and you know it. I like you, son. But I've waited long enough for my slice of Blackburn pie with nothing to show for it. So I'm going to take my slice now and start my own thing. No one will miss Lakes of Wonder. It's not part of the BBA portfolio."

"It has legions of fans," Ian protested. "It's a land-mark."

"It's a theme park. And now it will be a retail des-tination." Preston's gaze darted off camera. "We have to go now. You can have a few days to think about it. But then we vote with Harlan. Be seeing you, Ian."

"Ian?" Anna's voice brought him back to the dimly lit tunnel.

If they left the park now, he would have nothing but a tension-filled night ahead as he negotiated his uncle's and cousin's demands. Demands that would change Lakes of Wonder forever, should Ian be successful in acquiring the park for BBA. And he would be. He had no other choice.

He turned to her. "Up for an adventure?"

Her gaze narrowed. "What kind of an adventure?"

Ian indicated the door. "This tunnel exists because the gift shop was originally a private lounge for the original investors in Lakes of Wonder."

Anna's brow creased. "I thought the private lounge is located in Heroes Harbor, on the second level of Mount Stupendous."

"That was built shortly after the park opened, when the original lounge proved to be too small. And too easily seen by guests as they enter and exit the park."

"Okay, the shop was originally a lounge. Where does the adventure part come in?"

Ian motioned for Anna to follow him as he walked to the far wall where a simple schematic carved in metal was still in place. She traced the bas relief symbols with her fingers. "This tunnel leads to…" Her index finger followed the map's path and she turned to Ian. "The Lighthouse?"

He nodded. "So guests of the private lounge

could easily visit the even more exclusive residence inside the Lighthouse."

"Wait. You can go inside the Lighthouse? I thought it was a façade. Like a Hollywood prop, only three-dimensional and bigger."

"Real building. With real plumbing and electricity, even."

"Have you been inside the Lighthouse?"

"Never had the chance." And might not ever have the chance again, even if he successfully purchased the park. Not if Preston and Olive had their way.

"How do you know about it? I've read everything I could on Lakes of Wonder. Even read all the legal paperwork. There's no mention of the Lighthouse as a functional structure. It's just a...landmark." She smiled. "A weenie."

The warmth of her expression broke over him and he grinned back at her, to his chagrin. He didn't want to smile back at her. He didn't want to be friends with her. He was happy to flirt to get what he wanted and, sure, he'd be more than happy to repeat that night in his bed, but that was sex. He didn't need the sudden rush of...something, this inexplicable urge to bask in her light while building more in-jokes between them, more transparent lines of connection.

He cleared his throat, shoving the ball of something that felt very much like emotion back down, hopefully to dissolve for good. "Want to find out if I'm right?"

Her smile deepened, damn it, a pickax smashing holes in the thick walls he'd long ago built to ensure he only relied on his head, never his heart. Whenever he allowed his heart to lead, he always ended up looking like a fool.

"Let's go," she said.

They walked mostly in silence, Anna breaking it only to note where they were in relation to the theme park above them. Then the tunnel starting to slope upward, and they climbed until the passage came to an end at a heavy metal door.

Anna tried to turn the doorknob. "It's locked." She sighed. "Well, this was fun, anyway. I wonder when the last person walked this tunnel before us? But we should turn back. The park is going to close soon."

Ian dug into his pants' pocket and brought out a key. "I was once told this key could open all the doors in Lakes of Wonder."

She stared at him. "Where did you get that?"

He didn't answer. It had been a whim to pick up that key, all those years ago in his grandfather's home, and even more of a whim to carry it on him still. But Ian had grown used to its shape and weight. Some people carried lucky pennies; others bought charms. Ian didn't believe good fortune could be embodied in an item—you had to make your own luck—but whenever he left his house without the slight weight of the small metal object in his pocket, the world felt wrong, somehow. And once he knew Lakes of Wonder was in play and available for sale, he ensured he carried the key with him.

His grandfather had laughed when Ian had showed him his find, telling him the tale of how Archibald Lochlainn and Ian's great-grandfather, Cooper Blackburn, had had a falling out. The last item Cooper had taken from his office was the master key to Lakes of Wonder. Then his grandfather had chuckled and said it was no doubt useless now, so Ian was free to take it.

He found himself holding his breath as the key went into the lock. At first the lock wouldn't turn, which disappointed him more than he'd anticipated. He hadn't really expected his grandfather's story to be real, had he? Or, even if it had been a true story, for the locks to never have been changed in all the ensuing years? But then something gave, deep inside the tumbler, and the key turned with a loud click. The door fell ajar.

Anna's eyes widened. "Whoa…"

He took her elbow with his right hand to ensure she wouldn't stumble and, with his left, pushed the door further open. They encountered nothing but darkness. Fumbling with his free hand, he patted the wall until he located what felt like a light switch. Mentally crossing his fingers that the power hadn't been disconnected, he flipped it on.

She gasped from beside him.

An overhead light revealed they stood in the living area of an apartment that appeared as if it had been summoned directly from the set of a 1960's television series. In the middle of the room was a sofa, covered in a cheerful floral brocade. Oak bookcases contained porcelain knickknacks and ornately curlicued silver picture frames. A burled walnut coffee table held pastel-colored candy dishes—empty, thankfully—while the matching side tables were laden with jar-shaped lamps with fringed shades. Beyond, an open door provided a glimpse of a small kitchenette, complete with two-burner white range. Another door was closed—no doubt to the hallway that led to the bedrooms. Three of the walls were covered with ornate floral wallpaper, while the fourth wall was draped in floor-to-ceiling velvet curtains.

Anna slipped from his grip on her arm and began to explore, her smile broadening with each item she examined. "The chair—that's an original Eames. Oh! And this table is signed by Stickley." She turned to Ian. "This place is every antique hunter's dream. Where are we?"

Ian had remained still. Now that he was in the apartment, now that he had confirmation that it was real and not just a vague suspicion, he didn't know what to do next. Where to look next. It didn't help that the photos he'd seen had been in two-dimension black-and-white. Experiencing the apartment in three dimensions and in living color overwhelmed his senses. "This place? It was the apartment built by the creators of Lakes of Wonder for their families."

"So m—Archibald Lochlainn built this? For Keith?"

Ian nodded and then cleared his throat. "You could say that."

Her gaze flashed and she turned back to perusing the items on the bookshelves. He decided to explore what was behind the closed door and found a bathroom—luckily with running water—and two rooms emptied of furniture, although the mural of stylized planes, trains and cars that occupied the wall of one of the rooms suggested it had been meant as a young boy's bedroom. The other room had faded gilt-striped wallpaper where squares of bright color revealed where pictures had once hung.

He returned to the living area. Anna was where he had left her, still intent on picking up and examining the bookshelves' occupants. "Someone has been taking care of this place," she said without looking at him. "There's not much dust. It's been looked after."

"I agree." But who? he wondered. She was right that the apartment had been maintained, but it was also obvious no one had used it in a long time. Not only because the bedrooms were bare, but because the appliances were some fifty years out of date. Case in point, the television. It was a museum piece, a heavy hunk of furniture with a small, curved screen in the middle. He bet if the television did work—and could by some miracle receive an over-the-air broadcast signal—the picture would be in black-and-white.

Anna sniffed, breaking into his thoughts.

"You okay?" he asked.

"Must be the dust."

Ian frowned. "We just discussed how well-kept this room is."

"I guess I found what little still exists." She sniffed again.

That didn't sound like a suppressed sneeze. It sounded like...she was about to cry. He frowned. "You sure you're okay? You didn't hurt yourself while we were in the tunnel?"

Another sharp inhalation through her nose as she kept her face turned away from him, her eyes focused on an object in her hands. "I'm fine."

His gaze narrowed and he crossed the room to stand next to her, leaning over her shoulder to see what kept her so enraptured. A piece of memorabilia from the opening of Lakes of Wonder? But it was a photo of Keith Lochlainn with a small infant in his arms. "Oh. Do you always cry at photos of babies?" he teased.

She jumped. The photo slipped from her grasp and bounced on the carpet, landing face-down. Ian bent to pick it up before she could react.

It wasn't a particularly artful photo. The subjects were posed in front of the Lighthouse, and whoever had taken the photo hadn't accounted for the sun that day, as Keith was obviously squinting into bright light. But the sheer happiness on his face...

Ian began to understand why she'd found the photograph so compelling. This was not a side of Keith Lochlainn the public got to see often, if ever. Keith's public image was that of a taciturn, serious man who wore either scowls or amused smirks in his official photos. He would never appear so unguarded. So, well...joyful. It was the only word Ian could think of to describe the emotion pouring from Keith's two-dimensional expression.

Too bad he kept this side of himself under wraps in public, because Keith had a nice smile. It softened his square chin and the hard angles of his cheekbones. He appeared more approachable, more like someone who would lend you their umbrella instead of raising an eyebrow and asking why you hadn't thought ahead and been prepared. Someone who might care about one's well-being instead of silently calculating how much money they could take from you without it being called outright robbery. Someone like...

Anna.

She had the same smile as the Keith Lochlainn in the photography.

TEN

IAN PEERED CLOSER at the photo, mentally flipping through every image of Keith he could dredge up from his memory. Now that he saw the resemblance, it was all he could do to not unsee it. Anna not only had Keith's smile, she had his eyebrows: straight but with the slightest bend as they narrowed toward the outer edges of her eyes. She had his jaw, sharp and square.

Did she also have his killer instinct? His determination to find his opponent's jugular vein and slash it open at the precise time when the slice of the blade would hurt the most? Had the past several weeks been nothing but a setup?

Had that night been only a ploy?

Ian thought he had the upper hand. He was the game master. The pieces were falling into place at his instigation. He was in control and he dictated the moves.

The knowledge that he had been played from

the start crushed him, closing off his windpipe, caving in his chest, his breath coming in short pants as he guarded against the pain.

"May I have the photo back?" she asked.

With supreme effort, he dragged his gaze away from the framed image to meet hers. The room was still and dark, and so was she, hidden in the shadows. A perfect metaphor, he thought. What else was she concealing in those dim corners with her?

"It took me a while. But I figured it out."

"Figured what out?" She held out her hand.

He went to give the photo to her, but when she moved to take the frame from him, he found he couldn't let go. "Who you really are."

Her brow furrowed. "What are you talking about?"

"You. The Lochlainns. You're one of them. That's why you came in at the last minute to stop the Lakes of Wonder sale." He shook his head, his pulse ringing in his ears with the movement. "Now everything makes sense. I can't believe I didn't see it before, but then the family has kept your existence very quiet. The perfect stealth operative."

The only question was how she was related to the Lochlainns. Archibald had only one child,

Keith. And Keith's only child, Jamie, had died without producing children. A distant cousin? The result of a hush-hush affair?

Anna didn't move, her eyes wide, her mouth open in shock. Then her chest started to rise and fall in rapid motion. "What…how did you—"

"The photo." He finally released his grip on the frame. "The family resemblance is clear."

She grabbed the photo before it could hit the ground again. "It is?"

"The smile. Keith is rarely seen with one. You, on the other hand…" His stomach squeezed, harsh and painful, as memories of her smile flooded in. Anna gazing up at the fireworks, delight on her face. Anna laughing at him on the gondola then taking his hand in hers when she realized he wasn't faking his reaction to heights. Anna, pushing her hair off her face, her chest rising and falling against him, smiling with pure joy and delight after she came in his arms.

Anna traced Keith's frozen image with her index finger. "I haven't seen this photo before."

"I doubt many people have. Keith is particular about his public image. But then, you already know that. Since you're a Lochlainn." He folded his arms across his chest. It was either that or howl with the knowledge of just how much the Lochlainns had taken him for a ride. Had she been laughing at him with her family after their park excursions? Using their time together to probe for the chinks in his armor? Chinks, he had to admit, she'd caused to appear. "Were you going to tell me?"

"I...maybe. I guess. I don't know." She sank onto the sofa, under the floor lamp. The light lit her golden hair, almost as if she wore a halo. An angel of perfidy, perhaps.

"You don't know?" He crossed his arms and leaned against the bookcase. "Or you do know, but you're figuring out what to say next because your cover has been blown."

Her head snapped up. "Cover? What cover? May I remind you, *you* slept with *me* under false pretenses."

"False? I wasn't hiding who I am."

"Neither am I!" she shot back. "I've never pretended to be anyone but who I am." Then her shoulders fell. "Of course, how can I be who I am when I don't know who that is?" she mumbled under her breath.

The room wasn't large but the walls were thick and well-insulated from the noise of the theme park outside, so he heard her perfectly well. "You don't know who you are? Are you claiming amnesia now? What's next, the Lochlainns found you under a cabbage leaf and that's why no one has heard of you?"

She glared at him. "You wouldn't understand. How can you, when you've known all along who you are and where you belong? What is it like, being born a Blackburn, knowing you have a place in the family business?"

He stared at her. "What are talking about? The Lochlainns inserted you into the sale of Lakes of Wonder. You seem to have a place. The Stratford name, though, that's a nice touch."

Her head shook rapidly. "My name *is* Stratford. At least, that's the name I was born with. And I can't believe you would call me a, how did you put it, 'stealth operative.' I think it's been clear I am hopeless when it comes to understanding theme parks. Or billion-dollar negotiations."

She sounded sad. Exhausted. Frustrated. Not the emotions he expected from someone who had been beating him at his own game.

And she was right.

Not that she was hopeless at understanding the attractions industry – on the contrary, her insights were smart and incisive, even when he didn't agree with her — but that he was wrong to accuse her of operating in bad faith. Anna had been nothing but genuine with him, he realized. From the start.

From the night they shared together.

"I apologize," he said. "You've done nothing to earn doubts of your intentions. On the contrary. And you've made me look at theme parks in whole new ways."

"Thank you." She kept her gaze averted and he sat next to her on the sofa, almost but not quite touching.

"But you are a Lochlainn," he said.

She nodded, then shook her head. "Yes. No. It's complicated."

"Did Keith refuse to acknowledge he was your father until recently?" It was the only explanation that came to mind.

She laughed, but there was a frantic undertone to the sound. "Keith didn't refuse. He didn't know."

"Your mother never told him you were his daughter?"

Her laughter came harder. "You mean am I a secret baby kept from him? No. And Keith is my grandfather...well, biological grandfather. Jamie is my father. No, strike that, my sperm donor."

"What?"

Ian had been surprised before in his life. Shocked, even. Usually by something Harlan said or did in the name of BBA. But of all the things he'd expected to hear over the course of his lifetime, this didn't make the top ten thousand. "Jamie Lochlainn...is your father."

"My parents used a sperm donor to conceive me, yes. The donor was anonymous. They had no idea he was Jamie Lochlainn."

He blinked. "And how did you find out?"

She pushed a lock of hair behind her ear. "The Knock."

"Excuse me?"

"That's how I think of it. The Knock. With a capital *K*." She sighed, falling back against the sofa cushions. "Ever have one of those events that divide your life into before and after? Like, you were one person before the event happened and a different person after? And there's no going back to before?"

"Yes. I lost my father when I was twelve."

She sat up, her body twisting to face his. Her gaze, soft with empathy, locked onto his. "I'm so sorry."

He started to shrug, his usual response to expressions of sympathy. But there was something about the dark, still room, a now-secret shrine to lost family relationships, that caused him to rethink. Or maybe it was Anna and the fact she obviously had a complicated relationship with her parents, too.

"Thank you," he said simply. "It was a long time ago. But I know that feeling. That something immeasurable has changed and you can't return to being the same person as before, even if you want to."

"Precisely. Although, in my case, I didn't lose anyone. I guess you could say you I gained people." She bit her lower lip. "Thanks for putting it into perspective."

He shook his head. "If your life was impacted, it was impacted. That matters."

She picked up the photo of Keith and a baby Jamie from where she had placed it on the coffee table, running her fingers once more over their smiling faces before putting the framed picture back down. "And perhaps I did lose someone. I lost me. Or rather, who I thought I was." She glanced at him, her mouth twisting into a rueful smile. "I'm being so melodramatic. I apologize. Should we leave? The park must be shooing the last guests out of the gates right now."

He stayed where he was, stretching one arm out along the back edge of the sofa. "You haven't told me about the Knock."

"There's nothing to tell." When she could no longer hold his stare, she sighed. "It was a Monday morning. I was in my office—wait, I never told you what I do. I work for my family's furniture store as the in-house interior designer. The family that raised me, I mean. Not the Lochlainns, obviously."

"Now the excitement over the Eames chair makes sense. But I'm interrupting. Please, continue."

"At first I thought the person at the door was my mother. We were planning a trip to North Carolina for a furniture show. But when I answered the Knock, it was a man I'd never seen before. He asked if he could come into my office to speak in private. Over his shoulder, I could see both my parents. Their expressions... I'd never seen them appear so terrified."

She closed her eyes and leaned back against the cushions. He pulled her to him and she willingly went, his arms encircling her, lending her as much of his support as she wanted to take. "And they were afraid because?"

"Because they had to tell me the truth. My dad was not my father. Not my biological one."

"You learned this from a stranger?"

"No, my parents jumped in to tell me. But I wasn't given time to let it sink in. The man was from the Lochlainn Company, and he had a proposition for me." She lifted her head from his shoulder. "I'm not supposed to tell anyone the next part. If it gets out to the press, I'll lose."

"Lose?"

She sighed. "It's public knowledge Keith and Jamie were estranged for many years. When Jamie left as a teenager, Keith cut him off without a cent. But what people don't know is Jamie…well, he apparently earned money by…"

"Selling his sperm. I knew some guys in college who did the same thing."

She nodded and her head fell onto his shoulder again. He could smell her vanilla-scented shampoo, feel the warmth of her cheek where she lay against him. He shifted so he could take on more of her weight. "And I was the result." She lifted her head again. "Or one of the results. I haven't even thought about…" She swallowed.

He stroked her hair. The golden strands were silky-soft, the ends gently curling around his fingers. His chest walls ached, as if something deep inside was expanding and pushing against his limits. "That's an issue to figure out later. What happened when he told you? What's not supposed to get out? That Jamie sold his sperm, or you are his child?" He turned to look at her. "How did the lawyer know you are Jamie's child in the first place? Through the clinic?"

"The records are supposed to be sealed. My parents didn't know. They were shocked when the representative showed up."

"So how…?"

She sighed. "I took one of those DNA tests. I'd forgotten about it, until the Knock."

"And the Lochlainns found your results."

"Or they had the clinic's records unsealed. They wouldn't say."

"Trust Keith to make a mockery of privacy rules. And then the Lochlainns gave you Lakes of Wonder." He grunted. "Not a bad welcome-to-the-family gift."

"Oh, they didn't give it to me. I'm still proving myself."

What? "You're Keith's flesh and blood. You must prove yourself to him?"

"But that's the thing. We're related—I was required to take a more extensive paternity test—but he didn't raise me. He doesn't know me from a...hole in the wall."

"You carry his genes."

"So? Look at how often kids disappoint their parental figures."

"Or vice versa," Ian muttered.

Anna snorted. "True. But just because you're someone's child doesn't mean you grow up to be like them."

"Because you are raised by someone doesn't mean you'll be like them."

She glanced up at him. "You sound like you're speaking from experience."

He didn't want to think about his stepfather and his own tangled family issues. He tugged her head back onto his shoulder. "We're talking about you. Go on."

"Long story short, Keith gave me the sale of the theme park to oversee, to prove I have what it takes to be a Lochlainn. If I succeed to his standards—and who the hell knows what they are—then I will earn a place in his will. If I don't, I guess I go back to being some stranger he's never heard of." She laughed, but there was little humor in her expression. "I mean, who does that? Who decides if someone is worthy of being a relation based on a wholly arbitrary task?"

"A Lochlainn."

"Y'know, you've made several similar comments about the Lochlain family over our time together. Care to explain why you feel so strongly about them?" She straightened up to catch his gaze. Some of the despair that had been clouding her expression was starting to clear. Good.

"I suppose it's only fair I tell you my family story in return. So here's the Blackburns' secret—" He paused for dramatic effect. "Lakes of Wonder wasn't developed by Archibald Lochlainn. It was the creation of Cooper Blackburn—my great-grandfather."

She laughed. "C'mon. I've read as many books as I could find on Lakes of Wonder and—"

"History is written by the winners. And Archibald made it very clear that Cooper was to be exorcised from the history of Lakes of Wonder."

"That seems like something that would be difficult to cover up."

"I repeat, history is written by the winners. How did you think I knew about the Lighthouse? And the key?"

She pursed her lips into the most delectable shape. "I don't... I guess I think of you as the theme park guru who knows everything. Even to the point of magicking up a key. Rather silly, now that I think of it."

"I found the key in my grandfather's things. But my larger point is you're romanticizing something that isn't romantic. The Lochlainns don't care about people. They only care about profit. And they are ruthless about getting what they want."

Her gaze narrowed. "Then why did they come looking for me when they learned about my existence?"

"If I were a gambler, I'd bet Keith approached you as a form of proactive defense against you discovering the truth about your parentage. By approaching you first, he controls the narrative. He controls your place in the family." Too late, he realized he'd growled his words, his tone harsh and fierce. But Anna needed to know what she was up against. He had experience with the den of vipers a family-run conglomerate could be. She didn't.

"I don't..." She squeezed her eyes shut. "Okay. Fine. Maybe." She rose from the sofa, her movements jerky. "We should go. It's long past closing time. I don't want to explain to security why we are running around after the gates are shut."

The bright light that seemed to always illuminate her from within was extinguished. "Anna, I didn't mean to upset you—"

"You didn't." Her hunched shoulders and arms wrapped tightly around her chest said otherwise.

"I don't want you to get hurt. I've seen it happen too many times in families when there is a large company at stake. Believe me, the only ties that bind when it comes to business are contracts. Blood may be thicker than water, but paper is thicker than blood."

"Got it." She kept her eyes focused on the floor.

"The more knowledge you have, the better you can protect yourself. Did you sign anything? A nondisclosure agreement, perhaps? Have you to talked to lawyers?"

She shook her head, the movement small but shaky.

"I know some very good ones who would love to get their hands on anything regarding the Lochlainns. I can recommend—"

"No." The word reverberated in the small room. "No lawyers."

He stared at her. "Anna, you're not thinking clearly. There's a lot of money at stake and the Lochlainns threw you into the deep end without a net. You need to talk to—"

She scoffed. He'd never heard such a bitter sound from her. "I need. Yes, everyone is an expert on what I need. Or what I can or can't do. You know what I really need? To stop talking about this and to get out of here."

"Okay." He'd meant it when he'd said he didn't want to upset her. But on the other hand, the sooner she understood the truth about her birth family, the better life would be for her in the long run. He was doing her a favor, damn it. He stood. "Let's go. I know a shortcut to the park's exit."

She didn't answer, choosing instead to march to the door. She placed her hand on the doorknob and then turned to him, her gaze wide.

"The knob won't turn. The door is stuck."

ELEVEN

IAN MOTIONED FOR Anna to step aside. "Let me try."

She was right. The doorknob was frozen. He tried again, throwing his right shoulder against the thick door in the hope of jarring it loose. The only result was a sore shoulder.

"Use your key," she urged.

"I would if there were a keyhole on this side." And if he had the key. Too late, he remembered he'd left it in the lock on the other side of the door.

"I guess we'll have to call someone—" She brought out her cell phone and then groaned. "I don't have service. You?"

He looked at his screen. No bars appeared. "Lakes of Wonder's weak cell network and even weaker WiFi strike again."

"It's the twenty-first century. How can there be no signal?"

"I've told you. Keith has refused to invest in the park. It's falling down around your ears."

She narrowed her gaze. "Right. Convenient of this situation to remind me. I don't suppose this was your plan, to lock me up in this Lighthouse tower and feed me stories of my terrible family and their terrible custodianship of this park until I agree to sell?"

Ian had to laugh, despite their predicament. "No, Rapunzel, I did not plan this. I didn't know you were a Lochlainn until we arrived here."

She smirked. "I had to ask, in case I could persuade you to let me go early."

"Now you're telling me. If I knew all I had to do to get you to sell was to lock you in a lighthouse—" At her mock glare, he stopped. "Too soon?"

"Let's find another way out of here first, then the jokes. The park has security. And custodial staff. We just need to get their attention." She went to the curtains on the far wall and drew them back, revealing the large round window spanning from floor to ceiling that overlooked Seamus's Seaport.

He joined her. The view over the park was spectacular, especially with holiday lights outlining the buildings. And empty. Not a person could be seen. The pavement around the Lighthouse was wet, indicating the street sweeper had already made its rounds.

Anna pointed to a figure in the distance. "Look!" A man wearing the distinctive purple-and-gold uniform that marked the Lakes of Wonder private security force came into view. She waved furiously. "Hey! Up here!"

The man kept his gaze roving, but only on the storefronts at his eye level.

The window was not meant to be opened. She banged on the glass anyway. "Hey!" she shouted again.

"He's not going to hear you." Ian felt it was necessary to point out the obvious before his hearing was damaged. "The glass is thick, meant to withstand heavy storms and earthquakes. We're several stories above him. And all security guards wear a headpiece. You're going to hurt your hands."

"The balcony." She indicated the narrow walkway circling the exterior of the Lighthouse. "Is there a way to get to the balcony?"

"Right. Of course." He should have thought of that sooner. After some searching, they found the door, covered with the same wallpaper as the living area. The handle turned but the door only opened an inch.

"Hurry," she urged. "The security guard is about to finish his round of the plaza."

"I'm trying," he gritted. "Something is blocking—" Then the door suddenly gave way and he almost fell. Anna pushed past him and he stumbled onto the balcony after her.

"Hey! Help!" She grabbed onto the metal railing as she yelled. "Up here— No! Wait! Come back!"

The guard turned onto the path for Heroes Harbor and was soon out of view. Ian strained his vision, but he couldn't spot anyone else in the park.

"Looks like they cut the security budget," he murmured to Anna. "Another indication the park is in financial trouble."

If looks could incinerate, he would be a pile of smoking ash. "What are we going to do?" she asked.

She sounded as if she had learned an asteroid was on direct collision course with the planet and they had fifteen minutes to live. He touched her arm. "It's going to be okay. Worst-case scenario, we spend the night here. I'm supposed to be in a BBA executive committee meeting in

Los Angeles in the morning. Tai will send out a search party when I don't show up. They'll find us."

"Not until the morning?" She started to shiver. "Locked in here?"

He peered at her. Her pupils were dilated, and not because the evening sky was dark Her freckles stood out as dark smudges, her skin pale even for moonlight. The sharp rasp of her quickened breathing filled the air. This was not anger at the situation, nor frustration at being locked up with him. This was something deeper, more personal.

"We'll be fine. The plumbing works. There's even a couch for you to sleep on." He dug into his pockets. He'd worn these jeans on the plane earlier and hadn't had time to change before he'd met Anna. "And if we get hungry, I have a bag of airline snacks."

She took three gulping breaths. "You have your thing with gondolas. I…have a thing about locked rooms."

He reached out and took her hands in his. They were colder than if she had plunged them into a snowbank. "We'll be out of here in a matter of hours."

She started shaking her head even before he

finished speaking, her eyes becoming unfocused. Her legs trembled as if they were about to give out.

He steered her toward the sofa, guiding her to a seated position. "Don't faint until you feel the cushions."

That got a glare from her. Not a very strong one, but he was glad to see a spark in her gaze. "You don't need to coddle me. I'll be fine. I just need to get...accustomed."

"You don't look like you're getting over it."

"I'll be fine," she repeated. A faint sheen of perspiration appeared on her brow.

Something inside Ian's chest twisted, hard. He swallowed and pushed the pain down. He sat next to her. "Tell me something about your childhood."

"What?" But her head came up, her gaze catching his.

"Your childhood." He faked a yawn. "I'm bored and I doubt the TV works. Entertain me."

"Entertain you?" She laughed. "I doubt you'd find my life entertaining. I'm very boring. Well, except for the whole sperm donor thing, and you already know that."

He smiled, his gaze lingering on her blond

curls, her flushed cheeks, her perfectly normal nose, which shouldn't be as fascinating as it was and yet he couldn't take his eyes off how her features all came together in a compelling package. "Nothing about you is boring."

"You're only saying that because you want my theme park." She took several gulping breaths. "I'm merely an interior designer who works for her family's furniture store. The most interesting thing that happened to me before the Knock was winning a vacation in the Bahamas thanks to a charity raffle. But when my cousin and I went on the trip, the hotel was undergoing renovations and not only was the restaurant closed, but our window was covered by scaffolding, so we couldn't see the beach. See? Boring."

"You practice random acts of kindness. You whistle Broadway tunes. You bring a fresh perspective to Lakes of Wonder daily." She surprised and amazed him at every turn. He never tired of listening to her thoughts on the goings-on in the park. He found himself looking forward to the fresh ways she would challenge his long-held opinions. No one else made him laugh as much.

Being with her made him happy.

The realization took his breath way like a solid punch to his solar plexus.

"That's considerate of you to say—" She looked at him then did a double take. "Are you okay? Is saying nice things really that painful for you?"

"No, I—" He cleared his throat, hoping to buy time to restore the flow of oxygen to his brain. "I meant every word."

"Uh-huh." She snorted. "Your face looks like you bit into an entire crate of lemons."

"Are you accusing me of lying?" He wasn't. It shocked him how much he wasn't.

"It's fine. You don't need to butter me up to get what you want."

"Despite the phrase 'butter you up' creating very intriguing images—"

She laughed. "Are you never not flirting?"

"There was no buttering intended. Sadly." Her head was turned away from him and he couldn't see her expression. "Hey. Are you okay? How can I help?"

"You are helping. The talking is helping." She shifted on the cushions, turning so her body was angled toward him. Her eyes glistened in the dim light, but otherwise her signs of panic had vanished. A sense of calm settled in his limbs. "I find *you* fascinating, you know," she continued.

And just like that, her nearness made his veins sing, his nerves taut with heat. "Really." He kept his tone light, but it was a struggle. "Go on."

"Why is closing the deal with Lakes of Wonder so important to you? Why not walk away? BBA is doing fine. The company has two theme parks in Southern California, you don't need a third."

"Ah. It's not me you find fascinating, but BBA." The disappointment was crushing. Too crushing.

"Aren't they one and the same?"

"No—" He stopped. Were they? He'd been focusing on getting Harlan out of BBA for so long. Fighting Harlan's irrational directives and underhanded attacks. Concentrating on removing Harlan's influence not only from the company, but from his family, so that the lines between them blurred.

"You asked why closing the deal is so important. BBA is a family business. There's been a Blackburn at the helm of the company since my great-grandfather started it. But as I mentioned, my dad died young and my mother, in her grief, married a family friend because she wanted a male role model for me. But my step-father—Harlan—turned out to be anything but. She signed a very poorly written prenup that gave Harlan control of the shares she'd inherited from my father. And those shares got him on the board, where he consolidated power and became chairman. Long story somewhat shorter, I have the votes to force Harlan off the board, but only if I acquire Lakes of Wonder." That was the truth. Just not all of it.

"Then it comes down to family for you, as well."

"I suppose so. Yes." Not in the way she meant, but close enough. He was doing this to ensure Harlan stayed out of his family and his family's business. Stopped mentally torturing his mother at every company function.

"I always thought I knew where I belonged," she said softly. "Even as I went away to college, I knew I would come back home. Friends might come and go, even boyfriends, but my family... they're my rock. Were my rock." She blew out a puff of air. "Still are. But I used the Lakes of Wonder sale as an opportunity to run away. I... need space to figure out who I am."

He nodded. "My father worked long hours.

Then he had a heart attack. But I knew I belonged to BBA."

"Shouldn't that be the other way around? BBA belongs to you?"

He shook his head. "No. You spoke about your family as your rock. That's what BBA is to me. The one constant in my life." Another reason why Harlan needed to be thrown out. He was destroying that foundation.

"I don't think I'll ever belong to the Lochlainn Company. Not in that way. I only wish I knew where I belonged," Anna murmured. She leaned over to pick up the photo of Keith and Jamie from the coffee table, but it eluded her fingertips. Ian reached for the frame, intending to slide it closer to her, but she had already scooted to the edge of the sofa to extend her grasp.

Their hands collided, their fingers meeting. The resulting spark nearly short-circuited his brain. Her head flew up, her gaze meeting his. In the dim light, her eyes were dark and wide.

The room grew very quiet. The only sounds were her soft breaths and his heartbeat, a painful and rapid thump against his eardrums.

Her fingers relaxed, tangling with his, her warm touch soft at first, but increasing in in-

tensity until she held on to him as if he were
her only hope of not getting swept up in the
currents beginning to swirl around him.

But he was not her harbor of safety. Thanks
to Olive's and Preston's new demands, he would
be the unyielding rock upon which her ship
would crash.

He moved to take his hand away, but her
grasp only tightened. And, damn it, he didn't
want her to let go. He wanted to continue holding her hand. Wanted to hold more of her, to
press her soft length against him. Wanted to
rest his lips in the hollow of her throat to feel
her pulse leap, and then trace her shivers with
kisses down her beautiful full breasts and the
dip of her waist to her lusciously dimpled hips
and thighs and the delicious damp triangle between her legs.

Anna's gaze met his. He saw his desire re-
flecting from the bottomless blue depths—or
maybe it was hers. Theirs.

"Ian?" Her soft whisper reverberated in the
stillness. "I know we said…that one night
was…"

"Never to be repeated."

She nodded, her pink tongue briefly appearing to wet her lips. He was mesmerized by its

appearance. "But I...tonight... I..." She swallowed. "I want to kiss you. May I?"

He brushed an errant curl away from the curve of her cheek. "Of course. I'm happy help you take your mind off the locked room." He grinned. "Turnabout is fair play, after the gondola."

She shook her head, tiny rapid tremors. "No. I want to kiss *you*. Because you're you. Not because of the situation."

Ian's heart twinged, a painful, sharp twang that pulled all the oxygen out of his lungs. The lack of air made speaking difficult. But he could still move. He cupped her face with his hands and brought her closer to him.

He intended the kiss to be a gentle one. A comforting one, meant to reassure her she was safe despite her fear of locked rooms. He whispered his lips over hers, barely touching, letting her know he was there for her, however she needed him.

Then she moaned against his mouth, her own hot and warm and insistent, her tongue demanding he open to her. "I want you, Ian," she whispered. "Tonight. One more night."

TWELVE

IAN KNEW HOW good sex with Anna could be. That night in his hotel room would live in bright, unfading color in his memory until his deathbed. Being with her the last few weeks had been a supreme test of his self-control as he'd literally willed himself not to respond physically whenever her hand brushed his by accident. It was not an accident that he gave up his more tailored trousers for causal, loose pants or jeans when they were in the park, the better to hide when his self-control inevitably wasn't up for the challenge.

Anna's touch trailed streams of fire, her hands finding the hem of his shirt and tugging it over his head. He pushed her T-shirt up and off, making short work of her bra immediately after, and groaned when her breasts once more overflowed his hands, where they belonged. Her nipples were long and hard and he needed them in his mouth, now. He steered her toward the high-backed sofa, bending her backward until he could suit action to desire and finally claimed those tight buds, sucking and lathing while inhaling the clean, fresh scent that was uniquely hers. She moaned, moving against him, but when she would wrap herself against his leg to push her core against his thigh to relieve her pressure, he held her off. Tonight was about her. And he was going to make every second last as long he could. He stripped off her jeans and her panties in one motion, and then paused to take in the glory that was a nude Anna, her gaze warm with want, her arms reaching for him.

The pressure in his own jeans was becoming painful but he ignored it. His life had been spent pursuing control and while he'd rarely needed to deny himself in the bedroom, he was going to put that vaunted control of his to good use for Anna's sake. Because she hated being in a locked room. Because she wanted him.

Because he wanted to please her. Because he wanted her to know she was worthy of being worshipped. And he wanted to be the one who worshipped her.

"Turn around," he whispered to her, guiding

her to do so with his hands, helping her bend herself just so over the back of the sofa. Anna looked back at him as he dropped to his knees and she whimpered, her legs parting for him without needing to be asked.

God, she was beautiful, trembling for him, her hips bucking at his slightest touch. He adjusted himself. Yes, he was known for wielding his control but he feared this would test him beyond his limits. He breathed her in, reveling in her most intimate scent, relishing the slick proof of how much she desired his touch.

He kept his mouth on her, bringing her as close to the heights as he dared and then changing his rhythm to bring her back down, then driving her up again to glimpse the peak as many times as he could, finally allowing her to come apart on his tongue and lips as she shuddered and gasped, catching her in his arms as her legs finally gave out and settling them both on the sofa. She blinked up at him, her blue eyes dark and unfocused. "I changed my mind," she said, and his heart skipped a beat.

"What about?" he asked, hoping her mind hadn't changed about them, about this night.

"About locked rooms," she sighed, her eyes closing. "This isn't so bad." Then her breathing slowed and he smiled. He'd achieved his goal. She was relaxed enough to sleep.

Then one of her eyes opened. "I haven't forgotten you." Her hand drifted between them and found his erection, still pushing painfully against his zipper. "Just give me a few minutes,"

He laughed and gathered her close. "I've had more than my share of fun, believe me." Watching Anna come apart, knowing she trusted him enough to let go of her fears, was all the release he needed.

The bright morning light, no match for his closed eyelids, woke Ian. He blinked, confused at first as to why the hotel forgot to give him his customary early wake-up call. If the sun was shining this hot, the hour was long past his usual time to rise. He reached out for the phone on his bedside table, intending to call the front desk and demand to know what went wrong, but his hand encountered nothing but empty air.

He came fully awake and realized where he was. And with whom.

Anna was curled next to him on the wide sofa, her blond hair a wild cumulus cloud framing her peaceful face. He propped himself up on one elbow, his gaze loath to leave the relaxed planes of her face. He'd always found Anna attractive, as much for her disarming charm as her lush curves. But sleeping in the sunlight, with dust motes dancing around them as if they really were in an enchanted castle filled with pixie magic, she was beyond beautiful.

She was precious. Precious to him.

The realization was both awe-inspiring and humbling.

She sighed softly, her head stirring slightly. She would be fully awake any minute now. He both anticipated and regretted the moment they would need to leave the hidden apartment. Part of him wanted nothing more than to stay here, locked away from the world and their responsibilities and the demands placed on them. Another part was anxious to leave and tackle those very same demands—because while they existed, Ian and Anna would never be fully free to move forward and live the lives they wanted. A life, he was starting to realize, that would not be complete unless she continued to be in it. But they wouldn't—couldn't—even be friendly acquaintances if the deal remained a sword of Damocles hovering above their heads, threatening to sever the growing connection between them.

Ian prided himself on his strategic skillset. He'd never met a cake he couldn't have and also eat—it was a matter of figuring out the right solution. There had to be a way to oust Harlan from Blackburn Amusements without harming the relationship he had built with Anna. A way to get Olive and Preston on his side without agreeing to their demands to dismantle Lakes of Wonder and turn it into a retail site. But even as his mind raced through options, he discarded them before the thoughts could be fully formed.

Anna yawned and stretched, bringing him back to the present. The very pleasurable present. Hell, she was gorgeous waking up, her hair tumbled across her shoulders, her cheeks flushed, her mouth relaxed and softly parted. She sat up, the blanket Ian had found midway through the night falling away to reveal her rose-tipped breasts, and his hands begged anew to cup their glory.

But they had to get out of the Lighthouse sooner or later. And if he didn't maintain his focus on that goal, sooner would be later would be never. "What time is it?" she asked, her voice redolent with sleepy satisfaction, and though he was no longer looking at her, his cock grew even harder.

"A little after eight," he answered. Anna squeaked with surprise and the sounds of a frantic search for discarded articles of clothing soon followed. "We have an hour before the park opens, but the early morning crews should be here. Hopefully, I can get someone's attention." He crossed to the balcony door, half buttoning his shirt as he went, and pulled it open.

Anna gasped. "Wait. It's Saturday morning. Don't—"

Too late. He'd stepped onto the balcony.

And hundreds of park guests dressed in yoga wear, spaced evenly apart on the concourse that surrounded the Lighthouse, their arms raised in unison to begin a sun salutation sequence, stared back at him. Or so it seemed. Perhaps a few had their eyes closed or were focused on their alignment. But enough shocked gazes met his—and not a few of the guests immediately held up camera phones to memorialize his appearance—to assure him that their presence in the Lighthouse was no longer a secret.

He slammed the door shut and turned to face Anna. "The morning yoga in the park special event is today."

She nodded. "I'm sad I'm missing it," she said

with a straight face. "Do you think they'll re-
fund my fee?"

"I'm sure you can talk to management if you
run into problems. Speaking of, I'm guessing
security will show up here in the near future.

"It's okay, I'm related to the park's owner."
She smiled, and the room was bathed in light
brighter than the earlier morning sun. Then
the brilliance faded. "So. About last night—"

He crossed to where she stood, taking her
right hand in his. "I enjoyed every minute. I
enjoy being with you."

"Same here. But—"

"Last night was same as the gondola. Nothing changed," he stated, wanting to give her
the reassurance he assumed she needed. Even
though his recent epiphany meant his mouth
felt full of broken glass as he shaped the words.
"The deal is back on."

She shook her head. "No! Last night changes
everything."

Something blossomed in his chest. Something he had never experienced before. An
ache, equal parts pleasure and pain. "What do
you mean?" he asked, keeping his tone neutral, not sure how he wanted her to answer
the question.

She kept her head down as she finished buckling the strap of her second sandal. Then she lifted her gaze to his. "You're the only person I've told about my connection to the Lochlainns. Why I'm here. Why I'm obviously out of your league when it comes to the negotiation."

He sat down beside her, ignoring the rumpled cushions that still bore witness to their activities of the night before. "I'm honored you trusted me. Especially since I'm—" *The enemy.* He stopped himself before he revealed too much. "The other party in the deal."

"But you're more than that, right?" Her clear blue gaze searched his.

He wanted to be. The realization nearly made him fall off the sofa. Damn it, he wanted to be more. He had no idea how he could be.

"I mean, Lakes of Wonder is as much part of your DNA as it is part of mine," she continued. "It's your legacy, also."

His breath returned, his lungs inflating as normal again. Of course. That's what she meant. She was focused on the theme park, not him. Not *them.*

Who knew disappointment tasted as bitter as the old cliché asserted?

"Yeah, sure." He rubbed his temples, hoping she would take any dimness in his glance for tiredness. It's not like they'd gotten much sleep, after all. In fact, it was a relief to focus on the deal and not on any implications for his personal life. He didn't need the distraction. On the other hand, seeing her hopeful gaze as she reminded him Lakes of Wonder had been as much a Blackburn creation as a Lochlainn one, only reminded him he would wipe that light away for good once she learned what Preston and Olive planned to do with the acquisition once it was completed. "But I've had much longer to process my family's involvement—or lack thereof, when it comes to this park. I understand this is much newer to you."

"Right. And that's why we need to talk about the sale. Now that I know—"

A hard and insistent knock drowned out whatever she was about to say.

"Ian! You in there?" came a gruff shout.

THIRTEEN

"Ian?" A louder knock on the door. "I hope you're in there."

Tai. Ian couldn't decide if he had never been happier or more frustrated to hear his friend's voice. "We're here," he called back.

"We?" said Tai, and then he was opening the door. He smiled when he saw Ian and Anna sitting quietly on the sofa, the apartment in almost perfect order aside from a few cushions still on the floor. "Of course. Hello, Anna. Nice to see you again. We met at the closing—or rather, what wasn't the closing—"

Ian rose off the sofa. "Good to see you, too. We found ourselves locked in."

"Thought as much. The key was in the outer lock. Guess you discovered your lucky charm had a practical purpose after all." He tossed the slender item into the air and Anna caught it.

"How did you know we were here?" she

asked. "We can't get a cell signal and there's no WiFi."

Tai tried to hold back his smirk, but Ian saw it. "Seems there was a half-naked intruder at the Lighthouse. It's all over the internet. There are some very clever reactions on TikTok—"

Ian pinched the bridge of his nose. "Great."

"Hey, can't tell it was you in the video. But you didn't show up for our breakfast. And Maeve—that's my assistant," he said to Anna, "heard from friends at the Lochlainn Company that you didn't show up for the yoga event." He turned back to Ian. "And you know me. I'm a numbers guy. I knew you were meeting at the park last night and I know how to add two and two together. Or, in this case, one missing exec and another missing exec. Don't worry, we called off security. Your secret is safe."

"It's not what—" Ian paused. He didn't owe Tai an explanation. He and Anna were consenting adults. And Lakes of Wonder was hers… well, her grandfather's. They weren't theme park aficionados trying to pull one over on the park's security. She had every right to be there. And so did he, in a manner of speaking.

He spoke over Tai's knowing chuckle. "Let's

get out of here. I can still make the rest of the exec com meeting."

Tai's laughter died. "Yeah, about that." He threw a sideways glance at Anna, who was pretending to examine the contents of the bookshelf so Tai and Ian could have a semblance of privacy. "The meeting was canceled."

"What? But I didn't—"

"The conversations are happening above my pay level, which was made very clear to me every time I try to dig for more information. But I think you should return to Denver immediately. From what I gather, Harlan is planning a board coup. He got Russell to join his side, or so the rumor mill says."

"Russell?" The sun disappeared and Ian wondered if there had been an eclipse before he realized it was his vision turning blackly dark. "He's in the Caymans, counting his yachts or some similar nonsense."

"He showed up at the Denver office yesterday, according to Maeve. Look, I don't know Russell nearly as well as you do—"

"He's my second cousin and that's too close for comfort," Ian muttered.

"And I know swarm is Russell's default setting," Tai continued. "But Maeve said this wasn't his usual oily slither around the Black-burn executive suites. He was on a mission."

"Why would Russell…" Ian stopped when the answer hit him, hard. "Preston. Or Olive."

"Which one?" Tai asked.

"Both. Russell is looking for the best way to leverage the board's loyalties for his own gain. He's shopping for the best deal."

"Is there anything I can do?"

"Have Maeve book the BBA jet as soon as you can. I need to be in Denver ASAP."

Ian's gaze lingered on Anna. There was still so much for him to process, for him to sort through the emotions that threatened to swamp his usual excellent and coolly discerning strategic thought centers. So much to say. So much to discuss, like the future of Lakes of Wonder. The future of whatever they would be to each other—

No. *Stick to the plan*, he told himself. This was nothing but a speed bump. A very pleasurable one, but a minor inconvenience on his way to getting what he needed. Nothing positive ever came of allowing hormones to have a say in business relationships. It was a recipe for di-saster, and he refused to be the main course in the banquet of humiliation that Harlan would throw should Ian fail to remove him from the board of BBA.

And he was close. So close.

Anna looked over and caught his gaze, her smile so warm and bright, his jaw ached at having to leave her light behind. "You two all caught up? Are we ready to leave?"

"Yes. In more ways than one. Listen, I need to go to Denver."

The light in her expression dimmed, a mere cast of a shadow, but it was perceptible to him. "Of course. I was hoping we could have some of those Seamus-shaped waffles for breakfast, but business waits for no stomach."

"Something like that. I'm sorry."

She crossed to his side and picked up his hand, entwining her fingers with his. "Is there anything I can do to help?"

He blinked. People offering their assistance was new to him. "No," he responded, his mind already ninety-five percent occupied with his upcoming confrontation with Russell, Olive and Preston. If he lost their support, he was dead in the water. "This is a BBA issue. Nothing you have any insight into. I don't need anything."

Too late, he realized how his words sounded when she dropped his hand as if he had burned her. "Insight. Right. Of course, you don't need my help. I don't have the requisite experience. Nor, apparently, do you need any support from me, moral or otherwise." Her tone was ice-cold.

"That's not what I—"

"Ian, we need to go." Tai was staring at his phone.

"Wait, you have service?"

"Just a bar but enough to get text messages. Told you to switch providers."

"What is it?" Ian gritted.

"Harlan is having a hard time reaching Johnson Miller for the emergency board meeting. Probably on purpose. Johnson doesn't like being dictated to. He'll keep Harlan dangling for at least another half day, to show he's independent."

"But then he'll dance to Harlan's tune. As always."

"Tigers don't change their stripes," Tai agreed. "But he's buying us time, so don't look a gift jungle cat in the mouth."

"Right." Ian strode toward the door. But as he was about to cross the threshold, he realized Anna wasn't following him. "Aren't you coming?" he asked her. "I'd thought you be happy to get out of here."

Anna's gaze was distant. "You're obviously in a hurry. You go. I'll find my own way out. Don't worry, I'll have Teri from the Lochlainn Company set up the next meeting for this coming Friday."

"The next meeting? You and I can schedule that, you don't need Teri—"

"The last meeting," she clarified. "The sale."

"Ian, we need to go—" Tai started to say.

Ian cut him off with a shake of his head and turned to Anna. "We still have several weeks left. I thought we could—"

She shook her head. "I have all the information I need. And there's no need to extend my trip past Thanksgiving. Might as well put us both out of our misery, waiting for the inevitable." She smiled, but there was no brightness to it. "Thank you for bringing me to the Lighthouse. It sounds like a bad pun but being here put a lot of things in a new light."

"Ian." Tai's voice was firm. A tone he rarely took, considering Ian was formally his boss.

"It's okay," Anna said. "I'm okay. You have to leave. I understand." She tucked a curl behind her ear. "See you soon."

"You need to read the texts I received," Tai said, and there was a clear warning in his words.

Ian held up his left hand in acknowledgment of Tai but kept his gaze focused on Anna. "I'll call you from the road."

"You need to concentrate on whatever is going on at BBA," she said. "I'll see you soon." As if on impulse, she rose on her toes and brushed a kiss against his lips. "Good luck." Then she waved at Tai before walking back to peruse the dusty tomes on the bookshelf.

He couldn't be more dismissed if he were in a classroom and the bell rang. "Thanks," he said. "We'll talk. Soon."

He followed Tai out of the Lighthouse apartment. He couldn't stop himself from turning back for one last look at her. The sun streaming in from the window turned her hair to living gold before outlining her figure, her shoulders ramrod-straight and her chin held high.

He wanted nothing more than to reverse his steps and take her in his arms, lead her back to the sofa where they could once again shut out the world and lose themselves in each other. But one glance at Tai's set jaw and he knew that was an impossibility.

He would make it up to Anna. Once Lakes

of Wonder was his, he and Anna could figure out what they wanted to do about the crazy chemistry that ignited between them.

But if he didn't neutralize Harlan's threat, he would have no future to explore, with or without her.

Anna kept her gaze firmly fixed on the photo in her hands as Ian disappeared. Not for good—he would no doubt show up for the final meeting and the transfer of Lakes to Wonder to BBA— but his departure had an air of finality about it all the same. After last night, she thought...

Well. It didn't matter what she thought, did it? No doubt Ian viewed last night the same way he did the first time they slept together. A fun interlude, devoid of any meaning and certainly lacking any deeper emotion.

She sighed and carefully placed the photo back on its spot on the shelf. Unlike Ian, she didn't have urgent matters of multinational corporate concern to which to attend. She was just...someone who had a connection to Lakes of Wonder solely due to an accident of birth. She had no real role at the theme park, no corner office in which to ensconce herself. What she did have, in fact, was literally one job. And that job was to sign the papers selling the park to BBA.

She traced her way back through the tunnels and was soon slipping into the gift shop. No one noticed her entrance and she was quickly swept up in the crowd of guests eagerly rummaging around the new holiday-themed merchandise. She pushed her way through the shoppers and emerged onto Seamus's Seaport, blinking at the warm rays of sun on her face. Her phone was buzzing with missed calls, texts and alerts but she ignored them all in favor of hitting the button to video call Maritza. Voice wasn't enough. She needed to see the face of someone she knew loved her.

"Hey!" her cousin answered right away. "How's sunny California?" Behind Maritza, Anna could see Pepa playing with her dolls—who were currently attempting to ride on the back of a plush toy version of Seamus Sea Serpent.

"Fine," Anna said. "How's sunny Florida?"

"The same," Maritza said. She turned to Pepa and held the phone so Anna and Pepa could see each other. "Want to talk to Anna? Look, she's at Lakes of Wonder! You can see the Lighthouse of Amazement behind her."

Anna glanced over her shoulder and silently

cursed her choice of position. *"Hola, niñita,"* she called.

"Don't wanna talk to Anna!" Pepa turned her back to the phone screen, her tiny shoulders rigid.

Maritza came back into view. "Sorry," she said. "It's been a morning. She's really leaning into her drama queen phase."

"That's okay—"

Something crashed in the background. Her cousin disappeared, to be replaced by blurry movement and then a view of the kitchen's tiled floor as Maritza ran to the source of the noise. Anna glimpsed a spreading sea of cloudy white before her cousin reappeared. "Sorry, need to go. Milk emergency."

"Talk to you later—" But Maritza was gone.

Anna found an empty park bench and sat, the cool metal pressing into her legs. She should go back to the hotel, take a shower, maybe even a nap to catch up on the sleep she'd missed. But then what would she do? She'd explored most of Lakes of Wonder—and thanks to last night, even seen areas that weren't on the maps. She could continue to check out rival amusement parks in the area, but she'd seen enough to know that Ian was correct. Lakes of Wonder was special thanks to its history, but it lacked the well-honed whimsy and tightly maintained machinery of a Disney theme park. Or the stomach-flipping chills of a thirty-story roller coaster drop at a thrill park, like those owned by BBA. Or the crowd-pleasing ability to get up close with land and marine animals of the local zoos and aquatic parks.

Lakes of Wonder had nostalgia on its side and little more—and no investment from the Lochlainns, who obviously didn't care if the park thrived or died.

Why did she care so much? Was her pursuit of Lakes of Wonder because she was chasing a connection to the man whose DNA she shared? Or was her insistence on learning more about the park before selling it just a pretense to spend time with Ian? She could tell herself all she wanted that she was a sophisticated citizen of the world; one who indulged in one-night stands for fun and to assuage her curiosity about people she found sexually tempting. But if this trip had taught her one thing about herself, it was that she'd slept with Ian the first time because she not only found him attractive, but because she liked him. She'd slept with him last night because she…oh, she might as well acknowledge the truth her heart knew several weeks ago. She was falling in love with him.

And he couldn't get away from her faster if he were an Olympic gold medal sprinter.

She sighed, a long, loud exhale. She'd tried being someone other than who she was. She'd zigged where she would normally zag. She'd turned left instead of right. Yet she'd ended up making the same mistakes. Worse, she'd caused needless hurt and pain. She'd even made Pepa mad at her, although she knew Maritza was right and the five-year-old was milking—no pun intended—the drama for all she could. Yet Anna had ended up right back at the same square where she'd started, making the exact same mistakes.

Or worse ones. Because now she knew she could fall hard and fast for someone like Ian. Someone who made her laugh. Someone who made her legs weak with overwhelming desire, someone who took her breath away with a flash of his grin, someone who made her heart beat faster than a hummingbird's wings with one brush of his pinkie finger against hers.

Someone upon whose confidence and quietly commanding presence she'd grown to rely on, without realizing how much she'd come to accept him as a daily and much-looked-forward-to constant in her life. But that life, the one in which she and Ian had bantered as business rivals on the same equal footing, was not hers. Not really. She was borrowing it from the Lochlainns. Her actual life was in Florida.

In pieces.

She watched a family gather to take photos in front of the Lighthouse. The older daughter pouted, not wanting to waste time stopping. The younger daughter, around Pepa's age, refused to stand still and kept dancing out of the frame and having to be coaxed back by her father. The son had a Seamus-shaped bubble wand and wouldn't stop blowing cascades of bubbles in his older sister's face, irritating her more.

The parents looked hot and frustrated, despite the early hour. And yet, when the photos were finally taken, everyone broke into happy smiles. Their excitement at being at the park could be felt from where Anna sat.

Anna thought the park was magic. But watching the family walk off, the younger daughter still dancing, the older daughter now excitedly pointing out the sights to her brother, Anna finally understood: the real magic came from being with people you love. Family, whether by blood or by choice.

The photograph of Keith and Jamie in the Lighthouse floated in front of her vision. She had no way of knowing if she was right. But something—call it a Lochlainn intuition, per-haps the one thing she had inherited—told her the reason why Keith had let Lakes of Wonder fall into disrepair and that finally selling it was not because he'd fallen out of love with the park but because he'd lost the family he loved with whom to share it.

She still had no idea why Keith wanted her to handle the sale. But regardless of what happened between her and Ian personally, at least now she knew Lakes of Wonder would go to someone who also had a family tie to the park.

There was only one thing left for her to do.

Pick up the pieces.

She took out her phone again and searched her contacts. Her finger hovered over the screen. Finally, she pushed Call and listened to the phone ring on the other end, her hand trembling but successfully fighting the urge to hang up and pretend she'd dialed the number by accident.

After enough rings to make her wonder if she had left it too late—if they'd looked at the caller ID and refused to answer because she was now persona non grata—she heard the line connect.

"Anna?" her mother said. "Anna, honey, is that you?"

"Mom," Anna choked out before tears threatened to close her throat for good. "Mom, I've made so many mistakes. I'm so sorry. For running off to California without telling you directly, for refusing to talk to Dad when he tried. I don't know if you'll ever forgive me, but I'm coming home for Thanksgiving and I want to talk if you want—"

"Shh," her mom said, the same soft sound of comfort used to soothe Anna since she was a fractious toddler. "We love you, Anna bear. We know you're dealing with a lot. And we're sorry you've been so affected by our choices. We're so sorry. We only want you to be happy and healthy."

"I'm healthy." Anna sniffed and then she poured out most of the story of her time at Lakes of Wonder, keeping only the most private, treasured moments to herself.

She'd come to California hoping to discover who she was. Only to learn she couldn't continue to run from her past. Now it was time to determine who she wanted to be in the future.

And if that future could contain Ian Blackburn.

FOURTEEN

THE MORNING WAS crisp and cool, but the sharp bright sunlight outside his window promised a warm Southern Californian day ahead. Ian paced in his hotel suite, his gaze drawn more than he cared to the panoramic view of Lakes of Wonder below. He tried one last time to reach Anna before the meeting, but his call went immediately to voice mail. Damn it, now he was "it" in their game of phone tag. He could text, of course, but where would he start? How could he start?

A knock came at his door. He crossed to answer it, only realizing once he saw Tai that he had irrationally hoped Anna might be on his threshold instead. He nodded at his friend. "Hey."

"Hey back." Tai entered the suite, holding a paper bag in one hand and a tray of coffees in his other. "I brought bagels. Time to carbo load."

"You make it sound like we're about to run a marathon." Ian took one of the coffees.

Tai sat down on the sofa and starting to spread cream cheese on his bagel. "Well, it's the end of a very long chase. Sustenance is required."

Ian grunted, sipping his beverage.

Tai shot him a glance. "You sound more like a man going to his execution rather attaining his long-held desire. Great job with Russell, by the way. He's so on your side, I got an invite to join him on his yacht in Sardinia. Might even take him up on it. He said I can bring Linh."

Ian put down his coffee. His stomach roiled, hard, and the acidic beverage was making it worse. "Am I doing the right thing?"

Tai raised his eyebrows. "Do you think you're doing the right thing?"

"I love her, you know." He did. He'd realized it late one night, sitting in front of computer screen trying to make sense of numbers that refused to stay put, jumping around until all he saw was her face, flushed and relaxed, and her blue eyes staring into his.

He was an idiot for leaving her in the Lighthouse. For choosing BBA over her.

And, God help him, he was about to make the same mistake again.

"I know," Tai said. "So I'll ask again. Do you think you're doing the right thing?"

Ian didn't answer, choosing instead to dial Anna's number again. "C'mon, pick up," he said under his breath. But once again, only her voice mail answered.

"You're doing the right thing." Catalina Lochlainn poured more tea into the cup in front of Anna. "It's time for the Lochlainns to let go of Lakes of Wonder." She put the teapot down and smiled. "Thank you, again, for asking to meet. And for agreeing to have breakfast at this bistro. It's one of my favorite places."

"Of course. I know contacting you is against the terms of the Kno—the terms given to me by Bingham Lockwood when he discussed Keith's wishes." Anna picked up her cup. "But I couldn't leave California without at least trying to meet my new relatives. I'm only disappointed Keith didn't come with you. I would like to meet him."

"In time." Catalina's gaze warned Anna not to probe further. "But he wants you to know the sale remains wholly in your hands."

Anna placed her tea back on the table. "To be truthful, there's not much of an alternative if I didn't sign the sale documents, right? Like you said, the Lochlainn Company wants to be rid of the park."

"I wouldn't say 'rid,' exactly." Catalina cocked her head to the side. "More like it's been purposefully forgotten and needs to be rescued by someone else. And BBA is the only alternative to keep the park going. Otherwise, we've received many offers from developers to turn it into a golf course or shopping mall, something of that nature."

"And it's been forgotten because of Jamie. Because he cut off Keith, and then he died. And Lakes of Wonder is about families, but Keith no longer has one. Or at least, he no longer has his child."

The older woman maintained her pleasant expression, but a muscle jumped in her jaw. "You are very perceptive."

"I've learned a lot over these last weeks." Including that her heart was infinitely malleable and exponentially expandable. She'd had several long conversations with both her parents, full of tears and smiles and deep abiding love. No matter how they'd conceived her, the fact was she belonged to them and always would. But there was room for her Lochlainn relations, which was why she'd reached out to Catalina. She may never know if a certain trait was inherited from Jamie or instilled by her upbringing, but she was choosing the person she wanted to be.

And that person was in love with Ian.

She glanced at the clock on the bistro's wall. "Speaking of the sale, I should get going."

Catalina laid her hand over Anna's, stilling Anna's movements. "No matter what happens, I want you to know you have conducted yourself in this strange, unusual matter with grace. I am proud to call you my step-granddaughter."

"Thank you. And don't worry, the sale will go through. I'm sure of it."

Catalina shook her head. "Of course it will. I'm referring to the inheritance contest."

"The what? Contest?" Anna stared at Catalina, who for the very first time seemed to lose some of her equanimity.

"Oh, dear." Catalina swallowed. "You were not told by Bingham? You are in a contest. With Declan."

"Who is Declan?" Anna heard her voice as if coming from a faraway distance.

"Your half-brother. Also fathered by Jamie via donation. You honestly did not know?"

With supreme will, Anna managed to shake her head, tiny movements from side to side.

"Oh, dear," Catalina repeated. She took Anna's hands in hers, but Anna couldn't feel the older woman's grip. Her fingers were numb. "We have much to discuss."

Ian strode down the hallway of the Lakes of Wonder executive building, retracing his journey of...was it only four weeks ago? So little time, from one point of view. An entire lifetime from another.

His steps slowed as he approached the door, and he smoothed his hair before he knew what he was doing. The thud-thud-thud of his pulse drowned out any other noise that might be present.

He pushed the door open.

Ten heads swiveled in unison to watch him cross the threshold. He only cared about one. Anna. His gaze zeroed in on her like a person trapped in a desert who spotted a well. He smiled at her, but the smile faded as he took in her appearance.

Anna was wearing black. A tailored black-wool pantsuit, unadorned save for discreet silver buttons. Even the shoes peeking out from below her trousers were black. And the blouse under-neath the trim jacket was stark white. There wasn't a splash of Anna-characteristic color any-where. Her smile—her lovely, bright, irrepress-ible smile—was absent, while her blond curls were neatly combed back into a low ponytail. Worse, the light that usually suffused her from within, rendering her incandescent no matter the time of day or weather, was dim. Almost extinguished.

His pulse beat painfully against his eardrums. She nodded at him, once, then turned back to her discussion with Teri.

"Morning." He said hello to Tai, who had preceded him to the meeting, and nodded at the Lochlainn Company representatives. But his gaze never once left her. Every time he tried to take a step toward her, however, he was in-tercepted by one person after another. He ad-opted a close-lipped smile and listened patiently as they made small talk, the usual chitchat that precedes a much-longed-for but often-in-doubt closure of a business deal. Normally, he would revel in this moment, the calm after the storm, when both parties know the hard work of ne-gotiation is over and the only thing standing between them and a celebratory cocktail or two are a few signatures.

But he was anything but relaxed. He tried again to catch Anna's gaze. But she evaded his grasp in every sense of the word until time ran out and he found himself ushered to the chair next to hers. The déjà vu was strong as he sat down in the exact same spot as the first meeting, only so much had changed. Everything had changed.

"What's going on? Are you okay?" he whispered to her out of the side of his mouth.

She shook her head, a sharp movement almost too small to discern. "Later," she whispered back, but then she shot him a quick glance and he realized this was another one of her masks—one he hadn't seen before and hoped to never again—but the real Anna, his Anna, was still there. He smiled at her, a fast upturn of his lips meant as a reassurance, before she turned to the rest of the group now seated around the board table.

"Shall we begin?" she asked.

Ian moved through the next half hour as if in a repeated dream. This time, Anna signed the papers first. He watched her hand sign her name in bold, confident letters on the various documents. Then the documents were picked up, straightened, and placed in front of him.

Anna sat back in her chair and regarded him. Some of the tension had left her shoulders but her gaze remained wary and watchful.

This was it. The culmination of everything he had been working toward. The end of the Lochlainn/Blackburn feud, with victory firmly in the Blackburn camp. Preston, Olive and Russell would vote with him to remove Harlan. BBA would remain firmly in his hands, in Blackburn hands, as it was always meant to be.

And all he had to do was sign.

And Lakes of Wonder would go to Preston and Olive, who would destroy the park forever.

He turned to Anna. "We need to talk."

Her gaze darted around the room as she noted the avid stares of executives from both companies. "Now? Can't we talk after you sign?"

He shook his head. "No. It will be too late."

She licked her lips. "Okay. Where?"

He rose from the boardroom table and strode to the door, pausing only for her to catch up with him before he swept her out of the room and into the hallway. She ran-walked to keep up with him, taking two steps to his one. "Ian? Where are we going?"

He didn't answer, leading her down the corridor until they reached the elevator lobby. When a cab arrived, he ushered her inside—and pulled the stop button.

"Sorry. This was the only place I could think of where we would have privacy and no one would think to look for us," he said.

"What's going on?" Her gaze searched his expression. "Are you okay? Are you ill? Is something wrong at BBA?"

"Yes. No. Yes," he answered, drinking in the nearness of her presence. He'd missed her. Being close to her again, even if she remained on the other side of the elevator cab, was a restorative tonic for his soul. He could breathe easier, think clearer, now she was near. And now he knew what he had to do. What, really, was his only course of action. "BBA can't buy Lakes of Wonder."

She remained still, an Anna-shaped statue in the corner of the elevator. "Why?" she finally asked, her lips the only muscles she moved. "Lakes of Wonder is as much a Blackburn creation as a Lochlainn one. You're the perfect buyer. You're the only buyer."

"Remember I told you about my stepfather?"

Some color came back into her face. "Yes. Your awful stepfather."

"He is." Ian felt the tension of the last month—maybe even the last twenty years since his father had died—begin to leave his shoulders. "And he wants to remove me as CEO. I want to remove him as chairman of the board. We've been fighting for board votes this past week, with the vote next month. I have enough votes if the acquisition of Lakes of Wonder goes through. He has enough votes if it doesn't."

"I don't understand." Anna moved closer to him, her slender fingers coming to rest on his arm. Warmth radiated from her touch. "Then buy Lakes of Wonder. Why did you say BBA can't?"

"Because I only have enough votes if I give Lakes of Wonder to my cousin and uncle. And they have a deal to raze the park to the ground and build a live-work-retail complex. One of those shopping centers that looks like a fake Italian town." He raked a hand through his hair. "I know how much you love Lakes of Wonder. I can't let that happen."

Her hand dropped from his arm. "But your stepfather will win."

He closed his eyes. "Yes. And I'll lose my position. But BBA will survive Harlan. I'll fight my way back to the top again."

"But why?" She stared at him, her blue eyes dark and unreadable in the elevator's dim light. "You can save your job. Save BBA from your stepfather. I don't understand."

He swallowed. Hard. "Because I love you, Anna. And I can't destroy something you love." He cupped her face with his hands. "I've loved you since I saw you dancing to Halloween music wearing pink fairy wings. My only regret is I took too long to realize it."

"Ian, I—"

He kissed her, because he couldn't put off kissing her one second later. She made a sound deep in her throat and then she was kissing him back, her arms entwining around his neck as his hands molded her waist, her hips, pulling her to him so her soft curves met his hard planes, fitting together perfectly as they always had. He could have remained in the elevator forever, kissing his perfect partner, but she pulled back first.

He loved seeing her lips swollen, her gaze wide and wild. He burned the image on his memory. "So, we'll go back to the conference room and tell them the sale is off—"

"No." Anna smoothed her hair, restoring order. "You have to buy the park."

"Did you hear me? If BBA buys it—"

"Yes, I heard you!" Anger flashed in Anna's eyes. "And if BBA doesn't buy Lakes of Wonder, the park will be bought by golf course developers. Or residential developers. Or commercial developers. You know the Lochlainn Company won't spend the money needed to keep Lakes of Wonder running. You know Lakes of Wonder needs a buyer." She laughed, but there was no mirth in it. "You know it will take months, if not longer, to find another buyer while the park falls further into disrepair." She crossed her arms over chest, her gaze turning sharp and emotionless, like a shark seeking prey. "Is this a gambit to get Lakes of Wonder for an even lower price a year from now?"

What? "No, I'm not—" Not that he blamed her. That would be a trick worthy of BBA. Or a Lochlainn. "Where is this coming from?"

She sighed, her shoulders falling. "I had breakfast with Catalina Lochlainn this morning. And she told me… It doesn't matter what she told me, I don't want it anyway. But she also explained the history between BBA and the Lochlainn Company. From the Lochlainn perspective." She caught his gaze. "I don't blame you for playing games, including the night we met. I know you must to survive your world. But I'm tired, Ian. I'm not built to be a corporate player. I don't jump through hoops well. I'm terrible at machinations and intrigues."

"What did Catalina say to you?" He caressed her cheek and she leaned into his touch before straightening and putting distance between them.

He let his hand drop.

Anna smiled. There was no warmth in it. "The sale of Lakes of Wonder? Is an audition to be Keith Lochlainn's sole heir. He's pitted me against my half-brother—yes, I have a half-brother I didn't know about but Keith did, isn't that awesome?—and whoever performs the best at the task given to them will inherit the Lochlainn Company." She threw out her hands to the sides. "So, if you don't buy Lakes of Wonder, I am taken out of the running."

Ian inhaled. "Okay. We can figure this out."

She was shaking her head before he finished speaking. "I came to California because I didn't know who I was after the Knock. I thought I could reinvent myself, make myself into someone who was born a Lochlainn, not a Stratford."

Her right hand traced the line of Ian's jaw. "The type of person who meets an incredibly handsome and charismatic man and has amazing one-night stand sex."

He pressed a kiss into her palm. "You are that person. And more than a one-night stand."

"But I'm also still the same me who fled her friends and family in Florida. And that me is homesick—not for humidity and bugs the size of dinner plates, California has been a pleasant surprise on those fronts." She tried to smile, a real smile, but Ian could see the effort it cost her. "But I miss my family. I miss the me when I'm with my family. I could belong to the Lochlainn world. To the Blackburn world. But I choose not to."

"Anna, I love you." His heart beat a warning rhythm. He was losing control of the situation.

"And I love you. I've loved you since you put your jacket on my shoulders." Her blue eyes shone with unshed tears in the elevator's dim light. "But BBA is your world. Your legacy. Your family. And I can't ask you to leave it. I won't. Because I know how painful it is to cut yourself off. Just look at Lakes of Wonder. It's dying because Jamie cut himself off from Keith and his legacy."

"But if you love me..." His mind seized on the few words that still gave him hope, that provided a path that would allow him to maneuver. "If you love me, we can solve this."

"Oh, Ian." This time she kissed him. He gathered her closer, deepening the kiss, begging the seam of her lips to open to him, to acknowledge the truth between them, to stop denying the inevitable reality. She sighed, their bodies melting together as she responded, her mouth welcoming his, her tongue seeking and asking for a response he was all too happy to give. She tasted of sunlight and joy and hope. She tasted of Anna, of home and future and promise.

Too late, he realized the elevator was moving. The doors opened, depositing them in the ground-floor lobby. She stepped out of the circle of his arms, her regard steady but resolute. "Love isn't a problem to be solved. It just...is," she said. "A part of me will always love you, no matter what the future brings. But if I stay with you, I won't be me. I'll be a game pawn, to be used by you or the Lochlainns.

"No. You're wrong. You—"

"Ian." Her smile turned sad. "Who did you

think I was the night we met? What did you think I was?"

He couldn't hold her gaze.

She nodded. "I wish you nothing but happiness from now to eternity. Buy Lakes of Wonder. Save your company." She brushed her lips on his right cheek.

By the time his stunned limbs could respond to his brain's commands to go after her and make her stay, she was gone.

FIFTEEN

One month later

LAKES OF WONDER had never looked prettier.
Ian had seen photos of the theme park's opening
day when everything was new and fresh, and,
even so, the theme park outshone its previous
self. The buildings were draped in green-and-
purple bunting, disguising the patchy paint and
sun damage over the years. Flowers were everywhere—hanging from baskets in the Port of
Entry, overflowing from planters that lined the
walkway, peeking from vines twined together
to decorate the signs and way posts. The staff—
Seamus's attendants, in the vernacular of the
park—was smiling and waving at guests, their
costumes freshly washed and pressed. Even the
weather cooperated, a dark blue California sky
dotted with marshmallow clouds, appearing
like a painted backdrop made to order.

"You okay?" Tai materialized next to where

Ian stood on the main thoroughfare, munching on caramel popcorn from a Seamus-shaped plastic bucket.

"Never better."

Tai regarded him then nodded. "Yeah, I agree. You know how I know?"

"How?"

"You're not asking me if you're doing the right thing."

Ian chuckled. "No. I'm not. I have faith this time." Faith, and not much less. But he was good with that.

"I have to say, I'm going to miss this," Tai said, sweeping his hand to indicate the picture-perfect vista in front of them.

"You can take your pick of parks operated by BBA."

"Yeah, but none of them have a snack this good." Tai threw a piece of popcorn into the air and caught it in his mouth.

"It's the same vendor." Ian checked his smartwatch.

"Really?" Tai ate another piece. "Must be the Seamus bucket that makes it so tasty. And the time is five minutes past the last time you looked."

"Don't want to be late."

"Right. Late. That's the only reason why you're acting like a frog."

"A frog?" Ian turned to look at his friend.

"Jumpy." Tai threw another piece of popcorn in the air.

Ian shook his head and lifted his left wrist, only to put it back down when Tai shot him an amused look. "I'll see you later. Teri is looking for me. Last-minute changes."

"You've done everything you could that's in your power. It's out of your hands now, Kermit." Tai grinned at him.

"No one knows that better than me." Ian tossed Tai a quick salute and left to go find Teri. Tai was right, in some respects. The New Year's Eve party, which was doubling as the closing event for Lakes of Wonder was already a hit. The journalists handpicked to be there were thrilled with their access, the invited guests full of joy to be included. Oh, there were protests when they'd announced the park was going to shut down, and public sentiment was running very much against the decision, but if all went to plan, that would be the least of his concerns.

He took a deep breath. The future might be out of his control, but that didn't mean he couldn't attempt to tip the odds in his favor as much as possible.

★ ★ ★

Nothing brought Anna more joy than seeing Pepa's eyes widen when the five-year-
old caught her first glimpse of the Lighthouse
of Amazement in the distance. "Wow," Pepa
gasped, her always-in-motion feet glued to the
ground for once.

"Pretty cool, huh?" Anna smiled at her and
then exchanged glances with Maritza before
kneeling to address Pepa directly. "So, I have a
few errands I need to run. You're going to hang
with your mom and then I'll meet you in front
of the Lighthouse to watch the parade. Deal?"

"Deal!" Pepa gave Anna a high-five then
turned to her mother. "I wanna go on the Skyroute!"

"Hold on!" Maritza grabbed Pepa's hand
when she would dart off into the crowd. "You'll
be okay?" she asked Anna. "You sure you don't
want us to go with you?"

"I'll be fine." Anna hugged her cousin.
"Thank you for asking, though. It's a quick trip
in and out and then I'll join you, Pepa, and my
parents. Just save me a place in case the crowd
makes it difficult to get to you on time."

"Got it." Maritza hugged Anna back tightly.
Almost too tightly.

Anna drew back and regarded her cousin with her brows drawn. "Everything all right? Sure you don't want me to stay and help you corral Pepa?"

Maritza blinked. "No. Don't you dare not go to the Lighthouse. Right now. In fact, you should hurry. Get going, you!"

"O...kay." Anna drew out the word. Were Maritza's cheeks flushed? Was she coming down with something? "You sure you're all right?"

"Yes. I am." Maritza nodded rapidly. "I'm great. Since I'm here at the park. You know, a place I never thought I'd visit. Now go." She playfully shoved Anna. "See you later."

"All right. Have fun." Anna took a deep breath and then plunged into the gift shop, making her way to the hidden door without any difficulty. Before she knew it, she was in the tunnel and heading toward the Lighthouse.

Her heart stung more than she'd anticipated to be back at Lakes of Wonder, for the very last time. Everywhere she looked, she saw Ian. Even here in the tunnel, all she could see was Ian walking next to her, shortening his long strides to match hers, sneaking glances at her when she wasn't sneaking glances at him. His smile, tinged with cynicism in public, but always one-hundred-percent sincere when they were alone. The gleam of excitement in his eyes when they'd discovered the mythical door to the Lighthouse was real.

The sale to BBA had closed quickly after that month-ago meeting. Although media reports had been vague about what would happen to the park after today, she had no doubt Preston and Olive were looking at retail-center renderings at that very moment. So when the VIP invitation to attend the closing party arrived in her mailbox, she'd thought long and hard about accepting it. But her experience in California had showed her there was no running from who she was. She was a Stratford and a Lochlainn— even if she had called Catalina and politely but firmly declined participating in Keith's contest for an heir. She was done with families whose bonds were transactional only.

Before she knew it, she stood before the heavy metal door that led to the Lighthouse apartment. She reached beneath the collar of her mint-green dress and drew out the key she had snagged the morning she and Ian were "rescued." The doorknob turned without a protest and she stood on the threshold of the owner's apartment, which looked like no one had been there since—

No. Someone had been there. The cushions were back on the sofa in their respective corners. The blanket was folded neatly. And there wasn't a mote of dust anywhere to be found. The cleaning crew was apparently still cleaning, despite the park's eminent closure.

She entered the room, taking her time so she could savor the moment, soak up every impression while the room was intact, and the Lighthouse still stood. She brushed her fingers over upholstery on the couch, the smooth leather cool to her touch. Her gaze traced the worn beams of the ceiling and counted the cracks in the rough plaster cast of the walls. With her sandals slipped off, her toes gripped the worn Persian rug.

How was it possible to miss a place when she was presently standing in it?

But then, how was it possible to miss one person so much her heart threatened to crack like an egg under the weight of so much yearning?

She was still convinced she couldn't live in Ian's world. She'd made the right decision. She and her parents were communicating even better than ever. They'd offered her a partnership in Stratford's, but she'd turned them down in favor of finishing her college degree, in business this time, with plans to start her own independent interior-design business. But, oh, how she ached for Ian. And the ache gave no indication of diminishing any time soon.

She shook her head to clear it. She needed to hurry. If she lingered too long, she would miss meeting her family to watch the parade. Part of the reason why she'd agreed to the invitation to attend the closing party was the opportunity to share her Lochlainn heritage with her parents and her closest relatives, and she wanted to be there to see Pepa's eyes light up as the floats passed by. But she had one last piece of business before she could let Lake of Wonder go for good.

She found the bookshelf where the Lochlainn family photos continued to sit in their previous positions and picked up the picture of Keith holding a small Jamie's hand. She couldn't let such a precious memento fall into the hands of people who would only value for it for its collectible value, or worse, be destroyed along with the park.

Her gaze fell on frame holding a photo of Archibald with another man who could only be Cooper Blackburn. He had the same square chin as Ian, the same high cheekbones, the same patrician nose that gave them the appearance of a stern emperor deciding who should sit next to him at the banquet and who was being sent to the coliseum to face off with wild animals. In fact, dress Cooper Blackstone in a well-tailored suit and photograph him in color and it would be hard to tell the difference between him and his great-grandson.

She scooped up all the photos she could find and wrapped them in protective bubble wrap before placing them in her backpack, lingering on the photo of Jamie and Keith. Her biological grandfather still refused to meet her, leaving her to wonder why she had been chosen for the Lakes of Wonder task and not Declan. But maybe Keith had wanted one of his grandchildren to see the place Jamie had loved. Maybe that was all he'd wanted, to know one of Jamie's offspring had been there at the end.

She inhaled. This was it. Goodbye to Lakes of Wonder. But the park would live on in her memories. Memories that she was counting on to keep her warm for the rest of her life. Her relationship with Ian may have been brief, but was so intense, she knew she would be hard-pressed to find another partner with whom she fit so perfectly in so many ways—except when it came to what they wanted most out of life. Although her heart yearned to glimpse Ian while she was in the park, her brain told her it would be best to continue with the clean break that had started when she'd walked out of the elevator.

Her soul would always hurt for him.

She put her hand of the rough plaster of the wall next to the front door. "I'm sorry we're coming to end. But thank you for all you've given me—"

A loud bugle fanfare nearly caused her to jump out of her sandals. She checked the time on her phone. The parade wasn't supposed to start for another twenty minutes, according to the schedule of entertainment handed out at the gate when they'd entered the park. She should still have plenty of time to meet her family. Was there a special New Year's Eve event happening?

She made her way to the window and peered through the streaky glass. The plaza in front of the Lighthouse was packed with parkgoers, wearing the iconic lavender and mint hats decorated with Seamus's sea serpent scales. But she could see a path had been cleared from the Seaport entrance to the Lighthouse, the Lakes of Wonder staff doing its best to keep the crowd clear.

She squinted, trying to make out the activity in the far distance. There was a parade float, but not one she recognized from the parades she'd seen earlier. It looked like...a giant Seamus? A burst of flame erupted from the float and she jumped. It was Seamus! Had someone at Lakes of Wonder found the old parade vehicle? The sea serpent float was still a distance away but even from where she stood the float looked identical to the one in the photo that hung on the conference room wall—the float supposedly destroyed decades ago. What a fitting way to say goodbye to Lakes of Wonder, by bringing back its original iconic figure.

The music grew louder. She resisted the urge to step onto the balcony. Might was well find a comfy spot on the sofa—no matter that everywhere she looked she saw Ian. Couldn't run her hand along the leather whether remembering Ian's hands on her. Couldn't glance at the overstuffed decorative pillows without remembering how she'd fallen apart and flown with his mouth on her. How—

"Anna! Come to the balcony!"

Now she was even hearing his voice as well as reliving the glide of his skin against hers. She really wished the parade would go away—

"Anna! The balcony. Open the door and come out."

Her eyes flew open. She wasn't imagining Ian's voice. That really was him. What the…? She searched the wall and found the door, which opened easily—

And came face-to-face with Seamus, his mechanical head nodding and twisting from side to side in a slow rhythm. Her gaze traveled along Seamus's long neck to the sea serpent's back. And riding on Seamus…

She couldn't breathe. Her heart was in her throat.

She leaned over the balcony railing, ignoring the loud cheer that went up from the crowd when she made her appearance. "Do you have a death wish? What are you doing on Seamus— no, wait, where did you even get Seamus?—no, let's go back to the first question. That thing is breathing fire! And you're riding on it!"

"How else could I get your attention?" Ian flashed his grin.

"Maybe by saying hi? Buying me a frozen

custard? Ways that don't include putting your life in danger? She couldn't take her gaze off him. He looked good. So good. She drank in his appearance, not realizing until she could look her fill how starved she'd been. "You definitely have my attention now. Will you please get down from there?"

Ian's smile grew. "I have a better idea." He fiddled with something—controls of some kind, Anna surmised. Seamus's head stopped moving and froze into place. Then the sea serpent's neck started to elongate, until Seamus's massive head touched the wall of the lighthouse just below the balcony.

Surely, Ian didn't mean for her to hop over the railing and step onto a rickety mechanical sea serpent from the 1970s? She stared at him. "What are you…you're not expected me to…"

"Of course not." Ian scoffed. "I am."

He unbuckled himself from the seat at the back of Seamus's neck. Then he stood up and began to walk across Seamus's neck, his arms outstretched like a tightrope walker, his only concession to safety a thin guidewire attached to the mechanical serpent.

"Ian, stop! You hate heights!" Her heart beat hard and fast in her throat, almost choking her.

Her eyes squeezed shut. She was not going to watch him. She would not be a witness if the worst happened. "Don't—this isn't worth it—you're several stories above the ground, if you fall—"

"If I what?" Ian said from close by. "You can open your eyes. Because you are indeed worth it."

She did. The first thing she saw was Ian's dark gaze, warm with humor and joy. Her knees nearly gave out, both from relief and from the effect he always seemed to have on her bones' ability to remain solid.

Ian stood on Seamus's head, with only the thin metal railing separating them. Then she laughed, exhilarated both by his nearness and by the ridiculous and over-the-top situation they were now in. She indicated the crowd below them, a sea of faces partially concealed by the phones being used to record their meeting, with a sweep of her hand. No doubt they were being live-streamed around the world on multiple social media platforms. "What happened to keeping this room a secret?"

"No more secrets. You were right. I wasn't up-front and honest when we met. And that caused you to doubt my intentions throughout our relationship. So…"

Her head shook on its own. Her brain was still processing he was there, in front of her, and— "What are you wearing?"

"What?" He glanced down and a half-smile appeared on his face. "This old thing? I mean that literally. This costume is the same vintage as Seamus."

Ian's princely outfit glittered in the sunlight. The jacket and pants were a blinding white, with a crimson sash falling across Ian's chest from his right shoulder to end his left hip. A bright blue cape trimmed with gold braid was thrown over his left shoulder. Brass-plated medals set with large paste jewels in bold colors decorated almost every inch of the jacket's chest. He winked at her and pulled a red cap adorned with three fluffy white feather plumes out from under his jacket, perching the hat rakishly over his right eyebrow. "There. I didn't want it to fall off before you saw it.

"You're wearing colors. You're definitely not avoiding attention." She stated the obvious, simply because Ian's costume was so ridiculous, she could scarcely believe the evidence of her eyes. "You won't be able to sneak up on your prey."

She was joking, of course, because if she were to take the event's happening seriously, she might cry. Big, ugly, red-nosed crying, the kind that would wash away her waterproof mascara in three seconds flat. Besides, she wasn't quite sure if she could take what was happening at face value. This might all be a waking dream, her subconscious creating a happy ending to assuage her guilt over not securing a more positive outcome for Lakes of Wonder.

"You asked me to make you believe." Ian doffed his cap and bowed, causing the crowd to cheer. "How else than to show you I finally understand theme park magic is real?" He flashed his smile again, the smile he always kept for her.

"I don't understand," she said, her synapses beginning to fire again after recovering from her shock. "Preston and Olive…want a retail destination. Why…how…" She continued to sputter, finally seizing on a coherent sentence. "Ian, it's not practical or good business to bring the Seamus float out of mothballs and get it operational again if the park is going to be plowed…under…" Her words trailed off as

Ian's grin grew larger. "But...today is the closing party?"

Ian took her hands in his gloved ones. "Lakes of Wonder is closing. But only so I can get all the rides and experiences updated and up to code. Then it will reopen, better than before. I hope it will be a true Blackburn/Lochlainn collaboration this time."

Anna never knew hope could be so painful. Her chest was tight, her lungs struggling to bring in air. "Your plan to oust Harlan—"

"Worked," he said simply. "BBA bought Lakes of Wonder. Preston and Olive and, as it turns out, most of the board, voted with me."

"But—"

"And then I sold my shares in BBA and used the proceeds to buy Lakes of Wonder." He smiled at her. "The park is mine and mine alone. Tai is the new CEO of BBA"

"What?" Anna searched his face. His beloved, wonderful face. "But BBA is your family. Your legacy. Your inheritance. You said there had always been a Blackburn at the helm and always will be."

"I was wrong." He caressed her cheek with his white-gloved hand, then pulled the glove off with an expression of disgust. Then his fingers were wiping away the tears that had decided to appear after all. "BBA is a company. But that conversation in the elevator... I've thought long and hard about it ever since. You showed me that being true to oneself is a choice. Belonging to someone else, being in their life, is a choice. And I chose you, Anna. I want to be part of your family. And create one of our own, together. On our own terms, no games, no machinations. If you want me."

"I do," she choked out. "I always have."

His grin could rival the brightest fireworks. Then he dropped to one knee, her hands tightly clutched in his, his gaze shining so bright not even the fireworks could compete.

"Anna Stratford, heir of the Lochlainns, will you be my Lady of the Lakes?"

She could barely see him, despite holding both her eyes as open as wide she could so she could take in as much as she could, to hold the vision close in her heart forever. "Ian of the Blackburns, I accept, forever and ever."

And then his lips were on hers, a kiss of fire and heat carrying the promise of forever.

★ ★ ★ ★ ★

Seven Years Of Secrets

MILLS & BOON

Dear Reader,

Welcome back to the secrets and scandals of the Lochlainn family! This two-part series kicks off when Keith Lochlainn, a media mogul whose doctors say he is dying, decides to hold a contest to determine which one of his newly discovered grandchildren should inherit his empire by giving them each a business objective to complete. The first book, *More Than Rivals...*, is the story of Keith's granddaughter Anna.

Now it's his grandson Declan's turn. Declan, already a renowned investigative journalist, isn't interested in taking over the Lochlainn empire. But he has been carrying secrets of his own for seven years—secrets pertaining to his journalism school rival turned brief lover, Mara Schuyler. When Declan is given a news streaming service to run to see if he is worthy to inherit, he jumps at the opportunity to give Mara a job as a news correspondent to help relieve his conscience.

Declan broke Mara's heart when he ghosted her after their one week of passion seven years ago. She wants nothing to do with him. But when he makes her a job offer she can't refuse, it doesn't take long for her former feelings to resurface. However, even as Mara pursues the lead that could make her career, she can't help but feel that Declan is hiding something from her.

And when the secrets come tumbling out, Mara must choose between following her story and following her heart.

I hope you enjoy *Seven Years of Secrets*! And please feel free to get in touch. You can find me on Twitter, @susannaherwin; on Facebook at susannaherwinauthor; on BookBub, @susannaherwin; or at my website, www.susannaherwin.com.

Happy reading!

xoxo

Susannah

DEDICATION

For Lisa Lin,
for being the superstar that she is

ONE

THE MID-OCTOBER SKY was bright and clear, the slight breeze still held a touch of warmth but promised brisker days ahead and the maple trees lining the sidewalk wore crowns of fiery leaves. Autumnal wreaths of sunflowers, wheat stalks and colorful gourds hung on streetlights, while the windows of the quaint mix of shops and restaurants that comprised the small town's commercial district were decorated with pumpkins and straw bales.

Mara Schuyler couldn't ask for a more picture-perfect site from which to report on a harvest festival than Roseville, New York, situated forty miles south of the Canadian border and an entire mindset away from New York City. This was one of the more photogenic assignments she'd received since joining the five o'clock news team of WRZT-TV—the "Voice of North County."

Photogenic, but not earthshaking. Not that Mara minded. Much. She'd given up on her ambitions to be the next household name in broadcast journalism and left far behind her desire to be the host of her own television news magazine show watched by billions around the globe. She knew now that was the dream of a small child who never missed the Sunday evening ritual of watching *60 Minutes* with her grandparents.

She was grown now. A realist. And she was damn lucky to have any paying job in journalism, much less an on-air role as a correspondent for a local news station. Even if WRZT was the third-highest rated newscast in the 189th largest media market in the US. Even if her assignments to date mostly involved stories like interviewing the winner of the annual soap box car race and covering the town hall meeting where the public debated if city funds should be used to convert an unused lot into a skateboard park. The stories might not be holding heads of state accountable for their inequitable actions or taking down a drug cartel from within as an undercover investigator, but they mattered to the community.

Well, at least they mattered to the three viewers who commented online on her soap box story—no one commented on the skateboard park piece. Although, one viewer berated her for not giving his son, the second place winner, more airtime, and the next offered his opinion that she should smile more. The third comment detailed how to double one's current salary at home through data entry, so Mara suspected whoever wrote it may not have watched the segment.

"We all set?" she asked her photographer, Hank Yi.

Hank looked around at the picturesque main street and shrugged. "One spot is as good as another. Want to do your run-through?"

She took a deep breath, plastered a smile on her face and started speaking. "This is Mara Schuyler, coming to you live from downtown Roseville where the local merchants are preparing for the sixty-sixth annual Pumpkin Festival. Who will have the most impressive pumpkin display? Will Abe Nagasaki finally lose his crown as the carving pump-*King*?" She widened her grin as she hit the last syllable. Mara was twenty-eight years old, but dad jokes were becoming her trademark. Whether she liked it or not. "I know I'm on the edge of my seat—

Wait… That doesn't make sense. I'm standing, not sitting."

"It's a figure of speech." Hank lowered the Sony HDC-3500 camera that had been perched on his shoulder.

"But not accurate."

"So? No one's paying attention at five o'clock. They're doing homework or thinking about their workday."

She gave him an exaggerated eye roll. This was a familiar conversation. "We're reporting the news, Hank. Words matter. Precision matters."

"You'd think you were Declan Treharne, the way you obsess over every detail."

Her smile froze. Why did she ever tell Hank she once knew Treharne, the hot rising star of print and broadcast journalism? Damn that bottle of tequila after the ambulance story fiasco.

Not that she'd had much of a past with Declan. Just almost four years of intense rivalry in journalism school, then a week of even more intense passion, followed by devastating betrayal. Now Declan was winning plaudits and fame on both coasts for his hard-hitting investigative stories that led to the toppling of empires, both corporate and political, and she was—

"—it's a story that serves as background noise," Hank continued, unaware she had tuned him out. "We're going live for the teaser in five minutes. pick something and go with it."

"You never stop underestimating me." Mara dug into her pocket and brought out a pen. She tried to scratch out the offending phrase on her notes, but the pen didn't function without something solid to write on. "Do you have a clipboard?"

"Do I—No. Four minutes and counting."

"I'm on the edge…no. I'm breathless with anticipation…nuh-uh. The suspense is killing me?" She wrinkled her nose. "That's not only cliché but I'm obviously not dying. Um…" She continued to ponder.

"Two minutes."

"Creativity can't be rushed." She scrawled words on her hand, then rubbed them off.

"And we're live in four, three, two—" Hank pointed at her.

"This is Mara Schuyler, coming to you live from downtown Roseville where the local merchants are preparing for the sixty-sixth annual Pumpkin Festival. Who will have the most impressive harvest display? Will Abe Nagasaki finally lose his crown as the carving pump-

King? The suspense is thicker than a slice of three-time blue ribbon winner Betsy Goldstein's pumpkin pie! This year's festival will be held Thursday through Sunday. Don't forget to pick up your free tickets at your local Buy and Save supermarkets while supplies last. You don't want to miss this guaranteed *gourd* time!" She held her smile until Hank lowered his camera, indicating the signal had been cut and they were off the air.

Mara let her shoulders fall. She and Hank had twenty-eight minutes before interviewing the chairman of this year's festival for a short piece that would close out that day's half hour five o'clock news broadcast. She dug into her tote bag, searching for her phone and her electronic tablet so she could check messages and then review her notes.

"Angling for a piece of that pie? Is it really that 'gourd'?"

"Yeah, well, it never hurts to curry favor with the Roseville mayor in case we need access to her later. And she does bake a good pie." Mara scrolled through her phone, only half paying attention to Hank—

Wait.

Hank was already down the block, scouting for the best place to interview the chairman.

And she knew that voice. Seven years may have passed since she last heard him speak in person, but she'd had plenty of opportunities to listen to him expand on various topics of national importance over that time.

She kept her gaze on her phone, hoping against hope she was wrong, and the voice was a trick of her imagination brought on by Hank's mention earlier. But when he cleared his throat, she looked up and her hopes were dashed.

"Hello, Treharne."

Declan smiled and took off his mirrored aviator sunglasses. "Hey, Schuyler. You look great."

So did he. Damn, damn and double damn. Declan Treharne looked even better in the flesh than he did on television. The TV didn't bring out the highlights in his dark blond hair, cropped short these days with the barest hint of the tousle she remembered. The camera didn't capture the intense blueness of his eyes, the color fading inward from dark navy bands around the rims of his irises to a cerulean spring sky to the starburst of golden flecks surrounding his pupils. And no small screen could convey his sheer physicality. Declan wasn't the tallest man Mara had known—far from it—but he was certainly the most comfortable in his body. His leather jacket moved with him like a second skin. He appeared both wholly at home on Roseville's main street and yet completely otherworldly—a herald from a life Mara once dreamed of but had long given up on achieving.

And just like that, she was rocked back on her heels by his radiating charisma, as if she'd stepped through a rip in the space-time continuum and had sat down in the first row on the first day of Introduction to Journalism, confident she was going to rock the class hard—only for Declan to come through the door and all her concentration to go flying out of it.

She realized she was staring at Declan, her mouth opening and closing like a fish impaled on a hook but still eager to reach the worm, when his smile faded. "Everything okay?"

"Everything…" she repeated. Then she blinked, and then blushed, and then hated herself for doing both. "Everything is fine," she said, after taking a few beats to work moisture into her mouth.

"Good. Do you have a minute to talk? Can I take you out for coffee?" Declan motioned to a vehicle parked at the curb. She followed his gaze to a futuristic-looking two-seater sports coupé, sunlight bouncing off the silver metallic paint. She blinked several more times.

"You want me...to get in a car that costs more than the balance on my sizable student loans...with you?" Finally, her thoughts were slowing enough that she could form—well, almost form—complete sentences. Unfortunately, the next sentence that came out of her mouth was: "What the hell?"

"Is that a no on the coffee?"

"That's a 'what the hell!' As in 'what the hell are you doing here, Treharne?' And how did you know where to find me in the first place? In Roseville, I mean?"

"I looked you up in the alumni directory and then I called your station manager." Declan scratched the back of his neck. "I'm here to invite you to coffee."

She squeezed her eyes shut, not only to give her some space to make sense of the situation, but also because she forgot that looking at Declan for an extended period was like staring at the sun; his brilliance threatened to burn her retinas. "I can't get coffee. I'm working. I'm going on air with an interview in..." She opened her eyes to glance at her smart watch.

"Twenty-two minutes. And I need to review my notes beforehand."

"Coffee after your interview?"

At least one thing hadn't changed about Declan, despite his overwhelming success. He was still persistent. Probably why he was such a good journalist. "I'm going back to the television studio after I finish. To get notes and prep for tomorrow." She held up a hand when his mouth opened. "And I have plans tonight." She didn't, unless one counted watching *Jeopardy* and then binging the latest episodes of her favorite true crime documentary series, but he didn't need to know that.

"Breakfast tomorrow, then." It was his turn to shake his head when she tried to object. "You have to eat. You might as well eat with me." His grin was that of someone who rarely heard the word "no," especially not from people with whom he once shared a torrid week exploring their combustible chemistry. Just touching on the memory caused a rush of wetness between her legs. She'd had her share of dates since that lost week of debauchery—even had a boyfriend for nine months when she worked for the local paper in Hightown, some sixty miles away, until she got the call to join WRZT-TV and they both agreed the relationship was at best treading water—but while the sex had been good it hadn't been—

She was doing it again. She was letting Declan occupy her frontal lobe rent free. She spent months evicting thoughts of him from her brain. All he had to do was show up and boom! It was if he'd never left that comfy suite she'd created for him in her skull. "I'm not having breakfast, or coffee or any beverage or food substance with you. Not today, nor tomorrow nor any day for eternity until you tell me why you are here, at my shoot. And it's not because you have a hankering for Roseville's finest coffee, because it's mostly burnt water."

"Burnt water? How does that—" He stopped joking when she intensified her glare. "I'd like to explain, but perhaps our discussion should wait until you're less stressed—"

"Stressed? You think I'm stressed? Why? Because you deigned to show up in my life seven years after…?"

No. She would not let him know how much she cared. Not now, not with other memories flooding back, like how Declan always told her she worried too much and worked too hard on trivial details, leaving the bigger story untouched.

She shoved her tablet and phone back into her tote bag and began to march toward Hank, who was several blocks away chatting up the festival chairman in front of the Roseville city hall, draped in orange, brown and sunflower gold bunting for the festival. "I have work to do," she threw back at Declan over her shoulder. "You can vanish back to wherever you apparated from. We have nothing to discuss."

She left him standing on the sidewalk. And when she didn't hear footsteps pounding behind her and Declan's voice demanding she stop and talk to him, she lied to herself that was the outcome she wanted.

TWO

THE TWO-MINUTE LIVE interview with the chairman went smoothly. If Mara's hand holding the microphone shook, the viewers at home were none the wiser thanks to Hank's careful framing of the shot. She said her thank yous and goodbyes and refused Hank's offer to ride with him in the news van back to the studio. The viewers may not have noticed how affected she was by Declan's arrival out of the blue, but Hank could tell she was off her usual game and she was not in the mood to be interrogated on the drive. She told him she wanted to walk around Roseville and note any local color that might come in handy for the inevitable assignment to cover the Monarch of the Pumpkin Festival coronation next week. She'd call a rideshare service when she was ready to return to the station.

She sighed and walked toward the closest

bridge, intending to cross the river that ran through the center of the town for lack of a better destination, kicking at the fallen russet and yellow leaves as she went. She loved her job. She did. She just wished, perhaps, Declan Treharne didn't have to show up and rub her nose in the fact that he was a famous investigative journalist while she was…making bad puns about squash. Delicious squash, especially when made into pie, but she wasn't risking her life taking down a multinational organized crime ring from the inside, like Declan's latest exclusive story for *The New York Globe*. He even turned his story into an award-winning podcast. Of course.

She turned onto the side street that was her favorite shortcut to the river. At least she worked in a lovely part of the country. She set her smartwatch's meditation app to five minutes. Maybe if she stood here and breathed in the beauty, she would breathe out the frustration and, fine, the envy Declan's sudden arrival brought. She closed her eyes and inhaled, then exhaled. Inhaled, exhaled. Inhaled—

"How about that coffee now? Or something stronger? It's past five o'clock, after all."

Damn it. Even when she was meditating, her brain conjured him up.

"Your news director said you were done for the day, so you can't use work as an excuse this time."

Her eyes flew open. Declan's car, its motor a low purr, was parked at the curb next to her. She leaned down and peered through the rolled down passenger side window at him. "Isn't this the same model of car Tony Stark drove in the first *Iron Man* film?"

He grinned at her. "You know your cars. And your films."

She narrowed her gaze at him. "I knew you, and you haven't changed. Not interested, superhero. Go stalk someone else."

"Hear me out. I promise I'll disappear and leave you alone after we talk. If that's what you want."

"Let's pretend we did talk, and now is after. Guess I won't see you around." Mara straightened up and strode down the street.

Declan's car kept pace with her. "I'm sorry," he shouted through the open window.

She stopped, whirled and put her hands on her hips. "Sorry about *what*?"

She could think of many ways he could answer that. Sorry about letting her do all the heavy lifting on their joint project in sophomore year because he was being feted by the university's trustees for uncovering a ring of thieves who were stealing materials—and secrets—from the engineering research center. Sorry about scooping her on the story she worked so long and so hard on—the story that won him the IJAW fellowship that included an internship with a tech incubator focused on the next generation of journalism, which made him independently wealthy thanks to the app they devised now being used in newsrooms around the world. Although, to be fair, his scoop had been her fault. She let the story get away.

Sorry about dumping her and never looking back. That one was definitely on him.

Declan put the car in park and exited the driver's side. "Sorry I didn't get in touch sooner. I got your email about the class reunion. I kept meaning to respond, but—"

Her eyes would not stop blinking. "That's what you're sorry for? Not answering a mass mailing about our five year reunion? The reunion that was held over two years ago?"

Unbelievable.

He shrugged and gave her an apologetic

smile. "I still should have responded. Because the email came from you. We…we were friends. And our friendship meant something."

She was used to the confident Declan, the brash Declan, the take-no-prisoners Declan. She liked to believe herself finally immune to his charms. But a sheepish Declan, looking at her at her with…could that be regret in his eyes? Was Declan Treharne even capable of regret? That was new.

She was not immune to the charms of a Declan who apologized to her.

"That was a long time ago. As for the reunion, no one else wanted to be class secretary," she murmured. "It's not like I emailed you specifically. And we knew you weren't coming. You were in Kyrgyzstan covering postelection protests."

"You follow my stories?" A light flared in his gaze.

"Oh, please. You have the number one podcast in the country. You're on a different cable news show nightly. I am a journalist, too, y'know. I keep up."

Even as the words left her mouth, she realized how inane she sounded. And not a little jealous. She should leave before she dug her hole any deeper, which was a tremendous accomplishment considering she already had both her feet in her mouth. "Well, it's been nice catching up. Bye."

"Schuyler, wait." He placed his hand lightly on her arm. His touch burned through the layers of her blazer and button-down shirt. "I have a proposition for you I think you'll like."

He flashed his golden boy grin at her. She knew from experience how skilled he was at using that grin to get whatever he wanted. "Proposition? I'm not sleeping with you again," she blurted out.

His smile disappeared. "I wasn't...that's not the proposition. Although, I meant what I said. You look great."

"Good. I mean, good on the not propositioning thing." No, it was not so good. She'd only just then realized how much she'd held on to a fantasy that he would indeed appear out of the blue and confess that week had made as much of an impression on him as it did on her, haunting his dreams and his waking thoughts until he could no longer stand it, and so he had to find her so he could carry her off to his bed where they would stay—

Too late, she tuned into what he was saying. "—ork with me."

She held up a hand. "Wait. Maybe covering traffic accidents has done a number on my hearing, standing next to ambulances with their sirens on full blast, but did you say, 'work with you'?"

"Yes. Come work at LNT."

The events of the day must have done a number on her synapses because she could have sworn he said LNT.

"LNT? As in Lochlainn News Television?"

"The same."

"I thought you worked for *The New York Globe*."

Declan scratched the back of his neck—one of the two nervous tells she knew he possessed. "I do. But I'm on a leave of absence to pull together LNT's launch of its streaming news service. They want original programming for streaming only. And they've put together an extensive budget. I'm hiring journalists with unique points of views to create documentary specials and series. You can pursue whatever story you want. LNT has the resources for research, travel, you name it."

The world spun around her in a blur of red

and green and gold. "You want me—" she pointed to herself "—to work with you—" she pointed at him "—at LNT?"

"The LNT streaming service," he corrected. "Which is even better. We get to shape the future of news, Mara. You'll be a pioneer."

A pioneer. She always dreamed of being on the forefront of journalism, of blazing a trail for others to follow, especially for those who traditionally were shut out from receiving resources and advantages. But something about his offer didn't add up. "I don't understand. Why did LNT hire you? You're an investigative journalist. You're not a suit."

"What can I say? They told me they wanted a fresh perspective, so they looked outside the usual LNT suspects." Declan shrugged, but his gaze slid up to the left—his second tell: the one that said he wasn't being wholly truthful. Mara narrowed her gaze. That was interesting. "What do you say? I would need you in New York City by next week. The service is scheduled to launch in the beginning of January."

"January is three months away. And one of those months is December, when everybody is distracted by winter holidays. That's not very long. At all."

"Which is why I need an answer. Are you in?"

"I have a job here." That was the first thing that popped into her head. "I would have to give notice… I would have to move… Oh! And I would need to quit as the high school newspaper advisor…"

"Is that a yes?"

"No! Besides, you haven't told me the basics. Will I be paid? What about benefits?"

Declan named an annual starting salary number so stratospheric, Mara thought at first that he'd misspoke. Then he repeated it. When he said the amount for the fourth time, the numbers finally started to sink into her consciousness.

She could do a lot with that income. Like sponsor scholarships and grants for journalism students. Provide funding for outlets in underserved communities. Help underwrite a struggling local newspaper. So many possibilities.

"Why me?" she asked. "With that salary, you could have your pick of seasoned journalists with built-in national audiences."

He grinned. "LNT has their own stable of stars. But for the streaming service, we want new voices. Originality. That's you."

This was too good to be true. No matter

that she was eating up the compliments Declan was dishing her way. She'd had fantasies over the past years of what would happen when she saw Declan in person again—some more sexually graphic than others, she had to admit—but even when she pushed the limits of imagination, she never dreamed Declan would show up to hand her the keys to her very own documentary series.

There had to be a catch. Or an ulterior motive. Hidden agenda. Her journalistic nose could smell it.

"I cover harvest festivals and the high school team winning the state diving championship. Sure, sometimes I report on the occasional house fire or traffic accident when the senior reporters aren't available, and occasionally city council meetings can be a bit raucous—you should have been there when changing the Fourth of July parade route was discussed—but that's as hard-hitting as my stories get." She searched Declan's crystal blue gaze, as bottomless and clear as a mountain lake fed by newly melted pristine snow. "So, don't feed me a line about being impressed with my reporting. I'm not an inexperienced college freshman anymore. If you haven't noticed."

"I've noticed," he said, his tone low and suggestive, and that's when she realized his hand was still on her arm.

She shrugged off his touch. "Still not sleeping with you."

"Still haven't propositioned you in that way," he responded.

"Still waiting to hear why me for the LNT gig, after no word from you all these years," she retorted back. "I'm not buying you feel bad about not going to a reunion you weren't going to attend in the first place."

Declan scratched the back of his neck again. His smile faded, and his blue gaze turned up the intensity to eleven. "I'll be honest with you. There's a lot riding on the success of the streaming launch. And while I'm honored to be asked and can't turn the opportunity down, this is fresh territory for me." He reached out his hand and before she even knew her muscles were moving, she had entwined her fingers with his. "I could use a friend. Someone whose story instincts I trust. Someone who would want this to be a success as much as I do."

Her mind seized on one word. "Friend?"

"We were friends. Good friends."

"We *were*." She stressed the last word. "We're

nothing now. And that's because of you. You left. We graduated and you left and you never looked back. You didn't call, you didn't text or email and you outsourced your social media. Why should I accept your offer when, for all I know, you will walk out the door and disappear the next day?" Now it was her turn to cut him off when he would respond. "And no, this isn't about the fact we slept together right before graduation. That's on me. That was my mistake. But you leaving? That's on you."

His gaze was regretful, the expression on his face chagrined. She took a mental snapshot and filed it away in the easily accessible memories drawer. She doubted she would ever witness a regretful Declan again.

"I know," he said. "I am sorry. Sorrier than you can imagine. I thought—it doesn't matter what I thought."

"It does. It definitely matters."

He inhaled. "Cam Brower said you were taking the *Financial Times* postgrad internship. In London. For a year."

"Cam said…" She stared at him. "Why did you take Cam's word? Why didn't you ask me?"

"I saw the plane tickets to London on your computer. Cam was your roommate, so I figured he knew." He shrugged. "Graduation was nearing. You knew I was moving to New York City. You were entitled to go to the UK and start your own career. I knew I didn't have any say in the matter. And I didn't want to come across as if I presumed I did. So, I didn't ask. I figured you would tell me if you wanted me to know."

"I…" How Cam got that wrong was a mystery, but then Cam never did pay much attention to what his roommates said. Or what most people said. He had not been the most reliable source of school gossip. Or news reporting, for that matter. No wonder Cam was now working for *The National Inquisitor*, a tabloid known for its fake scurrilous rumors.

Declan was right. She didn't tell him a group of her high school friends had been planning a backpacking tour of Europe that summer. She bought the steeply discounted plane tickets just in case, but she wasn't sure if she would use them. Because she'd thought she might have a future with Declan. Or at least a relationship that would last beyond graduation.

As it turned out, neither the trip nor the future materialized.

"You still should have asked and not assumed.

And you could have called. You could have stayed in touch."

"So could you," he pointed out with impeccable logic. "Communication works both ways."

He was right. "I…you…" She opened and closed her mouth a few times. "I didn't think you…"

He put her out of his misery. "Let's relegate the past to the past. Please come to LNT."

She took a deep breath. Normally, the air would be filled with the sounds of the river rushing under the footbridge, birds calling to each other, the rustling of squirrels as they prepare for the coming winter and the occasional distant shouts of kids or the faint rumble of cars on the adjoining roads. But the only noise she heard was her heartbeat, a steady, loud thumping.

Was she going to accept his offer, no matter how incredulous she still found his reasons for asking her? Give up her job, her cozy apartment, her volunteer work with the high school newspaper?

"I need some time," she said.

"Of course. I'm still free for breakfast tomorrow morning if you want to discuss the opportunity more." His grin returned.

"Not necessary. I'll give you an answer to-night." She needed to check her contract with the station. And maybe see if one of the other reporters would take over advising the students.

"Take what time you need." He closed the distance between them.

She was very aware they were alone on the bridge. The sun's last streaks had turned the sky deep pink and purple, a few stars valiantly making their presence known. Her mouth was dry. Her palms were not. Despite her stern admonishment to ignore his magnetism for once, she couldn't help but sway in his direction.

He leaned in. Her breath caught. This close, despite the dim early evening light, she could still see the flecks of bullion that radiated around his pupils. His eyes had always fascinated her, the way they faded from a crystalline blue to burnished gold.

He tilted his head, as if preparing to slant his mouth over hers. "Thank you for considering the offer."

"Of course," she breathed back. Oh, she'd missed his mouth. His mouth was the stuff of fantasies at 3:00 a.m., when the world was silent and dark and her mind could run rampant over the most arousing images she could conjure.

Something about the way his lips fit with hers, just the right pressure, just the right firmness. His tongue...oh, his tongue. Her nipples contracted into aching hard points of need, making her grateful for the multiple layers she wore.

Declan bent his head. She inhaled, her eyes falling closed.

Then his mouth missed hers and traveled past her cheek. It stopped above her right ear. "Say yes," he rasped in her ear.

Sparks raced along her nervous system from the tips of her fingers to the soles of her feet, followed by chagrin at having even entertained the thought he might kiss her.

"I'll let you know," she managed to force out.

"I look forward to it." Then he straightened and smiled at her. "We made a great team. We will again." He turned and began walking back to the side of the road where he had parked his car.

"I could turn you down," she called after him.

"You won't," he called back. And then he disappeared into the lengthening evening shadows.

No, she wouldn't. She already knew she would accept.

But perhaps not for the reasons Declan suspected. There was more to the LTN offer than what he told her. Something he wasn't telling her.

She would uncover the truth, whether he wanted her to or not. She let him scoop her once; she wouldn't back down from a story again.

THREE

SEEING MARA AGAIN after seven years had been a gut punch in all the worst—and best—ways.

College-aged Mara had been pretty, all bouncy red hair and questioning green eyes and pale skin dusted with constellations of freckles. But adult Mara nearly brought him to his knees—her formerly coltish angles now lush curves, her sharp gaze filled with a confidence she'd been still developing as a student.

Not for the first time since a chance encounter with Mara's former roommate Cam had opened his eyes, he kicked himself, hard, for the choices he had made that last week of school. At the time, he'd seen no other path forward to attain his goals. But he knew now he had been selfish, prioritizing his own hurt and ambition over everything else, including her—

He sighed. Fine. He knew he'd been selfish then, too. He supposed he could blame his youth and general life inexperience, but Declan's late mother had always accused him of being an old soul and he'd certainly seen some of the worst the world had to offer by the time he started college.

So, instead of focusing on the past—and on the hurt and anger visible on Mara's face when she saw him—he would focus on the present. And on the challenge presented to him: successfully launch LNT's foray into streaming news so he would earn a place in Keith Lochlainn's will.

Declan had no affinity for video news. Sure, he did the occasional interview on air and lent his opinion to various network news programs, but he loved the freedom and creativity of using words to paint vivid pictures for his readers. He specialized in long-form journalism, his well-researched pieces running as features in *The New York Globe*'s Sunday magazine, and he loved nothing more than digging in deep and uncovering people's motives and dreams, focusing on the voices of those who were usually voiceless. And if he exposed the powerful and corrupt who would keep them voiceless, even better. He had yet to win a Pulitzer but he had a drawer stuffed with other prizes and besides, his career was still young.

He didn't want or need Keith's money. He only wanted one thing from the Lochlainn patriarch, and that was acknowledgment he was Jamie's flesh and blood. But he'd accepted Keith's challenge to launch LNT because the position would give him the power to right some of his past wrongs.

Like Mara.

Four weeks later, Declan wasn't sure if his plan had been a stroke of genius or irrational in the extreme.

He walked into his glass-walled office on the thirty-second floor of LNT's corporate head-quarters, a steel and glass skyscraper that dominated its section of Seventh Avenue despite being surrounded by other imposing buildings. The ground floors held the studios for the morning news and chat series aired on the Lochlainn Company's broadcast network, *Wake Up USA*. The top floors—with their expansive views across Manhattan—contained the executive offices with a Michelin-starred restaurant occupying the roof and adjoining terrace, and the cable news operation took up the middle floors. It was a longer elevator ride than those visiting the broadcast network, but when a fire drill occurred, it wasn't too taxing to walk down the emergency stairs.

The new LNT streaming app—there had been a debate about what to name the service but finally the execs landed on LNT Plus, following the naming convention of every other streaming service despite Declan arguing for something more distinctive—had been given the less desirable floors above the cable news operation. Longer elevator ride to get to the office, the fire drills were hell and they didn't have the views to compensate. Declan's office looked right into the office opposite him. He could predict the comings and goings of the woman who occupied the space with a ninety-seven percent accuracy rate.

This was why he shouldn't have a desk job. He didn't do well with predictability. Predictability made his skin itch. Predictability made him irritable with boredom, snappish with lack of new stimulation. He didn't fault those who sought a secure nine-to-six job, where the goal was to minimize how many fires one had to put out; he wished he'd been built that way. But he was an on-the-move kind of person, jumping from crisis to crisis.

As if the universe heard his thoughts, his

phone rang. Declan smiled when he saw the name on his screen. "Hi, Bobbi. No, I'm not ready to come back. Yet."

Bobbi James, the legendary editor of *The New York Globe* for the past thirty years, Declan's mentor since he won the IJAW fellowship seven years ago and his boss at the paper for the last four, sighed over the phone. "When will you be ready?"

"January 15. Launch day."

"I'm holding you to that. Still can't believe I lost my best reporter to broadcast."

"Not broadcast. Streaming."

"Does it matter? People watch pictures on a screen. Instead of reading words on a page, which is how the great deity in the sky designed news to be consumed."

He laughed. "If you say so. Listen, thanks for the check-in. I've got to run to a meeting."

"Wait." Bobbi's voice was oddly tentative. He frowned. "I'm hearing rumblings that all is not well with Keith Lochlainn's health. Serious rumblings. You okay?"

Declan took his phone away from his ear, his feet rooted to the ground. He didn't know what to say. He wasn't sure what he could say.

Bobbi was one of two people who knew of

Declan's connection to Keith Lochlainn. Well, he supposed, more must know now. There was the Lochlainn Company representative who came to his door with the offer to work at LNT. And Keith's current wife, Catalina, undoubtedly knew. But as far as people in whom Declan confided, there was his grandmother and Bobbi.

He held the phone back up. "I hear he's not in any immediate danger," he said, choosing his words carefully.

"I don't want to pry, kid," Bobbi said. "I know, I know. Funny thing for someone like me, infamous for snooping around, to say. But my concern is you. You okay?"

"Why would I be otherwise? I work for him. It's not like we have a relationship." The representative had been very clear. There was to be no contact between Declan and Keith until after Declan had completed the task set by the mogul.

He must have sounded more bitter than he intended, for Bobbi's tone shifted to gentle. And Bobbi James did not do gentle. "I'm sorry. Keith should have accepted you were his grandchild years ago when you first confronted him."

He closed his eyes. He hated to be reminded of how naive he had been. But he had been so excited when he put all the pieces of the puzzle together and contacted Keith's office. Only to be run off and threatened by a phalanx of lawyers who promised to bury his "charlatan fortune-seeking ghoulish ass for good" if he persisted in his efforts to meet the Lochlainn patriarch.

"My timing wasn't the best," he said. "I couldn't have known it at the time, but Jamie had just disappeared. And here I come, with the barest of circumstantial evidence Jamie was my biological father."

"But Keith is willing to acknowledge you now if you do this work at LNT? That's the part I'm unclear on."

"No. Only that Keith will grant me some sort of bequest when he passes on." Declan rubbed his forehead.

"That's bullshit," Bobbi huffed.

Declan agreed, yet hearing the sentiment from Bobbi made him oddly defensive of Keith. "I could see admitting that I'm the result of his son's hatred of him and the family legacy—since Jamie sold his sperm to help pay for college rather than accept any money from Keith—might not be something Keith wants to do publicly."

"He could still acknowledge you privately. You're his only grandchild. You're a good kid, kid. But if you tell anyone I said that I will have your head for my door decoration."

"I wouldn't be so quick to say I'm his only. When I spoke to the representative from the Lochlainn Company, I got the impression I'm in some sort of competition, although he didn't say in so many words."

Basic science and math dictated that if Declan had resulted from Jamie's sperm donation at a reputable fertility clinic, there was bound to be at least one other successful pregnancy out there. Not that Declan thought much about his possible half siblings. The mere fact that Jamie, who had been his journalistic idol long before Declan started to investigate the identity of his sperm donor, was his biological father was enough to occupy his mind.

"What does Louise have to say about all this?" Bobbi asked, who had met Declan's grandmother on several occasions.

"The clinic kept the sperm donor anonymous. My grandmother is glad my mom never knew I'm one-half Lochlainn, as people like Keith Lochlainn—who believed they owned the world and other people were placed on this planet to serve them—were the bane of her existence in the diplomatic corps." Declan chuckled, even as the wave of sadness at the loss of his mother when he was high school broke over him. The crest was smaller now but would never fully dissipate.

"Your mother would still be proud of you," Bobbi said.

"She would have told me to tell the Lochlainns to go to hell."

"So why didn't you when they came to you with the LNT assignment? Not going to lie, I could use you back."

Declan glanced at the glass wall of his office. People were gathering for the creative meeting. Mara's red waves were among the heads seated around the large conference table. "I have my reasons. Now I need to run."

"Fine, I know when I've been told that's enough prying for one day. Go to your meeting," she commanded.

"It's as if you still think you're my boss," he joked.

"Because I am. You're on loan. Don't forget it."

Declan ended the call as he walked into the conference room and took his seat at the head, aware he'd arrived two minutes early and thus, by his own standards, was late. Mara's gaze bore into him from her position several seats away, but he didn't turn to face her. A thick haze seemed to envelop his cognitive thinking center whenever she was near and that was not conducive to a productive meeting.

"Thanks, everyone, for coming. T minus eight weeks—less if we include the winter holidays—and counting to launch week. Let's run down what we have so far." He pointed at Mads Jefferson, the popular TikTok star he convinced to join LNT Plus as the inside expert on pop culture, and their producer, Adanna Obi. "You're up first."

Mads and Adanna detailed the stories confirmed for Mads's series on how Gen Z was changing entertainment. The hooks were solid, Mads's takes were well-founded and the guests lined up were stellar. One potential headache to strike off his list.

Next came Bryan Winner, a news anchor with over forty years of experience on the number one evening news broadcast. He'd been lured to LNT Plus with an unlimited budget to investigate anything he was interested in, which ended up being space exploration and the limits of earthly physics. At first, Declan was worried he'd made a mistake, especially when Bryan started to go deep into the math, but when he saw the final video Bryan had put together, he relaxed. The material was easily understood. And who knew Bryan was funny?

Declan continued to go around the table. Everyone was excited to be part of something with the potential to be groundbreaking and they were all bringing their A game to LNT Plus. With each report, Declan's shoulders fell another half inch. The launch would be a success. And Keith Lochlainn could go pound sand.

Declan didn't accept the LNT Plus assignment to win Keith's approval. He'd decided long ago, when Keith sicced his lawyers on him, that he would be a success without any Lochlainn help. He took the position for one reason.

And that reason was sitting by herself, the chairs on either side of her empty. His gaze narrowed. Mara returned his stare with equanimity. "By yourself today, Schuyler?"

"Yes." Still with the same calm expression.

"Was Tobey not able to make the meeting?" He'd paired Mara with Tobey Haulfield as her producer. Tobey was an old hand at producing news documentaries, having worked at NBC News on their prime-time news specials. While Declan had faith in Mara's ability to nail an on-air story, he'd thought Tobey's experience would offer additional value.

"Tobey...decided to seek opportunities elsewhere. The role might not have been the best use of his skills." She smiled at him.

The conference room, which had hummed with energy, went still. No one looked directly at him or Mara, but there were plenty of sideways glances and lifted eyebrows.

Declan's gaze battled with Mara's, neither of them giving an inch. "Tobey decided."

"Well, we decided. It was mutual."

"And were either of you going to fill me in?"

Mara lifted one shoulder with a delicate gesture. "You're being told now. I would have told you before the meeting, but you were late."

The room was so quiet, if a feather fell to the floor, the sound of its landing would echo like thunder. People were going to turn blue and pass out if they didn't start breathing soon. He stood up. "Good work, everyone. Meeting adjourned. I'll speak with the teams individually as needed, but for now, keep doing what you're doing."

The sounds of chairs being scraped back from the table filled the air, along with muted chatter. Declan kept his gaze focused on one person as she started to exit the room. "Schuyler, stay behind."

She froze where she was, her back stiff. Then she turned and faced him, her smile still plastered on her lips. "Anything wrong?"

"Please, sit." He sat and indicated the chair next to him.

"I assume this is about Tobey." She took her seat. "We had creative differences. This is for the best. My stories will be stronger, and the show will benefit as a result."

"What the hell is going on?"

That put a crack in her polite veneer. "What do you mean?"

"Tobey was your third producer. I get why the first two didn't work out. They were too inexperienced, and the chemistry wasn't there. But I paired you with Tobey because he complimented your strengths and weaknesses—"

Her smile disappeared. "How do you know what my strengths and weaknesses are?"

"C'mon. I know you—"

"No, you knew a college student, and it's evident you still think I'm one because you assigned Tobey to me. But just because you and I slept together doesn't mean you knew me then, and you don't know me now."

He'd always appreciated the way her green eyes flashed when she was amused or angry. She was the definitely the latter. "Is that what this is about? The past? If you can't put that behind you and make the most of the opportunity I'm handing you—"

"Handing me?" Too late, he realized he had gone too far. Much too far. Storms of lightning filled her gaze as she nodded, her head a blur. "Yes. Yes, that's what this about." She gathered up her laptop computer. "This is about me being unable to put a week of mostly mediocre sex seven years ago—"

He stared at her. Mediocre sex? What?

"—out of my head and unable to be oh so appreciative of—what did you call it?—an opportunity you're handing me." She snorted. "Handing me. So much for being impressed by my work at WRZT. I knew you had some sort of ulterior motive—"

He snapped out of his shock. "Wait. No. That's not what I meant. Bad choice of words—"

"You don't do bad choice of words," Mara

pointed out with cold precision. "You are an excellent word chooser."

"Not in this case, apparently," he muttered. "That's not—"

She stood up. "Do you want a formal resignation letter? Better we call this to an end before more time passes and we find ourselves too mired in a situation that becomes too difficult or painful to extricate ourselves from—"

He knew that speech. He blinked at her. "Are you throwing my words from the night before graduation at me?"

She held her arms out, palms to the ceiling. "Well, yes. I mean, you weren't wrong then. And I should've known better than to accept a job working with you. You and I are not able to—"

"I said that because you were going to London. I was saving you the trouble." And he had just opened the first of many letters from Keith Lochlainn's lawyers, his sense of self-worth pounded flatter than a paper towel. He hadn't been in any shape to be with anyone. Especially not Mara, who deserved more than he could give her at the time.

"Oh, so you were being chivalrous, breaking up with me." She threw her gaze to the ceiling. "Except I wasn't going to London."

"Regardless. When you didn't show up for the party that night or the traditional breakfast after graduation, that sent a clear message—"

"So now I'm the one who ghosted you? No. You always forgot. Not all of us had full ride scholarships that included room and board. Some of us had jobs." She stressed the last word. "I had to work early that morning. The rent didn't care I'd recently graduated." Her gaze met his, frank and not a little disappointed. "You could have called if you were so concerned. Communication goes both ways," she reminded him.

Touché. But that was the night the IJAW fellowship had been announced. When she didn't call *him* to congratulate his win, *he* had been miffed. He'd known she'd been up for the prize as well, but they had competed before and they'd always been happy for whoever came out on top.

Now he realized they'd not only parted less than amicably, but the story that won him the fellowship had originally been hers. He didn't know why she didn't publish what she had. She never said a word to him at the time, even though when she read his piece she must have known they had been pursuing the same leads.

But the result was the result. "You're right. I'm sorry. I should have remembered that you had a job and couldn't join us. I should've called you."

She blinked at him. "Wait. I'm right? You're sorry?" She looked around the conference room. "Are there hidden cameras in here?"

He laughed. "I can admit when I'm wrong."

"Really. I seem to recall someone who refused to admit he ate the last cookie at our study sessions even when he had crumbs all over his shirt."

He shrugged. "What can I say? I'm a bigger person now."

She smirked. "You were pretty big then." Then she clapped her hand over her mouth. "Sorry. That flew out. I've missed arguing with you, Treharne."

"I've missed this, too," he said, and he wasn't sure if he was referring to trading words with her, or the way warmth spread through him when she was near, or both. "But," he warned, bringing his mind back to the present, "you can't keep forcing your producers to quit. You'll get a reputation as being impossible to work with. And I know you're not."

"Right. About that." She sat in her chair again. "I should have said something sooner about Tobey and shouldn't have let it get to the point where one of us quit. I thought I could turn our relationship around, but this morning was the last straw."

"What happened?"

"Let's just say Tobey was patronizing."

He frowned. "Tobey has lots of experience, yes, but—"

"I have lots of experience, too. Only it was at a small team in a minor market, so obviously I must be treated as if I'd never seen a camera before. Then this morning, I saw his rough edit of our first story and…" Anger sparked back to life in her gaze. "He used nothing but outtakes. He made me look foolish. And incompetent. The other producers were laughing."

"What? That's—"

"Dishonest? Sexist? Condescending? Take your pick." She shook her head. "He didn't want to work with me. He took the job because he wanted to work with you. He shot all my pitches down and treated me like a puppet—just sit in the chair and ask the interview subjects the questions he came up with and nod my pretty little head as they answer. Do I look like I have strings?"

"Never." He caught her gaze. "I'm sorry Tobey was an ass. I should have vetted him better."

Their gazes held, tangled. The room faded

away, reduced to the sound of his own heart-beat as he stared into her forest green eyes. She always did have the most expressive eyes. He didn't realize until now how much he had missed watching her thoughts tumble and churn.

Then she averted her gaze. "Don't worry about it. On paper he was great. I was looking forward to working with him, until I wasn't. However…"

Her voice trailed off in a very uncharacteristic manner. He threw a sharp glance at her. "However, what?"

She inhaled, then blew out a long stream of air. "Tobey and I filmed footage for three pieces. Like I said, there's a rough cut of the first one, although it needs reediting. But the stories themselves…" She waved her right hand in the air as if shooing something away. "Boring. Old hat. Don't add a fresh perspective. I know we're under a time crunch until launch…"

There was an unspoken "but" hovering in the air. He leaned toward her. "What stories did Tobey shoot down?"

"Well." She pondered, pursuing her lips. The shape was imminently kissable. "Tobey told me I was insane for wanting to pursue this story—and I didn't appreciate him being a mental health ableist—but here goes. I'm not sure if you remember my brother Tim, but he married Lavinia Palmas."

Declan sat back in his chair. "Lavinia Palmas? As in Palmas Chicken? Tim married the poultry princess?"

Mara rolled her eyes. "She hates that nickname. A paparazzo called her that one night and it stuck."

"Wasn't there a scandal?" He rarely paid attention to the society pages—not his beat—but he couldn't help but overhear newsroom gossip.

"Her parents weren't happy she was marrying an environmental scientist whose work centers on how agribusiness is contributing to increased greenhouse gases, considering their major source of income—"

"Right. They cut her off."

Mara shook her head. "No. Lavinia cut them off. They live on Tim's salary. Lavinia was a management consultant, but she's pregnant and on bed rest now."

"You want to do a story on children who turn their backs on their wealthy families?" That might be cutting too close for comfort, considering Jamie Lochlainn had been one of

the best known scions of a billionaire to dis-
avow his father's riches.

"That could be another story down the road,
sure." She stopped, tilting her head to the side.
"Hmm. Kids who say no to their tainted inheritance because their family fortunes were
built on the broken backs of workers? Lavinia
is very vocal about how exploited laborers are
responsible for her family's wealth—she's donated much of her trust to farm worker unions
and cooperatives. Could be a great story. If we
could find more examples—which is a very big
if, but there must be others—"

"If Lavinia isn't your story, what is?"

"Right." She snapped back to the topic. "I
brought up Lavinia so you know where I got
the story tip. She really has given away most of
her trust but she hangs on to one thing from
her former life and that's the various fashion
weeks—"

"Ah. So, a story about couture fashion."

"No. And if you would stop interrupting, I'd
get to my point."

"Sorry."

"At the last New York Fashion Week, Lavinia
went to a party at Keith Lochlainn's penthouse
apartment—"

"Keith Lochlainn?" Judging by the look Mara shot him, Declan had spoken far too loudly. He lowered his voice. "I'm surprised Lochlainn has an interest in fashion."

"His wife Catalina, is a brand ambassador for House of Logan, so she hosted cocktails…" Mara stopped, her eyes lighting up. "You know who would also work for the kids who give up their inheritance story? Jamie Lochlainn. He was recently declared legally dead, but I wonder—"

"Your story," Declan bit out.

"So. Lavinia had been an art history major in college, and one of her favorite artists is Alain Robaire—"

"Like most people."

"Right. Well, she mentioned it to Catalina and this man that she described as, 'like, totally sketch' overheard her and they started talking about Keith Lochlainn's most recent acquisition, which Lavinia had never seen before and Lavinia likes art as much as she likes couture. She wrangles invites to private collections all the time. And this person—"

"The 'sketch' person?"

"Yes. He said the piece—a fifteen million dollar Robaire—came from a very private collector in Portugal and that's why the piece wasn't listed in any accounts of Robaire's paintings. They started arguing about it and he got very huffy. He said Keith Lochlainn is not the only Manhattan one percenter who is displaying art that was previously unknown and suddenly popped up. But then someone else entered the room and Lavinia said he turned white and he left the party. So, I did some deep digging. And there's a rumor—"

"This isn't already a rumor?"

"—there's a ring of people selling art with suspicious provenance as a money laundering scheme. And there's additional whispers the laundered money is then funneled into dark money campaigns, to buy judges and politicians." She stopped speaking, folding her arms across her chest and looking at him as if waiting for his reaction.

He frowned. "And?"

"That's the story I want to tell."

"You want to reveal that the wealthiest people in Manhattan—"

"And not just Manhattan. Lavinia said—"

"Including Keith Lochlainn. The owner of LNT." And his grandfather. Biologically speaking.

Keith was many things, not all of them nice.

Most, in fact, were on the ruthless and callous side. But hiding in the shadows to pull strings was not among them. Keith made his power moves in the open. "I don't think Keith would—"

"See, that's why Tobey shot it down. He thought you'd balk at—"

"—knowingly own counterfeit art that is a cover for laundering dark money."

Mara folded her arms and gave him a considering look. He knew that look. Her brain was making calculations. And he needed to head her off before she managed to add him and Keith Lochlainn together.

"This is based on your sister-in-law arguing with someone who is, and I quote, 'like, totally sketch'? The sketchy part is where I'm balking, not the involvement of Keith Lochlainn." Not completely.

"Lavinia thought he seemed totally sketch. But it turns out he's an art dealer. Alan Skacel. Owns a well-regarded gallery on the Upper East Side."

"Will Skacel go on record?"

She shook his head. "He disappeared. After the Lochlainn party. The gallery is closed, with a padlock on the door. Phone number goes to voice mail, which is full. He hasn't been home in weeks but his neighbors say he travels frequently and for long periods of time so they aren't concerned. No one seems to have seen him since the night at the Lochlainn penthouse."

"You want to do a story on his disappearance?" Audiences loved a true crime story. And this one had ties to the glittering masses of Manhattan's one percent. "Great," he continued. "We'll look for a new producer—"

"You agree? I should pursue the story?"

"When we find you a new producer—"

"No time. I need to go to the Poets and Artists Ball. This Friday. And I need you to get me an invite."

"The Poets and Artists Ball? Why?" The ball was one of the main events on the New York City social calendar. The event raised money to provide fellowships for promising young writers and artists, and everyone who was anyone clamored for a ticket and a chance to show off their finest couture for the cameras. "That's a hefty ask."

Mara bit her bottom lip, the first sign of uncertainty he'd seen since she entered the conference room. "I know. But Freja and Niels

Hansen are the chairpeople of the ball this year, and guess who also recently bought a Robaire from Alan Skacel?"

Declan leaned back in his chair and regarded her. His palms itched, a sign of his instinct telling him she had a story worth pursuing. There wasn't much to go on, but he'd broken stories that had less to begin. And if she could prove a conspiracy among the upper crust of Manhattan....Mara would have her pick of offers with which to build a spectacular career. Print, television, radio, long-form: the world would be her very comfortable oyster.

The involvement of the über wealthy Hansen twins sealed his approval, though they were far from Declan's favorite people. "Okay. But on one condition."

"Don't worry, I can provide an outfit. Lavinia has been begging me to borrow her fancy dresses since she won't be able to wear them for a while."

"Not the condition. But good to know because your expense account does not cover clothing."

She narrowed her gaze. "If you're going to continue to tell me I need a producer and I can't start to put the story together on my own until I have one—"

He shook his head. "No. Although we'll start interviewing tomorrow."

She crossed her arms over her chest. "Fine. What's the condition?"

He grinned. "The company isn't buying you a ticket to the Poets and Artists Ball. Seats start at fifteen thousand dollars even if there were tickets available, which there aren't." Getting her access to the event would be nearly impossible for most...but he wasn't most people. He raised his hand, cutting off the thunderclouds building on her expression. "Instead, you'll go as my plus one."

FOUR

MARA GLANCED UP from the note she was entering on her phone as the town car hired for the night glided to a stop at the curb. The door to where she sat in the backseat opened to reveal not the driver but Declan, holding his right hand out to help her exit. She eyed his hand with a slight frown.

Not for the first time, she wondered if she had made the right decision. Tobey hadn't been the only one who doubted if the story was real or merely a fun piece of scurrilous gossip told to her by Lavinia, although Alan Skacel's disappearance was an intriguing angle. But after that infuriating edit, Mara had no choice but to prove Tobey—and everyone else at LNT Plus who wondered out loud in her hearing why Declan had hired her—wrong.

One lesson was learned. She should have gone to Declan sooner. She let her pride trip

her up. If she'd told him sooner about her issues with Tobey, then perhaps there would have
been time to purchase her own ticket to the
Poets and Artists Ball. There was no way being
Declan's plus one for tonight would be benefi-
cial for her focus.

Take now, for example. Instead of concentrating on her notes and mentally reviewing everything she wanted to accomplish tonight, she
could only stare at the hand he offered, remembering how it felt to twine her fingers with his,
their palms fitting perfectly together, his grasp
warm and sure and offering strength. She had
other memories of those fingers, too: tracing
patterns on the sensitive skin of her stomach,
whispering over the tops of her thighs, parting
her slick folds and pressing and pulling until she
screamed his name…

"Mara?" Declan bent down and looked at
her. "You coming?"

Heat rose in her cheeks. Good thing he
couldn't read her thoughts.

Enough with strolling down memory lane.
Tonight was about showing Tobey and anyone
else who'd doubted her that she was a force to
be reckoned with. She put her hand in Declan's, ignoring the electrical charge when his

skin met hers, and allowed him to assist her out of the car.

His eyes widened when she straightened, revealing the transformation her appearance had undergone for tonight's event. While she wore makeup and took pains with her hair whenever she was on camera, tonight took worrying about how she looked to a whole 'nother level. Attending business luncheons and charity galas were one thing but attending a fundraising ball where the tickets started at fifteen thousand dollars a seat was a new experience. She'd spent valuable hours earlier that day, sitting in a salon chair being primped and polished, her friend Amaranth Thomas—one of the few new friends Mara had made since moving to the city—keeping her company and her nerves under control with jokes and banter. Amaranth had pronounced the result more than gala-worthy, fanning herself as she took in how the makeup artist made Mara's eyes seem wider and her lips fuller.

But when Declan remained still and silent, Mara wondered if perhaps Amaranth had been wrong in her assessment and Mara did not look as sophisticatedly glamorous as she'd intended. She patted her hair, ensuring the complicated updo was still intact, and then touched her ears to reassure herself that the diamond and opal earrings her parents had given her for her last birthday were still in place.

"Everything okay?" she asked. Maybe it was her dress. She checked the straps of the beaded emerald green chiffon gown Lavinia had overnighted to her. Nope, still on her shoulders. Lavinia had a larger bust than Mara and the thin straps holding up the loosely draped bodice had a bad habit of slipping. But if Mara remembered to hold her posture upright all evening, she should escape without any embarrassing wardrobe malfunctions.

Declan blinked, then his expression relaxed into his usual grin. "Everything's great," he said, offering his right arm to Mara. "But you're not wearing a coat. We better get you inside before you freeze."

She inhaled, hoping to breathe in courage along with the cold Manhattan evening air, and snaked her arm through his, giving herself a moment to balance on her precariously high stiletto heels. "Let's go."

Once inside the hotel, they joined the crowd ascending the wide, long stairs leading to the ballroom. Mara tried not to keep her head on constant swivel but she eventually gave up. Over there, wasn't that the actor from the television series about dragons? To her immediate right, she spotted a pop singer who recently made her smash debut on Broadway. And many more faces, recognized from studying the list of clients who bought art from Skacel.

Nor did Declan's presence go unnoticed. The paparazzi lining the lobby hoping for photos didn't call his name as loudly or as often as they did the other celebrities, but he was stopped to wave and pose for the occasional photo. Mara hung back in those moments. She wasn't Declan's date, as in a romantic connection. This was a work event. And Declan was her boss—technically —so she didn't want people, especially the stringers for the gossip websites, to get the wrong idea. Still, she couldn't help but feel proud of how well Declan handled the requests for his attention.

And how unbelievably handsome he appeared.

His dark blond hair was more closely cropped than six years ago, the deep grooves in his cheeks worn by his ever-present smile more pronounced. But his eyes were still the crystal blue of a spring-fed mountain lake, with similar depths in his gaze. Formal wear suited Declan, although, if she were honest, all forms of attire suited him. But there was something about the way his well-tailored jacket clung to his shoulders, then narrowed to fall over his slim waist. Beneath, trousers of the same silky black wool as his jacket hinted at the muscular legs underneath—he'd played tennis for fun in college and she'd spotted a racket in his office. She had no doubt the cut calves and hard, strong thighs she remembered were still present, and then shook a mental, chastising finger at herself. *Concentrate on getting the story.* She wrenched her gaze away from Declan and tried to find something else to focus on as a distraction.

But the crowd was growing thicker and each face that crossed her vision was more famous than the last. Her palms grew hot and she resisted the urge to wipe them on Lavinia's dress as her treacherous shoes started to slide on the polished marble floor. Declan tucked her hand firmly into the crook of his arm, ensuring she had enough support to stay upright. The crush of people kept her glued to his side.

She didn't mind. She took full advantage of the opportunity to catalog all the details she was curious about but didn't dare question. His bicep was warm and firm under the fine wool of his jacket, which rubbed like silk against her fingertips. He smelled… He smelled like Declan. She had to squeeze her eyes shut. He smelled like one of the best times of her life, of late night study sessions and early morning presentation rehearsals, like laughing in the library stacks despite the sign calling for "quiet," and like sneaking into the journalism school's video editing bays to make last minute changes to their stories for that day's school news broadcast. One inhale brought her back to the senior year apartment she'd shared with Cam, ordering pizza at eleven o'clock for the study session that turned into an all-night conversation she and Declan only ended when her alarm clock reminded her of her morning class.

The tall heavy doors to the ballroom opened and the crowd pressed forward, causing her to slip on the floor anew. Declan steadied her, his hand sure and strong, and kept a grip on her shoulders as they entered the cavernous space and began to search for the table to which they were assigned. The ballroom was carpeted, which Mara thought would be an improvement until her heels began to catch on the carpet's fibers. Thankfully, they didn't have far to walk. Declan had scored again; their table was in a prime location at the center of the room with a clear eyeline to tonight's speakers without being too close for comfort to the stage. She eyed her chair with yearning, eager to sit down and no longer worry about the torture instruments strapped to her feet. But the dinner was an hour away, which meant she would be wasting prime networking time. She sighed.

"Take off your shoes," Declan suggested. "Wear those flat slippers you have stashed in that purse."

She stared at him. How did he...? "You remember?"

"You hate high heels but insist on wearing them, so you carry backup shoes for when your feet hurt?" He grinned. "How could I forget? Freshman orientation. You changed shoes in the middle of questioning the health center representative about undergraduates' rights to free naloxone. Even I didn't know what naloxone was, that's how new it was."

"It helps to prevent death from fentanyl overdose, I thought the campus should make it available to students," Mara mumbled, her mind still marveling at the fact Declan recalled her habit of carrying spare slippers.

"And the campus eventually did. But that's when I knew."

The buzz of people chatting faded away, the whirl of brightly colored gowns and dark tuxedos replaced by utter stillness. The only sound she could discern was the bass thump of her heartbeat, reverberating against her eardrums. "Knew what?" she breathed.

Their gazes met and she drank in his clear blue depths. She wasn't sure how long they stood there—an hour? An eternity?—before he threw her his patented dazzling grin, the one that warned never to take him too seriously. The room spun to life around her as she dropped her gaze. Must have been only a minute after all.

"Knew I was going to sit next to you in class so I could crib from your notes," he said. "I thought, now there's someone who is not only prepared with a second set of shoes, but she's on top of current events that matter to students. She knows her audience." He nodded at her purse. "So do you have them?"

She opened the bag and showed him her foldable ballet slippers. His grin widened. "Go ahead. Put them on."

"Here?" Mara smiled at the couple who took

the chairs across the large round table from them, then turned to Declan. "With everyone looking?" she hissed.

"No one is looking."

"Well, yeah, I know I'm a nobody compared to you. But still—"

"That's not why no one is looking. Everyone here is concerned with how they look to the people they want to impress. So, they are not thinking about how you look to them. Take them off. If you want."

She bit her lip. He was right, no one was looking in their direction. Not even at Declan, and he was well-known. And her feet hated her footwear. Served her right for picking them out of Lavinia's closet during a video call based solely on the shoes' appearance. "I do want, but…"

"Here." He knelt. "Allow me to help."

Declan unbuckled the delicate strap around her left ankle. She steadied herself with a hand on the back of her chair and allowed him to slip her shoe off. The sense of relief was immediate, but the feeling warred with the awareness that had built as Declan's fingers brushed her skin. Who knew ankles were erogenous zones? Her nerves burned. He followed with her right shoe, and was it her imagination that his touch moved a tad higher than necessary, lingering a few seconds longer? She glanced down and the sight of Declan kneeling before her was superimposed on earlier memories, but his hands then were on her thighs, not her ankles. And his mouth was—

"There." He straightened and her memories fell away, although the wet warmth between her legs remained. "Shoes are under the table." His gaze flashed, focusing on a point over her shoulder, and he waved his hand in recognition before turning his attention back to her. "That's someone I need to talk to. See you back here for the dinner?"

"Of course. Happy hunting."

"More like 'happy keeping a source warm,' but same to you." He gave her a two-fingered salute and strode off.

He didn't seem hot and bothered at all, not even the smallest iota. She, on the other hand, needed a drink. Didn't matter what kind of drink, as long as it was ice cold and could counteract the heat still pumping through her veins. She swiveled her head, looking for the nearest bar—

Wait. Was that Freja Hansen standing near

the stage? Mara knew better than to stare, so she used her peripheral vision to confirm. The elegant blonde in the beaded champagne-colored gown had to be her. Mara had never met the billionaire heiress to a Danish retail empire, but she'd seen many photos online. And Freja and Lavinia used to run in the same general social circles, although they weren't close. Mara took a deep breath, rehearsing in her head how to introduce herself to the dinner's chairwoman. Did she lead with being a journalist working on a story? Or ease into it?

Freja was deep in discussion with a distinguished Black gentleman Mara recognized as the chairman of the board of trustees for the society that awarded the Poets and Artists fellowships. Good. That gave her time to prepare, to ensure she would make a calm, sophisticated impression. She planted herself in Freja's vicinity, waiting for her to finish her conversation. A waiter carrying a tray full of drinks passed by and Mara grabbed the first glass that came to hand, keeping her gaze on Freja and her companion. The two appeared to be wrapping up and Mara's mouth suddenly went dry. She took a large sip.

And she sputtered, choking as the strong alcohol burned the back of her throat while the overly sugary taste caused her to gag. She dabbed at her mouth with the cocktail napkin, hoping the neon aqua liquid hadn't dribbled and spilled on Lavinia's dress.

She glanced up, hoping no one saw her, only to discover a now alone Freja smiling at her. Mara tried not to grimace. Great. Busted. So much for making a good impression.

Still, she smiled back and walked over to join Freja. One good piece of luck—Lavinia was a few inches shorter than Mara so removing her heels meant the gown was now floor length and would hide her decidedly not fancy footwear. She held out her hand for a handshake. "Hi. I'm Mara Schuyler. Overly sweet cocktails and I do not get along."

The woman took Mara's hand, her grip cool and firm. "Freja Hansen. You communicated how I felt about the taste quite expressively."

"But I bet you didn't do a spit take in public."

"True. But I will have sharp words with the food and beverage committee tomorrow." She eyed Mara's gown. "Is your dress from Sadie Soho's fall collection? It's quite lovely."

Mara looked down and smoothed out imaginary wrinkles in the skirt. "I think so?" She smiled at Freja. "May I be frank? I borrowed the gown from Lavinia Palmas. Well, Lavinia Schuyler now. My sister-in-law."

"Lavinia!" Freja's expression shifted from obligatory politeness to sharpened awareness. "She sat next to me at Gary Habit's last show. Is she here?"

"No. She's on bed rest at the moment."

"I'd heard she was pregnant. Has she hired her plastic surgeon yet?"

Mara tried hard not to blink at the non sequitur. "Plastic surgeon?"

"For when she delivers." Freja's tone carried an implied "of course." When Mara continued to wear her puzzled expression, Freja added, "For the tummy tuck. Otherwise, as you know, she might as well say farewell to couture."

"Right," Mara said slowly. "I don't know if she's found a plastic surgeon yet. I'll ask her. But I'm glad we had a chance to speak tonight. I was wondering if I could ask you about—"

"Freja! Finally. There you are." A man who shared Freja's stunning ice blue eyes and sharp cheekbones joined Mara and her companion. "Before you say anything, the wine is as abysmal as the cocktails, hence I am empty handed," he said to Freja, and then turned to Mara. "Hello, I'm Niels. The brother of that one." He jerked his thumb at Freja.

"Mara Schuyler. Pleasure to meet you." Niels really was attractive, but in the way she found a piece of artwork attractive. She could admire how the various planes and angles came together to form an aesthetically pleasing picture on an intellectual level, but physically? Inside her, nothing happened. "I see you share my taste—or rather, distaste—for overly sweet cocktails."

Niels's expression lit up, his eyes flaring to sharp, appreciative life. Nope, still did nothing for her. "The blue drink is a crime against taste buds." He turned to Freja. "Shall we find our table? Simon wants to talk to you before the inevitable rubber chicken is served."

"Mara is Lavinia Palmas's sister-in-law," Freja said, her eyebrows arching high.

Niels's back straightened and he turned to Mara. "Lavinia! I was talking about her earlier today. We miss seeing her around town. Is she here at the dinner?"

"I was telling your sister she's currently on bed rest."

"I see." He and Freja exchanged a glance. "Nothing too serious, I hope?"

"Her doctor is being cautious. She's doing well."

"Good. But it's unforgivable she failed to tell me she has such a charming sister-in-law." His smile appeared, the wattage nearly blinding. If he had been dazzling before, now he was outright stunning. She could see why he had been named one of Europe's sexiest men by a leading London tabloid several years in a row. "Tell her I am deeply disappointed in her."

Mara laughed. "I will, although charming is not often a word applied to me. Thank you, however."

"I refuse to believe that." Niels's forehead creased. "You must not be traveling in the right circles."

"Or perhaps I am, and you don't know me well enough."

He waved off her comment. "Nonsense. I am an excellent judge of three things—wine, art and people. Especially enchanting women."

Mara ducked her head. She'd had her share of flirtatious conversations in her adult dating life, but never from someone whose photograph was featured on gossip websites from Paris to

Shanghai. "I trust your taste when it comes to cocktails, so I accept your word when it comes to wine," she said. "I would love to hear more about your taste in art. I understand you recently purchased a Robaire?"

His eyebrows rose. "I didn't think that was common knowledge. Are you a connoisseur of Robaire's work?"

"I wouldn't say a connoisseur. But you acquired a previously unknown painting of his? Recently discovered when a very private Portuguese collector needed to sell his estate?"

Niels regarded her. "Charming and an art aficionado who knows the market well."

"Isn't that why we're all here? To support the arts?" Mara smiled at him. "I would love to hear more—"

Freja cut short the conversation she was having and turned to Niels. "The meal is about to be served. We should take our seats." She nodded at Mara. "Pleasure to meet you. If you would excuse us?"

"Of course—" Mara started to say, but Niels interrupted her, bowing over her hand.

"Please, come join us at our table." He exchanged glances with Freja, who held his stare until she finally gave him a nod as she left.

Niels continued, "One of our guests couldn't make it at the last minute and we have an extra seat." His warm gaze ran over Mara, lingering perhaps a little too long over the bodice of her dress. She straightened up, and a shadow of disappointment passed over his expression. "We can become better acquainted between courses. And not to worry about the shameful wine on offer. I've arranged with the hotel staff to provide better alternatives for the meal."

"Thank you, but—"

He bent his head toward her ear. His warm breath wafted across her cheek, his low voice a husky timbre in her ear. "I won't take no for an answer."

Won't take no for an answer? That put his escapades with various women in the tabloids in a different perspective. Still, he was the lead she was here to pursue. "Well, I—"

She jumped as the heavy weight of a warm arm was slung across her shoulders. "Can't, because Mara is at my table tonight," Declan declared.

Niels blinked, and the connection between him and Mara was broken. She glared at Declan and tried to shrug his arm off, but he only tightened his grip on her shoulder in response. "I see," Niels said. "Treharne. Good to see you."

"You, too, Hansen. It's been a while since St. Alexander."

Mara's gaze ping-ponged between the two men, whose own gazes appeared to be locked in a battle for domination. St. Alexander was a prestigious boarding school in Switzerland. She knew Declan had been a student there, but that's about all she knew. He'd kept quiet when their friend group shared high school experiences. "You were at school together?"

"We overlapped." Declan's words were clipped.

Niels dropped contact first, and then turned to Mara. "I was a few forms ahead of Dec. And busy with sports and other social activities I'm afraid Dec didn't…partake in."

"He means I was there on scholarship," Declan explained to her.

"Well." Niels spread his hands in an apologetic gesture, although his expression was anything but. "Bygones and all that." He smiled, but his eyes stayed ice blue. "Good to see you, old chap. And how do you two know each other?"

"We're journali—" Mara began, but Declan's words drowned her out.

"We were college classmates." His tone left

no room for questioning. "And we've been close ever since, right, Mara?" His hip bumped hers, just a little, but enough to let her know he was asking her to play along.

She shot Declan a warning glare before smiling at Niels. "Yes, Declan and I met our freshman year. But I wouldn't say——"

"Looks like they are rounding people up to take their seats so dinner can be served. Mara, we should get back to our table. See you later, Hansen."

"But of course." Niels took Mara's hand and bowed low over it. No one had ever offered such a courtly gesture to her. She had to admit she found it a bit thrilling, even as Declan turned to stone next to her. "To furthering our acquaintance later," Niels said.

"I look forward to it." Mara said. She waited until he was safely across the room before shrugging off Declan's arm and whirling around to face him. "What the hell was that all about? You knew the Hansen siblings were at the top of my list of potential sources for the art forgery story——"

"You're going to thank me." Declan turned on his heels and started to beeline toward their table.

Mara ran after him as best she could in her

flat slippers, muttering "excuse me" and "coming through" as she darted around the celebrities and politicians wearing their finest. "What does that mean?"

"It means Hansen is spoiled and petty. I upped his interest in talking to you threefold."

She managed to get around Declan and plant herself directly in his way by darting in front of a film director well known for his blockbuster summer action flicks and almost causing him to spill his glass of red wine down the front of his suit. She ignored the scowl the director threw at her in favor of staring Declan down. "Wait. That chest thumping display back there... You think you were helping me? Look, superhero, I don't need you to fly in—"

Declan easily swerved around her and reached their table. "I don't think I was helping you. I know."

She rolled her eyes, made her way to her assigned seat and gripped the back of her chair so Declan couldn't pull it out for her. "I was doing fine without you. I was invited to sit at the Hansens' table before you showed up."

"Hansen likes to momentarily collect pretty things. But now he'll see you as someone to take seriously. Not as a piece of tissue."

"A piece of what?" Her hands dropped to her sides as she stored his use of the word "pretty" in the back of her mind, to be tossed around and examined from all sides when she was alone.

He pulled her chair out with ease. "Tissue. Something to be used and discarded."

"I'm a piece of trash?" She narrowed her gaze at Declan. "Tell me again why I'm supposed to thank you when the only person who has objectified me is you."

He sighed. "Look, I've seen Hansen in action quite a bit over the years. You want to talk to him about your art forgery story, fine. This will ensure he looks you in the eye and not—" His gaze dropped momentarily, his eyes widening before he returned his gaze to meet hers. "Lower."

She glanced down. What had caused his reaction—oh. The straps had shifted—the bodice falling precipitously low—and while there were young Hollywood up-and-comers at the party whose outfits were intentionally far more revealing, she was displaying far more of her upper body than she'd intended. Heat crept up her cheeks, but she tossed her head and held her chin high. "Oh, for heaven's sake, they're just breasts," she said. "I'm sure Niels has seen plenty of them. You, too. Half the world's population possesses mammary glands, you'll recall."

"Oh, I recall," he said, his tone low and rough, and she was transported to that week before graduation—that week when Declan had been particularly enthralled with her breasts, palming them with his large, sure hands, rubbing her nipples between his fingers and thumb, drawing the stone hard tips into his mouth, his tongue curling and swirling, his—

She blinked. She would not let Declan get into her head. And judging by the faint smile on his face as he watched her, he knew how his words affected her. How he meant for them to affect her.

Two could play at his game. She shrugged, and the straps fell farther down. She still technically wasn't breaking any decency laws, but Declan's gaze fell. And stayed.

"I'm parched. Aren't you?" She ran her left fingers lightly over her throat, allowing them to rest at the top of the shadowy valley between her breasts.

His Adam's apple bobbed as he swallowed. "Parched. That's a good word for it."

She knew what he meant as she struggled to work moisture into her own mouth. She let her fingers drift lower. Her nipples hardened, pushing against the thin fabric. He struggled to raise his gaze to lock on hers, but he finally gave up the battle.

She was teasing him. Flirting for fun. They both knew it. But she was enjoying his reaction. Enough to take the guardrails off and move closer to him, until her mouth found his ear. "And how do you propose we slack our thirst?" she whispered.

Declan's gaze snapped to a point over her shoulder. "If you want something to drink, there's a bottle of white wine in front of you. Excuse me. I see Bobbi James. I need to talk to her."

He left without helping her into her seat. Mara stared after him, her eyebrows raised high.

Ouch.

Well, at least she knew he wasn't wholly immune to her charms, such as they were. Useful information to have.

She turned back to face the table, only to catch the distinguished-looking gentleman from earlier sitting opposite her, also staring in the general vicinity of her chest. She shot him a narrow-eyed glare while she tugged her straps up and he turned back to his dinner companion, who also glared at him.

The rest of the dinner passed without incident, although Mara was careful to keep her posture rigid to ensure there was no further bodice slippage. Not that Declan seemed to care; upon his return to the table, he spent the entire meal engrossed in conversation with the woman seated on his other side. The man on Mara's left sat down, sipped some wine and then received a phone call that took him out of the ballroom—or at least away from the table— until well after dessert was served.

She stewed in silence. Her gaze returned more than once to the Hansens' table, where Niels and Freja appeared to be holding quite the merry court among the top of the crème guests. Once she caught Niels's gaze returning her glance, feeling her skin flush at getting caught.

Finally, the dinner ended after the honorees read from their works. Bright lights came up to flood the ballroom, letting the guests know the night was now over. As the room started to empty out, Mara pushed her chair back from the table.

Declan placed his hand over hers, warm and heavy. "Don't," he said.

"Don't what?"

"Don't go over to Niels." He threw a glance at her. "You've been too obvious with your interest as it was, although the blush was a nice touch."

"How... I wasn't..." She glared at him. "You didn't say one word to me all evening. How do you even—"

"Good. Keep that up. We look like we're fighting. He'll like that."

"You want to fight? We can fight. Why did you ignore me all dinner?"

He shrugged. "It's bad etiquette to talk to one's date exclusively at a social event."

She counted silently to ten. "We're not on a date. This is work."

"Agreed. But we arrived together. The etiquette still stands." He flicked his gaze toward the Hansen table. "Especially for those who expect us to play by their world's rules."

"I play by my own rules, and those rules are called politeness." She started, again, to rise from her chair. "I'm going to go over to the Hansens, thank them for a lovely evening and try to finagle an interview."

Declan rose with her. His left hand grasped her forearm. "Don't," he repeated.

"You really do want this to look like a fight,

don't you?" His grip was loose but sure, his hand warming her skin. She ignored the pops of electricity fizzing through her nerves and tried to surreptitiously shake herself free, careful not to cause anything resembling a scene. He did not take the hint. If anything, his grasp tightened, his fingers sliding along the sensitive skin below her elbow.

"I want you to get your story," he said in her ear, his breath hot on her cheek. Her pulse beat an answering staccato rhythm. "Niels does not like being pursued. He does the pursuing. I know him well. You will blow your chances if you approach him."

She stilled. "Okay. What do I do?"

"Give him a reason to come to you."

She gestured with her left hand, the one not attached to the arm he still held. "And how do I do that? Especially since you apparently aren't interested in letting me go."

He blinked hard. "What—oh. Sorry." His fingers relaxed. But she didn't move her arm. She told herself the ballroom was overly cool, especially now that most of the guests had left, and she appreciated the body heat he provided. That was all.

She was lying.

"So?" she asked. "What should I do?"

He scratched the back of his neck. "I have an idea. It's not the most professional. You won't like it. I'm not sure it's wise, myself. But it will cement Niels's interest."

Mara flicked her gaze toward the Hansens' table. Freja was kissing her table companions on both cheeks to say goodbye, while Niels was straightening his evening jacket as if preparing to leave. "What is it?" she hissed.

Declan's gaze was also focused on the Hansens. "We kiss."

"We what?" Mara whirled to face him, all thoughts of Niels and Freja flown from her head. "You can't be serious. That's going to bring Niels over here?"

"He likes to take things that belong to others," Declan said. "He especially likes my things. If he thinks we're together, it becomes a competition to see which one of us will be triumphant."

"Do we have to be together? What if we recently broke up?"

A steel shutter fell over Declan's expression. She'd never seen him so cold and still. Not even when he told her they were better off pursuing separate lives after graduation. "No. You'll be nothing but a plaything to be broken. He'll get even more joy out of destroying something that he thinks once belonged to me."

Mara narrowed her gaze. "That sounds very personal. You are going to have to fill me in on your history with Niels Hansen. Why didn't you say anything about him in college?"

"Why would I need to? I left St. Alexander. That was the past—" Declan grabbed her shoulders. "He's looking in our direction. Ready?"

"I am—" The rest of her words were swallowed as Declan's mouth closed over hers.

At first she was still, her lips shocked as overwhelming memories made it difficult to discern if the moment was real or a memory or just years of fantasies made viscerally real. Her synapses took a beat to catch up with her nerves, who were singing a sweet song of pure electricity. He was a polite kisser, not demanding, not trying to force a deeper connection, waiting for her to determine what was permissible and what was not. And for a second, she returned like for like, remaining passive and calm, a press of lips only. Then his right hand fell from her shoulder to her waist, resting there, not pulling her closer.

The hell with that. She was kissing Declan

Treharne for the first time in seven years and she would be damned if she let this opportunity go by without exploring what she dreamed of, late at night at her most alone.

She melted into him, entwining her arms around his neck. Her tongue traced the seam of his lips, begging him to let her in. He went still, his hands splayed motionless on her waist, but she sighed into his mouth and his fingers tightened, drawing her closer until only her dress and his suit was between them. His lips parted and finally, finally she was tasting Declan again, at once familiar and foreign, everything she remembered but tempered by the passage of time and the gaining of experience. Declan at twenty-two had been sure of himself with a ru-mored swathe of conquests through the under-grad and graduated programs; Mara tried very hard not to listen to gossip about which woman in the program he was dating that week.

The young man with whom she'd had a tor-rid, brief affair was still there. He was still De-clan, But now he was so much…more. More skilled, his tongue stroking hers and igniting nerve endings she didn't know existed. Stron-ger, more demanding, in control of what he liked and how to show her what he needed.

But also more aware of her, of how she wanted to be kissed, learning her responses and how to coax them from her.

Then she stopped comparing, stopped thinking at all as the embers kindling low in her belly erupted into pure conflagration and she could only feel. This was not good, the tiny corner of her brain still able to engage in rational thought tried to flag. She and Declan didn't work the first time. There was no way it would a second time. She didn't even want a relationship right now! She was building a career and couldn't get sidetracked.

She was—

"Excuse me." The low, cultured voice came from behind. "I hate to interrupt but I'm heading out. I'm taking an overnight flight to Europe I must catch, but I was wondering if I could have a word?"

Mara froze and then her eyes flew open. Declan disengaged first, his hands dropping from her waist so he could thrust them into his pants pockets. "What do you want, Niels?"

Mara slowly turned around. She must look a mess. Tendrils of hair that had escaped from her updo grazed her back. No doubt her lipstick was gone, as she could see traces of it on Declan's mouth. Too late, she realized her left strap had fallen down her shoulder and she tugged it back into place, trying not to shiver as the silky fabric shifted over her still hard and sensitive nipple.

Niels smiled as he addressed her. "You mentioned an interest in Robaire. Freja and I are having a small cocktail party, nothing too formal, at our place when we return to New York two weeks from now—a sort of private unveiling of the piece for our friends, as it were. Would you like to attend?"

She blinked, her brain racing to keep up with her ears. "I... I would be honored."

"Good." May I have your contact information so an invitation may be issued?"

"Um..." Her new business cards had yet to be printed. "I can write it for you on—"

Declan handed Niels one of his cards. "You can send the invite to me. I'll make sure Mara gets the information."

Niels's gaze turned frigid ice blue. "Of course. You're welcome to come as well, Treharne. Perhaps some culture might do you some good."

"I'll be there if Mara is."

"Of course." Niels turned back to Mara and the ice thawed. "I very much look forward to our next encounter. Perhaps we can have a real conversation—" he briefly turned his gaze on Declan "—alone, at the party. Until then." He bowed over her hand, nodded at Declan, turned on his heels and left.

Mara watched him go. She could either do that or look at Declan, and right now she wasn't sure if she could ever look him straight in the eye again. Not after that kiss. Not after she practically climbed him like he was a pole at a state fair climbing competition and she was trying to reach the prize on top.

"Right. That's settled then. Mission accomplished." Declan knelt, but before Mara could ask him what he was doing, he popped back up with her discarded shoes in his hand. "Here you go. Keep them off until you reach your car. Your driver is waiting for you downstairs."

She reached out automatically to take the shoes from him, her mind still trying to strategize how to explain away her reaction to his kiss. "Thanks. But we should—"

He cut her off. "I'll see you at LNT for the check in meeting on Wednesday. Have a good rest of your evening."

And then he was gone, swallowed up by the brightly dressed crowd as the partygoers slowly made their way to the exits.

Well, at least she didn't have to figure out what to say to him. She inhaled deeply, hoping oxygen would bring clarity to her disordered thoughts. She couldn't believe he just...walked off. But he'd been affected by the kiss as much as she had. She did not imagine his erection, pressing hard and heavy through the thin layers of their clothes.

Yet he acted as if the kiss never happened. Like how he ended their torrid week with a calm, unemotional speech about needing to pursue their own lives. Why should she expect today be any different than what happened seven years ago?

Honestly, she should be relieved. She finally had her big break in sight. The last thing she needed was to fall into another tangle of emotions over Declan Treharne. Even worse, seven years ago they had been fellow students, on an equal footing. Now, Declan called the shots when it came to which stories would air during launch week at LNT Plus.

She would never be taken seriously if people thought she'd slept her way into getting her story on air. Thank all the career gods that the ballroom had been nearly empty and no one—

well, except for Niels Hansen—seemed to be paying attention to them.

No, the best thing to do was to forget the kiss as fully as Declan apparently did.

She felt the pressure of his lips on hers through-out the rest of the night and into the weekend.

FIVE

DECLAN KEPT HIS gaze fixed out of the car window, keeping a close lookout for Mara, while attempting to also focus on his phone conversation with Bobbi. He wasn't doing a good job on either front.

"Could you repeat that?" he said, his attention momentarily diverted when the front door to Mara's apartment building opened, only for a man pushing a stroller to exit the building. He looked at his smart watch. The cocktail party at the Hansen twins' Upper East Side penthouse wasn't supposed to start for another half hour, and guests weren't supposed to arrive on time in the first place but were meant to be fashionably late. But he wanted to have a conversation with Mara—a good conversation, not the professional, stilted exchanges they'd had in meetings or in the hallways of LNT since the Poets and Artists Ball. He tried to find the right opportunity for a more personal discussion, but Mara was occupied getting up to speed with her new producer while Declan was needed to put out several urgent fires at the corporate level. But if Mara didn't get into the car he hired to drive them for the evening, there wouldn't be enough time to say the things he wanted to say.

To apologize.

Bobbi sighed over the phone. "That makes twice I've repeated myself. No more stalling. What's your answer?"

He blinked. "Answer?"

This time Bobbi's sigh was pure exasperation. "Answer to the assignment I'm offering you."

This was not good. He'd obviously blanked out on the main reason why Bobbi called him. And the one thing the famed and feared Bobbi James hated more than anything was to be ignored when she was speaking to one of her reporters. Maybe he could back into what he missed, ask enough questions to reconstruct the subject of their conversation. "What kind of time commitment do you think—"

"You weren't listening to me."

Declan tapped his fingers on the leather of the town car's rear passenger seat. He was alone in the vehicle. The driver was standing outside, at the ready to open the door for Mara who continued to be a no-show. "Sorry. You're right. I wasn't."

Bobbi snorted. "At least you admit it. What's going on with you, Dec? Did we not discuss you would be open to assignments from the *Globe* while you are at LNT? If I have that wrong, that's fine. But you need to let me know. I'm wasting time talking to you if you aren't available."

Declan pinched the bridge of his nose. "Yes, I'm open."

"Good. So—"

"But—" Declan hated to cut off Bobbi. He could see her now, pacing as she looked out over Midtown from the floor to ceiling window in her office, her favorite way to take phone calls. Her expression would be schooled not to show a single emotion in case some unknowing and unwise subordinate happened to look into her office through the glass walls, but a muscle jumping in her cheek would signify her displeasure. "—I'm not open now. And I'll be back in mid-January."

"I know." Bobbi was silent for a moment. "I'll hold the assignment as long as I can. It's mostly rumor anyway, although the sources are reliable. Maybe we can corroborate their information in the meantime. But if it heats up further, I'll have to get someone else."

He nodded. If tonight went well, Mara would be well on her way to having a story that could jump-start her career and help put her on the path to superstardom that should have been hers to begin with, and he could leave LNT. "That's fair. But can you repeat the assignment? I promise I'm listening."

Bobbie sighed. "You really weren't listening, were you? Monte Carlo."

Declan sat up straight. Monte Carlo was the home of the story that got away. The story that ended in tragedy. The one that still haunted him when he closed his eyes, whether daytime or night. "What? But she's—"

"Not dead. Or, at least, that's what we've been told. Would help if I had my top investigative reporter back in the bullpen, of course, but—"

He worked to get moisture into his mouth. "Alice de la Vigny has resurfaced."

"So said our source. We're working on confirmation. I can give you some time. But it might not be able to wait until February."

"De la Vigny is my story," Declan ground out.

"She was." Bobbi disconnected, a series of beeps in his ear letting him know she was gone. Declan allowed his hand holding the phone to fall, his gaze focused on the back of the seat in front of him but his mind seeing the manicured gardens and well-kept stone building facades of Monte Carlo.

"Hey." Mara stuck her head in the car. "Do you want to move over, or should I go around to the other side?"

With supreme effort, he dragged his focus back to the present. He trusted the team at the *Globe*. If anyone could confirm the source's story about Alice, they could. Might as well let them do the legwork for now. "I'll—"

Wow. Mara was stunning. Gone was the fancy updo and dramatic makeup. Tonight she wore her hair loose and down around her shoulders while her freckles were on full display. Although there had been nothing wrong with the glamorous Mara who attended the Poets and Artists Ball, not at all. He'd especially appreciated the dress she wore that night, the silky fabric skimming over her curves, hiding just enough that his imagination went into overdrive to fill in the missing details. And when they kissed and he knew there was nothing between his hands and her but that flimsy layer—

He cleared his throat and slid to the other side of the car. "Come on in."

She sat down next to him and buckled her seatbelt. The driver sat in his front seat, started the car and sped away from the curb. Her scent hung in the air, a light combination of lemon and strawberry. Her shampoo, he suddenly remembered. She must be still using the same brand. His hands tightened on the leather seat.

Mara looked out the window on her side, her head turned away from him. The silence stretched out, broken only by the sound of the car's engine and street noise from outside. He inhaled. He didn't have the time he wanted, but better to say something before they faced the Hansens.

Say something to her, before he started chasing other memories of Mara in college. Like Mara throwing on his shirt to fetch them coffee from the kitchen he shared with his three housemates, and when she didn't return to his bed in what he thought was adequate time, he ventured into the kitchen himself only to find her sitting on the counter, holding court with his friends—three avowed bachelors who had recently sworn off women for various reasons—eating out of her hand. She was delectable in the morning light, her tousled red hair glowing and her eyes shining, her long legs swinging as she exchanged baseball scores from the night before with the roommate who played club ball.

After his roommates left for their classes, he and Mara put that counter to good use…

Enough memories of the past. That was a distant country he would never visit again. "So—"

She spoke at the same time. "I knew it. There's something wrong. Am I not dressed right?"

"What? No. You're fine."

She glanced down at her navy blue dress, simple but elegant. "I spoke to Lavinia and she said not to try too hard, that people like the Hansens can smell desperation and fear. And that they definitely smell when you want something from them."

"You look great." And she did. So great, he was having a hard time looking at her, the way it was hard to look at the sun because the light was so bright. Mara would eclipse everyone at the party, he was sure. "Listen. We need to—"

"Because you hesitated when I came to the car. Like something was wrong."

"I…no. Nothing's wrong. At least, not with you," he said. Bobbi's news about Alice, on the other hand, had thrown him for a loop. Elegant and well-connected, Alice procured young women—very young women—for wealthy men. But she went to ground six months ago and the rumor was she was murdered because someone powerful got word she was about to expose the ring for whom she worked. The news she had resurfaced made his soul feel a little lighter—he hated thinking she was killed for talking to him—but that meant she was probably still involved in the same line of work. And that needed to be stopped.

"So something is wrong!" She shifted in her seat to face him. "What is it? Did you learn something new about the Hansens?"

"No. Not about the Hansens. Or tonight." He tried to smile at her, only to remember that Alice might still be out there, somewhere. And that he was wasting precious minutes not clearing the air with Mara. Traffic was not on his side for once; they were moving across town at a decent clip. "But we should—"

"You can tell me, you know." She faced front once more, her gaze fixed on the taillights of the cars in front of them that were visible through the windshield. "If something is wrong. We were good friends, once." He opened his mouth, but she continued. "If you need an ear, that is. Or if there's a problem."

Declan waited a beat. "Anything else?" he finally asked.

She glanced at him. "What? No."

"Good. Because we should talk. About the kiss at the Poets and Artists Ball. I went to HR and—"

"You went to HR?" She kept her gaze forward, but he saw her shoulders straighten. "The kiss was a ruse. It got us an invite to tonight's party. Why did you go to HR?"

"Because...we kissed. In public. And people might—"

"We kissed because it was an attempt to draw Niels's attention. Which worked." Her head tilted. "Unless it wasn't a ruse and there was another motivation."

"I—no." That had been the intent, but the result had shaken his soul to its core. However, since there wouldn't be a repeat, no need to say anything. He would be leaving LNT and Mara very soon as it was. "Good. We're on the same page about the kiss. And HR is aware that we had a prior relationship. LNT doesn't forbid dating—"

"We're not dating—"

"I know. But I want everything to be above-board. Workwise." Was it hot in the car? He should tell the driver to turn down the temperature setting. "But you and I should discuss—"

"Cliff!" she interjected. "Yes, we haven't talked much since Cliff came onboard to be my producer. He may not be as experienced as Tobey, but has a much better vision for the stories we can tell together. I think he's going to work out." She turned her head, giving him a brilliant smile that reflected the light from the streetlights flashing by outside the car windows. But her eyes remained shrouded in the shadows. "I appreciate your help. *Workwise*," she stressed.

Did the kiss leave her that unaffected? That was not the impression he got. She was pure flame in his arms, and he ignited right with her. "Glad Cliff will work out. But I want you to know that you are more than justified in going to HR yourself. If you wish to file a complaint over the kiss, I encourage you to do so. We work together and I control if your story will be on the air for launch week. There's a power imbalance—"

Mara snorted. "There's always been a power imbalance. At least this time the kiss was a means to an end that benefitted me as well." She waved a hand to indicate the car. "Like an invite to the Hansens'."

There had always been a power imbalance? "What do you mean—?"

"Oh, please." Mara turned a pitying eye on him. "You were the king of the castle, number one in the classroom and out of it. The golden boy. The kid who got all the prime slots. Being teamed with you on a project nearly always meant recognition by professors and school administrators. We all fought for you to pick us to be on your team, or more. Why do you think both Ahmed Shah and Julie Ting used to parade by your freshman dorm room on their way to the shower while wearing very little? They each hoped to catch your eye, and not because they admired your keen vision for stories."

"I thought they liked being clean," he mumbled. "I had a chance with Julie Ting?"

"You had a chance with Ahmed! I mean, you aren't exactly hard to look at, but Ahmed used to model in Italy. He was out of all our leagues. Anyway, my point is there has never been an equal playing field where you and I are concerned." The car began to slow, and

Mara glanced out the window. "Looks like we're here."

Declan didn't move. "I didn't know you felt that way."

"We all did." Her brow creased as she glanced at him. "C'mon, don't tell me your keen observational skills failed you back then. You had to be aware."

He thought back, his mind flipping through memories. Yes, he'd been highly successful in college—and since then—but that was the result of his hard work. His talent, which he honed. His skills, which he built and practiced with single-minded determination. That's what got him ahead…

Although. His innate aptitude was not why he earned an editor position on the school's newspaper as a freshman. He hadn't produced any work yet. But a classmate who had been a few years ahead of him at St. Alexander had got him the interview, when they had been reserved for upperclassman at the time. And he never looked back.

It never crossed his mind that Ahmed and Julie were pursuing him. Perhaps because he knew the professional life he wanted would have no space for a committed relationship. He was drawn to stories that required long stints of going undercover with dangerous organizations or being embedded in war-torn territories. His work was meant to bring the corruptly powerful to justice, to create so much evidence that legal enforcement could not ignore it or worse, be bought off. And with that came threats and near misses. Or outright assassinations.

Jamie Lochlainn died while investigating a drug cartel, his body never found. Declan assumed he wound eventually meet the same fate as his biological father. The only exception to his "casual flings only" rule had been Mara, and their sharp turn from friends to lovers had taken him by surprise. Taken both of them by surprise, or so he had thought.

"Is that why you…" No. That couldn't be why she came back with him to his apartment that night, why they fell into bed for one of the most glorious weeks of his life.

Her gaze struck sparks that lit the car's interior. "Are you asking if that is why I slept with you? To get ahead?" The car door next to her opened. The driver's hand extended into her space. She allowed him to help her exit the backseat.

Great. Just great. Awesome start to the evening, Treharne, he admonished himself.

Mara stuck her head back into the car. "For the record, if I had slept with you to get ahead in college, that would have been really, really stupid because it was the week before graduation and there was nothing left to get ahead on. So, thanks for insinuating my mental acuity, as well as my ethics, is suspect." She slammed the door.

Okay. He deserved that. And he had an evening of very sincere apologizing ahead of him. He reached for his door handle when Mara's door opened and she popped her head into the car's interior again. "We're still good for tonight though, right? That's the part I wanted to discuss. We have to be on the same page. Relationship-wise. Or fake relationship-wise, as the case may be. So…are we still dating? For Niels's sake, I mean?"

"Yes," he said, his tone brooking no disagreement. He exited the car and joined her on the sidewalk outside the tall, modern skyscraper that housed the Hansens' penthouse apartment. Mara was wearing flat-heeled shoes, he noticed with a smile. And also a note of regret, because it meant she wouldn't need to cling to him to change her shoes again. "And for the record, I have never questioned your mental acuity. Or your ethics. They have both been always top notch."

Her thin-lipped expression relaxed, and she came to take his proffered arm. "Thanks for that. But we are agreeing to pretend to be... together. So maybe they're a little suspect," she said with a small smile. "Y'know, you never did fill me in on your history with Niels."

She nodded at the security guard, who checked their identification and then led them to a private elevator that would whisk them to the Hansens' residence. Then she turned back to him. "Now would be a good time for the story."

"There's not much to tell." Declan kept his gaze fixed on the digital readout, flashing numbers as the elevator climbed higher. "We were at the same boarding school. I was on scholarship. Niels wasn't. But despite having everything money could buy, Niels didn't like his own possessions. He only wanted the possessions of others."

"And did he take yours?"

A flash of large brown eyes and an always laughing mouth seared across his mind. "What he wanted of mine he couldn't take. So, he hurt someone I was very fond of. Not physically. Emotionally and socially. She was never the same after. And he did it for sport."

Mara's eyes widened. "How terrible. Is she okay now?"

"I don't know. Her family moved away shortly after. She didn't return any of my texts or calls, and she isn't on social media that I can tell." They were almost at the penthouse. "The Hansens have riches and influence and they know how to wield their power effectively and decisively." And he wouldn't let Niels do to Mara what he did to Giulia. The situations were very different—Mara wasn't the daughter of one of the school's housekeepers and thus, she was not more vulnerable to the machinations of a student whose parents were on the board of directors of the institution—but he had no doubt Niels's tactics would be as cruel, if not more so, if he thought Mara was an easy target.

If that meant he and Mara had to pretend to be romantically together, well, he didn't mind the ruse. At all.

He might like it a little too much for comfort.

The elevator dinged and the doors opened directly into the foyer of the penthouse. Mara gasped. Even Declan, who was used to being in the gilded halls of the rich and powerful, had to the admit the foyer was a stunning piece of architectural art, from the honed marble floor to the lapis lazuli and gold mosaic walls and high arched ceiling. She grabbed his arm and whispered in his ear, "I feel like I'm inside a genie bottle."

A young woman in a formfitting black dress came forward to take Mara's coat. "Welcome. The Hansens are delighted you both could attend, Miss Schuyler, Mr. Treharne. If you would follow me, I'll show you to the party."

Mara raised an eyebrow at Declan as they followed the woman through a series of rooms, each more exquisitely decorated than the last. Eventually they reached a large open room with a terrace attached. The glass wall that would normally separate the two had been folded back upon itself so the party could flow indoors and outdoors at will. Declan wondered if he should ask for Mara's coat back, but quickly realized a series of cleverly hidden heaters kept the temperature outside pleasantly mild. Several groupings of tables and chairs had been set up for the guests on the terrace, while the left side of the room was dominated by a built-in bar, sleekly modern with shelves reaching to the ceiling of nothing but top tier alcohol.

On the right side of the room, the wall was severely bare except for one item: the previously unknown piece by Robaire.

Mara left Declan's side and went to stand in front of the painting. Declan had never been an art aficionado and modern art from the first half of the twentieth century left him especially confounded. What was so special about blocks of color or splattered paint? He could grab a canvas and some watercolors and produce the same result. But even he had to admit the Robaire was eye-catching—a six-foot by four-foot canvas that seemed to glow from within. He grabbed a drink from the bar and went to join her. "What do you think?"

"I haven't seen that many paintings by Robaire in person, but this looks on par with his best works," Mara said slowly.

"But of course it is."

Declan turned to see Niels standing behind them. The other man's gaze was fixed on Mara, whose cheeks filled with color.

"So happy to see you again," Niels said to her, stepping forward and positioning himself so his back was turned to Declan.

"Thank you so much for inviting me," she said, leaning forward as Niels greeted her with a kiss on both cheeks, European-style.

Declan failed to hide his eye roll. "Yes, we appreciated the invite," he said, shifting around Niels and then slugging his left arm around Mara while holding his right hand out for a handshake. She was warm and soft, and his hand drifted downward to rest on the curve of her lower back and bring her closer to his side. "We cancelled our five month anniversary dinner so we could attend. Isn't that right, sweetie?"

"Yes," she said, her smile wide. But her heel trod on his toes and he returned his hand to the neutral territory of her shoulders. Good thing she wore flats and not her spike heels tonight.

Niels perfunctorily shook his hand, then turned his attention back to Mara. "What makes you say this is one of Robaire's best works?"

"Well." Mara shrugged off Declan's arm and moved closer to the painting. "The use of contrast, of light and dark, to draw the observer's eye and ensure we look where he wants us to look. But of course, the areas that he wants us to overlook are where the profound meaning of the work can be found, in the emptiness and loneliness of the negative space. And the use of color—mimicking the observer's emotions as he takes us on this journey—is unparalleled."

Huh? Declan looked at the canvas. He saw nothing but amorphous blobs and blocks.

Niels was delighted. His fleshy lips curved in a smile that was half surprise, half leer. Declan resisted the urge to whisk Mara away from his assessing gaze. "Very good. You do appreciate Robaire."

"Very much. Although, I'm absolutely fascinated by this one. You recently acquired it?"

Niels inclined his head. "In the last few months."

"Interesting, I don't recall him ever using cobalt blue in such a manner. Also, the way he built up the pigment *here*." She indicated with her index finger but, for the life of him, Declan couldn't tell what distinguished the section she pointed out from the section next to it. "Very unusual for him."

Niels regarded the canvas with a frown. "Not so unusual," he said. "In *Woman on Staircase*, he used a similar technique."

"Did he?" Mara squinted at the painting. "Ah, I see what you're saying." She smiled at Niels. "What a find this is! You must have been so excited. I understand this came from the collection of a very private elderly gentlemen in Portugal who recently passed away?"

Niels nodded. "Yes. I was told he befriended Robaire at a time of need and was given several artworks in return."

Mara widened her eyes. "What a great story. Y'know, I recently started as a journalist for LNT and I'm researching a story on Robaire. I would love to interview you or your sister about this painting and the story behind it. I realize it's a big ask—"

Niels smiled tightly. "Too big of an ask, I'm afraid. You understand."

"Of course," Mara said, her smile never faltering. "I hope you understand I had to inquire. I'm so fascinated."

"But of course. Now, may I interest you in a drink on the terrace? There are some other art lovers whose acquaintance you should make. Perhaps they might wish to be interviewed. I would love to introduce you around."

"I would be delighted—" Mara stopped and threw a glance at Declan. "I mean, if that's okay with you, pookie?" She batted her eyelashes at him.

"Go ahead. I'll be enjoying the drinks inside

here, where it's warmer." It was true if anyone could be described to have a punchable face, Niels would fit the description. Declan didn't trust him for a nanosecond. But this was Mara's story, and he wasn't going to do anything that would jeopardize her ability to find the information she needed. Especially since his conversation with Bobbi put a fast-ticking clock on his time at LNT. He waved, a cheesy grin on his face, as Niels escorted Mara out to meet the other guests.

His face fell once they were on the terrace and other people blocked Mara from his sight. But this was good, right? Mara was ingratiating herself with the hoped-for source for her story. Sure, Niels said no, but that was only her first time asking him.

Watching her in action, her green eyes flashing and her red locks dancing as she tossed her head and laughed, he had no doubt she would eventually land her story—or any other story she wanted to tell. Before long, she would be an established star at LNT and from there, her career would be firmly in her hands.

And he could go back to doing what he did best: serving the world in his own way by uncovering corruption and injustice.

That was the future he wanted. A future where he was answerable only to his trusted editor and his own conscience. Where, if a compelling lead developed, he could drop everything to run around the world, chasing the information from dawn to dusk and all the hours beyond. If he was incommunicado for twelve days, no one would worry. Well, Bobbi might crease her brow, but she would also trust him to do what he thought needed to be done.

He didn't have to answer to anyone. He didn't bear any responsibilities except telling the truth and making the world a better place He knew some might sneer at his impossible, lofty goals—he'd been a quixotic fool several times—but he'd brought down a CEO who used his power to prey on women and non-binary individuals. The story he was pursuing involving Alice de la Vigny involved an international consortium of wealthy and powerful people who exploited refugees and desperate families in poverty. His life left no space to be shared.

Although—his gaze caught a flash of navy blue as Mara joined a small conversational group on the terrace, her red hair gleaming in the moonlight as she leaned her head back to laugh—he could see how developing a deeper, more intimate relationship with someone who shared his dreams, concerns and desires had a strong appeal.

He wrenched his gaze away. But not for him. Even though Mara understood his need to pursue stories and would probably dive headfirst into dangerous missions herself—intrepid didn't start to cover her courage—he couldn't ask her, or anyone, to share in the risks when he might not return home one day. He'd been devastated when he lost his mother and she didn't choose to be sick, while he was knowingly risking his life. He would not willingly put anyone else through that pain.

Perhaps Keith had been right to send him away when Declan appeared on this doorstep, all those years ago. No doubt, the loss of Jamie hit him hard, and here came someone claiming to be Jamie's blood, intent on following in Jamie's footsteps. Why put himself through the same loss twice?

His gaze found Mara again. Still, he couldn't deny he wanted her. Never stopped.

The sooner this story was over and she was established as a journalism star—and he could leave LNT and all the painful, conflicted mem-

ories being part of the Lochlainn empire stirred
up for him—the sooner he could return to his
old role and try to forget her all over again.

SIX

MARA JOINED IN the laughter, throwing her head back to chuckle loudly just as the man—wearing a suit that had to cost more than six months of her rent—next to her did, although she had no idea if what had been said had been funny or not. Apparently, there was a woman named Bunny and she lost her fur while visiting Gstaad? Or maybe the woman lived in Gstaad and her bunny lost its fur? She didn't know and frankly, she wasn't sure she would understand even if she did know. In-jokes were only funny when one was a member of the in-crowd, and it was clear Mara would not be invited to join.

The cocktail party was turning out to be a bust. While Niels had been overly solicitous when introducing her around to the other guests—a smorgasbord of international social-ites, captains of industry, current and retired politicians, and a few stage and screen stars sprinkled in for celebrity glamour—his interest seemed to wane once Declan was out of earshot. Freja was perfectly pleasant when Mara said hello to her, but her attitude clearly indicated Mara was there at Niels's insistence and not hers. Not that Mara blamed her. She and Declan were the only members of the press in attendance, and while the other guests did not shut her out of their conversational circles, neither did they relax their guard. Her attempts to draw various people out and move the conversation beyond small talk, into a discussion of the Robaire and the current art acquisitions being made by the Manhattan art crowd, were politely but firmly shut down.

She wondered if Declan was having better luck. This was his world, with his international upbringing and his Swiss prep school education. He grew up around diplomats and heads of state. He could converse with anyone—like the beautiful Black woman with whom he was currently deep in discussion, their heads so close together they were nearly touching. At first, Mara wondered if the woman had been at college with them, as she looked so familiar. Then she realized, no, he was speaking to Audrey Burt and she looked familiar because Audrey had recently won the Tony for Best Actress in a Musical. Mara was seeing her out of context.

She sighed. Of course, he would attract the attention of one of the most talented artists of their generation. That was Declan. Everyone gravitated to his sun, settled into orbit around his light. He seemed genuinely surprised when Mara mentioned Ahmed and Julie, but there was no way he wasn't aware of his effects on other people.

If only she had remembered that in college. At the time, she thought their friendship was sincere, the attraction that finally boiled over into that week of overwhelming passion mutual. Even now, it was hard to look back and realize how much she'd let herself believe Declan truly cared for her, that he hadn't only been interested in exploring the chemistry between them and then walking away. That she had been so wrong, so off in her reading of the situation.

She would not repeat her mistake.

Besides, she had much bigger fish to fry at the moment. And speaking of… She glanced around the terrace. Odd, she didn't spot Niels. Freja was nearby, speaking with the guest conductor for the Manhattan Symphony and a man Mara recognized from that morning's news program as a bestselling author from Brazil. Freja's calm, cool expression hadn't changed since Mara arrived, never slipping no matter who she talked to, but—Mara squinted—Freja's hands were clenched in tight fists. Rather unusual for someone who otherwise appeared relaxed and in charge.

Interesting. Mara sidled a little closer, pretending to admire the tall trees strung with small twinkling white lights lining the terrace's back wall. She strained to listen but could only hear an exasperated sigh followed by a hissed "Niels" before Freja turned on her heels and vanished deeper into the crowd.

Perhaps she wasn't the only person who had noticed Freja's twin brother was no longer on the terrace.

No use sticking around outside, making social small talk that went nowhere. Finding Niels and pinning him down for an interview went to the top of her list of things to accomplish at the party.

She passed Declan as she entered the penthouse. He didn't even flick a glance in her direction as she passed by. Good. Getting Niels to talk to her might be easier without Declan there, igniting the men's old rivalry. But Niels was not in the main living area, nor the chef's kitchen that would seem well-appointed even by Michelin-starred restaurant standards, nor the exquisite library off the foyer, nor the lavishly decorated dining room that appeared as if a party of twenty-five could be easily accommodated and still have room left over for dancing. She wandered through the rooms, taking mental notes of the other art pieces as she went.

Niels had not been lying. The Hansen twins' collection was indeed impressive. The stuff of which most museums could only dream. But of her host, Mara didn't spot one shining blond hair.

A sweeping staircase off the foyer indicated there was at least one more story to the penthouse, the stairs leading to a mezzanine that overlooked the room below. Mara hesitated, her hand lightly resting on the banister. Did she dare venture upstairs? There was nothing indicating the upper floor was off-limits to guests. But nor were people traipsing up and down the steps. The party was most definitely confined to the great room and the terrace.

The foyer was quiet, so quiet Mara swore she could hear the echo of her own breathing, bounced back by the marble floors and walls. She let her fingers trail along the polished mahogany wood. "Be bold," she heard her favorite journalism professor whisper in her left ear. "You dropped my name when you met the Hansens. Don't embarrass me," she heard Lavinia whisper in her right.

Venturing upstairs might be construed as an invasion of privacy. She turned to go, but glanced one more time at the staircase and the landing above.

Movement caught her eye. A person—dressed in khaki trousers and an oversize, rusty black jacket, their head of bushy gray curls bobbing— walked briskly along the mezzanine and disappeared into an open door. Mara swallowed, her heart pounding in her ears. She couldn't be sure from this distance and angle, but she could have sworn she'd spotted Alan Skacel, the missing art gallery owner.

She took out her phone and scrolled through her screenshots. She knew she had saved a photo of him…there. Yes, that shock of gray hair was distinctive. Not quite Albert Einstein, but close.

She was halfway up the stairs before she was aware she had moved. Oh, well. Score one for being bold. She hoped Lavinia would forgive her if necessary.

The man had disappeared into the second doorway on the left. Mara entered and found herself in what looked like another library. Only unlike the grand showcase of the room below, this library was human-sized and lived-in. An imposing dark wood pedestal desk dominated the room, papers stacked and sliding in various haphazard piles. Tall bookcases that matched the desk in color and ornateness lined two of the four walls, stuffed with books and photographs and small decorative pieces. Two large wing chairs covered in floral brocade flanked the fireplace on the third wall, and the floor was covered by what Mara recognized from visiting Lavinia's parents as an authentic, antique Aubusson rug. She almost didn't want to walk on it.

Between two of the bookcases on the opposite wall was another door, this one closed. Mara could hear voices. Male voices, muffled by the closed door, so the words were indistinct. Still, if she were in Vegas she'd take the odds that she had found both Niels and the person who resembled Skacel.

She crept closer. Eavesdropping wasn't polite, of course, and she would definitely disgrace Lavinia if she were to be found with her ear pressed to the door, but she sidled up close and listened as hard as she could, nonetheless. But the door was even thicker than it seemed at first—a good solid chunk of wood. The only silver lining was that if she couldn't hear them, speaking at a normal and, at times, louder register, then whoever was on the other side couldn't hear her breaths, which to her ears sounded raspier than an old car with a faulty muffler.

She pulled her hair away from her ear and pressed up against the door. "…onday," she was able to make out. And "…ant my mone…" There was the sound of something hard crashing to the floor—she winced at the noise—and the muffled shouts of two people arguing.

She put her hand on the doorknob and turned, ever so gently, but the knob didn't budge. Locked. Looked like she wasn't getting inside the room where it was happening. The only alternative appeared to be waiting for the two to finish their discussion and approaching them as they exited. Might as well settle in. She sat down on one of the chairs by the fireplace for the duration and hoped no one would miss her presence at the gathering below.

The chair's upholstery was scratchy against the back of her bare legs, the cushions firm—

too firm for comfort. The chair was obviously meant for decoration, not for sitting for long periods. She didn't want to drain her phone's battery, so all she had for entertainment was watching the minutes tick by on the grandfather clock in the corner as her legs grew numb. The room was warm and dark and quiet, and her eyelids started to droop—

A silhouetted figure appeared in the arched doorway to the mezzanine.

She jumped, her heart beating in her throat as her brain scrambled for answers as to what she was doing. As the figure advanced into the room, she shrank into the chair. Her heart beat in triple time as the silhouette came closer—

Declan. Of course.

She rose from the chair. "What are you doing here?" she hissed.

"What are you doing?" he countered in a normal voice, and she waved her hands in the universal signal to "lower your voice."

"I'm…" The journalistic ethics on snooping without having probable cause to believe a crime or some other danger was imminent were clear. And she wasn't about to tell him she spotted the missing art dealer when she wasn't sure she had spotted him herself. This was not a good look for her. She glanced around the room, hoping for inspiration. "Looking for an unoccupied bathroom."

He raised an eyebrow. "This does not appear to be one."

"Thank you, Captain Obvious. Now, if you'll excuse me, I really do need to find the ba—"

Muffled voices filled the air. Closer. More distinct. As if the people in the other room were moving toward the door. Mara stared at Declan. He stared back, understanding dawning in his gaze and a smirk started to form on his face. "Right. Bathroom. That's the reason why you're here."

She stepped closer to him, keeping her whisper barely audible. "Niels disappeared from the party. I wanted to pin him down for an interview. But when I went to look for him…" She shook her head. "I know you're going to think I'm seeing things, but I swear I saw Alan Skacel and he went into this room."

"Who?"

"Alan Skacel. The missing art dealer?"

The voices were louder. Whoever was on the other side of the room was right in front of the door.

"And you think Niels and Skacel are in the next room?"

She nodded her head rapidly. "But we should get out of here—"

The doorknob turned. Too late. Mara stared at Declan. "Would you mind?" she asked rapidly.

"Mind?"

"A repeat."

He nodded. "Sure. A repeat of what?"

The door started to open.

"You said yes. Remember that," she whispered against his lips. Then she kissed him.

Now she knew how she must have felt to him, that night at the party. He was still at first, his lips cool and firm, closed against hers.

Then, he wasn't. Not cool or closed, but hot and open, demanding entrance to her mouth which she willingly gave, sinking into his mouth like coming home after a very long, very lonely journey. The heat rose higher, faster than the kiss of the gala, for they had relearned each other, discovered how to coax sighs and clenched fingers and the desire to be closer— ever closer—from each other. They melted into one another as if they could take their bodies and form one, bigger and better than their individual selves.

She forgot where she was. She forgot why she was there. Niels and Skacel and mysterious paintings and dark web money flew out of her head as if they had never fully occupied it. All she knew, all she could feel, was right there, in her arms, under her fingers, his muscles bunching as she deepened the kiss.

His hands tightened at her waist, pulling her closer, spinning her into him, his hard length pressing against her. They bumped against something solid and a corner dug into her hip. The desk? She didn't know and she didn't care. Something fell to the floor with a crash but she paid the noise no heed as his knowing mouth built the flames higher and higher—

The door slammed and voices filled the room, dragging her back from the drug that was Declan's kiss. She stopped, her eyes flying open to meet his gaze, hooded and dark with dangerous lights glimmering far below the surface. "Follow my lead," he whispered against her lips and tucked her right against him before turning them both to face the newcomers.

Or rather, newcomer. Niels stood in the middle of the room, his arms folded across his chest, his eyebrows raised in question or scorn or both. Mara had a hard time reading his expression, both due to the dim light in the room and the fact that her sense still spun as if she had stepped off a merry-go-round set on high speed.

"Niels," Declan acknowledged. "Do you mind? We were busy."

Niels's eyebrows rose even higher. "I see that. But may I remind you this is my office. It is off-limits to guests."

"Can you blame me for looking for a quieter spot?" Declan indicated Mara as if she were a prize he won. She glared back at him. "I mean, look at her."

"My private office," Niels reiterated.

"Which is how I knew it would be unoccupied," Declan replied. "You and business, not much on speaking terms."

Niels smiled. It wasn't a nice smile. "I must ask you to leave," he said, his gaze never leaving Declan's.

Mara felt like she was another objet d'art for all the notice the men took of her. She cleared her throat and pushed herself away from Declan. "I am so sorry. I had no idea this was your personal space," she said to Niels. "I wanted to see the artworks you mentioned, and Declan offered to show me around. Believe me, I had no idea we would be doing…what we were doing…when I first entered the room."

That was the truth. She had no intention of kissing Declan when the evening started. Absolutely none. She enjoyed having a clear head and meant to keep one.

So much for good intentions. They truly were what paved the path to hell. Because now, when she finally found her bed later that night, she was going to do nothing but cloud her brain by reliving the kiss over and over again. Her vibrator hadn't seen so much action in years.

Niels ceased his battle of the stares with Declan and glanced over at Mara. "I know you are blameless, my dear," he said. "I would be happy to show you around. Perhaps I could give you a tour at another date? I must return to the other guests now."

"I would appreciate that. And while I know you don't want to be on camera, perhaps we could have a discussion on the record, for background purposes only. I'm sure I can learn so much from you and your perspective would be so valuable." She gave him her most blinding smile.

Pouring on the full wattage seemed to work.

Niels visibly softened. "Let's have the tour first. And then perhaps we can sit down if you are still interested." He ushered her toward the arched doorway, his hand coming very close to her waist. Declan trailed behind her. "I look forward to our next encounter."

"Same here." The three of them descended the stairs, Niels and Mara walking shoulder to shoulder, Declan a few steps behind. At the bottom of the stairs, Niels turned to Mara. "I will leave you both here. You are welcome to stay and enjoy more of the party," he said to her before turning a glare on Declan, "but as your original escort is leaving, if you wish to depart now, I understand."

"He's my ride," she said with a shrug. "And I have terrible luck with cabs and car services at night."

"Then, until I see you again, *à bientôt*." He kissed her on both cheeks again, and then shook Declan's hand for the briefest amount of time possible.

"Good night," she responded, and then she waited until Niels had disappeared into the next room before her shoulders collapsed and she exhaled an enormous sigh of relief. "That was harrowing."

"Yet you got the next invite and maybe even an interview. Let's get going," Declan pushed the button for the elevator, which arrived almost before the button lit up. They maintained their silence until they were seated in the rear seats of their town car, then he asked the driver to put on a classic rock radio station at medium volume.

"Led Zeppelin?" Mara asked. "At this hour?"

Declan kept his voice pitched low, so only Mara could hear him over the music. "I think you're right."

"Right about what?" She was still riding on the high of getting Niels Hansen to agree to talk to her. Sure, on background, but she could get him to go on record.

"About Alan Skacel."

She spun on the leather seat, not caring her skirt rode up as she searched his gaze. "You saw him? In the library?'

He shook his head. "No. Only Niels entered the room." He smiled, a hint of mischief in the closed set of his lips. "Of course, I was a tiny bit preoccupied. I might have missed something. For a second."

Two could play at this game. "Funny, it didn't feel like a tiny bit—"

His smile turned into a self-satisfied smirk.

She narrowed her gaze at him. "It felt like you were a *lot* preoccupied. I, on the other hand, can confirm I heard one step of footsteps enter the library."

She thought. She wasn't sure. Truthfully, an ambulance siren could have gone off beside her and the pulse of her racing heartbeat against her eardrums as he kissed her would have drowned it out. Not that Declan needed to know that.

His deepening smirk told her he didn't believe her. "Regardless. No, I did not see Skacel. But I found this while you and Niels were talking."

He reached into his suit pocket and pulled out a piece of paper which he offered to her. She took it and, using the flashlight on her phone, did her best to comprehend what it said. "This is a bill of sale. For an unspecified painting." She looked up. "So?"

"Read closer."

She reread the document. "To be delivered to..." She looked up at Declan. "Keith Lochlainn. That doesn't make sense. Why would Niels Hansen have a bill of sale for a painting sold to Lochlainn?"

"Keep going."

She scowled at him, then went back to the document. "Curiouser and curiouser. Why does Niels Hansen have a bill of sale to Keith Lochlainn signed by Skacel?"

"Check the date."

She blinked. "This is after Skacel disappeared."

"Don't know about you but seems interesting to me."

"It does, doesn't it? But—" she folded the paper and placed it in her purse. "—it's only interesting. It's not compelling evidence. It doesn't prove that was Skacel at the party tonight. Just that somehow Niels ended up with this document."

"And that somehow they are connected to Keith Lochlainn." He raised his eyebrows at her.

"Then what's the next step? Crash the home of the billionaire mogul who owns LNT and rifle through his art collection? That spells career longevity."

"What if you don't have to crash?"

"You are so buddy-buddy with Keith Lochlainn you can waltz into his home like a long-lost relative at any time?"

A shadow flashed across Declan's expression, so fleeting that if Mara had blinked she would have missed it. "No, I can't walk in," he said. "But we can go to the dedication of the new Jamie Lochlainn wing at the Museum of Contemporary Culture."

"Oh, right. That's the memorial Keith Lochlainn chose when Jamie was declared legally dead. And let me guess. You have an invite." Mara yawned, the adrenaline of the last hour draining and leaving her boneless. "You never did tell me how you got your position at LNT. Is it because you remind them of Jamie when he was alive? You have similar styles as journalists now that I think about it. Similar tastes in stories. You're both drawn to bleeding hearts, 'change the corrupt system' type of subjects."

That dark shadow dimmed Declan's gaze again, lingering perhaps a beat longer. And she wasn't imagining his stillness, his usually kinetic energy tamped down on low. She frowned. "Are you okay?"

He cleared his throat, shaking his head. "Sorry." His voice was rougher than usual. "Got something stuck in my throat. And no, I don't think that's the reason." He coughed, a dry sound that underscored his throat was irritated.

Mara pulled down the bulky armrest between her and Declan and exposed the compartment behind. The cars provided by LNT for their staff and on-air talent were usually stocked with water and breath mints, necessities for attending meetings or conducting interviews. Her eyebrows nearly hit her hairline when she saw what the compartment contained. This car had been supplied for someone who required stronger stuff. She pulled out two airline-sized bottles of whiskey and then folded the armrest back up.

She held up the bottles so Declan could see. "No water, but I found these. And no glasses. I think we're supposed to swig."

He snorted. "Do you know whose car this normally is? George Reynolds."

"No! Really?" Reynolds was LNT's legendary long-running six o'clock news anchor. "Will he mind us drinking his alcohol?"

"He's not going to say anything. Check your contract. No alcohol on LNT property, and that includes the company cars."

"Journalists with no alcohol? That's an oxymoron."

"There was an…incident…a few years ago. Involving Reynolds, by the way. Among others."

"Obviously he learned his lesson. And by

obviously I mean he didn't." She unscrewed the top off one bottle and handed it to Declan, then opened the second bottle for herself. "Here's to a successful evening." The straight whiskey left flames behind as it slid down her throat. "Thank you for the repeat. Niels would have caught me in the library and my excuse wouldn't have been anywhere near as convincing without you there."

He smiled. Not the smirk from before, but a real smile. Sincere. Warm. Her heart started to beat a little faster. She told herself the cause was the alcohol. For all that she had just joked about journalists and their reputation for being heavy drinkers, she mostly stuck to beer and wine, and even then that was occasionally. "Happy to help. Good instincts, but then you've always had them. You're amazing, always have been."

Her chest burned, and that wasn't the whiskey. "That's kind of you," she managed to choke out, her gaze fixed on the bare trees lining the sidewalk, counting the minutes until she could get out of a confined space with him and into her small studio apartment, where she could deal with the conflicting, visceral emotions his words raised. "Considering I launched myself at you without really getting your consent. Hope you don't regret saying yes."

"You can kiss me whenever you like, Schuyler."

His words were teasing, but his tone…his tone was raw. Sincere. Authentic. She whipped her head around to catch his gaze and inhaled a deep, shuddering breath.

His expression was still, his eyes dark and unreadable. Not banter, then. She could not tear her gaze away. Her pulse began a syncopated dance, a samba, heady yet hesitant. "Did you mean it?" she whispered into the quiet, broken only by the muffled hum of the car's engine.

"Which part?" he rumbled. "But the answer is yes. All of it."

"The part about how good I am. That you've always thought that."

"You blow me away, Schuyler."

"I do?"

Her hand was next to his on the smooth leather seat. He picked it up in his, his grasp warm and sure. She inhaled at the slide of his skin against hers, the sparks that trailed alongside it.

"My breath, gone," he continued. "From the moment I saw you arguing your point at orientation."

His gaze traced the contours of her face before coming to rest on her lips. Her mouth was suddenly dry and she licked them. The light in his eyes flared, and the desire that had never fully gone dormant since their kiss in the library leapt in answer.

The samba in her veins intensified, the hesitancy gone. She tightened her grip on his fingers as the car turned a corner, swaying in his direction even as he leaned into hers. "I've always been in awe of you," she murmured. "Never could quite believe you were real. I think that's why I hated you at first, so I wouldn't be overwhelmed by awe."

"I never hated you," he said, that hot light now sufficing his entire gaze. "But I never thought—"

The car slowed to a stop, cutting off his words. They must be at her building. She assumed, because she wasn't looking away from him now. "You never thought?"

His smile was slow, sure. Her stomach tensed with a delicious fluttering of a thousand wings. "That you would agree to come to my apartment that night," he said. "And stay." Her breathing sped up, but she couldn't get enough oxygen into her system. "Mara, I—"

The driver opened her door, cutting off

whatever Declan was going to say. She blinked, the rush of cold night air entering their formerly small, contained space acted like a bucket of water thrown on simmering embers. Right. This was Declan being charming again. It didn't mean anything.

She cleared her throat. "This is me. I should go."

She exited the car, the weight of Declan's gaze heavy on her back. She walked toward her building—one step, two steps—aware the closer she got to her apartment, the more things would stay the same, the more they would dance around their past in the hopes of not jeopardizing the present and possibly ruining the future.

But how could there be a future—much less a present—if they never dealt with the past?

She paused. She wasn't looking forward to another bout of sleeplessness, parsing every second of their kiss, examining every minute action or reaction from him for meaning and portents. She'd spent too much of her time since she arrived in New York City going over the same well-worn territory. To the point that her sister-in-law was threatening to make her give her a dollar every time his name came up on their phone calls. "One of us might as well get something valuable out of this," she'd said with a grin in her voice.

Plus, her vibrator wasn't going to cut it. Not tonight.

Turning on her heels, she walked around the rear of the car to Declan's side and tapped on his window. He rolled the glass down, a puzzled frown on his face. "Everything okay?

"The other part. Did you mean it, too?"

His gaze slightly narrowed in question, but he nodded. "I always mean what I say."

"Good. Because I feel like kissing you." She leaned in through the window and kissed him, openmouthed, hard and wanting. He was still, but only for the space of a sigh exhaled against her lips, and then he was open to her, tasting slightly of whiskey and wholly like him, a taste at once intimately familiar and excitingly new as she replaced her memories with the actuality of Declan now, seven years older, seven years more experienced.

With an effort, she broke contact and stepped back far enough so she could catch his gaze. "What were you about to say?"

"When? Got to tell you, my brain is lacking

oxygen right now." He grinned and reached for her.

She leaned back, just beyond the reach of this fingertips, no matter how much she wanted to lean into his touch "When the driver opened the door and cut you off. What were you about to say?"

The humor in his eyes fled. His gaze bore into hers, forceful, with sincerity. "I don't have regrets," he said. "Except one. How we ended."

She should be freezing. She was standing on a Manhattan street in December—the already cold breeze chilled further by the presence of the East River a few blocks away—in nothing but a thin cocktail dress and the barest minimum of wraps, her legs and arms mostly bare to the elements. But she burned, hot and bright and demanding more, demanding to be consumed entirely. "Because we never did end it, did we? Not properly."

"No."

"Right. As things stand now, I'll never be able to concentrate on the story when I'm around you. And this could be a very big story."

His brow creased. "I'm not sure I follow."

"I need to concentrate. You have the connections I need, but whenever we're together we always end up talking about what happened in college—"

"Talking? Interesting way to define—"

"Fine. Kissing," she agreed. "So, we should… clear the air."

"Clear the air. How?" Now both of his eyebrows were raised.

"By finally getting some closure," she said. "Tonight. Now. That is, if you want."

"Schuyler." He smiled, slow and dangerous. She couldn't suppress her shiver. "Are you inviting me to your place to talk?"

She shook her head. "No. I'm inviting you to my place for sex."

SEVEN

Kissing Mara was something Declan doubted he would ever tire of, not even if he lived to be one hundred and sixty.

Not that he had romanticized their past. They had been painfully young, still kids in so many ways, still not fully launched into the adult world. College had been a cocoon in which to experiment and try on different methods and ways of being. The seven years since graduation had been real in ways that college hadn't been for him: real obstacles, real challenges, real consequences for his actions.

But there had been one way in which school had painfully prepared him for life as a grown up, and that was the lesson that taught him to live by his morals, because the one time he didn't—the one time he decided to let his values slide and accept something that didn't fully belong to him, didn't do enough to make

everything right regardless of the circumstances—made him so incredibly ashamed that
he couldn't face Mara. Losing her was his pen-
ance, one he had been prepared to pay for the
rest of this life. Getting her the job at LNT was
the least he could do to begin leveling the playing field, only to discover the adult Mara ex-
ceeded everything he thought she would be and
more. He meant it when he said she blew him
away from their first meeting, but she knocked
him head over his ass now.

And her last words stole his breath…while
other parts of him were coming to hard, almost painful life.

"Sex," he repeated.

Her hands landed on her hips. Her curvy,
soft hips to which the silk of her dress clung.
He had his reasons for hanging back when he,
Mara and Niels descended the stairs. He wasn't
ashamed to admit that watching her hips sway
as she moved was one of them. "Is that such a
terrible offer?" she demanded.

"Terrible? No." He'd wanted to run his hands
over that dress all night. Bunch the skirt at her
waist, find out if the skin of her inner thigh was
still silkier than the fabric. He shifted in his seat.
"But have you thought—"

"Have I thought this through? Yes." She nodded. Then she shook her head. "No. Maybe. Look, I know this might make things more awkward. But truthfully, can they get any more awkward? We've been to two events and both times we ended up, well, kissing. And I need you to take me to the dedication of the museum wing next week, and I need a clear head while I'm there. Therefore, logically we should—"

She stopped as he opened his door and unfolded himself to stand next to her. So close that he could see the tiny bumps on her arms raised by the cold night breeze.

Or maybe something else.

The anticipation hanging heavy and sharp between them, the air almost visibly pulsating with static electricity, caused the hairs on his arms to rise as well.

"Didn't mean to interrupt you," he said. "We should what?"

"We should..." She swallowed. "Release the tension. So we can concentrate on our work."

"That's what this is? Tension?"

She moistened her lips, her tongue tracing a sensuous path. He called on his willpower reserves, resisting the demanding urge to replace her tongue with his, to feel those plump, pink lips under his. "Yes," she said. "Something physical we need to get out of our systems. A one and done."

He regarded her. She met his gaze, her chin held high, but he could see the slight wobble in her posture, her hands shaking in tiny quakes.

Growing up, Declan had seen old cartoons where Bugs Bunny or Mickey Mouse or whoever was caught on the horns of a moral dilemma, with an animated angel sitting on one shoulder and whispering "Don't do it!" while an animated devil sat on the other shoulder, telling the hero to go for broke. He never really grasped that visual metaphor until this very minute. Because he should listen to his inner angel. He should tell Mara kindly but firmly that sleeping together wouldn't resolve anything, certainly not the sexual tension that filled every molecule of air between them.

But his inner devil's whispers were seductive, tempting him with the promise of his most reliable fantasy of the last seven years come to life. Mara, naked and warm, her eyes heavy with desire, her legs wrapped around him. His to touch and caress and kiss and stroke until she fell apart in his arms, his name a screamed whisper on her lips.

Maybe she was right. Maybe this pull they exerted on each other would be lessened if they had sex. Maybe the force that kept bringing them together was merely curiosity. The natural response to seeing each other after all these years. It was inevitable sparks would fly.

Especially since the fire never had a chance to extinguish naturally.

"Well?" She raised her chin higher. "Offer is only good for tonight. You can take it," and she swept her arm, indicating herself. "All of it. Or leave it. And I'll find someone else who can get me into the Lochlainn event." She half smiled, half smirked, with a glint of mischief in her gaze that acted on his blood like a match touching gasoline. "Maybe Niels would like to escort me."

She fought dirty. He flicked his inner angel off his shoulder. Besides, he would be leaving LNT as soon as Mara was firmly established—if not sooner. His conversation with Bobbi echoed in his ears. There would be no harm, no foul, no lasting repercussions for either of them this time. They were going into this with eyes open.

And hearts closed.

"One time only, Schuyler," he growled, and

closed half the distance between them, the air practically crackling.

Her eyes widened, but she stood her ground. "One time. And we never talk of it again. So you better make it count, Treharne." She closed the remaining distance between them. "Of course, I could always use a new 'worst sex ever' story to amuse my friends. Either way."

He laughed. Sex with Mara had been far from the worst, and they had been much younger then. "Hold that thought," he said, and he stepped away to have a quick word with the driver. When the car sped away, he returned to Mara and pulled her tight against him. She let a soft yelp of surprise escape her, but then relaxed against him, her arms coming up to entwine around his neck, her soft curves short circuiting his ability to think. One thing was clear: whatever he wanted to give, she would willingly take and give back equally, if not more.

"Let's see where we land on the scale of worst to best," he said against her lips, and then he kissed her, hard and hot and openmouthed.

Somehow they made it into her building, Mara fumbling for her keys and turning the lock without ever losing contact, not that his grip on her would let her go very far. Somehow they made it up the four flights of stairs to her fifth-floor walk-up, Declan taking advantage of each landing to press her against the stairwell wall and devour her mouth and her neck, swallowing her gasps, keeping her hands locked in his because she had a very disconcerting and highly welcome tendency to find him, hard and heavy, through the fabric of his suit trousers. They might have remained in the stairwell if one of her neighbors didn't descend the stairs with full trash bags, calling out lewd encouragement as he passed them.

Once inside Mara's apartment, she seemed to gain inhibitions she previously didn't exhibit, even though they were safe from any prying eyes. She pulled her mouth from his and started to make apologies for the size of her studio apartment.

He didn't give a damn. What mattered to him was the bed at the far end of the space—a white cloud piled high with pillows—and a memory long suppressed came flooding back: Mara in her shared dorm room freshman year, her twin bed a smaller version of this one, laughing at something her roommate said with her head thrown back and her cheeks flushed and those glorious red curls contrasting with the bedding.

If he had been able to be honest with himself then, he would have admitted that was when he first fell in love—

Love?

Mara blinked up at him and then followed the line of his gaze to the bed. "I swear, the bedding is clean. I—okay, not that I thought this would be happening, or may be happening, but Fridays are my day to change my sheets. It's a habit I've gotten into, but if you want to go somewhere else, I'll understand. I know my place probably isn't what you're used to, especially after we just came from the Hansen penthouse—"

He shook his head to clear it, to bring his thoughts back to the here and now and the amazing woman in his arms. "I think," he said, backing her up deeper into her apartment until her legs hit the edge of her bed, "we both need to stop thinking." He kissed her again, his hands finding the curve of her waist, the soft globes of her ass, the elegant line of her spine.

She sighed and swayed into him, slightly stumbling, going limp in his arms as if trusting him to be the only reason why she was still upright. Then she yelped in surprise as he let go and she fell backward onto her bed, her legs bent and her feet on the ground. Before she could recover, he was on his knees, his hands running up the length of her calves, her thighs, persuading her to open for him, his hands finally free to push the silk of her dress up, up, up until she raised her arms and the garment slipped off.

Then it was his turn to gasp, a sharp inhale of breath, at seeing her exposed before him, only the tiniest, sheerest scrap of black lace covering her mound.

Mara raised herself on her elbows, her voice thick and slurred. "Please don't tear my panties, they cost more than my monthly grocery bill—oh!"

He kissed her inner thigh, once, twice, ten times, sucking and tasting and licking, moving ever higher to the most sensitive area of hers. "I won't," he said, his voice matching hers, and he pushed the scrap of lace to the side. One hand splayed on the warm silk across her belly as he brushed the thumb of his other hand over her stiff nub beneath. She jerked under his palm. A sharply inhaled hiss at his touch.

She was so warm and wet and welcoming,

her legs falling more open as he replaced his fingers with his mouth, tracing concentric circles around her sex and then delving into her opening, always paying careful, detailed attention to her clit, testing anew if she preferred featherlight strokes or more pressure. Mara didn't hesitate to let him know if his guesses were correct or wrong, her hand coming down to guide him to her favorite spot, her fingers urging him to faster or slower rhythms.

He became even harder, a feat previously thought impossible, as her hand stroked her clit as he teased her opening, her participation in her own pleasure heightening his. Then her hand fell to the side, her trembling legs beginning to stiffen, and he knew she was close.

He'd missed her. He hadn't realized how much until now—had kept himself too preoccupied, too busy for the last seven years to have space to contemplate what was missing from his life—but now he knew she was etched on his soul on an elemental level, as integral to him as water to drink or fire to keep warm. He slowed his ministrations, wanting the moment to last, wanting this time to never end.

She opened one angry eye. "I'm going to commit bodily damage if you don't go back to what you were doing," she said, her hips bucking against his hands, seeking the pressure she needed.

"I look forward to seeing what damage you can do," he said, and then sucked her into his mouth, laving her clit, tasting anew the sweetness that was Mara and Mara alone.

She screamed his name as she shuddered hard against him, and no sound had ever sounded better to his ears. He stayed where he was, reveling in her scent, her hot wetness, the knowledge he had caused her to fall to pieces, gentling his movements to match her slowing breathing.

When she started to emit tiny, breathy snores, he rose from his position, staring down at her. For the rest of his life, he would carry the impression of a sleeping, sated Mara, her limbs outstretched like a star, her skin pink and flushed, her red hair tousled and tossed. But when he would move away from the bed and leave her to her slumbers, a surprisingly strong grip on his arm stopped him.

"Oh, no, you don't," she said, blinking until the sleepiness disappeared to be replaced by bright mischief. Bright, somewhat evil mischief. She tugged at him until he lay beside her on the bed. Then she rose to her knees and looked down at him. "You're outrageously overdressed," she said. "Shy in your old age?"

"Ha. You know that's not true. Or should I go down on you again?" He rose on his elbows to grin at her.

"Nuh-uh," she said, pushing him back and straddling him before he could react.

There were erotic fantasies, and then there was a nude Mara Schuyler looking down on him, her beautiful rose-tipped breasts within easy reach, and he turned thought to action, reaching with his hands to bring her hard against him.

"Nuh-uh," she said again, and had his hands in hers and over his head before his surprised muscles could react. "Now. I could leave the bed and try to find my restraints, but I'm afraid this—"she rolled her core over the erection straining against his trousers "—might not like being left waiting. Or you could exercise that self-control of yours and grab onto my headboard until I tell you to let go."

"You own restraints?" His mind short-circuited with the images her words conjured.

"It's been seven years, Treharne. I like to keep up with the trends," she husked in his ear, the diamond-solid peaks of her breasts brushing against his shirt fabric. She guided his fingers to the metal bars of her Victorian-inspired bedframe. "You can let go when you want, of course." Mara started to kiss her way from his ear to his jaw, unbuttoning his shirt as she went. Then her mouth was on his throat, his own hard nipples, his belly, her knowing fingers following in her lips' wake to caress and tease until his skin was nothing but aching nerves.

Her hands found the zipper of his fly and pulled the tab down one metal tooth at time. His hips bucked and she placed her warm hand on his belly, holding him down. The look of pure satisfied power on her face almost sent him over the edge. Finally, his erection was freed and her soft gasp when he was finally bare to her sight made him feel pretty damn powerful, too.

"It's always nice when the reality is better than the memory," she said, her voice thick with an emotion he couldn't identify. Before he could ask her if she was okay, her mouth was on him and he forgot his own name. His universe narrowed to the hot, wet welcome he found, the sensations almost an unbearable pleasure-pain, as she learned him anew with her lips and tongue and gentle scrapes of her teeth.

"Mara," he panted, his eyes screwed shut, his hands gripping her headboard with all his strength, "if you're not careful—"

"I've got you," she said. She gave him one last tug with her mouth and then he heard the rip of a packet, followed by her fingers rolling the condom down his length. Her hand positioned him at her entrance and he opened his eyes so he could watch her sink down on him, her head tossed back to expose her throat, her chest rising and falling rapidly, her eyes wide with surprise and pleasure and something unreadable in their depths as he filled her. "Okay, let go," she breathed, her voice thick, and his hands flew up to hold her, to guide her, as she moved above him and he rose up to meet her.

When he came, he saw stars. And moons. An entire milky way as vast and as awe-inspiring as Mara. And as his vision cleared and his eyes met and tangled with her own passion-sated gaze, he saw home.

EIGHT

SUNLIGHT TICKLED DECLAN'S EYELIDS, the un-
familiar sensation teasing him awake. He normally slept with blackout curtains, a trick he
learned when working on stories around the
clock, to fool his brain into falling asleep no
matter the actual hour, so waking up to anything but dark shadows was disorienting. He
blinked...

And then he remembered.

He had to kick his left foot free from the tangle of the sheets. The bed resembled a battlefield
in which the two sides reached a most agree-
able compromise after several rounds of intense
skirmishing to determine who would end up
on top. Mara was curled up on her side, facing
away from him. The rays streaming through
the filmy white curtains turned her hair into a
red-gold cloud of tangles. The pale expanse of
her shoulders and back presented a strong temp-

tation to trace the knobs of her spine, kissing
his way as he discovered and named galaxies
of freckles.

He loved her skin in all its variations. The
soft smoothness of her inner thighs. The callous on the third finger of her right hand from
the wholly unique way she held writing instruments. The slight crinkles beginning to form
at the corners of her eyes, a testament to her
amazing, mobile expression and constant smile.

She needed her rest. So did he, come to think
of it. He always wondered why sex was referred
to as "sleeping together" when, in his experience and especially where Mara was concerned,
there was very little sleeping involved. But he
couldn't resist reaching out to run a finger
down her back. She sighed and stirred, and he
held himself up on one elbow to watch her eyelashes flutter. Then her eyes firmly closed and
her delightful snores—more like rusty squeaks
than a log being sawed—filled the air.

He found a pillow on the floor where it had
been tossed/kicked/thrown—he didn't remember which—and punched it back into shape, intending to join her in slumber, when a buzzing
noise jolted him wide awake.

A phone—set to vibrate instead of ring. Like

his. And the noise was coming from the corner of the room, where his pants were currently sprawled after she finally removed them.

He was conditioned to jump when a call came in. A source, a lead, a tip. If he didn't answer, he might lose out on the story of the century. But it was early Saturday morning, he wasn't on the tail of a story—well, not his story—and he wasn't on staff at the *Globe*. There could be a fire that needed to be put out at LNT, but he had very capable lieutenants and he couldn't think of anyone who would need him on the weekend.

A weekend he was beginning in Mara's bed, and he wasn't exiting his current situation for anyone. Besides, voice mail was invented for exactly this reason. The buzzing stopped and he closed his eyes.

The vibrations started again. Whoever was trying to reach him wasn't giving up easy. He muttered curses under his breath and retrieved his phone. If the caller was an LNT employee, they'd better have a very good reason to call or an ironclad contract if they didn't want to find themselves looking for a new gig. At least the noise didn't disturb Mara. She still slept, her mouth slightly open, an arm now flung over her eyes to block out the sunlight.

He'd never seen her look so delicious.

Then he glanced at the phone screen, at the caller's name, and all thoughts of sleep fled.

Mara's eyes fluttered open. She hadn't slept that hard or this long into the morning since... Since forever. She stretched, her muscles protesting in all sorts of new and rather wonderful ways, and for a second she wondered why—

Declan. She turned her head and the space next to her was empty, although there was evidence someone had been there recently. The sheets bore a vaguely human-shaped impression, but more than that, they bore his scent. She inhaled deeply before raising herself up on one elbow and scanning her tiny apartment. Nope. No sign of him. His clothes were no longer tossed to the furthest walls and he apparently even managed to find his shoes—she had a vague memory of someone's footwear flying into her kitchenette sink but it turned out those had been hers.

Oh, well. She tried not to be disappointed. It was probably for the best he left. They'd only promised each other one night and while she doubted the vivid memories created in the last eight hours or so would ever fade for her, better to not face him in the cold hard light of day and see regret—or worse, disappointment or pity—in his gaze. Seeing pity might literally dissolve her into sand.

A key sounded at her front door. She scrambled to clutch bedsheets to her bare chest, frantically trying to remember where she had stored her pepper spray, a gift from her brother when she announced she was moving to Manhattan. Who could possibly have a key and use it on a Saturday—

"I have pastries for you and bagels for me," she heard Declan announce as he entered, her ring of keys dangling from his left hand. "And coffee." He smiled when he caught her gaze. "Hope you don't mind. I borrowed your keys. Didn't want to leave your door unlocked while you were sleeping."

"I never kick out a person who brings pastries to my apartment. Even when I originally thought they were breaking in." She let the sheets fall as she stretched her arms overhead, aware the movement showed off her breasts to their best advantage, and was gratified by his quick inhale of breath. But when she would expect him to approach her—maybe even join her, naked and warm and willing on the bed—

he stayed where he was, then moved only to drop the bag and tray of coffee on the small table that pulled double duty as her desk and place to dine. She frowned at him as she reached for the blanket that had fallen to the floor and pulled it tight around her shoulders. The room had taken a chilly turn, and the change in temperature was only partially due to him letting in air from the outside. "You've got something on your mind."

"Do you still take two sugars in your coffee?" He concentrated on opening packets, neatly avoiding her gaze.

"Yes." She accepted the cup he handed her, but put it down on her bedside table, pressing her lips together tightly. It seemed there would be no repeat of last night. And that's what she wanted, right? He'd agreed to her terms. She should appreciate that he was a man of his word. "You can leave, y'know. The breakfast is great, don't get me wrong. But there's no need to do that awkward morning-after dance you do. After all, the sooner you leave, the sooner I can shower, which honestly sounds better than caffeine right now."

He half smiled, half grimaced. "That's not what I'm doing—"

"Maybe someone who doesn't recall you doing a very similar move seven years ago might be fooled, but not me." She tried to fully smile back, but she was pretty sure her expression matched his. "We said one night, we had one night—"

"A great night—" he started.

"Agreed." She cut him off. "Don't worry, last night will not come up when I'm asked to share my 'worst sex ever' stories."

"Wasn't worried, but thanks for the reassurance." He sat down on the other side of the bed. "This isn't seven years ago—"

"I know. I own restraints now. Even if I can't find them." By sheer force of will, her smile did not tremble. "So, we don't need to do this."

"Mara—" he started.

"We banged. It's out of our systems. We can now go about our lives as usual." She made a shooing motion with her hands. "I'll see you on Monday."

He regarded her through narrowed eyes. Then, finally, as if coming to an agreement with himself, he nodded. "If that's what you want."

"We were curious. Now we're not. It's just sex, Treharne. You're still taking me to the Lochlainn event, right?"

He stood up. Was it her imagination or a trick of the light that made his face suddenly seem ghostly pale? "About that. Listen, something—"

"Oh, no. No, you don't." Mara scrambled out of bed and wrapped the blanket around her like a makeshift toga. "You are not getting out of taking me."

"I'm not trying to. But there may not be an event." He walked to the table and opened the bag. "Pastry? I recall you prefer cherry strudel. No matter how cliché."

"Cherry strudel is the one true pastry. The rest are pale pretenders." Still, she wasn't going to be put off by food, even if the bag did come from her favorite local bakery. "What do you mean? Why won't the event take place?"

He opened a small container of cream cheese and began spreading it on a bagel. "Keith Lochlainn is in the hospital."

"Really?" She grabbed her phone and started scrolling through her social media accounts. "There's nothing on my feeds. Did someone at LNT tell you?"

"No, I—yes. Yes. Someone from the Lochlainn Company called."

"Is it serious?"

He shook his head. "A precaution. Or so they told me."

"Glad to hear it." She squinted at him. If she wasn't mistaken, that was the third time he'd put cream cheese on that bagel half. Either he really liked a healthy portion, or he was avoiding looking at her.

Interesting. This was turning into a pattern whenever the Lochlainns were mentioned.

Of course, Keith Lochlainn was the big boss. Declan wasn't one of his direct reports, but it made sense any employee of a Lochlainn business entity would be affected by news of Keith's hospitalization. But why was Declan specifically informed? The news wasn't public yet. Why did he need to know?

On the other hand, he was an executive with the news division, perhaps he needed to be standing by in case the "precaution" took a turn for the worse and some sort of tribute or obituary would need to be aired. But even as the thoughts formed, she rejected them. That was a decision for someone higher up the food chain to make, not him.

Something wasn't adding up. And that something started with the way Declan was currently avoiding her. She sipped her coffee, her brain chasing the puzzle.

"You seem far away," he said, his gaze finally meeting hers.

"I'm wondering why you rate a call from the Lochlainn Company."

"Why wouldn't I rate one?"

"Well, you're *you*, so of course you rate a call as a journalist, but at LNT you're just a producer—"

"Executive producer—"

"Right, but you're not the president of LNT or the executive in charge of news so…why?"

"Why not?" He bit into his bagel.

"I don't know, I…" She started to laugh. "You have cream cheese on your nose."

He rubbed the back of his hand across his nose. The cream cheese spread farther.

"Here, let me." She grabbed one of the thin paper napkins and dabbed at the offending spot. "There." She took a half step back to admire her handiwork, and her heart twinged—a painful pinch. He was so handsome. And he wasn't attractive because of the symmetry of his features or his chiseled bone structure, but because of his soul, for lack of a better word. The light that shone in his eyes when he was excited or interested, the slow smile that she could swear was just for her.

Like the smile he had now. Intimate, warm. Pure sex.

She was very aware she wore nothing but a blanket haphazardly wrapped around her. And the glint in his eyes told her he was very aware of her attire, too. The rush of hot moisture between her legs nearly made her knees buckle.

"Mara," he breathed, and she knew she was being weak, she knew she would regret doing so, but she swayed in his direction, her hands coming to rest on his chest. His firm, warm chest.

"Yes?" she said, her tone matching his.

"You have some cream cheese..." He motioned to the corner of his mouth.

"I do?" She reached up but didn't feel anything.

"Here," he said, and his thumb rubbed ever so softly over her lower lip, his gaze locked on hers. She inhaled sharply at his touch, the aching pressure building in her core—

Wait. She ate a cherry strudel, not a bagel. She smiled at him and leaned back, so that her hand could find the cream cheese container. She used her index finger to take a swipe and then, before he could react, she smeared the cream cheese across his upper lip. "Whoops. Looks like I didn't get all of it."

"You better get on that," he said, his thumb moving to the corner of her mouth, the curve of her jaw.

"Yeah, maybe I should," she said, and then she leaned up and kissed him, her tongue sweeping all evidence away before he pulled her to him and all thought of engaging in more food related pranks fled.

Forget breakfast. She hungered for only one thing and that was Declan. And judging by his hard length pressing against her, he had similar ideas. She tore her mouth from his. "One night. No more. And never to be discussed after."

He let his hands fall. She instantly regretted her words as his grip had been doing more to keep her upright than her own legs. "Right. Sorry, I—"

"But we didn't discuss the fine print."

"You want to discuss fine print?"

"We're not supposed to talk about sex after. So yes, now. To ensure all parties are on the same evidentiary page and all obligations are outlined."

His smile returned. "Wasn't aware you got a legal degree in the last seven years."

"They put me on the consumer affairs beat at the station," she said. "Anyway, 'night' was never defined. One could argue that a night is half a day, which makes it twelve hours long, and since we got back to my place at midnight, that means—"

"We have two and a half hours left." His arms wrapped around her and drew her right for a kiss so hard and deep she forgot her name. He broke off long enough to whisper, "That argument wouldn't stand up in court. But I accept the fine print." His left hand drew patterns on her spine, teasing swoops and swirls that caused her to shiver and laugh.

"What are you doing?"

"Signing my name on the dotted line," he responded, then covered her mouth with his again, his fingers traveling to explore the skin of her hip before cupping her ass and bringing her up hard against the proof he was more than ready to continue their "night."

She was so sensitive, craving him so much that when he slipped a hand between them to whisper over her mound, slipping his index finger inside her for the barest of touches to see if she was as ready as he was, she almost came.

But she didn't want to. She had clawed back

two and a half hours more with Declan and she wanted to make them count, not be dissolved in a boneless heap of pleasure for most of the time. And if she only had this time, then she was determined to use it to know him fully, storing up memories like so many hoarded jewels to be taken out and examined long into the future. Memories of him that, no matter where their lives might take them, would belong only to her.

"What was that you were saying about a bath?" he said into her neck, his hands now knowing how to roll and tweak her nipples, how much pressure to apply and when to back off, so that she nearly wept with pleasure.

"There's no way two of us are fitting in my shower," she gasped.

"Tsk-tsk." He clicked his tongue. "Where there's a will, there's a way." Kissing her the entire time, he guided her to her tiny bathroom, with its child-sized tub and handheld shower bracketed to the wall.

"See?" she said. "Let's go back to the bed." She used their time standing to undress him anew until they both stood nude, his skin warm and golden to her flushed and freckled pinkness.

He grinned at her and turned around until

they both faced her mirror, which ran the length of the room. "I think we should stay here," he said, stroking her skin as he held her gaze in the mirror. His hand came up to cup her breast before dipping between her legs. His erection pressed against the globes of her ass and she bit her lip as the Mara in the mirror bit hers.

He cupped her mound and the Mara in the mirror jumped, then relaxed into his touch. She started to close her eyes, the better to give herself over to the sensation his fingers created, but he tugged on her hair. "Watch," he said. "Watch yourself come apart." He pressed deeper inside her, finding just the right spot, caressing and retreating and caressing again. "Watch," he said again, his gaze never leaving hers, and she almost cried with how vulnerable she was—open not only to his sight but to her own—and yet how incredibly powerful she felt, watching him watching her in the mirror. He added a second finger and his thumb found her clit, circling and pressing until she couldn't take any more—

"Eyes open," he demanded. But she didn't watch herself. She found his gaze and held it as she flew apart in his arms, allowing another person—allowing him—to see her bared soul for the first time ever.

It wasn't until they were back in her bed, boneless and breathless and falling asleep, that she remembered he never did answer her question about why the Lochlainn Company called him about Keith.

The next time Mara woke up, the clock read one o'clock. Their night was well and truly over.

Declan's side was empty, any warmth he'd left behind long gone. There was a note on his pillow, however. His scrawled handwriting read simply, "See you on Monday."

She crumpled the piece of paper up, and then thought better of her actions and smoothed the note out. This wasn't seven years ago. She'd used her words like a big person and asked him for sex. And he, like an adult, respected the boundaries she set.

No one told her how much being a grown up could hurt.

NINE

Bobbi would not stop calling. Declan sent her latest phone call to voice mail and sat back in his chair in his office at LNT, contemplating his next moves. He didn't know where else to go on a Sunday. He used his apartment mostly for sleeping, showering and changing his clothes. He currently wasn't in the mood to stare at the blank walls he never did get around to decorating. He wasn't a film or television watcher, and his head was too full of Mara, too full of reliving every second he'd spent with her in the last twenty-four hours, to be able to concentrate on reading.

So, work it was. Work was familiar. Work was something within his control.

Leaving Mara's bed was one of the hardest things Declan had ever done, and he included being embedded with a small force that was fighting to liberate their invaded country when the enemy bombarded their position, forcing them to run. Then, he had been fighting for his life. Now he had a feeling he was fighting for something much more important and precious.

But impossible for him to reach. And perhaps, that was the best place for it.

He never tortured himself over things he couldn't obtain. By paying attention solely to what was possible in the present, he avoided remorse over the past and apprehension about the future. His ability to stay in the here and now was, in part, why he was an effective interviewer, keeping his subjects tightly focused on the subject at hand and steering them away from tangents that would derail their conversation.

Until he ran into Cam that fateful day and learned how much he had inadvertently screwed over Mara. Now, his thoughts were occupied more often than not with the past.

With what-might-have-been if he hadn't been so intent on proving Keith Lochlainn wrong, of demonstrating that Keith would be sorry he did not acknowledge Declan was Jamie's biological son. If he hadn't steamrollered his way to the fellowship, failing to ask questions about why the story fell into his lap at that particular time.

And for what? Keith might be dying that very second. Declan destroyed his then relationship with Mara to show up his biological grandfather, only for his grandfather to perhaps pass away without once acknowledging him. The closest he might ever get to being acknowledged as Jamie's son was his position at LNT, a position that came with strings attached and one Declan didn't want for himself in the first place.

But the past was just that. The past. He couldn't go backward, only forward. And dreams...of falling into bed with Mara every night, of sitting across from each other as they composed their stories, of tag teaming heads of state or going into battle zones side by side... were, well, dreams. They weren't reality.

Instead, reality was his phone ringing again. He exhaled before answering. "Yes, Bobbi."

"Do you want these tickets to Paris or what? Speak now or they will forever go to Griff Beachwood."

"Griff— You're not giving the story to Beachwood. This bluff is unworthy of you."

Bobbi sighed through the phone. "We're going to lose the de la Vigny story. *WaPo*, the *Guardian*, *Le Monde*—they're all sniffing. But we're the only ones with the solid lead. And we're the only ones who have you and all your previous work on this story. Or at least, we should have you. You promised if I gave you this leave of absence, you'd come back if the right story surfaced. And this is the right story."

He didn't respond, his gaze staring out of his window and into the office in the building next door. The occupant was doing what she always did at this time of day: concentrating on her computer screen, her fingers flying over her keyboard. Same old, same old. The idea of doing the same thing every workday still made his skin prickle. But then the door to her office opened and another woman appeared, holding the hand of a small child. The office occupant got up from her chair and embraced the new-comer, then knelt and gave the child a hug. Their joy could be felt even where he sat. The child squirmed free and made their way to the window, causing Declan to swiftly swivel his chair so he couldn't be caught observing them.

"Dec? You still there?" Bobbi barked into his ear. "Did you hear me? If you don't hustle your ass into action, we're going to be last in. We'll be scooped by the *Daily Mail*."

"The *Mail* only cares about the salacious bits. The rest of the story is safe." What was wrong with him? Why wasn't he already on the way to Paris? He lived for this kind of work. Forget blood—this was the substance that kept his heart pumping: running bad actors to ground, exposing their operations and providing so much sunlight they had nowhere else to hide and must face some sort of justice. But—his peripheral vision caught a glimpse of the family in the office across the way preparing to leave together, each woman holding one of the child's hands and swinging the kid between them—maybe one didn't have to live solely for work. Maybe there were other things in the world that could cause his heart to beat as fast.

"Last chance." Bobbi's voice wobbled. And while Declan often forgot she was in her seventies, for the first time she sounded like she would rather be enjoying her retirement than trying to sweet-talk a recalcitrant journalist. "I'd like to be the one to own this story. We've been following it for a long time. You've worked hard on it. But if you can't—"

"If I know Alice at all, she won't talk to the others," he said. "We have some time. I need to stay in New York through the weekend." Bobbi inhaled to speak, and he cut her off. "That's nonnegotiable. Then I'll give my resignation to

LNT and arrange to work through my notice period remotely from Paris. In the meantime, I'll share my notes with Beachwood, have him start working on background."

"You better get on that plane," Bobbi said right before she hung up, which Declan knew was her way of saying "thank you."

A week. He bought himself a week to wrap up what he wanted to accomplish at LNT and then turn his duties over to his lieutenants, who, if he were being honest, were doing the bulk of the heavy lifting anyway; he had been lucky and grateful to have been given a team who were all more experienced than he was and who were generous with their time and expert knowledge in putting together the launch schedule for the service. LNT Plus would be in excellent hands and he had no qualms on that front.

With regards to the Lochlainns, however... Leaving early would violate the terms of the challenge handed to him by Keith. Not that Declan was salivating to be included in the old man's will. He didn't need the Lochlainn money.

The one thing he did want was to be acknowledged as Jamie's son, but that had never been part of the LNT offer. Declan had hoped—well, he never really put his hopes into words, not even to himself, but he *supposed*—working for LNT would bring clarity about things he had long wondered about himself. Did he inherit his love of story, and putting puzzle pieces together into a coherent whole, from Jamie? Or his drive to expose and bring down those who would exploit and harm others? Jamie had reported on those same types of stories. But then where did Declan fit in with Keith? Could he have—would he have had—a better relationship with him, considering Jamie had renounced Keith?

If Keith died... Declan rubbed the back of his neck. If Keith died, there went his long-held but never voiced fantasy of bringing reconciliation to the Lochlainn family. Of stepping into the void Jamie left, unable to be Keith's son. Perhaps Declan would claim a true grandson-grandfather relationship.

He never thought he needed a father while growing up. His mother had given him a truly wonderful life, full of amazing experiences and constant exposure to new cultures and ways of thinking. His world had been truly vast.

But when his mother died and he discovered Jamie was his biological father... Well, he supposed it was only natural he wanted to get to know the people whose genes he carried. And wanted them to get to know him.

He picked up a ball made of multicolored rubber bands and began tossing it into the air. He had a mind for investigation. What made a family a family in the first place?

A light came on in the office opposite his and the family hurried back into the room. Apparently the child had forgotten something, for there was much kneeling on the floor and peering under office furniture. Finally, one of the women stood up and raised her arms in victory, a small object in her hand. The other woman picked up the child, who nestled into her shoulder. Their contented happiness was evident even from where Declan sat.

So what if Keith died without acknowledging him, a possibility that now was looming darkly? He didn't need to be a Lochlainn to have a family. He could choose to have a partner, a child, a life outside of work.

His gaze fell on his phone. He picked up the device and swiped to find his list of recent contacts. Mara's name was near the top—

Next to Bobbi's.

He put the phone down. He had commitments he couldn't ignore. Commitments that made the world safer for others. He'd fulfilled his main reason for accepting the challenge to work at LNT: Mara was on the path to career success that should have been hers all along. He had no reason to stay.

He nodded. He would make that plane to Paris.

And there were a million things he had to accomplish before he turned in his resignation. He turned on his computer and opened a new document, resolutely ignoring his phone. Mara made her terms clear. If she wanted to talk, she could call him.

But when he stared at his computer monitor, all he could see was Mara's gaze holding his in the mirror as he made her come, her need and want for him laid naked and bare before him. Not momentary sexual passion, but her soul, yearning for connction. Yearning for *him*.

As was his for her.

Mara did not see Declan on Monday. Her producer had lined up back-to-back interviews with a gallery owner in SoHo and an art history professor at Columbia for background on Robaire's life and his impact on both the art world and current pop culture. Both interviews were highly informative and full of sound bites that would be very helpful when pulling the edited story together, but both interviews also ran long. By the time Mara returned to the office, Declan had long left for what his assistant vaguely called, "a business thing."

Nor did she see him on Tuesday, Wednesday, Thursday or Friday as their schedules were similarly out of sync. She missed their staff meeting when her subway train broke down. Declan missed their weekly one-on-one check-in when one of the other correspondents angered a senator and Declan was needed to smooth over the relationship. They discussed meeting up at the LNT town hall, a mandatory all-hands gathering of the staff at which the company's goals for next year were presented, but a pipe burst in the apartment next to Mara's and the landlord needed access to her place to check for damage, while Declan had another "pressing engagement come up that couldn't be moved,", according to his assistant. Which meant her first time seeing him would be at the gallery dedication.

He wasn't wholly incommunicado, of course. He texted her several times. About work.

And he called. About work. Maybe the calls would have turned to more personal matters,

but they were cut off early because Declan had
to take care of a pressing office emergency or
Mara was about to sit down and talk to a source.

He didn't mention the hours in her apartment.
But then, neither did she.

Because she was a coward. Because she allowed her to see her deepest depths, but when
she next woke up, he was gone. Because she
feared that seeing her so nakedly laid bare before him, all pretense that their night was only
about sex torn to shreds, had driven him away.

Because she believed being that vulnerable to
him would ultimately lead to being hurt and
betrayed, and the devastation to her psyche
would be even more catastrophic than what
happened seven years ago.

By the time Saturday appeared on the calendar, Mara's nerves were strung tight. She threw
on her workout clothes and made one of her in-
frequent trips to the gym, a small, homey space
with the bare basics in terms of equipment. The
gym didn't have extended hours and that didn't
work with her schedule, but she liked the un-
pretentious atmosphere. It was a place to work
out and nothing more.

The speed bag was unoccupied, much to her
delight. Hitting something sounded like the

perfect match to her mood. She got into her stance, bouncing lightly on the balls of her feet, and settled into a rhythm. Before long, muscle memory took over the repetitive motion and her mind began to wander to the previous Saturday—the exact thing she was hoping to stop by coming to the gym.

Damn it. The whole purpose of sleeping together was to alleviate the tension between them. But that had obviously been a lie. So now, she found herself thinking of him at the most inopportune times, like in the middle of an interview question. The interview would be going swimmingly and then an image of Declan's fingers trailing a path from the underside of her breast to her stomach and beyond would cause her to sputter, her cheeks flushing hot. She'd been able to pass off her sudden lapses in attention as an irritation in her throat requiring a sip of water, which allowed her to regain her composure, but her producer and cameraperson were starting to raise their eyebrows at her when the flashes of memory happened.

Like now.

She hit the bag with more force than she intended.

"Whoa!" Amaranth Thomas, the gym's co-owner and Mara's closest friend in the city, appeared by Mara's side, her dark eyes wide. "Let the bag live to see another day."

"Sorry." Mara stepped away from the speed bag, much to the visible happiness of the young teenager waiting for her to finish her workout. "Lots on my mind."

"Want to talk about it? Or work more of it out?" Amaranth nodded at the boxing ring visible in the next room. "My client just cancelled their training. We can go a few rounds?"

Mara looked at the clock on the gym's wall. She still had many hours to go before she needed to shower and change for the Lochlainn event. "Sure. Give me ten minutes to get ready?"

"Seven," Amaranth responded. "You need as much time as possible in the ring."

"Five," Mara conceded, and ran-walked to the small dressing area where she kept a locker to store her gloves. Hands wrapped, hair pulled back anew, she was ready to go in four minutes.

Amaranth had her blue-tipped locks pulled back in a ponytail—an indication her friend was not going to take pity on her. Mara held up her gloved hands. "Go easy. I have to attend an event tonight."

"Another one? Let me guess—same guy?"

Amaranth bobbed on her feet, then threw a straightforward jab that Mara easily slipped. "Is that a problem?"

"Yes to all," Mara said, evading another jab and throwing her own punch. "It's complicated."

"What in life isn't?" Amaranth circled. Mara knew she was looking for chinks in her defense, of which there were many. "Rent is skyrocketing, my kid's best friend is suddenly ghosting him at school and the algorithms are burying this place on review sites. But you pick up and keep up." An intense jab-jab-cross combination had Mara heading toward the ropes.

"I hate to hear Trey is having problems with his friend," Mara said, somewhat breathless while trying to land her counterattack. "I sympathize. In fact, the guy in question? He ghosted me for seven years. Right after I slept with him."

Amaranth's feet stopped moving, but she still evaded Mara's right and left hook combo. "Okay. This might be beyond boxing. This might need a drink. Buy you a smoothie?"

"I thought you'd never ask." Mara climbed out of the ring, already sore despite the brief bout. She really had to come to the gym more often. Not only for the physical exercise, but because Amaranth was one of the few connections she'd made since moving to New York City. And she was only now realizing how much she missed having a friend to chat with in person. Zoom and FaceTime, although godsends when in person get togethers were impossible, were not great substitutions for being able to hang out in three-dimensional space.

Sitting at the juice bar counter over protein shakes, Mara poured out the entire story of her relationship with Declan, from their first meeting at college orientation to waking up to a note on her pillow last weekend. Amaranth listened, her calm gaze refusing to judge until, finally, Mara ran out of words. "What's tonight?" Amaranth asked. "The event?"

"It's another one of those 'rich people congratulating themselves on staying rich' things," Mara said. "The Lochlainn family is dedicating a wing of the Museum of Contemporary Culture in the name of Jamie Lochlainn."

"Lochlainn—as in Keith Lochlainn? Isn't he ill?"

Mara nodded. The news hit the media hours after Declan left her apartment. "He was. He's apparently better, so they are going ahead with the dedication, although I'm not sure if he will be there in person."

"And who's Jamie?"

"Keith's son. He disappeared seven years ago and was recently declared legally dead. Jamie was an investigative journalist—a legend, really, despite being relatively young—but his mother was a well-respected artist and Jamie was known as a big supporter of the arts, so I'm assuming that's why Keith chose a museum as a memorial."

"Sounds nice and cultural," Amaranth commented. "So, your problem isn't the event itself."

"Well, sort of." Mara chewed on her smoothie straw. "I'm playing a hunch. And if my hunch is right, this could be a huge story for me. Career-making. But I have no idea if I'm right. Or if the person I need to show up will show up. I'm going off only the flimsiest of evidence, plus my own gut."

"But that's not why you beat up on my poor innocent equipment."

Mara let her head hang forward so her hair, freed from her earlier ponytail, would hide her face. "No."

"So it's the guy."

"It's the guy," she admitted.

"Tell me something." Amaranth leaned her elbows on the counter. "Why does the guy have to be the problem?"

"What do you mean? He's the problem because he's the problem."

"Sure. But why does he have to be?" Amaranth took a contemplative sip. "Seems to me there's really not much of an issue between you two after all."

Mara straightened up. "He ghosted me seven years ago!"

"You told me. But that was a while ago. And he apologized, right?"

"Yes, but—"

"And you've slept with him since, both willing and consenting adults, and from the look on your face it was pretty damn good."

"It was, but—"

"And now you're going to yet another fancy event with him? And he doesn't have to go, right? He's only going because of you?"

"Well, yes, but—"

Amaranth held up a hand. "No buts. Your 'buts' don't work here. Look, I don't know Declan. But in my experience, single men don't get dressed up and go to boring society events with single women just out of some sort of obligation. He wants you. And you want him. So why does this have to be a problem?

Mara sat back on her stool. "He's my boss."

Amaranth opened her mouth, then closed it. "Oh."

"But he told HR we had previously dated, to prevent that from being something someone might try to hold over our heads," Mara rushed to add. "And after the second event, he suggested we sign consensual agreement contracts with HR, in case people thought we were dating." She put her smoothie down. "Huh. Guess he was psychic."

"Or hoping something would happen between the two of you." Amaranth waggled her eyebrows, earning a smirk from Mara. Then Amaranth turned sober. "And are you okay with dating your boss? That's hard because of the power differential. I don't date clients for that reason. Too many things can… go wonky."

Mara puffed air toward her forehead. "We're not dating."

Amaranth raised her eyebrows. "You get

dressed up and go out at night, and you've slept together. Is there another definition of dating I'm not familiar with?"

"Maybe the kind of dating where you both agree you are dating?"

Amaranth waved that off. "Technicality. I'll ask again. Why are you making this a problem? You want him, sounds like he wants you, you're squared away with your company—what's the issue? The real one this time."

Mara squeezed her eyes tight. "He might ghost me again."

"Good news—you already know you can survive that one. And you work together. Doubtful it would happen the same way it did before. Next?"

"I don't think... I mean, I..." Mara let her head fall. "I want to win Emmys. I want to win Pulitzers. I want to go on book tours promoting my latest book all about the amazing investigative reporting I did."

Amaranth squinted at her. "Sounds good. What does that have to do with dating him?"

"I don't want to give up my career. Not even for him."

A burst of laughter came from her friend.

"What makes you think you have to? Where did that come from?"

"From people I know! Well, people who identify as female. They all met someone, fell in love and gave up their passion to be with the other person."

"I didn't." Amaranth swiveled on her stool and indicated the boxing studio behind them. "I built this place when I was with Trey's dad. Next excuse."

Mara played with the empty straw wrapper. "I'm…afraid."

"Honey, we all are. But it's worth it. Even if it doesn't ultimately work out."

"We…had a moment. An intense moment." Mara shivered at the memory. "But he doesn't do intense. I don't do intense. We haven't really spoken since—" "But you'll see him tonight."

"Yes." Mara continued to play with the wrapper.

"At a fancy party with champagne and oysters." Amaranth clicked her tongue. "Still not hearing a problem."

That made Mara chuckle. "Don't know if there will be oysters."

"Then go and get some after. Add some dark chocolate and get your intense on. Problem solved." Amaranth pushed her stool out and slid back. "My next client will be here shortly. You coming to class on Tuesday?"

"I'll do my best to make it."

"Good, because I want to hear all about what happens tonight. The juicy stuff, too." She waggled her eyebrows at Mara and Mara laughed. "See you then."

"You will. And thanks." She stood up to give Amaranth a hug.

"Anytime." Amaranth smiled and then crossed the studio where she met a woman Mara recognized from her previous trips to the gym. She gave them both a wave before returning to her stool and her smoothie.

Was her friend right? Was Mara creating speed bumps in a flat, smooth road? Could she and Declan date—really date? Like lazy Sunday mornings competing to see who could complete the New York Times crossword first, late night discussions over a glass of wine and weekends at her family's farm upstate? Was that what he wanted?

Was that what she wanted?

Gods help her. She was back in love with Declan.

Oh, who was she kidding. She never fully fell out of love with him.

This was awful.

This was wonderful.

This had the potential to either make her the happiest she'd ever been or destroy her.

TEN

DECLAN ARRIVED AT the soon-to-be christened Jamie Lochlainn Gallery at the Museum of Contemporary Culture an hour before the ceremony was supposed to begin. The large, airy space buzzed with noise and bustle as the organizers and their staff ran around making last minute adjustments and ensuring all the details were buttoned down and taken care of. Swag bags were being carefully lined up on tables, tweaks were being made to floral arrangements and a woman with a clipboard and a light meter hurried from spot to spot, speaking with a low but firm voice into her wireless headset, ensuring the art was properly illuminated no matter where one stood. It was an educational glimpse into how much work went on behind the scenes to pull an event like this off and he found himself wishing Mara was with him to share in his observations. But when he received the request to arrive early, he held off asking her to join him and instead arranged to have a car pick her up closer to the ceremony's start time.

Not that he was trying to avoid spending more time with her. On the contrary, the more days that passed where they failed to make a connection, the more the acid in his stomach churned. If this kept up, he'd be looking at his first ulcer before thirty. They needed to talk. And soon. He would be handing in his resignation on Monday, and he didn't want her to be blindsided by the news. He knew he'd made an implicit promise to see her though the art forgery story, but she would be fine. Cliff was an excellent producer, and the piece was shaping up to be the breakout story of LNT's launch week.

In fact, he should have already called her and told her he was leaving. Sent a text. Left a voice mail. But every time he picked up his phone to tell her, he put it back down.

Telling her would make it real. Telling her would mean his time with her was over.

They'd see each other again, no doubt. They would run into each other at award ceremonies and conferences. They might even cover the same stories and find themselves sharing a drink as they discussed sources.

Thinking of that future depressed him. So, he'd hung on to the present as much as he could, doing his best to wrap up his loose ends at LNT while his night with Mara continued to play in his head, capturing more and more of his brain space with each vivid replay.

She was the first thing he thought about when he woke up, and the last image he saw behind his eyelids as he fell asleep. He wanted to know her thoughts: Did she read the front page story in the *Globe* about the latest privacy concerns for social media? What was her reaction to the two-part feature on their rival network ABN about the rising political power of people under the age of twenty? He found himself storing up funny things that happened over the course of the day to share with her later. When he ran into Mads and the author of the novel currently topping the bestseller list while they took a tour around the LNT studio, he broke every rule he had for himself about encountering celebrities and got her to sign an autographed copy for Mara because he knew it was a recent favorite read of hers.

He'd thought he'd have plenty of opportunities to give the book to her, but their paths seemed more divergent than ever, never crossing even in the hallways.

And now he was out of time.

His gaze was caught by the reason why he showed up to the dedication so early and he inclined his head in acknowledgment. Catalina Lochlainn smiled back and, after excusing herself, glided across the polished floor toward him. Hard to believe that in an alternate life, a life where Keith acknowledged he was Jamie's son when Declan reached out to Keith with his evidence, he might have had a relationship with her as his step-grandmother.

"Thank you for coming so early." Catalina's voice was husky, with a hint of her native Castilian accent. Declan knew from his research that she grew up in Madrid and spent several years working in advertising in the Spanish capital before meeting and marrying Keith.

"The invitation was irresistible," he said. "But then, you knew that. How is Keith? Has he settled in well at home after leaving the hospital?"

He kept his tone light and neutral. He'd learned not to expect much information from the Lochlainns. Even with accepting the challenge to program LNT Plus's launch week, he'd been given precious little insight into why Keith had chosen him for the assignment or to what end.

"He is recovering, but he won't be able to be here tonight."

"I hope he gets well soon," he said automatically, tamping the unexpected and unwanted disappointment down. "Anyway, I'm here as you asked. What can I do for you?"

Catalina looked around the space. "I was hoping preparations would be further along so you and I could have a good chat. Unfortunately, I still have much work do. So straight to the point, I want to persuade you to join me on the stage for the dedication in Keith's absence." Declan opened his mouth, but she cut him off with a quick shake of her head. "As someone who is following in Jamie's footsteps as a courageous journalist who fights for justice for those unable to fight. Jamie may be no longer with us, but you are carrying on his work."

Declan worked moisture back into his mouth. "I'm…" he searched for the right words to say. He settled on, "…flattered you would ask. But I don't know if that would be…" He searched again, "…appropriate, perhaps, is the best way to phrase it. It feels like a cheat. You and I know there is another connection. But Keith won't acknowledge it. Instead he plays his games, like his challenge at LNT, but only for a mention in his will." He hesitated. "Once upon a time, I would have jumped at the opportunity to be identified with the Lochlainn family. Even a connection as tenuous as the one you're offering. But I shouldn't need to remind you or Keith of Jamie. My existence should be enough. *I* should be enough."

"I know." Catalina tucked a lock of glossy black hair behind her ear. "You're right. And I am sorry. Keith is… Keith, and he has his reasons for acting the way he is, even though I have argued strenuously he is only hurting you and Anna—"

"Anna?" A hand squeezed his stomach, a most disorienting sensation. "Who is Anna?"

"Right. I've been so preoccupied with the dedication. I'm not thinking straight." Catalina inhaled, and then took his right hand in hers. "We discovered—well, Keith's investigator discovered—Jamie's sperm was used to conceive two children. You, and a daughter named Anna."

Declan blinked. That was the only muscle

group that seemed to be working. The rest of him was frozen, processing Catalina's words. "I have a half-sister," he said slowly. "And you and Keith knew."

Catalina moistened her lips. "Yes. But Keith didn't want either of you to feel as if you had to be in competition with each other. You understand, his father... Well, Archibald insisted on Keith earning his place at the Lochlainn Company, and with Jamie now officially gone, Keith is obsessed with passing on the company to an heir who has also earned it. So, he decided each of you would learn about the family business by being involved with an aspect of it that Jamie loved. Anna was sent to sell Lakes of Wonder, which was Jamie's favorite place growing up, and—"

"And I was sent to LNT. Because Jamie and I are both journalists."

She nodded. "I think Keith was hoping one of you, or both, would fall in love with the business you were sent to learn about. And then he would hand off the entirety of the Lochlainn Company to you or her."

Declan's head was shaking even before she finished speaking. "I'm leaving LNT. I'm announcing my resignation on Monday. And if

Keith wanted to know my thoughts about inheriting the entire company, he knew where to find me." He filed away the information about his half-sister to examine for later. He had enough issues to deal with for one night.

"I understand. I told Keith not to do this, but…" She bit her lower lip, and then shrugged. "Back to the matters directly at hand. I still believe having you on stage with me would be meaningful. And appropriate. Keith may have chosen an art gallery to honor Jamie, but we know Jamie's heart laid in his reporting. And even without your connection to Jamie being public, you are still the highest regarded heir to his journalism legacy."

"I'll think about it." He wished Mara was there to discuss Catalina's offer. On the one hand, being part of an event honoring his biological father—and more important, his professional hero—would be meaningful. But on the other, learning Keith was willing to hand over the Lochlainn Company to him or Anna, yet there was still no talk of recognizing his blood tie to Jamie… That hurt. More than he thought would be logically possible.

He could go public about his Lochlainn DNA on his own, of course. Announce to the

world he was Jamie's son. He had the paternity
tests to prove it; Keith demanded them before
Declan started work at LNT.

But he didn't need the world to acknowledge
his connection to Jamie.

Just his grandfather.

Which wasn't happening.

Catalina touched him on the arm. "Thank
you for considering my offer. I can ask for
nothing more, I know." Someone called her
name from behind Declan and she waved at
them. "That is the head curator. I must go."
She handed him her card. "This is my number.
Please text me and let me know your decision.
Even if the ceremony has already started."

"Wait," he called after her. "The Robaire
you're unveiling as part of the dedication—do
you know its provenance?"

Her brow wrinkled. "It came from a collection of a very private Portuguese collector,
which is why the painting hasn't been exhib-
ited in public before. It was quite the coup to
obtain the piece. I'm told the bidding was quite
intense, but Keith was determined to win the
artwork for Jamie's gallery. Why do you ask?"

He shrugged. "It's a previously unknown
piece and I'm a big fan of the artist."

"That's another thing you have in common with Jamie. Robaire was his favorite artist. Well, after his mother, Diana, of course. I am so sorry she died before she could meet you." She patted his arm lightly. "Please let me know."

"I will." And then Catalina was off in a cloud of subtle perfume that smelled mostly of expense.

So, the Robaire was yet another piece that came from the very private collector. Mara's story definitely had legs.

The frenetic activity that marked his arrival began to die down as the museum staff and the event organizers took their stations and the hour of the event drew close. Declan wandered the space and stopped to look at the various artwork on the wall—including a painting by Diana Lochlainn, his biological grandmother. The canvas was a cacophony of bold, dark strokes interspersed with touches of almost brilliant light. The result was an abstract piece that was wild and passionate, the emotions leaping off the canvas. A placard next to the painting informed him that Diana has created it the year Jamie disappeared, just two years before she died.

He stared at the photo of Diana with a young Jamie, fixed on the wall above the placard. He was glad the public would see this painting for years to come. He would never meet Diana or Jamie, but he felt close to them in this space. And maybe that was enough. Maybe that's all he ever wanted from the Lochlainns—to know them.

He checked his smart watch. Mara should be arriving any minute. Catalina's offer had thrown him off his game. He still hadn't rehearsed what he needed to say to Mara.

How to say goodbye.

Mara ran up the steps of the museum. Thankfully, tonight called for business instead of cocktail attire, so her shoes were sensible flats and her purse remained slipper-free. And she could wear her own clothes instead of formal wear borrowed from Lavinia, which was great because she'd already worn the two dresses her sister-in-law had mailed her. But she still spent far too much time trying to decide what to wear. By the time she left her apartment—the car Declan sent for her idling at the curb far longer than was good for the environment—most of her closet's contents were on the floor as she had tried on and rejected outfit after outfit. She smoothed her hand over the dark gray wool of her trousers and straightened her blazer. The pantsuit she settled on was serviceable if a little drab and utilitarian. But she paired it with her favorite blouse, an emerald green silk that she knew complimented her eyes and made them seem the same rich color. And if the silk was a bit transparent—especially with a black lace bra underneath—well, then she would keep her jacket on. Unless she was alone with Declan.

Her stomach squeezed as butterflies of anticipation danced up and down her nervous system. This was the first time she would see him since their night. Since she realized how deeply she loved him.

Should she tell him? How would he react? What if he looked at her and she saw nothing but rejection? Or pity?

She didn't think she could survive being the object of his pity.

She squeezed her way through the guests, scarcely noticing the stunning architecture nor the artwork on the walls. Normally, being allowed to wander a museum after hours at will, with elegantly prepared hors d'oeuvres and first-class wine hers for the taking, would be her happy place, but she only had eyes for one person and he was nowhere to be found—

There. He was in the corner, by what looked like a Mark Rothko painting. Now her heart took over, pumping erratically. She kept moving, her legs somehow bearing her weight, her brain insisting her knees stay solid and not disgrace her in front of New York's elite. He still hadn't seen her, intent on his conversation, but surely any minute—

"Ms. Schuyler." Niels Hansen appeared her in path, causing her to stop abruptly. He filled her field of vision, cutting off her view of Declan. "So good to see you again."

"H-Hi," she stuttered. "Nice to run into you again I hope you and Freja received the flowers I sent to thank you both for a wonderful evening?"

"The arrangement was lovely, but not as lovely as your company." He bowed over her hand.

Her breath started to come more easily. "That is very kind of you to say. And more than I deserve, well, considering. Again, I am so sorry—"

He pressed her right hand between the two of his. "No, no. There's no need to be sorry. I am well aware you are not the one who owes me their apologies."

"I don't know if it's fair to blame Declan—"

"Blood will tell. It always has with him." Niels waved his hand as if he smelled something unpleasant. "But that is not the reason I wish to talk to you. You've made quite the impression on me, Mara." His silvery gray eyes stared into hers.

She'd been concerned that seeing Declan for the first time since they slept together would be awkward, but whatever she imagined was nothing compared to this moment. "Oh. Thank you. But, um, I *am* with Declan—" At least as far as Niels was concerned. And maybe beyond? She hoped. "So I can't—I mean—"

Too late, she realized the slight shaking of Niels's shoulders meant he was laughing. "No, no, my dear Mara. I mean your questions about my new acquisition. You gave me much food for thought. You see, I was so enticed by the thought of finally adding a Robaire to my collection that I perhaps overlooked concerns about the painting's provenance. I sent the canvas out for analysis. And the results were…not pleasant. Apparently, you were right to suspect the cobalt blue pigment. The chemical report shows that particular pigment came on the market after the period when Robaire was active."

"Oh!" She scrambled for her phone in her purse and held it up. "May I record our conversation? You don't have to go on record if you don't wish."

"I would rather you didn't. Not at the moment. I am speaking with my lawyers. You understand."

"Of course." Mara put her phone down, keeping her expression neutral. "But I hope you will feel comfortable discussing your findings with me in the future."

Niels smiled. "I have asked for more studies. This was only one and I want to be sure the findings were correct. But I must thank you, my dear. You may have saved me and my family millions of dollars."

"Happy to be of service. And if you want to repay me, you know what I'd most like." She waved her phone.

"I'll do you one better," he said. "If the additional tests conclusively prove the Robaire is a forgery, I will appear on camera for your story."

"That's great." She swallowed. Having someone like Niels Hansen—a socially prominent billionaire and internationally renowned art collector—be in her story would be a publicity coup. He rarely granted interviews, so people would tune in just to see him. "I would appreciate that."

"I am in your debt. This would be the least I can do." He bowed over her hand again. "Now, if you will excuse me, I see some acquaintances I must greet. Until later."

"Until then." Mara watched him go, doing her best to keep a tight lid on her emotions. She wanted to jump up and down with excitement, yell her joy to the streets...

Kiss Declan senseless in celebration.

He was where she had last seen him, but now he was alone. Apparently he witnessed her encounter, for he used his chin to indicate Niels's retreating back and then raised his eyebrows at her in question. She nodded back at him, her lips pressed tightly together, but she was sure he'd read the happiness in her gaze when a broad smile broke across his own face. He started to weave his way through the crowd toward her and she did the same, so that they met in the middle of the gallery space. "Hey," he said. He gave her a smile, a lopsided one she'd noticed he saved only for her.

"Hey," she said back. Her gaze drank him in since touching him the way she wanted to would be highly inappropriate in public. Her heart stung with how much she'd missed seeing him in person since last week.

"I purposefully kept my distance," he said. "Didn't think you wanted me around when speaking to Hansen."

"Wise. Since you seem to set Niels off just by breathing."

"It's my talent and my gift," he joked. "So? Seems like you had a productive conversation."

She gave him a brief recap. "I'm still trying to track down Skacel," she concluded. "But if I can get Niels to go on camera…it could be a very solid story."

"Well done."

She basked in his praise. "It is, isn't it? I wasn't sure this story could come together under the time pressure, but I might have a compelling piece for launch week."

"You might."

"Might?" She raised her eyebrows.

"That…decision won't be up to me."

"What do you mean? Of course it's up to you. You're programming the launch." She took a step back so she could search his gaze. What she found wasn't reassuring. She wrapped her arms around herself. "Are you afraid people will think I traded sexual favors for professional advancement?"

"The story is good and your work speaks for itself. You deserve to be included. However..." He ran his left hand through his hair. Because he was Declan, the resulting hair tousle made him appear even more sexy and delectable. "Now is not the time, but we need to talk."

Mara may not have had many serious relationships, but she was well versed enough in dating-speak for the words, "we need to talk" to sends rivers of ice through her veins. "Okay," she said slowly.

His eyes flashed. "Not like that." He reconsidered. "Well, not in that way."

Declan was flustered. And the only other time she'd seen him flustered, he had been apologizing to her. Maybe this wasn't the disaster she was anticipating. "Consider my curiousity piqued."

"Good." His gaze was fixed on a point over her shoulder, and she turned to see what or who had caught his attention. Catalina Lochlainn was looking at him, her elegant eyebrows raised in a question. Declan gave her a rueful smile and a nod, and then turned his attention back to Mara. "I need to go. I've been asked to be part of the dedication ceremony."

"You were? You never mentioned that to me.

Not that you owe me a detailed account of your actions, you don't, but—"

"I would've told you. Catalina just asked me earlier this evening."

"She did? Why?"

He smirked at her. "Why not? Are you saying I'm not important enough? I am a journalist, like Jamie. And I do work for LNT."

She rolled her eyes. "Yes, I'm aware you are incredibly important, but when it comes to LNT, you work for a streaming service that hasn't launched yet." Mara glanced around the gallery. "Why not ask the president of LNT? He's by the bar. Or any number of Lochlainn Company executives? I think the entire board of directors is here."

He shrugged. "You'll have to ask Catalina why."

His eyes drifted up and to the left again. She seriously could not believe no one had told him about his tell. Or maybe no one else had gotten close enough to him to notice. The thought made her both warm with pleasure that he had let her in enough to notice and a little sad he apparently hadn't been close enough to anyone else in the last seven years who could have tipped him off. Like she was about to now. "You're doing that thing again, you know."

"What thing?"

"When you're not telling the entire truth. Your eyes slide, like this." She demonstrated.

He frowned. "They do not."

"Yes, they do. I first noticed when we were working on that project sophomore year—the one I had to step in and finish your work on because you were investigating the hack into the engineering school's IT system, but you wanted to keep your activities quiet because you hadn't identified the ringleader yet? You were so obviously leaving pertinent information out of your excuses. And your eyes slid." She demonstrated again.

She'd never seen him look so disgruntled. His grumpy expression caused her heart to squeeze.

That wasn't good. As Amaranth said, she knew she she could get over the overwhelming desire that threatened to capsize her equilibrium whenever he was near. She did before. But this deep-rooted fondness? Wanting to tease away his expression and make him laugh? This was new. And she feared it would be even more painful to weed out.

"I can't believe you never told me."

"Don't worry. Your secret is safe with me." She grinned at him, but her expression faded when he didn't return her smile. "Honest. I promise I won't squeal to your poker buddies."

"No, but we need to—damn it. I have to go. Catalina is signaling. Promise me you won't leave until we have a chance to talk."

She searched his gaze. "Okay. I wasn't planning on leaving immediately anyway. I'd love to talk to Catalina Lochlainn myself about the Robaire acquisition."

"She told me it's another piece from the, quote, private Portuguese collector."

"Oh, the Portuguese collector again. Quite the mystery person with the heretofore unknown treasure trove of art, yet not a single trace of this person can be found. Can you get me an interview with her?"

His expression relaxed. "I can ask."

On impulse, she leaned up to kiss his cheek. They had already cleared their relationship with HR, so she might as well take advantage of the corporate cover. "Break a leg up there."

She wasn't sure what she expected his response to be. Maybe a flirtatious grin, or a shrug to indicate he didn't need her good luck wishes or even perhaps a reciprocal kiss, a chaste one to reflect they were in public.

She did not expect him to cup her face with his hands, his fingers splayed warmly on her cheeks, as his gaze caught and held hers. "We'll talk. Right after this is over."

"I'll be here."

She watched him disappear into the crowd, admiring the way his trousers draped just so to show off his muscular thighs. Then she frowned. Interesting that Catalina Lochlainn had asked him to be up with her on the dais for the ceremony. Yet another inexplicable connection between him and the Lochlainns.

She couldn't shake off the foreboding feeling that the Lochlainn connection was one of the vital missing puzzle pieces of himself that Declan still withheld from her.

ELEVEN

THE DEDICATION CEREMONY came off flawlessly, despite the absence of Keith Lochlainn who, Mara was sure, had been the main draw for many of the guests. The crowd started to thin out soon after the short ceremony was concluded, people eager to enjoy what was left of their Saturday night.

Mara stayed at the gallery, waiting for Declan to finish making the rounds with Catalina to thank the donors and other guests who were still in attendance. She'd examined every piece on display, read every label tacked on the wall next to the artwork and was on her third tour of the space when she stopped in front of a painting by Diana Lochlainn.

She'd noticed the photograph placed on the wall next to the painting on an earlier round, of course. The black and white picture depicted Diana Lochlainn in her artist studio, complete with an artist smock and a painter's palette in one hand. But what caught her attention this time was the young boy who leaned against Diana's legs. He was fair-haired and compact in size, his expression intent as he stood in front of his own, smaller easel and canvas. Jamie.

She'd seen photographs and videos of Jamie, of course. What journalism student hadn't? He'd been widely admired for his calm, authoritative yet highly engaging presence on camera as well as his ability to draw out fresh, new insights from even the most jaded interview subjects. Hardened criminals found themselves crying on Jamie's shoulder; heads of state admitted their innermost personal secrets to him.

But she'd seen the older Jamie. The one who had cut himself off from his father when Keith divorced Diana. The man who had weathered several life shocks. This was the first time she'd seen a photo of a young, unguarded Jamie.

And she knew his expression.

She'd seen it in her apartment—on Declan as he propped himself up on one elbow and used his other hand to trace the freckles on her shoulders and chest, making her laugh with how serious he took his task.

She shook her head. No. She had to be imagining things. The last thing she'd consumed was the smoothie with Amaranth. She was dehydrated and needed more water. And her nerves were stretched taut with wanting things she knew she could not want, like Declan.

So clearly, she was seeing him everywhere.

Although... On her way to the bar her gaze sought out Declan, who was standing next to Catalina across the room. Then she turned her head to look back at Diana's and Jamie's photograph, not watching where she was going.

She ran into something hard and solid.

"Oh!" she exclaimed, concentrating on keeping her feet untangled before looking up to offer an apology. But the words died on her lips when she saw who had caused her to almost stumble and fall. "Cam Brower? Is that you?"

"Hey, Mara!" Her former college roommate embraced her with his beefy arms.

"Good to see you! Are you still with the *Inquisitor*?"

He held up his camera with a long lens attached. "You know it."

"I can't believe I ran into you." She grinned at him. "Literally."

"I believe it. You're here with Dec, right? I saw you two talking earlier."

She glanced away, hoping the muted light in the gallery that allowed the paintings to be displayed to their best effect wouldn't also display how red her cheeks must appear. "I'm here for work."

"Work. Right." Cam winked at her. "I saw that photo from the Poets and Artists Ball."

"Photo? What photo?" No one told her a photo existed. There had been nothing in the media.

"The picture was blurry and you mostly saw Declan's back so we didn't run it, but I should've recognized that red hair. That kiss looked hot." Cam grinned. Mara rolled her eyes and opened her mouth to deny being the woman in the photo, but Cam cut her off. "Y'know, Dec said he was going to look you up when we spoke. Glad to see he did."

Look her up? What did that mean? "You spoke to him tonight?"

"Nah. We spoke in…" Cam looked up at the ceiling while he counted on his fingers. "Late September? I interviewed him for the *Inquisitor.*"

"Wait, Declan agreed to be interviewed for the *Inquisitor*—never mind. Not important. What did he say about me?" Late September—that was before he showed up at her shoot in Roseville.

"Well, I wouldn't say he agreed. I ran into him at a coffee place and then I wrote down what he said after he left, but you have to grab the fish, right?"

Mara had forgotten talking to Cam was an exercise in going down several verbal rabbit holes that went nowhere fast. "Grab the fish?"

"Y'know...seize the carp."

"Carpe diem," she corrected. "Seize the day—again, not important. What did he say? Exact words. If you can."

Cam shrugged. "I don't recall exactly. We were talking about college and how the IJAW fellowship was the start of his career and I pointed out he stole it from you as it was really your story and then he said he would look you up."

She rubbed her temples. "You said what was my story?"

"The story that won him the fellowship? The campus gynecologist who was abusing female students? That was your story first. I saw your notes on your computer." Cam thumped his chest with his free fist. "I stick up for my friends. You're welcome, Mara."

"What?" She struggled to close her mouth. "No! You have it all wrong. Declan and I were both chasing that story. He scooped me by getting the confirming source on record before I did. I'll admit, it didn't feel good at the time, but he didn't steal anything."

Cam shrugged. "He seemed to feel differently. Anyway, glad to see you two have worked things out and you're together now—" His eyes lit up. "Hey, speaking of scoops, can I have this one? Y'know, you're the mystery woman in the photo? The one Declan Treharne is dating?"

"We're not dating." The last thing she needed was for...whatever was going on between her and Declan...to be splashed across the pages of a tabloid. "I told you. This is work."

"Uh huh. Sure." He winked at her again.

"Listen to me, Cam, and listen hard." She enunciated clearly. "I am not dating Declan and I never will. We were friendly rivals in college and now we're work colleagues. That's it. End of story."

Cam raised his hands as if in surrender. "Fine, if you say so." His gaze drifted over her shoulder. "Hey, Dec. Good to see you again."

Mara froze. "Declan is behind me," she said to Cam through numb lips.

"Yes. I am," Declan said. "Or rather, I was." He appeared at her side. "Good to see you, too, Cam."

Cam raised his camera and took a photo of Mara and Declan before Mara could react. "Got it in one," he said, examining the screen. "Thanks, you two. See you both around." He tipped two fingers to his brow in a salute and then took off.

"We're not—" But Mara's words fell into the empty air. Cam was gone. "We're not," she said helplessly to Declan. "I mean, at least as far as Cam is concerned, we're not. That's none of his business. And definitely not the *Inquisitor*'s business."

"Agreed," he said. "We're not."

Ouch. "Okay, yes, we aren't, but you don't have to agree so quickly," she said, trying to keep the hurt out of her voice.

"I'm agreeing that as far as Cam is concerned, we're not dating. As far as Niels Hansen is concerned, we are. I'm going to start requiring a scorecard, Schuyler." He grinned at her, but there was something missing. A spark of energy, perhaps. She took her first good long look at him since he'd joined her and her heart twinged at how exhausted he seemed.

"Must have been tiring, sitting on the dais," she tried to joke. "You look awful, Treharne."

"Thanks. Can't say the same. You continue to look amazing." He glanced around gallery. Only a few dozen people remained. "I suppose we should get out of here. Oh! Before I forget." He reached into his trouser pocket and pulled out a business card that he handed to her. "Here's Catalina Lochlainn's private cell phone. She's expecting your call about the Robaire."

"Private number? Wow. As always, you work miracles."

She threw her own glance around the gallery. Cam was gone. No one else was near. She cupped Declan's face with her hand and brought his lips down to hers. "Thank you," she whispered against his mouth. "I don't know how I would have gotten this far on this story without you. I'm so glad you asked me to come to LNT."

Then she kissed him. As always, the embers kindled whenever she was in his presence ignited instantaneously when their lips touched. Her bones dissolved and she melted into him, his arms gathering her close. But when she would deepen the kiss, he pulled back and their mouths disengaged. "Mara," he started, her name a warning.

"I know, I know, wait until we're not at a work event," she said. "Sorry. But I'm so happ—"

"Mara. I'm leaving LNT. I'm handing in my resignation on Monday."

She blinked at him. "I'm sorry. My ears must be playing tricks on me. I could swear you said you are resigning from LNT on Monday."

"Because that's what I said." He reached for her hands. She kept them by her sides, out of his reach.

"You are… I don't… Why? Before the launch? Before everything you… I…you worked for." She continued to blink. Maybe if she opened and closed her eyes enough times, she could reset the evening to before his pronouncement. But even if, by some feat of magical thinking, she managed to turn the clock back, she doubted she would ever be rid of the frost that invaded her heart and took hold.

Declan cleared his throat. "I have unfinished business elsewhere. As for LNT…" He shrugged, one-shouldered. "I accomplished what I set out to do."

He didn't intend to tell Mara here, in the museum gallery, with straggling guests passing by as they sought the exits. He planned to take her out for drinks.

Maybe even ask her to come back to his place. If she wanted. One last time, no misunderstandings muddying the next seven years and their eyes open.

Their hearts closed. As was necessary.

Mara was right. They weren't dating. She was pursuing a story and he made a convenient cover. And the sex was good, so no need for two consenting adults to deny themselves. Why not indulge?

That morning in her apartment would be seared on his soul forever, but that was his problem. Not hers.

Mara continued to stare at him, her green gaze searching his for uncomfortable minutes. "You're using weasel words," she said finally. "You're being vague. Talk to me. Why are you leaving LNT now?"

How could he stay, now that he knew what Keith wanted from him was something he couldn't fulfill? Didn't want to fulfill? He had no desire to run the Lochlainn Company.

Knowing that who he was would never be enough to earn Keith's approval and acknowledgement.

In some ways, the knowledge was like losing another parent all over again. Not exactly the same. Not as devastating. Not the howling, visceral pain that accompanied the loss of his mother.

But the conversation with Catalina had caused hope he didn't realize he carried—not much, and buried deep down in his subconscious—and that hope was gone now and he was forced to mourn its absence...

He did one thing right, however. He brought Mara to LNT and set her on the path that should have been hers all along. He took her unresisting hands in his. Her fingers were icy and he regretted, so much, being the cause. But she would thank him one day. He scratched the back of his neck. "I'm leaving for Paris on Monday. So, I'd like to—"

"Monday." She inhaled audibly. "Oh. That is soon."

"There's a story," he said. "An—"

"Important one," she finished for him. Her lips trembled into a semblance of a smile. "Always is, with you."

"A year ago, I was on the trail of Alice de la Vigny, who disappeared. But she's recently been spotted in France. She procures underage women for wealthy men. If I can finally get her to talk, to flip on the men she services—"

Mara's gaze softened. "That is important." She bit her lower lip. "But...the launch."

"The launch is in great shape. Brian, Mads, the wellness and health series, the morning global politics roundtable—all the heavy lifting is done." He gave her a smile, but even he knew his expression must appear strained. "I'm superfluous."

She didn't return the smile. "And me?" she asked softly. "What about me? Us? Are we superfluous?"

His gaze traced the contours of her face. He knew he didn't need to memorize her features— he would no doubt see her gracing screens big and small for years to come—but this might be his last chance to be this close to her. To watch her green gaze widen and narrow with her thoughts, her eyes truly the window to her expressive soul. To breathe in her scent, warm and lightly floral and all Mara. To zero in on his favorite freckles—the constellations that frosted the apples of her cheeks whenever she smiled.

"You're going to be a star," he said. "I've spoken to the president of LNT. Not just streaming, but the entire operation. She's seen rough cuts of your work and is very impressed."

Mara didn't react. Her gaze continued to hold his.

"Did you hear what I said? You're on track to obtain everything we talked about in college. Everything that should have been yours after graduation."

"I heard," she said slowly. "I heard that you didn't answer my question. And I was doing fine before coming to LNT. I was happy at WRZT."

"I know, but—" he gestured at the art gallery around them, at the Robaire—or supposed Robaire—painting hanging in the place of honor "—you could've been doing more. You are doing more. You deserve to do more."

"Covering local news is important—"

He scratched the back of his neck. "I didn't say it wasn't, just that I knew you had dreams to cover stories that mattered—"

"Local news matters. It matters a lot—"

"Of course it does. But I know you. We discussed many times what you dreamed of doing. And you never mentioned covering pumpkin pie contests." Why was she fighting him on this?

Declan was good at regulating his emotions. A childhood spent navigating the world with a single mother, who was also a skilled diplomat, taught him not to take offense at matters that were often cultural misunderstandings. And four years of boarding school with callous and cruel rich scions like Niels Hansen gave him much practice at keeping his cool and biding his time. But the last week—the hours with Mara in her apartment, planning his imminent trip to Paris to plunge back into the chase for Alice, his presence at a memorial to the man whose donated sperm gave him life, Catalina's kind insistence he sit on the dais with her but her firm regret that Keith had no interest in meeting him—had chipped away at his equilibrium until he was grasping at tatters.

"Then why—"

"Because I know you, Mara. You were the one who first uncovered the gynecologist scandal at the university. You were the one who found Jane Doe and spoke to her about going on record. That story changed the school. Laws were passed to ensure young women wouldn't be put in such vulnerable positions across the country. That's what kind of journalist you are. Those are the stories you should be covering—"

She was shaking her head so hard, her red locks bounced off her shoulders. "I didn't do that. You did that. That was your story. You scooped me, fair and square. I know it's been several years, but—"

"I got an anonymous tip about the gynecologist. I always thought the tip had been left by one of the victims. But now… I think I know who gave it to me." She couldn't hold his gaze. He may have a tell, but her entire expression gave her away. "You should have won the fellowship. Not me."

She tried to laugh off his suggestion. "Is this because Cam said something to you? I know you two had coffee a few weeks before you showed up in Roseville—" Then the color drained from her face. "Wait. Is this why you tracked me down and asked me to come to LNT? Because Cam Brower, of all people, said you stole from me?"

"He didn't say 'stole' in so many words—"

"Listen to me, Declan." She took a deep breath. "Yes, Jane Doe was my source first. Yes, I did a lot of the research that the 'anonymous tip'—" she made quotes in the air with her fingers "—left for you. But I couldn't complete the story. Some of the women he hurt were my friends. And so I chose to be their confidante, to hold their confessions private.

The story wasn't mine—it was theirs. Bringing the gynecologist's abuse to light required another writer, someone who could be objective and detached. And I was happy when your story came out. I cheered when it led to his dismissal and charges were brought against him."

"You didn't congratulate me—y'know what, never mind, it's a petty grudge to hold on to."

"You had just broken up with me! I wasn't exactly in a congratulatory mood."

"I thought...it doesn't matter."

"Did I want the fellowship? Did the story I submit pale in comparison to bringing down a predatory abuser in a position of trust at the university? Yes." She stepped closer to him. "But the story was yours." She poked him in the chest with her right index finger. "You wrote it." She poked him again. "You won. But me?" She poked herself in the chest. "Apparently, I have to be given opportunities out of pity, not because I earned them."

What the...? "You can't seriously think I brought you to LNT because I felt bad for you."

"Not any less than I think last weekend was a pity fuck." Her gaze widened. "Oh, God. It was, wasn't it? I mean, I propositioned you. At least you seemed to enjoy it, like last time. But now you're leaving. Like last time."

He grasped her shoulders. She stilled at his touch. "My leaving has nothing to do with you. Nothing. You would be the only reason I would stay."

Her chest rose and fell several times, and then she relaxed in his grip. "So why don't you? Stay, I mean."

He let his hands fall. "I told you. Alice. I can get her to talk."

"And no one else can? You're the only one who can report the story, or you don't want anyone else to get the story?" Her gaze sharpened. "Why did you come to LNT, if chasing Alice was so important?"

"I told you. She disappeared."

"If there's one thing you excel at, it's perseverance. Why do you think I tipped you off about the gynecologist? Because I knew you wouldn't let the university administration or donors hoping to head off bad publicity stop you."

He'd forgotten this about Mara: the way she could peel him like an onion, remove his protective layers. He did his best to keep them in place. "She was thought to be dead. And I was offered the LNT position."

"Right. LNT." Her gaze slid to a point over his shoulder. When he followed her gaze, he discovered she was looking at the painting by Diana Lochlainn. He frowned. "You never did tell me why LNT hired you."

"Pretty sure I did."

She shook her head. "No. You always managed to evade giving me a straight answer. Care to give me one now?"

He wanted to. He could tell Mara the entire story: How his mother wanted a child and decided to use an anonymous sperm donor. How he put two and two together and came up with Jamie Lochlainn as that sperm donor.

How Keith Lochlainn rejected him. And now, was using LNT for some sort of esoteric test of familial worthiness that Declan knew he was failing.

He opened his mouth. "Come with me. To Paris. Work on the story with me."

He wasn't sure where the invitation came from. He wasn't embarking on a sightseeing trip. He would be going into an unknown situation—he was certain that Alice wasn't dangerous, but she associated with people who had no qualms making problems disappear, and journalists fell into that category—and he didn't know how long he would need to stay in Paris. And if Alice decided to bolt, like she did last time, he would need to follow her.

But he couldn't leave things with Mara like this. Not with this artificial mask covering her features, with hurt that was still visible beneath. Not with her believing he only brought her to LNT to assuage his conscience. Yes, he might have driven to Roseville because he wanted to make things right, but as soon as he saw her...

As soon as he saw her, he realized how much he once cared for her. And still did. Would always.

He would make the situation right. He just needed time. "I can get you a ticket, arrange for time off—"

She looked at him with sorrow in her gaze. Sorrow for him, he realized. "I can't go to Paris. You know that."

"I know. You're in the middle of the art forgery story. But when you're done—"

She was shaking her head before he could finish. "I can't go because you break my heart. You don't mean to, but you do." For the first time that evening, moisture shimmered in her gaze.

"That morning in my apartment... If there's a piece of me you want, it's already yours. But it destroys me, knowing that you won't give me even a little piece of you." She leaned up and kissed him on the cheek. "Go save the world, superhero. Find Alice and stop the trafficking."

His world was slipping away from him. He tried to gather and hold what he could, but it was like trying to keep a sandcastle intact at high tides. "I'll call you."

She smiled sadly. "Don't make promises you can't keep, Treharne." Then she was gone.

Declan stayed in the gallery until the security personnel kicked him out. Going to Paris was the right decision. There was nothing for him at the Lochlainn Company, just the machinations of an old man who wanted an heir, but only on his own terms. While lives would be saved if Alice told the world what she knew.

Then why did he feel as if his own world stopped spinning once Mara left?

TWELVE

Two months later

LNT Plus was a bustling hive of activity. For once, the floors that contained its studios and offices weren't considered the hinterlands of the Lochlainn Company's empire. They were, instead, the epicenter of the multinational media conglomerate's universe. Rumor had it that there was more at stake than bragging rights to having the most popular streaming service in the cutthroat world of broadcast news; the whispers were that Keith Lochlainn himself had some sort of personal stake in the venture's success or failure and that the future of the entire company was somehow riding on how well LNT Plus performed.

Mara sat in a chair in the hair and makeup room, with one ear listening as the people dusting her face with powder and smoothing her hair so that no errant curl would appear on camera gossiped about her coworkers and the avalanche of positive press that had descended upon them once the opening lineup of stories for the launch had been announced. As she predicted, Mara did indeed land a prominent spot on the lineup. The head of LNT herself had personally congratulated her on the art forgery story and for bringing "culture, intrigue and wealthy people getting ripped off—the trifecta of attracting a broad viewership" to the service. In fact, she was so pleased with the story, she gave Mara a live segment for a follow-up interview with Niels Hansen, who had finally agreed to speak on camera about his counterfeit Robaire painting.

Her other ear was attuned to her phone. Niels was expected at the studio any moment, and security promised to call her as soon as his car pulled up to the building. She twisted her hands in her lap. Not that she was nervous—she had plenty of experience appearing live on camera, and she was relishing the adrenaline of knowing there were no second takes and she only had one opportunity to nail her interview—but for the first time since that evening at the gallery, she had space and time available for her mind to wander. She'd kept herself occupied nearly around the clock since his departure, nailing down the specifics, filling any holes and polishing her script and her delivery until they couldn't be perfected further. She'd worked on three more stories that were in contention for future slots. Her office was far more familiar to her than her apartment, and she hadn't joined Amaranth's boxing classes in forever. She hoped her friend would take pity on her whenever they got into the ring next, because Mara doubted she could throw a decent jab currently.

She'd been the first to raise her hand for a new assignment and the last to ask for time off, and while she told herself she was working her butt off to prove all the naysayers and gossip peddlers wrong about her, to demonstrate that she was at LNT Plus due to her own merits, she knew the real reason.

The more things she gave her brain to work on, the less she would obsess over Declan. Who did call her when he reached Paris, but had been radio silent the last few weeks. Not that she was counting the days. And not that his current silence wasn't to be expected. She knew his pursuit of Alice was at a critical juncture, and he had far more important things to do than to check in with her. Still...

"Any word?"

Mara startled. She caught the eye of Jack, the makeup artist, in the mirror. "I'm sorry?"

Jack nodded at the phone clutched in Mara's hand. "From your guest. We're ready for him." He dabbed at Mara's forehead, and then stepped back with a smile. "You're done."

Mara slipped from the chair. "Thank you. All looks great, as usual. And no. We're still waiting."

A production assistant bustled into the room. "Turn on the television." She pointed to the set in the corner, which was currently showing a Mexican telenovela. Everyone was addicted to the daily dose of drama, including Mara.

Jack frowned. "But we're waiting to see if Gabriel will recognize Yolanda after her make-over."

The production assistant grabbed the re-mote and changed the channel to NCN, LNT's main rival. Mara raised an eyebrow but leaned over the counter to examine a lock of hair that would not lie flat despite the best efforts of the hair stylist.

"—hanks for joining us on News Channel

Network," said the host of NCN's morning show in her soothing, low tones.

"Thank you for having me," said a voice Mara knew well. She straightened, her hair forgotten, and joined the others in the makeup room, staring at the television.

Niels Hansen was on the screen. He didn't have a gleaming blond hair out of place, Mara noted. He sat in a chair across from the NCN host, his suit perfectly tailored, the perfect picture of sophistication and elegance.

"Isn't he supposed to be here?" Jack stage-whispered to Mara. "Do you think he got the networks mixed up?"

"Not funny," Mara said back, not bothering to keep her voice low.

On screen, Niels addressed the camera. "It has come to my attention that there has been a concerted effort to discredit several major new art discoveries by claiming they are forgeries. This group is even targeting me and my sister, casting aspersions on our reputation as art collectors. I am convinced this is an attack on our honor by those who wish to do irreparable harm to the international art community—"

"But to what end?" asked the NCN host.

"Who would derive benefit from such a campaign? What reasons do they have?"

Niels leaned forward, the perfect picture of wounded innocence. "There are many reasons for such a nefarious scheme. To cause confusion in the market and to artificially manipulate art prices being main among them. An original Robaire painting is worth millions. But if its authenticity is questioned, then the price would plunge, leaving the owner with an investment that is worth less than the picture frame that contains it."

"Some of those frames are rather costly," said the host with a small laugh.

Niels did not appreciate her attempt at a joke. "This isn't a laughing matter. This is a blatant attempt by a small group to financially destroy their rivals."

The host frowned. "That is quite the accusation. Do you know who this group is?"

Niels smiled. It wasn't a very pleasant one. "Ask yourself who commissioned the story and whose company provides the platform to spread it, and you have your answer."

The makeup room erupted into loud buzzing. "Okay," Mara said. "We've seen enough. Turn off the channel." Her own pocket started to vibrate and she pulled out her phone. The caller was exactly who she expected to be calling her. "Yes, ma'am," she answered. "I'll come to the set right away."

Mara kept her head down as she made calls and then entered notes on her phone, her muscle memory allowing her to navigate the hallway to where it opened into the studio—a large, cavernous space that was split into realms: the dark shadows where the production crew lived, gathered around the playback monitors known as video village, and the well-lit set decorated in bright blue and metallic gold, the signature colors of the parent network LNT. Two modern easy chairs in shades of burnt orange were set up facing each other, while the tall backdrop was a high-definition video screen that would change scenes as Mara and her guest spoke.

"Hi. I know that sounded like a hit piece on the Lochlainn Company. And obviously, Hansen won't be joining us for the live segment, but I have—"

"Mara. It's good to see you."

Her gaze jerked up. That voice didn't sound like her producer. That voice sounded like...

Declan.

Oh, he looks good, her heart whispered. His

hair was longer, shaggy even, and in desperate need of a haircut. His skin was tanned and his dark blond hair sported the kind of highlights that only came from exposure to the sun. He hadn't shaved in at least a week, judging by the growth of his beard, and while his eyes drooped at the corners, indicating exhaustion, his smile was brighter than ever before.

She wanted to hug him and kiss him hello—okay, kiss him into oblivion for being there and in one piece and no longer the bane of her worry if she were being honest—but the set was bustling with people, from crew members to several LNT executives she rarely saw outside their offices.

"Hey, Declan. You look tired. Did you just get in?" She didn't know what else to say. What she wanted to say would probably get her fired, if that wasn't already the purpose of the executives descending on the set.

"You look amazing. As always." He grinned at her.

"Yes, yes, we all look great." Nan Greenwald, the president of LNT, approached them, several of her lieutenants by her side. Mara swallowed. She'd only met Nan once, and that had been a brief handshake at the launch party. Declan came to stand beside Mara, his nearness as comforting as it was distracting. What was he doing here?

"Is everything set?" Nan continued. She turned to the director. "I want everything perfect, understand?"

"Perfect for what?" Mara asked.

"For the live interview." Nan looked at Mara as if she had grown a second head.

"Right," Mara said slowly. "Well, I do have a backup ready." She checked her phone. "He'll be here in five minutes—"

Nan shot Mara another puzzled stare. "He's already here."

"What?"

Declan cleared his throat. "Hi."

Mara whirled to face him. "I'm not interviewing you."

"You can't have dead air. Niels isn't coming—"

"Obviously—"

"And you need a story big enough to distract from his accusations. So, here I am."

Mara started to laugh. "Look, superhero, I appreciate you swooping in out of the blue to save the day, yet again—and how did you know

Niels would pull this stunt, anyway?—but I've got it under control."

"The interview has been promoted for weeks. As soon as I heard Niels was your guest, I knew you needed a backup—"

"But you didn't bother to tell me—

"Because I wasn't sure if I would be able to pull this off." He shrugged, his grin slightly sheepish. Damn it, the expression made him seem even more appealing. Now that she had had some time to adjust to the fact that he was there, next to her, in person, her heart decided to react by beating in triple time.

"Pull what off? Flying in from Paris?"

"He means me," said a gruff male voice from the shadows on the edges of the studio. And then Keith Lochlainn came into view, leaning heavily on a cane.

Mara had never met the legendary mogul, but she had seen plenty of photos and watched many a video. Now the presence of Nan on the set made sense. "Is it weird I have an impulse to curtsy?" she whispered to Declan.

"I heard that," Keith said. "Go right ahead." Then he turned to Declan. "Redhead. Nice."

"She's more than nice. She's good," Declan said. "Ready to be miked up?"

"Time out." Mara made a "T" sign with her hands. "What the hell is going on?"

"I'm going to give you the scoop of the century. I'm—"

"A Lochlainn," Mara said. "I figured it out the night of the gallery dedication. And having Mr. Lochlainn here—" she bobbed, if not a curtsy, then a short bow "—confirms it." She glanced at her phone. There was still thirty minutes to go before she was supposed to go on air. She pointed at Declan. "You. Me. Private conversation. Now." She looked at Keith and Nan. "If you two will excuse us."

Keith shrugged while Nan waved them off. Mara left the set, pulling Declan down the hallway to her small dressing room. She waited until the door was firmly shut behind them before turning on him. "What the hell, Declan!"

"Hello to you, too, Mara."

"What do you think you're doing?" A new thought hit her. "And what about the Alice story? How could you leave that? Now?"

"Griff Beachwood has secured Alice's cooperation. His story should run in the *Globe*'s next Sunday magazine."

"Griff— But that's your story! You've worked so hard—"

Declan closed half the distance between them. She swallowed her words, her synapses, as always, scrambled by his nearness. She had missed him so much. Her gaze traced his face, his broad shoulders, his narrow hips and powerful thighs. How could one human look so amazing? She licked her lips, hoping to work moisture back into her mouth.

"And Griff will do an excellent job with it. I realized, sitting in the South of France—"

"Oh, poor baby," Mara tried to joke, hoping to leaven the tension that always sprung to life whenever they were alone together, her nipples already contracting to points of need. "What a terrible assignment…" Her words trailed off as he closed the distance again. Now he was within easy reach. All she had do was lift her hand and she could reassure herself he really was there, with her, and not just a very realistic waking dream.

"As I was saying," he said, and then his hand did touch her, his fingers finding hers and squeezing, "I was sitting at a café, alone, discussing with Bobbi which stories to submit for consideration for various prizes, when I realized—the only person whose opinion really mattered was you. Always has been."

"Me?" There must be something wrong with the ventilation system in her dressing room. She could scarcely breathe. "Always? But that week in college…and then you walked away…"

"I don't know if you remember, but I did a story on Jamie Lochlainn for the alumni magazine. After talking to some of his buddies, and putting a few hunches together, I was pretty sure Jamie Lochlainn was the anonymous donor my mother used to conceive me. That week coincided with Keith telling me to get lost when I brought him my evidence."

"Oh, Declan. I'm so sorry." She reached for his other hand with her free one and brought the distance between them to scant inches.

"I was hurt. Ashamed. The fellowship promised a way to prove myself worthy to him. I took it and never looked back. I didn't want to look back. Can you forgive me for walking out on the best thing that ever happened to me? Because it's you, Mara. Always has been. Always will be."

It wasn't possible for birds to be singing in her windowless dressing room. But she heard them. She smelled roses, too. And felt fresh summer breezes. Or maybe that was Declan, bringing the joy and hopefulness of a bright spring day with him. "You were forgiven the first minute you showed up in Roseville." She dropped his hands, but only so she could entwine her arms around his neck. "Thank you for telling me about Jamie. Are you and Keith reconciled now?"

He rested his forehead against hers. "I've spent my adult life chasing Keith's approval. It wasn't until I refused to jump through his hoops and told him he was going to acknowledge me as Jamie's son, live on air, that I earned a modicum of respect."

"You confronted Keith for me?" She pulled back enough so she could catch and hold Declan's gaze. "Thank you."

"I love you," he said simply. "I offer you one psyche, a bit battered and bruised, but all yours. If you want it."

The entirety of the sun filled her heart, hot and glowing and all encompassing. "I'll always want you. All of you. Then, now, forever. I love you so much."

But when Declan would kiss her, she pulled back, regret making her eyes wide as she pulled out her buzzing phone. "I have to be on the set in ten minutes."

"Right. That means I do, too."

She shook her head. "Actually, no, you don't. Because my backup guest is ready to go." She turned her phone around so Declan could see the messages on her phone.

"Skacel? You found Alan Skacel?"

"Found him, and he's more than willing to go on record that the forgery ring was being run by Niels. We thought he might pull something like this, to not only throw suspicion off himself but to also target you. Alan was waiting at a coffee shop around the corner in case I needed him as a special guest when Niels was scheduled to be my guest. Now he will spill all the details and then it will be up to the authorities."

Declan was shaking his head. "You're very sexy when you talk about nailing a story. Did you know that?"

She looked at her phone again. "Seven minutes until I need to go live. So that gives you five minutes to show me how sexy I am."

"How about the rest of our lives?" he said against her lips.

"Challenge accepted," she replied, and she kissed him.

EPILOGUE

One year later

KEITH LOCHLAINN WAS DYING.

But not today. And not this year.

Not for the foreseeable future, in fact.

He read the medical report for the fourteenth time that day. During his recent sojourn in the hospital, a doctor that was new to Keith's care reexamined his charts and ordered a new battery of tests. It turned out that what his old—and now fired—doctor thought had signaled the beginning of the end for Keith's life was something the new—and now hired—personal physician had developed a procedure to fix. Keith wasn't clear on the details, but he didn't need to be. All that mattered was that he felt better than he had in the last seven years—ever since Jamie died.

And while he gave his new doctor full credit

for his clean medical bill of health, Keith suspected the true cause of his renewed good health was sitting around the Thanksgiving table with him.

To his left sat his granddaughter Anna, beautiful and golden-haired. She was laughing at something her husband, Ian, said, her smile as wide and as open as her heart. Of course, Keith still couldn't believe he was now related to a Blackburn, after decades of trying to squash the upstart rival family. He even believed he had been on the opposite side of the table from young Ian himself, and of course came out the winner. He always did.

Still, Ian appeared to make Anna very happy, even if Anna decided to forego her Lochlainn inheritance in order to run the Lakes of Wonder theme park with her husband. Keith couldn't be too angry that Anna had eschewed his offer to be a key part of the Lochlainn Company, however. Lakes of Wonder had been very special to Jamie—so special, that Keith could barely stand to hear the park's name mentioned once Jamie cut himself off from Keith. So having Anna run the theme park—with photographs of Jamie decorating not only the executive board rooms but also the private apartment in Lakes of Wonder's iconic Lighthouse, which was now available for very special guests such as children suffering from chronic illnesses to stay in—felt…right…to Keith.

Seated on the other side of Ian was Mara, Keith's newest grandchild-in-law. She and Declan were in New York City as a pit stop between covering the meeting of the G6 in Europe to observing what promised to be a contentious election in South Asia. Mara's sharp wit and ability to keep Declan and all of them, for that matter, on their toes was appreciated by Keith. He'd always had a weakness for redheads, anyway.

And there was Declan. Keith didn't do regrets. If he did, he wouldn't be able to get out of bed in the morning with the thought of the years he lost with Jamie. *You always think you have time to reconcile, to explain, to make up for things said and done*, Keith thought, *until you don't*. If he dwelled on everything he lost when Jamie died, the gulf between still death, Keith would be catatonic. So he kept moving and never looked back.

But if he did do regrets…then, next to Jamie, his treatment of Declan would be up there. He supposed Declan reminded him too much of his lost son—from his dark blond hair to his choice of profession—and so even though he knew Declan was in the right about Jamie being his birth father all those years ago, he pushed him away. Slammed the door right in that face with the determined expression that was a carbon copy of Jamie's and wiped the encounter out of his heart.

Keith was too late to be a father—a real father—to Jamie.

But he finally learned it wasn't too late to be a grandfather to Declan and Anna.

Even if neither of his grandchildren wanted anything to do with his pride and joy, the Lochlainn Company. The future of his company after he was gone still rested heavily on Keith's shoulders.

"Everything alright?" asked Catalina. "Here. Chef made this special for you." She placed a plate of plain white turkey and steamed brussels sprouts in front of him. Everyone else around the table dug into plates piled high with mashed potatoes swimming in butter, brussels sprouts roasted with bacon and turkey with all the trimmings, from cranberry orange relish to decadent stuffing.

"Bah," Keith said, pushing a sprout around

with his fork. Then he looked over at Catalina and gave her a smile. A rusty one, no doubt, but sincere. "Never better."

Catalina arched an eyebrow and picked up her fork. "Good to hear. I have to admit, family dinners are more congenial since you stopped badgering Anna and Declan about joining you at the Lochlainn Company."

"They don't want to be involved. I respect that."

Catalina blinked at him, then smiled. "That's very mature of you, Keith. Good on you."

"Bah," he said again, but there was no heat in it. Even he had to admit it was nice to have peace at the dinner table.

He took a bite of turkey. It wasn't half bad. The bird was juicy and flavorful. He didn't miss the stuffing after all. If eating like his doctors ordered would help him live another twenty or thirty years, then this was how he would eat.

After all, if he wasn't mistaken, Anna was pregnant. She refused wine with dinner and she and Ian kept sneaking glances at each other as if they had a secret they were bursting to tell but couldn't just yet. Mara was drinking champagne like there was no tomorrow—she might as well drink his good stuff since he wasn't able to—

but Keith was confident in his ability to talk her into giving him great-grandchildren, too.

Before long, there would be new heirs to the Lochlainn dynasty. And he knew just the way to determine which heir should inherit his empire.

* * * * *

DESIRE

Scandalous world of the elite.

Available Next Month

All titles available in Larger Print

Matched By Mistake Katherine Garbera
The Rancher Meets His Match J. Margot Critch

From Highrise To High Country Barbara Dunlop
Bad Boy Gone Good Katie Frey

Just A Few Fake Kisses... Jayci Lee
The True Love Experiment Anne Marsh

Keep reading for an excerpt of a new title
from the Western Romance series,
FORTUNE'S RUNAWAY BRIDE by Allison Leigh

CHAPTER ONE

No CHURCH HAD ever looked so beautiful.

White flowers cascaded from every pew and loose petals artfully outlined the aisle. The occasional disarray from the sweep of the ten bridesmaids' gowns only enhanced the lovely vision.

The music from the pipe organ swelled, and the late afternoon sun streamed through the clerestory windows at just the right angle.

It had all been perfectly timed and coordinated to achieve the most perfect result.

Timing. To the minute.

Decor. White. More white.

Gowns. Lilac. Couture.

Tuxes. Black. Custom.

Visually, it was stunning.

Isabel Banninger's father stood ten paces away, his arm at the ready to escort her up that long aisle to marry Trey Fitzgerald III. Charismatic. Handsome TFIII.

He stood at the end of the aisle wearing the tux that fit his tall, lean body to perfection. His confident, blindingly white smile was directed to the guests. To his raft of groomsmen. To her bridesmaids, arranging themselves exactly where they'd practiced just two days earlier.

Confident. That was Trey.

Everything always worked out for him.

Always.

The matron of honor—Isabel's sister Ronnie—had reached the end of the aisle and was moving into place. The guests all rose to their feet. A sea of faces turned toward her.

The music seemed to reach a fevered pitch.

Isabel took a first step and felt the hushed anticipation of the guests like a palpable thing.

Don't do this!

The thought that had been a hesitant whisper in the back of her mind suddenly eclipsed the gasp and wheeze of the pipe organ. It screamed through her head.

Unescapable. Undeniable.

She whirled, the skinny heels of her custom-dyed silk sandals slipping a little as she raced away from that confident smile.

Not always, Trey.

Not this time.

The doors slammed open under her palms and she was out. Out onto the wide, shallow steps of the Third Community Church of Corpus Christi. Her heart hammered.

Now what?

She looked left. Cars parked nose to end all the way down the block.

She looked right. A parking lot just as full as the pews inside the church behind her.

The limousine that was to transport the newly married Mr. and Mrs. Fitzgerald on the long drive to their lavish reception at the prestigious LC Club on Lake Chatelaine was parked at the ready. But the driver was conspicuously absent.

She turned to the left again, charging blindly down the steps. She just needed to get to the end of the block. She'd duck into the convenience store and—

Do what?

The bus stop. She'd get to the bus stop and—

Do what?

Her head whirled. She'd run, but now what was she supposed to do? Where was she supposed to go? All of her family and friends were back there in the church and—

The wall came out of nowhere.

She hit it with no finesse whatsoever.

Flowers burst free from her enormous bouquet like a flock of flushed birds.

The wall's cell phone flew, too.

It dived straight to the cement.

"Sorry," she gasped. It was hard to lean over with Italian silk constricting her from breasts to knees, but she did it anyway. Light prickled behind her eyes, and she wobbled precariously, but the wall's hand caught her bare arm, keeping her from total ignominy.

"Careful there."

His deep voice barely registered as she found the hard edges of the slender phone and straightened again.

Dark suit. White shirt. Silver tie shoved haphazardly into his lapel pocket like he had every intention of putting it on but hadn't gotten around to it yet.

Probably because he'd been more interested in the picture on his cell phone.

She'd left a smear of Number 879 Red on the front of his shirt. Like he'd been nicked with a little dagger at the center of his chest.

She looked up even farther and met a pair of bluer-than-blue eyes, and she very nearly dropped the phone all over again.

Could the day get *any* worse?

"What're you doing here?"

Reeve Fortune raised an eyebrow, managing to look

amused and cynical at the same time. Which, in her limited experience, seemed to be his usual expression.

"More to the point," he said, jerking his chin toward the church behind her, "what are you *not* doing in there?"

She ignored the question and pushed past him.

Since he was basically a human wall, solidly built and nearly a foot taller than her even with her treacherously high heels, he didn't move much.

She realized he hadn't taken his phone back, either.

The cracked screen did nothing to obscure the image of Trey Fitzgerald III, surrounded by his laughing groomsmen, beer mugs in their hands, raised in salute. The only thing in Trey's hands, however, was the naked woman he was kissing.

A naked woman who was most assuredly *not* his intended bride.

The social media post didn't shock Isabel. Not like it had when she'd seen it first thing that morning.

Happy wedding day to you, Isabel Banninger.

"Not marrying your *buddy*," she finally told Reeve.

He played basketball with Trey nearly every week. For all she knew, he'd been the one behind the camera.

She slapped the phone against Reeve's chest, and he barely caught it before it fell to the ground a second time. She gave him a wide berth as she tottered down another two steps.

Any minute now, Trey would come after her, and if she had to listen to another dose of his "but princess, it didn't mean anything," she would lose her mind. "It was just the guys and me having a last hurrah before you and I tie the knot," he'd said when she confronted him that morning with the evidence.

She should have called off the wedding right then.

But no. She'd let Trey convince her otherwise.

"You know me." His persuasive tone had been pitch-perfect. "I love you. You love me. Don't overreact to something that doesn't mean anything."

If this had been the only time that wasn't supposed to mean anything, maybe she'd still be in the church, holding her father's arm as she walked toward her future as Trey's wife.

The slick sole of her shoe slipped on the cement and she stumbled yet again.

Reeve caught her arm once more but she yanked free. A few more flowers escaped.

She glared at the bouquet. The base of it was so thick she couldn't even wrap her fingers all the way around it. She wanted to throw it to the ground altogether. Maybe even grind her slippery shoe on top of it for good measure.

But she was still at the church. The church where she'd once gone to Sunday school as a child. "Tossing" a bouquet was one thing. Throwing it away was just…littering.

"I s'pose you were there last night." She pointed her bouquet accusingly. Taking the photograph and then posting it for all the world to see.

As if what he'd done to her already wasn't enough.

"Where?"

"The bachelor pa-arty." She hated that her voice hitched. It made it sound like she wanted to cry, and crying was the last thing she felt like doing.

Screaming her outrage? Closer.

"I didn't make it."

She heard a commotion behind them and didn't look back to see who was coming out of the church. It felt like forever since she'd run out, but she knew it could only have been a minute or two.

She sucked in another uneven breath that was nowhere

as deep as she needed thanks to the viselike dress and kept going, even though her wrenched ankle screamed at her.

She'd deal with her parents later. And her sisters. They'd be shocked, but they'd understand. There might not be a lot of them, but the Banningers were tight. Unlike the Fitzgeralds. Most of the three hundred guests inside the church were from the groom's side of the equation, whether family or friends or business acquaintances. Yet Trey had told her some of them didn't talk for months on end.

She realized Reeve was keeping pace with her. Almost as if he expected her to fall on her butt. Or her face.

And why not? He'd already kept her from doing both.

For a guy who'd threatened to sue her for libel, he was being suspiciously solicitous.

She wrote an online community blog. Just last month he'd taken issue with something she'd written regarding his family and a letter from his lawyer had immediately arrived, warning *The Chatelaine Report* to cease and desist.

When she'd told Trey about it, he'd just laughed it off. Told her he'd take care of it with his *buddy* and not to worry.

She watched Reeve from the corner of her eye as they reached the bottom of the shallow steps.

Not worry? A few weeks ago, the company that published her blog, Stellar Productions, had been bought out by FortuneMedia. Which meant that the head of FortuneMedia—none other than the human wall named Reeve Fortune—now held her very livelihood in his hands.

If his threat of a lawsuit didn't succeed in quashing any mention of the wildly extensive Fortune family—who were movers and shakers all over the entire state of Texas—then he would put her in the unemployment line instead.

A late-model Mercedes had been parked in the loading zone, blocking her path.

No driver there, either.

Probably having a smoke around the corner with the limousine driver while they snickered over Trey's "just boys being boys" antics the night before.

She had no money with her. No cell phone. No purse. All of that was back in the bride's room at the church, and Ronnie would bring it, along with Isabel's overnight bag, to the reception. The only thing Isabel possessed besides the wedding finery she wore was her grandmother's hanky with the pretty bluebonnets embroidered in one corner that she'd tucked into her garter.

Granny Sophia had carried the hanky when she'd married Isabel's grandfather along with a book of prayers and poems that *her* mother had written. In turn, Isabel's mother had done the same thing when she'd married Isabel's father.

Isabel had planned to follow tradition. But she'd had to improvise because of the massive bouquet. She couldn't carry both.

If she'd insisted on her granny's book and a single stemmed flower like she'd wanted, would everything have turned out all right?

She looked over her shoulder to see how close the pursuit might be. But Reeve's body blocked her view and all she accomplished was hitting her hip painfully against the corner of the car.

She sucked in, winced at the pinch in her ribs, and slapped her bouquet against the offensive vehicle.

More flowers flew and she heard Reeve swear under his breath. He grabbed the bouquet from her. "You're dangerous with that thing." He yanked open the passenger door of the Mercedes and tossed the bouquet inside.

"I should have known you'd park in a loading zone. You think you can just do anything, don't you?"

"I think you just need to be quiet and get in before you

really hurt yourself. Or do you want to go back into the church?" He didn't wait for an answer but pushed her down inside the car as unceremoniously as he'd dispatched the bouquet.

She was so shocked she didn't even try to resist. But she also could finally see the doors of the church open.

She pulled the long veil free where it was trapped behind her and yanked her feet inside the car while he shoved at the mass of organza ruffles sprouting voluminously from her knees down.

"It's like trying to smash clouds," he muttered. Their hands knocked against each other when she tried to help.

But she gasped when Trey appeared in the doorway of the church, and she instinctively dived out of view, leaving Reeve to deal with the problem of her dress.

It had been hard to breathe standing straight. It was even harder hunched over in the car with her forehead pressed against the soft leather of the driver's seat.

Don't see me. Don't see me. Don't see me. The chant inside her head was accompanied by the drumming of her heart.

She didn't even realize that Reeve had closed the passenger door until he opened the driver's side next to her head. He leaned down and lifted her head just enough to slide behind the wheel as nonchalantly as he pleased.

Then he let go and her head landed unceremoniously on his leg.

And there she was. In the blink of an eye. Staring up at the underside of his dashboard, feeling surrounded by the warmth and scent of him.

What was worse? This…or Trey?

He was Trey's friend. "Why are you helping me?"

His arm brushed against her shoulder as he put the car

in motion. "There's got to be a rule somewhere to always help a bride on the run."

He was just as slick a talker as Trey. She started to move but his hand settled on her head.

"Hold tight," he murmured, and she nearly passed out when she realized he was rolling down his window. He braked and called out the window. "Trey!"

She knocked her head against the steering wheel when she tried lifting up. "You vile sna—"

His hand unceremoniously covered her mouth. "Be still or he'll see you," he said under his breath.

She subsided, but only because she couldn't actually sink her teeth into the palm of his hand.

He raised his voice again. "Ceremony over already or is it just running late?" His tone was easy. Buddy to buddy.

"We're delayed a few minutes," Trey called back. "Nothing to worry about. See you inside?"

She ground her teeth together. *Nothing* to worry about?

"Can't." Reeve didn't sound regretful in the least. "Business emergency. You know how it goes."

Trey laughed. Confident. As if his bride hadn't just run out on him for all the wedding guests to see. "Maybe I'll see you at the reception, then. Got a helluva party planned. It'll be worth the drive. Fireworks on the lake."

"That's what I hear," Reeve returned.

"Even the governor's coming," Trey added. "Got confirmation just this afternoon."

"Bet your dad's pleased," Reeve responded.

"You know it!"

She heard the soft whir of the window closing again. Trey's sheer nerve infuriated her. Did he intend to have the reception without her?

"Hold on," Reeve murmured for her ears only when

she tried to lift her head again. "He's still in the doorway looking."

She subsided but there was still a growl building in her throat.

Reeve's thigh shifted again, and the steering wheel brushed her forehead as he turned the car. She tried to imagine herself anywhere other than where she was. Anywhere other than with this man who was *not* her friend.

"Have to say this wedding is turning out more interesting than I expected." He sounded disgustingly cheerful. "And you're safe, by the way. He's gone back inside the church."

She did growl then and peeled his fingers away from her mouth. "Glad you're amused." She angled her head, trying to avoid the steering wheel as she awkwardly scooched away from his leg.

"Didn't say it was funny. I said it was interesting."

He lifted his arm and the edge of her veil caught on his cuff link. She ruthlessly wrenched it free and with one hand on the console, managed to lever herself upright into her seat. She leaned as far away from him as she possibly could, though he didn't even seem to notice.

He was too busy grimacing at his palm as he wiped off a smear of Number 879 Red with the tie he yanked from his pocket. When he was finished, he tossed the tie in the back seat as if it were a spent tissue. "So, what made you change your mind? Didn't like the shade of Trey's tux?"

"How can you even ask that? I know you saw the picture of him." She flicked his cracked phone where it sat on the console between them. "Kissing that naked girl."

"So?" His gaze ran over her face.

She gaped. *"So?"*

He frowned slightly as he braked before turning out onto

the busy street. "What's so different about this girl from the others? Trey said you two had an open arrangement."

She blinked. "He said...*what?*"

He glanced at her as if he were suddenly reevaluating something. "No arrangement, I take it," he said after a moment.

"No," she confirmed through her teeth.

He shook his head and sighed. "Always help a bride on the run."

She waited for him to say something else. Something about the lawsuit. About buying Stellar Productions. Something that would put the bow on the big black funereal ribbon wrapped around the worst day of her life.

But he didn't say anything at all.

So neither did she.

One disaster for the day was enough.

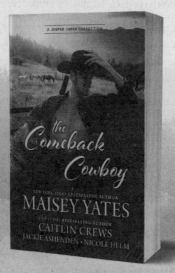